AUG 17 2018

DATE DUE			

STARLESS

STARLESS

JACQUELINE CAREY

A TOM DOHERTY ASSOCIATES BOOK  NEW YORK

STARLESS

Copyright © 2018 by Jacqueline Carey

All rights reserved.

A Tor Book
Published by Tom Doherty Associates
175 Fifth Avenue
New York, NY 10010

www.tor-forge.com

Tor® is a registered trademark of Macmillan Publishing Group, LLC.

The Library of Congress Cataloging-in-Publication Data is available upon request.

ISBN 978-0-7653-8682-3 (hardcover)
ISBN 978-0-7653-8683-0 (ebook)

Our books may be purchased in bulk for promotional, educational, or business use. Please contact your local bookseller or the Macmillan Corporate and Premium Sales Department at 1-800-221-7945, extension 5442, or by email at MacmillanSpecialMarkets@macmillan.com.

Printed in the United States of America

0 9 8 7 6 5 4 3 2

CAST OF CHARACTERS

Desert
Khai
Brother Saan—Seer
Brothers: Merik, Drajan, Ehudan, Jawal, Tekel, Hakan, Ramil, Eresh,
    Karal
Brother Yarit of Clan Shahalim
Jakhan, chieftain of Black Sands Clan (sons Yasif, Khisan)
Vironesh the Shadow

Court
King Azarkal
Princes: Kazaran (deceased), Elizar, Tazaresh, Dozaren, Kozar, Bazar
Princess Zariya
Queens: Adinah, Makesha, Rashina, Kayaresh, Sanala
Princesses: Nizara, Izaria, Fazarah (husband Tarkhal)
Tarshim—captain of the Queen's Guard
Prince Heshari of Barakhar—suitor
Lord Rygil of Therin—suitor
Varkas Long-Arm and Sandrath the Quiet of Granth—suitors

Sea
Jahno the Seeker
Tarrok of Trask, the Thunderclap
Evene of Drogalia, Opener of Ways
Elehuddin: Essee, Kooie, Keeik, Seeak, Tiiklit, Tliksee
Eeeio and Aiiiaii—sea-wyrms

Lirios the Mayfly, the Quick

Yaruna—the Green Mother of Papa-ka-hondras

Deities

Zar the Sun, Nim the Bright Moon, Shahal the Dark Moon, and Eshen
   the Wandering Moon

Pahrkun the Scouring Wind and Anamuht the Purging Fire—Zarkhoum

Droth the Great Thunder—Granth

Ilharis the Two-Faced—Therin

Lishan the Graceful—Barakhar

Obid the Stern—Itarran

Dulumu the Deep—Elehud

Quellin-Who-Is-Everywhere—Drogalia

Luhdo the Loud—Trask

Ishfahel the Gentle Rain—Verdant Isle

Selerian the Light-Footed—Chalcedony Isle

Shambloth the Inchoate Terror—Papa-ka-hondras

Galdano the Shrewd—Tukkan

Johina the Mirthful—Kerreman

STARLESS

DESERT

ONE

I was nine years old the first time I tried to kill a man, and although in the end I was glad my attempt failed, I had been looking forward to the opportunity for quite some months. That is only natural, I think, when one is raised as I was; although as I grow older, I am less and less sure what that means. All things proceed from nature—if one thing alters the course of another's growth, is that not yet within the accordance of nature? A vine trained to climb a trellis remains a vine.

And I am Khai, and remain myself, whatever that means.

It is a good name; strong and bold, a name like the sound of a desert hawk's cry. A fitting name for a child of the desert; a fitting name for a child whose destiny was determined by a single feather.

But that is not the whole truth, and Brother Saan, who is our Seer and the wisest among us, says truth must be laid bare, as clean as a corpse flensed to the bone by Pahrkun the Scouring Wind.

So.

This was the truth as I knew it: Nine years ago in the realm of Zarkhoum, such an event transpired as had not taken place for a hundred and fifty years. At the precise moment that Nim the Bright Moon obscured Shahal the Dark Moon, a child was born to the House of the Ageless, whose members are also known as the Sun-Blessed.

The priestesses of Anamuht the Purging Fire are great keepers of records, and the lore of the realm holds that when a child of the royal house is born during a lunar eclipse, so too is his or her shadow.

I was not the only such child born at that precise moment. According to

Brother Saan, the priestesses of Anamuht spent almost a year consulting midwives across the length and breadth of Zarkhoum. In the end, they discovered thirteen of us.

Hence, the feather.

I remember it.

I do not remember the mother or father to whom I was born. I do not know if I was high-born or low, or if I was born to the fierce desert nomads who acknowledge no rank save that which personal honor won in their own vendettas accords them. Brother Saan does not know, either, but he tells me that the priestesses of Anamuht will have that information recorded in their scrolls, and I may seek it for myself when I come of age, if the Sun-Blessed princess who is the light to my shadow allows it.

Perhaps I shall; perhaps not. After all, does it matter? In the end, I was the one who was chosen.

A feather.

It took place in the portion of the Fortress of the Winds that we call the Dancing Bowl, although that I do not remember; I know only because I have been told. It is a hard, stony basin that the men use for sparring practice. There are three tunnels that open onto its sloping sides, and many more riddling the cliffs that rise to tower over it. High above the basin, there is a thin stone bridge that arches across it—nothing built by human hands, but a structure etched into being by Pahrkun the Scouring Wind some thousands of years gone by.

I know it well, for I have crossed it many times. I have felt its faint tremor beneath my bare feet; I have felt the wind tug at my garments, threatening to unbalance me. Ah, but the wind . . . I must learn to embrace it.

And so I shall, for I am pledged to Pahrkun the Scouring Wind, and it is all because of the feather.

I remember.

I do.

There were thirteen of us, all babes. Thirteen carpets were laid on the floor of the Dancing Bowl; thirteen babes were set upon the carpets. I do not remember that part, but Brother Saan has told me many times. It was mid-morning in high spring, and the heat would have been rising like an oven, only a slight breeze swirling in the basin. I can imagine it well. Atop the arched bridge, Brother Saan opened his hand and let fall a single hawk feather.

When I close my eyes, I can see it still: blue sky and a lone feather, a pale brown with darker brown stripes. I see it fall, drifting on the breeze, turning in circles as it falls. I see the breeze carry it west, then north; east, then south. I see the edge of the vanes catch the light like the honed edge of a blade, I see the hollow shaft glow with a milky translucence.

Brother Saan watched from atop the bridge. The figures of the other brothers and a cluster of veiled priestesses in their bright red robes dotted the tunnel mouths above the Dancing Bowl, waiting, waiting, to see where the feather would fall, which babe would be marked by Pahrkun's favor, chosen to be the shadow to the bright Sun-Blessed princess in the faraway city of Merabaht.

Along the walls of the Dancing Bowl, the families watched and waited to see who among them would return to their far-flung homes less one babe, bragging of the honor bestowed upon them.

The feather drifted and drifted, circling down above me. I waved my hands in the air and caught it in one chubby fist.

A great cheer went up; that, too, I do not remember.

But I remember the feather. I have it still.

And so it came to pass that I was raised in the Fortress of the Winds by the Brotherhood of Pahrkun, raised to be a warrior.

Of course, at nine years of age, I was not yet fully versed in the traditional weapons of the brotherhood. I lacked the strength to effectively wield the curved sword known as *yakhan,* or wind-cutter, as well as the three-pronged *kopar* that served as a weapon of both offense and defense, but that, I was promised, would come in time. I was quick and wiry, hardened to the elements by going shirtless and barefoot in summer and winter alike, and I could take down a mountain goat with a single, swift blow to the jugular with the slender dagger that had been given me on my seventh birthday.

And so, when a caravan escorting a supplicant to attempt the Trial of Pahrkun appeared on the horizon, I begged to be allowed to take part. Understand that there was no malice in it. This was simply our way in

Zarkhoum; and indeed, I believed that there was both purpose and mercy in it. It was a harsh mercy, but then the desert is a harsh place.

The nature of the Trial of Pahrkun was this: Any man convicted of an offense deserving of execution could choose instead to undertake the trial, upon which he would be escorted by the Royal Guard across the deep desert to the Fortress of the Winds. At the entrance to the fortress—which, like the bridge above the Dancing Bowl, is no man-made edifice, but a vast series of caverns and tunnels—the supplicant would strike the sounding-bowl and announce his intention.

To pass the trial, the supplicant had to do but one thing: make his way past three brothers in the Hall of Proving. If he succeeded in emerging alive into open air, he was reckoned scoured of his sins by Pahrkun, accepted into the brotherhood, given a new name and a new life.

Very few men attempted this.

Even fewer succeeded, for the fighting skills of the brothers who were born into this warrior caste and pledged to its service as young men—though none so young as I—were not only honed by decades of practice and centuries of tradition, but augmented by the skills of those few who did succeed.

There was much debate around the supper table the evening before the supplicant's arrival.

"Khai is young," Brother Drajan said in his slow, implacable manner. He served as cook to the brotherhood, and although I was often grateful for his considered way, on that occasion it made me impatient. He glanced at me out of the corner of his eye, one corner of his mouth tugging downward in an apologetic grimace. "Let him be a boy while he may. It is too soon for him to wrestle with mortality."

Brother Jawal made a lightning-quick gesture as though flicking away a fly. "Are we raising a warrior or not? Death is no respecter of age."

"Therein lies *my* concern." Elderly Brother Ehudan, who taught me my characters and numbers, knit his brow. "What would come to pass if the shadow of the Sun-Blessed met an untimely demise?"

Everyone looked to Brother Saan, including me.

Brother Saan's face was tranquil. He was old, too; older than Brother

Ehudan, although it seemed to me that age had visited him in a different way. There was nothing crabbed or querulous about him, only a deep stillness none of us could yet emulate. "Khai might die in a dozen ways in our care before the princess comes of age," he said mildly. "One wrong step in the heights, and he would plunge to his death. We cannot allow that fear to hobble us."

I stifled an indignant protest at the notion that I might perish due to a careless misstep.

Brother Saan's gaze rested on me. "You are eager to undertake this challenge?"

I placed my palms together and touched my thumbs to my brow in a gesture of respect. "I am, Elder Brother."

"Then it shall be so," he said. "On the morrow, Khai will take the third and final post in the Hall of Proving."

My heart quickened. "Thank you, Elder Brother!"

"It is no gift I give you, but a grave charge," Brother Saan said to me. "Tomorrow, a man's life hangs in the balance. It is Pahrkun who decides his fate; know that you are but an instrument."

I touched my brow again. "Yes, Elder Brother."

Brother Saan's eyelids crinkled. "What is a warrior's first and greatest weapon, young Khai?"

"It is his mind, Elder Brother," I said.

"Very good." Rising from the table, Brother Saan laid a hand on my shoulder. "Conduct yourself with honor."

I inclined my head. "Always, Elder Brother."

My sleep that night was restless. I rose at dawn to offer my prayers in the privacy of the small cavern that was my bedchamber; four genuflections for Zar the Sun, Nim the Bright Moon, Shahal the Dark Moon, and Eshen the Wandering Moon; two genuflections for Anamuht the Purging Fire and Pahrkun the Scouring Wind; and at last four genuflections for the four great currents, east, west, north, and south.

Brother Jawal poked his head in the opening of my cavern. "Are you done?" he inquired. "Come, let's get a look at this supplicant."

I scrambled to my feet. "Yes, brother."

Atop the western lookout, the wind was brisk and buffeting. I stood beside Brother Jawal, knees flexed to maintain my balance.

Let your mind be like the eye of the hawk.

So Brother Saan had taught me. I gazed at the party making its way toward the Fortress of the Winds. Six men in the crimson-and-gold silks of the Royal Guard riding hardy, sure-footed steeds. One man in the center of them; a portly fellow clad in rich brocade robes, several purses and a long sword with a gem-encrusted pommel dangling from his waist-sash. Their shadows stretched westward behind them.

Brother Jawal made a disparaging sound. "A merchant," he said in a dismissive tone. "Soft and rich. Like as not, he'll try to bribe us."

I was shocked. "Is that permitted?"

"No." Brother Jawal shook his head. "But that's the way city folk are."

I supposed it must be true, and I shook my head too at the folly of city folk. To think that one could *bribe* us!

It made me wonder, though, what the princess would be like. I thought of her often; the light to my shadow. It was the first time in recorded history that a daughter of the Sun-Blessed had been born with a shadow. Zariya was her name; all of the Sun-Blessed bear the name of the Sun in their own names. Zariya of the House of the Ageless, the seventeenth child born to His Majesty King Azarkal, who had reigned for three hundred years; the third child born to his fifth wife. Sun-Blessed, because Zarkhoum lies the farthest east of any nation beneath the starless sky; the House of the Ageless, because the sacred *rhamanthus* seeds that are quickened by Anamuht the Purging Fire bestow great longevity upon its members.

These things I knew because Brother Ehudan taught them to me, but I could not imagine what such a person would be like. I knew the desert and hawks and wind; I did not know cities.

I imagined there must be color, a great deal of color, like the silks the Royal Guards wore; or like the robes the fat merchant wore, all blue and green with gold stitching, robes that were wholly unsuited for the desert.

As they drew near, I saw that he was sweating in the heat, the poor foolish fellow. "Why would he wear such garments?" I asked Brother Jawal.

He shrugged; he was desert-born, a son of one of the nomadic tribes, and pledged to Pahrkun's service by birthright, not trial. "Among the city folk, such garments indicate wealth and status."

I squatted on my haunches, leaning over the ledge of the lookout. "I wonder what his crime was."

Brother Jawal shrugged again. "Whatever it was, he'll meet his final judgment today."

"Or not," I reminded him.

He laughed and caressed the hilt of his *yakhan*. "Oh, I think a mighty wind is coming for this fat man, little brother. I've been given the first post."

I glanced over my shoulder toward the east. Beyond the peaks and valleys of the Fortress of the Winds lay the deepest desert. It was the domain of the Sacred Twins, for there Pahrkun stalked the sands, raising them into a killing gyre as tall as mountains, blotting out the sky. There Anamuht strode veiled in sheets of flame from head to toe, lightning bolts in her hands.

From time to time, we caught glimpses of them in the deep distance, but not today.

My weight shifted as I looked back, and my left foot dislodged a pebble. It rattled down the cliff.

Far below, the fat merchant and his escort were arriving. The merchant glanced up. Rivulets of sweat ran down his plump cheeks, but his gaze was unexpectedly sharp. He glanced away and twitched the long sleeves of his robes to better cover his hands on the reins. His mount tossed its head in a fretful response and something tickled at my thoughts, making me frown.

Let your mind be like the eye of the hawk . . .

But then Brother Jawal's hand was on my elbow, urging me backward. "Come," he said. "It's almost time to take up our posts."

The sounding-bowl rang as we withdrew, a single chiming note that seemed to hang forever in the bright air.

As was the custom, the supplicant was given leave to rest and refresh himself before attempting the trial. The fat man, I thought, would be grateful for such a respite even if they had made camp within an hour's ride of the fortress. I wondered if it were true that he would attempt a bribe.

His hands, though . . . why did he seek to conceal his hands?

I shook my head; whatever thought I'd had was gone. I had made my stance at the third post in the Hall of Proving. It was warm, the breath of the desert stirring faintly here. Behind me, the cavern opened onto daylight.

Daylight; for the supplicant, freedom and life.

For me, it meant I would be silhouetted in light, giving the fat man an advantage. Oh, but he wouldn't get this far, would he?

No, it seemed impossible. Brother Jawal was fast and ruthless; the fat man stood no chance of defeating him in combat or evading him with speed. Even if by some miracle he passed the first post, Brother Merik stood at the second post. He was not as fast as Brother Jawal, but he was a seasoned warrior who fought with deadly efficiency, never a single move wasted.

Still, I had to be prepared. "Pahrkun, I am your instrument today," I whispered, drawing my dagger. My hand was sweating and slippery on the hilt. "If it is your will, use me."

Silence.

Hands, the fat man's hands.

Maybe it was another odd custom of city folk. My mind drifted, drifted like the hawk's feather.

Zariya.

I closed my eyes, letting my gaze adjust to the darkness before me. When I opened them, I could make out the crooked stalagmite at the bend that marked the threshold between the second and third posts.

The sounding-bowl rang again, its chiming note muted by the stone walls around me. I heard Brother Saan's voice announcing that the Trial of Pahrkun had begun.

I heard Brother Jawal begin to utter his tribal war-cry, high and fierce— but then the cry was abruptly muffled. I listened for the sound of clashing blades and heard nothing. My palms began to itch and I had a taste like metal in my mouth. Brother Jawal . . . no. It was not possible.

I waited.

In the darkness ahead of me, there was a faint, familiar sound, followed by an unexpected flare of light that nearly made me cry out in alarm. Blinking ferociously against the dazzle behind my eyes, I heard a thump and a grunt of pain, then the sound of Brother Merik's voice uttering low curses and the clatter of a blade against . . . what? Not metal, but stone, I thought.

The air around me eddied.

He was coming.

The fat man was coming, and now, at last I was afraid. My knees shook and every fiber of my being urged me to hide, hide and conceal myself in the shadows, and let the fat man pass.

No.

There was no honor in hiding. And yet here at the third and final post, how was I to prevail against a man with the skill and cunning to make it past Brother Jawal and Brother Merik? The dagger in my hand felt puny and inadequate; *I* felt puny and inadequate.

I recalled Brother Saan's words again: *What is a warrior's first and greatest weapon?*

I shoved my dagger into my sash and unwound the *heshkrat* that was tied around my waist; three lengths of thin rope, the strands joined at one end, stones knotted at the other. It was a hunting weapon, not a combat weapon; one used by tribesmen to bring down antelope in the desert.

Brother Jawal had taught me to use it. I prayed to Pahrkun to guide my hand.

The flare of light around the bend in the cavern had died and something was moving in the shadows. A man; not a fat man in robes, but a slender one clad in close-fitting black attire, staying close to the walls and walking as soft-footed as a desert cat, with throwing daggers in both his hands.

I saw him see me and throw with one hand and then the other, flicking his daggers in my direction as quick as the blink of an eye, but the wind of his motion warned me and I was already moving, the ropes of my *heshkrat* whirling overhead; one turn before I loosed it, aiming low.

The man was moving too, but the *heshkrat* was designed to bring down prey on the run. It tangled his legs and he fell hard.

A gust of wind blew through the Hall of Proving and a hard, fierce joy suffused me. Drawing my dagger, I fell on the man, thinking to stab him in the jugular. Agile as a snake, he twisted beneath me and the point of my dagger struck the stone floor of the cavern, jarring my arm.

I swore.

Still, he was unarmed, and if I could only stab him before his greater strength prevailed . . . but no, as we grappled, somehow his hands were no longer empty, somehow there was a cord wrapped around my throat, and his hands were drawing the ends tight. His hands; his strong, slender hands. That was why he'd hidden them. They were not the hands of a fat man. It had been a disguise.

Interesting.

It was a pity that my throat was burning, my chest was heaving for lack of air, and my vision was blurring.

"Watery hell!" The not-fat man's eyes widened. "You're just a kid!" He let go the cord, kicked free of the ropes of the *heshkrat,* and backed away from me; backed away toward sunlight and salvation. "I'm not killing a fucking kid!" he called out.

I got to my hands and knees, wheezing.

Brother Saan entered the Hall of Proving, his features as calm and grave as ever. He regarded the not-fat man who now stood beyond the threshold of the cavern in broad daylight, wind ruffling his hair. "I am pleased to hear it," he said in his mild voice. "Whatever sins you have committed, Pahrkun the Scouring Wind has cleansed you of them. Welcome to the brotherhood."

TWO

Brother Merik was merely injured, having taken a throwing dagger to the forearm he raised against the unexpected brightness; a dagger expertly placed between the steel prongs of the *kopar*. After that, the supplicant had slipped past him while he blundered blindly in the darkness, his sword clattering against the stone walls.

Brother Jawal was dead, his neck broken. The supplicant had flung his robe over him and taken him by surprise.

The impossible had come to pass.

We laid his body, stripped bare save for a loincloth, on a bier atop a high plateau. Once the hawks and vultures and carrion beetles, all creatures of Pahrkun, had picked the flesh from his bones, they would be returned to his clan.

Although I had no right to be angry, I was; angry at the supplicant for his trickery, angry at Brother Jawal for letting himself get killed. I was angry at myself for seeing too late through the supplicant's disguise, angry at myself for failing to kill him, angry that I owed him my life.

That night the king's guardsmen dined with us. I saw them glance at me with open curiosity, but the mood was a mixture of somber mourning and quiet acceptance, and they did nothing to disturb it.

The supplicant—whatever his name had been, he was a man with no name now, and would remain thus until Brother Saan gave him a new one—kept his head low and ate quickly and deftly. Out of his disguise, he looked younger than I had first thought. Otherwise there was nothing remarkable to the eye about the nameless man, and it seemed wrong that such an ordinary-looking fellow should be responsible for killing Brother Jawal.

When our meal of stewed goat and calabash squash had been consumed, Brother Saan poured cups of mint tea. "By your skills at deception and subterfuge, I take it you are a member of the Shahalim Clan from the city of Merabaht," he said, passing a cup to the nameless man. "It is said that they are thieves and spies without peer."

"I was," he said in a curt tone.

Brother Saan blew on his tea. "I thought the Shahalim never got caught."

The nameless man grimaced. "Never spite a Shahalim woman, Elder Brother. I was betrayed." He lifted his cup, then set it down. "That's the princess's shadow, isn't it?" He pointed at me. "I can't believe you damned near let me kill a Sun-Blessed's shadow."

There were a few murmurs of agreement, and I flushed with embarrassment and anger.

"Yet you did not," Brother Saan said calmly. "It seems Pahrkun wishes you to teach Khai your ways."

The nameless man stared at him. "Teach clan secrets to an outsider? Never. It is forbidden."

Brother Saan took a sip of his tea. "Your former clan betrayed you. The Brotherhood of Pahrkun is your clan now."

The nameless man got to his feet. "I won't—"

The six guards and several of the brothers rose, hands reaching for sword hilts. The nameless man sat back down.

"I don't *want* to learn his ways!" The words burst from me. "They're nothing but trickery! It's dishonorable!"

Brother Saan eyed me. "Khai, it is your grief that speaks. Go, retire for the night. We will speak more of this on the morrow."

I hesitated.

"It is an order, young one," he said.

I went reluctantly. Behind me, I could hear the tenor of the conversation change. There was a part of me that was tempted to creep back and listen, but that seemed the sort of unworthy thing the nameless man would do, and so I obeyed Brother Saan and retired to my chamber.

In the morning, Brother Jawal was still dead and my anger was still with me. Brother Ehudan dismissed me within mere minutes. "You're not fit to study today," he said irritably. "Take your foul temper elsewhere. Take it out on the spinning devil."

Since it was as good a suggestion as any, I went.

The spinning devil was a contraption of the nomadic tribesfolk, designed to train young men in the art of weaponless combat they called "thunder and lightning." It consisted of a tall, sturdy central shaft planted firmly in the earth—or in this instance, wedged firmly in a deep crevice in the floor of a cavern—and four leather-bound paddles of varying length that spun around it like wheels around the axle of a cart. It was a cunning device, and one that Brother Jawal said could be easily disassembled and transported. He was the one who taught me to use it, as he taught me to throw the *heshkrat*.

A grown man could set all four paddles in motion so that the device resembled the spinning dust devils from which it took its name. I could only strike the lower two with any force, but it was enough for now. *Boom*, I threw a punch with my fist that was thunder, and the paddle spun; *flash*, I struck an angled blow with the side of my hand that was lightning, and the paddle spun the other way. *Boom*, a direct forward kick to the lowest paddle, and *flash*, a side kick with the blade of my foot.

Boom, flash flash, boom boom flash, flash boom boom, flash flash. The spinning devil spun and spun and creaked, the paddles a blur. Brother Jawal had told me that the nomads invented thunder and lightning many, many years ago as a way for hot-blooded young men to fight without killing one another.

Once they got very, very good at it, that didn't always hold true.

Brother Jawal said that there was a ritual to challenging a tribesman to fight with thunder and lightning, a ritual that involved clapping your hands and stamping your feet. Clap-clap-stamp on the right, clap-clap-stamp on the left. If you wanted to insult your opponent and imply that he was unworthy, you clap-clap-stamped twice on the left instead. He had laughed when he told me that, and although he did not say it, I knew that he had done it, and won his challenge.

And now Brother Jawal was dead at the hands of a nameless man who knew nothing of ritual or honor.

Flash flash flash boom boom.

I fought the spinning devil with grim determination, sweat stinging my eyes and dampening my hair. I was still battling it when Brother Saan entered the training chamber, a rolled wool carpet under one arm. When I paused, he gestured for me to continue and set about unrolling the carpet. I launched a final flurry of blows at the spinning devil, then stepped back, panting hard. The paddles continued to drift in circles, creaking slowly to a halt.

Brother Saan sat cross-legged on the carpet awaiting me, a leather-wrapped bundle before him. I folded my legs to sit opposite him, pressing my palms together and touching my brow. My breathing sounded loud in the quiet cavern. Brother Saan waited for me to find stillness. Except for the slight rise and fall of his chest, he might have been carved out of stone. Even though time had touched his flesh with the slackness of age, the muscles beneath were lean and ropy.

At last my breathing slowed, and I found stillness. A shaft of sunlight angled through the cavern from an aperture above us and dust motes sparkled within it. All was quiet.

"Once upon a time, there were stars in the night sky," Brother Saan began, then paused when an involuntary sound escaped me. I was in no mood for tales of wonder from days of yore.

"Forgive me, Elder Brother," I murmured. "I meant no disrespect."

He waited another long moment. "Once upon a time, there were stars in the night sky," he began again. "Thousands and thousands of them, shining as bright as diamonds. And those stars were the flashing eyes and teeth and the fierce beating hearts of the thousand children of Zar the Sun, Nim the Bright Moon, Shahal the Dark Moon, and fickle Eshen the Wandering Moon, and we revered them all. The stars in the night sky let us guide our steps on land, and allowed mariners at sea to find their way on the four great currents." He lifted one finger. "But the children of heaven were not content to keep their places while the Sun and the Moons traveled freely, and so they rose up and sought to overthrow their parents. Chaos reigned in heaven; fiery stones fell to earth in the battle, and the great currents and tides ran wild in the seas."

I nodded; all this I knew.

"Until Zar the Sun said *enough*." Brother Saan made a sweeping gesture. "In anger, he cast down his thousand rebellious children and they fell from the heavens to earth. Here they are bound and here they remain, and the night sky is empty of stars." He regarded me. "Do you suppose that all the fallen children of the heavens shall remain content that it should ever be thus?"

"I . . ." I blinked; I had not anticipated the question. "I beg your pardon, Elder Brother. What?"

Brother Saan rested his hands on his knees. "Here in Zarkhoum, we are fortunate. Even though they raised their hands against him, Anamuht the Purging Fire and Pahrkun the Scouring Wind are two of Zar's best-beloved children; his brother and sister twins born to different mothers," he said. "Zar the Sun saw to it that they fell to the land where they might be the first of his children he gazes upon when he begins his journey across the sky, and the Sacred Twins have pledged to protect the land to which they are bound, and never again defy their father."

All this, too, I knew. "Do you say this is untrue elsewhere?" It was a difficult idea for my mind to encompass; although I had been taught that there were other realms and other gods beneath the starless skies, the desert and the Sacred Twins were all that I had ever known. I could not imagine other gods.

His gaze was troubled. "I fear it may be so. The priestesses of Anamuht claim that there is a prophecy that when darkness rises in the west, one of the Sun-Blessed will stand against it."

My breath caught in my throat. "Zariya?"

"It is *highly* unlikely." Brother Saan's voice took on a rare acerbic note, and his gaze cleared. "The daughters of the House of the Ageless are cherished and sheltered. Still, when one of the Sun-Blessed is born with a shadow, we must avail ourselves of every form of training that presents itself."

My sullen anger, forgotten in my battle with the spinning devil, stirred. "You speak of these Shahalim."

"I do." Brother Saan gave me a sharp look. "Do you know what happened the last time a shadow was born?"

I shook my head. "Only that it happened a hundred and fifty years before my birth, Elder Brother."

"Yes, and some forty years ago, his Sun-Blessed charge died in his care," he said simply.

I tallied the figures in my head and frowned. "But how could that be? He would have been a hundred and twenty."

"The shadow of one of the Sun-Blessed is allowed to partake of the *rhamanthus* seeds," Brother Saan said. "He did not begin to age until his charge died."

My head was spinning like the spinning devil. "Forgive me, Elder Brother, but what has that to do with the Shahalim?"

He did not answer my question directly. "I myself was not yet born when that shadow's training took place," he said. "But I was newly appointed as Seer when his charge died, and it fell to me to question him about what happened. The shadow was a broken man, filled with bitterness and fury."

"Why?" I whispered.

"Because he failed to prevent it." Brother Saan gazed into the distance. "His charge was poisoned."

I let out my breath in a hiss.

"Yes." Brother Saan nodded. "A most dishonorable means of attack; and yet, it proved effective. Brother Vironesh—for that was the shadow's name—had no means by which to anticipate it. He spoke passionately to me about the need for *honor beyond honor*."

"Honor beyond honor," I echoed.

He nodded again. "That is what it meant to him to keep his charge alive at any cost. Honor beyond honor. We failed to prepare him for it. And so I do not think it is any accident that Pahrkun has accepted one of the Shahalim into our brotherhood; one from whom you might learn a great many things we cannot teach you. They are sneaks and thieves, but they are highly skilled in their arts. These are things that you might reckon dishonorable; only know, they are in the service of honor beyond honor. As a shadow, nothing else must matter to you."

I was silent.

"Do you understand?" Brother Saan asked me.

Bowing my head, I touched my brow with the thumbs of my folded hands. "Yes, Elder Brother. I do."

"Good." He unfolded the bundle before him to reveal Brother Jawal's fighting weapons; his sharp-whetted *yakhan* with its worn leather-wrapped hilt and curved blade, and the three-pronged *kopar*. "You have stood a post in the Trial of Pahrkun. It is only fitting that these are yours now."

I took them up with reverence, feeling the weight of them. I could not resist a few trial passes, weaving the *yakhan* in the complicated figure-eight pattern favored by the desert tribesfolk, spinning and reversing the *kopar* so its prongs lay flat along my forearm. It made my wrists ache.

Brother Saan smiled, his eyelids crinkling. "Here," he said, plucking two more items from his bundle. They were fist-sized rocks.

I eyed him. "Elder Brother?"

"Squeeze them," he said, fitting actions to words to demonstrate. Beneath his wrinkled skin, the muscles in his wrists and forearms stood out like cords. "Three thousand times a day."

I inclined my head. "Yes, Elder Brother."

He folded his empty bundle, rolled his carpet, and rose. "On the morrow, after your lesson with Brother Ehudan, you will begin training with Brother Yarit, and obey him in every particular whether it seems honorable or not."

I glanced up at him. "Brother Yarit?"

"The Shahalim." He smiled again, this time wryly. "We held a naming ceremony for him today. Whether he likes it or not, and at the moment, he likes it no more than you do, he is one of us now."

A thought came to me as I rose. "Elder Brother . . . are there other shadows yet among the living?"

"No." He shook his head. "The last born before Vironesh was some seven hundred years ago. His charge came into *khementaran* centuries ago."

"*Khementaran?*" I did not know the word.

"The point of return." Brother Saan rubbed his chin thoughtfully. "Members of the House of the Ageless live very long lives, if those lives are not cut short by violence or illness, but they do not live forever. Sooner or later, each comes to the point they call *khementaran*, when they desire to return to the natural rhythms of the mortal world, to allow themselves to age with the passing of the seasons."

I eyed him, thinking it seemed unlikely to me.

He favored me with another wry look in return. "It may be that you will find out for yourself one day, young Khai."

I tucked that thought away to ponder later, but I was not quite done yet. "Elder Brother . . . what became of Vironesh? The broken shadow?"

"Ah." His expression changed. "Well you might inquire, for I have been endeavoring to learn that very thing. There are rumors. It may be that he yet lives, for his body was decades younger than my own when he began to age." He shook his head. "But if it is so, thus far he does not wish to be found." He raised his brows at me. "Have you other questions for me today, young Khai?"

I touched my forehead with one thumb, Brother Jawal's weapons tucked under my other arm. "No, Elder Brother."

"Very good."

I returned to my chamber to stow my new possessions and began squeezing rocks, but it was later than I'd reckoned. The midday heat was oppressive, and my limbs were weary from my battle with the spinning devil. By the time I reached five hundred, my eyelids were growing heavy. Still, I kept going until I reached a thousand. I would do the rest after a midday nap, when the air would be cooler.

Thoughts drifted through my mind; drifted, drifted like a hawk's feather on the wind. Falling stars, *rhamanthus* seeds. *Khementaran*, the point of return . . . who would seek to return to death and decay?

And yet death and decay were a part of nature and the purview of Pahrkun the Scouring Wind . . .

Poison; a broken and bitter shadow, his charge slain by dishonorable means. Who were the enemies of the Sun-Blessed? Who would seek their lives?

One day I would know.

Whatever might come, I resolved that I would strive to attain honor beyond honor. Brother Jawal, I thought, would understand.

THREE

"Right." On the floor of the Dancing Bowl, Brother Yarit looked me up and down, a sour expression on his face. "Here's your first lesson, kid." With a deft twist, he unwound the tie that bound his hair back. "Catch."

Something tumbled through the air; I caught it by reflex. It was a length of tightly braided leather cord with bone pegs at either end.

"Always keep a garrote handy," Brother Yarit advised me. "That's what I damn near used to kill you."

Oh, I remembered.

"Here," he said. "Let me show you how to do it."

Honor beyond honor.

Those were the words I whispered in my thoughts as I suffered Brother Yarit to lay his hands on me and demonstrate, pulling my hair back into a tail and winding the cord and the pegs around it, releasing it with a twist. Those were the words I whispered to myself as he made me practice it over and over.

Several of the brothers watched from the mouths of tunnels above the Dancing Floor. It made Brother Yarit uneasy.

"I agreed to train the kid!" he shouted up at them. "I never agreed to share clan secrets with *all* of you!"

None of the brothers responded.

"You agreed to everything when you undertook the Trial of Pahrkun," I murmured, twisting and untwisting the garrote around my hair. "You are Pahrkun's instrument now, brother."

Brother Yarit glared at me. "Let me see you jump."

"Jump?" I repeated.

"Jump." Suiting actions to words, he ran lightly toward the western wall of the Dancing Bowl, launching himself with a prodigious leap; high, higher than I would have thought possible. He caught an outcropping with both hands, hauled himself up, and launched himself again with a standing leap. Wedging fingers and toes into narrow crevices, he scrambled up the face of the bowl to the mouth of an unoccupied tunnel, then sat on the ledge with his feet dangling. "Come on, kid!" he called down to me. "Jump!"

I took a running start and did my best.

Brother Yarit snorted in disgust as I slid futilely down the face of the bowl, scraping my hands. "You've got the legs of a seven-year-old." Dropping into a low crouch, he launched himself from the ledge. I heard someone above him make a muttered sound of alarm, but he landed safely, hands and feet braced against the stony ground, flexed limbs absorbing the impact. Shaking out his hands, he straightened. "Right, then. Jumping practice it is." Glancing around, he led me over to a staircase etched into the wall that led to one of the middle tunnels, this one carved by human hands. "Hop up it."

Feeling foolish, I hopped onto the first step.

"No, no, no." Brother Yarit shook his head. "You pushed off on your right leg. Hop with both legs, feet together." I did as he said, finding it considerably more difficult. "All right, keep going." He clapped his hands together. "Hop like you're a desert toad with a . . . what eats toads?"

"Hawks," I replied, slightly breathless.

"Hop like you're a desert toad with a hawk on its tail," he said. "Do toads have tails? Never mind. All the way to the top."

It was twenty steps to the top, and when I reached it, he ordered me to turn around and hop back down. When I regained the floor of the Dancing Bowl, the muscles of my legs felt wobbly.

"Good. Do that . . ." Brother Yarit considered the staircase. "We'll start with ten times a day. Five in the morning and five in the evening."

I pushed down a wave of resentment. "Hop."

"Hop," he said. "You want to learn to run? You start by walking. You want to learn to jump, you start by hopping." He clapped his hands again. "Go on, kid! Hop to it."

I turned back to the staircase.

"Hold, Khai." Brother Merik emerged from the mouth of one of the lower tunnels. He folded his arms over his chest. There was a bloodstained white bandage around his left forearm. Sunlight glinted on his *kopar* and the pommel of his *yakhan*. "Do you seek to mock us?" he asked Brother Yarit in a grim tone, dropping one hand to his hilt. "Because I would welcome a, shall we say, friendly rematch in the broad light of day, with no trickery between us."

Brother Yarit grimaced. "I'm sure you would, brother. I've heard the tales."

"What tales?" There was a dangerous edge to Brother Merik's voice.

"They say the warriors of Pahrkun are as fierce and deadly as the desert. They say the wind itself warns them of a blow before it lands." Brother Yarit shrugged. "Make no mistake, I am no warrior. And yet I am here. Shall I tell you what defeated you the other day?"

"I know what defeated me," Brother Merik said. "And I know what slew Brother Jawal. Trickery."

I glanced uneasily from one to the other. Sparring was permitted among the brothers; feuding was not.

But Brother Yarit was shaking his head. "No, what defeated you was your own expectations. Brother Jawal expected a fat merchant who would be easy prey; he did not expect that merchant to spit out the wads of cotton wedged in his cheeks and use his fine robe as a weapon. You, Brother . . . Merik, is it? You expected the advantage of darkness, not the glare of an oil-wood knot. Brother Khai . . ." He glanced at me. "You expected me to be weaponless when I was not."

Brother Merik regarded the smaller man with narrowed eyes. "It is not our way."

"Shall I apologize for not dying?" Brother Yarit said dryly. "I will not. The Shahalim are thieves and spies, yes, but we take our name from the Dark Moon herself, and we are not without pride. Our weapons are disguise, stealth, distraction, and agility; an agility won through strength. I'm trying to teach the kid the latter." He made a show of adjusting the sleeves of the loose tunic of the brotherhood that he had adopted. "Believe me, it wasn't my idea. If you don't like it, speak to your Seer."

Remembering the throwing knives he had wielded in the Hall of Proving, I had a strong suspicion his hands were no longer empty. I stepped between them, facing Brother Merik. "I like this no better than you do," I said to him. "But I think it is Pahrkun's will that I learn from this man." I made myself smile. "Brother Saan has me squeezing rocks. Shall I balk at hopping?"

After a long moment, Brother Merik gave me a brief nod. "I will be watching you," he said to Brother Yarit. "I do not trust you."

Brother Yarit shrugged. "I'll do my best to defy your expectations. Again."

I expected Brother Merik to bristle at that, but he merely shook his head and walked away.

Brother Yarit smoothed his sleeves. "All right. Get hopping, kid."

I pointed at his nearest sleeve with my chin. "Would you have thrown on him?"

"You saw that?" One corner of his mouth curved in a faint smile. "You're observant. Good. No, not unless he'd drawn on me."

"May I see?" I asked.

He hesitated a moment, then pushed up one sleeve to show me a brace of three throwing knives strapped to his forearm; odd, flat little knives wrought of blackened steel nested in a cunning sheath. "They're called *zims*. Hornets, in the traders' tongue."

Honor beyond honor, I told myself.

"Will you teach me to use them?" I asked. "To throw like you do?"

Brother Yarit stared at me for a moment. "What happened to all that high-and-mighty palaver about dishonorable ways? When all's said and done, you're a violent little bugger." He nodded at the *heshkrat* knotted around my waist. "Will you teach me how to use that whatsit?"

I saw no reason to refuse. "Yes."

"Then we've a bargain," he said. "Now get hopping."

I hopped; hopped and hopped up the staircase and down until my thighs were burning. After the midday rest, Brother Yarit made me hop the staircase three more times before taking pity on me.

"Let's try something else." He spilled a satchel of loose pebbles and gravel over the floor of the Dancing Bowl, spreading it about judiciously. "Can you walk across it without making a sound?"

I walked across it as light-footed as I could, but even so, the gravel shifted and crunched under my weight.

Brother Yarit took a deep breath. "Watch." Standing at the edge of the gravel patch, he flexed his knees deeply, centering his weight above his left leg. His right foot reached out slowly, little toe descending first, then the outer blade of his foot. The ball of his foot, then the sole and heel descended with a slow, rolling motion. There was not a single crunch as he shifted his weight from his left to his right leg, then repeated the motion on the other side. Again and again, until he'd crossed the entire distance without a sound.

For the first time, I found myself truly *wanting* to learn what Brother Yarit could teach me. He was strange to me with his dishonorable ways and his coarse language—and I could not yet bring myself to forgive him for Brother Jawal's death—but Brother Saan was right. There were things I could learn from him that I could not learn from anyone else.

Still, I was not quite ready to give him the satisfaction of knowing it. "You wouldn't want to be in a hurry," I observed. "Takes a long time to cross a patch of ground that way."

Brother Yarit snorted. "Yes, and there are different ways of silent walking for different circumstances, most of them faster. But if you need to move over that kind of turf without making a sound, you'd damn well *better* take your time." He nodded at the gravel patch. "Try it again."

It took a lot of effort to move in a deep crouch, but it was the only way to truly control the shift of one's weight from one leg to the other. I began to see the point of Brother Yarit's hopping exercise. I practiced until the shadows grew long and Brother Drajan blew the horn summoning us to dinner.

"You did well, kid," Brother Yarit said to me, genuine sincerity in his voice. "I know it's hard. But give it a month, and you'll be amazed at the progress you make. Give it a year, and you'll be walking like you were born to the clan."

I felt a surge of pride that was not wholly welcome; but not unwelcome, either. I touched my thumbs to my brow in respect, reckoning he was owed that much. "Thank you, brother."

That night I fell aching onto the carpet in my chamber. It was verging into autumn and the day's heat gave way to a chill. I pulled a thick wool blanket over my sore body and slept deep and hard.

I awoke in the small hours before dawn to Brother Saan stooping over me with an oil-wood torch and shaking my shoulder. "Khai," he murmured. "Brother Yarit is gone."

"Gone?" I sat up. "What do you mean *gone*?"

In the torchlight, Brother Saan's pupils were strangely wide and blurred. "He stole a horse and fled when the Bright Moon was yet high. As those who stood the Trial of Pahrkun for him, the duty falls to you and Brother Merik to retrieve him."

Stifling a groan, I crawled out from beneath my blanket. My legs were so sore, I feared at first that they would not hold me. "Yes, Elder Brother."

Brother Saan lit the wick of the little oil lamp in my alcove with his torch. "We will meet at the horse canyon."

My legs wobbled. "Yes, Elder Brother."

I dressed as swiftly as I could, donning a loose-fitting tunic that fell to my knees, wrapping my sash and my *heshkrat* around it and thrusting my dagger into the sash. In the Fortress of the Winds, we were shielded from the worst of the sun's rays, but it would be different in the open desert. I wound a long scarf around my head and neck, securing it with Brother Yarit's—curse him!—garrote, and laced my feet into tough camel-hide sandals. Throwing on my plain white woolen robe, I blew out the lamp and hobbled through the fortress in near darkness, making my way outside and down the long carved stone stairways to the horse canyon, where a cluster of men with torches was gathered.

The crescent of the Bright Moon was visible on the western horizon, and high overhead, the Dark Moon was full, a glowing sphere of ruddy ochre that laid a bloody pall over the landscape.

The horse canyon was long and narrow. Scrub grass and gorse grew there, and there was a brackish watering hole; enough to sustain the few hardy mounts—anywhere from four to six—that the brotherhood kept on hand for errands. There was a wooden gate across its opening and it had been left ajar, but it seemed the remaining horses had better sense than to flee into the open desert. Two of them were saddled and waiting. Brother Tekel, who tended them, stood at their heads.

"Khai." Brother Merik noticed my limping approach and frowned. "Can you ride?"

I made an effort to straighten my stride. "Yes, brother."

Brother Drajan patted a bag lashed behind the cantle of the nearest horse's saddle. "You've two water-skins apiece, dried meat, and a satchel of grain," he said. "I reckon you won't want to stop to forage."

Brother Merik gave a brusque nod of assent and swung effortlessly astride his mount. I followed suit gracelessly, assisted by a boost from Brother Tekel. To be fair, it was a longer step up for me.

"He will have gone due west toward the supplicants' campsite." Brother Saan hoisted his torch and pointed. "It's the nearest watering hole, the only one he can be sure of. By the time you reach it, it should be light enough to pick up his trail. I suspect he will bear northwest and attempt to make his way to Merabaht."

"I trust you want him brought back alive?" Brother Merik sounded as though he hoped otherwise as he took up the reins.

"Yes." Brother Saan turned his strange, blurred gaze on him. "Have a care. The Sacred Twins have left the deep desert and are abroad in the west. I have Seen it."

My breath quickened, wisps of frost escaping my parted lips. Brother Merik was less enthralled by the notion. "I mean no disrespect, Elder Brother, but I would that you'd Seen the villain's escape before it happened," he said in a dour tone.

Brother Saan smiled, and his smile was as uncanny as his gaze. "What makes you think I did not?"

My skin prickled at his words, and Brother Merik's expression changed. He touched his brow with the thumb of one hand. "Forgive me, Elder Brother," he said. "We go forth to do your bidding."

Brother Saan returned his salute with both hands. "Ride with my blessing."

We set out at a slow, steady trot. I had ridden out from the fortress before, but never farther than a hunting excursion and never at this hour. Everything looked strange and unfamiliar in the bloody light of the

Dark Moon. I gazed at the sky overhead, trying to imagine it filled with a thousand upon a thousand sparkling lights, and could not. The air was still, not a hint of breeze, and the sound of the horses' hooves on the arid, stony ground seemed unnaturally loud to me. Then again, perhaps yesterday's lesson with Brother Yarit had made me particularly sensitive to the sound.

I couldn't believe he'd *fled*. It felt like a betrayal, especially after I'd worked so hard yesterday.

I wondered what Brother Saan had meant. If he'd Seen Brother Yarit's escape, why hadn't he prevented it? I pondered these matters in silence, hoping that Brother Merik would weigh in on them. When he didn't, I broke my silence to ask him.

"There's no merit in trying to guess at the Seer's reasoning," he said. "I doubt he could even explain it to the likes of you and me. But as for the Shahalim . . ." He shrugged. "Well, he's a thief, isn't he? I reckon he thought he'd try to steal his life back from Pahrkun."

I frowned. "And cheat the god of his due?"

Brother Merik's teeth flashed in a bloody-looking grin. "I didn't say it could be done, little brother."

As Brother Saan had estimated, although the sun had not yet cleared the mountains behind us, the sky was beginning to pale by the time we reached the supplicants' campsite nearest the fortress. There was a small watering hole in a patch of greenery. It was mostly silted over, but when I dismounted to dig, I saw someone else had done the same not long before me.

"Look." I pointed to the piles of wet sand.

Brother Merik sifted a handful of it through his fingers. "That's our man, all right. I'd say he's a couple hours ahead of us."

I watered the horses, their sweat-dampened hides steaming in the dawn air, while Brother Merik scoured the area for signs of Brother Yarit's passage.

"Looks like he's following the tracks of the king's guardsmen." Brother Merik remounted. "The Bright Moon must have been high enough to make them out when he came through. Why do you suppose he'd head straight back to Merabaht where he was caught?"

I clambered into the saddle, my thighs protesting at the effort. "Maybe he thinks to enter in disguise."

Brother Merik grunted, displeased at the reminder. "Let's make time before the sun catches us, little brother."

In the desert we say *Make haste slowly.* Brother Merik and I resumed our ride at a brisk walking pace as the sun cleared the mountains and began to climb overhead, dispelling the night's chill. Heat began to mount. I shrugged out of my woolen robe, lashing it to the packs behind me.

There was no outrunning the sun. As the morning wore on toward noon, Brother Merik began casting about for shelter. "There should be . . . ah!" Standing in the stirrups, he pointed toward a rocky formation shimmering through the rising heat haze in the distance. "There's an overhang on the leeward side."

It was large enough to provide shade for at least a half a dozen men and horses, but there was no evidence that it had been used in recent days. On Brother Merik's orders, I gave the horses each a handful of grain, then a few mouthfuls of water in a leather bucket. While I tended to them, he stretched out in the shade, crossing his feet at the ankles, folding his arms behind his head, and closing his eyes.

Make haste slowly.

My duties done, I sat in the shadow of the overhang with my arms wrapped around my knees and gazed out at the desert. It shimmered in the heat of the midday sun, dun-colored sandstone interspersed with outcroppings of ochre deepening to rust-red in places.

"Do you suppose Brother Yarit is taking shelter?" I asked.

"If he's got any sense, yes," Brother Merik said without opening his eyes. "He made the crossing with the king's guardsmen, he ought to have learned a thing or two. If he didn't, he's a fool."

I tipped a water-skin and took a mouthful, swishing it around before letting it trickle down my throat. "What if he reckons it's worth the risk to . . . to make haste swiftly?"

Brother Merik cracked open one eye. "Do you think we'll lose him? If the Shahalim is pushing his stolen horse in this heat, it will founder; and we will catch up to him sooner rather than later if it does. We're on his trail.

Trust me, we *will* catch him." He yawned and closed his eyes. "Let the desert teach you patience, little brother."

Brother Merik slept, snoring faintly.

The horses cocked their hips and dozed, heads hanging low. I chewed a meditative strip of dried goat.

The desert shimmered with heat.

I rested my head against my knees and dozed, too.

The rising wind woke me. There was something in it that called to me, that tugged at me, saying *Now now now*.

Brother Merik awoke and caught my sense of urgency. We mounted and began riding westward into the teeth of the wind, moving again at a steady trot. Sand swirled around the horses' legs, plumes dancing across the floor of the desert.

Pahrkun.

I was at once exhilarated and scared. It was one thing to catch a glimpse of one of the Sacred Twins in the distance from the safety of the fortress; it was quite another to face the prospect of encountering one or both in the open desert. Pahrkun and Anamuht guarded the realm to which they were bound, but that didn't mean it was *safe* to be in their presence, no more than it was safe to encounter lightning or a sandstorm or any great force of nature.

The wind toyed with us, rising and falling, changing directions. It rattled pebbles and raised eddies of sand, erasing the signs of the trail we were following. More and more frequently, Brother Merik was forced to dismount to examine the ground at close range, searching for the various signs, the fresh scrapes and gouges and overturned stones, that indicated recent passage; signs that became increasingly scarce. An hour or so after we'd resumed our pursuit, he rose from a futile search and shook his head in a reluctant admission of defeat.

"I'm sorry, little brother," he said. "Either we've lost his trail or it's gone for good. Maybe we should have ridden through the heat of the day." He dusted his hands with a grimace. "Or maybe Pahrkun doesn't want the Shahalim in his service after all."

"Brother Saan wouldn't have sent us on a fool's errand." Out of the corner of my eye, I saw movement. "Look."

There was a column of carrion beetles making their way in a northwest-erly direction. While I watched, a scorpion emerged wriggling from its bur-row and began scuttling across the sand in the same direction.

Brother Merik glanced at me, and there was something in his expression that reminded me of the way he'd looked at Brother Saan. There was a mea-sure of respect in it. I was young, but I was Pahrkun's chosen. I had caught a hawk's feather in my fist. "We follow them?"

I nodded, feeling sure. "We follow them."

The wind continued to rise as we followed the desert insects that were creatures of Pahrkun. Now sand filled the air, dimming the sun. The horses became balky, until at last Brother Merik and I had to dismount and lead them on foot.

"We can't keep this up, Khai!" Brother Merik shouted to me above the roaring wind. "Time to take shelter or—" He halted mid-sentence, craning his neck and staring past me.

I followed his gaze.

A hundred yards from us, Pahrkun the Scouring Wind loomed out of the desert. For the space of a few heartbeats, my wits ceased to function alto-gether. Cloaked in swirling sand, Pahrkun stood mountain-tall. High in the sky, his great black head, long and inhuman, turned this way and that, glowing green eyes set in deep hollows surveying the landscape. I dropped the reins in my hand and fell to one knee, genuflecting without thinking. Beside me, Brother Merik did the same.

I forced myself to my feet, only to fall and genuflect again as Pahrkun moved with slow, graceful strides to reveal a vast tower of flame behind him: Anamuht the Purging Fire. One skeletal bone-white arm emerged from the flames to lift high, lightning crackling in her fist.

Brother Merik was shouting in my ear and pointing.

Anamuht flung her arm forward and a bolt of blue-white lightning struck the barren earth between us. In its sudden glare, the small figure of a man struggling to keep his seat in the saddle of a terrified horse was illuminated.

Brother Yarit.

". . . with the horses!" Brother Merik shouted. "I'll get him!"

Dumbstruck and nigh frozen, I did as he said, gathering up the fallen reins. The horses tossed their heads in protest, fretful and fearful. Brother Merik ran unerringly toward the Shahalim, unwinding his head-scarf as he ran. He wrapped it around Brother Yarit's mount's eyes and began leading them back.

The wind howled.

"Let's go!" Brother Merik cried. "Go, go, ride!"

I tossed his reins to him. Carrion beetles crunched underfoot as I hopped about in an effort to mount my horse. A strong hand grabbed the back of my tunic and hauled me belly-down across my saddle. From this undignified perch, I managed to scramble upright, my feet fishing for the stirrups.

"Watery hell!" Brother Yarit wheezed. His face was coated with a rime of dried sweat and sand, his eyes bleary and bloodshot. "All right, kid. I guess we're stuck with each other."

We rode, the wind dying in our wake.

I glanced over my shoulder once as we fled. The Sacred Twins had vanished into the desert.

FOUR

That night we made camp beneath the overhang where Brother Merik and I had taken shelter at midday.

"Do we need to stand watch over you tonight?" Brother Merik asked Brother Yarit in a weary voice.

The latter smiled without any humor. "I don't expect you to take me at my word, but no. The Sacred Twins' will is clear. I won't be leaving this desert without their consent."

"You accept this as a given truth?" Brother Merik pressed him.

"Yes, brother." Brother Yarit touched his thumbs to his brow, somehow making the gesture a mocking one. "I do not like it, but I accept it." He paused, then continued in a different tone. "I very likely would have died out there if you hadn't come for me. Thank you."

"Thank Brother Saan," Brother Merik said. "It's the Seer who divines Pahrkun's will. *I* wouldn't have bothered."

Brother Yarit shrugged. "Nonetheless." Warming his hands at our small campfire of gorse and dried dung, he gazed westward. "By all the fallen stars, that was a thing to see, wasn't it?" He shuddered. "I thought I was done for."

"I think they just wanted you to turn back," I said. "If the Sacred Twins wanted you dead, you would be." I was still angry at him. "You said we had a bargain."

He stared at me. "What?"

"You said we had a bargain," I repeated. "That you would teach me to throw *zims* if I taught you to use a *heshkrat*."

Brother Yarit let out his breath in a long sigh. "You don't know much about the world, do you, kid? First of all, no one has a bargain with one of the Shahalim if it's not sealed in blood." Pulling out his belt-dagger, he pricked the ball of his right thumb with the point. "Here, give me your hand." I let him prick my thumb in turn, a bead of blood welling. He clasped my hand, pressing the ball of his thumb against mine, our blood smearing together. "In the name of Shahal the Dark Moon, I pledge to honor our bargain. There you are, then."

"That is not our way," Brother Merik said with disapproval.

Brother Yarit gave him a dour look before returning his gaze to the western horizon. "It's been a long time since the Sacred Twins left the deep desert. Do you suppose they mean to continue on to Merabaht?"

"That's a question for the Seer." Brother Merik's frown deepened. "Why? Is the city threatened?"

"Not by outside enemies, no." Brother Yarit scratched his chin. "I'm just wondering. Rumor has it that *rhamanthus* seeds are running in short supply. Anamuht hasn't quickened the Garden of Sowing Time since . . ." He counted on his fingers. "It must be going on a dozen years now."

"What happens if they run out?" I asked.

He gave a short laugh. "Well, then I reckon the House of the Ageless will start aging, won't they? But that's no concern of mine anymore."

I cocked my head. "Was it ever?"

Brother Yarit gave me a shrewd glance. "You *are* an observant one. Yes, little brother. It became a concern of mine when I accepted a commission to attempt to steal a cache of *rhamanthus* seeds."

"Pahrkun has scoured you clean of your sins," Brother Merik said. "We do not speak of what lies in the past."

"Is there anything of interest that isn't more or less forbidden to you lot? Small wonder that I wanted to escape this forsaken place." Brother Yarit stifled a yawn. "Suffice it to say that if I'm ever able to go back to Merabaht, there's a member of the House of the Ageless who owes me a *very* large favor for refusing to divulge her name on pain of death."

So that was why he'd been planning to return. I wanted to hear more, but the look on Brother Merik's face dissuaded me from pursuing the matter.

"Enough," he said firmly. "Today has been a long and arduous one. It is time and more that we slept. Especially you, Khai."

As much as I longed to protest, he was right; as soon as I wrapped my robe tight around me and pillowed my head on my arm, my eyelids grew heavy. I was stiff and sore from the long day's ride as well as yesterday's exertions, and my mind was still reeling from the sheer awe of our encounter with Pahrkun and Anamuht.

Despite Brother Merik's admonition, the men continued to talk in low voices. I caught bits and snatches of their conversation as I drifted in and out of sleep, interspersed with the faint crackling of the fire and the occasional stamp and snort of the hobbled horses.

". . . teach him about the world at some point if he's bound for the House of the Ageless, brother."

Sleep, drifting like a hawk's feather on the wind.

". . . purity in the desert." That was Brother Merik's voice, deep and adamant. "Let him be forged in it. There's time enough for the world."

Drifting.

Drifting.

". . . been cut yet? Pity, but he'll have to be to serve as the princess's shadow," Brother Yarit mused. "Though I suppose it makes sense to wait until he's got his full growth."

Cut?

There was a long pause, long enough that I drifted back down toward sleep, before Brother Merik said, "Khai is *bhazim*."

It was not a word I recognized. Brother Yarit drew in a sharp, surprised breath. "Does he know?"

"No. There is time enough for that, too." Brother Merik's voice took on a note of finality. "Go to sleep."

It was a strange conversation and one I wanted to remember, but exhaustion smoothed the edges of my thoughts, wearing them away like the wind wearing down sandstone.

And, too, there was the memory of Anamuht the Purging Fire and Pahrkun the Scouring Wind towering over everything.

In the first light of dawn there were chores to do; the last of the grain doled out to our mounts; the second-to-last water-skin to be shared among men and horses alike; hobbles to be untied; tack to be secured. Brother Yarit's mount had been in rough shape by the time we made camp, but he hadn't foundered and a night's rest had done him a world of good. We set out for the fortress at a jogging trot, making the most of our time before the sun cleared the mountains in the east. It was a good hour before that half-remembered conversation flickered through my thoughts. In the light of day, my thumb sweating on the reins and stinging where Brother Yarit had pricked it with his dagger, it seemed to me that any reference to cutting must be some further Shahalim custom of blood-letting, one from which I ought to be exempt.

As for the word "*bhazim*," I forgot it entirely. It would be quite some time before I heard it again.

Our return to the Fortress of the Winds was received without fanfare, although Brother Saan met with all three of us separately. I do not know what he said to the others, but Brother Yarit seemed as chastened as I could imagine him. Brother Merik was quietly pleased.

To me, Brother Saan said, "And how did you find your encounter with Pahrkun and Anamuht?"

"Oh!" Words went clean out of my head at the thought of trying to describe it. "It was . . . They were . . ."

He chuckled.

"It was awe-inspiring, Elder Brother," I managed at last. "It was like seeing the very heart and soul of the desert made flesh."

Brother Saan nodded in approval. "Well said, young Khai. The children of the heavens embody the places to which they are bound."

A creeping sense of shame nagged at me. "And yet I stood frozen in their presence, Elder Brother," I confessed. "I dared go no further. It was Brother Merik who led Brother Yarit to safety."

"Yes, and you who led Brother Merik to find him," Brother Saan said. "For now it is enough."

"But one day it will not be?" I asked him.

"You are pledged to Pahrkun the Scouring Wind," he said. "One day you will undergo a trial to determine if that pledge is worthy of being fulfilled. But that day is far from now."

"What manner of trial? Am I to attempt the Hall of Proving?" It surprised me a bit, as it was not required of the desert tribesmen, only criminals like Brother Yarit convicted by the royal judiciary. But then, I was different from both of them. I had been born at the height of the lunar eclipse; I had grasped the hawk's feather.

"No." Brother Saan shook his head. "No, in the end it is Pahrkun himself who will determine whether or not to accept your pledge, not those of us who serve him. You will venture into the deepest desert and seek to encounter the Scouring Wind face-to-face."

I could not help but swallow hard at the prospect. "Did you undergo such a trial, Elder Brother?"

"No." His eyes crinkled with sympathy. "A Seer is born every lifetime. Less is asked of us than of a shadow, whose birth is far more rare. The last man to stand such a trial was Vironesh."

I took a deep breath. "I see."

"Khai." Brother Saan laid his hands over mine. "You did well. Trust. Have patience. Be content to learn."

I bowed my head to him. "Yes, Elder Brother."

My training resumed. I squeezed rocks and hopped up and down the staircase, and bit by bit, the muscles of my wrists and forearms and legs acquired new strength. The three-pronged *kopar* was still too unwieldy for me to use, but I reached the point where Brother Merik deemed me capable of learning the rudiments of the *yakhan* and began teaching me.

There was a great deal to learn. There was a complicated series of slashing strikes one made with the curved outer edge of the blade and straightforward thrusts with the tip. In close quarters, there were reverse thrusts with the spiked pommel, though one had to be careful to avoid fouling the blade. There were backward blows to be struck with the blunt inner curve of the blade. Brother Merik made me practice each and every one of them over and over, first with my right hand, then with my left. I did so with diligence, working toward the day when I should be allowed to spar like a true warrior-in-training. Brother Hakan, who was the smallest in stature, had promised to give me my first bout as soon as Brother Merik consented.

From Brother Yarit, I learned stealth.

I learned the Shahalim ways of walking: the silent toe-rolling step he had first demonstrated to me, the back-to-the-wall crossing walk, the swift heel-toe glide, the crouching walk, the crouching frog walk with splayed fingers and toes. On Brother Saan's orders, Brother Hakan and a few of the other young brothers studied with us, so that the skills might be preserved and passed on within the Brotherhood of Pahrkun.

No one trained harder than I did, for the other warriors were already well versed in the usage of a wind-cutter sword. They needed only to keep the edge of their skills honed, while my fledgling skills were like a blade with no edge that must be ground on the wheel. At least that was how Brother Drajan put it, for he was as at home in a smithy as a kitchen, and taught me how to sharpen and maintain a blade.

When it came to Brother Yarit's teachings, it was another matter altogether, in that I had the advantage of the grown men, who had started training far too late to ever gain full mastery of Shahalim methods. Brother Yarit took a certain grim satisfaction in the knowledge, for he maintained a degree of resentment at being forced to reveal his clan's secrets. But with me, he did not stint; he pushed me harder than he pushed any of the other warriors.

And so it was that I spent every waking hour save my morning lesson with Brother Ehudan and the midday rest training, training, training.

When I slept, I dreamed of training, my limbs twitching in my sleep like one of the dogs the tribesfolk used for hunting.

I grew stronger.

I grew taller, tall enough to deal a solid blow to the third paddle on the spinning devil.

Brother Merik measured the length of my arms and deemed me ready to begin learning to use the *kopar*.

Brother Yarit honored his bargain and began teaching me to throw *zims*, training my hand and eye and mind to work in concert.

I exulted and despaired in these fresh challenges. The *kopar* was a tricky weapon with a long, sharpened prong in the middle flanked by two shorter prongs on either side. Its usage wasn't native to the desert tribesfolk, but rather the city guardsmen of Merabaht. As a defensive weapon, it could be used to deflect or trap other weapons or an opponent's limb at close range; it could be reversed to lay flat along one's forearm to deflect a blow thusly. As an offensive weapon, it could be used to stab and pierce, or to strike with blunt force like a truncheon. When reversed, the heavy pommel could also be used to strike a crushing blow.

Throwing *zims* was easier, at least at first. Oh, but throwing *zims* with anything like the speed and accuracy that Brother Yarit demonstrated—with equal ease with both his right hand and his left—would require years of practice. There was scant consolation in discovering that Brother Yarit found the *heshkrat* a good deal more difficult than he expected.

There were some elements of Shahalim training that Brother Yarit was unable to teach for lack of supplies. As winter gave way to spring, he became more vociferous in his complaints.

"There are no doors in these damned caves," he said to Brother Saan. "How am I supposed to teach Khai to pick a lock? And I need bells and rope and . . . watery hell, the kid's going to need a whole set of his own tools if we're going to make a proper thief out of him."

Brother Merik thumped his fist on the dinner table. "Elder Brother! Surely there must be a limit to this madness. Khai is to serve in a position of honor! Why would he need to know how to pick a lock?"

"I do not know," Brother Saan said mildly. "Only that Pahrkun's will in the matter is clear. What Brother Yarit has to teach, Khai will learn, and it will become a part of our lore. Perhaps it will be important one day. The last shadow failed due to a lack of knowledge regarding poisons." He raised his brows at Brother Yarit. "Can you teach us about poisons?"

"How should I know about poisons?" Brother Yarit said. "The Shahalim are thieves, not assassins."

Brother Saan shrugged. "I had hoped. Perhaps you know someone who does?"

"I—" Brother Yarit paused. "I've heard rumors regarding certain apothecaries, Elder Brother. Send me to Merabaht with your blessing, and I'll find you one."

There was no disguising the note of naked hunger in his voice. Brother Saan shook his head gently. "One day, perhaps, but neither now nor soon, brother. But I *will* send to Merabaht for the supplies you desire. Give Brother Drajan a list of all that you require, and the names of these apothecaries."

"They won't talk to just anyone. You need to send someone who knows the ways of the city." Brother Yarit was not yet ready to admit defeat.

"Brother Drajan is familiar with its ways," Brother Saan said calmly. "Give him your list."

Thus it was determined. Brother Drajan—patient, steady Brother Drajan, whom I had no idea was familiar with the city of Merabaht—was gone for fifteen days, leaving the cooking to his assistant.

It put Brother Yarit in a foul mood. "I hope he brings the oranges I asked for," he grumbled. "Don't you ever get tired of goat meat and stewed squash?"

"No," I said honestly. "What's it like?"

"Oranges?"

I shook my head. "The city."

Brother Yarit glanced around, but we were alone in the Dancing Bowl that afternoon. "It's a glorious place, little brother, filled with taverns where for the price of a bowl of spicy crab noodles and a flagon of date-palm wine, you can hear some of the greatest musicians in the land perform. And the dancing girls!" He kissed his fingertips. "They wear robes and veils of the finest silk from Barakhar, so thin and fine you can almost see right through it."

"Do the Sun-Blessed?" I asked.

"I'm told that in the privacy of the women's quarter, they wear the finest silks of all," Brother Yarit said. "Red and gold, the colors of fire. They wear gold bangles on their wrists and gold anklets with tinkling bells. When they venture out of the Palace of the Sun, they're carried on golden litters, so their precious feet need never touch the ground."

I tried to envision it. "What are they like? Are they very different from you and me?"

"Not as much as they like to imagine," he said dryly. "A long life doesn't always grant wisdom."

"Like the one who commissioned you to steal *rhamanthus* seeds?" I'd been wanting to ask him about it for months. "What was she like? It seems a foolish thing to do."

"Ah." Brother Yarit gave me a wry look. "If you think I was so privileged as to meet a daughter of the Sun-Blessed in the flesh, you're mistaken. The royal women are cloistered in their quarters. Not even Princess Fazarah would deign to meet with the likes of me."

"Which one is she?" I asked.

"The only member of the House of the Ageless to turn her back on the gift of the *rhamanthus*. But that's not something that need concern you right now." He pointed at the throwing target. "Get practicing, Khai. You've got a lot of catching up to do."

Reluctantly, I obeyed.

FIVE

Brother Drajan returned with a string of laden pack-horses, but no apothecary. "These things take time," he said in his unflustered way when Brother Yarit grumbled about it. "They're suspicious. If I return next year with gold in hand, they'll be less so."

It was the only cause Brother Yarit had to gripe, for Brother Drajan had brought everything else he requested, including a sack of oranges. There were padlocks of varying shapes and sizes. There was an array of used garments. There were grappling hooks, yards and yards of rope, and dozens of brass bells, the purpose of which mystified me. There were several sets of *zims* and slender probes for picking locks.

Among the new assignments that these supplies portended, I found picking locks to be the easiest. According to Brother Yarit, it required keen ears and a delicate touch, both of which I had. Beneath Brother Saan's tolerant gaze and Brother Merik's disapproving one, the younger brothers and I practiced picking locks while Brother Yarit stalked the ground of the Fortress of the Winds, wearing coils of rope over his shoulders and muttering to himself.

I tried to imagine under what circumstances I would need to pick a lock in the service of Princess Zariya. What if she ordered me to steal something? That I could not in conscience do.

Or could I?

Oh, but what if she were abducted or falsely accused and I needed to rescue her? That would be an honorable use of my skill. But then, if such a thing came to pass, I would already have failed her, would I not?

One could go mad wondering about the unknowable, so I gave up wondering about it and wondered about the princess instead. Was she vain, riding in her golden litter with her silk robes and veils, her precious feet never touching the ground?

I wondered what Zariya looked like. Was she pretty? What did a pretty girl look like?

What did a *girl* look like?

I had no memory of women or girls; I knew only the men of the Brotherhood of Pahrkun. I had some idea that they were small and fragile, like the desert flowers that blossomed after the spring rains, and must be protected.

I wondered if she wondered about me, her shadow. I wondered if she wondered what *I* was like.

I hoped so.

At length we learned what Brother Yarit was about with the ropes. First, we were to learn to climb them, throwing the grappling hooks and scrambling up sheer cliff faces that afforded no grip to fingers and toes, hauling ourselves up the ropes with strong arms and nimble feet.

Second, we were to learn to walk across a rope that was secured at both ends above the ground.

It should not have been so different than crossing the stone bridge above the Dancing Bowl, and yet it was. Stone stayed put. It might evince a faint tremor beneath bare feet, but it did not *sway*. Rope swayed. No matter how tightly it was tied, it stretched and gave under the weight of a human body, even my lesser weight. It was a good thing Brother Yarit found outcroppings to which to secure his rope that were not high above the ground.

I fell.

Often.

And yet there was something in it, something of balance and wind and the abyss of the fall, that spoke to me.

For the third thing, Brother Yarit begged permission of Brother Saan to use the Hall of Proving. There he tied ropes across it at all manner of angles, low and high and angling in between, and to the ropes, he strung brass bells.

"All you have to do is cross the hall without ringing any bells, kid." He gave me a pat on the shoulder. "Think you can manage?"

I stood straighter. "I do."

"Good." Brother Yarit unwound a scarf from about his neck and tied it around my eyes, then spun me around three times for good measure. "Did I mention you'll be doing it blindfolded?"

I sighed. "No, brother."

I did not succeed the first time or the fifth, but neither did Brother Hakan or any of the others. Still, it taught us to focus and apply the tenets of stealth that he had imparted to us. Blind and disoriented, we crouch-walked through the Hall of Proving, keeping our bodies low and centered, outstretched hands feeling for the first brush of a rope obstacle. We crawled on our bellies beneath some; we high-stepped as carefully as the cranes that Brother Yarit had described to us over others.

None of this sat well with Brother Merik, and he was not alone in his disapproval. One night, returning from a late visit to the privy, I chanced to overhear him lingering over the dinner table in conversation with Brother Drajan and Brother Saan.

My first instinct, learned from my earliest and most honored teachers, was to withdraw out of respect, as I had always done in the past. My second, learned from my latest, was to be silent and listen.

This time, I heeded the latter.

". . . forget the purpose of the Brotherhood of Pahrkun," Brother Merik was saying in a low tone. "First and foremost, it is under our auspices, and ours alone, that the desert tribes will unite to defend Zarkhoum in a time of need."

"I forget nothing," Brother Saan said. "But if Zarkhoum is threatened at the moment, it is from within, not without."

"Because of the *rhamanthus* seeds?"

That was a piece of news Brother Drajan had brought back with him. Anamuht the Purging Fire had not been seen in the city to quicken seeds in the Garden of Sowing Time, and the shortage continued.

"It may be a sign that change is on the horizon," Brother Saan said. "There is discord in the House of the Ageless."

"There is always discord in the House of the Ageless, is there not?" Brother Merik said wryly. "The king's heirs are restless. They are always eager to kill one another, and they have been waiting on *khementaran* to come upon him for the past fifty years."

"Yes, and they may wait another fifty," Brother Saan said. "Regardless, those are the circumstances for which we are training Khai." His voice took on a rare fretful note. "I would that we could locate Vironesh! Broken or not, he is the only living soul who knows what it truly means to serve as a shadow to one of the Sun-Blessed."

"If he yet lives," Brother Merik reminded him.

"I have Seen him in my dreams," Brother Saan murmured. "And I do believe he has a role to play. But wherever he is, it is beyond the scope of my Sight at this time."

Brother Drajan cleared his throat. "A thought, Elder Brother. What if Brother Vironesh is no longer in Zarkhoum?"

There was a pause.

"Where would he go?" Brother Merik asked in an incredulous voice. "Why? And how? In a *boat*?"

"I do not know," Brother Drajan said apologetically. "But it is the one thing we have not considered. Many outland traders hire mercenaries to guard their ships. It is not inconceivable that Vironesh followed this path."

Another pause ensued as they pondered the conceivability of anyone willingly departing Zarkhoum; on a boat, of all things. I will own, I could not conceive it myself.

"It would explain why he has not been seen anywhere in Zarkhoum," Brother Saan mused at length. "Surely, a purple man should not be so difficult to locate otherwise."

A *purple* man? I shook my head, thinking I must have misheard him.

". . . *if* he yet lives," Brother Merik was repeating.

"Yes, yes." Brother Saan's voice took on a more decisive tone. "Brother

Drajan, when you return to Merabaht next spring, you will make extensive inquiries of outland traders."

"Yes, Elder Brother."

"And the concerns I voiced?" Brother Merik inquired.

There was yet another pause. "I do not take them lightly." Brother Saan sounded troubled. "Indeed, in some ways I share them."

"What we discussed, Elder Brother," Brother Merik said. "If we do not take this opportunity to send Khai, there may not be another for some years. If it were to be done, it would be best done before—"

"Yes, yes," Brother Saan said again, interrupting him. "I think we all know what deadline nature imposes upon us." A note of finality entered his voice. "I will think and pray upon the matter."

It was my cue to depart and I took it, my bare feet moving silently on the stone passageways.

In the morning, after I had concluded my lesson with Brother Ehudan, Brother Merik consented to allow me my first genuine bout with Brother Hakan.

It made me forget all thoughts of overheard conversations. Brother Hakan was nineteen years of age, slight of build and only a head and a half taller than me. Being desert-born and reared to it, he was more skilled than I with the *yakhan*, but he wielded the *kopar* no better than me.

We faced off on the floor of the Dancing Bowl with the entire Brother-hood gathered around the perimeter and above to watch. I willed my mind to stillness and took slow, deep breaths, preparing to channel Pahrkun's wind, feeling its warm breath on the bare skin of my chest and arms. Sunlight glinted on our weapons and my blood quickened in my veins. I had fought practice bouts with wooden weapons before, of course, but never steel upon steel.

Brother Hakan . . .

Brother Hakan, whom I thought of as a friend, looked down his nose at me. He was a handsome fellow, usually quick with a smile or a jest, but not today. Today there was contempt in his dark eyes.

He touched the blade of his *yakhan* against the central prong of his *kopar* so lightly that it might almost have been an accident, except that he did it twice, tapping his left foot on the floor of the Dancing Bowl. Click-click-tap.

He did it again.

Click-click-tap.

It was a variant of the traditional tribal challenge of thunder and lightning against an unworthy opponent. One of the watching brothers chuckled, and I felt myself flush with anger and embarrassment.

"To first blood!" Brother Merik raised one arm, fist clenched. "Try not to maim each other, please. Go!"

Filled with fury, I launched a flurry of blows at Brother Hakan. He fell back before my onslaught, deflecting it with ease. I needed to get inside his reach, but his footwork was better than mine. I had spent too much time on stealth-walking, not enough time on fighting. Every time I tried, he pivoted deftly away from me, the blade of my wind-cutter sliding harmlessly off the tines of his *kopar*.

Still, I was faster than him; I *knew* I was faster. I feinted and lunged, only to find him side-stepping with a half turn to avoid my thrust, and that I was already past him and overextended.

Brother Hakan's *kopar* smacked the back of my skull like a truncheon. I staggered, my arms wheeling like the paddles of the spinning devil. With an effort, I managed to catch my balance and turn to face him.

"You—" I began angrily.

He smiled, but it was not his usual smile. His *yakhan* wove in a lazy figure-eight pattern, slow and insulting. "Yes, little brother?"

I trapped his blade with my *kopar*. "Ha!"

That was the last syllable I spoke before Brother Hakan struck me a smart blow to the center of the forehead with the butt-end of his *kopar*; a blow that raised a lump and split the skin.

I dropped like a stone.

The blue sky was black and full of spangles, and there was no feather floating in it. I had not earned Pahrkun's favor today, that was certain. My head was ringing like a sounding-bowl. I blinked my eyes, trying to clear my vision. Something dark loomed between me and the sun. I couldn't make out Brother Saan's face, but I knew the shape of his head.

His voice drifted down from above me. "What is a warrior's first and greatest weapon, young Khai?"

I winced. He was right, of course. I'd allowed myself to lose my temper and fight from a place of anger. "His mind, Elder Brother."

"Even so." The dark shape withdrew.

I lay on my back and waited for the world to stop spinning. When at last I managed to sit upright, Brother Hakan extended a helping hand to me. His disdainful expression had given way to an apologetic one. I gave him a sour look in return. "Did Brother Saan bid you to bait me?"

"No," he said. "Brother Merik."

I accepted his hand and let him help me to my feet. I could feel warm blood trickling down my forehead, parting over my nose to form rivulets on either side. "Well done, then."

"There's more to a true warrior's skill than mastery of weapons." Brother Merik came over to clap me on the back. "And now you'll have a scar to remind you. Come, let's get you bandaged."

I did my best to receive the lesson with humility, but it stung.

In some ways, I suppose it put me in a more receptive mood for that afternoon's lesson with Brother Yarit. Mindful of the lingering dizziness from my injury, he elected to forgo the usual grueling physical challenges to take a new approach, gathering our small group in the relative coolness of the training chamber.

"Let us have an exercise in thought," he said. "You've all learned certain skills. What do you suppose would be the best way to, shall we say, infiltrate the Palace of the Sun?"

"Scale the walls under the cover of night," Brother Hakan offered with the prompt confidence of a man who was having a particularly good day.

"Wrong." Brother Yarit upended a satchel, dumping out the clothing and various other implements that Brother Drajan had brought from Merabaht. "Attention is like water. It goes where it is directed." Picking through the garments, he selected a white tunic and a wide-legged pair of breeches, and a long woolen sash striped with crimson and gold, the nap worn thin in places. "This is the standard livery of palace servants." He tossed the garments to Brother Hakan. "Put it on."

Somewhat disgruntled, Brother Hakan complied.

"Congratulations," Brother Yarit said. "You're now invisible." He handed Brother Hakan a silver platter. "Now pretend you're about some important errand on which your master has sent you."

Brother Hakan's nostrils flared. "My *master?*"

"And now you're no longer invisible," Brother Yarit said wryly. "Now you've drawn attention to yourself."

"I am a proud son of the Standing Rock Clan, not some errand boy," Brother Hakan retorted.

"Right." Brother Yarit took the platter from him. "Attention flows like water. Direct it away from you." Balancing the platter on one hand, he crossed the floor of the training chamber with quick, purposeful steps, his gaze alert and watchful, yet averted in a deferential manner. "See?"

I saw.

Brother Yarit set down the platter. "Suppose you wish to go unseen on the streets of Merabaht in broad daylight," he suggested. "How do you propose to accomplish *that?*"

"Another guise?" I frowned. "But I do not know the city to guess what guise may pass unnoticed."

"Fair point, kid." Rummaging through the attire, he picked out a hooded cloak of ragged dun-colored wool. He rolled his shoulders, cocked his head from side to side, and then pulled the hood over his head and hunched, hobbling forward with bent spine and bowed legs. "Where the House of the Ageless rules, youth, or at least the semblance of it, is prized." He poked his face out from the hood's shadow. "People look away from those who are old and impoverished, and do not have the luxury of awaiting *khementaran* to come upon them."

Out of the corner of my eye, I caught sight of Brother Saan pausing to watch from one of the passageways, and I felt bad knowing that he was hearing this, for it seemed disrespectful to me.

In that, I was not alone.

"It is not so in the desert," Brother Eresh, who was only a few years older than Brother Hakan, said in a heated tone. "We are wise enough to revere the wisdom of our elders!"

In the background, Brother Saan raised his eyebrows. His expression was thoughtful and troubled.

Brother Yarit straightened. "Did I say you weren't? I'm just doing what I understand to be my duty." He shrugged out of the cloak and held it out. "Who's ready to give it a try?"

I glanced toward Brother Saan, but he was gone.

SIX

On the following day, Brother Saan announced that he intended to retreat from the world and hold a vigil to allow Pahrkun's will to manifest with greater clarity.

For three days, he would seclude himself atop a high butte in contemplation, taking neither food nor water.

Brother Yarit was beside himself, railing. "Do you understand that he will *die* out there, kid?" he demanded. "Look, I know he's a tough old buzzard, but three days in the desert heat without shade or water?" He shook his head. "He won't survive it."

"Brother Saan knows what he is doing," I said loyally.

"Does he?" he asked me, then whirled on Brother Merik, who was passing. "Does he? Or is this some . . . I don't know, some grandstanding form of mystical self-immolation?"

Brother Merik frowned; I was not sure he understood precisely what Brother Yarit was suggesting any more than I did. "It is dangerous, yes. But he is the Seer."

"And how, exactly, will that prevent him from dying of thirst or exposure?" Brother Yarit inquired.

"He is the Seer," Brother Merik repeated. "If Brother Saan's death were upon him in this venture, he would have Seen it."

"And yet by his own admission, he's going out there because his Sight lacks clarity." Brother Yarit threw up his hands in disgust. "I swear by all the fallen stars, you people are addled. It would serve you right if Elder Brother dies out there and leaves you without a Seer."

I caught my breath at his words, but Brother Merik only regarded him with weary patience. "So long as Pahrkun the Scouring Wind abides in the deserts of Zarkhoum, there will be a Seer. Have no fear, Brother Saan's successor has already been chosen."

"He has?" This was news to me. "Who is it?"

Brother Merik spared me a small smile. "As to that, I cannot say, young Khai. When Elder Brother's death comes for him, his gift will pass to another; but who that will be, only Pahrkun knows."

Thus it was a relief when Brother Saan returned from his vigil on the morning of the fourth day. We gathered in the Dancing Bowl to await him, leaving off our training at the first sight of him. He made the long, slow descent from the high butte with careful steps. Brother Eresh ran to assist him, and I chided myself for not doing the same when Brother Saan accepted his assistance, leaning on his arm.

For the first time, Brother Saan looked *old*; old and worn and frail, his lean, ropy muscles withered on his bones. His brown skin was burned darker by the unrelenting sun. And yet his sunken eyes were wide and strange and blurred, and there was a brightness upon him, a brightness that seemed to emanate from the very marrow of his fragile old bones, as though the desert had worn him to his finest essence.

In the Dancing Bowl, we fell silent.

"Such an audience!" Brother Saan laughed a parched, creaky laugh, a laugh that gave way to a cough. "Water?"

Brother Merik proffered a water-skin. "Elder Brother."

He drank deep, rivulets spilling on either side of his chin, then wiped his mouth. "Ah, that's good." His gaze settled upon me. "Khai."

I placed my palms together and saluted him, touching my thumbs to my brow. "Yes, Elder Brother?"

"Khai." He lifted his vision-filled gaze to the sky, the empty sky. "Oh, Khai! Perhaps Zar the Sun in his heaven can see the pattern of the path that lies before you in its entirety, but I cannot. It is filled with strange turns and branchings, and where it will lead you will depend upon the choices you make. Therefore, I deem it fitting that you continue to study any such skills as may assist you on your path."

"Then I shall." I did not know what else to say.

"Good." He drank again, coughed again. "But before one may aspire to such a thing as honor beyond honor, there must be an understanding of *honor*. I have made a decision. In a month's time, the gathering of the clans will take place, and there is a matter of honor to be addressed. " He pointed at me. "You will return Brother Jawal's bones to his family and inform them that he perished in the service of Pahrkun."

I saluted again. "Yes, Elder Brother."

"You will accompany him." Brother Saan's wavering finger pointed at Brother Merik, who saluted him. His finger wavered, wavered, and steadied to point at Brother Yarit. "And you."

"Oh, watery hell!" Brother Yarit muttered.

Despite the grave matter of the undertaking, I was excited. From time to time, folk from the desert tribes visited to trade or seek the Seer's counsel or escort one of their members into Pahrkun's service, and they seemed very glamorous to me with their hunting dogs and falcons, and the tall camels with their great fatty humps and long, swaying necks. The gathering of the clans took place in the mild days of autumn at the great oasis that was a ten-day ride to the southeast. It was a time to trade, to settle blood-feuds, and to arrange marriages. On Brother Saan's orders, I spent the days prior to our departure concentrating on training with the *yakhan* and *kopar*, which irked Brother Yarit, who complained of the interruption to my studies of the Shahalim arts.

On the day before our departure, we retrieved Brother Jawal's bones from the bier atop the high plateau where they rested. It had been almost a year since his death and the desert had done its work; his bones had long since been picked clean by scavengers and bleached by the sun.

Brother Saan wrapped them reverently in a soft piece of tanned goat hide. "Jawal of the Ardu, son of the Black Sands Clan, Pahrkun the Scouring Wind honors your service and your sacrifice," he said in a formal tone. "Khai, you knew him well. Do you accept the task I lay upon you?"

"I do," I said.

He laid the packet in my arms. It was unwieldy, but it weighed a good deal less than I would have guessed. "Then I charge you with returning

Brother Jawal's bones to his family." He paused, studying me. "Honor his memory."

"I will, Elder Brother," I promised.

For a moment, it seemed that Brother Saan meant to say something further. The strange inward brightness that had been upon him since his vigil had never quite left, and his gaze was unsettling. But in the end, he glanced at the sky and shook his head, then smiled at me with surpassing gentleness, placed his hands on my shoulders, and kissed my brow with wrinkled lips.

"Pahrkun guide your steps, young Khai," he said to me, then saluted. "We will await your return."

Tears stung my eyes; I didn't know why.

It was an arduous journey, but an uneventful one. Brother Merik used the time to further my instruction in the ways of surviving and negotiating the harsh conditions of the desert, pointing out landmarks where they existed, demonstrating methods of triangulating around the trackless sand where they did not.

Brother Yarit . . .

Well, he complained a fair amount, which I expected. But eventually he grew weary of his own complaining, and instead chose to regale us with tales of his former life in Merabaht, all the myriad charms the city had to offer, and his prowess as a master thief of the Shahalim.

I did not always believe him, for some of the tales he told seemed impossible; and yet I will own, I enjoyed them.

Brother Merik was less amused. "Why, in Anamuht's holy name, would *anyone* want a Granthian stink-lizard?" he inquired after one particularly unlikely story unfolded on the fifth day.

"People want what they cannot have." Brother Yarit shrugged. "The Shahalim do not ask why. We ask *how*."

Brother Merik grunted. "I would ask *why*. Do you forget that Granthian stink-lizards nearly destroyed this realm?"

"Yes, well, that was a long time ago." Brother Yarit flashed him an impertinent grin. "It was only one little egg. Once it hatched, the client paid double to have it returned."

So passed our journey. On the tenth day, we spotted the oasis. It shimmered on the horizon like a mirage, except it did not vanish as we drew near.

Water.

It was a vast expanse of water, more water than I had ever seen in one place, low and flat, reflecting the sky like a great blue eye—the Eye of Zar, the tribesfolk called it. It was ringed around with date palms and greenery, tents and standards and camels and horses and goats and dogs and men. I stood in my stirrups and stared, awed by the sight.

As we drew near, Brother Merik unfurled our standard and held it aloft to reveal the carrion beetle that symbolized the Brotherhood of Pahrkun. I wondered, not for the first time, why one of Pahrkun's nobler creatures had not been chosen to represent him. Brother Saan had told me that one day I would understand.

A pair of riders peeled away from the nearest verge of the campsite and came to intercept us. "Good greetings and welcome!" one of them called. "What brings the Brotherhood to the gathering of the clans?"

"A matter of honor," Brother Merik replied. "We come bearing the bones of a son of the desert. He was an Ardu of the Black Sands Clan."

"Ah." The other rider nodded in sympathetic understanding. "You'll find the Ardu camp on the eastern side of the lake."

We thanked them and rode onward. I could not keep from staring. There was so much to see, so many people and animals! The men wore white tunics and breeches like my own, but their robes and sashes and head-scarves flaunted bright colors and intricate embroidery.

Children darted underfoot, and here and there . . . women.

The women wore long robes of white and blue and yellow, and elaborate headpieces that rose to a point, with long veils that covered their faces and shoulders, embroidered in patterns meant to evoke the flames of Anamuht. The folds of their veils swayed as they walked, dark eyes gleaming behind the oblong holes cut out of the fabric to allow them to see.

Brother Yarit heaved a wistful sigh. "It's been a long time."

Brother Merik gave him a sharp look. "Don't even think it unless you want to lose a limb."

Brother Yarit raised his hands. "Merely an observation."

In the encampment of the Ardu tribesfolk, we found the standard of the Black Sands Clan, black and white with a yellow circle, planted outside a large tent. There was a leather strip with bells attached to it affixed to the poles of the doorway. Brother Merik dismounted and shook the strip, causing the bells to jingle.

A young man emerged. Seeing the standard of the Brotherhood, he touched his brow in respect. "Yes, brothers?"

"We come on a matter of honor," Brother Merik repeated in a formal tone. "Bearing the bones of a son of the desert."

The young man's expression changed. "I will fetch my father."

"Brother Saan laid this charge upon you, Khai," Brother Merik said quietly. "The task is yours to complete."

Now it truly seemed a heavy burden to bear. I dismounted and unlashed the bundle of Brother Jawal's bones from the pack-horse that bore them. Brother Yarit dismounted, too. The three of us stood waiting, while I held forth Brother Jawal's bones on my outstretched arms like some dire offering.

A man of middle years emerged from the tent. His features were weathered, but he had strong black brows that dipped to meet over the beak of his nose. "I am Jakhan of the Ardu, chieftain of the Black Sands Clan." He looked askance at the bundle I bore. "I fear you bring grave tidings."

Now I did not want to be the one to inform this man that his son was dead, but Brother Merik stood silent beside me. And Brother Yarit . . . well, Brother Yarit had killed him.

I had accepted this duty; it was mine.

"I am Khai of the Fortress of the Winds," I said. "We come bearing the bones of Jawal of the Ardu, son of the Black Sands Clan. He perished in the service of Pahrkun the Scouring Wind."

"Oh, my son," the chieftain murmured. He took the bundle from my arms, cradling it in his own. "My son!"

"I am sorry," I said to him. "He was my friend and teacher."

His gaze searched my face, fierce and anguished. "Did my son die with honor?"

"Yes." I did not hesitate. If there was dishonor in the manner of Brother

Jawal's death, it was through no fault of his. "He was slain at the first post in the Trial of Pahrkun."

Chieftain Jakhan's eyes flashed. "The villain who killed my eldest son must have been a very great warrior!"

This time, I did hesitate.

"Not really, no," Brother Yarit said in an unsteady voice. "But he possessed great cunning and did not wish to die."

The chieftain's right hand fell to the hilt of his *yakhan,* his left arm yet cradling his son's bones. "You."

Brother Yarit folded his palms and touched his brow. "Yes."

"Cunning." The chieftain's upper lip curled in disdain at the word. He glanced at Brother Merik. "You are desert-born, are you not?"

Brother Merik inclined his head. "Merik of the Sanu, son of the Hot Spring Clan."

"Tell me, Merik of the Sanu, why does the Seer send me the bones of my son in the arms of a mere child?" Chieftain Jakhan inquired in a cool tone. "Why does he insult my clan and my tribe by sending this cunning man who killed him?"

Until this moment, it had not occurred to me that our mission was a dangerous one, save for the usual dangers of the desert. After all, we were conducting Pahrkun's business at Brother Saan's bidding, were we not?

And yet Brother Saan had allowed Brother Yarit to escape. It was true, there was no guessing at the Seer's reasoning.

"Have the tribesfolk forgotten that there was a shadow born to the Princess Zariya the Sun-Blessed?" Brother Merik asked. "One day, young Brother Khai will serve in the court of the House of the Ageless in Merabaht. Before that day comes, the Seer would have him understand the honor of the desert."

"Ah." The chieftain nodded. "There is wisdom in that. But what of the cunning man?"

Brother Merik shook his head. "I cannot say."

"Neither can I," Brother Yarit muttered. "I'm sorry for your son's death, but I won't apologize for not dying." He lifted his chin in a defiant jerk. "I didn't make the fucking rules!"

People were beginning to look, and the air felt tight and tense, making my shoulder blades prickle. "None of us understand the whole of the Seer's mind save Pahrkun himself," I heard myself say. "We are here. We have brought your son's bones. Will you dishonor *his* memory and deny us hospitality?"

For a long moment, Chieftain Jakhan glowered at me. "Do you think to test me, young shadow?"

I stood my ground. "Brother Jawal was my friend and teacher. He taught me to throw the *heshkrat.*"

An unexpected hint of tears glimmered in the chieftain's eyes. "My eldest had a good arm, did he not?"

I nodded. "The best."

Still cradling the bundle of his son's bones in his left arm, Chieftain Jakhan took his right hand from the hilt of his *yakhan* and swept aside the flap closing the doorway of his tent, opening it wide. "I will see that your horses are tended to. Come and be welcome, brothers of Pahrkun."

SEVEN

Inside the tent, it was warm and spacious. It smelled of good meat seasoned with unfamiliar spices. There was an elaborate tea service on the carpet-lined floor and a curtain of felt that hung from the midpoint, dividing the tent in two parts. Behind it were voices; women's voices, higher-pitched and more melodious than men's, engaged in some manner of singing game.

Two young men rose as we entered; the one who had first greeted us and another who had his father's strong brows.

"Yasif, Khisan," the chieftain said to them. "Make our guests welcome, serve them tea. I must speak to your brother's mother."

One inclined his head.

The other scowled at us.

Chieftain Jakhan ducked behind the curtain. The sound of laughter and singing stopped. There was a single wail, cut short and muffled as though whoever uttered it had clamped a hand over her mouth.

"Please, sit and drink, brothers." Fine beads of sweat formed on Yasif's brow. "May I pour you tea?"

I glanced at Brother Merik, who knew the ways of the tribesfolk. He demurred three times, accepting on the fourth. Brother Yarit and I did the same. We sat cross-legged on the carpets and sipped mint tea.

Behind the curtain, low murmuring voices and a few quiet sobs broke the uncomfortable silence.

Khisan of the strong brows continued to scowl. "You've come at an inauspicious time."

"There is no good time to deliver such tidings," Brother Merik replied.

"But the gathering of the clans is the only time we might be certain of finding your people."

"Yes, of course." Yasif sounded as though he'd like to apologize for his brother's rudeness. "It is only that we have declared blood-feud against the Sweet Meadow Clan. The Matriarch of the Ardu has granted our petition to redeem our honor this very day. We fight at dawn."

"How many?" Brother Merik inquired.

"We are eight men of fighting age." Khisan glanced at his brother. "They are nine."

Brother Merik sipped his tea. "A pity."

Khisan eyed him. "Yes." Without excusing himself, he rose and went to join his father behind the curtain.

"Forgive his manners," Yasif said. "My brother has always been hot-headed."

"Tempers run high on the eve of battle," Brother Merik said. "What is the cause of this blood-feud?"

Yasif poured more tea for us. "My father refused their suit for our eldest sister's hand. They stole his prized camel and slaughtered it in retaliation."

It all seemed strange and exotic to me, this business of mothers and sisters and marriage suits. I glanced at the hanging curtain, wondering about the world of womenfolk and family that existed behind it. I wished we had not come on such a grave errand and at such an inauspicious time.

"Why did your father refuse their suit?" Brother Yarit sounded genuinely curious.

Yasif's expression darkened. "Because the chieftain of Sweet Meadow Clan is the sort of man who would steal a camel and slaughter it simply because he did not get his way," he said. "Our sister deserves better."

His father and brother returned. "There is food prepared," Chieftain Jakhan announced. "You will dine with us now."

A great platter of roasted goat meat and rice was brought out to us by one of the women. Wife or daughter, I could not guess at first, for although she did not wear the tall headdress indoors, her scarf was wrapped around her face to veil her features all the same. Then I thought to look to her hands, for as Brother Yarit had taught me, the hands do not lie. Her hands were worn with age in much the same way that the chieftain's face was weathered, and I guessed then that she must be his wife. I wondered if Yasif and Khisan were grateful to have a mother, to have sisters. I wondered if I were sorry that I did not; or at least that I did not know them if I did. I could not say.

The food was tasty. I watched Brother Merik out of the corner of my eye to make sure I took no more than was seemly, and saw Brother Yarit do the same. Even so, it was an uncomfortable meal, and I was glad when I saw Brother Merik wipe his fingers on his sash to indicate that he was finished.

"An excellent meal, Chieftain Jakhan," he said politely. "We thank you for your hospitality."

The chieftain looked surprised. "You cannot mean to leave yet!" He nodded in my direction, and his voice took on an edge. "Not when your own shadow has reminded me of my duty. You will sleep beneath our tent tonight."

"I cannot ask you to house us when I have kin of my own in the Sanu camp," Brother Merik demurred. "Certainly not on the eve of battle."

"Battle, yes." The chieftain's features hardened, and I realized that this wasn't about hospitality after all, but something far more serious. "*Battle* is exactly what I wish to discuss with you, brother." He pointed at Brother Yarit. "You have brought this man who killed my son into my tent, this cunning man with his disrespectful tongue."

"I've barely said a fucking thing!" Brother Yarit protested.

"See?" the chieftain said grimly. "*I* say there is a debt of honor owing between us. Tomorrow one of you will stand and fight with the Black Sands Clan, Merik of the Sanu; you or the cunning man."

Something tickled at my thoughts . . .

Brother Merik was shaking his head. ". . . know as well as I do that that is impossible. We are sworn to Pahrkun's service. We are forbidden to take part in tribal blood-feuds."

I followed the thing tickling at my thoughts as though it were a hawk's feather, drifting, drifting, ignoring the rising voices.

". . . *cunning* man . . ."

". . . the fucking rules!"

"... son's bones ..."

Yasif and Khisan were glancing back and forth, following the argument with fascination.

"I will do it!" I announced. Everyone ignored me. I rose to my feet and repeated it. "I will do it!"

They fell silent. A slit in the curtain dividing the tent stirred and I had the impression of unseen eyes watching.

"Khai, you cannot," Brother Merik said to me. "You are sworn to—"

"No," I interrupted him. "I am pledged to Pahrkun's service, but he has not yet accepted it. There is a trial I must yet stand before he deems me worthy. Brother Saan told me so."

"Still—"

"He bade me honor Jawal's memory," I said. "He sent me here to gain an understanding of honor. He Saw this."

Brother Merik took a long, slow breath but made no response. The chieftain looked thoughtful.

"You cannot be serious!" Khisan said incredulously, gesturing dismissively toward me. "He's only a boy. He's nowhere near fighting age. He'll only get in our way and worsen our odds."

Chieftain Jakhan turned his deep-set gaze on me. "Is that so?"

There was no wind in the tent. I wished I could feel its touch against my skin. Pahrkun's breath was always stirring in the Fortress of the Winds. I thought about Brother Jawal's grin as he taught me the ways of thunder and lightning, and I thought about Brother Hakan baiting me.

Shifting to confront Khisan, who was still seated, I clapped my hands together twice and stamped my left foot on the carpet, then repeated the gesture; clap-clap-stamp, clap-clap-stamp.

Khisan leapt to his feet, blood suffusing his face. "You little—"

"Khisan, *sit*!" His father's voice was sharp with command. Khisan hesitated, then obeyed grudgingly. "You challenge my son to thunder and lightning?"

I withdrew my *yakhan* and my *kopar* from my sash, laying them both on the carpet, then touched my brow in salute. "I do."

"So be it." Chieftain Jakhan rose. "Let us see if you are fighter enough to stand with the Black Sands Clan on the morrow."

Outdoors, we gathered in an open area between tents where the sandy soil was packed hard and flat. Word of the challenge spread quickly throughout the camp, and within minutes, a crowd had gathered.

In the center of the ring that had formed, Khisan unwound his head-scarf. His bristly black hair was cut short and close to his skull. He kicked off his sandals, shrugged off his robe, untied his *heshkrat* and sash, and stripped off his tunic, tossing everything aside. He was a young man of prime fighting age, his lean brown body corded with muscle, and he paraded around the ring to shouts and cheers.

I slid loose the garrote that bound my hair back and unobtrusively unbuckled the braces of *zims* concealed beneath my sleeves. Brother Yarit was on hand to take them from me. "You only get one chance to play the element of surprise, kid," he muttered. "Remember what I taught you."

Nodding, I shed my sandals and sash and tunic, handing them to him. "I'll do my best."

A wave of laughter, mostly good-natured, arose from the tribesfolk as I stepped into the ring opposite Khisan. A few people called out for him to take it easy on me; others taunted him, which made him clench his jaw. But there were other murmurs that ran beneath the current, murmurs that spoke of the Sun-Blessed and a shadow.

I stooped to touch the sandy soil, letting a few grains run through my fingers. "Pahrkun, I am your instrument," I whispered. "If it is your will I do here today, grant me honor."

"Are we fighting or not, little boy?" Khisan spread his arms wide. "I'm ready when you are."

I straightened. "I am ready."

The sun was hovering above the western horizon. Khisan sidled sideways, forcing me to either take a stand or retreat so that the sun was in my eyes, thinking to play on my youth and inexperience.

I retreated, letting him think he had won that small victory. Light filled my eyes, and Khisan's figure was a black silhouette before me. Still, it was enough that I could tell by his flex-legged stance that he expected me to strike low and fast, trying to use my quickness and small stature to get inside his greater reach, just as I had tried with Brother Hakan. That, then, was exactly what I would *not* do. I darted forward and feinted to the right; the chieftain's son threw a great, buffeting blow that would have knocked me to the ground if it had landed.

It didn't, for I had never actually intended to be there.

Overbalanced, Khisan stumbled, cursed, and recovered; too late. From a standstill, I launched myself skyward, higher than he could have guessed, lashing my left leg out in a simple forward kick.

Boom.

The ball of my left foot thundered against his chin. I heard his teeth click together. His eyes rolled up in his head as he crumpled to the ground.

There was a brief stunned silence followed by laughter and cheers. "Does that answer your question?" I asked Chieftain Jakhan.

He smiled wryly. "At the expense of my son's pride, yes. We welcome your aid. Will you not sleep beneath our tent tonight?"

I glanced at Brother Merik, but he offered no response and his expression gave me no indication. I pondered the matter. In the ring, Yasif was helping his brother to his feet. Khisan looked furious and embarrassed, and I had no great wish to sleep in his company that night.

"I would not presume upon your hospitality while there is a debt of honor between us," I said, choosing my words with care. "And I know Brother Merik is eager to see his kin. Thus we will pass this night with the Hot Spring Clan. If we are victorious on the morrow, do you declare the debt between us settled?"

"I do," the chieftain said.

"Then we will be grateful to accept your hospitality," I said.

He gave a nod of approval. "Fairly spoken. I will send Yasif for you at dawn. We fight on foot," he added. "The Matriarch has decreed no further livestock shall be slain in the settling of this feud."

Retrieving my weapons and our mounts, we rode to the southern side of the oasis, where the Sanu clans were camped. Brother Yarit—who, in fairness, had been reasonably close-mouthed in the presence of Jawal's kin—was filled with chatter and questions, the latter of which Brother Merik fielded with terse answers, his thoughts obviously elsewhere.

"Given that your people are nomads, why is it that all the clans are named after places?" It was the fourth or fifth such question that Brother Yarit had posed. "It seems a bit contradictory if you ask me."

Brother Merik sighed. "Which I did not do." Turning in the saddle, he rounded on me. "Khai, do you have *any* idea how lucky you were?"

"I was no such thing!" I said indignantly. Having spent countless hours hopping up and down stairs, I reckoned my leaping ability was more than fairly won. "I did what he didn't expect."

"I am not speaking of *that*," Brother Merik said grimly. "I am speaking of tomorrow's battle. Did you hear what the chieftain said?"

"I . . . yes."

He fixed me with a hard stare. "I don't love your chances, little brother, but I don't hate them, either. The tribesfolk don't use the *kopar*. But if this battle were fought on horseback . . ." He shook his head. "You'd be dead."

I licked my lips, which had gone dry. "The possibility hadn't occurred to me, brother."

"Nor me," Brother Merik said. "But it should have. I've gotten soft in the ways of the desert."

"Would you have forbidden Khai if it *had* occurred to you?" Brother Yarit inquired.

Brother Merik shot him a dour look. "Of course."

"Then maybe it's for the best it didn't." Brother Yarit grinned. "Did you see how high the kid jumped? That hothead never saw it coming."

A faint smile tugged at the corner of Brother Merik's mouth. "No, he most surely did not." We rode in silence for a few paces. "There isn't sufficient grazing for any clan to stay in one place," he added presently. "That's why we travel. But every clan has one campsite we consider home. That's where we bring the bones of our dead. That's the place from which we take our names."

"I see." Brother Yarit flashed another impudent grin. "That wasn't so hard, was it, brother?"

Brother Merik ignored the comment. "Khai, there is a thing I must ask of you. When you need to relieve yourself, let me know, and Brother Yarit or I will accompany you to the latrine." He hesitated. "The men of the tribesfolk do not hold privacy in these matters in high regard as we do in the Fortress of the Winds, and . . . and it is possible you have made enemies here today."

"A man's never so vulnerable as when he's shitting," Brother Yarit added. "Which is also a handy thing to remember."

"And as for you." Brother Merik pointed at him. "*You* will exercise some of that famous Shahalim discipline and keep a civil tongue in your mouth. I don't care how city folk talk. This is the desert and every curse word you utter is a slap in your host's face. Understood?"

"Yes, brother." He seemed genuinely chastened.

"Khai?"

I saluted with one hand. "Yes, brother."

Our welcome in the camp of the Hot Spring Clan could not have been more different from the one we received from the Black Sands; although to be sure, we were about a very different mission. In the light of the setting sun, Brother Merik's kinfolk spilled out of their tents to greet him with shouts and warm embraces. So many introductions were made, my head spun at the thought of remembering everyone's names. Our mounts were whisked away to be untacked and pastured in a patch of scrubby grass that was allocated to the clan, and we were ushered into the largest tent in short order. Offers of tea and food were pressed upon us, and when we demurred and said we'd already eaten, they insisted on bringing out a platter of sweets made of almond paste.

I will own, it was a bit overwhelming. There were men and boys of all ages crowded into the tent, and silky-haired hunting dogs with lean bellies that lay where they pleased; and yet there was a certain comfort in the chaos.

Chieftain Saronesh, Brother Merik's uncle, was an elegant old man with a long silver beard that was much admired as a sign of virility among the tribesfolk.

"So, young shadow," he addressed me when Brother Merik ducked behind the dividing curtain to pay his respects to his female kin. "We hear you fought quite the bout of thunder and lightning today."

I opened my mouth to reply, then paused to consider. I did not like Khisan, or at least what little I knew of him, but it would be unkind to disrespect him further. "My opponent fought in the heat of anger and grief. Another day, it might have gone differently."

He clapped his hands. "Well spoken! I am pleased to know that my nephew has taught you good manners."

I smiled at the old chieftain. "It is an honor to hear you say so."

Brother Yarit shoved a square of almond paste into his mouth and muttered something inaudible.

"Father!" A young man—a boy, really—who couldn't have been more than a year or so older than me burst into the tent. "The Wandering Moon is rising!" He was breathless with excitement, his eyes sparkling. "That means all three will be on high! Vahalan of Tall Grove Clan sent me to tell you the Matriarch of the Sanu says anyone who wishes to bathe in the waters of the Eye of Zar and seek the Three-Moon Blessing tonight may do so."

The old chieftain raised his brows. "Is that so?"

The boy flung himself at his father's feet, clasping his ankles in an exaggerated gesture of pleading. "Can we go, Father? Please?"

Chieftain Saronesh chuckled. "So much passion to expend over a little splashing in the moonlight! Yes, I suppose so. Go tell your mother."

"Thank you, Father!" Leaping to his feet, the boy planted a resounding kiss on his father's cheek, then dashed past the curtain.

Within minutes, the entire lot of us were traipsing through the camp toward the lake, men and women separating into two streams; and it seemed nigh every single one of the clans was doing the same. In the sky above us, Nim the Bright Moon was full, bathing the oasis in silvery light. Shahal the waning Dark Moon shone red as a garnet, and there on the eastern horizon was Eshen the Wandering Moon, a pale blue crescent, speckled like an egg and surrounded by a faint nimbus. All three of their faces were reflected in the shimmering black expanse of the water, and it was a magical sight, as though the faces of Zar's three divine lovers were reflected in the pupil of his vast eye.

Following the lead of the others, I took off my scarf and sandals in the thick sedge grass around the edge of the lake and hiked my breeches to my knees before wading into the calf-deep water. The night air was cool, but the water retained the warmth of the day's sun. It felt strange to be immersed in it, my feet and shins moving sluggishly against the resistance of so much liquid.

All around, people were laughing and splashing, scooping up handfuls of water and pouring them over one another's heads.

"You're the shadow, right?" The boy who'd brought the news addressed me. "Do me, and I'll do you."

"Do what?" I asked in confusion.

"Offer the Three-Moon Blessing!" He cupped his hands and filled them with water. "Bow your head." I did, and he poured water over my head, repeating the gesture twice more. It ran down my neck and into my eyes, turning cool against my skin. "Now me!"

I did the same.

He laughed and shook his head when I'd finished, water spraying. "Ah, that's good!" He thrust out one hand. "I'm Ahran."

I clasped his forearm. "Khai."

His eyes sparkled in the moonlight as he returned my clasp; he had a merry face. "Well met, Khai! Will you be staying with us for a time? There's such fun to be had at the gathering!"

"No, I don't think so," I said. "We're here on a matter of honor."

Ahran's face fell. "Oh, that's right. Forgive me, I'd forgotten for a moment. Is it true you're going to fight beside the Black Sands Clan tomorrow?"

"Yes."

He glanced around and lowered his voice. "Are you scared?"

A year ago, when Brother Yarit undertook the Trial of Pahrkun, I had been eager to prove myself a warrior capable of dealing death to an opponent; and a year ago, I had failed. Whatever I felt now, it wasn't eagerness. With the three moons overhead in the starless sky shining down their blessing upon this gathering, all the tribesfolk laughing and chatting and splashing in this inconceivable abundance of water, it seemed impossible that come dawn, some of these very same people would be immersed in deadly combat, and I among them.

Was I scared?

"I don't know," I said honestly. "Right now, it doesn't seem real. But I imagine that will change tomorrow."

Ahran nodded sagely. "I imagine it will."

EIGHT

"Khai." Brother Merik's lips were close to my ear as he shook me awake. "It's time."

I sat up and rubbed my eyes. "Already?"

"Yasif is waiting," he said.

It was not yet dawn and the floor of the tent was strewn with the sleeping bodies of men and boys and dogs. I picked my way among them.

Outside in the low grey light, Yasif was awaiting me atop a tall camel, his left leg hooked over the pommel of its saddle. He had a second camel on a lead-line. "Are you ready?"

I was not.

My bladder felt full and my bowels felt loose, and there was a part of me that wished that this was not my destiny, that I was not the shadow of one of the Sun-Blessed, that I was still asleep among the warm and comforting sprawl of bodies inside the tent, and that I would awake with nothing more to do than discover what manner of fun and mischief a boy of the Hot Spring Clan might find during the gathering.

I cleared my throat. "I need to use the privy."

"Hurry."

A yawning Brother Yarit accompanied me, while Brother Merik went to fetch their mounts.

Afterward, I felt better, as though my body, purged, was prepared for the coming battle.

We rode through the camp. Although most of the men and boys were yet sleeping, a number of women were already about the day's chores, tending to their cooking fires and milking goats. They watched us pass silently, and I wondered if they were grateful or envious at being spared a warrior's lot.

The feuding clans were gathered in the empty desert a few hundred yards beyond the verge of the campsite, presided over by a black-robed figure seated atop a milk-white camel, a pair of men holding its reins. By the exceptionally tall embroidered black headdress she wore, I took her to be the Matriarch of the Ardu.

Yasif tapped his camel on the shoulder and it knelt so he could dismount. I did the same. A young boy took charge of our camels, and we went to stand with the fighting members of the Black Sands Clan. Khisan gave me a grudging nod. Today, we were brothers.

"Chieftain Jakhan of the Ardu, son of the Black Sands Clan, you have declared blood-feud against the Sweet Meadow Clan," the Matriarch announced. "Do you recant your claim?"

He squared his shoulders. "I do not."

The Matriarch turned to the chieftain of the opposing clan. "Chieftain Nahbin of the Sweet Meadow Clan, do you offer redress for his claim?"

Chieftain Nahbin spat contemptuously into the sandy soil. "I deny his claim! He has no proof."

The Matriarch of the Ardu raised one hand. "Then I decree that this matter of honor will be settled with steel, for honor is more precious than gold, more valuable than rubies. Without honor, we are nothing." Her veiled gaze turned in my direction. "Who is this who would stand with the Black Sands Clan?"

I took a step forward. "Khai of the Fortress of the Winds. I fight in memory of Jawal of the Ardu, son of the Black Sands Clan, who perished in the service of Pahrkun. The weapons I bear were his."

Her gaze shifted toward Brother Merik. "And you have sanctioned this, brother?"

"I have, lady," he said in a reluctant tone. "Khai is not yet formally sworn into Pahrkun's service."

"Very well." The Matriarch glanced eastward. "When the sun breaches the horizon, the horn will sound and the battle will commence. Whosoever calls for surrender concedes the point of honor. Is this understood?"

"It is," Chieftain Jakhan said, and Chieftain Nahbin spat on the ground once more before agreeing.

The Matriarch lowered her hand. "Then we will withdraw, and leave you to await the signal."

Brother Merik looked over his shoulder at me as they rode some distance away, mouthing some final piece of advice to me, touching the hilt of his *kopar* with exaggerated significance.

The clans faced off in two loose rows, no more than ten yards separating us. Our numbers were evenly matched, which meant that the man I was facing would likely be my opponent. He looked like a seasoned warrior, his stance loose and relaxed, but his *yakhan* held in a grip that suggested he wasn't about to get careless and lower his guard, even against a much smaller opponent.

Now I knew the answer to the question Ahran had asked me last night. I *should* have been scared, and yet I was not. I felt strangely calm. My mind was keen and clear, my body honed and ready. I held my *yakhan* in my right hand, my *kopar* in my left. My palms were dry and my grip was sure.

The wind stirred and my spirits rose with it, rising, rising.

Today was my day.

Overhead, a hawk drifting on the dawn breeze angled its wings and let out a single piercing cry. The crown of Zar's golden head appeared over the ridge of mountains in the distance.

A horn sounded, echoed by battle-cries from both clans as we broke ranks and ran toward one another.

My opponent aimed a great, slashing blow at me as we met in the middle, intending to take advantage of his greater height and reach to dispatch me at the outset. I held my ground, which he did not anticipate, and caught his blade in the tines of my *kopar,* trapping it with a deft twist that took a good deal of wrist strength to execute. He blinked in confusion. I brought the curved edge of my *yakhan* down hard on the meat of his left thigh and he cried out with pain, his leg crumpling beneath him, red blood soaking the cloth of his breeches.

His blade slid free of my *kopar.* Braced on one knee, he bared his teeth and essayed a direct thrust. I turned my torso to evade it and slit his throat open with a back-handed blow.

He died looking surprised.

My blood was singing in my veins, and all around me was the sound of blades clashing. To my right, a pale-faced Yasif was retreating before the on-slaught of a skilled and determined opponent.

I could have struck the man from behind, but I did not. That would not have honored Brother Jawal's memory.

"Hey!" I shouted. "Here!"

Yasif's opponent turned to level a blow at me; I reversed my *kopar* so that it lay the length of my forearm and parried it, then thrust the point of my *yakhan* into his belly. He dropped his blade and sank to his knees, hands covering the wound, eyes wide with shock. I let Yasif deliver the killing blow. He gave me a quick, hard grin, and the two of us plunged back into the fray.

Cut, slash, thrust; parry and trap. It was a terrible, deadly dance, and I reveled in my skill at it.

Somewhere someone was shouting something, but I couldn't make it out over the pounding blood beating against my eardrums. It wasn't until the horn sounded again that I understood that the chieftain of the Sweet Meadow Clan was calling for surrender and the battle was over.

I lowered my weapons.

Four men of the Sweet Meadow Clan were dead or dying on the desert floor. There were injuries on the side of the Black Sands Clan, but no fatalities. As for me, I didn't have a scratch on me.

The Matriarch of the Ardu returned, along with the other witnesses. I wondered what expression she wore beneath the folds of her tall headdress as she surveyed the carnage.

"Nahbin of the Ardu, you have brought death and dishonor upon your clan," she said in a severe voice, and the chieftain bowed his head in shame. "It is my judgment that in pride and anger, you or your sons committed this crime of which your clan is accused. You thought to prevail today by dint of numbers, but Pahrkun the Scouring Wind saw fit to redress the balance. As a forfeit, I decree that you will give your finest camel to the Black Sands Clan. Is this understood?"

He mumbled agreement.

She turned to Chieftain Jakhan. "Is your honor satisfied?"

He saluted her. "It is, lady."

The Matriarch swept her veiled gaze over the battlefield one last time, then dusted her hands together in a gesture of finality. "This matter is finished." Escorted by her clansmen, she rode away, swaying atop her white camel and leaving the rest of us to attend to the casualties of our battle; one clan jubilant in victory, the other sullen and somber in defeat.

Brother Merik jogged his horse over and tossed me a woolen rag. "Clean your weapons, young Khai."

I set about doing so. "Is that all you have to say, brother?"

He eyed me. "Do you seek praise? I do not mean to begrudge it. You fought well, Khai. You brought honor to Brother Jawal's memory. Today, you are a warrior blooded in the heat of battle. But tell me, what did you learn?"

"*I'd* say we learned that our young Khai's pretty damned good at killing," Brother Yarit observed in a caustic tone.

Ignoring his comment, I watched the members of the Sweet Meadow Clan gathering their dead. "I think this is not only about the merits of honor, brother. It is about the cost of *dishonor,* is it not?"

Brother Merik nodded. "Even so."

There was a great feast that evening in the camp of the Black Sands Clan, one to which we were welcomed as honorary kin; even Brother Yarit. It seemed I had acquitted myself well enough on the battlefield that the chieftain and the majority of the clan had determined that all that had transpired, including Brother Jawal's death, was in accordance with Pahrkun's will.

The mood was very different than it had been upon our arrival. It was not a joyous occasion—not with the news of Jawal's death, not with the injuries that had been sustained—and yet there was a certain fierce merriment to the proceedings, born out of victory and the restoration of honor. There were flagons of date-palm wine, which Brother Merik cautioned me to sip sparingly. And the single greatest difference was that now that we had been declared honorary members of the clan, the girls and women mingled among the men and boys, and while they yet covered their heads with colorful scarves inside the tent, the scarves were unwrapped to bare their faces.

I was a bit disappointed.

The women of Zarkhoum veiled their faces in honor of Anamuht, who it was said showed her true face only to Pahrkun; somehow, I had imagined that women must be as different from men as the Sacred Twins were from each other. And yet it was not so. I suppose it was foolish to think so. After all, Anamuht and Pahrkun were gods, children of the heavens fallen to earth, fallen stars taken shapes that embodied the land unto which they had fallen.

We, we were merely human.

Still, I studied them, searching for differences. There were some, most pronounced among the young women and older girls. Women's features were more delicately molded, their lips fuller. Beneath their robes, there was a suggestion of curves that men did not possess. Their interactions were different, with subtle glances and murmurs and gestures I could not interpret. They—

"Hey!" Khisan's belligerent voice broke my reverie. "That's my sister you're staring at."

"Forgive me," I apologized. "It's just—"

He scowled at me. "If you're old enough to fight beside men, you're too old to ogle a man's sister or wife."

"I didn't mean to," I said. "Only—"

"Do I need to defend her honor and challenge you to another bout of thunder and lightning?" Khisan's face was flushed and his voice loose and slurry; he had not drunk sparingly of the date-palm wine. "I warn you, I'll not be caught unawares a second time, hopping toad."

I glanced around the tent, hoping someone, perhaps Chieftain Jakhan, would intervene, but it seemed that this, too, was a matter of honor. The tribesfolk watched with curiosity and the young woman at whom Khisan had caught me gazing drew her scarf over her lower face in reproach.

I had given offense.

"Come, little shadow, little brother." Khisan got to his feet, wavering a bit. "A friendly bout to avenge the insult."

"You're drunk," Yasif murmured. "Sit. Khai meant no insult."

His brother paid him no heed. "A friendly bout to restore *my* honor, eh? You owe me that much."

I did not want to fight him again, not least of all because I was fairly sure

I could best him in this condition with or without the element of surprise, and thus embarrass him further. "Can we not simply—"

Khisan clapped twice, then stamped his left foot; but before he could complete the challenge, Brother Merik rose smoothly from the carpet on which he was seated, his hand closing on the younger man's wrist.

"A word outside, kinsman," he said in an even tone that brooked no objection, steering Khisan toward the outdoors. "Indulge me."

They departed the tent, leaving an awkward silence in their wake.

"Customs, how they do vary!" Brother Yarit said in a bright, cheerful voice. He refilled his cup with date-palm wine and downed a gulp. "Elsewhere in Zarkhoum, the king's word is law. Tell me, how is it that among the desert tribes, a woman is the final arbiter of justice?"

His query at once eased the tension and evoked a handful of ambiguous sounds in response.

"The king!" an older woman said scornfully; I recognized her eyes and her time-worn hands, and thought she was the chieftain's wife who had served us yesterday. "What does King Azarkal know of life and death?"

Brother Yarit quaffed his wine. "Well, as to life, he's led a long one; as to death, it hasn't called his name yet. Do you disparage his rule?"

"We do not hold the Sun-Blessed in light regard." Chieftain Jakhan raised one hand to emphasize his point. "We do not forget that it is they who had the wisdom to worship the Sacred Twins and win their favor; favor that has resulted in the long-standing rule of the House of the Ageless. It is why we have always rallied to the banner of the Brotherhood of Pahrkun when you have called upon us to defend Zarkhoum." He glanced at me. "And we do not forget that it is foretold that one day, there will arise a darkness in the west against which only one of the Sun-Blessed may stand."

The others murmured in agreement. Brother Saan had mentioned such a prophecy to me. I wondered if the desert folk might tell us more of it, but now was no time to interrupt.

"I sense a 'but' coming," Brother Yarit muttered into his cup before upending the dregs into his mouth.

"But the law of the desert is survival," the chieftain continued in a firm manner. "Women bring life into this world. They understand the value of it, the cost in blood and suffering. Who better to pass judgment in matters of life and death?"

Brother Yarit shrugged and reached for the nearest flagon. "When you put it that way, it almost makes sense."

The chieftain eyed him. "You are a rather strange man."

Brother Yarit raised his cup in a salute. "I've heard worse."

The women laughed and murmured under their breath, exchanging confidences I couldn't make out.

Khisan and Brother Merik returned, the latter looking grave and the former looking surprisingly subdued.

"I beg your pardon, Khai." Khisan's gaze searched my face, his hawk-winged brows drawing together over the bridge of his nose in a perplexed frown. He blinked a few times, then rubbed his eyes with the heel of one hand. "I . . . there are things I did not know. I drank too much date-palm wine. I understand now that you meant no offense. You fought bravely beside us today, and I am grateful for it." He paused again, then extended his hand to me. "Ahh . . . brothers?"

I wasn't feeling exactly brotherly toward him, but I was happy to keep the peace. "Brothers."

In the morning, we departed, stopping to say our farewells to Brother Merik's kin. I was sorry to take my leave of them so soon, and yet it seemed to me that between one day and the next, a door had closed. Ahran and some of the other boys near my age were playing some game of chase around the tents, whipping their *heshkrats* at each other's legs, tolerated by the adults with a mixture of indulgence and annoyance.

Today I understood in my heart that I would never be one of those boys. I was the shadow of one of the Sun-Blessed, pledged to Pahrkun the Scouring Wind, and now I was a blooded warrior. It made for a distance between us that could not be bridged; but that was my destiny, and a source of pride and honor, too.

"What did you say to Khisan last night to bring him to his senses?" I asked Brother Merik as we headed into the desert.

"Oh, I merely explained to him that there are no women at the Fortress of the Winds," he said. "That you didn't mean to give offense, it was only that you'd never seen women before, or at least not since you were a babe in arms."

"That's what *I* was trying to tell him," I said. "Only he wouldn't let me get the words out."

Brother Merik shrugged. "Men will heed words spoken from one in a position of authority that they disdain from other sources."

"That's foolish," I said with some irritation.

"But true," Brother Yarit noted. "So what did you think of them?"

"Of what?" I said.

"Women," he said. "Girls and women."

"Oh." I considered the matter. "I thought they would be different. *More* different, I mean. I thought that men and women would be as different from each other as Pahrkun and Anamuht."

Brother Yarit snorted. "I take it you didn't get close enough for a good look at the face of Pahrkun the Scouring Wind when you two came to fetch me back to exile at the fortress last year."

"No." I was stung by the reminder of how I'd frozen. "Why?"

"Because you'd never have thought such a thing if you had," he replied.

"Let him be," Brother Merik said mildly. "Khai's day to face the Scouring Wind will come, and no one save Pahrkun truly knows what face Anamuht wears beneath her veils of fire. Or," he added, "if she wears any face at all. Tradition holds it is so, but no one has ever seen it, and there are some who believe that the flames themselves are her true face."

Over the course of days, I thought about these things, and wondered what forms the gods of other lands might take. We Zarkhoumi are not adventurers to sail the great currents and bring back tales of far-flung isles and the gods who inhabit them. From the Zarkhoumi history that Brother Ehudan had taught me, I knew of Droth the Great Thunder who held aegis in the nearby realm of Granth—the great dragon whose offspring were the terrible stink-lizards that had once nearly succeeded in conquering Zarkhoum—but even Brother Ehudan was vague on the details of the myriad lands that lay beyond our watery borders.

We might be the people of Zar's favorite children, but we were an isolated folk here in the uttermost east.

Although Brother Yarit had never left Zarkhoumi soil, at least he had tales of other realms to share; tales garnered from traders and sailors on the docks of Merabaht. On the isle of Therin, he told us, Ilharis the Two-Faced was a marble statue with one face that looked east and one that looked west, and on those rare occasions when Eshen the Wandering Moon was full and visible in the night sky, it wept crystal tears that could change a man's luck; crystals that were both prized and feared, for one's luck might change for the worse as easily as the better.

In Barakhar, he said, they worship Lishan the Graceful, who took the form of a tree called a willow which could pull up its roots and wander about the land, showering dew imbued with enduring grace on her chosen.

When I said I could see nothing great or terrible about a wandering tree, Brother Yarit informed me that I was a fool to underestimate any of the children of the heavens or their gifts. "Anything can be a weapon, kid," he said wryly. "Grace and guile can be deadlier than a stink-lizard's bile, and luck can change any outcome."

"What about this business of a darkness arising in the west one day?" I asked him. "What sort of darkness?"

Brother Yarit and Brother Merik exchanged a glance. "No one knows for sure," the latter admitted. "Only that the earliest origins of the legend can be found in the fall of the children of heaven. But that's a matter best left to discuss with Brother Saan when he sees fit."

"Leave it to the Seer," Brother Yarit agreed. "I daresay he knows more about it than the rest of us. But let me tell you, I once saw a grace-touched Barakhan dancer perform, and every single man in that audience—"

"Enough," Brother Merit interrupted him in a firm tone. "Khai doesn't need to hear this."

"Just trying to pass the time," Brother Yarit replied with an edge to his voice. "The kid's got to learn about the world beyond the desert someday."

"Yes, and as I've told you, that day too will come when Brother Saan sees fit," Brother Merit said impatiently. "Would you see Khai armed against such weapons as grace and guile? His first defense will forever be the lessons of honor and survival learned in the crucible of the desert of Zarkhoum."

"Spoken like a true—" Brother Yarit halted mid-sentence, staring into the distance.

I followed his gaze and saw nothing but sand and scrub and rocky outcroppings. The sun was riding low in the west, but not so low that we need think of finding shelter for another few hours. "What is it?" I asked, bewildered. "I see nothing." He gave no answer. I glanced at Brother Merik, who shook his head. "Brother Yarit? Brother Yarit, what is it?"

"Ahhhh!" A terrible cry emerged from Brother Yarit's throat and he lurched backward as though struck, toppling from the saddle.

"Brother Yarit!" I shouted in alarm, dismounting. "What *is* it?"

"No, no, no, no, no!" He thrashed and writhed on the ground, tangling the folds of his robe and panicking his mount. His hands rose, fingers clawed, to cover his eyes. "Oh, fuck me! No!"

Squatting beside him, I tried in vain to tug his hands down to see what was wrong. "Are you hurt?"

His mount's panic infected mine; I heard Brother Merik mutter a curse as he sought to secure two sets of reins before they could bolt.

Brother Yarit kicked at me, scrabbling backward, one hand still clamped over his eyes. "It can't be it can't be it can't be!" he groaned. "Oh, fuck me, fuck me to eternity, no, no, no!"

I followed him. "Brother, what—"

"Khai!"

Something in Brother Merik's voice stopped me in my tracks. I glanced at him and saw him pointing. Brother Yarit's thrashing had disturbed the burrow of a banded onyx scorpion. Most of the things that crawl and creep on the floor of the desert will bite or sting; only two are fatal. One is the blind shadow-viper, a sinuous black-scaled nocturnal snake that hunts by scent.

The other is the banded onyx scorpion.

It had emerged fully from its burrow, less than a foot away from where I crouched, frozen. It was fully as long as my forearm. Its black carapace was shiny, the lower thorax striped with the crimson bands that fairly shouted *danger, poison, run away*; and oh, believe me, with the blood running cold with instinctual terror in my veins, I would have liked to do nothing more.

"Khai, back away from it," Brother Merik said quietly. "Slowly, as slowly as you can."

Brother Yarit was still thrashing and moaning. The banded onyx was poised almost motionless between us on its segmented legs, its tail curved over its back, the deadly stinger quivering.

"I can't," I whispered. "Brother Yarit—"

"Khai, *get away*!"

But I couldn't, I couldn't abandon Brother Yarit in the throes of whatever fit had overcome him, his sandaled heels drumming against the sandy soil; too near, the scorpion's pincers beginning to twitch . . .

Gathering my legs beneath me, I dove the length of Brother Yarit's body, landing gracelessly on my hands and feet and whirling to grab the collar of his robe, digging my own heels into the sand and dragging him a few yards away with fear-driven strength. It was a near thing and it was not over. For the space of a heartbeat, I saw the banded onyx scuttling toward us, impossibly fast, and I despaired in the knowledge that I lacked the strength to haul Brother Yarit out of its path a second time; and then his mount, still loose, crashed between us and the scorpion.

I got a grip under Brother Yarit's arms. "Help me, damn you!" I shouted at him. "Help me!"

He understood enough to use my grip to lever his body and get his feet under him, pushing at the ground and helping me haul him to a safe distance, where I collapsed in the sand. There was stomping, the sound of Brother Merik shouting, and then an awful equine squeal.

I saw Brother Yarit's horse go down and fall heavily on its side, squealing and twitching in agony; later, I would learn that the scorpion stung it on the fetlock. I saw Brother Merik draw his *yakhan* and cut its throat, putting it out of its misery, blood spilling onto the thirsty sand. I saw the banded onyx scorpion retreat backward into its burrow, content that it had defended its territory. Perhaps it had even done Pahrkun's bidding, for it was one of his creatures to command. If there was a purpose in it, I could not guess at it.

All the while, Brother Yarit bowed his head, covered his eyes, and keened, rocking back and forth on his knees. He would not respond to my worried queries, and I did not know what to do.

It took Brother Merik some doing to collect and calm the surviving horses. He came over limping—one of the horses had stepped on his foot—and squatted before Brother Yarit. "All right now," he said gently, taking hold of Brother Yarit's wrists. "Come, let's have a look. What happened to you? What's all this fuss about?"

I watched over his shoulder as Brother Yarit suffered him to lower his hands, and lifted his head to meet our gazes. His face was gouged by the marks of his own fingernails and his eyes were wide and wild and strange, his too-large pupils blurred.

My skin prickled.

Brother Yarit drew a long, shuddering breath and laughed; it was a cracked, desperate sound. "Brother Saan . . . Brother Saan is dead," he said in a ragged voice, and the lowering light of the sun was reflected like twin flames in his eyes. "And I'm your new Seer."

NINE

No one knew what to say, least of all me. The enormity and impossibility of it was too great to comprehend.

Brother Saan, dead.

Brother Yarit, the *Seer*. City-born Brother Yarit with his careless, profane tongue; Brother Yarit the master thief of the Shahalim Clan. Brother Yarit who had killed Brother Jawal through dishonorable means; Brother Yarit who had sought to flee from Pahrkun's service.

And yet it was so.

I did not doubt it. While Brother Merik and I went about the business of redistributing our supplies so that we might free up a pack-horse for Brother Yarit to ride, he sat mumbling to himself, sketching in the hard-packed sand with the point of his dagger.

"So if this, then that; but if *this,* then *that.*" He shook his head and drew a series of sweeping lines that looked like snakes chasing each other's tails. "I can't see it all. It's too big."

"What is that?" I asked, hoping to draw him out of his vision and back into the world. Seer or not, we needed him fit to ride. "It looks like Brother Ehudan's map of the four great currents."

"It's too big," he repeated to himself as though I hadn't spoken, erasing the drawing with an impatient swipe of his left arm, then slashing at the sand, back and forth, up and down, to create a burst of lines radiating from a single point, which he circled violently. "Miasmus," he muttered. "The Maw, the Abyss that Abides . . ." He shook his head again. "No, no, no, too soon." He pressed the heels of his hands against the sockets of his eyes. "Oh, fuck me!"

I gave up and went to ask Brother Merik if we should butcher the dead horse.

"No." He tightened a girth strap. "We've no room to spare and fresh meat's like to draw predators. Let the desert take it as an offering to Pahrkun."

I lowered my voice. "I don't understand, brother. How can it be . . . him? Brother Yarit?"

Brother Merik cinched the strap. "I wish I knew, little brother," he said. "And I wish even more that we could ask Brother Saan. But we must trust that Pahrkun has his reasons."

I nodded, my throat tightening at the mention of Brother Saan.

"Come," he said. "We can't stay here, not atop the burrow of a banded onyx. Help me get Brother Yarit astride."

It wasn't easy, but we managed it. Once in the saddle, Brother Yarit sat slumped, his hands lax on the reins, continuing to mutter to himself. Fortunately the pack-horse he now rode was trained to follow and it plodded obediently enough in our wake. In light of what had transpired, Brother Merik pushed us harder than he might have otherwise, anxious to return to the Fortress of the Winds as soon as possible. The night's chill was not yet so severe that we needed shelter and fire as soon as the sun's warmth departed, and Nim the Bright Moon was only a week past fullness.

It seemed a great deal longer to me that I had waded into the Eye of Zar and sought the Three-Moon Blessing.

I said as much to Brother Merik when at last we made camp.

"That's the way of time, Khai," he said. "According to the marks on a sundial, it all moves apace, but a single heartbeat may seem like an eternity when you're staring down a banded onyx poised to sting; and a week may pass in the blink of an eye when great events are afoot."

I wrapped my hands around a battered tin cup filled with mint tea to warm them. Nearby, Brother Yarit tossed and cried out in a restless sleep. He hadn't acknowledged any offer of food or drink.

"Do you think he'll be all right?" I asked. "Or has this driven him clean out of his wits?"

"I don't know, little brother," Brother Merik murmured. He looked up at the starless sky where Eshen the Wandering Moon now stood overhead, waxing toward half. "They say strange things happen under the Wandering Moon." He turned his own tin cup in his hands and glanced downward. "You were right. I thought the burden of this gift would fall to me, and I was prepared to bear it. Brother Saan and I did not always agree on your training, but we spoke often of it."

I was silent a moment. "Before we left . . . what he said to me, it felt like a farewell blessing. Do you think he knew?"

Brother Merik sighed. "I'm sure of it." He downed the remains of his tea. "Try to get some sleep."

I expected Brother Yarit to awaken as strange and addled as he'd been, but somewhere in the small hours of the night he ceased his thrashing and muttering to fall silent, and dawn found him alert and clear-eyed.

"I'm sorry if I scared you," he apologized to us, and although his clothing was filthy with grime and there were raw gouges on his face, there was something of the bone-deep brightness that had been upon Brother Saan when he descended from the mountain upon him. "It's just that it came upon me all at once, and . . . it's like trying to drink from a torrent in full flood."

"What did you See?" Brother Merik couldn't keep a sour note from his voice. "Other than a gift you sought to refuse."

"You've got that right." Brother Yarit scrubbed at his face with both hands, but in an ordinary way. "Is there tea?" I filled a tin cup and handed it to him. He slurped his tea. "Ah, that's good." He took another long drink, his throat working, then lowered the cup. "Look, I know you hoped this gift would pass to you, and believe me, I'd give it to you if I could," he said to Brother Merik with a hint of undisguised bitterness. "But I can't. As to what I Saw . . ." He took a deep breath. "It's going to take me some time to make sense of it, if that's even possible. But one thing I do understand is that El-der Brother Saan wasn't trying to be secretive when he kept his visions to himself. It's like . . ." Setting the tin cup on the ground, he raised both hands palm-upward. "Scales."

"Scales," Brother Merik echoed.

"Right." Brother Yarit nodded. "At every crossroads, something hangs in the balance. It might go this way . . ." He lifted his right palm, then alternated to lift his left. "Or that way."

Brother Merik frowned. "But surely one outcome is more desirable than another."

"It may seem that way," Brother Yarit agreed. "But beyond every crossroad lies another, and another, and another. To use the Sight to attempt to tip the scales in any given instance . . ." He let both hands fall in a crashing gesture, overturning his cup of tea. "Upsets the balance of everything."

Spilled tea sank into the sand, making a damp patch.

Brother Saan's words about my path being filled with strange turns and branchings came back to me. I wished I'd paid greater heed to them.

"Is this . . ." I cleared my throat. "Is this about me?"

"Not exactly, kid," Brother Yarit said ruefully. "It's about *all* of us." He dusted his hands together and glanced around. "Watery hell, I'm famished! Tell me there's something to eat, eh?"

Four days later, we returned to find the Fortress of the Winds in a state of mourning and confusion.

Despite everything, there was a very small part of me that had held out hope against hope that Brother Yarit was wrong, that he had suffered sunstroke in the desert, that we would return to find Brother Saan alive and well, his eyes crinkling with amusement at the notion that he had perished while we were away.

It was not so.

I visited his body, which had been laid atop a bier in the heights. It looked small and shrunken, but the expression on his face was one of peace. As though to express their respect, none of Pahrkun's creatures had yet troubled his flesh.

Beside his bier, I wept.

He had been a father to me; father, grandfather, mother . . . everything.

The hawk's feather I had caught as a babe had fallen from his hand, and I did not know how to be in this world without him.

On the high plateau where we laid our dead to rest, Brother Yarit touched my shoulder. "I'm sorry, kid."

"I know," I whispered.

And yet life continued, as it must.

If Brother Yarit was unhappy about Brother Saan's gift of Sight passing to him, he was surely not alone. No one was pleased to hear it, and a good many of the brothers doubted it. In the end, Brother Yarit called a meeting, addressing the entirety of the brotherhood from the narrow stone bridge that spanned the Dancing Bowl while we gathered below.

"I get it," he said to us. "You don't like this. Well, I don't like it, either. But you know what? That's too damn bad. None of us gets a choice in this matter. I don't imagine I'll ever be as wise as Brother Saan was, but for whatever reason, Pahrkun's chosen me for this. All I can tell you is that I'll do my best. All I ask is that you do the same. All right?"

It wasn't eloquent, but it was honest and it did the job; for the most part the grumbling ceased and we returned to our regular regimen of training. If I had thought that becoming the Seer would alter Brother Yarit's demeanor in any significant way, I was soon disabused of the notion. After that first day in the desert when the Sight had come upon him, he spoke little of it.

Autumn gave way to the chill winds of winter. I continued to squeeze rocks and pick locks; to hop up and down steps and shinny up and down ropes; to practice walking soundlessly and navigate sightlessly. I threw *zims* and the *heshkrat*; I trained with the *yakhan* and *kopar,* both of which became easier to wield as I continued to build strength in my wrists and forearms. I practiced the art of disguise. I sparred with Brother Hakan and a few of the others, acquiring and bestowing more than a few new scars in the process.

As spring and my eleventh birthday approached, I grew taller by several inches, though no broader of shoulder; impatient, I despaired of gaining the physique of a grown man.

"When will I come into my full growth, do you think?" I asked Brother Yarit one day in the Hall of Proving. "Next year? Or the next?"

I expected him to counsel patience; instead, he opened and closed his mouth a few times and eyed me with an unreadable look. "Frankly, kid, that's something I'd like to know myself."

It wasn't the answer I'd expected. "Why? What do you mean?"

Brother Yarit shook his head. "Never mind, I'm just thinking out loud, wondering how long we have before you turn sixteen and it's time to send you to serve the House of the Ageless. This business of the Sight's no use when it comes to practical matters," he added. "It's enough to drive a man mad."

I might have thought nothing further of it if Brother Yarit hadn't summoned the senior brothers to a meeting in his chamber that evening. He did it discreetly, but that was the very thing that caught my notice. He had taught me too well how to notice when one's attention was being diverted.

The days when I would have scrupled at eavesdropping were long gone. Since Brother Yarit's tenure, the entrance to the cavern that served as the Seer's chamber had been hung with thick carpets to keep out the wind, for when it came to the elements, he was not as hardy as desert-born Brother Saan. The good thing was that meant I had no need to conceal myself; the unfortunate one was that it meant the voices of the men within were muffled.

I strained my ears to hear. At first I could make nothing of the murmurs, but as the conversation grew heated, voices rose; especially Brother Yarit's.

"No, I haven't *Seen* it!" he said in annoyance. "I don't need the Sight to show me what common sense makes perfectly clear. Or are you planning to wait until the kid starts sprouting tits?"

Someone shushed him then; Brother Ehudan, I thought. I frowned, trying to make sense of Brother Yarit's words. Was he speaking of me? Milking she-goats and camels had tits; I could no more see why the flat nipples that adorned my narrow chest would sprout them than I would grow horns or hooves.

After a prolonged spell of inaudible discussion, it was Brother Drajan's deep voice that rose above the fray. "All right, all right," he said in a conciliatory tone. "I'm returning to Merabaht next month. I'll do whatever you ask in order to procure an apothecary's services, but only if you promise to await my return before you do anything rash."

There was some low muttering, which I guessed by the general tenor to be Brother Yarit agreeing to something he'd prefer not to do, and then Brother Merik's voice. "Very well, brothers," he said formally. "I do believe we're in agreement."

It was the sound of a discussion coming to a conclusion, and I crept away.

A month passed and Brother Drajan set out for Merabaht once more, in search of a willing apothecary and any rumor of the long-missing Brother Vironesh, the broken shadow. This time he was armed with mysterious letters of instruction written by Brother Yarit, as well as fistfuls of gold from the brotherhood's coffers.

Since I couldn't satisfy my curiosity regarding the matter that piqued me most, I chose to satisfy it regarding another matter. "Elder Brother," I said to Brother Yarit; after half a year, it still felt strange to address him thusly. "I chanced to overhear a conversation some time ago."

He raised his eyebrows at me. "Oh, you did, did you?"

"Yes," I said. "And there is something I've been wondering about ever since. Last spring, when they were speculating about Brother Vironesh's whereabouts, Brother Saan said it should be easier to find a *purple* man. What did he mean?"

"Ah." Brother Yarit relaxed a bit; whatever he had expected me to ask, that wasn't it. "As to that, it happened before I was born, but I know the tale. You know that his charge was killed?"

I nodded. "Poisoned."

"Right," he said. "Prince Kazaran, the king's third-born son and his favorite. He had a name for being a great swordsman. Someone slipped death-bladder venom in his wine." He raised his brows again. "Do you know how death-bladder venom kills?"

I shook my head.

"It causes all your veins to burst," he informed me with a certain macabre relish. "It's called the Purple Death."

"But Brother Vironesh didn't *do* it, did he?" I was confused. "Brother Saan said he was devastated."

"No, no, of course not," Brother Yarit assured me. "The thing is, *his* wine, Vironesh's wine, was poisoned, too. Only he didn't die. He was proof against the poison, at least in part. Only the little veins in his skin burst. Like a bruise," he added. "Except it never healed."

"So he really is . . . purple?" I asked.

"So says the legend," he said. "And Brother Ehudan, who is the only one among us old enough to remember him now that Brother Saan has passed, confirms the truth of it."

"He doesn't remember Brother Vironesh's training, though, right?" I asked.

Brother Yarit laughed. "Are you joking? None of us mere mortals outside the House of the Ageless was alive when that took place. We have only the lore passed down through generations."

"Who poisoned the prince and why?" I asked. "And why was Brother Vironesh proof against the poison?"

He grimaced at me. "You're full of questions today, kid. And I suppose you're owed some answers. The prince's killer was never caught, but if I were to put money on it, I'd bet on one of his two older brothers. You know King Azarkal hasn't declared an heir?" I nodded. "Well, the story goes that forty-odd years ago, he was close to naming Prince Kazaran. You see, the prince was betrothed to a Granthian woman."

"Granth!" From what little I knew of Granth, I couldn't imagine it. "Why?"

"Ah!" Brother Yarit raised one finger, warming to his tale. "Because Granth has no hereditary monarchy. They're a warrior folk."

"Like the desert tribesfolk?" I asked.

"Even more so," he said. "I'm not saying they're better warriors, mind you—the desert's a harsh proving ground—but the tribesfolk fight as a matter of honor, and frankly, I think they're wise to let their Matriarchs serve as arbiters of bloodshed and justice. Granthians . . . Well, let me put it this way. Every seven years, they hold a tourney. The strongest warriors in the nation gather and fight to the death. It's more slaughtering ground than battlefield, and the last man standing is crowned the Kagan. He gets to rule for seven years, and while he does, his word is absolute law. The stink-lizards are his to command, and he gets his pick of any woman he wants. Not a bad gig while it lasts."

"But he has to defend his crown in seven years?" I asked.

"Right." Brother Yarit nodded. "There have been a few who succeeded, none more than once. There's always someone younger and quicker and stronger barking at their heels. But it might be another story if, say, a member of the House of the Ageless took the crown."

I put the pieces together. "Prince Kazaran meant to try to become the Kagan?"

Brother Yarit grinned at me. "You've got it, kid. With a Granthian bride, he'd have been eligible to fight in the tourney. It's a fair bet that King Azarkal would have named him his heir if he had won and laid claim to Granth. And with the *rhamanthus* seeds, he might have been able to hold the crown indefinitely."

"I wonder how Brother Vironesh felt about it," I mused. "He wouldn't have been able to protect him in a tourney to the death."

Brother Yarit shrugged. "If we ever find him, you can ask him for yourself," he said pragmatically. "Whatever he felt, I imagine it would have been better than what *did* happen."

"True." I shuddered, then recalled an earlier question. "Elder Brother, you never answered. Do you know *why* Brother Vironesh was proof against the death-bladder venom?"

He hesitated. "That, young Khai, I cannot answer. It's a mystery you'll have to discover for yourself."

"Does it have to do with an apothecary?" I asked.

"No." Brother Yarit's voice was unwontedly gentle. "No, it's absolutely nothing of the sort."

TEN

"Is it true that you remember Brother Vironesh?" I asked Brother Ehudan during our study session the next morning. "And that he's *purple*?"

"Yes, yes." He flapped one gnarled hand at me. "The broken shadow, I remember him well."

"Did he speak to you of honor beyond honor?" I asked.

"He didn't speak to me at all," Brother Ehudan said wryly. "Only to Brother Saan, to whom the gift of Sight had quite recently passed. But one does not forget a purple man, nor a man whose entire purpose in life has been destroyed."

"Did—"

"Khai." He took a seat on a carpet in the study chamber, gesturing at me to do the same. I sat cross-legged opposite him across from the low table, which was spread with a map of the world. "Brother Yarit gauges it is time you learned something more of the world."

My pulse quickened. "Yes, brother."

"You have heard how the children of the heavens rebelled against the Sun and the Moons, until Zar the Sun cast them down to earth," he said. "And that Anamuht and Pahrkun were Zar's best beloved, and the first to repent of their rebellion."

"Yes, brother." I did my best not to sound disappointed, having hoped to learn something new and interesting.

"Attend." Brother Ehudan touched the map with one crooked finger. "You do not know the whole of the tale, young Khai, for there is a portion we do not tell to children, and this is what I will tell you today. Before the rebellion began, Zar saw that the heavens were growing crowded and his children restless. He declared that the Moons would bring forth no more new life; but he did not know that Eshen the Wandering Moon was already with child. No one noticed when she hid herself to bring forth this child, for Eshen was ever fickle in her ways. This child she cloaked in darkness and hid from Zar's eyes."

"Why?" I asked.

"She was afraid," he said simply. "And so the child Miasmus grew in darkness and knew nothing of the bright lights of its brethren—"

"Miasmus?" Something tickled at my memory; it was a name Brother Yarit had uttered in his ravings when the Sight first came upon him.

"So Eshen named the child," Brother Ehudan said. "And Miasmus took no part in the rebellion, but when the children of heaven were cast down, there was nowhere left for Eshen to hide her last-born. Angry at her defiance, Zar cast Miasmus from the heavens, the last to fall."

"That wasn't fair," I said.

"Perhaps not," Brother Ehudan agreed. "But it was done." He touched the map again, pointing out a blot of darkness on the farthest western verge of the world. "And here is where Miasmus fell to earth."

The west.

"What form did he take?" I asked. "Or . . . she?"

"No one knows," Brother Ehudan said. "I was once told that many have sought to explore, and sailors from distant realms tell tales of a great abyss capable of swallowing entire fleets of ships, but no one has ever returned to confirm it."

"The Abyss that Abides," I murmured. "The Maw."

"You know of it?" Brother Ehudan sounded surprised.

I shook my head. "Not really, no. Brother . . ." I swallowed. "There is a prophecy that one day a darkness will arise in the west against which one of the Sun-Blessed will stand. Is it Miasmus?"

"That, too, is unknown," he said. "Some of the priestesses of Anamuht believe it to be so; others believe it is a force of darkness to which Miasmus will give birth after these many centuries, for it is said that Miasmus is male and female alike." He rolled up the map carefully. "Understand, Khai, that it is exceedingly unlikely that this will come to pass in your lifetime," he said kindly. "The princess Zariya, whom you will serve one day, is surely neither a warrior nor an adventurer, and I can conceive of no reason for her to leave Zarkhoum, let alone journey to the far reaches of the world. We are not a nation of sojourners. Like as not, she'll be wed to some distant kinsman, and you'll be guarding her from nothing more challenging than petty squabbles in the House of the Ageless."

"And all my training will be for naught?" I couldn't keep a faint note of bitterness from my voice.

"If it is so, you may count it a blessing," Brother Ehudan said sharply. "Don't go begging for trouble, Khai. I've seen one broken shadow; I've no wish to see another."

Abashed, I saluted him. "Forgive me, brother. I will pray for an uneventful life and do my best to be grateful for it."

His wrinkled face creased in a smile. "It is the province of youth to dream of battle and glory. May you live a long and rich life, and one day in truth be grateful that those wishes were not granted."

In many ways, the tale Brother Ehudan told me changed nothing; and yet I felt different for knowing it. I might be years away yet from being a man grown, but I was no longer a mere child.

There was darkness in the world, and it had a name: Miasmus.

I remembered how Brother Saan had spoken to me of the fall of the children of heaven the day after Brother Yarit's trial, when I was angry and grieving. He had spoken of how they were bound to the earth, and the night sky was empty of stars, and I had not forgotten another thing he said to me. *Do you suppose that all the fallen children of the heavens shall remain content that it should ever be thus?*

I would not be content if I were Miasmus, raised in darkness and secrecy, cast down from the heavens for a sin I had not committed. No, I would not be content at all, but filled with a bitter and long-simmering fury; and I thought this, perhaps, was the reason this portion of the tale was not told to children. It was a grave thing for a child's mind to encompass.

On that same day, Brother Saan had spoken for the first time of the prophecy, of the Sun-Blessed and the darkness rising in the west. Of course, he'd also said much the same thing that Brother Ehudan had, that it was highly unlikely it had anything to do with the princess Zariya.

No doubt it was true, and it was foolish of me to entertain the idea that it might be otherwise; no, if there were a hero born to the Sun-Blessed, it would be someone like the slain Prince Kazaran, a great warrior with a bold and adventurous spirit, not the seventeenth child and youngest daughter.

Still, I allowed myself to daydream from time to time, and I was determined to continue training as though it might be true.

Honor beyond honor.

Whatever came, I would not fail Zariya for lack of preparation; and if it were to prove in vain, so be it.

It was some weeks before Brother Drajan returned from his errands in Merabaht, but he came with an apothecary in tow, a dusty-looking fellow in drab clothes. Even his skin seemed to hold a tinge of grey. Still, he knew his business. Ostensibly, that was the preparation and prescription of tinctures and powders to treat all manner of ailments; in practical terms, it included the administration of poisons, though in my particular instance it was to be constrained to recognition of the distinctive qualities of various poisonous substances.

Nazim was the apothecary's name, and although he had consented to accept this assignment for a considerable amount of gold, he remained reluctant and apprehensive regarding it.

"I tell you, there's no point in it," he informed Brother Yarit in a querulous voice upon the day of his arrival at the Fortress of the Winds. "Members of the House of the Ageless have long memories. Forty-odd years since Prince Kazaran's death and there's not one of the Sun-Blessed would allow a morsel of food or a sip of drink to pass his or her lips without a taster."

"And what of the piercing toxins?" Brother Yarit inquired. "Those administered by breaking the skin?"

Nazim the apothecary sighed. "I suppose it's possible, but I can conceive no reason that anyone would want to poison the young princess. She's of no political value."

Brother Yarit folded his arms and looked impassive. "Nonetheless."

And so the apothecary was given a spacious cavern overlooking the

Dancing Bowl in which to unpack his wares, spreading a large carpet and setting forth vials and pouches of philtres and powders.

It was all very complicated.

One of the deadliest poisons native to Zarkhoum was the venom of the blind shadow-viper—harmless if ingested, fatal if administered by stab wound. However, a blade needed to be coated in a fair amount to deliver a fatal dosage, and the venom caused the metal to take on a telltale tarnish. Another was the innocuous green manchi-fruit that grew in abundance on the southern coast of Zarkhoum. The juice and flesh, which had a faint, pleasant aroma, produced a mild stinging sensation in the mouth upon tasting and closed the airways within minutes of being consumed.

I would have thought the venom of the banded onyx scorpion could be found among Zarkhoum's deadliest poisons, but Nazim gave a dry laugh when I inquired, and informed me that few people had ever been foolish enough to attempt to harvest a banded onyx's venom, and none had ever succeeded.

Most of the poisons about which Nazim taught me came from Barakhar, where guile and grace were valued over martial skills and poisoning was considered something of an art form. I learned to recognize tam-tam nuts, the husk of which could be ground to deadly powder; the sap of creeping prickleback vines; a vile paste made of hairy caterpillars; the paralysis-inducing spines of the black rock-urchin; the pungent leaves of the calanath shrub; the fragrant dried petals of lovers' doom flowers; the viscous harvested slime of the ring-toothed eel.

All of these things I memorized by sight, scent, and effect. All of them were deadly in certain quantities, and none had antidotes.

One thing Nazim the apothecary didn't possess was the death-bladder venom that induced the Purple Death. When I asked him about it, he merely responded with his dusty, coughing laugh. "Are you joking? It would be worth my life to be caught with death-bladder venom."

"Because of Prince Kazaran's death," I hazarded. "But what is it? Where does it come from?"

"Death-bladders are kin to jellyfish . . . you've no idea what a jellyfish is, have you?" he asked. I shook my head. "Well, they're translucent bladders of flesh, with stinging tentacles. Most are quite harmless. Death-bladders are another matter. Traders say the waters around Papa-ka-hondras are filled with them."

"Papa-ka-hondras?" I echoed.

"It's an island far to the southwest." Nazim gave me a thin smile. "Even here in Zarkhoum, its name is known to apothecaries. According to legend, it means 'A Thousand Ways to Kill.'"

I groaned. "Does that mean a thousand more poisons to memorize?"

"No, I don't believe anyone's ever gotten more than half a league or so into the interior." He shuddered. "And I can't imagine why anyone would want to try."

The other thing Brother Drajan had brought back from Merabaht was news, and it was exciting news. Brother Vironesh had been found, or at least his whereabouts had been determined. Brother Drajan had guessed aright when he suspected that Brother Vironesh was no longer in Zarkhoum, and although he was not employed as a mercenary on the ship of some outland trader, it was an outland trader who recalled seeing him.

Brother Vironesh, it transpired, had become a courser in the service of Obid the Stern, sailing the four great currents in pursuit of pirates.

According to Brother Yarit, the coursers were a peculiar lot. Itarran was a realm over which Obid the Stern held aegis. It lay to the northwest, and its people were much consumed by justice—so much so that they had no ruler by right of birth or age or conquest, neither king nor Matriarch nor Kagan. No, every ten years, the entire adult populace cast a vote to elect the person they deemed most worthy of governing them. That person, man or woman, best exemplified the principles of justice laid down by Obid the Stern, which included the solemn task of attempting to root out piracy on the lawless seas.

A thankless task, too, one might surmise; but apparently other realms, including Zarkhoum, were willing to pay a tithe to Itarran for their efforts.

It seemed a strange choice indeed for anyone born to Zarkhoum and pledged to the service of Pahrkun. I could not fathom serving a strange god, but then there was a great deal I could not yet fathom. At any rate, Brother Drajan had paid good coin to the captains of any trade ships he could find to carry word to the coursers of Obid that the Seer of the Brotherhood of

Pahrkun required Brother Vironesh's return. There was naught to do but wait and hope on that score, for the coursers of Obid sailed everywhere and Brother Vironesh might be thousands of leagues away.

Some days it seemed as though my world had grown by leaps and bounds since I gained eleven years of age.

But there were mysteries that remained, including the full purpose of Brother Drajan's mission to Merabaht and the missives he carried from Brother Yarit. That, I could not determine. Brother Yarit had grown cagey in the matter of eavesdropping, and I only caught the merest hints of conversation here or there. If I had not had so much to learn and consider, it would have made me impatient.

And, too, Brother Drajan had brought other news with him.

Some of it was much the same. Anamuht had not appeared in Merabaht to quicken the Garden of Sowing Time, and the supply of *rhamanthus* seeds continued to dwindle and grow ever more precious; *khementaran*, the point of return, had not yet come upon King Azarkal. Both of these things continued to be a source of increasing strife in the House of the Ageless.

One day these things might be of great meaning to me, but not yet. They did not touch upon life at the Fortress of the Winds.

Another piece of news did.

It had been two years since Brother Yarit came to us; two years since he undertook the Trial of Pahrkun and succeeded against all expectations. No one had attempted it since, but that was rumored to change. According to Brother Drajan, the Royal Guard was expected to escort another prisoner to the Fortress of the Winds to undertake the Trial of Pahrkun before spring turned to summer.

And this time, it was one of their own.

ELEVEN

"Elder Brother, I respectfully request the right to stand first post," I said to Brother Yarit, saluting him.

"Of course you do." He eyed me. "You and all the other lunatics in this place. It's not going to be an easy decision. Brother Drajan shouldn't have let the news slip."

"He said the city was abuzz with it." I lowered my voice. "He said the guard preyed on little boys."

"Yeah." Brother Yarit ran his hand over his hair. "I'm pretty sure it's been going on for years. There were rumors among the beggar kids; find a safe place to sleep at night or the bad man will take you." He grimaced. "And it would probably have gone on for years more if he hadn't gotten careless and gone after the son of a well-connected merchant."

I was shocked. "Who would let such a thing happen?"

"People cover for their own," he said cynically. "That includes the king's guardsmen. You can't tell me *someone* didn't know."

"What did he do to them?" I asked in a hushed tone. "The boys he took?"

Brother Yarit regarded me. "Watery hell, you're an innocent, kid! Let's just say he hurt them, and when he was done with them, he killed them."

I considered this. "Will you grant me first post?"

He shook his head. "No, you had the chance to blood your sword last fall at the gathering of the clans. I'll grant you second post, Khai; you've earned the right and there's merit in the training if it comes to it. But first should go to someone untried like Hakan or Ramil." He smiled without any mirth. "Give them a chance to slay the monster."

I was disappointed, but it was fair. I touched my brow in acknowledgment. "Thank you, Elder Brother."

It was some weeks into my apprenticeship with Nazim the apothecary when the caravan was spotted on the horizon, and it took the better part of a day to dismantle the elaborate course of ropes and bells and obstacles that had been strung throughout the Hall of Proving. In the end, Brother Yarit had given the first post to Brother Hakan, who was eager to prove himself. The second post was mine, and Brother Merik would anchor the third and final post.

I could not help but wonder what would happen if the supplicant won his way past us as Brother Yarit had done. Brother Yarit had spoken truly: we were not meant to know a supplicant's crimes. Indeed, Brother Merik had once chided him for speaking of his own. And yet in this instance, we knew; we knew, and it was vile. A league away, the caravan made camp at the nearest watering hole. My thoughts drifted, drifted, a hawk's feather on the wind. Could Pahrkun the Scouring Wind truly cleanse a man of such a sin? Did he come seeking absolution in earnest, or did he mean to attempt the trial because it was his only chance of survival? Brother Yarit had come for the latter reason; come and succeeded, and become the Seer. What if Pahrkun had a similar purpose for this unknown king's guardsman?

The prospect made my flesh creep; and yet if it were to come to pass, we would have no choice but to accept it.

I prayed it would not.

Two years ago, it was Brother Jawal who had come to fetch me to get a look at the supplicant before the trial began; this time, it was me that rose before dawn, made my genuflections, and stole quick-footed through the caverns to summon Brother Hakan to the heights. Although he was the older, I had been more years than him in the Fortress of the Winds and it seemed my place to do so. Side by side atop the western lookout, we squatted on our haunches and watched the caravan approach.

There was no guise here and no mistaking the supplicant. Although he sat tall in the saddle with his head held high, eyes glaring at the world, his mount was on a lead-line and his wrists were bound behind his back.

"He looks strong," Brother Hakan mused. "Strong and fit. Not one to go down easily."

"He'll know how to wield a *kopar*," I reminded him.

He nodded. "So no advantage there."

Below us, the caravan drew rein and halted. One of the Royal Guard in his gold and crimson silks dismounted and unsheathed a dagger to cut the rope that bound the supplicant's wrists behind him. The supplicant took his time, rolling his shoulders and stretching out his cramped arms, but eventually he dismounted and took up the hammer to ring the sounding-bowl. Brother Tekel and Brother Drajan came to assist in taking their mounts to the horse canyon and escorting them to the fortress where the supplicant might slake his thirst and hunger before the trial began.

Brother Hakan touched my elbow. "We'd best take our places, Khai. Pahrkun's blessing on you."

I squeezed his forearm in return. "And you."

For the first time in two years, the Hall of Proving felt like a solemn and sacred place once more; although now it was one that I knew forward and back, blindfolded or open-eyed. I took my place at the bend in the center, some yards in front of the crooked stalagmite that marked the borderline between the second and third posts. It was the darkest of the three posts and I closed my eyes to let them adjust, although I remained mindful of the trick Brother Yarit had played in this very spot, blinding Brother Merik with the unexpected dazzle of an oil-wood knot. I doubted the supplicant would think to do the same—manipulating light and shadow was a Shahalim art—but I would be prepared for it if he did.

Before me, Brother Hakan's figure was silhouetted in the entrance. I recognized the outline of Brother Yarit's figure as he approached, and I tensed for the second chime of the sounding-bowl, but the supplicant was not with him yet and it did not come.

Instead, Brother Yarit beckoned to me.

I went to him and saw that his eyes were wide and strange with the Sight. "Yes, Elder Brother?"

"Khai." Even his voice sounded different, as though it came from some deep place. "I have changed my mind. You'll stand first post."

I touched my brow. "Yes, Elder Brother."

"Oh, but—" Brother Hakan began in protest. Brother Yarit turned his uncanny gaze on him, and he fell silent.

"I do not do this lightly," Brother Yarit said to both of us. "Nor do I do it in the knowledge that the outcome is sure. But I have Seen the faces of this man's dead, and of this I am sure. Today, you are the instrument of Pahrkun's will, Khai." He laid a hand on my shoulder, and there was something in the gentleness of his touch that reminded me of Brother Saan. "May he guide your blade."

And so Brother Hakan and I traded places, and it was I who stood in the gathering shadows just beyond the mouth of the great cavern, my *yakhan* in my right hand and my *kopar* in my left, and watched the supplicant strike the sounding-bowl a second time, Brother Yarit standing before him.

The chime echoed across the desert, high and clear. Beyond the Hall of Proving, it was a fine, bright morning. The supplicant's weapons had been returned to him and he drew them now, his movements fluid and sure.

"The Trial of Pahrkun has begun!" Brother Yarit announced, and stepped aside.

The supplicant rolled his shoulders again and flexed his grip on the hilts of his *yakhan* and *kopar*. As Brother Hakan and I had seen, he was a tall fellow and well built, broad through the shoulders. Handsome, too, with strongly carved features and a narrow beard groomed to a point. He'd splashed cool spring water on his face. I could see droplets clinging to his beard and glinting in the sunlight.

He had not seen me in the shadows, not yet.

I felt a stirring within me like the wind rising. My body felt as keen as a blade, my bare feet light on the cavern floor.

One stride, two, three . . . the supplicant passed the threshold of the Hall of Proving, passed from sunlight to shadow, his features taking on a different cast without the sun to gild them.

He paused to let his eyes adjust and saw me. I saw the shock of it go through him, fear and anger and uncertainty chasing across his face, and I understood, then. I was a boy, not a man.

I wore the face of his victims.

"Is this some manner of jest?" the supplicant demanded, lowering his guard unwittingly.

I could have advanced and dealt him a mortal blow in that moment, but I did not. It would not have been honorable, and although this man might not deserve an honorable death, I would conduct myself as though he did. For the sake of the boys he had killed, this man would die as Pahrkun the Scouring Wind intended, and he would know it before the end.

"No jest," I said. "This is the Trial of Pahrkun." I turned slightly, gesturing with my *kopar* and leaving my left side exposed. "Will you seek to pass?"

In a flurry of long strides, he was on me, seizing the opening I'd feigned far more swiftly than I'd reckoned. I barely managed to raise my *kopar* in time to deflect his blow and catch his blade in its tines. He parried the jab I essayed with his own *kopar,* trapping my blade and rendering us at a stalemate, my arms spread wide. It was not one that would last long, for he had the advantage of me in reach and strength; already, I could feel my left wrist beginning to tremble with the effort of keeping his blade averted.

We were near enough that I could smell the rancid tang of the supplicant's sweat, see the pores of his skin. A slow, cruel smile curved his lips. "Did the Brotherhood of Pahrkun think to use you as an instrument of vengeance?" he taunted me, using his greater strength and reach to force my arms farther apart. "I think not, little boy. If I am to die today, it won't be by your hand."

I gritted my teeth. I shouldn't have let him close with me. Now I could no longer use my greatest advantage, my knowledge of the terrain. I had been careless and overconfident, relying on my speed, too sure of Pahrkun's favor.

The supplicant's smile widened, his eyes gleaming in the dim light. "Have you anything to say before I kill you?"

I could feel his muscles tensing to move and knew I'd been a fool; but it was not too late. He shouldn't have taken the time to taunt me. I let him see fear in my eyes and shifted my weight onto my rear foot as though I meant to seek to disengage and retreat. I felt him readjust and brace to press forward when I did. Instead, I brought my right knee up hard and sharp into his groin with all the force I could muster.

It connected with solid bone and spongy flesh, and he let out an involuntary groan and doubled over. Not for long—he was too well seasoned a warrior for that—but it was enough. Freeing my weapons, I took a single step backward, planted my feet, and thrust the central tine of my *kopar* into his right shoulder.

It felt good.

My *kopar* slid out red with his blood. He straightened with another groan, attempting in vain to raise his blade. His right arm wasn't working properly. Blood pulsed from the deep puncture at a rapid rate, darkening the crimson sleeve of his guardsman's tunic. It wasn't a mortal wound, but it was enough to end the contest between us, and he knew it. His mouth twisted as he dropped the *kopar* and switched his *yakhan* to his good left hand, angling it between us.

I regarded him. "Have you anything to say before I kill you?"

"Fuck you." The supplicant raised his blade high overhead and lunged at me, intent on taking me with him. I ducked and whirled to the left, catching him across the midriff with a slashing blow as I did.

The supplicant fell heavily to the floor of the cavern, his blade beneath him. He scrabbled at the ground with his elbows and knees, trying to regain his feet, but there was a pool of blood spreading across the stone. I hooked one foot beneath him and rolled him onto his back, which was a good deal harder than it sounds. He was a big man, but he was a dying man now.

He did not attempt to rise again, only lay breathing in short, quick gasps. The warm breath of the desert whispered in the entrance to the Hall of Proving. "Do you hear that?" I stood over him and placed the point of my *kopar* on his breastbone. "Pahrkun is calling your name."

His only reply was to bare his teeth at me in a grimace. There was blood staining them, too.

I drove the point home, and he died. Slow blood continued to seep from his wounds, his empty eyes staring.

It was finished. The Trial of Pahrkun was over.

I emerged from the Hall of Proving to inform Brother Yarit. The strangeness of the Sight had passed from him, but he still looked unwontedly grave. "Well done, Khai," he said to me. "The shades of his dead will rest easier tonight."

There would be no funeral bier for a supplicant who had failed the Trial of Pahrkun. His body was thrown into a gorge, the distant floor littered with the old bones of other supplicants who had failed over the centuries.

The king's guardsmen dined with us that night as they had when Brother Yarit had come to us. Despite what he had said about people covering for their own, none chosen for this escort detail seemed to mourn the passing of their brother-in-arms. Indeed, there were a few who took a certain grim satisfaction in the manner of his passing, especially after they prevailed upon me to recount the details of our brief battle. "Kneed him right in the bollocks!" One of the guards elbowed the fellow next to him. "If that's not fitting, I don't know what is, eh?"

I frowned in confusion, unsure what he meant. "Why?"

The guard blinked at me. "Well, because he was buggering—"

"Cease." Brother Merik's voice held a warning note. "We do not speak of a man's sins here. There is only the Trial. If a supplicant succeeds, he is scoured of his sins; if he fails, then we may know Pahrkun the Scouring Wind has passed judgment on him and speak no more of it."

"It's just . . . Sun-Blessed shadow or not, he's a kid! That's fitting, right?" the guard protested. "Isn't that why you chose him?"

"Khai was the Seer's choice to stand first post today," Brother Merik said. "And the Seer chooses as either wisdom or Pahrkun's guidance dictates." He glanced at Brother Yarit, who was paying scant heed to the conversation. "Is that not so, Elder Brother?"

"What's that?" Brother Yarit's head slewed around. "Oh, yes. You know, it's a funny business, the Sight," he said in a conversational manner. "It's not like watching players on a stage act out a story, you see; it comes in bits and pieces. Sometimes images of people and places and things that are happening or might happen, but sometimes nothing more than words and impressions. Sometimes not even that, sometimes just symbols. And it's hard to tell *when* you're Seeing, or whether a thing might actually happen or not, because so much depends on everything else."

There was a moment of silence around the table. It was probably a great deal more than any Seer had ever said regarding the gift to outsiders in the history of the brotherhood; it was surely a great deal more candid.

But then I doubted there had ever been a Seer as conflicted at being chosen as Brother Yarit.

"So . . . what *did* you see, Elder Brother?" one of the guards inquired with cautious curiosity.

"Dead children." Brother Yarit fixed him with a bleak look. Atop the table, he drummed and twitched the fingers of his left hand restlessly. "But I'm not supposed to talk about *that*, am I?"

Awkward glances were exchanged. I watched Brother Yarit's left hand and did a surreptitious survey to see if anyone else was doing the same. Although he had not yet taught it to me, I remembered Brother Yarit mentioning that the Shahalim had a secret language of hand signs. I didn't catch anyone out at it, but I had a strong sense my hunch was right. Brother Yarit wasn't given to drumming his fingers.

And if I was right, that meant one of the guards was a member of the Shahalim. It seemed the Seer's former clan had not forsaken him after all.

Brother Yarit cleared his throat, breaking the uncomfortable silence. "Forgive me, it's been a trying day. I think it's best if I retire for the evening."

"I think it's best if we all retire, Elder Brother." Brother Merik sounded relieved to have an excuse to disperse this particular gathering. "It's growing late and our guests have a long journey ahead of them."

In my chamber, I waited until I could hear neither footsteps nor words carried on the night winds that soughed through the halls and caverns. It was pitch black in the fortress when I slipped out of my chamber and I dared not light a torch, but crept soundlessly in the dark through the labyrinth of halls toward the empty cavern on one of the lower levels where guests bunked. Outside the entrance, I made myself small in a shallow, rocky alcove.

I could have been wrong, of course; and even if I was right about the hand signs, I could be wrong that they betokened a clandestine meeting. I was only guessing, but it was a guess informed by the training of a man who taught me to be observant.

I waited.

By my reckoning, the better part of an hour passed before I heard the faintest scrape of sandy grit displaced by a near-silent footfall. If I hadn't been straining my ears, I wouldn't have heard it at all. Although I could not see in the dark, the wind currents in the passageway eddied.

I rose and stole noiselessly in their wake.

One turn, then another and another, and I knew that we were bound for the Dancing Bowl. I hung back, letting the stealthy figure precede me. His pace quickened as he glimpsed moonlight beyond the opening before him. I waited until he emerged into the Dancing Bowl, then put my back against the wall of the broad tunnel and sidled through the shadows. Only Eshen the Wandering Moon was full in the night sky overhead, but after the total blackness of the fortress, it was easy to see in the dim bluish light that she shed upon the land, and I made out the shape of Brother Yarit waiting in the moon-shadow of the stone bridge.

The guard crossed to greet him, and the two of them clasped forearms in a familiar manner. "It's good to see you, Amal," Brother Yarit murmured. "Were you able to do as I asked?"

The other glanced behind him. "The shadows have ears, cousin."

With a silent curse, I plastered myself tighter against the wall.

"Khai!" Brother Yarit called. "It's all right, you can come out. Come, meet my kinsman."

I waited for the space of a few heartbeats before emerging sheepishly into the moonlight. "What was it that gave me away?"

"Your footwork was excellent." Brother Yarit's cousin looked much like him, which was to say ordinary; there was nothing in his features one would remark on, and I could not even recall where he'd been sitting at the dinner table. "But you were careless with your breathing."

"You're Shahalim?" I asked.

He did not answer.

"I called in a favor," Brother Yarit said. "More than one, actually, but I was owed a few. Did it pay off?"

"Not easily." His cousin withdrew a small wooden box from a purse hanging from his sash and handed it over. "But yes, it did."

"Ah." Brother Yarit lifted the lid of the box. Soft amber-gold light emanated from it. He beckoned to me. "Do you know what this is, Khai?" I shook my head, peering into the box. There on a cushion of satin rested a single teardrop-shaped gem the rich honey-colored hue of the light it emitted, no bigger than the nail of my littlest finger.

"No, Elder Brother," I said honestly. "I've no idea. Should I?"

"I suppose not," Brother Yarit admitted. "No reason you would. It's a piece of amber from the Lone Tree of the Barren Isle, which produces a single drop of resin every century. It takes another five centuries to harden into stone."

"Long ago, it belonged to a famous courtesan-queen of Barakhar," his cousin Amal added. "According to legend, she once took a thousand lovers over the course of a single year."

I was confused. "I don't understand."

"I know." Brother Yarit replaced the lid, extinguishing the gem's soft golden glow. Now there was only the lone full moon overhead, Eshen the Wandering Moon, mother of the dark-shrouded Miasmus, her dim blue light making indigo hollows of his eyes. "Khai . . . there is a thing I must tell you. Our success in procuring this gem, I think, is a sign that it is so. But not here, not tonight." He took a deep breath. "Tomorrow at midday, we will meet in the Seer's chamber and speak, you and I. Tell no one what you saw tonight."

I saluted him; what else was I to do? "Yes, Elder Brother."

TWELVE

My sleep that night was restless, filled with swords and shadows, glowing gems and the faces of dead boys.

I awoke feeling strange to myself. The king's guardsmen took their leave, and neither Brother Yarit nor his cousin gave the slightest indication of knowing each other. It almost seemed I might have dreamed the encounter. Yet I had not, which meant I was keeping a secret from the rest of the brotherhood, and that was an uncomfortable thought. But Brother Drajan had carried letters to Merabaht; surely the appearance of Brother Yarit's cousin and the mysterious gem he brought could not be unrelated.

So perhaps the senior members of the brotherhood knew after all, or at least knew more than anyone was saying.

My mind chased itself in circles trying to guess what Brother Yarit meant to impart to me. Brother Ehudan chided me for inattentiveness during our morning lesson. It made me careless in a sparring match and I ceded first blood to Brother Hakan, who caught me wrong-footing a turn and scored my backside with the central tine of his *kopar*. He teased me for it until I was very nearly ready to throttle him. Another day, the teasing would not have stung so much, and I understood that Brother Hakan was envious that I'd taken his post yesterday, but today, it was nigh unbearable. Although I had been trained to be patient, it seemed like midday would never come.

When at last it did, I presented myself at the entrance to the Seer's chamber. Brother Yarit was there, and Brother Merik, too. Three carpets had been laid out in a formal arrangement, a tea service in the center.

"Come in," Brother Yarit said to me, pouring a cup of tea. "Sit."

I entered warily and accepted the tea. "Have I done something wrong, Elder Brother?" I hesitated. "Is this about last night?"

"No." Brother Yarit folded his hands in his lap. "I thought someone who'd known you since you were a babe should be present for this discussion, so I asked Brother Merik. I hope you don't mind."

I held my tea untasted. "No, of course not."

They exchanged a glance, and Brother Merik inclined his head slightly to Brother Yarit, who sighed and rubbed his hands over his face before returning them to his lap. "Khai . . . do you know what it means to be *bhazim*?"

I shook my head. It was on the tip of my tongue to say that I'd never heard the word, but a feather of memory brushed my thoughts. Night and the desert, voices heard half-asleep.

. . . has he been cut yet?

Khai is bhazim.

Does he know?

No.

It was midday and wind-still; not a breeze was stirring, and it was hot and stifling in the Seer's chamber. Nonetheless, I felt a chill, the sweat on my skin turning cold. "What does it mean?" I whispered.

Brother Merik took pity on Brother Yarit and answered. "It's a very old practice, Khai. I cannot speak to how it is in the city or the coastal villages, but in the desert, sons are prized above daughters. Sons grow up to become warriors and bestow honor upon the clan. Daughters are expensive; daughters require dowries. A man without sons is to be pitied. A woman without sons is reckoned less than a woman."

No.

I did not understand what he was saying, did not want to understand. "What has this to do with me?"

They exchanged another glance.

"Sometimes a couple that has borne no sons will declare one of their daughters to be *bhazim,* an honorary boy," Brother Merik said in a gentle tone. "The child will be raised as a boy, dressed as a boy—"

"It's much the same in the city," Brother Yarit interrupted him. "I don't know about the villages."

Brother Merik ignored the interruption. "Sometimes a couple will conceive a son within a few years and declare their *bhazim* child a girl again. Sometimes—"

"I don't care about that!" I shouted at him, slamming down my cup of tea. "What are you saying? Are you telling me that *I'm bhazim*? Why? I'm pledged to the Brotherhood of Pahrkun! How can I *not* be a boy? I don't even *know* my parents! Why would they care if I were a son or a daughter?"

"Khai, be calm and listen," he said.

"No." I was on my feet with no memory of having risen, pacing the Seer's chamber. "No, no, no!"

"It wasn't your parents, Khai," Brother Yarit said to me. "It was Brother Saan's decision."

That brought me up short. "Brother Saan? *Why?*"

"All of us men, and none of us blood-kin to you? No one knew how else to raise you without dishonor in the brotherhood," Brother Merik said simply. "There's never been a female shadow before; nor a shadow born to a female member of the Sun-Blessed."

Brother Yarit's expression was sympathetic. "I can't tell you what Brother Saan may have Seen, Khai. It's in the past."

I stared at my hands as though they were a stranger's. They were strong and sinewy and callused, but they were slender. A boy's hands, I'd thought; hands that would lengthen and broaden into a man's when I came of age.

No.

A *girl's* hands.

I clenched them into fists. "So you're telling me that I'm a *girl*?"

"We are telling you that you're *bhazim*, Khai," Brother Merik said. "In the tribes, yes, most *bhazim* choose to live as women when they come of age. Not all. Some choose to remain *bhazim*."

I looked at Brother Yarit. "But I'll never be a grown man."

He did not equivocate. "No."

Now I was no longer chilled. Instead, it felt hot and claustrophobic in the Seer's chamber, and my skin was too tight. I plucked at my clothing. "So what . . . by all the fallen stars, what happens when I *do* come of age?" I remembered a snatch of their conversation I'd overheard with horror, unwanted tears stinging my eyes. "Ah, no! Will I sprout tits like a milking goat?"

Brother Merik flushed to the roots of his grizzled hair.

"No." Brother Yarit rose and laid firm hands on my shoulders, grounding me. "Your body will change, yes. But I promise, you won't sprout tits like a milking goat."

I gazed at him through my tears. "I don't want this, Elder Brother! If I won't grow into a man, I don't want my body to change!"

He shook his head. "I'm sorry, kid. Nature will take its course whether you like it or not. But look, it's not all bad. If you *were* born with a boy's kit and tackle, you wouldn't be able to serve as the princess's shadow without having your privy bits lopped off."

I looked blankly at him. "What?"

Brother Yarit gave my shoulders a little shake. "Ah, come on! I know the brotherhood's been careful about protecting your innocence, but you've seen plenty a pizzle and bollocks on livestock, haven't you? Did you really think human males were any different?"

"No." I remembered the sensation of my knee connecting with spongy flesh at the supplicant's groin yesterday. "I don't know. I never thought about it."

"Well, trust me, if you had 'em, you wouldn't want to lose 'em," he said. "Better *bhazim* than a eunuch."

Although I could tell it was meant to comfort me, it did not. I backed away from him, wrapping my arms around myself. "Why did you lie to me? Why did you *all* lie to me?"

Brother Yarit angled his head toward Brother Merik, clearly unwilling to take the blame for that decision. "No one meant to lie to you," the latter said quietly. "Khai . . . we meant to raise a warrior."

"But you *did* lie to me," I whispered. "All of you."

Brother Yarit took a step toward me. "Khai—"

"No." I backed farther away from him toward the entrance. "I've heard enough. I don't want to hear any more."

"Khai, listen—" Brother Merik began.

Brother Yarit raised his hand. "Let him go."

I fled.

Half-blind with tears of grief and fury, I blundered through the halls of the fortress, emerging from one of the eastern egresses. The sun was high overhead and the sky was a hard blue tinged with bronze, the kind of sky that promised a sandstorm in the offing. I ran along the ridge of the mountain range that held the Fortress of the Winds, ran beneath the hard blue sky, scrambling over crags, up and down peaks, loose rocks sliding beneath my bare feet; ran until my breath was sobbing in my lungs and it felt as though my pounding heart would burst through my ribcage.

I ran until I could run no farther, and flung myself to the ground atop a high plateau.

Bhazim.

I could not run away from the word. I could not run away from the thing I was.

Bit by bit, my heart ceased its pounding and my breathing slowed. I rolled onto my back and shielded my eyes from the sun's glare with my right forearm. Behind my closed eyelids, I saw red.

I was not a boy.

I would never be a man.

The unfairness of it was so vast I could not encompass it. I wished Brother Saan were alive, so I might ask him *why*. Oh, I supposed I could come to understand the decision in time, but why did he not tell me the truth? Why did they lie to me? Now I knew; and yet, I did not know who I was anymore.

Sweat evaporated from my skin, leaving a rime of salt behind, and my mouth was as dry as dust.

I licked my dry lips. "Why did you do it, Elder Brother?" I whispered. "Why did you lie to me?"

Somewhere nearby, a hawk gave its fierce hunting cry.

I remembered a hawk's feather, drifting, drifting. It must have caused the brotherhood great consternation that the babe who seized it in one chubby fist was a girl-child.

Had all of us been girl-children, or was I the only one?

Why had Pahrkun chosen me?

I pushed myself upright and scrubbed at my face, dried sweat and tears ribboning under my fingers. The sun was beating like a hammer and tongs on the baking anvil of the earth. I'd fled without a head-scarf or a water-skin, and there was no shelter in the heights. If I wasn't careful, I'd get sunstroke and die out here. A childish part of me thought it would serve them all right if I did, but no, that was not a thought befitting a blooded warrior. And whatever else I was, Brother Merik was right; I *was* a warrior. A young one, yes, but a warrior nonetheless. It was the only thing I'd ever known.

I could not stay here and sulk like a child. I had to go back, to face them; to face the thing I had become.

Nothing has changed, I imagined Brother Saan's voice saying. *You were Khai yesterday; you are Khai today.*

And yet everything *had* changed. Yesterday I was a boy impatient to become a man.

Today I was not. Today I was something I did not recognize.

My legs were wobbly when I rose. Still, I made myself walk to the edge of the plateau. It was a good vantage point, high enough that the hawk I'd heard was gliding on the thermal winds in the canyon below me. I could see the ochre desert spread out in every direction, dotted here and there with patches of late-blooming spring flowers, carpets of blue heliotrope and bright yellow splashes of poppies. In the deep distance, I could see a gyre of sand, so far away that I could not tell if it was an ordinary dust devil or Pahrkun himself.

Either way, it was a sign of the storm to come. I turned away from the abyss before me and made my way back to the Fortress of the Winds with a great deal more care than I'd left it, feeling the rising wind pushing at my back, picking up loose sand and grit and stinging my skin. The ignominious wound that Brother Hakan had dealt me had stiffened, causing me to limp. It was a considerably longer journey than my headlong outbound flight, but I managed to return before the storm broke, filthy and exhausted.

I went to the mountain spring that supplied the fortress with fresh water, thinking to slake my parched throat and wash the grime from my skin before I saw or spoke to anyone, only to find a dozen or so members of the brotherhood waiting in line, buckets in hand. I should have expected as much. The spring was located in a sheltered grotto on the northern slope and it was a good, reliable source that never ran dry—during the rainy season, water cascaded from it in a generous rivulet—but it could be silted over during a sandstorm, and clearing it was a day's work. Filling the fortress's cisterns in advance of a storm was a sensible precaution.

Brother Ramil caught sight of me before I could beat a stealthy retreat. He murmured something too low to hear, and the brothers stepped back, offering me a clear path to the spring.

They knew.

All this while, they had known what I did not; that I was not what I believed myself to be. It was the reason for the strict discipline of privacy in matters of the latrine that did not exist elsewhere among men of the desert folk. They had always known it. And now they knew that I knew it, too.

Most of them had schooled their faces to expressionlessness, but on a few I saw looks of pity, and that I hated the most. Although I would have preferred to flee, I steeled my nerves and approached the spring. Brother Hakan handed me the dipper without a word. I filled it and drank deeply, then poured several dippersful of cool water over my head.

"Thank you." I returned the dipper to him. "Do you know where Brother Yarit is?"

"In his chamber, I think. He let us out of training to prepare for the storm." Brother Hakan cocked an eyebrow at me. "Did I mention that I'm sorry about that scratch on your arse this morning, brother?"

If there was a right thing to say under the circumstances, that was it, for behind the brotherly guise of Brother Hakan's mocking apology I heard his assurance that nothing had changed between us; that he regarded me no differently this afternoon than he had this morning.

"Don't worry." I clapped a hand on his shoulder. "I'm sure you'll get a chance to fight a *real* battle someday."

There was a ripple of laughter in response and Brother Hakan scowled, but with a quirk to one corner of his mouth that told me he didn't mean it. I nodded my thanks to him and went to find Brother Yarit.

"Khai." He greeted me with undisguised relief. "I'm glad you're back. There's a sandstorm coming."

"I know," I said. "I saw it gathering."

He waved me into his chamber for the second time that day. "Come, sit."

I entered, but remained standing. "So, Elder Brother, now that we are alone, tell me what has any of this to do with the gemstone your cousin brought?"

Brother Yarit pursed his lips and regarded me, hands folded, index fingers pressed against his chin. "Sit," he repeated, and this time it was a command, not an invitation. "Before I answer your question, there are some things you need to know."

I sat.

Outside the winds gathered and sand darkened the sky, blotting out the sun and fulfilling the promise of the bronze-tinged skies. Inside the fortress, oil lamps and oil-wood torches were kindled, and the heavy hanging woolen carpets that kept out the cold winds of winter were drawn against the driven sand.

In the Seer's chamber, I sat quietly and listened while Brother Yarit explained to me in detail the differences between men and women, how they coupled for pleasure and procreation, and exactly what that entailed. He explained to me that in Zarkhoum, any unwed woman engaging in such activities—or even suspected of doing so—would bring dishonor on her family and be cast out for her sins; and that yet, there were always unscrupulous men who would press them to do so. He explained, too, that there were men whose desires ran perversely counter to nature; men who desired other men as a man ought to desire a woman; or worse, men who desired young children, girls or even boys.

Sick at heart, I understood then what the guardsman I'd slain had done, and why his fellows had reckoned his end a fitting one.

In a dispassionate tone, Brother Yarit described the changes that would occur to my body as I matured. Despite his assurances that a woman's breasts were things of grace and beauty and nothing at all like a milking goat's udder, I was unconvinced, and I was appalled at the notion that my narrow hips would widen into curves. Perhaps if I had been raised in the presence of women, I would not have been so disdainful of the female form that day; yet I suspect not. Even if I'd had a greater understanding of what my body would become, I cannot help but think it would be no less a betrayal to learn that I was *bhazim*, that I would never become a man.

Lastly Brother Yarit explained to me that a woman's fertility was not a constant thing, but ebbed and flowed like the tides, and that once a month my body would produce an effluence of blood.

"I'm not afraid of blood," I said dismissively.

He smiled a little. "I know."

I considered him. "How is it that you know so much about women?"

"Ah." Brother Yarit shrugged, his smile vanishing. "Well, I was married to one, kid."

"You were?" It surprised me, then I remembered something he'd said long ago, when he first came to us. "Was she a member of the Shahalim Clan? Is she the one who betrayed you?"

"My wife?" He ran a hand over his hair. "No. No, she died some five years ago. Dhanbu fever. There was an epidemic in the city," he said. "A lot of people died, and those that survived were left crippled. Children, mostly. In Merabaht, you see them begging in the streets."

It was humbling to be reminded that Brother Yarit had had a whole different life once; and, too, that I knew so very little about the world outside the desert. "I'm sorry."

His smile returned, lopsided and rueful. "You're a good kid, Khai. I'm sorry we lied to you. In my opinion, you deserved better from us. But like I said, I have no way of knowing what Brother Saan may have Seen. I do know he loved you," he added. "And he would never have wanted to hurt you. So I can only believe there must have been a good reason for it."

I looked away, my eyes stinging. "When will it happen? These . . . changes?"

There was a rustling sound as Brother Yarit shook his head. "No telling. Twelve or thirteen's pretty standard, I reckon, but it can begin earlier, as early as ten or eleven. Or later. It could be later."

So I likely had a year, maybe two, before I had to contend with unwanted changes in my body.

"All right." I looked back at Brother Yarit. "Now will you tell me what this has to do with the gemstone?"

He hesitated. "Maybe that's a discussion for another day. You've had quite enough to think about today."

"*No.*" The word emerged hard and low; I found my fists clenched again and made myself relax them, place my palms together and touch my thumbs to my brow in salute, changing my tone to one of respect. "Elder Brother, forgive me, but I would prefer to know."

"Fair enough." Brother Yarit rose and retrieved the small wooden box from a cubbyhole. He sat back down, placed it on the carpet before him, and lifted the lid. The golden glow that emanated from the gem wasn't as bright in the light of the oil lamp as it was beneath the starless sky, but it was just as rich and warm. "I told you where it comes from. It's called a Barren Teardrop. Do you remember what my cousin Amal said about it?"

I did, and I understood it a great deal better today than I had last night. "He said it belonged to a famous courtesan-queen of Barakhar," I said. "Who once took a thousand lovers in a single year."

"Right." Brother Yarit poked the gem with one finger. "Whether or not it's an accurate figure is debatable. Most women of my acquaintance deem it excessive. But this is what she used to keep from getting with child until she'd chosen a consort she deemed worthy; and that portion of her legend I do believe has been substantiated."

"How?" I asked.

"There are written records," he said.

I shook my head. "No, how did she use the gem? Did she wear it around her neck, or . . ." I lowered my voice and gestured vaguely toward the nether regions I wasn't sure I fully understood yet. "Put it somewhere down there?"

Brother Yarit's expression was impossible to decipher. "Ah, no. Actually, it was sewn into her flesh." He craned his head around and indicated a spot on the back of his neck. "Here."

I clapped a hand to the back of my own neck and stared at the gem. "Why are you telling me this, Elder Brother? Have you Seen that I will have need of it?" A terrible notion struck me. "Have you Seen that I will be . . . assaulted?" Dropping my hand, I hugged my knees to my chest, unconsciously protecting a body that felt considerably more vulnerable than it had yesterday.

"No, no, no, no!" Brother Yarit raised both hands in denial. "Nothing like that, I promise. I *did* See the Teardrop, Khai, but I've no idea what it betokens, only that it's important."

I couldn't stop staring at it. "And you want to sew it into my flesh?"

"Well, first of all, I wanted to procure it," he said dryly. "Which was no easy task, as it was in the possession of Prince Elizar, the king's eldest, who has a great passion for collecting valuable curios."

"So you called in a favor and had your cousin steal it?" Brother Saan, I thought, would have been mortified at the notion; but then, Brother Saan might not have recognized a vision of the Barren Teardrop in the first place.

It was an interesting thought, and for the first time, it occurred to me that there may have been deep-laid reasons why the Sight had passed to Brother Yarit.

Brother Yarit lifted one shoulder in a half-shrug. "Just doing my duty, the way I reckon it."

I loosened my grip on my knees. "May I see it?"

"Sure."

I picked up the Teardrop and held it in the palm of my hand. Although I'd expected it to be warm, it wasn't. "It must be quite valuable."

"Ah . . . yes." Brother Yarit's tone told me that was a considerable understatement. "I don't know why you're meant to have it, but it's yours."

I glanced up at him. "Do you think I ought to . . . to have it sewn into my flesh like the Barakhan queen?"

"I wish I knew." His expression was troubled. "I'll be honest, Khai; if the Teardrop has a purpose beyond preventing unwanted pregnancies, I don't know it. For all I know, it does, and you're meant to carry it in your pocket or wear it on a chain around your neck. But if you *do* choose to have it implanted, it will offer you a measure of protection in case—"

My shoulders tightened. "In case I *am* assaulted."

"That would take a very brave and foolhardy man, kid," Brother Yarit observed. "No, I was going to say in case you needed it. Who knows, you might choose to wed someday; as far as I know, there's no proscription against it." I stared at him in horror. "Or maybe not," he added hastily. "But at a minimum, it would keep your monthly courses at bay."

A faint spark of hope kindled in me. "Would it let me stay a boy? Would it keep my body from changing?"

"No." Brother Yarit shook his head. "I'm sorry, kid. Only in the matter of fertility."

"Oh."

"Look, you don't need to decide this anytime soon. In fact, I'd rather you waited at least a year." He handed me the wooden box. "Keep the Teardrop. Don't mention it to anyone. We'll see, maybe in a year's time we'll know more."

I placed the Teardrop in its box and saluted him. "Thank you, Elder Brother."

Brother Yarit rose and I followed suit, preparing to take my leave. "Khai." He called me back. His eyes were kind and concerned. "Are you all right?"

I didn't know how to answer his question. I was angry and confused; yes, and hurt, too. The most elemental thing I had believed about myself was a lie, and I did not know how to be this different thing.

"No," I said at last. "I don't think so."

"Ah, come here." Brother Yarit pulled me into an unexpected embrace, wrapping his arms around me and resting his chin atop my head. It felt warm and solid and reassuring to be held thusly, and I couldn't remember if anyone had ever done such a thing to me before. "You will be. I promise." He took a deep breath, then let me go and wrinkled his nose. "But watery hell, kid! You *stink*. After the storm passes, have a proper wash, will you?"

Despite everything, it made me smile. "Yes, Elder Brother."

THIRTEEN

Bhazim.

No one spoke of it, but the word plagued me. I flung myself into training with redoubled ardor, doing my best to forget it, but all the while it was there, throbbing like a heartbeat at the back of my thoughts: *bhazim, bhazim, bhazim.*

Everything had changed.

Everything was different.

To their credit, the members of the brotherhood treated me no differently. Then again, why should they? They had always known. No, the difference was inside me, and it could not be undone.

Bhazim.

Sometimes I *was* able to forget for hours at a time, especially when Brother Yarit set us some new skill to master, such as picking pockets and stealing purses, or Brother Merik determined it was time for me to learn to fight on horseback. But always, the word came crashing back over me.

Lest I forget for any length of time, the box containing the Teardrop sat in an alcove in my chamber to remind me. Sometimes I took it out to look at it, wondering if it was more than a harbinger of the changes to come.

My body had become suspect, a traitor in waiting. Although my chest remained as flat and narrow as a boy's, I grew fearful of the mysterious swell of breasts lurking in my future, and was no longer comfortable going shirtless. No one commented on it, but I had no doubt that it was noticed.

Bhazim.

If I had envied the men who surrounded me their growth before, it was nothing to what I felt now. Before, it was only a natural impatience at being a boy among men that galled me. Before, I believed it was only a matter of time before I would attain the attributes I coveted: the broad shoulders and deep voice, the burgeoning muscles, the height and reach, the wiry black hair that sprouted on forearms and shins, the beards on those lucky and virile enough to grow them.

Now I knew otherwise. None of those things would happen to me. When my body changed, it would become a stranger's.

And yet Pahrkun the Scouring Wind had chosen me.

Me, Khai.

It was one of the few thoughts that gave me strength when fury and despair threatened to overwhelm me in the early days following the unwelcome revelation; but I thought about Zariya, too. I had a duty to her, a sacred duty. In light of that fact, perhaps it made sense that I was *bhazim*. I did not have to like it, or even accept it, to understand it on that level.

And so I did the only thing I knew to do, which was to train harder and harder and harder.

The sandstorm had erased the last vestiges of spring; summer passed and gave way to autumn. Nazim the apothecary pronounced me as well versed as he could make me in the art of detecting poison for what it was worth, which was in his opinion nothing, and packed his vials and pouches and tinctures.

Brother Drajan escorted him back to Merabaht and returned with a long-awaited piece of news.

Brother Vironesh was coming.

Vironesh, the broken shadow. Not yet, but soon; he had sent word through the coursers of Obid that he had received the message and would return to Zarkhoum in the spring.

It was a welcome piece of news, for it provided me with a much-needed distraction from my woes. Discovering that I was *bhazim* set me apart from the rest of the brotherhood, but it was not the only thing; it had never been the only thing. First and foremost, I was a shadow. The other brothers might fight at the king's command if the need arose, or they might spend their lives training for a battle that never came, passing on their lore to the next generation. I, and I alone, would go to serve in the court of the House of the Ageless, bound to a single charge. I, and I alone, would be privileged to partake of the *rhamanthus* seeds alongside the princess Zariya and know what it was like to live without aging.

No one could prepare me for that but Brother Vironesh. No one else alive knew what it was like to be a shadow to one of the Sun-Blessed or even to serve in the House of the Ageless.

Thus I anticipated his arrival with great eagerness. I thought that perhaps with Brother Vironesh, I would not care so much that I was *bhazim,* for the thing that we shared in common was so much greater than the differences between men and women. It pained me to recall how ignorant I had been at the gathering of the clans, studying the girls and women of the Black Sands Clan as though they were a foreign species, unwitting of the fact that beneath our robes, we were the same. There was a part of me that wished I *had* known at the time. I could have gone behind the curtain; I could have had a greater glimpse of what the world of women was like.

I said as much to Brother Merik, who nodded in understanding. "That's true, Khai. But like as not, the tribesfolk wouldn't have let you join in the fight to settle the blood-feud if they'd known you were *bhazim.* Which would you have chosen?"

"I would have chosen to fight," I admitted.

He nodded again. "Exactly so."

It sparked another memory: Brother Merik ushering the belligerent Khisan out of the tent when I'd given offense by studying the women too closely, and the strange way Khisan had regarded me upon their return. "But you told Khisan, didn't you?" I said. "The chieftain's son, that night after the battle. You told him I was *bhazim.*"

Brother Merik had the grace to look abashed. "Only to keep the peace. It didn't matter at that point, Khai. You'd already had your first battle and become a blooded warrior."

I looked away. "It matters to me, brother. I feel a fool for not knowing what I was, and doubly so for knowing others did."

To that, he could do nothing save offer an apology.

The winter months dragged mercilessly. Brother Yarit undertook to teach us the subtle and complex system of hand signs that the Shahalim used to communicate silently with each other.

I learned that his cousin Amal's mission to steal the Teardrop was not unknown to the senior members of the brotherhood. As I had suspected, it was entailed in the missives that Brother Drajan had carried to Merabaht. The secrecy that Brother Yarit had employed was to protect his cousin from exposure within the Royal Guard itself, an extremely useful position for a thief. The Shahalim were willing to aid Brother Yarit—and even to forgive him for sharing clan training with me and the brotherhood—in exchange for the secrets he kept.

The spring rains came and the desert bloomed anew. I gained twelve years of age, and despite my fears, my body had yet to betray me.

At last, Brother Vironesh came.

We had warning, for Brother Yarit had Seen his impending arrival and posted a lookout. It rained that morning, a single hard downpour that darkened the skies for less than an hour and passed, leaving the world bright and refreshed, yellow gorse and snakeweed blossoming in its wake.

It seemed to me that the arrival of the only other living shadow in the world should be a grand affair. After all, he had been an honorary member of the House of the Ageless for more than a century. I expected him to arrive in state, perhaps escorted by an honor guard of the king's men.

I was wrong.

Brother Vironesh came alone, riding at an unhurried pace across the desert, no pack-horse in tow. I should have liked to get a better look at him before he entered the Fortress of the Winds, but Brother Yarit forbade it, ordering us to train as usual in the Dancing Bowl while he sent a delegation to greet the returning shadow and usher him into the fortress.

I spent the morning training in a fever of impatience, expecting Brother Vironesh to enter the Dancing Bowl at any moment, but the sun climbed high into the sky without any sign of him. It was not until after the midday rest, when we resumed our training, that Brother Yarit escorted him into our midst. I cannot recall who spotted them first, but word raced around in a hushed whisper, until everyone ceased whatever activities in which they were engaged.

"All right!" Brother Yarit called. "Put down your weapons and come welcome the esteemed shadow Brother Vironesh back to the Fortress of the Winds after so many years."

Sheathing our *yakhans* and *kopars,* we gathered in an attentive semicircle, folding our palms and touching our brows in salute, murmuring respectful greetings: *welcome, Brother Vironesh, well met, Brother Vironesh, we are honored, Brother Vironesh.*

It was hard not to stare.

Rumors of his appearance had not been exaggerated. Brother Vironesh's skin was an unmistakable bluish-purple, the hue of a three-day-old bruise. His eyes were set deep in their hollows, and there were strange silvery, slashing lines below them that glittered faintly like mica, one on each cheek. It was hard to gauge his age, but he was older than I'd expected, which was foolish. Of course he would have aged in the forty-some years since Prince Kazaran died; by now, he would have the body of a man in his sixties. He was tall and heavyset, broad-shouldered but thick around the middle. He wore faded indigo blue robes, and it was hard to say whether they disguised or emphasized the odd hue of his skin. A *yakhan* with a well-worn hilt protruded from a scabbard hanging from his sash, but I could see no other weapon.

He did not look pleased to see us. "Just Vironesh," he said curtly. "Been a long time since I counted myself a member of the brotherhood."

"And yet here you are," Brother Yarit observed in a neutral tone.

Brother Vironesh—Vironesh—looked sidelong at him. "I thought it was Brother Saan who summoned me."

"Brother Saan had been seeking you for years," Brother Ehudan assured him. "Ever since Khai was chosen."

"Khai." Vironesh's jaw worked as though he were chewing on a wad of something. His disinterested gaze settled on me. "That's you."

I offered him another salute. "Yes, brother."

"Huh." He looked back at Brother Yarit. "And you want me to train him."

"It seems fitting, yes," Brother Yarit said. "I presume there are things you can teach him that we cannot."

"Why?" Vironesh asked bluntly. "What I learned, I learned from the Brotherhood of Pahrkun. There was no living shadow to train *me*."

Brother Yarit's nostrils flared; he was nearing the end of his patience. "And look at how well that ended for you," he murmured with acid politeness.

I caught my breath. It struck me as a mortal insult, the kind of thing a man could die for uttering. I was not alone, for around me, I heard feet shifting on the sand, hands dropping to hilts, preparing to defend the Seer from the violent outburst sure to come. But the blue man, the hulking shadow, only lifted his gaze to the empty sky as though looking for answers there.

"All right," he said eventually, shifting the unseen wad in his mouth to the other cheek. "But only the boy. The girl, that is. Whatever you call him. Her."

It was a thing no one had dared say in my presence, and it hit me like a blow to the gut. I found myself trembling with unexpected fury. Out of the corner of one eye, I saw Brother Yarit's hand move at his side, giving me a sign that meant *Wait, be patient, do nothing.*

"Khai," he said mildly. "We call him Khai."

"Khai," Vironesh repeated for a second time. He gave me a brusque nod. "We'll start tomorrow. See to it that no one disturbs me in the meantime," he added to the brotherhood in general.

With that, he turned and walked away unbidden, the hem of his blue robe brushing the floor of the Dancing Bowl.

I waited until he was out of earshot to let out my breath in a long hiss. "Elder Brother—"

Brother Yarit held up a hand to forestall me. "Come with me. We'll talk in my chamber."

Inside the Seer's chamber I paced as though my anger had caused my heels to sprout wings, complaining bitterly of Vironesh's callous demeanor, his unthinking incivility, his disinterest and discourtesy. Brother Yarit leaned against a wall of the cavern, picking at his nails, and suffered me to carry on until I'd talked myself dry.

"Are you quite finished?" he asked when I had.

I was ashamed. "Yes, Elder Brother. Forgive me, I didn't mean to be disrespectful. It's just—"

"I know. You're disappointed."

"I'm *angry*!"

"You're angry because you're disappointed," he said. "You expected a warrior out of legend, someone who could teach you what it meant to be a shadow, teach you about honor beyond honor, be a mentor to you in a way that no one since Brother Saan has truly been."

I lowered my gaze. "You've taught me a great deal, Elder Brother."

"But not necessarily what you *wanted* to learn," Brother Yarit said. "It's all right. I know. But Khai . . . listen. You've heard from the beginning that Vironesh was a broken shadow. I don't think you can begin to understand what that means. I'm not sure any of us can, but I've been reading Brother Saan's notes. Do you know what Vironesh said about the moment he met Prince Kazaran for the first time?" He checked himself. "No, of course you don't. He said that the only way to describe it was that it felt like his heart had begun to beat in another's breast."

"Oh," I murmured.

Brother Yarit nodded. "And he said that when Kazaran was poisoned, it was as though his own heart had stopped beating, and his dumb, useless body went on living without it."

I stole a glance at him. "You're telling me to be compassionate?"

"I'm telling you to try," he said dryly. "I'm not saying he's making it easy; all the fallen stars under heaven know I'm struggling. But you can't expect him to take pleasure in your existence. Everything you are, everything that lies before you, reminds him of everything that he's lost, reminds him that he failed at his sole purpose in life."

I shook my head. "I understand what you're saying, Elder Brother, but it doesn't even seem like he *cares*."

"Oh, he cares," Brother Yarit said. "Far too much to bear the pain. I'd lay you a thousand-to-one odds that's why he's chewing *gahlba*."

"*Gahlba?*"

He cocked an eyebrow at me. "You didn't notice?"

"I noticed the chewing," I assured him. "But *gahlba* isn't anything the apothecary taught me about. What is it?"

"It's a leaf," he said. "It dulls the emotions while leaving the senses unimpaired. Right now, trust me, Brother Vironesh—Vironesh, that is—isn't feeling *anything*. Probably hasn't for years, maybe decades." Brother Yarit pushed himself away from the cavern wall, his dark eyes intent in his plain, forgettable face. "Here's the thing, Khai. I've Seen that Vironesh is meant to be here at the Fortress of the Winds, that Pahrkun himself wills it. Of that much, I'm sure. Brother Saan Saw the same thing. But what if he's not meant to be here for your sake?"

I was confused. "Whose, then?"

"His own," he said simply. "Maybe Vironesh is meant to find healing here in the desert. Maybe you're meant to aid him."

It was a humbling change in perspective, and perhaps all the more valuable for it. "I will try," I promised. "But there was no call for him to insult me as he did."

"To insult . . ." Brother Yarit paused. "Ah. First of all, there's no shame in being a woman, Khai."

"I didn't mean it thusly," I muttered.

"But you feel he disrespected you as a warrior by referring to you as a girl," he said shrewdly. "I doubt he meant to. When I told him you were *bhazim*, he barely recognized the word. Remember, Vironesh has been away from Zarkhoum for a long time. Among the coursers of Obid, there are women who sail and fight alongside the men."

I stared at him. "*What?*"

He laughed. "Different realms, different customs, kid. You didn't figure that out when I mentioned that Barakhan courtesan-queen with a thousand lovers?"

"Oh." I flushed. It had never occurred to me that there were different ways of being a woman in the world beyond Zarkhoum, that a woman might even be reckoned a warrior. "Yes, I suppose I should have."

"That's all right." Brother Yarit extended his arm. "Listen, kid. You do your best to be patient and respectful with Vironesh, and I'll do the same. Do we have a bargain?"

I clasped his forearm. "We do."

FOURTEEN

I had my first lesson with Vironesh the next day.

It did not go well.

Mindful of my promise to Brother Yarit, I was resolved to be polite and respectful no matter how Vironesh treated me. I presented myself before him in the Dancing Bowl and saluted him.

Vironesh regarded me impassively. "Very well." He drew his *yakhan*, holding it loosely in his right hand. "Try me."

I hesitated. "You wish me to attack you?"

"Yes."

I glanced around. "Would you like a *kopar*, brother?"

"No."

"All right." I drew my weapons and took a stance. Vironesh stood motionless. I felt awkward about launching an attack on him. I had two weapons to his one, and although he had the reach of me, I had youth and speed on my side. Still, it was what he'd bade me to do, and to disobey would be disrespectful. I essayed a low jab with my *kopar*, only to find it parried with a turn of wrist so subtle I barely saw it; not to the outside as I'd expected, but to the inside. His left hand closed on the central tine, and with another deft twist, Vironesh wrenched the *kopar* from my grip, using it to parry the sweeping slash of my blade. He took a single unhurried step backward and flipped the *kopar*, catching it by the hilt.

No question, I was overmatched; and I didn't even know how he'd done it. Every motion had seemed so slight, almost negligible, and yet here I stood, half disarmed. I didn't bother trying to press the attack with my remaining weapon. "How did you do that?"

Instead of answering, Vironesh tossed my *kopar* to me. "Try again."

I did.

I tried a dozen times, using a dozen different attacks, and not a single one of them went anywhere. It was maddening and bewildering. It didn't seem as though Vironesh's defense should be so effective, so impenetrable. His movements appeared slow and deliberate, and yet when I played them over in my head, I could see that he somehow managed to anticipate my every move.

"How do you do it?" I asked again after another failed attempt. "It's like you know what I'm going to do before I do."

"I've had a century and a half's worth of practice." He shrugged. "That's nothing you can teach. It comes with time and experience."

Impatience rose in me, and I tamped it down. Vironesh had neither asked nor volunteered to teach me; maybe he didn't even know how to be a teacher. Maybe my role was to help him discover it. After all, at least I had plenty of experience being a student.

"What of the inside parry?" I asked humbly, miming the motion. "That's a move I've never seen. Can you teach it to me?"

He shrugged again. "I can try."

It's fair to say that in the days that followed, Vironesh *did* attempt to teach me. He had been at the craft of battle for a long, long time. Like me, he had been raised from a babe by the Brotherhood of Pahrkun, but he had also studied Granthian fighting techniques in the service of Prince Kazaran. He had sailed the four great currents of the world with the coursers of Obid, learning their skills; and, too, encountering the fighting techniques of the pirates and smugglers and raiders the coursers sought to police.

In many of the sparring sequences in which we engaged—I will not call them matches, for our exchanges were not worthy of the name—there was some element with which I was unfamiliar; a parry, a pivot, a two-handed blow. These things Vironesh deigned to teach me when I succeeded in identifying them. The other brothers gathered around to watch and learn when he did so, and although Vironesh had said he would train only me, he did not seem to care if they studied his technique any more than he paid heed to the buzzing flies that the summer's heat brought.

I learned the mechanics of each unfamiliar maneuver, but it availed naught. I was no closer to determining how Vironesh was able to anticipate my every move than I had been at the beginning.

There was something that evaded me, and I had no idea what it was. Vironesh the broken shadow was a lock I could not pick.

"Brother Vironesh is holding back," Brother Merik observed in a conversation I chanced—well, not chanced, exactly—to overhear among the senior brothers.

"But what?" Brother Drajan asked in bewilderment. "And why?"

"I'm not sure he even knows himself," Brother Yarit said thoughtfully. "On either count."

While it was somewhat reassuring to hear that not even the Seer and the senior brothers could solve the mystery of Vironesh, it was also discouraging. I did not know what any of us could do.

Especially me.

If my existence galled Vironesh, he did not say so. Still, it felt very much as though he disliked me, although in truth Vironesh didn't care enough to dislike or like anyone or anything, unless it was his ever-present wad of *gahlba*. He interacted with members of the brotherhood as little as possible, disdaining the common dining hall to take his meals in his private chamber. I tried to maintain sympathy for him, and if I did not always succeed, at least I managed to remain respectful, hoping that one day there might be a crack in his uncaring façade.

As time wore on, it began to seem less and less likely. I found myself spending evenings after training had ended venting my frustration on the spinning devil by the light of an oil-wood torch. At times I could not help but wonder if it would have been different if Brother Saan were still alive. Vironesh had respected him, that was clear; it was the only reason he had come. It was equally clear that he had little or no respect for Brother Yarit. Brother Saan with his kind, gentle, insightful manner might have been able to find a chink in the broken shadow's armor and ease his way inside, to coax him into lowering his guard and seek healing in the desert.

One thing was certain, he wouldn't have done what Brother Yarit did.

To say that Brother Yarit was an impatient man is to do him a disservice. In matters of his own craft of stealth and thievery—and of imparting it to others—he was capable of endless patience. When it came to enduring the foibles of others . . . well, that was another matter.

It was some six weeks into Vironesh's time at the Fortress of the Winds. Brother Yarit told no one what he intended; none of us had the slightest inkling of what he'd done until we entered the Dancing Bowl one morning to find him kneeling in the center beneath the shadow of the stone bridge, tending to a brazier from which a foul-smelling smoke billowed.

"Elder Brother," I said cautiously. "What is it that you're burning?"

Brother Yarit got to his feet and grinned. "Oh, I expect you'll find out soon enough."

That we did.

In six weeks' time, Vironesh had shown no emotion. This morning, it was different. This morning, he entered the Dancing Bowl like a thundercloud, his brow furrowed as he stalked the grounds. Catching sight of the brazier, he halted. "What have you done?" he asked in a low, dangerous voice.

Despite the morning's heat, Brother Yarit made as if to warm his hands over the brazier. "Can't you guess?"

Vironesh's shoulders tensed. "You had no right."

Brother Yarit raised his chin. "I am the Seer."

In a few swift strides, Vironesh was upon him; but no, it wasn't Brother Yarit he was after. Not yet. He kicked over the brazier with one sandaled foot. Ashes of *gahlba* spilled across the ground, a few embers yet glowing. Brother Yarit retreated several discreet paces, hands twitching toward his sleeves.

"You had no right!" Vironesh repeated, his voice rising to an anguished shout. It was like hearing a boulder crack; it seemed mountains should crumble in its wake. *"No right!"*

Brother Yarit stood his ground, hands low at his sides, concealing the deadly *zims* I was sure they held. "You need to *feel*, brother!" he said. "You're no good to anyone if you can't!"

I moved to place myself between them. Across the Dancing Bowl, I saw Brothers Hakan and Ramil exchanging hand signs, signaling their intent to flank Vironesh from behind.

Vironesh glanced around, a great beast brought to bay. His broad shoulders slumped in defeat. "You are mistaken," he said to Brother Yarit with quiet dignity. "The coursers of Obid valued my service. I think it best if I return to them."

It was a statement on which to make an exit and Vironesh turned to do so, but Brother Yarit wasn't done with him yet. "The coursers must value it indeed to overlook your use of *gahlba*," he called. "Do not the followers of Obid disdain the use of any substance that might impair judgment?"

A shudder ran through the purple man's flesh, as though Brother Yarit's words had struck home. Still, it was not enough to sway him from his course. "I'm sorry, Khai," he said as he passed me, and it felt as though he were truly seeing me for the first time. "I pray you never have cause to understand the choices I have made."

No one made a move to halt or dissuade him. We stood and exchanged uncertain glances, looking to Brother Yarit for guidance. Brother Yarit's hands passed under his sleeves once more, sheathing the hidden *zims*. His expression was unreadable.

Once Vironesh had vanished into the interior of the fortress, it was Brother Merik who broke the silence. "Please tell me this scheme of yours is in accordance with the Sight, Elder Brother," he said in a formal tone that nonetheless managed to convey a considerable amount of disapproval.

Brother Yarit grimaced. "'Accordance' is a strong word. Let us say I'm attempting to nudge events in the right direction."

Brother Merik stared at him. "Nudge? When the Sight first came upon you, I seem to recall you saying that attempting to tip the scales upsets the balance of everything. Everything! Am *I* mistaken?"

"No," Brother Yarit admitted. "But something needed to be done, and quite frankly, it was the only thing I could think of. We'll see whether or not it bears fruit."

"And how, exactly, might that come to pass?" Brother Merik demanded.

He gestured toward the west. "Even as we speak, the only other living shadow in existence is gathering his things and preparing to depart for good!"

"Yeah." Brother Yarit cocked his head. "I tried that once, too. Remember?"

An errant breeze skirled through the Dancing Bowl, raising puffs of dust. It stirred my memories.

Rising wind, lowering sun.

"Do you think Pahrkun will turn him back as he did when you sought to flee?" I asked Brother Yarit.

"Turn him back?" He shook his head. "Not in the same way, no. But I'm gambling on the hope that Pahrkun the Scouring Wind is long overdue for a word with his eldest chosen."

Brother Yarit was right.

In the uncertainty that followed Vironesh's abrupt departure, Brother Merik assigned us sparring matches. I was matched with Brother Drajan and used one of the maneuvers I'd learned from Vironesh to catch him wrong-footed and slip inside his guard, but I was too distracted to press my advantage.

The wind continued to rise, and my skin was prickling. Brother Drajan walloped me alongside the head with his *kopar*. "Don't lose focus, Khai!" he chided me. "If I were an enemy, you'd be dead."

"Ow!" I rubbed my stinging ear; it would be swollen by nightfall. A nest of red ants emerged from a crevice in the floor of the Dancing Bowl and scurried toward the east in a straight line. I watched the line veer gradually southward as they progressed.

"Khai?" Brother Drajan tapped his weapons together, gesturing for me to resume our bout.

"Your pardon, brother," I said to him. "It's just . . . I think Pahrkun is coming."

He stared at me. "Here? Now?"

I shook my head and pointed at the ants. "No, but near. Soon."

Brother Drajan lowered his weapons and let out a shout. "Brothers! The Scouring Wind draws nigh!"

He sent me to fetch Brother Yarit, who summoned us to gather atop one of the high lookouts. Although the mounted figure of Vironesh appeared small in the distance, he hadn't gotten far from the fortress yet; there simply hadn't been enough time. I reckoned the distance was less than half a league.

In the east, the storm that was Pahrkun was approaching, a tall figure looming in a wall of moving sand. Though we had the benefit of our high vantage, it seemed impossible to me that Vironesh had not yet seen or sensed him. Even as I thought it, I realized that I was mistaken. Vironesh was making for a stunted thorn tree. Dismounting, he tied his horse's reins to a low branch, then made his way toward the east on foot, putting some distance between himself and his mount.

Atop the lookout, we watched.

At what he gauged to be a safe distance, Vironesh halted and genuflected three times, then sat cross-legged on the stony ground and waited with his head bowed, patient and still. Whatever else one might say of him, he didn't lack for courage.

I rubbed the prickling skin on my arms and wondered if I would be brave enough to do so when my time came.

Pahrkun the Scouring Wind came, crossing the desert with great strides, robed in blowing sand. Although the sandstorm of his approach blotted out the sun, it was there behind him, causing his immense shadow to stretch before him for leagues and leagues, darkening the ochre terrain and falling over the seated figure of Vironesh. Pahrkun's long, dark, misshapen head moved to and fro as he came, green eyes in deep-set sockets glowing through the veils of sand as he surveyed the desert. Although he was too far away to see clearly, it seemed almost that the very flesh of his face was in a strange state of constant motion.

One day, I would encounter him face-to-face.

But not today, no. Today, he had come for Vironesh.

The winds atop the lookout were buffeting. I braced myself against them and squinted into the sand-stinging gusts.

The Scouring Wind came and came across the desert and halted at last.

One enormous figure standing, long, inhuman head held high; one tiny figure seated, head bowed in submission.

"*That* is what I Saw," Brother Yarit murmured to no one in particular.

Pahrkun spoke to Vironesh.

If there were words, we could not hear them; and yet I sensed them. I felt them buzzing against the drums of my ears; I felt them in the low rumble of the earth against the soles of my bare feet.

I felt . . . what? Awe. Terror.

Envy.

Yes, envy.

Vironesh listened; Vironesh lifted his gaze to meet Pahrkun's immense green-glowing eyes. Vironesh put his palms together and touched his thumbs to his brow in salute.

I released a breath I hadn't known I was holding.

Pahrkun the Scouring Wind turned and departed, striding back toward the deep eastern desert. The winds died in the wake of his departure and the blowing sand fell and settled. The sun shone brightly once more. Beneath the thorn tree, Vironesh's mount stamped its hooves and gave a plaintive whicker that carried over the now wind-still distance, tossing its head and tugging restlessly against the reins.

Unfolding his legs beneath him, Vironesh rose with an effort and trudged back toward his horse.

We waited long enough to see that he meant to return to the Fortress of the Winds before Brother Yarit ordered us to disperse. It would have been foolish to pretend that the Brotherhood of Pahrkun did not know what had transpired; and while Brother Yarit might lack tact, he was surely no one's fool. He bade me accompany him to welcome Vironesh upon his return.

"Elder Brother," Vironesh addressed him from the saddle. It was the first time he had used the term of respect. "It seems I am meant to be here."

"Yes," Brother Yarit said simply.

Light glinted on the strange, mica-flecked scars beneath Vironesh's eyes. "You sought to manipulate fate based on the gift of Sight. I bear a message for you. Pahrkun the Scouring Wind says, *Do not attempt the like again*."

Brother Yarit inclined his head. "I will not."

Vironesh dismounted. "Good." He looked at me, a reluctant spark of life in his gaze. "Khai."

I saluted him. "Yes, brother?"

"I will spend the rest of today in contemplation," he said to me. "Tomorrow morning we begin anew."

FIFTEEN

Things were very different the next morning. When I emerged from my lesson with Brother Ehudan, the fortress was nearly empty, the grounds deserted. Vironesh was waiting for me alone in the Dancing Bowl.

"Where is everyone?" I asked him.

"Brother Yarit arranged a hunting expedition," Vironesh said. "I wished to speak with you without the distraction of the entire brotherhood around us."

"I see." I was disappointed to miss a hunting party, which was always a welcome relief from the eternal regimen of training, but I tried not to let it show.

Vironesh noticed anyway and essayed a faint smile; it seemed a great effort for him. "Come. Walk with me."

I fell in beside him. We climbed the stairway to the stone bridge, and I followed as he set out across the narrow structure.

Halfway across, Vironesh halted, gazing down at the Dancing Bowl below us. The expression on his strange bruise-colored face was unreadable. "Do you remember catching the hawk's feather?"

My pulse quickened; I'd never known anyone who shared the same experience. "Yes," I said. "Do you?"

"Oh, yes," he said quietly. "Vividly."

We stood together in silence for a moment. The breeze tugged at my tunic, stirred his robes. I was confident in my balance, but Vironesh seemed as immovable as a mountain atop the slender span of stone.

"Brother Yarit tells me that despite your youth, you are a blooded warrior," he said at length. "That you have fought and killed."

"Yes," I said. "Twice."

He looked at me. "And when you did, did you have a sense within you like a rising wind?"

I met his gaze. "Yes, I did."

Vironesh nodded. "It is the essence of Pahrkun's spirit coursing through you. *That* is what you must learn to harness and channel, Khai."

"How?" I asked him.

"By dint of long practice," he said dryly. "But one must begin somewhere. If it is mortal stakes that you require to evoke it, so be it." Shifting to face me, he drew his *yakhan*. "Let us spar."

I gaped at him. *"Here?"*

Sunlight ran like water along the edge of his blade. "Here."

"No." Shaking my head, I took a careful step backward. "As much as I wish to learn from you, I'm not mad enough to court death, brother."

Vironesh laughed, a sound like rocks grating. "You, who fought your first battle at the tender age of ten? You, who stood first post in the Trial of Pahrkun at eleven? It seems to me you are *eager* to court death."

"That was different," I said stubbornly. "This . . ." I gestured around. "There's no purpose in it."

"But I have told you the purpose." Vironesh cocked his head. "Are you afraid?" There was a genuine note of curiosity in his voice.

"Common sense is not fear," I retorted. "And if you think to provoke me into losing my temper, I've seen that trick before." I tapped my temple. "Brother Saan taught me that a warrior's first and greatest weapon is his mind."

"You do not trust me." Vironesh lowered his blade and rested the tip on the stone. "That is fair; I have given you no reason to do so." He hesitated. "You cannot truly know what it is to be a shadow, not until you've been paired with your charge. But suppose . . . suppose someone you loved lay injured and dying on the other side of this bridge. Brother Saan, were he still alive. Would you not do everything in your power to reach him?"

I felt the sense of which he had spoken stirring within me at the notion. "Of course."

"Good, good." Vironesh raised his *yakhan*. "Now suppose I am the only thing that stands between you and saving Brother Saan's life."

Common sense told me I should abandon this mad endeavor; but common sense had never availed me in learning whatever it was that Vironesh had to teach me. The rising wind inside me owed nothing to common sense.

And Pahrkun had sent the broken shadow here.

I drew my weapons. "As you will, brother."

We sparred atop the high, narrow arch, blades clashing, the drop looming beneath our feet, and a sense of exhilaration filled me. It *was* madness, but oh, what a glorious madness it was!

"That's it!" Unexpectedly, Vironesh was grinning; a hard, fierce grin that showed all his teeth. "Channel it, harness it!" Pressed by my attack, he retreated a step, then parried my follow-up blow with enough force that I nearly lost my balance, teetering on the stone bridge. I glanced down involuntarily and felt my heart leap into my throat at the sight of the ground far beneath me. "Don't look down! You know damn well how far a fall it is. Keep your eyes on me!" I regained my balance and acknowledged him with a grim nod. His blade feinted and teased, hinting at openings that never quite materialized. "Let the wind guide you, Khai. Look for the spaces *between* things."

"I don't understand," I said through gritted teeth.

"Oh, but you do." His blade flicked mine away with one of those infuriatingly subtle parries. "Wind will blow through any chink it can find, flow around any obstacle in its course. Follow the wind's example and let it guide you into those spaces. Between a strike and a parry, between a step and a turn, between a thought and its execution, between one breath and the next—ow!"

I'd caught Vironesh on the knuckles of his right hand with the blunt inner edge of my *yakhan* in a backward-sweeping blow. He dropped his blade out of sheer surprise, and it fell glinting through the sunlight to clatter onto the ground below.

Breathing hard, I stepped back and put up my weapons. "May I presume Brother Saan is saved?"

"You may." Vironesh shook out his hand, regarding me. "Congratulations. That's the first time a lone opponent has landed a blow against me since . . . well, it's been a very long time."

"I am not so vain as to believe I could have done so if you were not intent on instructing me at the time," I said wryly, sheathing my *yakhan* and thrusting my *kopar* into my sash.

"True." He was not given to false modesty. "But what I spoke of . . . you understood it, did you not?"

I hesitated. "Let us say I have the first inkling of understanding."

"An inkling is more than I possessed at your age," Vironesh observed. "In time, you will come to understand and channel Pahrkun's wind at will. You will find that time itself seems to slow when you do, and you will develop a greater facility for seeing the spaces between one thing and another."

It was a beginning.

I should like to say it was a beginning that changed everything, that the spark of insight I'd gained atop the stone bridge that day was transformative. Alas, it was not. In the days that followed, I was no more able to summon the essence of Pahrkun's spirit at will than I was able to summon Anamuht's lightning from an upraised fist. It was a spark that needed to be carefully tended and fed. But it *was* a spark, and it was the beginning of my true training with Vironesh.

He pushed me; he pushed me hard in an effort to provoke me into channeling the wind. It did not always work. Unless we were sparring atop a deadly precipice—and Brother Yarit, when he learned of it, made it clear that was *not* to be an everyday occurrence—I was too aware of Vironesh's superior skill to believe that my life was at stake in the battle. He was just that much better than me, better than all of us. Vironesh might deal me the odd injury to remind me that it was serious business we were about, but I didn't believe he would truly do me a grievous harm. I was far more likely to suffer a serious injury at the hands of a less skilled opponent.

But sometimes . . . sometimes in the heat of the moment I was able to forget, and that sense would fill me, a sense like a wind rising from the soles of my feet, spiraling through me to the tips of my fingers.

And bit by bit, the spark was nurtured into a flame, albeit a small one. At those times when I was able to channel Pahrkun's wind, I began to see what

Vironesh meant about the spaces *between*. Brother Saan's counsel notwithstanding, as warriors, we trained our bodies to react quicker than thought
in battle; but we were human and imperfect. One motion did not always
blend seamlessly into the next.

Sometimes there were missteps.

Sometimes there were misjudgments.

It could be something as significant as wrongly anticipating an opponent's
next maneuver; it could be something as small and simple as misgauging an
opponent's angle of attack by a few degrees.

And there were spaces in between those things, spaces into which one
could flow like the wind.

This, I began to see.

It set me apart from the rest of the brotherhood, which was a thing I
regretted. In the depths of winter that first year, there was a revolt led by
Brother Hakan, a dozen of the younger brothers complaining in an aggrieved
manner that Vironesh was withholding valuable secrets, demanding that
they be allowed to train with him in the same fashion. Brother Yarit heard
them out and met privately with Vironesh, urging him to meet their demands.

To my surprise, Vironesh agreed.

It was to no avail, a thing he had known. None of them were able to channel Pahrkun's wind or even understand what it meant to do so.

None of them had caught a hawk's feather in an infant fist.

None of them were shadows.

"What makes *you* so damned special, Khai?" Brother Hakan spat at me
after a failed attempt. "Why *you*?"

"Brother . . ." I spread my hands helplessly. "Nothing. I was born at the
right moment. I cannot say why Pahrkun chose me."

Angry tears glittered in his eyes. "It's not fair!"

"Life is unfair, young brother," Vironesh said impassively. "But if you
think to envy Khai, you are a fool."

Such dour pronouncements were as close as Vironesh came to speaking
of the pain of his loss, though it was obvious to all that he carried it inside
him like a stone. My hope that he would share insights with me on what it
was like to be a shadow had proved a vain one thus far; he spoke only in the

most general of terms, never mentioning Prince Kazaran by name. Brother Yarit cautioned me to be patient, and I reluctantly obeyed.

My progress seemed to please Vironesh, insofar as anything pleased the man. When his fierce battle-grin emerged in the midst of a training session, I knew I might take pride in my efforts. I no longer had the sense that he disliked me, but I could not say that I had the sense that he harbored any fondness for me, either. Having gone for decades without allowing himself to feel, Vironesh seemed determined to avoid any emotional attachment to another living being.

It made me lonely.

Being the only child in a brotherhood of grown men had never troubled me before; it was all I had ever known. But now I was three times set apart from the brotherhood. I was young. I was *bhazim*. And the further I progressed in my training with Vironesh, the further apart I grew from the others, a solitary young warrior learning a skill that was not afforded to my companions.

The more proficient I became, the more evident it grew; not only in sparring matches, but in some of the arts of the Shahalim Clan in which Brother Yarit continued to train us. When I was able to channel Pahrkun's wind, I could see the spaces between attention and distraction so clearly, I was able to slip unnoticed by an observer or pick a pocket so deftly that even Brother Yarit had to own himself impressed. I was grateful for his praise; and yet, it drove home the point that I was at an ever-increasing remove from the brotherhood.

Were it not for that, I cannot say whether I would have made the choice I did when the inevitable happened and my body betrayed me.

I was some months past my thirteenth birthday when it began. Shallow swellings of soft useless flesh emerged on my narrow, sturdy chest.

I hated it.

I hated them.

Bhazim, bhazim, bhazim. The word from which I could not flee, the thing I did not want to be. An honorary boy, yes. But I was unable to deny the unsaid truth beneath it: My body was a girl's.

No one commented, but I saw in Brother Yarit's shrewd, sympathetic gaze that he noticed and knew.

I took to winding a length of cloth around my chest, binding my bud-
ding breasts so that they lay as flat as possible. As though rebelling against
my attempts at constriction, my narrow hips widened.

Not a great deal, in truth; later, when I knew more about men and women
and the ways of the world, I would understand that the exhaustive training
I had undergone from a young age kept my body far more lean and muscular than most. But I did not know that, then. I only knew that the betrayal
had begun, setting me yet further apart from my brethren.

Alone at night in my chamber, I would take the Teardrop from its wooden
box and contemplate it, its deep honey-gold light illuminating the creases
and callused ridges of my palm. According to Brother Yarit, the Lone Tree
of the Barren Isle was one of the children of heaven, but if it had a name, no
one knew it.

A single drop of resin every hundred years, and five hundred more for it to
petrify; its worth, I thought, must be incalculable. Were it to be sewn into
my flesh, that would be yet another way in which I was different. No one
else in the brotherhood would have a gem worth a prince's ransom hidden
beneath their skin.

And yet . . . it would allow me to keep from crossing the final threshold
that divided women from men. I would not be subject to the tides of fertility that Brother Yarit had described; I would not be transformed into an
unfamiliar creature suited to the world of childbearing and nursemaiding.

It would make *bhazim* more than a word I despised; something, perhaps,
of value. I would be a thing apart, but that was already true.

At last I spoke to Brother Yarit about it, hoping that the Sight might have
afforded him a greater understanding of the Teardrop's purpose in the year
that had passed since he gave it to me.

"No." Brother Yarit shook his head when I asked him about it. "I wish it
had, but no." He paused. "You're considering it?"

I fidgeted. "Do you think I should do it?"

"I cannot make that choice for you, Khai," he said gently. "You had no
voice in the decision to raise you as *bhazim*, and that cannot be undone. But
this . . . this you must choose for yourself."

"Does everyone know about this, too?" I asked him, unable to keep a hint of bitterness from my tone.

"No." Brother Yarit understood. "No, only the senior brothers. And Brother Karal will have to be told if you decide to do it," he added. Brother Karal had some knowledge of healing herb lore and a neat hand with a needle and thread; he was the one who patched our wounds and saw to it that they didn't fester. "I wouldn't trust the job to anyone else. But I'd very much prefer it went no further." He ran a hand over his hair. "None of the brothers knows that the Teardrop was stolen from a member of the House of the Ageless, but it's not exactly a safe item to have in your possession. Prince Elizar was, ah, considerably dismayed by the loss."

"Is your cousin in trouble?" To my chagrin, I realized I hadn't even considered the possibility.

"Amal would have been on our doorstep attempting the Trial of Pahrkun if he'd been caught," he said dryly. "And wouldn't *that* have posed me an interesting moral quandary. No, he's fine, but—" He cut himself off.

"But what?" I asked when it was apparent that he didn't intend to finish the thought.

Brother Yarit hesitated, clearly reluctant to tell me. "Someone else paid a price for it," he admitted at length. "I learned some time ago that Prince Elizar had his chamberlain executed."

It shocked me. "Was the man guilty?"

"Only of failing to protect the prince's collection," he said. "It's not an offense deserving of execution, but . . . nerves are strung tighter than an over-tuned harp in the House of the Ageless these days."

"Because of the *rhamanthus* seeds?"

He nodded. "That, and the matter of succession. It has been thus for a very, very long time."

It reminded me that the world I was being prepared to enter was one wholly unfamiliar to me. "So it would be worth my life to be caught with the Teardrop, wouldn't it?"

Brother Yarit did not mince words. "Probably."

It was strange to think that an innocent man had died so that I might possess this gem for an unknown purpose, simply because Brother Yarit had Seen it in an unclear and imperfect vision. The knowledge made my heart ache and pricked my sense of honor. "I didn't *ask* for this, Elder Brother. You have brought dishonor upon me."

"I'm sorry, Khai," he said quietly to me. "It's not a consequence I foresaw. All I know is that you're meant to have it. I can only believe it is in the service of the Sight and that honor beyond honor of which Vironesh once spoke."

"Does it have anything to do with the prophecy?" I asked him. "Miasmus and the darkness that will one day rise in the west?"

Again, he hesitated, his brow furrowing in consternation and genuine perplexity. "That's not a question I can answer."

So it *was* possible, then. I wondered what would have happened if Brother Yarit had simply asked for the Teardrop, had told the prince in his capacity as the Seer that it was a necessary sacrifice. Likely it was a naive notion; likely there was a reason that Pahrkun the Scouring Wind had chosen a master thief to succeed Brother Saan as the Seer. And anyway, it was done. Whatever its ultimate purpose, the Teardrop would be safer hidden in my flesh than on my person.

Brother Yarit was watching me.

I made a decision. "I want to do it."

SIXTEEN

Two days later, it was done.

It hurt. It hurt quite a bit more than I'd anticipated. I'd sustained worse injuries while sparring, but one doesn't feel pain as much when one's blood is high. This was a measured and deliberate carving of my flesh.

It took place outdoors in the protected gorge where the banked embers of Brother Drajan's cookfire burned. Several of the senior brothers stood guard to ensure our privacy. I knelt on the ground beneath the bright sun, biting down on a strip of worn leather while Brother Karal made a careful incision between the cords at the back of my neck and slipped the Teardrop in place.

"Am I doing this right?" he asked Brother Yarit.

"Hell if I know," Brother Yarit said. "Looks good to me."

"Very well." Brother Karal swabbed the back of my neck. "I'm going to close it, then. Pinch the edges of the wound shut."

I clenched my teeth on the leather strip and let out my breath in a hiss as the needle bit into my flesh; once, twice, three times. Brother Karal sluiced my skin with a dipperful of water, swabbed it again, then slathered it with salve from a clay pot and bandaged it with a clean length of cloth.

"Done," he said. I felt at the back of my neck, fingers prodding at the bandage. Beneath the tender flesh, I couldn't even feel the Teardrop. He swatted my hand away. "Leave it be, Khai."

Brother Yarit crouched before me, his fingers wet and red with my blood. "How do you feel?"

It was a fair question. I'd just had the petrified sap of a living god sewn into my flesh. "Fine." It seemed like I ought to feel something more powerful, some change within myself, but I didn't. "I mean, it hurts, but . . . otherwise, I don't feel any different."

"All right." He nodded. "I'll take that as a good thing." Straightening, he gave everyone present a significant glance. "Remember, this never happened."

And that was that.

No one commented on the bandage wrapped around my neck; injuries were commonplace. No doubt the younger brothers assumed I'd gotten it in the course of training with Vironesh, while Vironesh assumed the opposite to be true.

I will own, it *was* strange knowing the Teardrop was there, even if I didn't feel any different. I would find myself fingering the site without realizing I'd raised my hand, especially after the swelling went down and Brother Karal took out the stitches; reaching beneath my hair to finger the tender skin and the slight ridge of healing scar tissue, feeling for the faint bump of the luminescent amber Teardrop nestled in my flesh.

A man had died because of it.

I couldn't leave it alone.

After catching me at it for the third or fourth time, Brother Yarit summoned me to his chamber. "You're developing a habit, kid," he said bluntly to me. "You've got to stop. It's a telltale."

Telltales gave away thieves, liars, and prisoners of war. I clasped my hands together in my lap. "I'm sorry."

Brother Yarit sighed. "Look, I get it. It's . . . well, it's got to be damned odd. But it's done. So do us all a favor and forget it's there."

"I'll try," I said.

He shook his head. "You've got to do better than try, Khai. Forget it. Put it clean out of your thoughts. Forget it ever happened, forget what you know about how it came into your possession. Forget it."

I hesitated, and pulled my hair aside. "Tell me one thing, Elder Brother. What does it look like?"

Brother Yarit peered at my nape. "It's healing nice and clean. Brother Karal did a fine job."

"You can't see it . . . glowing . . . or anything?" I pressed him.

He laughed. "What, like your moment of *khementaran* is upon you?"

"What?"

He sobered. "You didn't know? That's what happens when it comes upon one of the House of the Ageless." He touched the insides of his wrists, the hollow of his throat. "It's the essence of Anamuht the Purging Fire that quickens the *rhamanthus* seeds and burns in the veins of the Sun-Blessed. They say you can see it glowing at the pulse-points when *khementaran* comes upon them."

"Oh."

Brother Yarit shrugged. "So the stories tell. But no, Khai. There's nothing to see. It's hidden. Safe. And if you can manage to forget about it like I asked, it will stay that way until the time comes."

I pricked up my ears. "What time might that be, Elder Brother?"

He regarded me with a mixture of wry affection and the Seer's obliqueness. "Tell me and we'll both know. You've got a formidable will, kid. Can you manage to apply it to this task?"

I saluted him. "I'll do my best."

"Good."

Once I set my mind to it, it wasn't as hard as I imagined. Brother Yarit was right: I had a formidable will and it was constantly being honed and challenged by Vironesh's training. I concentrated on learning to channel Pahrkun's wind at will and forced myself to forget about the Teardrop. I trained my hands not to reach for the back of my neck, and once my body learned to obey and abandon the impulse, my thoughts followed and the Teardrop ceased to plague me.

Forget it's there.

Forget, forget it ever happened.

I turned fourteen and encountered a spurt of growth, gaining several inches in what felt like weeks. It forced me to learn to concentrate anew, retraining these longer limbs, this elongated torso, building new lean muscle so that mind and body might work in effortless tandem. Vironesh was surprisingly sympathetic. To say he warmed to me would be an exaggeration, but he saw when I struggled with the ongoing changes in my body, and he developed a shrewd sense of when to press me and when to step backward and allow me time to adjust.

He opened up a little.

There were topics that were forbidden to me; this, he made clear. First and foremost of these was the poisoned Prince Kazaran, his Sun-Blessed charge. Vironesh gave me no insight into the profound relationship between a shadow and his charge. He spoke to me in the broadest possible terms of what life in the eternally complicated court of the House of the Ageless was like, preparing me for a vipers' nest of intrigue, yet stressing that he knew nothing of what I might expect of life in the women's quarter. He gave me no insight into what it was like to partake of the *rhamanthus* seeds and live for decades without aging, Anamuht's fire coursing in one's veins.

Vironesh would not explain why he was proof against death-bladder poison and its ensuing Purple Death.

Vironesh would not discuss the strange glittering scars on his cheeks.

But there were things he deigned to discuss in time, giving in to my curiosity—and to be sure, that of the entire brotherhood—about his long tenure among the coursers of Obid. None of us could fathom what would cause a man of Zarkhoum to take to the sea in the service of a strange god.

"Justice," Vironesh said simply. "I hungered for it. Since I did not find it in Zarkhoum, I sought it elsewhere."

He told us of the code of Obid the Stern, which the coursers followed in meting out justice on the high seas; stark principles reflected in the black-and-white-striped sails that adorned their ships, striking terror into the hearts of pirates. It was hard to quarrel with most of their principles—though I had to fight the dormant urge to finger the back of my neck when Vironesh condemned theft—but Brother Yarit couldn't resist taking issue with the coursers' stance on intoxication.

"Surely there's no harm in indulging in the occasional flagon of date-palm wine or a pipe of hashish," he remarked. "You yourself—"

Vironesh's jaw tightened. "Contrary to your belief, the coursers do not condemn the use of *gahlba*," he said curtly. "One's judgment is clearer when not hampered by useless emotions."

Brother Yarit opened his mouth to argue. I gave him a discreet hand sign begging him to stand down. He scratched his cheek. "If you say so, brother."

Vironesh relaxed a measure. "It is not only justice the coursers pursue," he said. "There is a prophecy that when the children of Miasmus sow darkness in the world, the coursers of Obid will stem the tide."

My pulse quickened. "The *children* of Miasmus?"

Vironesh inclined his head. "So they say."

"But what of the prophecy of the Sun-Blessed?" I asked in confusion. "Surely you know—"

"Yes, Khai." He cut me off. "Believe me when I say I am well aware of it. Understand . . ." He paused in search of the right words, a complex look of sympathy in his eyes. "Zarkhoum is only one realm. There are a great many pieces of prophecy beneath the starless sky, and no one knows exactly how they fit together. There are some who call it the Scattered Prophecy, for it is broken into a multitude of pieces, and no one can see the whole of it."

"That's for damn sure," Brother Yarit muttered into his tea.

Many prophecies.

It was a staggering thought, something I had never considered. Of course, I knew that Zarkhoum was not the center of the world. Brother Ehudan had taught me in my studies that that was the Nexus, the central point around which the lesser currents and counter-currents swirled. Indeed, according to Vironesh, the Nexus was a place of great consternation to the coursers of Obid, for it was surrounded by a vast archipelago of scattered islands that provided shelter and safe harbor to pirates, rife with backwaters and counter-currents. At the innermost heart of the place, a many-limbed god known as the Oracle of the Nexus held aegis and offered sage advice to those pilgrims who came seeking it. The Nexus was one of the few places where the efforts of the coursers were rendered nigh futile.

But Zarkhoum was the center of *my* world.

Zarkhoum the easternmost; Zarkhoum that lay beneath the aegis of Anamuht the Purging Fire and Pahrkun the Scouring Wind, the Sacred Twins, the children of heaven best beloved of Zar the Sun.

It was difficult for me to think that the wheel of fate might not revolve around Zarkhoum.

So it was that my notion of the world grew more vast even as my skills became more refined. There were weeks on end where it seemed to me that I did nothing but eat, sleep, and breathe Pahrkun's wind, until channeling it became almost instinctive. I no longer fought individual sparring matches with the other brothers. In consultation with Brother Merik, Vironesh staged matches for me with multiple opponents; at first two, then three. This I found exhilarating, for there was genuine danger in it and I could feel Pahrkun's wind vibrating in the marrow of my bones as I whirled like the spinning devil itself, parrying blows and seeing things they did not, my tines and blade flashing into the spaces between, the chinks in my opponents' attacks.

It did not endear me to my brethren.

Despite Vironesh's counsel, they envied me, or at least the younger ones did. It was different for the senior brothers, who had known me since I was a babe—training me to be a warrior had been their sole purpose for a long time. But for those such as Brother Hakan, who had come to the Fortress of the Winds when I was already a boy, it was galling.

At first it galled me in turn, for I would have traded places with any one of them if it meant I were not *bhazim*. But as time passed, I grew less sure. It was the dearest wish of my heart, and yet I could not imagine relinquishing the ability.

If Pahrkun himself appeared to me and offered to make me a boy in exchange for his gift . . . what would I say?

And what if that very choice was the Trial of Pahrkun I would one day undergo? It was a thought that haunted me until at last I dared to ask Vironesh about it. He fixed me with an incredulous stare. "Whatever gave you that idea?"

"Nothing," I said. "It just came to me. I know you cannot speak of what the trial *is*, but . . ." I considered how to phrase my question. "If this is something that it *isn't*, can you tell me?"

Vironesh eyed me. "Have I not told you that the code of Obid the Stern holds that men and women are equal in merit and should be gauged according to their skills?"

I looked down at my bare, dusty feet. "Yes, brother."

"Have I not told you of the valiant women who fight and sail among the coursers?" he asked.

"You have," I admitted.

"And yet you persist in this disdain," Vironesh observed. "How do you suppose that will make the princess feel?"

Stung by indignation, I raised my head. "That is unfair!"

"Is it?" he asked.

Emotions to which I could not give voice roiled within me and I looked away, unwanted tears pricking my eyes. Vironesh knew many things, but he did not know what it was like to discover he'd been lied to for his entire life, to discover that he was the opposite of what he'd believed himself to be. "May I be excused from training this afternoon?"

"Very well," he said.

I was halfway across the Dancing Bowl when he called me back.

"Khai?"

I turned.

Sunlight glittered on the unnatural slanting scars beneath his eyes. "No," he said. "That is not the nature of the trial."

SEVENTEEN

I turned fifteen years of age.

In a year's time, on the event of our shared day of birth, I would be presented to Princess Zariya; assuming I succeeded in passing my own personal Trial of Pahrkun.

During the course of that year, I thought about what Vironesh had said to me.

Disdain.

It was a harsh word, and yet he was not wholly wrong. If I disdained what *I* was, how could I respect it in another? Because it was a question I could not answer, I set it aside.

In the summer of that year, Brother Yarit grew impatient with the restlessness of the younger brothers and took to the heights to spend a vigil in contemplation of the matter. He was not gone three full days like Brother Saan, but a single day and night in the full heat of the desert in midsummer was enough to make me nervous for him. Nonetheless, he returned safely, his eyes wide and blurred with the Sight.

"I have made a decision," he announced after gathering the brotherhood in the Dancing Bowl. "We will hold a lottery." A low murmur of confusion ran through those assembled. Brother Yarit gestured toward an empty urn and a pile of potsherds. "Any man among you who wishes to be released from your vow, come forward and scratch your name on a shard. I will draw ten names from the urn. At the gathering of the clans, you will return to your kin and your tribes will choose replacements to send to the Fortress of the Winds in your stead."

"Elder Brother, there is no precedent for this!" Brother Merik said in dismay. "Will you allow them to dishonor Pahrkun's service?"

With the Sight upon him, Brother Yarit was impervious to protest. "There is no honor in service given unwillingly," he said. "Others will prove eager to come." He beckoned. "Well?"

The young rebels hemmed and hawed, reluctant now that their bluff had been called, but at length Brother Hakan strode from their midst. He wrote his name on a shard with the point of his dagger, then dropped it in the urn and saluted Brother Yarit. "Forgive me, Elder Brother," he said respectfully. "I have no wish to dishonor the brotherhood, but I am twenty-three years of age and not yet a blooded warrior. I see no purpose in my presence here save to serve as one of Khai's training dummies."

"It may be that that is purpose enough," Brother Yarit observed. "But it may also be that Pahrkun has another purpose in mind for you. Who's next?"

A few more came forward, but many of the most vocal complainers hung back.

"There's no trick here," Brother Yarit said irritably. "If I draw your name, you're free to go home to fight and fuck and herd camels to your heart's content. I just spent a day and a night baking on a mountaintop, waiting for the Sight to show me how to make you whiny little bastards happy in accordance with Pahrkun's will. This is it, so come write down your damned names."

Brother Ramil raised a hand in inquiry. "Elder Brother?"

"What?"

"I cannot write," he said simply, and a number of others echoed their agreement.

"Huh." This, the Seer had not expected. "How many of you?" A dozen hands went up. He tilted his head and contemplated them. "All right. Any who choose to stay will be taught to read and write. There will be another lottery in . . . ah . . . three years' time."

Brother Merik looked aghast. "You would turn the Fortress of the Winds into an academy of letters?"

Brother Yarit shrugged. "Why not? There aren't enough supplicants to satisfy their bloodthirsty hearts during peacetime." He looked at Brother Ehudan. "Are you willing to take on new students?"

"I am." The most senior member of the brotherhood sounded almost surprised at his own answer. "Khai has learned as much as I have to teach him. I would welcome it."

"Then it's decided," Brother Yarit said. "Right now, those of you who can write assist those who cannot."

When all was said and done, there were exactly ten names placed into the urn. Brother Yarit drew out each shard and read the name aloud.

The chosen brothers exchanged uneasy glances, no longer certain that they'd done the right thing.

Brother Yarit dusted his hands in satisfaction. "Well, that's that, then."

Needless to say, it changed the tenor of life in the Fortress of the Winds, but after the initial awkwardness had passed, even Brother Merik had to agree that it was for the better. Those of the younger brothers who had chosen to stay found a new purpose and challenge in Brother Ehudan's lessons; those who had chosen to leave no longer had cause for complaint.

As for me, I spent more and more time in the company of Vironesh, and if our relationship grew no warmer, we developed a certain wordless accord born of long training and the silent brotherhood of Pahrkun's wind.

We sparred in the Dancing Bowl.

We sparred on mountaintops.

We sparred with weapons that were unfamiliar to me, spears and shields, and with things that were not weapons at all, torches and platters and urns, so that I might come to understand in my flesh and bones that anything, anything at all, might become a weapon at need.

We sparred empty-handed.

And then summer gave way to autumn and the gathering of the clans was upon us. Brother Yarit decreed that a farewell feast would be held, assuring those who were leaving that there was no ill will between us. The defectors toasted his generosity and wisdom, promising to sing the praises of the Brotherhood of Pahrkun. The following morning they left, escorted by Brother Merik, and the Fortress of the Winds felt undermanned in their absence. But in two weeks' time replacements arrived, eager young tribesmen drawn by the promise of literacy as well as the honor of serving Pahrkun—and, too, by tales of Vironesh the purple man, the great living shadow, and his student, Khai, who was learning to channel Pahrkun's wind.

Although the new brothers were older than me—the youngest was seventeen—it didn't feel that way. Having known only tents and a nomad's lifestyle, they marveled at the vast caverns and passageways that honeycombed the fortress.

They marveled at Vironesh.

And they marveled at *me*, for none of them knew me as the little brother who had grown up training alongside them. Brother Hakan had given me my first real sparring match and my first scar to remember it by; any of the new brothers could reckon himself lucky to land a blow against me.

I suppose it was nice to be respected, but it was isolating, too. The gap between us would never be bridged; and in less time than seemed possible, it would grow even wider.

When Shahal the Dark Moon first swelled to fullness come the spring rains, the trial would take place.

As to the nature of the trial, I knew little more than what Brother Saan had told me many years ago. I was to venture into the deep desert and seek to encounter Pahrkun face-to-face so that the Scouring Wind might determine whether my pledge was worthy of being fulfilled. Oh, there was more to it, of that I was sure; but *what*, I didn't know. I toyed with the notion that I would be required to defeat Vironesh in single combat, thus demonstrating that I had surpassed my mentor; but no, that made no sense. There had been no living shadow to train Vironesh or those who had come before him.

Still, there must be a test of some manner, else why call it a trial? What was to be tested? My courage? My honor? My loyalty?

And what would become of me if I failed?

Sometimes when I could find no respite from my own thoughts, I would take to the heights and sit beside Brother Saan's bier in contemplation.

Although he had been desert-born, it had been his wish that his bones remain at the Fortress of the Winds, for he deemed the brotherhood his true clan.

In the years since Brother Saan's death, his flesh had remained undisturbed by Pahrkun's scavengers, but it had withered and hardened onto his bones. Even so, there was something peaceful about his presence, and I took comfort in it.

That winter, Brother Yarit spent a number of evenings interviewing me about Vironesh's training, taking copious notes as I described what it was like to channel Pahrkun's wind and learn to see the spaces between things, the various methods Vironesh had used to coax forth my ability, and how and why I thought they may have proved effective.

"I don't think this is the sort of thing that can be learned from a scroll, Elder Brother," I said one evening, watching him write in his scrawling hand. "I'm not sure what good it will do."

"Neither am I," he said without looking up. "But there should at least be a record, don't you think?" He dipped his quill and finished a sentence. "It never occurred to me that the brotherhood probably had so few written records because so many of our past Seers couldn't read or write."

"Brother Saan could," I said.

"Yes, and his notes have been helpful to me," Brother Yarit said. "But Brother Saan never had the chance to observe one living shadow passing on a lifetime's worth of accumulated wisdom to another, and I'd prefer that knowledge not be lost." He stoppered his inkwell. "It may prove useful to another Seer in the future."

"Have you Seen it?" I asked.

He gave me a wry, crooked smile. "No, I'm just playing the odds, kid."

I sighed. "I should have guessed."

Brother Yarit studied me, his gaze shrewd. "Are you all right, Khai? Everything well with you?"

"Fine, Elder Brother." The urge to finger the back of my neck surfaced and I resisted it. "I'm lonely," I admitted. "And I'm scared."

"I'll grant you lonely," he said. "Under the circumstances, lonely is understandable. Why scared? It's unlike you."

"The trial," I murmured. "I just wish I knew what to expect."

"I'd tell you more if I could, kid." There was sympathy in Brother Yarit's tone, but no yielding. "But I can't."

"Because it would tip the balance of what might come to pass?" I asked him. "Or just because tradition forbids it?"

He raised his eyebrows at me. "When have you ever known me to be a slave to tradition? But as it happens, it's both."

"Fair enough." I took a deep breath. "Maybe you can tell me *this*, Elder Brother. What happens if I fail? If Pahrkun finds me unworthy? No one's ever spoken of the possibility. Where would I go? What would I do? The Fortress of the Winds is the only home I've ever known, but there wouldn't be any point in staying. Brother Jawal's clan named me honorary kin. Should I throw myself on their mercy and ask them to take me in? Or should I run off with Vironesh to join the coursers of Obid?" I gave a humorless laugh. "I can't fathom leaving Zarkhoum, but the way he speaks of them—" It struck me that Brother Yarit was gazing at me with grave compassion, and I realized what I should have known all along.

If I failed the Trial of Pahrkun, I would die, just like any ordinary supplicant in the Hall of Proving.

"Oh." My voice sounded small to my own ears. "That . . . that isn't something I need to worry about, is it?"

"I didn't think you needed to know until the time was nigh," Brother Yarit said quietly. "That was my judgment. If I erred, I beg your forgiveness."

"No." I shook my head. "No, I understand." Rising, I saluted him. "Thank you, Elder Brother."

"Are you angry?" he asked me with rare uncertainty. "I'm sorry, Khai. I was just trying to protect you as long as I could."

It was a sincere question, and I realized that my answer mattered to him. Gazing at Brother Yarit, I saw the spaces between that existed in him; the space between his unwanted destiny and the life he'd been forced to leave behind; the space between the Sight and his instinctive cunning; the space between his brusque manner and the well-guarded tenderness of his heart.

I saw that he had done the best he could in the spaces between those things, and that he had come to love me there.

And I could not help but love him for it.

"No, Elder Brother," I said to him. "No, I am not angry."

EIGHTEEN

My trial was to take place in the Mirror of Heaven.

It was a desolate place a day's ride east of the mountains that housed the Fortress of the Winds; a flat, empty expanse of plain that glittered with flakes of salt and mica under the hot sun.

Not even the spring rains could coax a single plant to blossom in the Mirror. Animals avoided it.

I might die there.

We made camp in the shadow of an unfamiliar peak, Brother Yarit, Brother Merik, Vironesh, and me. There was no watering hole and the skies were clear, so we were forced to rely on what we carried or could harvest from the morning dew, but there was enough scrubby gorse for two or three days' worth of grazing.

At dawn, I would walk into the desert on foot. I would carry nothing but a full skin of water, my dagger, and the hawk's feather I had caught so long ago. I would walk due east across the Mirror until Zar the Sun had vanished over the western horizon. Then while Shahal the Dark Moon rose full and red, I would wait.

That much I knew. After that . . . nothing.

It was strange to think that the last time this place had been used as a campsite was when Vironesh underwent his own trial. We gathered stalks of dried gorse and chunks of near-petrified dung to build a campfire just large enough to brew a pot of mint tea, then sat around the campfire sipping tea from tin cups. It was comforting to have something familiar to do.

"This must take you back," Brother Merik remarked to Vironesh. The purple man grunted in assent.

We drank tea.

Nim the Bright Moon rose, just waning and pale. Dark Shahal followed, very nearly full. The tethered horses dozed cock-hipped beneath their light, giving the occasional stamp or whuffle. It was all very peaceful, and it was hard to believe this might be my last night of existence.

Wrapping myself in my robe, I slept.

Although I had hoped for rain, morning dawned bright and clear. Brother Merik rekindled the fire and brewed another pot of tea. I drank from my tin cup and gnawed on strips of dried goat meat. The mint tea was at once warming and refreshing. The goat meat was hard and tough, but it yielded a smoky savor after long chewing. I found myself acutely conscious of these things. I tried not to think about *why*.

And then there was nothing left to do, no cause to delay. It was time. Time to venture across the Mirror; time to undertake the trial.

Brother Merik withdrew a small pot of kohl from some inner pocket of his robe and offered it to me. "It will help keep you from going desert-blind."

I dipped my forefinger into the black paste and smeared it over my eyelids and all around the sockets of my eyes. "Thank you, brother."

He saluted me. "I wish you luck."

I wrapped my head-scarf low over my eyes and high over the lower part of my face, the better to shade my eyes and keep from losing my breath's moisture. I touched the shaft of the feather thrust through my sash to make sure it was secure, and settled the weight of the water-skin strapped across my chest.

"Khai." Brother Yarit took a shaky breath and gazed at me with tear-bright eyes. "See you tomorrow, kid."

I swallowed and nodded before turning to Vironesh. "Do you have any final counsel for me?"

My mentor gave me a long, impassive look. "Don't flinch."

Thus armed, I set forth across the Mirror of Heaven, heading in a straight line toward the rising sun.

For the first couple of hours, I felt strong and fresh. I kept a slow, steady pace. I kept my head low, shielding my eyes from the sun's glare. Although I was mindful of the desert's peril, I was young and strong and fit. A day's walk, even through the worst heat of the day, should not be too difficult to bear. I needn't worry about keeping watch for snakes or scorpions in the Mirror. Sunstroke and heat prostration were the only things I need fear, and so long as I was careful not to overexert myself and to drink sparingly at regular intervals, I would be fine.

Or at least so I thought.

As the sun climbed higher, it became obvious that I had greatly underestimated the effect of the Mirror. The glittering white plain reflected the sun's light until it became a dazzling glare from which there was no escape; and as the sun traveled across the sky, I could no longer use it as a guidepost toward due east, but must rely on landmarks. While there were none in the Mirror itself, there was a two-pronged mountain peak in the distance that Brother Merik had told me I could use to orient myself. It had seemed an easy enough thing to do in the gentle grey light of dawn, but in the blinding light of midday, my vision swam and I feared to trust it.

Brightness above, brightness below. I thought of those mariners from days of old who were accustomed to navigate by the stars, and how they must have felt when the children of heaven fell to earth and darkness swallowed the night skies, leaving them directionless and lost.

I . . . I was being swallowed by light.

Still, I kept going, squinting through tear-stinging eyes at the distant peak and readjusting my course.

When the sun stood high overhead, every instinct within me told me to halt, to rest and take shelter. Of course, there was no shelter to be had, but I might pause, might make a canopy of my scarf and robe. I might close my eyes beneath the shade they provided and take a brief respite.

No one had said it was forbidden.

No one had said it wasn't, either.

I had wondered what it was that would be tested within me; well, now I could guess. My will. Ignoring my instincts, I hunched my shoulders against the beating hammer of the sun and kept walking.

From a distance, the Mirror of Heaven looked to be one flat, uniform surface. At close range it was not so. There were expanses of soft white sand that sank and yielded beneath my feet so that each step became more arduous than the last. I trudged across them, feeling the effort sap my muscles. There were patches covered with a thin, brittle veneer of salt that cracked beneath my sandaled feet. If I stepped carelessly, the sharp, broken edges scored the bare flesh of my ankles.

The tang of salt and minerals hung in the forge-hot air above the Mirror. It sucked the moisture from my skin and left me parch-mouthed.

I sipped warm water that tasted of goat's bladder, swishing it around my mouth before letting it trickle down my throat.

I kept going.

I kept going.

By the time Zar the Sun was behind me, I was staggering. My aching head was swimming and my eyes were filled with dazzling brightness. The distant peaks faded in and out of my vision. I only hoped I was still headed due east.

Stretching before me, my shadow told me otherwise. Oh, but I *had* a shadow, and the respite from the endless brilliance it afforded filled me with gratitude. Wiping the salt-stinging sweat from my eyes with my sleeve, I summoned the dwindling reserves of my will, adjusted my course, and followed my shadow eastward, step by unsteady step, until the sun vanished in the west and the outlines of my shadow became vague.

Wait.

Were I not fairly certain the true trial was yet to come, I could have wept with relief upon allowing myself to fold my legs and sit.

Willing my mind to stillness, I waited. The day's heat dissipated with surprising speed. I touched the hawk's feather in my sash, hefted my water-skin to gauge its fullness and reckoned it nearly half empty. I drank no more. Nim the Bright Moon rose, a silvery crescent in the dark sky, transforming the landscape around me. I was a single point of life in a strange barren sea.

I waited, my mind drifting.

Shahal the Dark Moon rose full and round and crimson, drenching the plain in bloody light. As it climbed higher into the sky, the wind began to stir, and I felt an answering stirring within my blood.

Pahrkun the Scouring Wind was coming.

There were no scuttling ants or creatures of the desert to give warning here in the Mirror, but I felt it in the touch of the wind against my skin, in the rustle of the sand, in the vibrations deep within the desert that spoke to me and said, *He comes, he comes, he comes.*

And soon I saw him, a looming figure in the distance, eyes like twin sparks of green fire.

Remembering what Vironesh had done, I rose on shaking legs and genuflected three times toward the east, bowing my head and stretching out my hands to touch the ground before me as my knee brushed the sand. I sat once more. My mouth had gone dry again, this time with fear and awe. Stride by stride, Pahrkun drew nearer, his immense form cloaked in folds of swirling sand that shifted and flared around him. Buffeted by the rising winds, I squinted through the sandstorm. My heart was racing and I could feel my pulse thudding in my throat. I fought the urge to fling myself facedown upon the desert and hope he would pass me by.

The wind faded as Pahrkun planted his feet in the sand and halted before me, bringing me into the stillness at the center of his being. At close range, his massive limbs and torso appeared man-shaped, albeit wrought of basalt or obsidian. The Dark Moon made a crimson nimbus around his vast head.

Pahrkun's face . . .

It was not a *face* as we understand such a thing to be. It seethed with life, the life of the thousands upon thousands of carrion beetles of which it was comprised, crawling over each other in a writhing mass, black carapaces touched with a hint of green iridescence in the bloody moonlight.

For a delirious instant, I wondered if I had suffered sunstroke after all.

Deep-set green eyes regarded me from on high. The mass of beetles shifted to form a mouth that opened and spoke with the voice of the desert; the soughing of a sandstorm, the rasp of a snake's scales, the dry whirring of a beetle's wings. *"Khai."*

My name drew me to my feet with an unexpected surge of joy. Standing in the eye of the storm that was Pahrkun the Scouring Wind, I pressed my palms together and touched my thumbs to my brow in fervent salute. "Yes, my lord Pahrkun!"

Could such a mouth smile? It almost seemed to me that it did. *"Do you bear my token?"*

I drew forth the hawk's feather. "I do, my lord."

Stretching his right arm down from the sky, Pahrkun opened . . . not a hand, no. Where a hand would be was a banded onyx scorpion, three times larger than life. I gulped involuntarily, my mouth making a dry clicking sound. Vironesh's warning took on new meaning. The stinger at the end of the scorpion's tail quivered as it opened and closed its claws.

My hand trembling, I placed the hawk's feather in the scorpion's claw. Pahrkun raised it to his seething face, opened his mouth that was not a mouth, and blew out a breath of air hotter than the midday sun. The feather glowed white for the space of a heartbeat then disintegrated, minute flecks of silvery ash drifting down around me inside the column of wind that surrounded us.

"Breathe," said Pahrkun, and I drew a deep breath in response, filling my lungs. *"Know that to wear my mark is to carry my token within you. To carry the breath of the desert inside you. Do you understand?"*

"I think so, my lord," I said.

Pahrkun's immense head lifted, green-glowing eyes in their deep crawling sockets gazing toward the west. *"Life and death. Fire and wind. These are the things over which my sister Anamuht and I hold dominion in Zarkhoum."*

"Yes, my lord."

His head dipped, his gaze returning to me. *"If the time is upon us, these are the gifts you and your soul's twin will carry to the end of the earth. These are the gifts you will summon, Sun-Blessed and shadow. Remember this."*

"Yes, my lord." I hesitated. "My lord Pahrkun, how am I to know if the time *is* upon us?"

"Do not concern yourself about this, for they are events beyond your control," he said, and there was a strange reassurance in it. *"Concern yourself only with events over which you may exert control. Above all, concern yourself with your charge."*

I inclined my head. "Yes, my lord."

"Is it your will to wear my mark?" Pahrkun the Scouring Wind asked me. *"Is it your will to fulfill your pledge?"*

To wear his mark . . . it was the second time the god had spoken of it. The sandstorm howled around us. I thought of the odd glittering scars that marked Vironesh's face and swallowed again. "It is, my lord," I whispered.

"Then kneel."

I knelt on the white sands of the Mirror and Pahrkun went to one enormous knee before me, and although he did it with such deliberate grace that it made no sound, I felt the earth nonetheless shudder beneath the impact. His hands—no, not hands, not even close—reached toward my face. The banded onyx scorpion on the right, and on the left . . . the left was a shadow-viper, eyes milky and blind. Red moonlight glistened on its black scales and its forked tongue tasted the wind.

"Khai of the Fortress of the Winds, from you I require the gift of perfect trust." There was a gentleness like the softness of a spring breeze to Pahrkun's mighty voice. *"Do you give it to me?"*

The scorpion's eyes glittered in the bloody moonlight, the scarlet bands on its thorax muted by the Dark Moon. The segmented tail that curved over its back twitched, the wicked stinger as long as my forefinger. The shadow-viper's head wove back and forth, its sinuous, muscular length describing coils in the air, its tongue flickering.

I was afraid.

I was *very* afraid, for this was madness by any measure. And yet, as when Vironesh challenged me to spar on the bridge above the Dancing Floor, there was a certain wild exhilaration in the terror. Vironesh had stood where I stood; Vironesh had done this. Here in the heart of the Mirror, Vironesh had received Pahrkun's mark and been rendered proof against the poison that killed his charge.

I could do no less.

"Yes, my lord." I lifted my face to meet Pahrkun's gaze. "I do."

"So be it," said Pahrkun the Scouring Wind. *"I accept your pledge."*

The shadow-viper swayed, drawing back its head and raising its blunt nose. Its forked tongue flickered. The banded onyx's tail twitched.

I closed my eyes.

Don't flinch.

They struck at the same time, twin lines of fire raking across my cheekbones. Not to kill, only to score, but oh, by all the fallen stars, it hurt! And as the venom entered my blood, I understood that this was only the very beginning of pain. Opening my eyes, I saw the scorpion and the serpent withdrawing as Pahrkun rose to his feet, his distant head once more blotting out the night sky.

"Khai of the Fortress of the Winds, you have my blessing," the god said to me. *"May you survive it."*

I gave no answer but a grim nod, for a spasm of pain gripped me and rendered the muscles of my face too rigid for speech. Pahrkun the Scouring Wind took his leave and the sandstorm of his wake engulfed me, flaying my skin as he departed.

The storm of Pahrkun's passage abated.

The storm within my body continued to rise. Somehow, I had fallen onto my side. I curled into myself. Poison raced through my veins, agony contorted my limbs. I fought to draw breath; one, then the next, then the next. If I lived to see the dawn, perhaps I would survive.

Instead, darkness dragged me down.

NINETEEN

My eyelids flickered.

"Khai?"

It was Vironesh's voice; and impossibly, there was a note of genuine concern in it. I forced my heavy eyelids open. "Am I alive?"

The purple man raised his eyebrows at me. "Barely. How do you feel?"

"I don't know." I took stock. No water-skin, no dagger, no hawk's feather . . . no, that was gone forever. My face ached; my entire body ached. My skin was tender. I touched my cheekbones and felt the raised lines of twin scars, rough with embedded bits of sand and mica. "Where am I?" Glancing around, I realized I was lying on my carpet in my own cavern in the Fortress of the Winds. I wrinkled my brow, feeling the gesture tug at my fresh scars. "How?"

"Oh, we rode into the Mirror to fetch you," Vironesh said. "Dead or alive, that was always the plan."

I prodded my cheekbones. "Good to know."

"You did it," he said quietly. "You've been insensible for a few days, but here you are."

"Alive," I said.

Vironesh nodded. "Alive."

So.

I was alive; I was a shadow. Pahrkun had found me worthy of my pledge; Pahrkun the Scouring Wind had marked me as his own. Wherever I'd been born, I was a true child of the desert now. The poison of a banded onyx scorpion and a shadow-viper had coursed through my veins, and I had survived.

Vironesh left to procure a bowl of broth for me. I was standing on wobbly legs and testing my strength when Brother Yarit entered my chamber and gave me a broad grin. "Hey, kid. I heard you were awake."

I eyed him. "More or less, but I'm as weak as a babe."

"Well, you very nearly died," he said in a pragmatic tone. "Vironesh is of the opinion that the Scouring Wind dosed you with a bit more venom than he ought, you being *bhazim*."

I frowned, feeling the flesh of my face tug on my unfamiliar scars again. "And weaker because of it?"

Brother Yarit raised a forfending hand. "Just smaller, Khai. You're a fair height, but there's less mass to you. Don't worry, you're young and resilient. You'll get your strength back."

Abashed, I saluted him. "Forgive me, Elder Brother. I don't mean to be rude."

"It's all right." Brother Yarit shrugged. "You've been through an ordeal." He lowered his voice. "And you've been initiated into one of the world's great mysteries. Keep it close to your heart."

"I will." My legs were beginning to tremble with the effort of standing. Folding them, I gazed up at him. "So what happens now, Elder Brother?"

"Rest," he said. "Regain your strength. Resume training when you're ready. In ten days' time, we ride for Merabaht."

Merabaht.

With the prospect of the Trial of Pahrkun hanging over me, I hadn't allowed myself to think about what came next if I survived. Now I did, and it made the blood quicken in my veins. "Truly?"

"Truly," Brother Yarit assured me.

I spent that day abed and I daresay I should have spent the next, but I was too excited by the prospect of the future unfolding before me to allow myself to convalesce a moment longer than was absolutely necessary. Vironesh made no comment, merely allowed me to batter myself into exhaustion against his defenses. On the third day I paid a price for my folly, but I persevered, pushing past the lingering aches and weariness that plagued my flesh. I took my temporary weakness as a lesson and concentrated on finding the spaces *between* into which an angle of attack might flow, and I was rewarded by Vironesh's nod of approval.

Day by day, the scars on my cheeks healed; my body regained the strength and quickness that the poison had sapped.

In a week's time, I felt nearly myself.

Preparations for the journey were under way. Brother Yarit had decreed that there would be ten of us going, for we had but a dozen mounts between us, the largest number of animals that the grazing and the watering hole of the horse canyon of the Fortress of the Winds could sustain.

I took it as a given that Brother Yarit would be one of our number, and was surprised when he told me otherwise. "But why, Elder Brother?" I asked him in bewilderment. "Surely this is the opportunity for which you've longed!"

"It is." He gave a wry half shrug and his crooked smile. "And that's why I dare not take it, Khai."

"But—"

Brother Yarit sighed and ran a hand over his hair. "Like it or not, for now my place is here in the desert. If I leave, I might never come back."

"You've Seen it?" I asked respectfully.

"I've Seen . . . possibilities," he murmured. "The Brotherhood of Pahrkun may yet have another role to play, and that cannot come to pass if the Seer abandons his post." His mouth quirked. "And the truth of it is that I know my own limitations. So yes, I will remain at the Fortress of the Winds."

The remaining days dwindled; three, then two, then one. On the day before we were to depart, Brother Merik presented me with an unworn set of clothing: a tunic, robe, breeches, and head-scarf wrought of fine-combed white wool. "A last gift from Brother Saan," he told me.

Everything fit perfectly. "How did he know?"

Brother Merik smiled. "I daresay he Saw it, or at least a vision he hoped would come to pass."

Among the senior members of the brotherhood, Brother Merik and Brother Drajan would accompany me to Merabaht, and Vironesh, too. Brother Tekel would tend to the horses. It shames me to confess that I do not recall all the names of the young brothers chosen to fill the remaining five places, for although they were as naive and excited as I was at the prospect of seeing the great city for the first time, the gulf that had ever existed between us had only grown more vast since I had undergone the trial.

My last night in the Fortress of the Winds was a bittersweet affair, for it came home to me that I was leaving everything I had ever known.

My home.

My family.

I knew nothing of cities; I knew nothing of courts or palaces save what Vironesh had told me. I knew nothing of women.

I was embarking into a world that encompassed all of these things.

It seemed at some point, Brother Yarit had succeeded in trading for several flagons of date-palm wine, and it flowed freely that last night. I drank sparingly of it, but others indulged more deeply; somewhat to my surprise, Vironesh was among them, although it seemed to bring him no pleasure. Still, he stayed long enough to drink to my health when Brother Yarit toasted me, which was convivial by his standards.

When our final evening meal was concluded, Brother Yarit escorted me back to my chamber for one last word in private.

"I wish I had some really damn sage advice for you, kid," he said wistfully. "But the fucking truth is the Sight just doesn't work that way. If I try warning you about the different crossroads that might or might not lie ahead of you, I'll just fuck everything up."

"I know," I said. "I remember."

"Brother Saan would have had something profound to say," he mused. "Some piece of deep desert wisdom."

I smiled a little. "Let your mind be like the eye of a hawk."

Brother Yarit nodded. "Yeah, that's good. Listen, my cousin Amal in the Royal Guard will keep an eye out for you, but don't risk contacting him. If you need the Shahalim Clan's help for any reason, go to the Lucky Tortoise teahouse and ask if they carry three-moon blend."

"Three-moon blend," I repeated. "I thought you called in whatever favor you were owed."

"I did," he said. "But for better or worse, I *am* the Seer of the Brotherhood of Pahrkun, and that's good for some credit."

"You're the Seer that Pahrkun chose to guide me into adulthood," I said softly. "You've taught me things that no one else could have, Elder Brother." I brushed the nape of my neck with one finger. "You've given me a gift that no one else could have."

"Yeah, there's that." He took a deep breath. "I'm proud of you, Khai. And I hope I did right by you."

"You did," I said to him. "I'm sure of it."

"How in the watery hell would you know?" Brother Yarit laughed and pulled me into a warm embrace, the first since the day he'd told me that I was *bhazim*. Then, I'd been small enough that he could rest his chin atop my head; today we were nearly of a height. "Ah, kid!" He turned me loose. "All right, get some sleep. I'll see you off in the morning."

It was actually some hours before dawn when our company gathered and made ready to depart. In what seemed a happy omen, all three moons were overhead with Nim the Bright Moon waxing toward fullness and shedding plenty of light by which to travel. I was touched to see that even though we'd had our farewell feast the night before, the entirety of the brotherhood turned out to watch us take our leave, figures dotting the entryways and lookouts of the western face of the fortress.

The moonlight lent Brother Yarit's plain features an unaccustomed dignity. "Khai of the Fortress of the Winds, we send you forth to serve as a shadow to the Sun-Blessed Princess Zariya of the House of the Ageless," he said in a formal tone, placing his hands on my shoulders. "May you attain honor beyond honor."

Swallowing, I nodded and saluted him. "Thank you, Elder Brother."

After so long, it seemed impossible to believe that the moment was upon me; and yet it was.

Brother Yarit, the first man I'd tried to kill, the most unlikely of Seers, kissed my brow and released me. "May Pahrkun guide your steps." He saluted me, and the rest of the brotherhood followed suit.

I swung myself astride my horse. I was a blooded warrior. I had my *yakhan* and my *kopar* thrust through my sash, a brace of *zims* strapped to my left forearm, my *heshkrat* knotted around my waist, and a garrote tying back my hair. In my packs were a grappling hook and a length of rope and a set of lock-picks. I bore the marks of Pahrkun's favor etched on my cheekbones and the Teardrop hidden in my flesh. I could move silent and unseen through shadows, leap astonishing heights, pick a pocket so deftly its bearer would never know I'd been there, and channel Pahrkun's wind.

I was ready.

Even so, I could not help but glance backward as Brother Merik gave the command and we set out across the desert at a steady trot. Bit by bit, the figures of Brother Yarit and the rest of the brotherhood were swallowed by the distance, and I set my gaze on the western horizon and ceased looking backward.

There was little in the way of conversation on our first leg of the journey, which I suspect may have been due in part to the after-effects of the date-palm wine, but when we resumed our sojourn after the midday rest, Vironesh brought his mount alongside mine.

"As I have said, you'll find the court is rife with factions," he said without preamble. "But I fear that I cannot tell you what those factions may be. I've been gone too long. In my day, the princes Elizar and Tazaresh, who are the king's first- and second-born sons, made common cause against Prince Kazaran, for it was well known the king favored his third-born son." A muscle in his jaw twitched. "However, I do not see that alliance enduring beyond Kazaran's death, and I suspect you will find them at odds."

It was the first time Vironesh had spoken his Sun-Blessed charge's name aloud. "I am listening," I said carefully.

He gave a brusque nod without looking at me. "I'd be surprised if one of the younger sons wasn't angling for the throne. Not the twins, they struck me as fairly simple souls. Good foot soldiers in someone else's campaign, not likely to spearhead their own. No, my money's on Dozaren."

"Dozaren," I repeated.

"That's Rashina's boy," Vironesh said. "Fourth-born son. A quiet type, but charming when he wants to be, and he's not one to miss an opportunity. And his mother's ambitious."

I did my best to recall the genealogy that Brother Ehudan had taught me. "That's His Majesty's fourth queen?"

"Third queen, fourth-born son," Vironesh corrected me. "Look, Khai . . .

the truth is, your girl's not likely to be a threat to anyone. She's the king's last-born, the youngest of eleven daughters."

I raised my brows in his direction. "Daughters aren't a threat?"

"Not to ascend to the throne, not in Zarkhoum," he said bluntly. "Most of the king's daughters are already wed and have households of their own. They received the allotment of *rhamanthus* seeds they were to be given throughout their lifetime as their dowry to bestow as they or their husbands choose. Most of the House of the Ageless have chosen to hold off on bearing children."

I pondered this, thinking about the crime for which Brother Yarit was caught and convicted. "And if they're not content with their allotted share?"

Vironesh smiled humorlessly. "Then they scheme and intrigue on behalf of whatever aspirant to the throne promised them more. The women's quarter is a world unto itself and I spoke truly when I told you that I've very little idea what transpires in it. Even so, I can't imagine there's much of anything the young princess can do to influence the succession. But if your girl has enemies, it's because she's a member of someone's faction. And if you can find out who it is," he added, "I'll do my best to convince His Majesty to assign me to a rival faction's personal guard and help you protect her."

It surprised me. "You're *staying*?"

The purple man's broad shoulders rose and fell in a heavy shrug. "If the king will have me."

I hesitated. "Does he . . . does His Majesty blame you for what happened?"

"Not as much as I blame myself." Vironesh's tone brooked no further questions, and I asked none.

Still, I thought about it as we rode across the desert.

My mind was awhirl with the names and connections I should have memorized, abstractions that were to become real flesh-and-blood people and relationships in a short amount of time.

Six sons, one dead.

Eleven daughters; eight of them wed, the eldest serving as the High Priestess of Anamuht.

Zariya.

What was she like, the king's youngest? Like me, she was on the cusp of turning sixteen years of age. Powerless, according to Vironesh; and like as not it was true. Yet there was one thing of which he had not spoken.

On the third day of our journey, I broached the silence between us to ask him, "Brother Vironesh, what of the prophecy?"

"The prophecy?" He laughed, but it was a hollow sound. "Oh, Khai! I've told you, there are many pieces of prophecy beneath the starless skies. You cannot imagine this girl-child is the one to fulfill ours."

"Why not?" I asked stubbornly.

For a long moment, I thought he would not answer, but then he did. "Because if it were anyone, it should have been Kazaran," he said with un-expected savagery, the outburst provoking startled murmurs among the rest of our company. "*He* had a vision! He had strength and courage and nobil-ity . . ." Vironesh shook his head, jaw tight. "Prince Kazaran was born to be a hero, and I would have helped him build an empire. One that would have stood against any darkness that might rise."

Ahead of us, Brother Merik drew rein. "Khai bears Pahrkun's mark as surely as you do, brother," he said in a reproving tone. "And a duty to the House of the Ageless yet to be fulfilled. I am sympathetic to your loss, but he has the right to ask such questions."

Vironesh took a ragged breath. "You are right," he said, inclining his head toward Brother Merik. "Forgive me, Khai. Prince Kazaran's death . . . I fear it is a wound that will never heal. As we ride toward the Palace of the Sun, I feel it anew."

"I am sorry," I said quietly. "I do not mean to trouble your heart. You should not do this if it pains you so."

He favored me with one of his grim smiles. "There is a part of me that would like nothing better than to return to the coursers of Obid the Stern, for there is a certain stark purity in their code that I find makes the disgrace of my failure easier to bear. But there is another part that wonders . . . What if there is a measure of redemption in this for me?" He paused. "Unless you object, I will stay."

"I welcome it," I assured him.

For the remainder of the journey, we spoke no more of prophecy, nor of the slain Prince Kazaran.

Merabaht had always seemed to me to be such a faraway place, it was strange to realize that in truth it was a mere week's ride from the Fortress of the Winds. To be sure, it was a forbidding ride, but the rigors of the desert held few terrors for the Brotherhood of Pahrkun.

On the fifth day, we reached the River Ouris.

Never in my life had I seen such a thing! Its slow-moving bronze waters cut a vast swath through the desert, nearly as wide across as the Eye of Zar, but stretching endlessly before us toward the west and behind us toward the northeast. Moisture hung in the air. Acres upon acres of green fields of wheat and rice lined its banks, and date palms rose to curve over the flowing water; water upon which men on flat-bottomed boats called skiffs cast nets and hauled in catches of silvery fish.

I stared and stared.

Brother Drajan leaned over in the saddle and clapped a hand on my shoulder. "Wait until you see the city!"

For two days, we followed the river, riding along a well-graded path, a road on which other travelers and traders journeyed. Brother Merik brought forth the standard of Pahrkun, and we rode beneath the sign of the carrion beetle, folk saluting us as we passed, thumbs pressed to brows. Villages of palm-thatched huts were clustered along the river every half a league or so. When we made camp on a trampled patch of land that had been used by countless travelers before us, shy villagers came to offer us wooden bowls full of slippery noodles and cooked fish in exchange for our blessing. The fare was unfamiliar to me, but I ate it with relish.

On the last day . . .

Merabaht.

On the far side of the river, the city sprawled before us. It occupied a hill, and atop the hill were the honey-colored marble walls of the Palace of the Sun. At the very apex of the hill was the Garden of Sowing Time, the crown-shaped fronds of the *rhamanthus* trees reaching toward the sun.

I gawped at it.

In this I was not alone, for the younger members of the brotherhood gawped, too. Even Brother Merik stared, although he winked at me when he saw me notice. "A far cry from the desert, eh, Khai?"

I smiled at him. "Indeed, brother."

We crossed the river on a conveyance called a ferry, a great floating plat-form of wood that was drawn back and forth across the wide expanse by means of half a dozen stalwart men hauling on a great length of rope. Brother Drajan paid a fare to the fellow in charge and we led our mounts and the two pack-horses onto the ferry.

It was strange indeed to be standing upon water, more water than I'd ever seen in my lifetime. Oh, but that was only the beginning, for as we gained the far bank and the outskirts of the city, the vista opened onto the ocean.

Of course, I had known from Brother Ehudan's maps that the ocean was vast, but it was one thing to know it and quite another to *see* it. It was as vast as the desert, but it was *water*. Even at a distance I could see that it was in a state of constant motion, sunlight sparkling on gentle waves, all manner of ships large and small following the course of the great western current.

"Who are they all?" I asked Brother Drajan. "Where do they come from and what do they do?"

"Traders, for the most part," he said. "Some official delegations from our nearest neighbors. Others, like the Tukkani, engage in commerce wherever the four great currents will carry them. Zarkhoum is rich in gold and grain and livestock," he added. "But for aught else, we needs must trade."

"Like what?" I could not think of what else one might need.

"Iron, for one thing," Vironesh said. "Where do you think the iron that forged your weapons comes from?"

"I don't know." It had never occurred to me to wonder. "Where?"

"Granth," he said in a sour tone. "That's why, like it or not, our realms need each other."

"Oh." Once again, I had the sense of the world and my understanding of it growing and expanding.

"And silk," Brother Drajan said cheerfully. "Heaven knows, our fine lords and ladies and rich merchants need their Barakhan silk!"

There were no fine lords or ladies in evidence at the ferry landing. Instead there was a market where dozens of peasant farmers from the countryside along the river offered goods for purchase—wheat and rice, squash and other vegetables I did not recognize, live birds. Women in plain-spun robes and

simple veils traveled in pairs or groups of three or four, perusing the se-
lection.

"Come." Vironesh nudged his mount. "We're bound for the barracks of
the Royal Guard."

We made our way upward.

The city of Merabaht was laid out in concentric circles. From a distance,
it had looked as though it would be fairly easy to navigate. In practice, it
was a complicated maze, at least in the lower levels. The cobbled streets were
narrow, lined with multi-storied sandstone dwellings that leaned inward to
block out the sun, and thronged with people going to and fro on foot. Many
of them saluted when they saw Pahrkun's banner and sought to let us pass,
but at times we simply had to wait for the knots of foot traffic to dissolve. It
smelled of sweat and spices and ordure, and I found myself overwhelmed by
the crush of humanity and longing for the purity of the desert.

Wherever the streets gave way to a crowded square, there were markets.
Here were different goods on offer, items of clothing and household goods,
baskets and pots and pans. I saw crippled boys begging in the squares, leaning
on crutches and dragging wasted legs, and I remembered that Brother Yarit
had told me of such things. Seeing the abundance that surrounded the city,
it seemed shameful to me that there were children forced to beg for subsis-
tence.

From my mounted vantage point, I saw pickpockets and cut-purses sliding like deft shadows through the throngs, and I wondered if any of them
were part of the Shahalim Clan.

I saw members of the City Guard, clad in long black tunics and white
breeches, an emblem of a wheat sheaf on their breasts. They did not carry edged
blades, but a pair of *kopars* thrust through their sashes. The Royal Guard,
Brother Drajan told me, was tasked with carrying out the king's justice; the
City Guard was tasked with maintaining order in the streets of Merabaht.

The sun was climbing overhead by the time we gained a broad rampway
that led to the next level, and I was sweating beneath my tunic. The streets
grew wider, the buildings that lined them shaded with palms and other
lush vegetation. Here there were shops that catered to a more wealthy clientele: jewelers' shops, teahouses, wine taverns.

I looked for the Lucky Tortoise to no avail, but I did see something that caught my eye.

A harried gem merchant was conversing with a city guardsman, gesticulating in an animated fashion. On the wall outside his shop, there was a scrawled symbol—a black burst of lines radiating from a single point.

I had seen it before. Brother Yarit had drawn it in the desert when the Sight first came upon him.

"Brother Drajan?" I pointed. "What does that symbol mean?"

Brother Drajan frowned. "I've no idea. You?" He glanced at Vironesh, who shook his head.

Brother Merik hoisted the standard of Pahrkun. "Hey!" he called. "What passes here?"

The guard saluted him. "Nothing of import, brother," he said in a respectful manner. "Vandals, nothing more."

"This symbol." I edged my mount closer. "What does it betoken?"

The guard's eyes widened as he looked up at me. "You're the young princess's shadow!" He took notice of Vironesh and his eyes went even wider. "And you must be—" Wisely, he didn't finish his thought. He saluted us. "The black star? It's the mark of some foolish troublemakers, that's all. A disgruntled lot who care about nothing but overturning the order of the world." He grimaced in distaste. "They call themselves the Children of Miasmus."

TWENTY

The Children of Miasmus.

Despite the day's heat, I felt a chill run the length of my spine. I glanced at Vironesh. "It's just a name, Khai," he said dismissively. "I daresay they took it to give people a fright." He addressed the guard. "What's their quarrel with the order of the world?"

The guard looked uneasy. "I really couldn't say, brother."

"Well, I will if you won't!" the gem merchant said angrily. "They're just a handful of ungrateful rabble who resent their betters. And they're using the fact that Anamuht hasn't appeared in the city to quicken the Garden of Sowing Time for over twenty years to claim the House of the Ageless has lost favor with the Sacred Twins."

The guard put a hand to the hilt of one of his *kopars*. "That's treason you're talking."

"*I'm* not saying it," the merchant retorted. "The ruffians calling themselves the Children of Miasmus are. And I'd like to know why the City Guard can't seem to do anything about it!"

"Do you think we've got enough men to patrol the streets morning and night and catch every low-born agitator able to lay his hands on a tar bucket and a brush?" the guard said in an aggrieved tone. "If you want to protect your shop at all hours, open your fat purse and hire someone to do it for you!"

At Brother Merik's signal, we rode onward, the sounds of their quarrel fading behind us. Here the streets were wide enough for me to bring my mount alongside his. "That symbol, the black star. Brother Yarit drew it in the desert on the day that the Sight passed to him. Do you remember?"

"He did?" Brother Merik looked surprised. "No, I can't say I do. But if it were something you needed to know about, I'm sure he would have told you."

"Not if he couldn't," I said. "Not if it would upset the balance of what might come to pass."

"And not if it meant nothing," Vironesh said wearily. "I spent years sailing among the coursers of Obid. Trust me when I say I'm quite sure that this business has nothing to do with their prophecy."

"How can you be sure?" I challenged him. "Do *you* know how all the pieces fit together?"

He sighed. "Let it go, Khai."

Although I was not convinced, I set the matter aside for the moment.

We reached another rampway and ascended another level, our horses' hooves clopping on the paving stones. Below us the harbor glistened, filled with ships rendered tiny by the distance, and the sea breeze cooled our skin. Now the streets were even broader, and they were lined with gracious residences set back behind fretted gates; homes that featured roofs of red clay tiles and abundant gardens. The hustle and bustle of the lower levels seemed remote, a thing best forgotten in the heights. Our company fanned out, riding four abreast. What little foot traffic there was, Brother Drajan informed us, were servants trekking to and from the marketplaces: clusters of veiled women with baskets on their arms, trudging men with lowered heads hauling long-poled carts heaped with produce behind them.

From time to time, we saw curtained litters carried by strapping servants, their occupants hidden from sight.

It was all very strange.

On the penultimate level of the city of Merabaht, we reached the barracks of the Royal Guard, an imposing sandstone structure. At least it was a fortress of sorts, and thus familiar to me.

The king's guardsmen had seen us coming and they flung open the doors to their barracks. Servants were summoned to lead our horses to the stables and cart our belongings inside, and we were escorted to the Common Hall, where the captain of the Royal Guard greeted us.

Captain Laaren was a tall, lean fellow with grizzled grey hair he wore cropped short. "Welcome, brothers," he said with a salute, then stopped short at the sight of Vironesh. "You. I've heard tell of you."

"I'm here to serve if the king will have me," Vironesh said quietly.

The captain shrugged. "Well then, I reckon that's for His Majesty to decide." His gaze settled on me. "Khai, is it?"

I saluted him. "Yes, brother."

At me, he smiled. "His Majesty is eager to meet you. Princess Zariya is quite a favorite of his, you know. I'll send word to the palace that you've arrived. All of you are welcome to share our quarters. Please take refreshment, rest, and avail yourselves of the baths until the king is ready to receive you."

"We will require a private chamber for Khai," Brother Merik said, prompting a perplexed look from the captain.

"I am *bhazim*." The word tasted bitter on my tongue, but I was weary of having others explain it for me.

"Ha! I assumed—" Captain Laaren scratched his chin and regarded me as though I'd sprouted a second head. "Well, no mind. You'll take my chamber, I'll have a basin sent so you can bathe. We've no proper women's quarter here except in the servants' lodgings, and that's no way to offer hospitality to the shadow of one of the Sun-Blessed."

I inclined my head. "My thanks."

The captain beckoned to one of the guards who'd escorted us into the hall. "Tell His Majesty that the delegation from the Brotherhood of Pahrkun has arrived. And please ensure that he's aware of the, ah, particulars of the situation."

In the captain's chamber, servants brought a basin of water, a jar of soap, and a strange porous object that I might scrub myself, a clean length of cloth with which to dry myself, as well as a platter of food and a pot of mint tea. I removed my weapons, stripped off my clothing, and washed quickly, feeling self-conscious about the whole process. So much water just for the purpose of bathing! It would have been unthinkable in the desert. Still, it did feel good to don the new clothing that Brother Merik had presented me over clean skin, and stow my dusty, worn, and sweat-stained garments in my pack.

After sampling the food the servants had brought, I lay down on the captain's pallet and dozed through the midday heat, awakening to the unfamiliar salt tang of ocean breezes sighing through the open window.

In the Fortress of the Winds, this would have been the hour when we resumed our training, but when I ventured into the Common Hall, I found the off-duty guardsmen idle, tossing knucklebones and wagering with each other in a game of chance that Brother Yarit had told me about.

"Is that customary?" I asked Vironesh.

"In most parts of the world, yes." He smiled wryly. "Although the coursers of Obid frown upon it."

I smiled, too. "I do not doubt it."

Vironesh eyed me. "Shall we have a bout?"

"Here?"

He nodded. "Here."

"I don't think it's a bad idea to remind these city-born fellows what kind of warriors the desert gives birth to," observed Brother Merik, who'd overheard us. "Or what a pair of shadows are capable of."

The guards left off their games to watch as Vironesh and I faced off in the center of the Common Hall. To be fair, it was more a demonstration than a proper bout, but it was a good one nonetheless. We exchanged blows almost too quick for the ordinary mortal eye to follow as I danced around him, Pahrkun's wind singing in my veins, using my youthful energy and speed to prod at his deceptively impenetrable defenses.

When we halted in unspoken accord, the watching guards whistled and clapped their hands in applause.

"Very impressive," Captain Laaren said in a neutral tone. I hadn't known he was there. "Are you finished? King Azarkal will see you now."

I sheathed my weapons. "Of course."

There was no outer road from the barracks of the Royal Guard to the palace, but rather a broad tunnel carved into the hillside proper, illuminated by periodic shafts of light from strategically placed apertures overhead. Although the tunnel and the ensuing rampway that led to the uppermost circle of the city of Merabaht were tall and wide enough to accommodate horses, we progressed on foot, emerging into a heavily guarded courtyard. Zar the

Sun was setting in the west, and the honey-colored walls of the palace glowed in the evening light.

Men built this, I thought; and marveled at the thought.

And then I thought of the crippled boys I had seen begging in the marketplace, and I marveled less.

Captain Laaren strode up to the tall doors of the palace, and the palace doors swung open wide.

We followed him inside.

It was an immense place, and I was grateful to have a knowing guide. Among us, only Vironesh did not gape at the splendor, at the high ceilings, marbled floors, and frescoed walls.

Here and there, guards strolled.

Here and there, servants scuttled, keeping their heads down, meeting no one's gaze, nigh invisible.

I thought about Brother Yarit.

I missed him.

The captain led us to the throne hall, where he announced us in ringing tones. "Your Sun-Blessed Majesty King Azarkal, foremost of the House of the Ageless, ruler of Zarkhoum! I present to you the delegation of the Brotherhood of Pahrkun the Scouring Wind, and among them Khai of the Fortress of the Winds, who would serve as shadow to the Princess Zariya."

Seated on his throne, the back of which was rendered in the shape of a vast golden sunburst, the king beckoned us forward.

At a glance, King Azarkal looked youthful, a man in the prime of his fighting years, no more than thirty . . . but only at a glance. There was nothing obvious that belied the semblance. His face was unlined, and the skin of his hands was smooth. There was no trace of grey in his black hair or his neatly trimmed beard, and his body beneath the flowing golden silk robes he wore looked fit and hale. But he wore a crown set with clusters of glowing red stones I knew without being told were *rhamanthus* seeds, light shifting like embers in their depths, and somehow one could see in his stillness that it was a weight he had carried for a very long time.

"Khai," he said to me. "Approach the throne." I found my knees trembling slightly as I obeyed and saluted him. King Azarkal's gaze searched my face, dark and penetrating. "Yes," he mused. "Your features are delicate for a boy's. But I am not sure I would have seen if I were not looking."

Not knowing what to say, I said nothing.

"You bear Pahrkun's mark." The king leaned forward on his throne. "Tell me, did the Scouring Wind reveal to you why the Sacred Twins chose to bestow a shadow upon my youngest?"

There was a strange combination of hunger and bitterness in his voice. I shook my head. "No, Your Majesty."

"A pity." He sat back, his gaze shifting. "Vironesh. I did not think to see you again in my lifetime."

"Nor I to find myself in this position, Your Majesty," the purple man said with quiet dignity. "But it was Pahrkun's will that I train Khai." He hesitated. "I do not exaggerate when I tell you that because of it Khai possesses skills that it took me many more years to acquire."

King Azarkal drummed the fingers of his right hand against his thigh. "And yet I find myself wondering *why*; and wondering, too, would my third-born son have become such a target had the Sacred Twins not shown him such favor? What does it betoken for my youngest daughter? What need has a girl-child of a desert-trained shadow?"

I drew in a sharp, involuntary breath at the notion that the king would challenge Pahrkun's very will.

He glanced back at me. "That strikes you as blasphemous?"

I looked around for assistance, but Brother Merik gave me a slight gesture with one hand, indicating the question was mine to answer. "I think it is a fair question for a grieving father to ponder, Your Majesty." I saw that there were three empty settings in a cluster on the left of his crown where *rhamanthus* seeds had been pried loose; and I saw the king see me notice. The shortage must be grave indeed if they were desecrating the royal crown. "But if I were a member of the House of the Ageless, I do not think I would choose this moment in time to question the will of the Sacred Twins."

I felt rather than saw a shock ripple through the members of the Royal Guard in attendance.

King Azarkal lifted one hand, bidding them to stillness. "So the young

shadow dares say to my face what members of my household do not," he said.
"Very well. I shall emulate those touched by Lishan the Graceful in Barakhar
and bow before the winds of fate like a veritable willow tree. Thank you,
brothers, for delivering your charge. Your duty is fulfilled. In the morning,
Khai will be presented to Princess Zariya on the occasion of their shared
day of birth."

A wave of relief washed over me at hearing an outcome I had never suspected was uncertain.

"On behalf of the Brotherhood of Pahrkun, I thank you, Your Majesty,"
Brother Merik said with a respectful salute. "I believe your decision is the
right one, and I can assure you the Seer agrees."

"The Seer, yes." The king regarded him. "I'm given to understand that a
convicted *thief* of the Shahalim Clan serves as Seer. Is this so?"

"It is." Brother Merik couldn't keep a stiff note from his voice, but he
didn't back down, either. "I was there when Brother Yarit passed the Trial
of Pahrkun and was scoured of his sins, and I was there when the Sight came
upon him, Your Majesty. It is not a thing that could be feigned. As unlikely
as it seems, he is Pahrkun's chosen."

"Yes, I recall the fellow, though by a different name." King Azarkal
drummed his fingers against his thigh again. "He was caught attempting
to steal *rhamanthus* seeds from the royal treasury. Of course, he failed; but
strange to say, there was another theft in the palace, almost as grave, that succeeded some years ago. An item of great value was stolen from my eldest son."
He raised his brows at Brother Merik. "I don't suppose your Seer knows
aught about it?"

Brother Merik stared at the king with unfeigned astonishment. "Your
Majesty! No, certainly not."

"No?"

My fingertips itched with the perverse urge to feel the slight rise at the
nape of my neck where the Teardrop was buried in my flesh, and I was sur-
passingly glad that the question had not been directed at me.

"No," Brother Merik said firmly. "There was no opportunity. On the sole
occasion that Brother Yarit sought to flee the Fortress of the Winds, it was

the Sacred Twins themselves who turned him back. Since he became the Seer, he has conducted himself with . . ." He paused, then nodded to himself. "I will not say propriety, but I believe *integrity* is a fair word to use."

In a way, he wasn't wrong.

Just doing my duty, the way I reckon it, Brother Yarit had said to me.

Even so, I was grateful when the king flicked his fingers and dismissed the matter. "On the morrow, then."

Vironesh stepped forward and saluted. "Begging Your Majesty's pardon, I seek a post in the Royal Guard. Do you consent, it would allow me to be of service to the House of the Ageless and continue Khai's training."

King Azarkal considered him, then beckoned to Captain Laaren, who approached and bent his head.

The two of them conferred in low tones.

"The Royal Guard has no shortage of able-bodied men of good birth willing to serve," the king announced. "But I will gladly offer you a post in the City Guard." His mouth hardened. "Of late, Merabaht is afflicted by a scourge of malcontents, looters, and vandals calling themselves the Children of Miasmus. Perhaps you are familiar with the name? I hear tell you served amongst the coursers of Obid."

Vironesh shot me a wry look. "I did and I am, Your Majesty."

"It's merely a name chosen to sow fear and chaos, of course," King Azarkal said. "Still, they are a thorn in our side, and I would see them rooted out and brought to justice. Do you accept?"

"Yes, Your Majesty," he said. "I do."

It was not exactly what we had sought, but it meant Vironesh would be staying in Merabaht, and I was glad of it.

I had the uneasy feeling that we had only heard the beginning of the Children of Miasmus.

TWENTY-ONE

Although I was offered a guest chamber in the palace proper, I chose to pass the night in the barracks. Captain Laaren was somewhat disgruntled at having to surrender his chamber for the entire night, but he bore it graciously enough.

In the morning, everything would be different.

In the morning, my entire life would change.

And so I clung to this last bit of familiarity, this last piece of brotherly solidarity, before it all changed. For the most part, the guards kept a respectful distance and allowed us our night of camaraderie, though I could see that they looked at me differently here in Merabaht than any guards to visit the Fortress of the Winds had ever done. There, none of them had known I was *bhazim*; here, all of them did. I caught one assessing my body beneath my loose woolen garments, although he flushed and looked away quickly when I did. I wondered if he had doubts, if he was uncertain what lay beneath my clothing. I was glad that Vironesh had suggested we spar earlier, for if any man here were minded to find out firsthand, that would surely cause him to think twice.

Less than a day in the palace made me realize that for all the strictness and discipline that my life at the Fortress of the Winds entailed, in some ways, I had been very well protected. What dangers existed were simple and straightforward—heatstroke, predators, a fall from the heights, a sparring accident, a successful supplicant. I would have trusted any one of the brothers with my life.

And for my entire life, that had been the bedrock of my existence.

Here, the terrain was unfamiliar and the footing was treacherous. I would have to be very circumspect.

The Brotherhood departed at dawn. "If you have need of us, know that we are always there for you," Brother Merik said softly, his callused hand squeezing my forearm. "You are one of us. You have but to send word."

I returned his grip. "I draw strength and comfort from the knowledge, brother."

Once they had gone, Captain Laaren informed Vironesh that he was to report to the barracks of the City Guard, on the second level.

Vironesh fixed him with a level stare. "If you don't mind, I'll wait with Khai until he's summoned."

The captain shrugged. "As you will."

I was grateful for his company, for it was some hours before the summons came; not, as I expected, from one of the king's guardsmen, but a quartet of guards in white linen robes with golden sashes, each one carrying a spear with a gilded, leaf-shaped blade. Although they were all well above fighting age, all of them were smooth-faced and beardless and lacked the broad-shouldered physiques of the warriors with which I was familiar.

"Those are members of the Queen's Guard," Vironesh murmured to me. "Cut at an early age so they might serve in the women's quarter."

I swallowed, understanding that would have been my fate had I been born into a boy's body. "I see."

"Khai of the Fortress of the Winds." The fellow who addressed me wore a gold collar inlaid with pale gems around his neck. He planted the butt of his spear on the floor. "I am Tarshim, captain of the Queen's Guard. We are bidden to escort you to the Hall of Pleasant Accord."

I saluted him, then turned to Vironesh. "I'll see you anon?"

The purple man nodded, then caught my arm. "Khai, listen. I know I haven't been as forthcoming as you might have wished, but there's nothing I could say to prepare you for what you're about to experience. But when it comes to life within the court, trust no one save your charge," he said in a low voice. "And even then . . ." He paused. "Listen to your head as well as your heart."

"I will," I promised.

"You'll try." Vironesh put on one of his humorless smiles. "But you'll find it more difficult than you think. Do your best, and I'll tell you what I learn of the Children of Miasmus."

With that, we parted ways.

The Queen's Guard escorted me through the same tunnel passage. When we emerged into the bright morning light, I noted that there were additional gates to either side that led into the main courtyard, manned by members of the Royal Guard who searched every cart that sought entry. I surmised that there must be roads from this uppermost level to the lower levels on which merchants or servants traveled to and from the market, supplying goods to the palace.

Inside the palace, Captain Tarshim set a brisk pace through the honey-colored marble halls and up a series of broad staircases. "As you are desert-born, may I assume you are ignorant of the ways of the court?" he inquired.

It sounded like a cutting comment, and yet I sensed no edge to it, only a blunt pragmatism. "You may."

"The Hall of Pleasant Accord lies between the women's quarter and the rest of the palace," he said. "It is a place where the Sun-Blessed fathers and sons and brothers, mothers and sisters and daughters of the House of the Ageless, as well as other esteemed and privileged members of the court, may freely commingle."

"Only there?" I asked.

The captain of the Queen's Guard gave me a sidelong glance. "Within the bounds of propriety, yes. It is also one of the only places within the palace walls where the Sun-Blessed are oath-sworn to conduct themselves in a spirit of harmony. Neither violence nor intrigue is permitted."

It was telling that such a place needed to be designated. "And is this oath honored?"

Captain Tarshim hesitated. "To the best of my knowledge, yes. No one has ever violated the proscription against violence. I would not swear upon my life that the same holds true for intrigue." It was a sensible answer, and I was glad that he was willing to be honest with me; I was not so glad when he continued. "You'll need to be examined before you enter, of course."

I halted. Servants with downcast eyes detoured around us. "Examined?"

"To confirm you're what they say," Captain Tarshim said impatiently. "*Bhazim*, or at least cut. We cannot afford to take you at your word. Shadow or no, it must be confirmed before you're allowed to serve in the women's quarter, let alone allowed to bear weapons there." He gestured toward the door ahead of us. "Unless you're deceiving us, it will take but a moment."

"I am not lying," I said. "And no one told me of this."

"No doubt it was assumed you would expect it," he said. "These are the royal women of the House of the Ageless. Did you think to find us careless of their safety?"

"I did not think to find such mistrust leveled at one chosen by Pahrkun himself," I retorted.

He gave a thin smile in reply. "Then you are naive."

And so I allowed myself to be escorted into the antechamber of the Hall of Pleasant Accord. There, behind a silk-paneled screen, I untied the drawstring of my breeches and let them fall to the floor. The captain examined me with an impersonal gaze, gesturing for me to widen my stance as he lifted the hem of my tunic and peered between my thighs to make sure I was hiding nothing.

Humiliated, I endured it, gazing at the top of Captain Tarshim's bent head and thinking how easy it would be to kill him. I reminded myself that he was merely doing his duty, and of how Brother Yarit had said it was better to be *bhazim* than a eunuch. Satisfied that I was what I claimed, the captain retreated to allow me the small dignity of pulling up my breeches in private.

My physical nature confirmed, I was permitted to bear my weapons into the Hall of Pleasant Accord. Four men in the crimson-and-gold silks of the Royal Guard were posted on either side of the entrance that led to the hall beyond. At a word from Captain Tarshim, they opened the doors to admit us.

Did I gape? I'm sure I must have, for it was a splendid space. Later, I came to know it well, but my memories of that first glimpse are bright and fractured like shards of broken glass. I recall sunlight spilling through the tall windows. I recall there were a dozen or so members of the royal family in attendance, their robes seeming to glow in the light. Sun-Blessed, indeed. I recall there was a long carpet covered with so many shining pitchers and heaped platters that they obscured its intricate design. There were cushions strewn around the edge of the carpet. Some of the Sun-Blessed were lounging at their ease, laughing and picking delicacies from the platters. The women were unveiled and wore their hair in ornate braids, with gold bangles on their arms and anklets with tinkling bells as Brother Yarit had told me long ago.

I recall plants in great pots, date palms and others I did not know by name. I recall King Azarkal, his crowned head bowed as he spoke to a small figure seated on a low stool with curved sides.

Zariya.

Although I had tried in vain to picture her a thousand times, I knew her at a glance, I knew the attentive angle at which she held her head. Everything changed in that instant; *everything*. I felt myself turned inside out. Vironesh was right, nothing could have prepared me for what I felt. I was dumbstruck by tenderness, I was honed to a fierce, keen edge with protectiveness. I knew her; I knew the curve of her cheek and brow, I knew the tilt of her chin. I could have picked her out of a crowd a hundred times this size.

Oh, I wanted to say, *it's* you.

King Azarkal straightened at our entrance and clapped his hands. The murmur of conversation died. The captain and his guards joined others posted around the perimeter of the hall, gazing straight ahead. The king made an announcement, but he may as well have been speaking Granthian for all that I heard of it. The focus of my world had narrowed to a single living being.

Zariya.

My heart ached at the sight of her. It seemed an invisible cord stretched between us, drawing us together as inexorably as the moons beneath which we were born draw the tides, binding us together with ties stronger than iron. The Sun-Blessed watched in silence as we gazed at each other in wonder. Zariya leaned forward on her stool, hands gripping the curved sides. Her kohl-lined eyes were dark and lustrous and awestruck, her carmine-painted lips parted in amazement.

I daresay my own expression looked much the same. Every empty space within me that loneliness had carved out was being filled at once, and it felt as though my heart could barely contain it. I could have laughed aloud for the sheer joy of it and wept with grief at the enormity.

I had found the light to my shadow, the fire to my wind.

Somehow I made my way across the hall and knelt on the tiled floor before the stool on which she sat.

"Oh," she whispered. "It's *you!*"

"Your Highness, I would give my life for you," I said simply to her. "All that I am is yours."

"I know." Her slender hands rose to cup my face, thumbs stroking the mica-flecked scars on my cheekbones. "And I yours. We belong to each other now, don't we?" A delicate furrow of concern emerged between her finely arched brows. "Oh, my poor darling! Did it hurt?"

I gazed up at her. "It doesn't matter."

"It matters to me." Zariya's voice was soft, but firm. She took her hands away. "But you must know the whole truth from the beginning. We must never be less than honest with each other. Nalah, my canes?" A maidservant in a white linen dress and a sheer veil over the lower half of her face stepped forward to present the princess with a pair of gilded canes. Zariya used them to lever herself to her feet with difficulty. I rose with alacrity to assist her, but she shook her head at me. "No, you must let me do it," she said breathlessly.

"My youngest contracted Dhanbu fever as a child." King Azarkal came over to place a gentle hand on her shoulder. "It left her thus. But as you can see, she has the heart of a lion nonetheless. Lest it need be said, do not speak of her condition," he added. "No one outside the palace walls is aware of it."

"I hope you are not disappointed," Zariya said to me.

"In *you?*" I stared at her in disbelief. "Never! I could *never* be disappointed in you!"

"Well, I trust you were not expecting to find me a warrior," she said. "But I'm sure you were not expecting a cripple, either."

There was a touch of wry, self-deprecating humor in her tone that reminded me of Brother Yarit. "I had no idea what to expect, Your Highness, and thus no expectations," I said to her. "You are beautiful and gracious, while I am a child of the desert and ignorant of the ways of court. Are *you* disappointed?"

"In *you*?" A hint of color flushed Princess Zariya's cheeks. Leaning on her canes, she laughed, eyes sparkling at me. "Khai of the Fortress of the Winds, you are the fiercest and most wonderful thing I have ever seen! Do not ask me foolish questions, my shadow."

The remainder of that morning passed in a blur.

Let your mind be like the eye of a hawk, Brother Saan had taught me, but my heart was too full of strange new feelings to allow my mind to soar impartially above the fray I had entered.

Oh, and it *was* a fray. Despite the sumptuous setting and the courteous manners on display, there was no mistaking it for aught else. Everyone was pleasant enough to me, but I could sense the mixture of curiosity and resentment lurking beneath the superficial politeness. All five queens including Zariya's mother were in attendance; I know that because the Palace of the Sun was their permanent dwelling. King Azarkal, of course. His eldest surviving sons, Elizar the collector from whom the Teardrop had been stolen, and Tazaresh the second-born. I do not recall that Dozaren was present that day, though I could be mistaken. There were so many unfamiliar faces, and so many of them possessed an uncanny youthfulness at odds with the subtle markers of age in their demeanor. It was disconcerting.

The one member of the House of the Ageless to whom I took an immediate liking was Princess Nizara. A tall woman in crimson silk robes, she was the king's eldest daughter, the one who served as the High Priestess of Anamuht. She wore a headdress like the matriarchs of the desert tribesfolk, although the veil was pinned back. It was strange to me to see so many women's unveiled faces, but Nizara's features were grave and kind, and it was obvious that she bore genuine affection for her youngest sister.

"The bond between Sun-Blessed and shadow is forged in accordance with the will of the Sacred Twins," she said to Zariya and me. "I am pleased to bestow my blessing upon it in the name of Anamuht the Purging Fire."

I saluted her. "Thank you, Your Highness."

Princess Nizara smiled. "I have held the role of priestess far longer than that of a princess. I was there when Pahrkun the Scouring Wind chose you, Khai. You may call me Elder Sister if you like."

It made me feel a little less adrift, and I was grateful for it.

Once introductions had been made, all the Sun-Blessed sat on low cushions around the elegant carpet to enjoy the repast.

"How shall I attend you, Your Highness?" I asked Zariya uncertainly. "I have been trained to detect poisons."

"You have?" Her eyes widened. "Oh, but we do not speak of such things in this hall, my shadow."

"But—"

"Every dish has been tasted, young Khai," Sister Nizara said in a quiet voice. "Do not fear."

The apothecary had said as much to me. Feeling rude and uncouth, I inclined my head in apology. "Then I shall abide with the Queen's Guard until you have need of me, Your Highness."

"What?" Zariya laughed. "You will do no such thing. You are my shadow, not my servant." She patted the cushion beside her. "You will sit next to me and tell me every last little thing about you."

I sat.

What did we speak of that first morning? I recall that I did my best to heed Vironesh's warning and be circumspect; I had already been unwise in blurting out that I had been taught to detect poison. I was out of my depth here. And so I was careful to say nothing of my training in the ways of the Shahalim Clan, speaking lightly instead of such things as Brother Saan's injunction to squeeze rocks three thousand times a day.

It was difficult, for I *wanted* to tell Zariya every last little thing. And I wanted to know every last little thing about her.

But no, this was neither the time nor the place for such candor; and despite what Zariya had said to me, I was quite certain she was more than aware of it. By all the fallen stars, I wanted to be *alone* with her! I wanted to be free to talk and talk and talk . . . what a strange feeling.

Prince Tazaresh, who had a warrior's keen gaze, asked me questions regarding the weapons with which I had trained; I spoke of the *yakhan* and *kopar,* and nothing else, mindful of the brace of throwing knives strapped to my left forearm, the garrote that tied back my hair.

Prince Elizar the collector stroked the trim mustache that adorned his upper lip and looked bored by the entire affair. He would not be so bored if he knew what was hidden in my flesh, I thought.

Whatever factions existed, they were not in evidence that morning in the Hall of Pleasant Accord. Still, it was a profound relief when the interminable gathering was dismissed.

Zariya allowed me to help her rise from the low cushion. Farewells were exchanged and the Queen's Guard escorted the women in attendance into the guarded sanctuary of the women's quarter.

I had entered a world within a world.

COURT

TWENTY-TWO

In the Hall of Pleasant Accord, the demeanor of the royal women had been reserved and demure, deferential to King Azarkal and the princes of the Sun-Blessed. All of that changed the moment the doors to the women's quarter closed behind us.

"Well, you got what you wanted," Queen Adinah said tartly to Sanala, who was Zariya's mother and the most junior of the queens. "I daresay your broken-winged dove is officially his favorite pet. May it bring you more joy than it did me."

"Yes, and a target painted on her back," Queen Sanala retorted. "*I* didn't ask for this." She looked me up and down. "We'll have to procure proper attire. She looks like some desert chieftain's son. It's unseemly."

"Khai is *bhazim* and a trained warrior marked by Pahrkun himself." Sister Nizara folded her hands in the sleeves of her crimson robes. "His attire is appropriate."

Someone gave a humorless snort. "*Bhazim*, is it?"

"It's unseemly," Sanala repeated in a fretful tone.

I glanced at Zariya and saw her flushed with anger and embarrassment, and suddenly I was angry, too; anger rising in me like Pahrkun's wind. I looked for the spaces between that existed in this bickering exchange and drove words into them like a blade. "I do not answer to you, Your Majesties," I said to both Adinah and Sanala in the coldest voice I could muster. "Not in this or any matter. I do not answer to anyone save Pahrkun the Scouring Wind."

For the first time since I'd caught sight of Merabaht, I was not the one gaping.

"You dare!" Queen Adinah recovered first, striding forward to strike at my face with an open palm. I angled away from the blow, causing her to stumble. She drew in an outraged breath. "Guards!"

Captain Tarshim stepped forward, signaling to the others. As their gilded spears leveled at me, I braced myself and tried to gauge whether I could take out all four without bloodshed.

"No!" It was Sister Nizara who countermanded them in a forceful tone. "Mother, Anamuht is displeased with the House of the Ageless. Will you worsen matters by incurring the outright wrath of the Sacred Twins?"

The guards stood down and I breathed more easily.

Queen Adinah summoned her dignity with an effort. "Because you are young and ignorant, I will forgive the offense you have given me today," she said to me. "And I will tell you to choose wisely before you make enemies at court."

I inclined my head to her.

She beckoned to a maidservant. "I will retire to my chambers for the midday rest."

Following her lead, the others dispersed save for Sister Nizara, whom I saluted. "Thank you, Elder Sister."

She frowned. "My mother is in the wrong, but there is merit to her advice . . . Zariya, are you *laughing*?"

"No, sister," Zariya said in a choked voice, her shoulders shaking. "I am trying very hard *not* to."

Sister Nizara cast her gaze heavenward. "Would that I understood the will of the gods better! Khai, in a day or so when you are settled, I ask that you call upon me at the High Temple of Anamuht. I would speak with you there about what knowledge the brotherhood may share."

"Yes, of course," I said.

"Try not to kill anyone in the meantime," she said wryly.

By the time she took her leave, Zariya had regained her composure. "Come," she said to me. "You're to stay in my chambers."

I followed her through the vast labyrinth of the women's quarter, Zariya leaning on her canes, the maidservant Nalah accompanying us. It seemed to me that her chambers were rather far.

"Yes," she said when I remarked on it, her breath coming short again with the effort of walking. "Because I had to be kept isolated from the others when I was sick as a child. But I stayed because I like it."

When we reached Zariya's chambers, I understood why. The sitting room wasn't large, but it was light and airy and filled with birdsong. An elaborate wooden cage with half a dozen birds with green and blue and yellow feathers, an unfamiliar species to me, took up an entire corner.

"Those are my little friends," Zariya said with a smile, sitting on a divan. "I hope you don't mind birds."

I shook my head. "Not at all."

While she caught her breath and Nalah bustled around, tidying things and pouring water into a washbasin, I took stock. In addition to birds, there were books and scrolls, a great many of them stacked on shelves and nestled into rows of cubbyholes. There was a desk with a low stool with curved sides like the one in the Hall of Pleasant Accord, and a low table flanked by a pair of hassocks. The sitting room opened onto a private garden with a high wall around it. In addition to the sitting room and a privy closet, there was a sleeping chamber with a carved wooden bed. There was an additional cushioned pallet on the carpet beside it, and the leather satchel containing my belongings sat on a trunk at the foot of the bed.

It should have been disorienting to think, *Oh, this is my new home*; and yet it wasn't.

Zariya was my new home.

"It's lovely," I said to her when I'd completed my inspection. "I take it you like to read?"

"You have two strong legs to carry you across the world, my shadow," she said. "I have words."

It touched on a matter that was troubling me. "My lady . . . how is it that one as well protected as you contracted Dhanbu fever?"

Zariya did not answer, glancing instead at the maidservant. "Thank you, Nalah. You may leave us now."

It was careless of me to think I could speak freely in front of the servants,

I realized. I was unaccustomed to this business of mistrust. Nalah saluted and departed, closing the door with its fretted panels behind her. I heard the soft steps of her slippered feet departing, and the even softer steps of her return.

"It is not a matter of which I would speak—" Zariya began.

I touched one finger to my lips and pointed to the door. There was a shadow visible behind the fretwork of the lowest panel. I crossed the floor soundlessly and yanked the door open. The maidservant Nalah, kneeling with one ear pressed to the panel, nearly fell into the room.

She scrambled to her feet. "Forgive me, my—" Uncertain how to address me, she checked herself. "I only thought to remain in earshot lest you and Her Highness require anything."

"We do not," Zariya said. "Thank you for your concern, but please retire to the servants' quarter until the midday rest is ended."

I folded my arms, and Nalah beat a hasty retreat.

Zariya sighed. "I should have found a way to warn you—most of the servants are in Adinah's pocket. But I did not think Nalah would stoop to spying outright. I suppose things have changed now that you are here."

"I should not have spoken heedlessly," I said. "I have a great deal to learn."

"Come." With the aid of both hands, Zariya lifted her legs one by one onto the divan and shifted to recline upon it, propping her head on one hand. "Lie beside me and we will whisper secrets into each other's ears."

I hesitated.

"I have made you uncomfortable." There was acute understanding in her dark eyes. "Forgive me."

"It is only that I am unfamiliar with the ways of women," I said to her. "You are the first one I have known."

"I have a great deal to learn, too," Zariya observed. "It's so peculiar, is it not? I feel as though I've known you forever. I would trust you with my life without a moment's hesitation. And yet in truth, we come from very different worlds and know almost nothing of each other."

I smiled at her in relief. "Yes, exactly."

She returned my smile. "Well, let us make a beginning before we plunge into the noisome depths of courtly intrigue. Tell me, what was it like to be raised *bhazim*?"

Sitting cross-legged on the carpet beside her divan, I explained to Zariya that I had not been knowingly raised *bhazim*, but had believed myself to be a boy until I was on the cusp of adolescence.

She listened attentively. "It must have come as a terrible shock."

I hugged my knees to my chest. "It did."

"How do you think of yourself now?" she asked curiously. "As a boy or a girl?"

I thought about it. "Neither, I suppose. I don't know *how* to be a girl, but I don't want to, either." Realizing how insulting that sounded, I made a face. "I'm sorry, I didn't mean it."

"You did, but no mind," Zariya said mildly. "If I were you, I'm sure I'd feel the same way. In Zarkhoum, women are not warriors. To be considered a girl . . . it feels like an insult to your spirit and training, does it not? To the very essence of you?"

It was as though she'd laid a finger upon my heart, and I glanced away to hide the unexpected sting of tears. "Yes."

"Well, I will simply consider you Khai, my shadow; unique unto yourself," she said in a gentle voice. "But tell me, lest I offend, would you rather I say *he* or *she* when I refer to you?"

I wiped my eyes on my sleeve, a ragged laugh escaping me. "I do not know how to answer, my lady. Sometimes it seems to me that to be *bhazim* truly *is* a thing unto itself, and there should be some other term for one such as me."

"The Elehuddin have such a term," Zariya said, surprising me.

"The Elehuddin?" I echoed.

She nodded. "The sea-folk, those who can breathe water as well as air. Do you not know of them? I've never met one, of course—they do not venture to the shores of our desert realm—but I've read about them. According to Liko of Koronis, there are words in their language one uses to refer to a person who is neither a man nor a woman. Or possibly both," she added. "He was never entirely clear on that point. At any rate, I fear I cannot tell you what those words may be, my darling, for the language of the Elehuddin is composed of whistles and trills and clicks."

I frowned. "Who is Liko of Koronis and how does he know what the Elehuddin are saying if all they do is click and whistle?"

"Liko of Koronis was a great scholar and a prophecy-hunter. He lived among the Elehuddin and learned to speak their tongue." Zariya smiled wistfully. "I should have liked to be a prophecy-hunter."

"Vironesh says there are a great many pieces of prophecy beneath the starless sky," I said. "But no one knows how they all fit together."

"Vironesh." Her brows drew together. "He was my brother Kazaran's shadow, was he not?"

"Yes," I said. "And my mentor, too. Before that he spent the decades following your brother's death among the coursers of Obid. Now he is here in the city . . . my lady, do you know there is a faction calling themselves the Children of Miasmus wreaking havoc in Merabaht?"

Zariya's eyes widened. "No! Is it true?"

I shrugged. "So I was told. At your father's behest, Vironesh will serve in the City Guard and learn what he might. He thinks it is but a name chosen to sow fear," I added.

"Like as not," she mused. "Still . . ."

"I know."

We thought together in silence for a moment.

"What pieces of prophecy did this Liko of Koronis succeed in finding?" I asked her presently.

"Ah." Sorrow touched Zariya's features. "Therein lies the tragedy, my heart. Liko wrote many treatises regarding his studies among the Elehuddin and other peoples, but his writings on the scattered pieces of prophecy he uncovered were a close-guarded secret, kept hidden in the state library. All the Koronians were great scholars, for the realm of Koronis lay under the aegis of Enayo the Speaking Stone, who declared that a scion of Koronis would be the one to assemble the puzzle."

"Liko didn't succeed?" I guessed.

Zariya shook her head. "Koronis sank beneath the waves a hundred years ago," she said. "The library was lost."

"How can an entire realm sink beneath the sea?" I asked in astonishment.

"It was caused by the eruption of a volcano," she said. "Koronis was a small island, nothing like Zarkhoum. The entire population perished."

"Then how is a scion of Koronis to assemble the pieces of prophecy?" I asked.

"That is a very good question," Zariya said. "But you haven't answered mine."

"What's that?" I was so distracted by this talk of sea-folk and scholars and sunken islands, I'd nearly forgotten. "Oh. *He,* my lady; it is what I am used to. And you haven't answered my question, either."

"Dhanbu fever." Zariya pronounced the words with distaste. "Yes, my shadow. It is quite unlikely that I, and I alone among the Sun-Blessed, should have contracted it." She paused, lowering her voice. "The apothecaries believe it is spread by bed-mites, and indeed, my pallet was found to be infested with them. Mine, and mine alone."

"You think it was done a-purpose?" Despite the midday heat, I shivered. "Oh, but my lady! You would have been a child of . . . what would it be, no more than six years old. You could not possibly have posed a threat to anyone. Who would do such a thing?"

Her expression was too cynical for her sixteen years. "Someone who resented the fact that my father favored his youngest," she said. "Someone who hoped that my death might bring on *khementaran.*"

I took a long, slow breath. "Do you know who?"

"No," she said wryly. "But there is no shortage of candidates. It was cleverly orchestrated," she added. "I am given to understand that the entire servants' quarter was put to harsh questioning. None of them confessed to any knowledge of how such a thing might have come to pass. I had a nursemaid of whom I was very fond. She was executed for carelessness."

"And now I am here." Too restless to sit, I rose to pace. "Your mother said my presence painted a target on your back. Your father made much the same speculation yesterday." My throat tightened. "Maybe . . . maybe you would be safer if you did not have a shadow. Maybe I should leave."

"*No!*" Zariya's eyes flashed. She pushed herself upright on the divan. "We've only just found each other. Tell me, Khai of the Fortress of the Winds, is there *any* part of you that feels as though we ought to separate?"

"No," I admitted. "My heart feels as though it will shatter into a thousand pieces at the thought of it. But Vironesh told me to listen to my head as well as my heart."

Her gaze was fierce. "And what does your head tell you?"

I stopped pacing and put my wits to work. "The person—or persons—who poisoned your brother were never caught, were they?"

"No."

"That must have been cleverly orchestrated, too," I mused. "And death-bladder venom would not have been easy to obtain. What of your brother Elizar? I hear he is a great collector of curios."

Zariya nodded. "It is the logical thought. Then again, a clever conspirator might think so, too, and plot accordingly. Kazaran's death happened long before I was born, but I am told every apothecary in Merabaht was put to harsh questioning. As with my illness, none confessed to having sold the death-bladder venom to Elizar, nor to anyone from whom he might have obtained it." She shuddered. "I do not know why anyone would possess such a thing in the first place."

"In very, very minute doses, it is said to ease inflammation of the joints," I informed her. "There are many potentially deadly substances that have useful properties."

"Ah, you were trained to know such things," she observed. "It is clear that our educations have been very different."

"Were any members of the House of the Ageless put to this famous harsh questioning?" I inquired.

Zariya hesitated, then shook her head. "No."

"Why?" I asked. "Surely, it is obvious that one or more of them are behind these incidents."

"It is not an easy thing to explain, my heart," she said to me. "Among the Sun-Blessed, it is said to the lion go the spoils. In Granth, warriors battle to the death to earn the title of Kagan. In the House of the Ageless, we are simply a great deal more subtle about it."

I stared at her. "Are you saying that the king *sanctions* this kind of deadly intrigue?"

She pursed her lips. "Not exactly. But it is understood that the throne shall pass by right to the one strong enough to seize it; to the boldest and brightest, the most ruthless and cunning of all the king's heirs. Commoners may be put to questioning or executed, but the Sun-Blessed are permitted their intrigues, assuming they are clever enough not to get caught."

"Even though such intrigues cost him the life of his favorite son?" I asked in disbelief.

"Yes," she said. "Even though it breaks his heart."

"That seems an incredibly foolish way to manage the business of succession," I said bluntly, then clamped my mouth shut tight lest it utter further indiscretions.

"There are too many of us and we live too long," Zariya murmured. "I do not think it was meant to be thus."

It was treason she was speaking, and I saw in her steady gaze that she knew it; Zariya was indeed trusting me with her life. I returned to sit on the carpet beside her divan, keeping my voice low. "With whom are you aligned?"

She shifted back onto her side. "I have done my best to avoid entanglements. My mother bore only girls, and none of us are reckoned of any particular value as allies, least of all me."

"Only as a weapon capable of causing your father pain," I said slowly.

"It is possible." Her eyelids flickered. "Less now than once, I think. Before I was ill . . . I think perhaps there was a part of him that hoped, somehow, I *had* been chosen for something special. I suppose it's why I entertain fanciful dreams of having been a prophecy-hunter. But since it happened . . ." She gave a low, mirthless laugh. "You have seen me, my shadow. I am hardly capable of *standing* against any darkness that might rise."

I remembered the strange mixture of hunger and bitterness in the king's voice at our first audience. "Even so, to lose a second child thus favored—"

"Do not speak again of leaving me!" Leaning over, Zariya reached for my hands and caught them in a surprisingly strong grip.

"I was only speculating, my lady," I assured her. "If you are in danger, we must be prepared for it."

"Speculate to your heart's content, only promise me that you will never leave me." Her grip tightened on my hands, dark eyes gazing into mine. "The Sacred Twins joined our fates together when we were born. In the entirety of my young life, that is the first and only thing I trust with my whole heart. Promise me."

I could no more deny her than I could cut out my heart and present it to her on a platter. "I promise."

Zariya sighed with relief, her breath wheezing slightly. She let go of my hands and closed her eyes. "Thank you."

"I have wearied you," I said with remorse. "Forgive me."

"No, I have talked overmuch," she said without opening her eyes. "The cursed fever left me with a weakness in my lungs. I will rest for a while. Tell me more about yourself while I do." Her eyes flickered open and she reached over to stroke the scars on my cheekbones. "Tell me about these."

I did.

It was a mystery to keep close to my heart, Brother Yarit had told me; but he did not understand the bond between Sun-Blessed and shadow. Zariya's eyes glimmered with wonder as I told her about my journey across the Mirror of Heaven to undertake Pahrkun's challenge, and tears when I related the words the Scouring Wind had spoken to me.

"'If the time is upon us, these are the gifts you and your soul's twin will carry to the end of the world,'" she whispered. "Oh, Khai! Only imagine if it were true. But what about the marks you bear?"

I told her about that, too; and I will own, it was gratifying to see the awe and horror in her gaze.

"I am quite sure I would have screamed," she said. "Screamed and hobbled away as fast as my canes could bear me."

"I am not so sure of that, my lady," I said to her. "There is fire inside you. I can see it."

Her eyes had closed again. "They say Zar's fire runs in the veins of the Sun-Blessed," she murmured. "But I have never felt it. Perhaps it is because I am too young to partake of the *rhamanthus*. Oh, but perhaps I will declare myself *bhazim*—can one do such a thing? And we will run away together, you and I, to the ends of the earth. We will swim with the Elehuddin and learn to speak their whistling tongue, consult with the Oracle of the Nexus, seek the Speaking Stone in the drowned ruins of Koronis, and pluck a drop of amber from the Lone Tree of the Barren Isle . . ."

My skin prickled with alarm at the mention; but no, Zariya was merely dreaming aloud. Her voice drifted off as she fell into slumber, her breathing coming easier as she slept.

I gazed at her for a time, overwhelmed at the nearness of her, at the flesh-and-blood realness of her.

My soul's twin.

I wished I had Zariya's effortless gift of affection to tell her how I felt, to bestow careless endearments and touches; and yet at the same time, it was unnecessary. She knew. We knew. And no matter what counsel Vironesh had given me, Zariya was right. The Sacred Twins had joined our fates. My place was at her side. Honor beyond honor; I did not question it now. It seemed impossible that we had known each other in the flesh for less than a day, for we belonged to each other forever.

I would do anything to keep her safe.

Anything.

My heart too full for sleep, I rose and prowled her chambers on soundless feet. The blue and green and yellow birds twittered, fluttering from perch to perch in their wooden cage, cocking their heads and watching me. Unable to resist, I poked my fingers through the bars, smiling as the birds nibbled at them with their hard little beaks. I tested the latch on the door to the sitting room and determined it could be a good deal stronger. I peered at the fretwork, thinking about things that could be passed through it—noxious vapors, a slender serpent.

In the sleeping chamber, I stowed my battered leather satchel in a corner and made a note to drag my pallet in front of the doorway when we slept, so that anyone attempting to enter unbidden would encounter me first.

There were no latches securing the doors and shuttered windows that led into the garden. I explored the garden, rubbing leaves of unfamiliar plants between my fingers and sniffing them. I found nothing harmful.

The wall concerned me, though. From the inside, it was no higher than twice my height. If the same held true for the outside, it would be easily scaled by any would-be intruder.

Mindful of Zariya sleeping on the divan, I held off attempting it, returning instead to sit cross-legged beside her. There was no breeze, and the midday heat was oppressive. I leaned my head against the wall and dozed.

I awoke to a tickling sensation beneath my nose and sneezed, springing to my feet in a blind panic, my hands reaching for my weapons.

"Oh, Khai!" Zariya caught her breath with a laugh. She waved a small blue feather with downy tufts at the base in one hand. "I'm so sorry. It's only that you looked so peaceful, I couldn't help myself."

Feeling foolish, I scowled at her. "Does it amuse you to mock me, my lady?"

"A little." Refreshed by sleep, her eyes sparkled unrepentantly. "You are so *very* serious, my shadow."

I could not be angry at her.

One day that would change, I guessed. We were human, with human weaknesses and foibles. Right now, our bond was too new, too precious, too overwhelming to allow for criticism. One day we might quarrel, but not today. Thinking on what Vironesh had said to me, I suspected he had let his heart give way to his head while serving as Prince Kazaran's shadow; thinking on what Zariya had told me, I suspected that while Kazaran may have been the brightest and boldest of King Azarkal's sons, he had not been the most cunning.

To the lion go the spoils . . .

Vironesh had regrets.

I did not want to have regrets. And I did not ever want to see the sparkle in Zariya's eyes dimmed. "Forgive me, I am unaccustomed to such teasing." I smiled at her. "Will you think me too serious altogether if I tell you that I am concerned about the wall enclosing the garden? Begging your indulgence, I would survey it."

She sobered. "Of course."

Leaning on her canes, Zariya followed me into the garden and peered up at the wall with a frown. "I believe there is a considerable drop on the far side, but you're right, I cannot attest to it. Shall I send for a ladder?"

"A ladder?" I laughed. "No."

After more hours of inactivity than I could remember, it was a blessed relief to scale the wall. I took a running leap at the northwestern corner and propelled myself upward with a couple quick toe-holds, catching the top of the wall and hauling myself upright atop it. From this vantage point, I could see much of the city of Merabaht spread out before me, and the ocean shining in the distance. A pleasant breeze tugged at my hair and clothing. I saw that Zariya was right: There was indeed a steep drop to the rocks below, perhaps some fifty feet or so. One could scale it with a grappling hook, but it would not be easy and access was guarded by the barracks of the Royal Guard.

"Khai! *Khai!*"

Glancing down, I saw Zariya looking pale. "My lady?"

Her voice trembled. "Please come down from there before you fall to your death, you mad thing!"

I nearly laughed again at the thought of it before realizing that she was genuinely terrified. "In a trice, my lady," I said with a respectful salute. "Only allow me to ensure the whole perimeter is safe."

I completed a circuit of the three walls enclosing the garden as quickly as I dared, conscious all the while of Zariya's fear-stricken gaze fixed upon me, then lowered myself by my arms to drop lightly to the ground.

Zariya sighed with relief. "There *is* a considerable drop, isn't there?" I nodded. She gave me a complicated look. "Oh, my poor darling. We've caged a hawk, haven't we? I pray you can bear it here."

"For your sake, I can bear anything," I said.

"I hope so." Her demeanor eased. "Well, I've never seen anyone run up a wall before! Tell me, what other skills are you hiding?"

I smiled.

TWENTY-THREE

I told Zariya everything; or almost everything.

I did not tell her about the Teardrop, for I could see no point to it. An innocent man had died for it, and it was not a secret with which I wanted to burden her. But I told her about Brother Yarit and the Shahalim Clan training I had undergone.

Zariya listened to it wide-eyed. "It's like something out of an old story," she murmured when I had finished. "Though I'm not sure to what use we might put such skills . . . Khai, does anyone outside the Brotherhood of Pahrkun know about this?"

I shook my head. "No."

"Tell no one," she said decisively. "Whether there's a purpose to be discovered or not, it's best no one knows what you're capable of."

"I wasn't planning to," I assured her.

She gave me a rueful smile. "So many skills! I feel more inadequate than ever, my shadow."

"Oh, but you *know* so much more than me!" I said in surprise. "I have never heard of the Elehuddin or Liko of Koronis or . . . my lady, I do not know what a volcano is or why it should cause an island to sink beneath the sea."

"It's a mountain that breathes fire," Zariya said. "This one erupted in gouts of molten stone, causing the earth to shake and the seas to rise . . . you needn't call me 'my lady,' you know."

"Shall I call you 'Your Highness,' then?" I asked. "I'm sorry, no one knew what the protocol among the royal women might be."

She wrinkled her nose at me. "Call me by my name."

"Zariya." Although I had known her name all my life, it felt strangely intimate to say it to her face.

Still, it made her smile; and that made my heart sing. "Better." There was a tentative rapping at the door to her chambers. "Yes?"

"Your Highness?" It was the maidservant Nalah's voice, sounding contrite. "Your lady mother bids me summon you to the baths."

"Ah." Zariya reached for her canes. "Then I suppose I must go. Come with me, my heart."

Nothing in my experience had prepared me for such a thing as the baths in the women's quarter in the Palace of the Sun, and to this day, I blush to remember it. Oh, it was no fault of mine; nor, truly, that of the brothers who raised me. When Brother Saan made the choice to raise me as *bhazim*, he implemented a strict code of modesty when it came to such matters, one to which the entire brotherhood adhered. And, too, the desert imposed its own strictures. Water was precious and used sparingly. Prior to my brief stay in the barracks of the Royal Guard, in my experience, bathing entailed a brisk scrub with a dipperful of water and a handful of clean sand.

Here . . .

It was an immense space lit from above by high windows, the walls covered with smooth tiles with intricate, colorful designs. Water spilled from an unseen source into a vast marble pool that was somehow heated from below, for steam rose from its surface, making the air dense and moist with its vapors. And although the steam caught in my throat, I was grateful for its presence, for the wreathing curls served to partially shroud the figures of at least half a dozen naked women.

If I had been shocked at seeing so many women's unveiled faces, it was nothing to this.

Panic rose in me. "I cannot do this," I whispered to Zariya, who was seated on a low stool, allowing Nalah to divest her of her silk robes. "Please do not ask it of me."

"Of course I will not force you," she said in a pragmatic tone. "But the baths are the heart and soul of the women's quarter. Sooner or later, you're going to have to confront them."

I said nothing.

There was nowhere safe to rest my gaze. This was wholly a women's place, where not even members of the Queen's Guard were admitted. Female servants in thin linen shifts poured ewers of scented water over the bathers, undid their braids and combed out their hair, rubbed their skin with pumice, offered them delicacies on platters. The royal women laughed and chatted in deceptively amicable accord, though I suspected there were subtle barbs aplenty in those exchanges.

Out of the corner of my eye, I saw Nalah finish undressing Zariya and fold her clothing away neatly. She took Zariya's elbow to steady her as they crossed the slippery marble floor, helping her step carefully into the hot pool and ease herself to sit in the waist-deep water.

My place was at Zariya's side, and yet every part of my upbringing was insisting that I should not be here.

Her mistress safely ensconced in the pool, Nalah approached me. "May I assist you, chosen?" she inquired. It seemed a term of address had been selected for me. "It would be my honor."

"No." I shook my head at her. "Thank you."

She inclined her head, but it seemed to me that there was the slightest hint of contempt in her eyes. "As you will."

I felt an uncivilized fool standing there in my woolen desert garb, weapons hanging from my sash. I wondered if Vironesh had dealt with such a quandary; but no, he was not *bhazim*. In the barracks of the Royal Guard, he'd not hesitated to attend the baths. It *was* foolish. Until I was eleven years of age and learned I was not a boy, I'd prided myself on going barechested in all manner of weather. In the Fortress of the Winds, modesty applied only to the body's intimate functions, not the body itself.

And yet . . . to be wholly naked, a woman among women? The thought of it was profoundly uncomfortable.

I tried and failed to think what Brother Saan would say to me at this moment. Instead, I found myself envisioning Brother Yarit's incredulous expression and hearing his voice in my thoughts. *Are you serious, kid? What the watery hell are you waiting for? Get the fuck in there!*

It made me smile. "You *would* say that, Elder Brother," I murmured.

Nalah turned back, brows raised. "Your pardon, chosen?"

"Nothing," I said to her. "I will attend to myself, thank you. Please leave my things undisturbed."

Again she inclined her head. "Of course, chosen."

I unwound the *heshkrat* from my sash, untied my sash, and leaned my *yakhan* and *kopar* carefully against a stool. I removed my sandals and stepped out of my woolen breeches. With the quick dexterity that Brother Yarit had taught me, I unbuckled the brace of *zims* on my left forearm and hid them beneath my breeches, then pulled my tunic over my head. I folded the tunic, unwound the length of cloth that bound my breasts, and folded that, too.

So.

Behind me, the interplay of gossip and banter had fallen silent. Even without looking, I knew the royal women of the House of the Ageless were appraising my naked form; speculating, analyzing, passing judgment. I slid the garrote from my hair with another dexterous twist, concealing it in my right hand and tucking it under my tunic. I shook my hair loose, letting it fall over my shoulders.

So.

Naked and unarmed, I strode across the marble floor.

Stepping into the bath felt like crossing a threshold from which there was no return. I sank down into the hot water, resisting the urge to draw my knees up to hide my breasts.

Zariya reached over and squeezed my hand. "We were just talking about Izaria's betrothed," she said in a casual tone. "They're to wed in a fortnight. Rumor has it that he's quite handsome." One of the women giggled—Izaria, that was the sister closest to her in age, the only eligible one yet unwed.

"He'd better have something to recommend him, my darling," another woman said smoothly. "Since all the fallen stars know it's not his family's wealth."

"At least he comes from a good lineage, Rashina." That was Zariya's mother, Sanala. "Some of us value breeding over wealth."

I let the conversation wash over me, filtering away bits of knowledge. Queen Rashina; she was the one that Vironesh said was ambitious. Although I was careful not to look directly at any of the women's bodies, there was such an abundance of flesh on display, it was impossible to avoid. Having only ever seen my own woman's body, it was disconcerting to catch a glimpse of the more fulsome figures, of heavy breasts as full and round as ripe squashes, tipped with large, dark nipples that seemed to spread across their flesh like puddles of oil on a hot rock.

A maidservant with a ewer approached me. "Shall I wash your hair, chosen?"

That much I could bear, and at least it might serve to distract me from my discomfort. "Yes, thank you."

I will own, it was not unpleasant. The maidservant's touch was deft and impersonal as she rubbed fragrant soap into my hair and poured water over my head. It was the first time I'd been immersed in water since I'd waded into the Eye of Zar the night of the Three-Moon Blessing, and I liked the feel of it against my skin. The warmth was relaxing, and I was growing accustomed to the dense steam.

"Khai of the Fortress of the Winds, I do believe you're enjoying this," Zariya teased me. "We'll convert you to courtly ways yet!"

I stole a sidelong glance at her, smiling a bit. "Some, maybe."

"I swear, it's like watching a charming little romance blossom," Rashina said in a studied drawl. "My dear Sanala, you'd best see Zariya betrothed before she becomes enamored of her own shadow."

I flushed.

Zariya tilted her head. "Whatsoever you wish to call it, there's nothing little or charming about it, Aunt," she said calmly. "In fact, it's like nothing *you* could possibly imagine."

Her candor took Queen Rashina aback; I don't know why, since it seemed to me that what was obvious to the king should have been obvious to all. My soul's twin had the heart of a lion. "Darling . . ." Queen Sanala said ineffectually to no one in particular, then let the remainder of her words trail away unspoken. Queen Adinah wore a private smile; the other two, Queen Makesha and Queen Kayaresh, were murmuring together and laughing.

There are too many of us, and we live too long.

True words, I thought. I had been raised to hold the Sun-Blessed in reverence; I had not thought to find them so . . . petty.

"Oh, please!" Izaria clapped her hands together, her expression imploring. "Can we not go a day without quarreling?" She glanced at her younger sister. "Tell me, my heart, would you rather wed a handsome man or a wealthy one?"

Zariya considered the question. "If I had the luxury of choice, I would choose a kind man."

"A wise choice given your circumstances," Rashina observed. "Your betrothed may be disappointed to find his bride is damaged goods."

"The physicians are quite certain that Zariya is capable of bearing children," her mother said indignantly. It seemed a familiar argument between them.

"Is that her only worth?" I asked, the words escaping me before I could think to censor them. Zariya ducked her head and smiled. Beneath the water, her knee nudged mine.

"Of course not." Queen Adinah raised her brows. "But it cannot be denied that it is an important measure."

"I'm sure Father will choose wisely for me when the time comes." Zariya changed the subject. "Khai tells me there is a faction of troublemakers in the city calling themselves the Children of Miasmus. Have you heard of such a thing?"

"The king may have mentioned it in passing," Queen Adinah said. "But he did not seem overly concerned."

"What a dreadful name." Izaria shuddered. "What sort of trouble are they causing?"

I told them about the vandalism I had witnessed outside the gem merchant's shop, though at least I managed to be circumspect enough not to pass on any treasonous speculation. I certainly did not say anything about the fact that Brother Yarit had drawn the black star symbol on the day the Sight passed to him. The matter was of sufficient interest that they discussed it at some length; and yet with a curious indifference, too. It might all have been taking place in some distant realm, not the streets of this very city, and they could not seem to fathom why some denizens of Merabaht might be unhappy with their lot. Gazing at the faces of the servants, schooled to a careful impassivity, I guessed some of them might feel differently, but none of them would dare show it.

After an interminable amount of time in which I provoked a minor scandal by declining to allow one of the maidservants to scour the hair from my pubis and armpits using caustic pumice, the bath was concluded. Wrapped in robes of white linen, the royal women took turns shedding their robes to recline on a divan, where they were massaged with warm, scented oil by an elderly maidservant whose hands were as strong and gnarled as tree roots.

I slipped into my familiar attire, feeling much more myself at having my weapons about me.

As the youngest, Zariya was the last to take her turn, but the old servant took the most care with her, squeezing and kneading the muscles of her legs; and to my pleasure, the other women withdrew.

"I'm quite sure that Soresh here is the only reason I'm able to walk at all," Zariya said drowsily, lying on her stomach. "She insisted on pummeling a spark of life back into my legs."

The elderly servant gave a cackle and slapped Zariya's thigh. "I beat you like a tough cut of meat!"

I overcame my self-consciousness enough to actually look at her legs. They were thin and the muscles were underdeveloped, but they were not wasted. "Is there pain?"

"No." Zariya shook her head. "There's a lack of sensation; not wholly, but enough to make walking difficult. Breathing pains me more." She smiled wryly. "Damaged goods."

"Do not listen to that one," Soresh said in disapproval. "Do not take her words into your heart and make them yours."

That struck me as good advice. "I saw crippled boys begging in the markets," I said. "Dragging their legs behind them."

"And the Sun-Blessed wonder that there is unrest in the city," Zariya murmured. "I am aware that I am more fortunate than most, my darling. I do not mean to complain about my lot."

"No, I only meant . . ." I wasn't sure in truth why I'd said it. "It seems something could be done."

"Ah, you're a reformer!" She gave me a shrewd look. "You'll have to meet my sister Fazarah."

The name rang a bell in my memory. "Your mother's eldest?" I didn't have them straight yet.

"No, Makesha's eldest," Zariya said.

"Queen Makesha is the fair-skinned one?" That much I remembered; she had skin the color of pale sand.

"Yes, and not likely to let anyone forget it," Zariya said acerbically. "Her family claims a Therinian prince in their lineage, but there's nothing in the records to support it. I suspect a buried scandal. Anyway, Fazarah's the rebel of the family."

Now I remembered; Brother Yarit had spoken of her once. She had refused the gift of the *rhamanthus*. I glanced at Soresh, unsure how freely I ought to speak before her. "What did she do that was so rebellious?"

Zariya followed my gaze. "Don't worry, my darling, this is all common knowledge in the women's quarter. Fifteen years ago, Father wed Fazarah to a man he thought was biddable, the High Judiciary's son. It turns out he was something of a firebrand in disguise." Common knowledge or not, she lowered her voice. "He refused her dowry of *rhamanthus* seeds. A week later, Fazarah entered *khementaran*. A year later, she bore a child."

"There aren't a great many royal grandchildren, are there?" I asked, recalling that Vironesh had said as much.

"No." Her tone was sober. "The *rhamanthus* shortage . . . it's been going on for longer than people realize."

"I saw your father's crown," I said.

She nodded. "The others have held off; hoping Anamuht would quicken the Garden of Sowing Time, hoping Father would enter *khementaran*, hoping not to bear children and be forced to choose between inducting them into the House of the Ageless and growing old themselves, or watching their children age while they remained youthful."

"A difficult choice." I was just beginning to grasp why the shortage had sown such unrest among the Sun-Blessed. "And yet the king continued to take wives and beget children."

"Yes."

Something in Zariya's voice warned me against pursuing that line of thought aloud, so I chose another. "Still, one cannot *choose* to enter *khementaran,* can you?" I frowned. "I thought it was a state that came upon you unbidden."

"It is, my heart, but no one can say how or why it happens when it does. Usually it does not happen for at least two centuries." She shrugged. "Fazarah was born under the Wandering Moon, and the children of Eshen are known to be unpredictable."

"And yet it sounded as though you rather admired her," I observed.

She smiled at me. "I do, but we say such things quietly here." Soresh muttered something under her breath, and Zariya glanced over her shoulder at her. "Yes, yes, I know, she's your favorite, too."

"*You* are my favorite, little lioness," the old woman retorted. "But she is the best of the lot of you."

It shocked me, but Zariya was unperturbed. "Well, I'd like to think that's yet to be determined. But you *should* meet Fazarah, Khai. Now that I think on it, if anyone's likely to know aught about this business of the Children of Miasmus, it's her."

Soresh let out her breath in a huff and muttered something else I couldn't make out, something about prophecies and meddling, her gnarled hands kneading Zariya's flesh like dough.

"I am *not* meddling," Zariya said over her shoulder. "I'm . . . curious, that's all. Some of us actually do wish to know what passes in this city." She looked back at me. "We'll ask my sister Nizara to arrange a meeting when we pay her a visit at the Temple of Anamuht tomorrow. As the High Priestess, she may do such a thing without reproach from my father." Her eyes shone at me. "Khai, my darling, you can go where I cannot. You are *bhazim* and a warrior, you can pass between the worlds of women and men, between the worlds of the palace and the marketplace. Are you willing to be my eyes and ears in the city of Merabaht?"

My heart simultaneously leapt at the prospect of being freed from the oppressive confinement of the women's quarter and constricted with a pang at the prospect of being parted from Zariya. "Oh, but now that I am here, I do not think I should leave your side!"

Her gaze was steady, and I saw in it a silent reminder of everything I had told her earlier today. "Are you sure?"

I was not.

I was trained to be a warrior, yes; and a thief and a spy. I was her shadow, and the Brotherhood of Pahrkun had determined such skills as I possessed might be needful.

We were only just discovering what a gift the gods had given us in each other.

I inclined my head to her. "My lady."

TWENTY-FOUR

The High Temple of Anamuht was located on the foothill of the Garden of Sowing Time.

There was a private path from the women's quarter that led directly to it, ascending the heights above the city. Although it was flanked on the right by a secondary path, that path was protected by walls and gates attended by unseen members of the Royal Guard.

It was the Queen's Guard who attended us, four of them carrying Zariya in a litter with the curtains drawn.

I walked beside it, accompanied by Captain Tarshim. He seemed as glad to be free of the women's quarter as I was. "Perhaps you and I and a few of your men might spar sometime?" I suggested to him. "I do not know when my mentor Vironesh will be freed from his duties in the City Guard, and I do not wish to let my training lapse."

Captain Tarshim gave me a quizzical look. "A *few* of my men?"

I shrugged. "More if you wish, but I do not promise I can accommodate more than five at a time, especially without doing serious injury. Forgive me, but I am still learning," I added in explanation.

He stared at me, then shook himself like a dog. "I'm sure it can be arranged, chosen."

Inside the litter, Zariya gave a soft laugh.

The temple was splendid, but the *rhamanthus* trees dwarfed its splendor. Like Merabaht itself, the Garden of Sowing Time rose in tiers. When I had my first glimpse of the *rhamanthus* from the far banks of the river, I should have guessed at their scale, but it caught me unprepared. Their silvery-grey trunks were large enough in diameter that two men's arms could not reach around them, and they stretched high, high into the heavens. Like palm trees, the trunks had ridges and no branches; unlike a palm they were straight and unyielding. Their deep green crowns of foliage were silhouetted against the bright blue sky, and I could barely make out the fist-sized clusters of crimson seeds nestled against the top of their trunks. There was a grandeur to them that reminded me of being in the presence of the Sacred Twins.

"Oh, they're beautiful!" I said in awe. "I didn't expect them to be so beautiful!"

"They are, aren't they?" Sister Nizara had emerged from the temple to greet us. "It's a pleasure to see them through new eyes."

From far below, it was difficult to estimate how many seeds each cluster held, but I guessed at least fifty, and there looked to be at least seven to a tree. I began counting trees.

Sister Nizara read my thoughts. "There are twelve *rhamanthus,*" she said. "The harvest, when it comes, will be bountiful; enough to sustain the House of the Ageless for many years." She beckoned. "Come inside. If you wish, we will tour the garden after we've taken some refreshment."

I assisted Zariya out of the litter and handed her canes to her, and we followed her sister the High Priestess into the temple. She led us to the windowless innermost sanctum, lit by a dozen or more oil lamps and a single tall flame that burned on a dais, fueled from beneath by a hidden source. The walls of the sanctum were carved with images of the Sacred Twins and smaller human figures I did not recognize. Several sisters in red robes were kneeling in supplication before the dais, murmuring prayers.

"That flame was lit by our ancestress Azaria, the first High Priestess of Anamuht," Sister Nizara said quietly. "Kindled from the lingering fires that burned after Anamuht the Purging Fire first quickened the *rhamanthus.* In thousands of years, it has never been extinguished."

"Shall we offer our prayers?" Zariya asked me, and I helped her kneel on the carpet before taking my place beside her.

Belatedly, it came to me that I knew no prayers. In the Fortress of the Winds, we began each day with wordless genuflection; our prayers to Pahrkun were offered in feats of steel and muscle and bone.

I bowed forward until my brow touched the carpet and spoke the words that were in my heart. "Anamuht, I beg you to grant me wisdom," I whispered. "Guide me that I might best serve this youngest daughter of the Sun-Blessed and keep her safe from harm."

Beside me, Zariya whispered words too soft to hear.

It seemed it sufficed, for Sister Nizara touched us both on the shoulder. "Come, we'll speak on the terrace."

When I moved to help Zariya rise, she shook her head at me. "Up is easier than down," she said in a practical tone, using her canes to pry herself to her feet. "I told you, you must let me do for myself whenever possible."

The terrace to which Sister Nizara led us overlooked the sprawling city of Merabaht, its harbor, and the ocean beyond. To our right, cataracts of water spilled over a series of broad marble steps that led to a vast pool below, the level of which was controlled by a great gate that could be raised or lowered to supply water to the entire palace.

There was a low table on the terrace set with a tea service and a platter of fried balls of dough drizzled with honey. Sister Nizara poured three cups of tea and invited us to sit and partake. "Khai, I will speak frankly," she said. "It was my hope that you came bearing a message for me, either from the Seer or from the Sacred Twins themselves, but I sense it is not so."

"I wish it were, Elder Sister," I said to her. "But no, I was given no message for you."

Her gaze was intent. "But you *were* given a message?"

I hesitated. "I mean no disrespect, but it is in my heart that what Pahrkun said to me when I underwent his trial was not meant for any ears save mine and Zariya's."

"Did they have any bearing on the *rhamanthus*?" Sister Nizara asked me. "Anything that might indicate why Anamuht is displeased with us?"

"No."

"Has the Seer ever spoken of the matter?" she pressed me.

"Only that the shortage existed," I said. "If he Saw anything, he said nothing of it; nor would he be likely to do so."

Sister Nizara sighed. "Ah yes, the famous crypticism of desert mystics."

"Brother Yarit is the least likely desert mystic one could imagine," I said. "But I was there when the Sight came upon him and there is no doubt that Pahrkun chose him. If he is cryptic, it is out of necessity, not any desire on his part. Elder Sister . . . is there not a Seer among the priestesses of Anamuht?"

"No." She took a sip of tea. "There is a saying; sword and Sight for the brethren, stylus and scroll for the sistren."

"Nizara's role is a hereditary one," Zariya added. "Bequeathed to the eldest daughter of our line from time out of mind."

"I have seen to it that the records are kept," Sister Nizara said wistfully. "Every seed to quicken and fall has been recorded; every seed that has been consumed. Every appearance of Anamuht within the city has been noted. Had she spoken, every word would have been recorded, but Anamuht has spoken only in tongues of fire during my long tenure here. I have tended the Sacred Flame faithfully. When another child of the Sun-Blessed was born beneath the convergence of Nim the Bright Moon and Shahal the Dark Moon, I led the search to scour the realm for one who might prove to be her shadow. I have pored over the records of those who held this post before me for a clue, any clue, to where I might have gone astray, and found nothing. I do not know how I have failed her."

"I'm sorry," I said humbly. "I wish I did know something that might help." A thought struck me, one that seemed so obvious I hesitated to give voice to it. "Elder Sister, have you asked Anamuht herself?"

She gave me a look that, while not unkind, suggested I had indeed voiced the obvious. "I pray for her guidance every day, Khai."

I shook my head. "No, I mean . . . when the Sight was unclear, Brother Saan retreated to the high places of the desert to seek clarity in solitary contemplation. Even Brother Yarit, too. This temple . . ." I waved my hand. "It is beautiful and splendid, but it is not the heart of Zarkhoum. The desert is the heart of Zarkhoum."

Sister Nizara stared at me. "You propose that I should leave Merabaht for the desert?"

Feeling foolish, I shrugged. "All these years you have been waiting and waiting for Anamuht the Purging Fire. What if *she* has been waiting for you?"

Her lips parted as she continued to stare at me. "What if *she* has been waiting for *me*?" she echoed in a tone of wonderment.

"It is only a thought," I muttered. "One I'm sure you've entertained a thousand times over. Forgive me."

"Ah, no!" Sister Nizara uttered a startled laugh and leaned forward to take my face in her hands, planting a kiss on my brow. "Khai, my darling, it is a thought that cuts like a blade through the endless knot of speculation. And I must confess that it is one that never occurred to me."

I blinked. "It didn't?"

"No, for there is no precedent for it." She released me. "But there is no proscription against it, either. I have not undertaken a pilgrimage since the day you were chosen. Perhaps *you* are the message for which I have yearned."

"Will you take to the desert, then?" Zariya asked with interest. She popped a honey-soaked dough ball into her mouth, chewed it, and swallowed. "Because I've a favor to ask ere you do."

By the time we took our leave, it was determined that Sister Nizara would arrange a meeting between me and the rebel Princess Fazarah, whose firebrand husband Tarkhal had chosen a career advocating for the poor and downtrodden in the halls of the king's justice.

"Do you know, he was even responsible for the conviction of a member of the Royal Guard? It seems the fellow had been preying on helpless children in the streets and inflicting grievous harm upon them." Sister Nizara shuddered. "One day he overstepped his bounds, though. Oh, but you may even have encountered him, Khai," she added, remembering who I was and where I came from. "For he chose the Trial of Pahrkun over execution." The thought caused her to frown in dismay. "I sincerely pray he did not succeed in it."

"He did not," I assured her. "I stood first post myself. The guardsman did not pass me."

She stared at me again. "But you would have been no more than a child yourself!"

"I was eleven and a blooded warrior." A hint of indignation crept into my voice. "Though Brother Yarit did not intend to give me first post," I admitted. "Not until he Saw that it was fitting that I should be the one to serve as Pahrkun's instrument, because I wore the face of the guard's victims."

"The sword and the Sight," Sister Nizara murmured. "I do wonder what I shall find in the desert."

Another thought came to me. "Elder Sister . . . the records that you keep. Brother Saan once told me that the priestesses would have recorded the information of my birth and parentage. Is that true?"

"Of course," she said in surprise. "You mean you don't know?"

I shook my head. "The brotherhood does not record such things. Or they didn't then."

She clicked her tongue in mild disapproval. "Of course. I don't remember the details at the moment—there were thirteen babes altogether—but I'll look in the archives and find out for you."

Caught up in her plans to stage a retreat after the upcoming royal wedding, she bade Zariya and me to explore the Garden of Sowing Time at our leisure. I would have spared Zariya the effort, but she insisted on accompanying me, and so I confined my exploration to the lowest tier. At close range, the *rhamanthus* trees were not as unyielding as I'd thought, swaying ever so slightly, silvery trunks creaking in the sea breeze. I craned my neck to gaze at their distant green crowns and the tantalizing clusters of crimson seeds tucked securely beneath them.

"What's it like when it happens, do you suppose?" I wondered aloud.

"Splendid and terrible," Zariya breathed, leaning on her canes. "From what I'm told."

I tried to imagine it, quickened seeds raining down like thousands upon thousands of embers. "They must be as hard as gems to be set in your father's crown. How did the Sun-Blessed know to eat them?"

"You touch upon the matter of prophecy, my heart," Zariya observed. "This is what Anamuht the Purging Fire said to Azaria, the first of our line: 'As I am my father's daughter, each seed now bears a spark of the sun's fire. Partake of them, you and your descendants, that his blessing might dwell in your flesh and blood, and lead long and virtuous lives. For one day a darkness that threatens will arise in the west, a darkness that threatens to swallow all that exists beneath the starless skies, and one of the lineage of the *rhamanthus* will stand against it.'"

Hearing her recite the words with such surety made me wonder if I should not have told Sister Nizara what Pahrkun the Scouring Wind had said to me in the Mirror of Heaven, that it might be preserved in the priestesses' records; and yet it still seemed to me that those words were meant to be held close. I resolved to think on it.

"Surely, we have led long lives," Zariya mused. "I do not know if we can claim to have led virtuous ones. Did you really kill that guardsman, my darling?"

"Yes."

She cocked her head at me. "What did it feel like?"

I could not lie to my soul's twin. "I knew what he had done," I said to her. "It felt good."

Zariya looked thoughtful. "I expect it would."

Several days passed without incident. I received word neither from Vironesh nor from Princess Fazarah.

I learned many things, though.

I learned from Sister Nizara that I was neither city- nor desert-bred, but had been born to a family of fisher-folk on the southern coast, a revelation that came as a surprise to me. Zariya laughed at the thought of me mending fishing nets, and promised that I might send word to my family if I wished. In turn I promised that I would do so once I'd had time to accustom myself to my new life.

I learned that in the women's quarter in the Palace of the Sun, one was expected to bathe *every day*; and that this daily ritual was just as prolonged as it had been the first time. I learned that one was expected to don fresh attire *every day*, no matter how wasteful or unnecessary it seemed, which meant I had to supplement my meager stores with the linen robes of the Queen's Guard.

I learned that the eunuchs of the Queen's Guard served in a largely ceremonial capacity and were not highly skilled fighters. It was not their fault, for none of them had chosen their lots; all had been sold into servitude at a young age. Still, they made for unsatisfactory sparring partners.

To his credit, Captain Tarshim did not disagree, and welcomed my offer to provide additional training; but I learned to my dismay, for I appreciated his candor, that he was enamored of Queen Rashina, who was my least favorite of the king's wives.

I learned that it was understood that neither the king's wives nor his unwed daughters would venture beyond the Hall of Pleasant Accord unless it was for an affair of state.

I learned that a night spent with King Azarkal was an occasion for preening and gloating.

I learned that it was widely believed that the warrior Prince Tazaresh was the son that the king was most likely to name his successor.

I learned that among her half brothers, Zariya was fondest of Prince Dozaren, who brought her a yellow bird with a sweet song to join her little friends, and I learned that Dozaren had a subtle charm I did not trust.

It was such a strange place to me, the women's quarter, perpetually suspended between tedium and tension, between lassitude and spite. Oh, there were aspects I did not mind, especially when there were musicians or poets or storytellers to entertain us as we idled in the baths or the great sitting room, which bore the ironic title of the Hall of Harmonious Beauty, and I liked best of all the times when Zariya and I were alone together and able to talk about anything under the sun. I began teaching her the Shahalim language of hand signs, and her facility at it delighted both of us. But she had spoken truly when she had named me a caged hawk.

Thus it came as a relief when I received an invitation from Princess Fazarah to call upon her.

Already, I had been in the Palace of the Sun long enough that it felt strange to escape from it; strange, too, to be on my own, and strangest of all to be parted from Zariya's presence. As I departed the palace, I became aware of a hollowness inside me, an ache that deepened with every step I took. The ties with which Pahrkun and Anamuht had joined us were powerful.

Still, I went, wondering if it was the same for her.

I went on foot, for the mount I'd ridden here had returned to the desert as a pack-horse with Brother Merik and the others; and, too, it was easier to navigate the crowded streets of Merabaht as a pedestrian. Not wanting to draw attention to myself, I wrapped my head-scarf around the lower part of my face to hide the marks of Pahrkun that glittered on my cheekbones.

Fazarah and Tarkhal's household was located in a sprawling residence in a neighborhood that occupied a space between the second and third tiers of the city. It was far lower than one would expect for one of her stature, but the location allowed his clientele among the less-fortunate denizens of the city easier access to his services. Upon presenting myself at the doorstep of the upper level, I was ushered into a parlor room with alacrity; Princess Fazarah herself welcomed me shortly thereafter with gracious curiosity. In appearance, she looked to be somewhere in her midthirties, a good ten years older than her mother. At the pulse-points of her wrists and the sides of her throat, her blood glowed beneath her skin in a steady beat.

Khementaran.

"Khai of the Fortress of the Winds," she said, sounding bemused. "I must confess, I am intrigued by your presence. How may I be of service to my youngest sister's shadow?"

"I understand that you and your husband concern yourselves with the business of the poor and oppressed, my lady," I said to her. "Is there aught you can tell me about the faction calling themselves the Children of Miasmus?"

She frowned and avoided answering my question. "I do care a great deal for Zariya, you know. She's a sweet child, and a bright one, too. But she has suffered since her illness. Zariya dreams of things that cannot be. I would rather not give fuel to her fantasies."

I raised my eyebrows. "Which are?"

Fazarah returned my look in a steadfast manner. "Will you pretend not to know, my sister's shadow?"

"You speak of prophecy," I said. "You are aware, I trust, that the coursers of Obid have a prophecy regarding the Children of Miasmus?"

She sighed. "You're as young as Zariya and as easily beguiled by the romance of prophecy, aren't you?"

I ignored the comment and gazed at her, sensing uncertainty in the spaces between one thought and another. "You're frightened," I said softly. "My lady, I am not here on some childish fancy. I have been chosen by Pahrkun himself to protect your youngest sister from all threats, and I would know what manner of threat these Children of Miasmus pose. What do you know that you are reluctant to tell me?"

Fazarah looked away. "There are rumors of a man that they call the Priest of the Black Star or the Mad Priest," she said. "I have not encountered him, but I have heard tales from those who claim to have seen him. It is said that he walks the streets of Merabaht and preaches in the poorest quarters of the city, claiming that Miasmus comes to him in his dreams, that Miasmus shows him visions of how it will rise and swallow the world in darkness. The Mad Priest advocates . . . upheaval."

"Upheaval," I echoed.

She nodded. "Chaos. Mayhem. The overturning of the law of order. He exhorts them to rise up and overthrow the ruling class."

"To what end?" I asked.

"To seize whatever they may before the world ends," she said soberly. "May I show you something?"

"Of course."

Donning a gauzy veil, Fazarah led me through their residence to a balcony overlooking a courtyard on the lower level. A long line of people snaked through the courtyard; men in ragged garb, veiled women with children in their arms or clinging to their skirts. They looked up as we appeared, many of them saluting her. She returned their salute respectfully. "This, young Khai, is the number of people clamoring for my husband's services on an ordinary day," she said to me. "Some of them bear grievances against each other, but most bear grievances against someone wealthier or more power-ful. Many of them will sleep here overnight in the hopes of having their cases heard. Many of them will go without food."

"That's a lot of people," I murmured.

"Yes," she said. "We do what we can to feed them, especially the women and children, but there are simply too many. Now, look there." She pointed toward the street to the south. From our vantage, I saw a line of men hauling the long-poled carts I had noticed before, carts piled high with wheat and rice, barrels of fish and cages of chickens, stacked pyramids of squash and fruit, the carters' heads lowered as they trudged up the rampway between the second and third tiers of Merabaht. "All that is bound for the Palace of the Sun," she said quietly. "Enough to feed every hungry man, woman, and child in this courtyard a dozen times over. Do you wonder that the poor of this city can be incited to violence?"

"No, my lady," I said. "I do not. Has it always been thus?"

"It has grown worse as the Sun-Blessed grow more desperate," she said. "Once, my father paid greater heed to the affairs of the realm; once, he cared about rooting out corruption in the Royal and City Guards. Would you see a prophecy fulfilled, my sister's shadow? I tell you this: If Zarkhoum were to embrace many of the worthy and just principles of the code of Obid the Stern, there would be no uprising of the Children of Miasmus."

It was a startling thought, not least of all because it had merit. "Zariya said that you were a reformer," I said. "Do you believe that is the true meaning of the prophecy of the coursers of Obid?"

Fazarah hesitated, then shook her head. "It may be that all prophecy is merely veiled symbolism, but I cannot claim to speak for any of the children of heaven." She held out her overturned hands, and a soft blood-glow pulsed at her wrists. "I will not dissemble. I believe my father, King Azarkal, has made unwise choices," she said with dignity. "I believe in seeking to create a better society here in Zarkhoum. But I do not believe it can be accomplished through the weapon of chaos."

I looked ruefully at her. "I would that your father would name *you* his successor, my lady."

"For both of our sakes, that is a thought best kept to yourself, young Khai. This is Zarkhoum," she said wryly. "In Zarkhoum, women do not rule."

"That's not entirely true," I observed. "Among the desert tribes, each individual clan is ruled by a chieftain, but a Matriarch presides over decisions concerning life and death for each of the three great tribes." I tried to remember what Chieftain Jakhan had said about it long ago. "In the desert, they say women bring life into this world and understand the cost in blood and suffering, so are best suited to pass judgment in such matters."

Fazarah gazed at me in surprise, her breath stirring the sheer veil. "Is this true?"

"I am not given to lying," I said with a touch of stiffness. "I was raised to revere honor, my lady."

She smiled. "Forgive me, I meant no offense. It is only that I have never heard such a thing."

Once again, I thought that the Sun-Blessed were entirely too unfamiliar with the desert; and I understood better why the desert tribes acknowledged no authority save their own. "Well, I assure you, it is true. My lady, do you know where I might find this Mad Priest?"

"If I had that knowledge, I would share it with the City Guard," Fazarah said. "For I am sure they have heard the same rumors. I know only the places the Mad Priest is said to have been seen preaching; at the wharves, in Three-Copper Quarter, in Kabhat Square . . ." She regarded me with a worried expression. "Do you mean to search for him?"

I shrugged. "Perhaps."

Fazarah's grave look deepened. "I would ask you to reconsider. These are dangerous places for a single young . . . person. You should not venture into them alone. And is your place not at my sister's side?"

"I am a dangerous young person," I reminded her. "And I am doing this at your sister's behest."

"That," she said, "is what concerns me."

TWENTY-FIVE

I made my way through the crowded streets of lower Merabaht to Three-Copper Quarter; so named, Fazarah had told me in parting, because that was what the worth of a human life was reckoned there.

If she was trying to dissuade me, she failed. Oh, I understood her concerns. *Khementaran* notwithstanding, she was a member of the House of the Ageless, and she had been alive for longer than Brother Saan had been when he passed from this world. To her, Zariya and I must appear as wishful children dabbling in matters we were too young to understand.

Perhaps we were.

And yet . . . I had knelt before Pahrkun the Scouring Wind on the sands of the Mirror of Heaven, closed my eyes, and offered up the gift of perfect trust. The mark of that moment was forever etched upon my face. We had to be true to ourselves, Zariya and I; we had to trust what we were. If she dreamed of being a prophecy-hunter, well, then, I would hunt prophecy for her.

I succeeded in finding my way to Three-Copper Quarter, mostly by virtue of the fact that I had but to go downward and south until there was nowhere else to go. Once there, I found myself hopelessly lost in its winding streets. It was a squalid labyrinth of unpaved alleys and crumbling clay-brick buildings. There was refuse underfoot, vegetable peelings and picked bones, and slab-sided dogs and scrawny boys fighting for the best scraps. Veiled women in homespun robes hurried about their business in knots of three or four, whispering to each other. Gaunt men with feverish eyes muttered offers of hashish at every corner.

Let your mind be like the eye of the hawk . . .

I slowed my steps, closed my eyes, and let my perceptions drift, drift like a hawk's feather on the wind. I felt the breeze of a reaching hand at my side and turned to catch the wrist of the boy angling for the pocket of my robe.

"I didn't do anything!" he said in a pleading whine, tugging against my grip. "Let me go!"

"I will if you can answer a question." I lowered the scarf muffling my words. "Do you know where I might find the Mad Priest? The Priest of the Black Star?"

"Why should I?" His eyes widened. "Watery hell! You're the royal shadow, aren't you?"

Silently, I cursed myself for carelessness; Brother Yarit would have been disappointed. "Will you answer my question or shall I turn you over to the City Guard for thieving?"

The boy spat on the ground between us. "Do what you like, I can't tell you what I don't know!"

As far as I could tell, he was telling the truth. A bribe might have elicited more information than a threat, but as he would have discovered, there was no purse in the pockets of my robe. "Then get out of here before I decide to give you a lesson in manners," I said, turning him loose.

He pelted away on bare, grimy feet. Under covert stares from onlookers, I pulled my scarf into place. Even as I considered asking them, the way their gazes slid away from mine told me that the royal shadow would find no assistance in this quarter.

This place, I thought, had a rhythm and a pulse all its own. I needed to learn to attune myself to it. I closed my eyes again and listened. I listened to the whispers, I listened to the muttering, to the hacking of wet coughs and the subsequent hawking of spittle. At last, I heard the distant thread of a voice that was none of these things. It was urgent and strident, a call to arms that cut through the somnolence of the city's most impoverished quarter.

It was what I imagined a Mad Priest might sound like, and since I had no other leads, I followed the thread of the voice through the endless warren of cluttered streets, backtracking whenever an alley led to a dead end.

I was almost close enough to make out words when I began to notice figures atop the roofs.

"Shadow!" a voice hissed, and then another and another. *"Shadow!"*

The first rock struck me on my left shoulder, and it was followed by
others. The voice in the distance was cut off mid-sentence.

Damn.

I ran forward, following the trail of figures on the rooftops, dodging
rocks and veering from side to side to present a more difficult target. Rocks.
I'd never considered rocks. Trusting to my fighting skills, I had been a fool
to underestimate the dangers of the quarter. If I encountered enough men
with enough rocks at the end of this chase, I was in serious trouble.

Instead I emerged into an empty square of hard-packed dirt. If the Mad
Priest had been there, he was gone. There were more figures on the surrounding roofs, but they melted away. I learned why soon enough, and it
had naught to do with any threat I posed. As I stood in the center of the
square attempting to determine which way the Mad Priest and his protec-
tors may have gone, a score of City Guardsmen entered the square from the
opposite direction, Vironesh among them.

"Khai!" He strode across the square and grabbed my shoulders to shake
me. "Are you addled? You have no business being here."

"There's a man they call the Mad Priest," I informed him. "Or the Priest
of the Black Star. He's the one inciting the Children of Miasmus to violence."

"Yes, I know." Vironesh's tone was heavy with disapproval. "Why else do
you suppose we're here?"

"How should I know?" I countered. "I've had no word from you since the
day we parted."

"Forgive me for assuming that your new duties would occupy you for at
least a week's time," he said sardonically. "May I ask why you're delinquent
in attending to your charge?"

Because my new duties in the women's quarter consist of endless rounds
of bathing and gossip, I wanted to say; something you cannot possibly understand. Because my lion-hearted princess is a prisoner thrice over; a pris-

oner of her status and her gender, a prisoner of her own poor damaged body.

Because whether you like it or not, it appears there are pieces of prophecy in play.

Because it is Zariya's heart's desire that I do what she cannot. Because honor beyond honor may mean something more than simply keeping her alive.

In the end, I said none of these things; and yet I think Vironesh read them in my face.

He loosed my shoulders with a sigh. Behind us, members of the City Guard were pounding on doors and interrogating denizens of the quarter. "Did you at least see this Mad Priest?"

"No," I admitted. "Have you seen him?"

Vironesh shook his head. "There are always lookouts posted. Anytime we get close, he vanishes." He glanced behind him. "The Guard is riddled with corruption. I daresay half of them are extracting bribes this very moment. I haven't figured out who I can trust. No one, maybe." He looked back at me. "You're bleeding."

Now that he mentioned it, I had felt a sharp blow to the temple. I touched my skin and my fingers came away bloody. "The lookouts threw rocks at me."

"Welcome to Three-Copper Quarter," he said. "Do I need to elaborate on the depths of your folly today?"

I looked away. "No."

"Good. Once we're done here, we'll escort you back to the palace, and you can tell me how the hell you found out about the Priest of the Black Star." Vironesh's voice took on a gentler note, one tinged with sorrow. "And how you're finding it to be paired with the young princess Zariya."

That was a thing too big for words. All I could do was glance back at him with tears in my eyes.

He nodded. "I know."

As we drew near the palace, I felt the hollowness within me begin to ease. Even so, it wasn't until I was reunited with Zariya in her chambers in the women's quarter that it was replaced with a profound rush of relief and elation.

I needn't have wondered if she felt the same way. "Oh, my darling!" Her eyes glistened. "I hadn't known it would be so difficult!" Her gaze sharpened. "And you're hurt. What happened? You were gone so long! Who dared to hurt you?"

I smiled at her ferocity. "It's nothing, truly. But I have a great deal to tell you."

Zariya's face lit up. "Tell me *everything*!"

After making sure no one was spying outside the door to her chambers, I sat on the carpet beside her divan and related the day's events to her. She reclined on her side and listened intently, waiting until I had finished to comment; and if there was something of a child's wonder in her listening, there was an equal measure of a keen intellect at work.

"How exciting!" She let out a soft breath of laughter. "I'm not sure which name I prefer best, the Mad Priest or the Priest of the Black Star! They're both so . . . evocative, aren't they? I wish you'd managed to catch a glimpse of the fellow and learn something about him."

"So do I," I said. "But I was impulsive and careless. I should have heeded Brother Yarit's training and waited until I was able to enter the quarter in a guise that would deflect attention from my presence." I felt at the mica-flecked scars on my cheekbones. "Though he did not reckon on these."

"Well, you were careless to lower your scarf," Zariya said in a practical tone. "But even had you not, you look every inch the desert warrior." She paused. "Have you considered women's attire?"

I tensed. "No."

"It is only that I am thinking a veil would hide the marks of Pahrkun without seeming out of place," she said apologetically.

I said nothing.

"Ah, I have made you uncomfortable again," Zariya said. "And I have broken my vow to myself and told you a lie."

I raised my brows at her. "Oh?"

"Do not be angry at me, my darling," she said. "You are a splendid boy. But the choice to raise you as *bhazim* was made for you, and because it was kept from your knowledge, it carries the sting of betrayal. There is a part of me that cannot help but wonder what choice you would make if you allowed yourself to explore the possibilities available to you." She smiled gently at me. "Because I think you would make a lovely girl, too."

Something in her words made my stomach flutter, and I drew in a long, shaking breath. "I don't know."

Zariya waved one hand. "Consider the Elehuddin! You could be both, my heart. A double-edged blade."

"Or neither," I reminded her. "You said that Liko of Koronis was unclear on that point."

"True." Her gaze was disconcertingly direct. "Either way, you would still be *you*. Will you at least think on it?"

I nodded.

Zariya closed her eyes. "Good."

She was right, of course; I would be far less obtrusive in Three-Copper Quarter as a woman in a veil. A part of me rebelled at the notion, but Zariya was right about that, too. The sense of betrayal I felt cut deep, and a measure of my reaction to the thought of donning women's attire was born of it. But that was foolish. Disguise was a tool, one I had been taught to use. It would be short sighted of me not to use the best possible tool for the job.

And if I were absolutely honest, there was a small part of me that was curious. What *would* it feel like to be a girl for a day? It was not something I would have wondered about a week ago, but my life had changed since then. "All right," I said to Zariya when she awoke from her nap. "I will do it. But I will need to acquire such clothing as will not draw attention in the poor quarters of the city."

"I will ask Nalah—" She paused. "No, I think it is best if no one knows of our plans. But one can buy such things in the markets, can you not?"

"One could if one had money," I said. "I fear the brothers did not think to provide me with a purse."

Zariya slid a thin gold bangle from her wrist. "Here. I daresay this will purchase an ensemble or two. Oh, but we don't want it noised around the city that the princess's shadow was seen bartering peasant rags in the marketplace, do we?" She considered me. "Suppose we dressed you in something finer for the excursion? My mother's dying to see you draped in silks."

I hesitated. "That's not why you're suggesting this, is it?"

"Not even the slightest little bit, my darling." Her reply was swift and sure, and I could tell the question injured her.

"Forgive me," I apologized. "I fear I am overly sensitive in the matter."

"Yes, and not without cause," Zariya observed. "It was a thoughtless thing to say, and I'm sorry for it." She glanced toward the door. "Nalah will be coming to summon us to the baths any minute, but I had another thought regarding the death-bladder venom that killed my brother Kazaran."

The way her thoughts darted so quickly from topic to topic made me smile. "Which is?"

"What if it were stolen?" she said. "You said it was a member of the House of the Ageless that commissioned your Brother Yarit to steal *rhamanthus* seeds. What if it wasn't the first time the Shahalim Clan had undertaken such a commission?"

"It would explain why none of the apothecaries would confess to having sold the venom," I said slowly.

Zariya nodded. "Because none of them did."

"It would have been some fifty years ago," I said. "If it were true, whoever stole it may not even be alive."

She shrugged. "I expect that the Shahalim would keep a record of such a thing. It's a powerful piece of knowledge. You said Brother Yarit gave you a means of contacting his clan?"

I nodded. "The Lucky Tortoise teahouse. I'm to ask if they carry three-moon blend."

Zariya smiled at me. "Something to consider."

I was grateful to have something to contemplate in the baths, for it served to distract me from the unbridled glee exhibited by the royal women when Zariya mentioned that I had consented to be dressed in women's finery, as though it were some victory that they had won.

You would be less gleeful if you knew why, I thought.

For her part, Zariya was protective. "Khai has agreed to attempt this," she warned them. "But if it does not suit him, so be it. There will be no further discussion of the matter."

Her mother ignored her warning. "Oh, I'm sure it will suit you beautifully, my darling!" she said to me, patting my hand. "You'll see, Khai! You'll finally be comfortable in the skin into which you were born."

I pulled my hand away. "Perhaps."

From thence, the conversation turned to Izaria's impending wedding, now merely a week away, and I was glad of the reprieve. The ceremony was to take place in the High Temple of Anamuht, and would be followed by a procession through the city in which the might and majesty of the House of the Ageless would be on full display, reminding the citizens of Merabaht that they had been chosen to rule Zarkhoum by Anamuht the Purging Fire herself.

"It will be good to have an occasion for the Sun-Blessed to make a show of force," Queen Adinah noted, and for once, none of the royal women disagreed with the sentiment she expressed.

I wondered what any of them would make of Three-Copper Quarter, or if they had any idea such a place existed.

I thought about the queue of men and women in Fazarah and Tarkhal's courtyard, and the line of carters trudging up the ramps.

I thought about stolen venom, and wondered if the Shahalim Clan would be willing to give up their secrets if it were true.

In the morning, there was a pair of seamstresses in the Hall of Harmonious Beauty. A stunning array of Barakhan silks was spread over every available surface, and the royal women were already perusing them with delight. Although I had hoped that this would be a more private undertaking, it was clear from the outset that that was not to be. Izaria took me by the hand the moment Zariya and I entered the hall.

"Come, my darling, you must choose which ones you like best," she announced. "I will show you the ones *I* think will suit you."

I was not insensible to the beauty of the fabric. I had always admired the crimson-and-gold silks of the Royal Guard. These were every bit as vibrant and far more intricate in design, gold thread creating patterns of flowers and waves and shells and leaves against backgrounds of turquoise, purple, orange, and green, as well as the familiar crimson and gold.

Izaria held up a bolt of bright orange silk with a border of gold in the shape of waves. "This would complement your skin tone."

"Yes, one needs a darker tone to wear that hue," Queen Makesha observed. "It doesn't flatter me, obviously."

I shot a glance at Zariya, who hid a smile and made the hand sign that meant *Be patient and hold your ground.*

"And I thought this one would echo those strange scars of yours." Izaria raised a length of lavender silk with a silvery undertone alongside my face.

"Those are the marks of Pahrkun the Scouring Wind," Zariya said from the divan on which she had reclined. "You might wish to speak of them with a measure of respect, dearest."

"I'm only trying to help, my darling," her sister replied, unperturbed. "Khai, do you like them?"

I nodded.

"Good." She beckoned to one of the seamstresses. "Then let us begin, shall we?"

Had I not grown somewhat accustomed to the ritual of the daily bath, I would have found the business of stripping naked to be draped and measured and pinned before so many onlookers a difficult ordeal to bear; as it was, I surely cannot say I was comfortable with it. But I will own that the sensation of silk against my bare skin, soft and flowing as water, was a pleasant one.

"What is it made of?" I asked Zariya, running a fold between my forefinger and thumb. It was so fine it caught on my callused fingertips. "Surely no animal has a coat so soft."

"It is woven of thread spun by silk-worms," she said. "Silk-worms which eat a particular kind of leaf from a tree that grows only in Barakhar."

Thread from worms! I shook my head in wonder.

Once the seamstresses had done with me and set about their work, it seemed it was not enough that I should don women's attire; it was also expected that I would be oiled and braided and painted in the manner reckoned essential to a woman of the upper classes of Zarkhoum.

I scowled at Zariya. "This, we did not discuss."

She looked contrite. "It is part and parcel of the whole, my heart. I assumed you knew. But you needn't do it if you don't want to." Someone snickered, and I understood that if I did not do this, I would be nothing more than a jest in these clothes, a desert barbarian dressed in women's finery.

And so I consented.

While the seamstresses' needles flew and the royal women gossiped, maidservants attended to me. They rubbed the skin of my face and arms and hands with scented oil, combed and braided my hair, and twined fine lengths of thread to pluck hairs from my eyebrows.

"Not too much," Zariya cautioned them. "Khai will want to keep his fine strong brows."

When the plucking was done, the maidservants lined my eyes with kohl and painted my lips with carmine. I did not mind the kohl, which felt like nothing once it was done, but the carmine felt thick and greasy on my lips. Such was the length of the procedure and the speed of the seamstresses that by the time they had finished, the orange silk dress and an outer robe were ready for a preliminary fitting.

I put them on.

The royal women oohed and cooed over the transformation, loaning me bangles for my wrists.

Zariya said nothing.

I felt uncertain and strange to myself. "Well?"

"You should see for yourself, my darling," she said. "Aunt, may we borrow your mirror for the occasion?"

"Of course." Queen Adinah summoned a pair of guards to fetch the tall standing mirror from her chambers.

I approached it with apprehension.

In the mirror, a woman walked toward me. The folds of her silk garments swayed as she did, hinting at the curves of her figure beneath them. The woman's brown skin had a luminous sheen, and her black hair was coiled and looped in elegant braids. Gold clinked and glinted at her wrists. The strong lines of her eyebrows had undergone a subtle refinement. The woman's kohl-lined eyes, wide with astonishment, appeared twice the size of my own, and her red lips, parted in awe, were generous and startling.

If it had not been for the glittering slashes on my cheekbones and the graze on my temple, I would have doubted it was me.

"Oh," I whispered. "Oh!"

I was a girl.

By all the fallen stars, I was a rather *pretty* one.

Leaning on her canes, Zariya came alongside me. "I told you that you would make a lovely girl," she murmured. "How do you feel?"

I touched my reflected face in the mirror. "Honestly? I don't know. Like a stranger to myself."

She tilted her head at me. "A stranger you would like to get to know better or a stranger you hope never to see again?"

I couldn't stop staring at the mirror. How *did* I feel? This was a vision of myself I had rejected with disdain and loathing since I was eleven years old, reckoning it weak and soft and everything a warrior was not.

And yet . . .

In our brief time together, Zariya had shown me that one need not be a warrior to possess a warrior's heart. One need not be a *man* to possess a warrior's heart.

"I think . . ." I paused. "'Like' is a strong word. I think it is a stranger I am *willing* to get to know better. And I think . . . I think perhaps I am grateful to you for introducing me to her."

She sighed with relief. "And I am grateful to hear it, my heart. I feared you would be unhappy with me."

I smiled at her. "That, I cannot imagine."

TWENTY-SIX

Can one be two things at once?

It seemed to me that day that one could, for I felt myself to be two things in one skin. The royal women quickly lost interest in my transformation; as far as they were concerned, I had been nothing more than a girl dressed in boys' clothing, and now I was properly attired.

For me, the matter went far deeper. When Zariya wrapped a scarf of the shimmering orange silk around my head and pinned a veil of the same material in place, I no longer saw anything of myself that I recognized. Khai the warrior, Khai the honorary boy, had vanished, replaced by an anonymous pair of kohl-lined eyes.

No one would recognize the royal shadow, that much was certain, and there was a certain exhilarating freedom in the knowledge.

While Zariya sorted through the remaining silks, I practiced walking. I had noticed a gait particular to the women of Merabaht; a shortened stride that placed one foot directly in front of the other, causing their garments to sway slightly from side to side as they walked.

"One would almost think you've had practice," Zariya observed. Selecting a bolt of unadorned dark blue silk, she called the seamstresses over. "Let's do something a bit more modest with this one," she said to them so naturally one would never suspect there was an ulterior motive behind it. "Something a well-bred woman's maidservant might wear in public."

One would almost think you've *had practice*, I thought silently, but then I supposed in a sense, she had. Growing up in the court of the Sun-Blessed, she'd had as much practice in dissembling as I'd had mastering different gaits under Brother Yarit's tutelage.

Resigned to the fact that it would be too late to venture to the market by the time the more modest blue ensemble would be finished, I spent the day in the women's quarter. And that afternoon, for the first time, I enjoyed a measure of comfort in the ritual of the daily bath.

For better or worse, I had earned the right to be there, a woman among women; at least for the moment. But when it was over, when the cosmetics were scrubbed from my face and my elaborate braids undone, I donned my old attire. I claimed it was because I intended to hold a training session with a handful of the Queen's Guard, which was true enough, but it was not the whole reason.

I wanted to know what it felt like to slip from one identity to another in the same skin.

I wanted to see myself anew.

Queen Adinah's mirror yet stood in the Hall of Harmonious Beauty. I approached it a second time.

This time I saw a fierce scowling boy in a rough-spun white woolen tunic and breeches, ready to take on the world, hands callused from squeezing rocks and gripping the hilts of the weapons that hung about him. A young man armed to the teeth, a young man who had knelt to Pahrkun the Scouring Wind and offered up his face in perfect trust, awaiting the sting of the viper's tooth and the scorpion's tail and their deadly venom coursing through his bloodstream.

A boy who had not flinched, and lived to bear the shining marks on his cheeks because of it.

As before, Zariya came alongside me, and this time our gazes met in the mirror in silent understanding. "You know I adore you both, don't you?" she said softly to me.

I nodded. "I do."

The following morning, I transformed back into a girl.

The dark blue dress and outer robe were indeed more modest. It was a thicker weave of silk and the material did not cling and flow in such a suggestive manner. Zariya painted my eyes and braided my hair herself, as expert as any maidservant. "Be careful," she said before pinning my veil in place. "Don't do anything foolhardy out there."

"I won't," I promised. "I'll have no safe means of changing disguises, so I won't be searching for the Mad Priest today. I'll see what the Shahalim have to say regarding the death-bladder venom instead."

While I was able to conceal my *zims* under the dress's generous sleeves and my dagger under my robe, as well as twine the garrote around my braids and my *heshkrat* around my sash, dressing in women's attire meant I had to forgo my *yakhan* and *kopar*. Still, after being pelted with rocks, I thought I would be safer venturing into the city partially armed and unrecognizable than I would be with my familiar weapons.

Yesterday, I had told the Queen's Guardsmen on duty at the door to the women's quarter that I was leaving to meet with my mentor, Vironesh, and they had not questioned it.

Today, when I told them I was about an errand, it was different. They looked uncertainly at each other and bade me wait while one of them fetched Captain Tarshim, who eyed me up and down.

"What's this errand you're after?" he asked me.

"It is no concern of yours," I said coolly. "Am I not free to come and go as I please?"

Captain Tarshim frowned. "Under the circumstances, I'm not sure what the protocol ought to be. It may be reckoned unseemly."

Anger stirred in me. "I am the same person I was yesterday, Captain. I am not one of the royal women of the House of the Ageless. I am Princess Zariya's shadow, the chosen servant of Pahrkun the Scouring Wind, and I could kill you in a dozen different ways without breaking a sweat. Do not think to dictate my comings and goings."

With a grimace, he gestured for me to go.

No one spared me a second glance after I left the women's quarter. The Royal Guards I passed in the halls of the palace gave me cursory looks, but there was nothing of interest in a lone woman in modest attire. Once I gained the streets of Merabaht, the same held true.

During Brother Yarit's training in the Fortress of the Winds, I'd never developed a full appreciation for the power of disguise. Oh, I understood it on an intellectual level—it was Brother Yarit's disguise that had allowed him to take Brother Jawal by surprise in the Trial of Pahrkun—but I'd never *felt* it. After all, we all knew one another in the brotherhood, so it was just so much play-acting.

Today I understood.

Nothing about me stood out; nothing about me drew attention. I was an ordinary woman in a city teeming with people, faceless and anonymous behind my veil. I could be anyone.

It was a heady feeling, tempered only by the gnawing hollowness I felt at being parted from Zariya.

I made my way past the gracious houses of the third tier and the fine shops and teahouses of the second tier to the sprawl below them, wandering the crowded marketplaces and observing what manner of goods and services were on offer and how the less fortunate citizens of Merabaht bartered for them; trying to grasp the rhythm of their transactions, trying to get a sense of what the single gold bangle Zariya had given me might be worth.

Once I was satisfied that I wouldn't make an utter fool of myself in the transaction, I chose an old rag merchant whose eyes were shrewd but kind above her veil. One thin gold bangle bought me a drab brown ensemble of coarse linen, a woven basket in which to carry the items, and a handful of silver and copper coins in change.

"My thanks, old mother." I settled the basket in the crook of my arm and stowed the coins in an inner pocket of my robe. "Do you know where I might find the Lucky Tortoise teahouse?"

She pointed toward the northeast. "Somewhere over there on the second tier, I think."

The desert tribesfolk navigate by way of fixed landmarks, and Brother Merik had taught me to do the same. I had allowed myself to be overwhelmed by the city on my first outing.

Now, I paid closer attention and felt a sense of the city's staggered landscape begin to settle into me.

Many of the establishments billing themselves as teahouses were clearly serving more than tea. These were the places of which Brother Yarit had spoken with such fondness, the sound of music and laughter spilling from their open doors along with clouds of hashish smoke and the lingering scent of savory foods and date-palm wine, indicating much merriment was to be found within.

When I found the Lucky Tortoise, I saw that it was not such a place. It was a quiet, staid establishment tucked into the northeasternmost corner of the second tier. A hanging sign with a creature I took to be a tortoise marked its presence.

I entered it and saw clay jars of tea labeled with painstakingly written signs lining the shelves behind the proprietor's counter. Men and a few women sat cross-legged at low tables, sipping tea and murmuring together.

The proprietor, an ordinary-looking man of middling years, glanced up at my approach. "Yes?"

I cleared my throat. "I beg your pardon, but do you carry three-moon blend?"

His gaze sharpened. "For special occasions, yes." He beckoned to a veiled woman who was attending to the clients. "Belisha, escort the lady into the storeroom and show her our selections."

She saluted him, and indicated that I should follow her.

There was no storeroom, but rather a passageway that led to a residence surrounded by high walls. In an antechamber, Belisha made a palm-downward gesture indicating that I should wait there. I did, and presently she returned to escort me into a sitting room where an elderly man awaited me.

Despite the wrinkles that lined his face, his eyes were clear and keen and markedly suspicious. "Welcome, my lady. Who are you and why do you come seeking the three-moon blend?"

Taking a seat on the carpet across from him, I unpinned my veil and revealed my face.

He drew in his breath in a sharp hiss. "Lukhan's shadow! I know who you are. Why are you here?"

I blinked. "Lukhan?"

The old man shrugged, his narrow shoulders rising and falling. "You know him by another name, of course. So. What is it you seek of the Shahalim?"

"Fifty years ago, Prince Kazaran was poisoned with death-bladder venom," I said. "I wish to know if someone commissioned the Shahalim to steal the venom, and if so, who it was."

The old man's eyes were as hard as pebbles. "Do you know so little of the Shahalim Clan that you actually think I would answer that question?" he asked me with contempt.

"I am only trying to protect my charge," I said to him. "Brother Yarit—Lukhan—said I could ask the clan for help if I needed it."

"Help, yes." He shook his head. "This is not asking for our services. This is asking us to betray the bedrock of the principles by which our clan has lived and prospered for hundreds of years. Our silence is a sacred trust, a matter of gravest honor. And *you* should know it," he added in an accusatory tone. "Your own Brother Yarit, my favorite nephew, Lukhan, chose to face the Trial of Pahrkun rather than betray a client." He jerked his chin at me. "Do you suppose the Royal Guards did not come asking questions of the Shahalim when the Barren Teardrop was stolen? Should I have answered *their* questions? It would have saved an innocent man's life."

What he said was true, and I realized that it had been a mistake to come here in the naïve hope that the Shahalim would aid me, but his demeanor angered me. "You are quick to boast of your clan's honor," I said. "And yet it was one of your own who betrayed Brother Yarit, was it not?"

The old man's face hardened further. "That is a clan matter and it has been dealt with accordingly. Belisha! Show her."

The silent woman came over and lifted her veil. Opening her mouth, she showed me the stump of her severed tongue.

I felt sick. In the desert, a matter of honor would be settled with fists or swords, but never this deliberate mutilation. The woman lowered her veil, and now I saw that her eyes above it were filled with sorrow and regret.

I pinned my own veil back in place and rose. "I am sorry for wasting your time," I said to the old man. "I did not mean to impugn the honor of the Shahalim Clan. I do but seek to fulfill the duty with which Pahrkun the Scouring Wind charged me, by any means possible." I paused. "My mentor, the last living shadow, has a term for this. Honor beyond honor, he calls it."

Unimpressed, the old clan leader shrugged again. "If there is nothing else, Belisha will escort you out."

She led me back the way we'd come. Now I felt awkward in her presence. What did one say to someone who'd committed such a profound betrayal and been punished so grievously for it?

And yet had she not done so, Brother Yarit wouldn't have been caught. Seven years ago, someone in the House of the Ageless would have taken possession of the remaining cache of *rhamanthus* seeds, and the balance of power among the Sun-Blessed would have shifted.

Brother Yarit would never have stood the Trial of Pahrkun and been chosen by the Scouring Wind as the next Seer.

I would never have been trained in the arts of the Shahalim Clan.

These were thoughts that made me shiver to my core. I remembered the madness that Brother Yarit had displayed when the Sight came upon him, the way he drew feverishly in the sand with his dagger, muttering, *So if this, then that; but if* this, *then* that, trying to puzzle out a future too vast and shifting for a mortal mind to encompass.

I wondered if Brother Saan had Seen Belisha's betrayal and what would come of it among the glimpses he had been afforded.

At the door to the teahouse, the maimed woman turned to me, positioning herself in such a manner that my body blocked hers from the view of the proprietor or any of their clients. Her gaze caught mine, then she blinked once and glanced downward in a deliberate gesture.

I followed her gaze.

Come tomorrow, she signed with her right hand. *Drink. Do you understand?*

I inclined my head to her. "Thank you for your time."

Taking my leave of the Lucky Tortoise, I returned to the Palace of the Sun to report my findings to Zariya.

She listened with appalled fascination. "Well, I suppose the clan had to punish her, but how awful! Why do you suppose she's willing to take the risk of betraying them again to aid you? Revenge?"

"I don't know," I said. "I don't see how this amounts to revenge. After all, she doesn't even know what I mean to do with the information."

"Why, then? And what *do* you mean to do with the information, my darling?" Zariya added. "Tell my father?"

"That's a good question," I said slowly. "It's not as though we'll have *proof,* she wouldn't even have been alive at the time. And I don't want to do anything that would get her punished or killed for trying to help us." I thought about it. "I'll tell Vironesh and let him decide. He has the right to know."

"Very well, then. I must confess, *I* don't want the responsibility." Zariya examined the basket full of garments I'd purchased, wrinkling her nose. "I don't suppose these have been washed in recent memory, have they?"

"I doubt it," I said. "That's part of what will make them an effective disguise."

She set them aside. "Let's store these in the garden where Nalah won't come across them."

I returned to the Lucky Tortoise the following morning and ordered a pot of hibiscus tea. I kept my eyes lowered and affected a whispery tone, concerned that the proprietor would recognize me as the woman who'd inquired about three-moon blend yesterday, but the famed Shahalim powers of observation didn't extend beyond a veil. He bade me seat myself, and in a few moments, Belisha brought over my pot of tea and a cup on a wooden tray. She set it down and left without any indication that she'd recognized me, but when I lifted the brass teapot to pour myself a cup, I found a scrap of paper folded small beneath it.

I palmed it unobtrusively and sat sipping tea, listening to the conversation in the teahouse. It seemed the Children of Miasmus had struck twice in the night, dumping a shipment of Barakhan silks into the harbor and overturning a wagonload of wheat intended for the palace.

Tomorrow, I thought, I would resume my search for the Mad Priest; today, I was anxious to know what information Belisha had imparted to me. I finished my tea and took my leave.

I was tempted to read the scrap as soon as I was clear of the place, but I gauged it wiser to be circumspect. That being the case, I reckoned I might as well wait to share the moment with Zariya.

In the sleepy hours of the midday rest, it was quiet in the women's quarter. Cicadas droned in the garden, and occasionally one of Zariya's little birds uttered a chirp or an unexpected burst of song. I unfolded the scrap of paper and smoothed it, and we leaned our heads together to read what was written on it.

One word.

A name, written small but clear in the same painstaking hand that had labeled the jars of tea at the Lucky Tortoise.

Tazaresh.

"Tazaresh!" Zariya breathed.

"You're surprised?" I asked her.

She nodded. "I hadn't thought him so . . . subtle. Do you suppose it's true?"

I shrugged. "They say he's favored to be named as heir, don't they?"

"Yes, they do." Her dark eyes were grave. "You're right, it's not proof. But it's something. You'll speak to Vironesh?"

I nodded. "I will."

That afternoon, I met with Vironesh in the barracks of the City Guard, finding him in a foul mood after the latest escapades of the Children of Miasmus. At least it made for a good training bout, something of which I was in much need. When we were both exhausted and panting, leaning on our blades, I informed him that I had something of import to tell him.

Vironesh heard me out, his expression growing increasingly stormy. "Khai, I told you—"

I interrupted him. "She gave me a name."

He hesitated, and I could see the desire to know warring on his features with the desire to reprimand me for careless meddling. "Whose?"

I told him.

Vironesh took a slow, shuddering breath and closed his eyes. "If it's true, I will kill him for it. Is it?"

"I cannot swear to it," I murmured. "Everything I know, you now know. What will you do? Will you tell the king?"

He opened his eyes and gazed into the distance. "No. Once this latest impending royal wedding has passed, I will find an opportunity to confront Prince Tazaresh. I will give him a chance to confess and explain himself. If I am not satisfied, I *will* kill him."

"King Azarkal might very well have you executed for it," I said to him.

Vironesh gave me one of his hard, mirthless smiles. "If it comes to it, I would welcome it."

TWENTY-SEVEN

The Mad Priest had vanished.

My disguise proved effective. The blue outer robe and headwear were generous enough to cover the ragged brown garments I'd purchased in the market, allowing me to leave the palace dressed as a well-bred lady's maidservant. Once out of sight of the palace, I had but to shed my outer layers and stow them in my basket to transform into one of the city's less fortunate denizens.

It served me well in the places that Fazarah had mentioned: Three-Copper Quarter, the large marketplace in Kabhat Square, the wharves. As she had warned me, these were not places where it was safe for a single woman, but I developed a trick of identifying a pair or trio of women headed in the same general direction and hovering just close enough that a casual viewer would assume I was a member of their company.

And yet it was all to no avail, for the Priest of the Black Star was nowhere to be found. At least I had become circumspect enough to keep my mouth closed and my ears open. Although there was surprisingly little talk of the fellow or the Children of Miasmus on the streets of the lower levels, the sailors in the harbor were given to exchanging gossip and speculation. From what I could gather, there had been no sightings of the priest since the day I'd been stoned by his supporters.

If my outings were fruitless, they afforded me a chance to marvel at the rich and varied sights of the city. The harbor with its impossibly tall lighthouse was a source of particular fascination to me. I was still awestruck by the vast expanse of the ocean, and if I had no news to report to Zariya, I could bring her tales.

I told her about the day a ship with the black-and-white-striped sails of the coursers of Obid docked at the harbor, and how the coursers strode the wharves with more authority than the City Guard, examining shipments and manifests. I told her about the nimble Barakhan sailors who scrambled up and down the rigging of their ships with careless grace, and the Granthian ship with a leathery stink-lizard with a long neck and folded wings perched on its prow to guard its cargo, an incredible sight to see.

"Oh, I should so like to see such things for myself!" Zariya said wistfully. "If I had two good legs, you could find a way to smuggle me out, couldn't you, my darling? Think what adventures we could have!"

The thought of the two of us exploring the dangerous quarters of the city was an alarming one, giving me cause to sympathize with Vironesh's concerns. "You'll have more freedom when you're wed," I said to her. "You can venture out in a litter with your own household guard."

"If my husband permits it," she reminded me. "And never on my own two feet. Not unless . . ." She fell silent.

I waited a moment. "Unless what?"

Zariya gave me an apologetic glance. "There is one thing I have not told you, only because it is so dear a hope that I fear even to give voice to it. But I do not want secrets between us." She rubbed the tops of her thighs in an uncharacteristically restless gesture. "There is the slightest, *slightest* possibility that partaking of the *rhamanthus* may heal me." She shook her head at me as I opened my mouth to reply. "No, don't even speak of it. I can't bear it."

It was a grave revelation, but I nodded in understanding and changed the topic.

In the final days leading up to the royal wedding, I gave up my futile quest. There was so much activity in the women's quarter, seamstresses and jewel merchants and flower vendors and purveyors of cosmetics coming and going at all hours, that I was loath to leave Zariya unguarded.

My own wedding attire was a matter of much heated debate. The royal women assumed I would wear one of my fine new gowns and were shocked when I refused outright, but there was no way I was attending Zariya at a crowded ceremony and a public procession less than fully armed. It would be Khai the warrior, Khai the shadow at her side, not this girl-Khai I barely understood other than as a useful disguise. The royal women were adamant that there must be finery, and for once, Zariya sided with them. In the end, we settled on a compromise in the form of a new tunic and breeches in a rich gold silk brocade.

The wedding was held in the High Temple of Anamuht with Sister Nizara presiding over the ceremony, the Sacred Flame stretching toward the ceiling behind her, dozens of oil lamps casting their lesser glows over the proceedings. Women sat veiled on the left side of the carpeted floor, men on the right, while Princess Izaria and her groom, a minor lord's eldest son, stood before us.

I sat beside Zariya, a bare-faced anomaly on the left side of the sanctum. Her breath was coming quick and shallow, and I was concerned lest she overtax herself, but when I gave her a concerned look, she dismissed it with a quick shake of her head.

During the long invocation, I stole glances at the men's side of the sanctum, especially at Prince Tazaresh, wondering about his guilt. He sat straight-backed with a warrior's discipline, his features fixed forward.

The bride and groom exchanged the traditional blessing gifts, she offering him honey in a gilded bowl to symbolize the sweetness she would bring to the marriage, he offering her a pile of salt on a gilded platter as a symbol that he would provide for her. The groom—Parvesh was his name—took a spoonful of honey, and beneath her veil, Izaria lifted a few crystals of salt to her lips.

And then it was time for the *rhamanthus*.

There would be no dowry, only the promise of a dowry when the harvest came, but each would partake of a single seed pried from the king's crown.

Sister Nizara held them forth on a cushion of gold silk, glowing like living garnets. "Each of these seeds has been quickened by Anamuht the

Purging Fire. Each bears a spark of the sun's fire; each represents a year of enduring youth and vitality. Partake, my Sun-Blessed sister, and lead a long and virtuous life. Partake, my brother, and enter the House of the Ageless."

A soft murmur ran through the sanctum as they accepted the seeds; envy, perhaps. There were so very few quickened seeds remaining.

Beside me, Zariya leaned forward.

I could not see Izaria's face behind her veil, but I watched the groom, Parvesh, as he put the seed into his mouth and swallowed. For a moment, there was no reaction, but then color suffused his features and his lips parted in wonder. "Oh," he said. *"Oh!"*

Did it hurt, I wondered? No, it seemed some other sensation entirely, one to which one could not put a name. And knowing what I knew, I envied him on Zariya's behalf. We had not spoken further of the matter, but I had learned that she would not be allowed to partake of the *rhamanthus* until she turned eighteen or was wed herself, whichever occasion came first. Since the Sun-Blessed wed later than most, it was likely to be the former.

If Anamuht came to quicken the harvest; if the king's crown was not stripped bare by that day.

Sister Nizara invoked a final blessing and pronounced the pair wed in the name of the Sacred Twins. Izaria unpinned her veil, and she and her groom embraced in the sight of all assembled. She looked happy; he was indeed a well-favored young fellow. I hoped for her sake that he was kind, too.

Thence, the procession.

It was in truth a splendid sight, at least from my perspective at the rear. King Azarkal led it astride a fine black horse. Behind him, his two eldest sons rode beside uncurtained litters carrying the two senior-most queens, Adinah and Makesha. The litters were borne by members of the Queen's Guard, spears in their free hands, and flanked by a score of Royal Guardsmen on foot. Behind them was the new royal couple in a shared litter, given special pride of place for the occasion, then came the daughters and husbands of the senior queens, although I noted that Princess Fazarah was not among them. Next were the junior queens and the sons they had borne, followed by their daughters and husbands. Another two score of Royal Guardsmen were staggered along their length on either side.

Because she was the junior-most queen and had borne only daughters, Zariya's mother, Sanala, was the last of the royal women in the procession; because she was a daughter and the youngest of the Sun-Blessed, Zariya's litter was last of all. A quartet of mounted Royal Guardsmen rode behind us.

I walked beside Zariya's litter, watching the procession snake down the mountainside before us. In the west, the sun laid a shining path across the ocean. Although the sun was still high in the sky, a soft blue twilight was gathering in the shadowed streets, dispelled by the oil-wood torches carried by the Royal Guardsmen who were on foot.

The plan was that the procession would descend to the second level of the city and return to the palace by sundown. In less fraught times, it would have ventured to the very base of Merabaht. Having spent a number of days haunting those quarters, I was glad it was going no lower.

We descended past the fourth level, which was largely occupied by the barracks of the Royal Guard.

On the third level, the denizens of the stately houses there turned out to cheer the newly wedded couple and throw orange blossom petals; in turn, the new royal couple tossed out silver coins that were received with a laugh and a salute.

On the second level of Merabaht, it was an even livelier affair. As a precaution, members of the City Guard were stationed along the main thoroughfare, but folks spilled out of the teahouses that lined it, calling out blessings and begging for coins. It was reckoned good luck to catch a coin thrown by a member of a royal wedding, and everyone in the procession had been given a purse of copper for the occasion.

Zariya leaned out from her litter to toss her coins, laughing with delight, her breath catching in her throat.

My skin prickled.

There were too many people lining the streets, and among the revelers were scores of silent and robed figures, hanging back behind the City Guardsmen.

I felt Pahrkun's wind rising, rising within me.

I tasted violence in the air.

Zariya caught my expression and sobered. "What is it, my darling? You look grim."

"Something's wrong," I said in a low tone. "There are—"

"Children of Miasmus!" a voice thundered behind us. *"Rise!"*

The mob swarmed out of the shadows. There weren't scores of them, there were hundreds; and they were armed with daggers, not rocks. They took out dozens of the City Guardsmen from behind, stabbing backs and slitting throats, revelry turning to slaughter in the blink of an eye.

Zariya.

I was in motion without thinking, my *yakhan* and *kopar* in my hands with no recollection of having drawn them. Zariya's litter clattered to the ground, dropped by the terrified guards carrying it.

"Children of Miasmus, the end is nigh!" the voice called out in the traders' tongue. "Rise up against those who oppress you! Seize *what* you can *while* you can!"

One, two, three . . . I lost count of the number of men I killed after three. There was no artistry or finesse to my fighting. It didn't matter. All that mattered was that no one harmed Zariya, because if they did, my heart would die inside me. The cobbled street was growing slippery with blood and crowded with corpses. Zariya's litter-bearers had rallied enough to put their backs to the conveyance and level their spears, helping keep the mob at bay and giving me space to work.

Only there were so *many* of them, and they kept coming.

Behind us a horse was screaming in pain, hamstrung and floundering, throwing the quartet of Royal Guardsmen into chaos. Out of the corner of one eye, I saw a darting figure low to the ground, the flash of a blade, and another horse down in agony. I didn't dare abandon my defense of Zariya, but I shoved my *yakhan* into an assailant's dead body, freeing my right hand to whip one of my *zims* into the back of the horse-mutilator's neck, taking vicious pleasure in seeing him fall.

"Do the Sun-Blessed not live by the sweat of your brow? I have seen nothing else since I set foot on Zarkhoum's shores! Have they not taken from you, taken and taken and taken? Children of Miasmus, it is *your* turn to take! Take now, before it is too late, for the world *will* be swallowed in darkness!"

"Get the priest!" I shouted at the guardsmen, yanking my blade out of the corpse.

"Fuck the priest!" one shouted back at me. "Ward the king!"

The two guardsmen with hale mounts left to them pounded past Zariya's litter on either side, flesh and bone crunching beneath the horses' hooves. For the first time, I was left with a clear view of the Mad Priest.

The Priest of the Black Star.

Based on the fact that he spoke the traders' tongue, I had guessed he wasn't Zarkhoumi. The Mad Priest was younger than I had expected, fair-skinned as a Therinian, with long, unkempt black hair and a thin scruff of beard clinging to his cheeks and chin. He wore ragged breeches and a filthy vest that hung open to reveal a black starburst symbol etched into his pale chest.

A second mob stood behind him.

Someone to my right launched himself at me with a blood-curdling scream, dagger raised high; I slashed his midsection open absentmindedly with a back-handed blow of my *yakhan*, spilling his bowels onto the street.

The Mad Priest pointed at me. "Kill the shadow!" he cried. "It is the will of Miasmus! Kill the shadow and seize the princess!"

With a roar, the mob behind him raced forward, hurdling the floundering horses, bowling over the remaining guardsmen.

I fought like a spinning devil, Pahrkun's wind blowing through me in a gale, finding the spaces between; between the mind's intention and a dagger's blow, between incitement and hesitation, between rage and fear.

I built a wall of corpses.

They came and came and came until there were no more of them.

At the forefront of the procession, I could hear the sounds of battle subsiding; the groans of the surviving wounded, the exhausted utterance of orders, and a rising ululation of grief.

Alone in the thoroughfare, every supporter to his cause slain or fled, the Mad Priest wavered on his feet.

I crouched beside Zariya's fallen litter and peered into the window, filled with the urgent need to know that she was alive and unharmed. "My lady?"

"I am fine." Her tone was shaken and furious, her eyes flashing. "Do what you must, my heart. Take the priest alive if you can."

I straightened and took stock of the scene. There were no more assailants. The battle had ended, and it had ended badly for them. "Ward the princess," I said to her litter-bearers. "Ward her with your lives."

I vaulted over the wall of corpses I had built. Shoving my *yakhan* into my sash, I unwound my *heshkrat*.

The Mad Priest gave me a strange, tranquil look. His lips were parched and bitten, and the black starburst etched on his chest seemed to pulse with the beat of his heart. "This is only the beginning. You cannot stop it, you know. Miasmus will swallow the world in darkness."

I twirled the *heshkrat*. "We'll see."

His eyes rolled up to show the whites and he crumpled to the ground as I released my *heshkrat*, its lines twining around his throat as he fell, rather than his legs as I'd intended. He lay motionless on the street.

I hesitated.

Behind me, the ululation continued to rise as though sparks were passing from throat to throat and kindling a blaze of grief. There was no one here, I thought, to mourn the slain Children of Miasmus; that meant there had been a death in the House of the Ageless.

I dashed back to Zariya's litter and saw Vironesh coming toward me through the carnage in his City Guard uniform, blood-splattered and limping. Of course, he would have been posted among them; later, I learned that his efforts had broken the spine of the attack in the middle of the procession. Even so, it had not been enough to prevent a royal casualty.

"Who is it?" I asked.

Vironesh met my gaze. "Prince Tazaresh."

Inside the litter, Zariya drew in a sharp breath, but she did not lend her voice to mourning him.

"You didn't—" It was a dishonorable thought and I didn't complete it. "No, of course not."

"What became of the Mad Priest?" he asked.

I pointed past the wall of corpses. "He collapsed. Dead or alive, I don't know."

"Let's find out." Vironesh called over an additional handful of guardsmen to stand watch over Zariya's litter and I hauled dead men out of the way so he wouldn't have to clamber over them.

The Mad Priest was lying motionless where he'd fallen, my *heshkrat* wrapped around his throat, a trickle of blood that looked black in the gathering dusk at one corner of his mouth. At close range, the symbol on his chest was a more gruesome thing than I'd reckoned, a craterous pit of a wound with radiating lines. Although his chest did not rise and fall with breath, the black star continued to pulse.

I reached to prod it with the central tine of my *kopar*, and Vironesh caught my wrist. "Don't touch him. There's something unnatural about this. Go find a torch." There were a number of oil-wood torches still burning where they'd been dropped. I grabbed the nearest, and Vironesh and I bent low over the still figure.

Something was crawling out of the abscess in the Mad Priest's chest, one spindly black leg at a time.

Vironesh and I watched in horrified fascination. It looked like a black spider the size of a man's hand, with a tiny body and a profusion of long, skinny legs. It dragged itself out of the priest's chest, crawled down the right side of his torso, and crouched on the cobblestones, pulsing up and down on its splayed legs, its carapace glinting in the torchlight.

Both of us backed away from it.

"What the watery hell is that?" I whispered to Vironesh, hoping he had an answer.

He shook his head. "It looks like a sea-spider, but I've never seen a black one; and anyway, they're harmless. I've never heard of anything like this."

I gazed at the ruin of the Mad Priest's chest and swallowed. "Brother, I think we'd best kill this thing, and quickly."

Vironesh drew his *kopar*. "Be ready with the torch in case steel's not enough, Khai."

The spider-thing shuddered when Vironesh drove the point of his weapon into its body; shuddered, and began hunching its way *up* the tine, the ends of its legs somehow gripping the smooth steel.

I thrust the torch at it, bathing it in flames. For a long moment it seemed not even fire would deter the thing, then at last came a sizzling sound and it stopped moving. After another moment, its long legs shriveled and curled in against themselves. Still, I held the flame to it until Vironesh bade me cease. He used the blade of his *yakhan* to scrape the burnt black remnant of the thing free.

I glanced back to assure myself that Zariya was being well guarded. "What about the Mad Priest?"

Vironesh grunted. "I think it's fair to assume he's dead. Bring the torch over here, let's make certain there isn't another one of those things inside him." I let the torchlight play over the priest's pale torso. Nothing pulsed within the abscess, and I was beginning to think about reclaiming my *heshkrat* when Vironesh swore under his breath. "Raise the torch, let me see his face."

I obeyed and watched him study the priest's features. "What is it?"

He looked up at me. "I've seen this man before. When I was with the coursers of Obid. He was first mate on a pirate ship we chased and lost in the Nexus on more than one occasion."

I shivered in the warm evening air. "Whatever he was, he wanted me dead. 'Kill the shadow,' he said; 'kill the shadow and seize the princess.' He said nothing of Prince Tazaresh."

Vironesh lowered his voice. "Someone armed this mob with daggers wrought of Granthian steel, and that doesn't come cheap. You've been in Three-Copper Quarter. No one living there could afford such a thing, let alone hundreds of them. I am not sure it was one of the Children of Miasmus who killed Tazaresh."

"A conspiracy, then?" My clothing and my hair were drenched with blood; my fingers were sticky with it.

He shrugged. "Perhaps."

I pointed at the dead priest or pirate with his ruined crater of a chest, his chapped and bitten lips. "And him? He kept a second mob in reserve, brother. He sent them after Zariya and me and claimed it was the will of Miasmus. Are you still so very sure there is no prophecy at work here?"

In the torchlight, Vironesh looked old; old and weary. "No."

TWENTY-EIGHT

In the aftermath of the attack, the scene on the thoroughfare was one of chaos. I would have liked nothing better than to get Zariya back to the relative safety of the palace, but the streets were clogged with dead or dying men, dead or dying horses, unmanned litters, and panicked revelers fleeing.

She insisted on getting out of the litter to survey it, and although it was against my better judgment, I understood.

"By all the fallen stars!" Zariya leaned on her canes, looking pale. *"Why?"*

I shook my head.

There were hoofbeats and King Azarkal loomed out of the dusk astride his fine black mount, his face taut with grief and fury and fear. "Zariya! Zariya!"

"Here, Father!" she called to him. "We are here."

He dismounted and enfolded her in a crushing embrace. "Thank the gods that you're safe. You heard?"

She nodded when he released her. "Yes, it's terrible. Was anyone else in the family harmed?"

"Minor injuries among the fighting men." He looked past her, only now registering the number of slain attackers. King Azarkal had ruled for three hundred years and I do not think he was often dumbstruck. Tonight he was. "Ah, gods! I'd no idea they'd mounted such an attack on the rear of the procession." His gaze settled on Vironesh, standing quietly by. "Your handiwork?"

"No, Your Majesty. I was stationed among the City Guard, and nearest the newly wedded pair when the attack came. This was Khai's doing." My mentor's expression was tinged with regret and bitter pride. "The Scouring Wind's youngest chosen reaped a bloody harvest tonight."

King Azarkal's gaze shifted to me. "So it seems. And if I'd heeded your request and placed you in the Royal Guard, Vironesh, I might not have lost a son tonight. I will not make that mistake again."

"I am resigning from your service, Your Majesty," Vironesh said to him. "I will be rejoining the coursers of Obid."

"Are you mad?" The king stared at him. "After what happened here tonight? You're needed *here*!"

Vironesh beckoned to him. "What's needed is an answer to a mystery. There is something I would show you."

When we showed King Azarkal the Mad Priest's body and the charred remnants of the thing that had crawled out of his chest, he stood without speaking, his mouth compressed into a tight line. At length, he lifted his head and began giving orders to the surviving members of the Royal Guard. "I want this priest's body taken to the palace and examined by physicians!" he shouted. "I want this *thing* that inhabited him preserved and examined by the royal zoologist! I want the streets cleared for passage, but I want every last dead Child of Miasmus identified before a single corpse is claimed! Is that understood?"

There were murmurs of agreement; the Royal Guard was beginning to regroup, and set about obeying his commands. Within a quarter of an hour, the thoroughfare was clear enough to allow the royal procession to retreat to the palace.

I had never thought to find myself so relieved to enter the confines of the women's quarter.

A day of celebration had turned into a night of mourning. Everyone in the procession was profoundly shaken, and Queen Makesha, mother of Prince Tazaresh, was inconsolable. In the hour of her loss, the others offered comfort and attempted to piece together the details of what had befallen him. The only point on which all agreed was that one of the assailants had hamstrung his mount. Beyond that, no one knew for sure who had planted a dagger between his ribs.

Listening to them made my head swim.

"Khai, my love," Zariya said firmly to me, "you're covered in blood. You need to bathe."

For once, I agreed.

Her maidservant Nalah lit the lamps in the baths. I sent her for some rags that I might clean my weapons, which I did sitting on the broad lip of the warm bathing pool before disrobing. My *yakhan* would need whetting on the morrow, and I'd forgotten to retrieve the throwing dagger I'd used on the assailant crippling the guards' mounts.

Prince Tazaresh's horse had been hamstrung, too. But the king's had not, nor had Prince Elizar's; and they had been in close proximity.

I mulled over these facts, and Zariya watched me, her dark eyes lustrous and grave, thinking the same thoughts.

Once I had undressed, Nalah gathered my blood-soaked attire with a grimace and took it away.

I sank into the warm water, plumes of crimson trailing from my hair. Zariya lowered herself carefully to the edge of the bathing pool. She took up a ewer and poured water over my head, then found soap and began washing my hair with gentle hands. "Tell me what you're thinking, my darling."

"I am certain Vironesh is right about one thing," I murmured. "Someone paid to arm and organize that mob, using it toward their own ends; and whoever it was, they had reason to benefit from Prince Tazaresh's death."

Zariya slid her arms around my neck, putting her lips close to my left ear. "But there is more, is there not?"

Not so very long ago, I would have flinched at the intimacy of such an embrace; now, I merely turned my face toward hers. "There is the fact that I do not think the Mad Priest had any interest in conspiring against the House of the Ageless. He believed what he said."

"Do you?" she asked.

"Do I believe Miasmus will swallow the world in darkness?" I summoned a tired smile. "I surely hope not. But I'd like to know what in the name of all the children of heaven that *thing* was that crawled out of his chest."

"It sounds like the sort of nightmarish creature one might find in Papa-ka-hondras." Zariya resumed scrubbing my hair. "We'll consult Liko of Koronis in the morning. He catalogued a hundred and seventy different deadly plants and animals on the outskirts of the island and the surrounding waters."

Papa-ka-hondras . . . I remembered the name. The apothecary Nazim had told me about it; it meant "A Thousand Ways to Kill."

"The waters around that island are infested with death-bladders, aren't they?"

Her hands went still for a moment, then continued scrubbing. "I do believe you're right. That would be an unlikely coincidence if it proves true, would it not?"

"It would," I agreed.

As grateful as I was for the shelter of the women's quarter that night, by midmorning the next day I was chafing once more at its confinement, yearning to know what passed in the city. But I saw alarm in Zariya's eyes when I suggested I venture out to explore, and so I abandoned the notion. As courageous as she was, I needed to be mindful of the fact that nothing in her life's experience had prepared her for the horrific violence of the attack. Still, when Vironesh paid a call on me, she insisted that I ought to meet with him. I left her poring over the lists of deadly things her beloved Liko of Koronis had compiled.

After his heroic defense of the procession, it seemed a tacit agreement had been reached that Vironesh be restored to his former status of an honorary member of the House of the Ageless, and he was granted admittance to the Hall of Pleasant Accord. Veiled servants brought us tea and pastries, and a pair of the Queen's Guard stood in attendance.

"You may leave us," Vironesh informed them. "Thank you, but your presence is not required."

They departed after a mere moment's hesitation, and it galled me to note how much more readily they ceded to his wishes than mine.

I poured tea for us both. "What passes in the city?"

"Nothing good." The purple man looked grim. "Guards are breaking bones and cracking skulls in the lower level, but if there are leaders to this conspiracy, no one's given them up yet."

"Have the slain assailants been identified?" I asked him.

He shrugged. "Some. But by my count, there were perhaps three hundred men in the mob that attacked us. There are at least ten thousand people living in Three-Copper Quarter alone, and they protect their own."

"You don't think the City Guard will be able to uncover the truth," I observed.

"No," Vironesh said bluntly. "And I'm of no use in the effort, for neither side trusts me."

I sipped my tea. "And that's why you mean to rejoin the coursers of Obid?"

"The coursers of Obid know more about what passes beneath the starless skies than anyone else to sail the four great currents," he said. "I have seen a great many things in their company. I have seen a wyrm-raider ship cutting across the currents, yoked serpents towing it like cart-horses. I have seen winged sharks that launch themselves above the waves, and I have seen patches of strangling kelp capable of bringing down a great tusked whale. But I have never seen a sea-spider burrow into a man's chest. I have never heard a madman claim to speak for Miasmus."

I was silent.

Vironesh sighed. "Khai . . . what passed last night may have naught to do with any prophecy. It may simply be that the Mad Priest and his followers targeted you because you are a symbol of the order he opposes. It may be that they reckoned you young and untried, and the rearguard of the procession vulnerable. But it has been four years and more since I sailed with the coursers. I would learn what they have encountered since I left them."

"I think it wise, brother," I said quietly to him. "It is only that I will miss my mentor."

He looked surprised, then favored me with a fierce grin that showed his teeth white against his bruise-colored skin. "After last night, I think you have scant need of my training."

I turned my hands palm-upward on my crossed knees. "I had Zariya to protect."

Vironesh nodded. "Even so." He paused. "I spoke to King Azarkal earlier this morning."

"Oh?"

"I told him I had reason to believe that Prince Tazaresh was responsible for Prince Kazaran's death, in the hope that it might ease his grief a measure," he murmured. "I did not tell him *why*, and he did not ask. After all, it matters naught now."

"It matters who was responsible for Tazaresh's death," I reminded him. "If one of the Sun-Blessed was behind it, he or she has an army of ten thousand angry and impoverished denizens of Merabaht awaiting orders."

"Yes, and I told the king to look to the shipping manifests," Vironesh said. "As I said last night, that's a considerable amount of good Granthian steel. Whoever armed that mob had to have imported those weapons at some point, and somewhere, there ought to be a record of it."

I nodded. "A good thought."

Another silence fell between us, a silence stretching toward awkwardness. After four years, it seemed there ought to be more to say; and yet, I could not think what it might be. And then it came to me.

I rose first. "I know you were hoping for redemption, brother," I said to Vironesh. "Or failing that, perhaps revenge. I fear that neither opportunity has presented itself. I hope it is yet to come. And I hope that my actions as your pupil may in some small part give honor to you."

"Khai . . ." Vironesh shook his head at me, then climbed heavily to his feet and reached out to clasp my forearm in a firm grip. "In *no* small part, little brother. I'm shipping out as a hired sword with a Tukkani trader tomorrow morning. I'll rejoin the first coursers' ship to cross our path and return in less than a year's time. No more prowling the city while I'm gone. Stay out of harm's way and keep your charge alive, eh?"

I saluted him. "Be well."

It felt strange to know that Vironesh was leaving. Our relationship had never been a warm one, but there was depth to it. He was my last connection in Merabaht to the Fortress of the Winds, and the only other living soul who understood what it meant to be a shadow to one of the Sun-Blessed.

Still, it was in my heart that it was the right choice for him; and having found nothing in the annals of Liko of Koronis to suggest that the black

star spider had come from Papa-ka-hondras—or any other place the esteemed scholar had studied—Zariya was of the same opinion.

In the days following Vironesh's departure, we received precious little
information about events outside the women's quarter. King Azarkal had insisted on increased security measures, and the usual networks of spies who
served as sources of information in the quarter—the servants who owed
fealty to Queen Adinah, Captain Tarshim, and those of his men who were
loyal to Queen Rashina—were disrupted. We knew only that the city was
in upheaval; and meanwhile, Sister Nizara's planned retreat to hold a vigil
in the desert must be postponed until a funeral could be held for Tazaresh,
whose body must first be prepared for the pyre.

In the desert, we gave the bodies of the dead into the care of Pahrkun the
Scouring Wind and his creatures; in the city, the dead were consecrated to
Anamuht the Purging Fire. Or at least among those who could afford it.
The bodies of the guards who had been killed in the attack would be given
a place of honor in the base of Prince Tazaresh's pyre. I wondered what was
to become of the dead assailants, but no one in the women's quarter knew.

Seven days after the attack, the House of the Ageless gathered in the
Garden of Sowing Time. The pyre had been constructed on the highest tier
beneath the lone *rhamanthus* tree that towered atop it, which seemed to me
a dangerous prospect.

"Is there no concern that the tree will catch fire?" I murmured to Zariya.
"Or that the heat will damage the seeds?"

She shook her head. "The seeds can only be quickened by lightning cast
by Anamuht herself. The *rhamanthus* are impervious to ordinary heat and
flame."

Twilight was falling when Sister Nizara gave a brief invocation, a torch
kindled from the Sacred Flame in her hand. "Prince Tazaresh of the House
of the Ageless, Sun-Blessed son and brother, may Zar the Sun, father of us
all, receive your spirit, and the spirits of your brave companions, with kindness and mercy."

She lit the pyre, thrusting the torch into the southwestern corner of the
structure. By design, the pyre burned slowly at first, until the creeping
flames reached the portion wrought of oil-wood. Then it spread in a rush,

gouts of flame rising upward. Once it was well and truly ablaze, the pyre burned hotter than a forge. I could make out the bodies of the guards, embalmed in sweet oils and wrapped in linens, twisting in the flames at the base of the pyre. On a platform at the very top, the shrouded figure of Tazaresh had not yet been touched by the fire.

Above the pyre, the tallest *rhamanthus* stretched into the sky, the sun's light yet gilding its crown; impervious to heat and flame; impervious to the petty machinations and griefs of the long-lived mortals clustered around its base; impervious to all save the will of Anamuht the Purging Fire.

"What is it that you require of us, Anamuht?" I whispered, gazing upward at the tree. "Only tell us, and I will see it is done." Beside me, Zariya slipped her hand into mine and squeezed it.

The flames reached Tazaresh's body. Save for Zariya, the royal women wailed and rent their garments in mourning, some of it genuine. Princess Fazarah was among them; of course, she was Makesha's daughter, too. The soft glow of *khementaran* pulsed at her wrists and her throat, rendered faint by the pyre's blaze. I had asked Vironesh once why he had not entered *khementaran* when Prince Kazaran died; he told me that it only came upon the Sun-Blessed.

Why? I wondered. Because of Zar's fire that was said to run in their veins?

All the fragrant oils beneath the starless sky could not entirely disguise the scent of charred flesh. King Azarkal's face was impassive as he watched his son's body burn; the son he favored, the son who might have been responsible for the death of the son the king had favored over him. The son who might have been murdered in turn, the victim of yet another endless conspiracy.

There are too many of us, and we live too long.

I had a wild urge to seize Zariya and flee from this place, flee to the depths of the desert where honor and status were cleaner and simpler things. We could live among the tribesfolk.

Zariya had said that given the choice, she would wed a kind man. Unexpectedly, I thought of the boy Ahran whom I'd met at the gathering of the clans, the lively, laughing boy who'd waded into the Eye of Zar with me and poured water over my head in the Three-Moon Blessing. I'd wager he was growing into a kind young man, one who would see the bright spirit within her and treasure it.

And there in the desert, I would . . . what? Ah, there my vision went dark. I could not see a place for myself.

As though sensing my unspoken thoughts, Zariya gave my hand another reassuring squeeze.

Her place was here.

And mine was beside her, no matter what dreams of the desert I might harbor; here, and nowhere else.

Despite the size of the structure, it burned more quickly than I would have guessed, collapsing onto itself and sending a vast shower of sparks into the darkening sky, accompanied by the ululations of the royal women. The sight would be visible clear down to the lowest level of Merabaht. In other times, I understood, it would allow the denizens of the city to mourn along with the House of the Ageless. I doubted many of them were mourning to-night.

Once the pyre had burned down to embers and the charred bones of the dead were indistinguishable from the handful of beams that continued to smolder, most of the royal family retreated to the Hall of Pleasant Accord, where a feast was to be held in Tazaresh's honor. As High Priestess, Sister Nizara would remain behind to hold a vigil until the last ember died. In the morning, she and the other priestesses would spread the ashes throughout the Garden of Sowing Time and gather the bones that they might be ground into a coarse meal to fertilize the *rhamanthus* trees.

I would rather have been gathering bones in the garden than attending that feast. It began civilly enough, with platters of lamb stew cooked with saffron and dates served over a soft grain, flagons of palm wine and toasts to Tazaresh's memory, many of them offered by Kozar and Bazar, the twin sons of Kayaresh, who was the second-junior-most queen. Simple souls, I remembered Vironesh had deemed them; good foot soldiers in someone else's campaign. Based on the genuine quality of their grief, it seemed that someone had been Prince Tazaresh.

If King Azarkal was unwontedly reserved, no one noticed. It was after the meal had concluded, when talk turned to the attacks and their after-math, that the mood of the occasion changed.

I could see a storm gathering on Princess Fazarah's features, the pulse-points of *khementaran* beating more rapidly as the twins argued heatedly for doubling the City Guard and taking more aggressive measures in the lower levels. Seated beside her, her husband, Tarkhal, stroked her back in an ef-fort to calm her.

It was to no avail.

"You are wrong," she announced, unable to hold her tongue any longer. "Don't you understand, the City Guard is part of the problem! Everyone knows they're riddled with corruption." She turned to the king. "Father, if you want to root out the malcontents, a show of beneficence and the offer of a reward would do a great deal more than an increased show of force."

King Azarkal gave her a brooding look. "Do you say so? The time for this counsel would have been before the Children of Miasmus attacked our household, daughter, not after."

Fazarah's color rose. "I tried to offer you counsel, Father!" she said with dogged persistence. "You would not hear it. It has taken my brother's death to give me a chance to speak!"

The king's features, unlined features that appeared younger than his own daughter's, hardened. "You overstep your bounds."

"She speaks the truth, Your Majesty," her husband, Tarkhal, murmured. His gaze was downcast, but the line of his jaw was stubborn. "Fazarah and I know the hearts of the less fortunate of Merabaht in a way that you can-not. Will you not at least listen to her?"

Back and forth they went, voices rising with increased passion and acri-mony, other voices chiming in as the argument escalated, Queen Makesha wailing at the desecration of her son's funeral feast and the other royal women pleading for an end to the unpleasantness.

Me, I wished I was elsewhere, and I knew Zariya did, too. As much as she admired her rebel sister, she loved her royal father, and it grieved her to hear them quarrel so violently.

While the discussion raged, Prince Dozaren seated himself on a cushion next to Zariya. "I have a gift for you, little sister," he whispered, holding his cupped hands out to her. "'Tis but a trifling thing. I meant to give it to you the night of Izaria's wedding. Perhaps it will give you at least one happy memory of tonight."

She took a shallow breath. "Not another bird, surely!"

"Oh, but it is!" Dozaren made his hands flutter like wings, then opened them to reveal a wooden whistle carved in the shape of a bird. He put the mouthpiece to his lips and blew a warbling tune, then gave it to her. "Now when your little friends sing their merry songs, you can join them."

Zariya examined the whistle with delight. "It's so cleverly made! Wherever did you find such a thing?"

Prince Dozaren smiled at her. "I met a cunning carver in the market one day and thought of you. Do you like it?"

She kissed his cheek. "Very much so, my darling. Thank you."

Unexpectedly, Dozaren's gaze shifted to me, his expression turning to one of grave respect. He moved his cushion so that he and Zariya and I were seated in a cluster. "Forgive me, chosen. I have been remiss in not thanking you for your service. I have heard wondrous tales of your prowess during the attack." He offered me a salute, then took my right hand in his, clasping it warmly and looking into my eyes. "I have no words to tell you how grateful I am that my favorite sister has such a protector."

Although his tone was utterly sincere, I was uncomfortable. It was the first time I'd been the recipient of his attention, and I discovered he had an unnerving way of looking at a person as though no one else in the world existed. He had fine features with lashes as long as a girl's, and he wore the mask of his youth more lightly than most members of the House of the Ageless. I had to remind myself that this smooth-skinned young man was at least seventy-five years of age.

I inclined my head to him. "It is my honor."

Dozaren's thumb stroked the back of my hand in a manner that was unsettling and intimate. "I am not the warrior that my brother Tazaresh was, but I have some skill with a blade. Perhaps you would consent to school me in the techniques of the brotherhood?"

I fought the urge to yank my hand away. I didn't know what game the prince was playing at, but it stirred strange sensations in me and made me uneasy. "Of course."

"My thanks." He turned my hand over, running his thumb over the thick ridge of callus below the base of my fingers. "Here's to the hand that saved Zariya's life. I would kiss it if I dared."

"Leave Khai be, my dearest." There was a rare edge to Zariya's voice. "It's disrespectful of you to flirt at our brother's funeral. And where is your lady wife this evening, anyway?"

Dozaren released my hand and smiled at her. "Eilish is indisposed. And flirting with your shadow is more respectful than arguing with Father, little sister. Tazaresh would certainly have preferred the former." He rose gracefully. "I'll arrange a time when we might spar, chosen."

I managed a nod. When he had withdrawn to his own seat, I gave Zariya an inquiring look.

She responded with the Shahalim hand signal that meant *later*.

At the head of the low table, King Azarkal was declaring a forcible resolution to the argument with his rebel daughter, who bowed her head in a gesture of acquiescence that did little to conceal the fact that her anger continued to smolder as surely as her brother's funeral pyre. The king surveyed his unruly household, and the mask of *his* youth weighed heavy on his features.

"My son is dead," he said in a harsh voice. "Let us offer one last toast to his memory." He hoisted his goblet. "To Tazaresh!"

"To Tazaresh," we echoed, and drank.

TWENTY-NINE

While Prince Tazaresh's funeral pyre crumbled into ashes in the Garden of Sowing Time, Zariya and I whispered in her chambers.

"I am sorry if Dozaren disturbed you." Her eyes glimmered in the light of a single oil lamp. I sat cross-legged on my pallet, resting my chin on folded arms on the edge of her bed. "He meant no harm by it."

I could still feel his thumb stroking my hand, and the unsettling sensations it stirred in me. "Why, then?"

Zariya hesitated. "Dozaren takes his pleasure with men as well as women," she said quietly. "It is why our father has never favored him."

I said nothing.

Her gaze was shrewd. "Have I shocked you?"

I shook my head. "No, I knew such things existed. Brother Yarit told me so. But why me?"

"Oh, my lovely boy!" Zariya gave her soft, breathless laugh. "Need you ask?" She touched my cheek. "You combine the best attributes of both. I daresay my brother looked upon you tonight, took notice, and desired you. But we have never spoken of desire, you and I, have we?"

My shoulders tensed. "No."

She regarded me. "I often know your thoughts before you give voice to them, my darling. And yet, I know nothing of your desires. It is a closed door I have not attempted to open."

I looked away. "There is nothing to tell."

"Have you never considered your body as aught but a weapon, Khai?"

There was genuine curiosity in Zariya's voice. "Have you never considered it as an instrument of pleasure?"

I flushed and looked back at her in the flickering lamplight. "Have *you*?"

"Ah, well, it is a damaged instrument," she said wryly. "But yes, of course, I have considered it."

"Of course?" I echoed.

"I am crippled in body, my darling, not in desire or imagination," Zariya said. "Do you not know that most of the royal women, including my own mother, are convinced I've already taken you as a lover?"

I stared at her in disbelief. "Is such a thing even permitted?"

"Permitted?" Zariya laughed. "Oh, gods, no! But that's never stopped such dalliances from happening in the women's quarter, and it's considerably less risky than dallying with the captain of the Queen's Guard like Rashina. You've never noticed?" I shook my head mutely. "Ah, and now I *have* shocked you," she observed. "Though perhaps that is not altogether a bad thing. As charming as I find your innocence, it may be to your benefit if you were not quite so naive in the ways of the world."

"Shall I take your brother for a lover, then?" I said stiffly. "Or both of you?"

"Don't be angry with me, my shadow," she said. "It is only that desire is a part of being human, and I would not have you deprive yourself of such knowledge, or be discomfited by its existence." She yawned. "Forgive me, but it has been a long and difficult day."

I dragged my pallet to block the door to Zariya's bedchamber and blew out the lamp, but sleep evaded me.

Desire.

Was that what I felt when Dozaren stroked my hand? I didn't trust him; and yet something within me had responded to his touch, to the way that he had looked at me. And something within me had been profoundly shocked by the ease with which Zariya had said the royal women believed us lovers. What she referenced with such careless ease seemed a world-shattering notion to me.

At length, I did sleep; and in the morning, I found that I looked at the world a little bit differently.

I discerned relationships between the king's wives that had utterly evaded me before, affinities and jealousies that were owed to more than just ambition, rivalry, and shifting alliances. I saw the indulgent assumptions that they made when they looked at Zariya and me.

Zariya . . . yes, I looked at her differently, too. My soul's twin, the reality of her presence still so new to me. I saw her fierceness, her delicate beauty, and her courage in a different way. I considered the shape of her lips, the subtle hollow at the base of her throat. At unexpected times, my heart gave a strange, startled flutter within my breast at the sight of her.

I could not help it.

She bore it with quiet amusement.

I had assumed that Sister Nizara would postpone her retreat for at least a day after holding vigil over Prince Tazaresh's pyre, but she paid a visit to the women's quarter to offer a final word of condolence to her mother and bid us farewell before venturing into the desert.

"Are you sure it's wise?" Queen Makesha fretted. "If anything were to happen to you . . ." She did not finish her thought.

"I am sure of nothing, Mother," Sister Nizara said somberly, her eyes red-rimmed with sleeplessness. "And that is why I must do this."

The High Priestess meant to ride to the Fortress of the Winds to take counsel with Brother Yarit and retreat to one of the high places in the mountains where the Seers sought clarity, hoping that Anamuht might find her there. A handful of priestesses and two score of the Royal Guard would accompany her.

"Have you any words for the Seer, Khai?" Sister Nizara asked me.

"Tell him about the Mad Priest and the sign of the black star." I paused, remembering the maimed woman at the Lucky Tortoise. Why *had* she aided me? Unless it was for some deeper reason that had not yet been revealed, it could only be out of a sense of guilt at having betrayed Brother Yarit. "And tell him . . . tell him I think that Belisha did her best to make amends."

The High Priestess looked bemused. "Belisha?"

I nodded. "He will know what it means."

In the wake of shocking violence and unexpected grief, the women's quarter settled slowly into a new pattern of normalcy. I spent more time training the Queen's Guard and recommended to Captain Tarshim that he replace their ceremonial spears, which were impractical in close quarters, with *yakhans* or a serviceable short sword. He gave me a dour look and informed me that the procurement of steel weaponry was a sensitive topic at the moment. It was a pity, but I did my best with what Vironesh had taught me of the tactics of fighting with a spear.

At least it helped hone their skills and it kept me from losing my wits at the sheer tedium. Within days of the funeral, I would have welcomed the opportunity to spar with Prince Dozaren no matter how disconcerting I found the experience, but he had not contacted me.

Eventually Zariya took pity on me and dispatched me to the city to learn what I might.

The lower levels of Merabaht were in a sullen mood. It had been almost two weeks since the attack, but the City Guard was still out in force, swaggering through the streets, hands on the hilts of their *kopars*. There were few women venturing out in public, and those who were hurried about their business. Here and there I saw the sign of the black star painted on walls and doors, and it seemed to me that it had gone from a symbol of desecration to one of defiance. For the first time since I'd been pelted with rocks in Three-Copper Quarter, I felt apprehensive.

"Hey, girl!" The leader of a squadron of City Guardsmen hailed me. "What are you doing out here on your own? Don't you know it's dangerous?" He sauntered over and looked me up and down, his men gathered behind him. "Looking to put a bit of food on the table, are you?" He jingled a purse at his belt. "We'll help you out in exchange for a bit of sport."

"No, thank you," I murmured, and moved to pass him.

He moved to block me, his men fanning out. "Be polite, eh? I made you a generous offer."

I eyed him. "And I am not who or what you think I am. Step aside."

The guard leader laughed and raised both hands in a gesture of mock fear. "Oh, dear! What is it I've found here? A mouse with the heart of a lion?"

What little patience I possessed deserted me. I plucked his twin *kopars* from his sash and bashed him neatly on either side of the head. He went down like a sack of rocks. The other guards stood stunned.

"*Shadow,*" someone whispered from an alley; I'd betrayed the guise of my women's garments with a single display of prowess. "*Shadow!*"

The back of my neck prickled. The Mad Priest had exhorted his followers to kill me; I could not guess if they yet wanted me dead, or if in defying the City Guard, I might, like the black star sign, become a symbol of something else. And I did not mean to stay and find out. "Stand down or face the Scouring Wind's wrath," I said softly to the remaining guards. They moved out of my way with alacrity. I tossed their leader's *kopars* on the hard-packed dirt of the street and made my way out of Three-Copper Quarter, heading for the wharves.

In the harbor, I found more guards—Royal Guardsmen this time—and a commotion.

"I am a man of Granth and an honest trader!" a thickset Granthian fellow was shouting in fury. "You have no right to detain me! No right!"

Intrigued, I sidled closer.

"No one is saying you are guilty of wrongdoing, messire." The assurance was uttered by a slender, nervous-looking Zarkhoumi in robes befitting a wealthy merchant or a palace official. "But I have been tasked by the king with examining the manifests for cargo delivered within these past six months." He waved a piece of parchment. "According to this, Prince Elizar of the House of the Ageless commissioned and accepted delivery of a shipment of Granthian daggers from you."

The Granthian glowered. "What of it? Do you say that if a crown prince of Zarkhoum wants to buy five hundred pig-stickers, I should refuse him?"

"Again, no one says such a thing," the official assured him. "It is only that King Azarkal wishes to know more of this bargain."

"Well, tell him to ask his bloody damn son!" the Granthian said in an aggrieved tone.

Prince Elizar.

That was news in truth, and a greater piece of it than I had expected to learn; and if it had not been for my encounter with the City Guard, I would not have been in a position to learn it before it reached the court. I did not wait to see how events played out with the Granthian, but made a hasty retreat back to the palace.

I found Zariya in the Hall of Harmonious Beauty and signed *talk privately* to her; she excused herself to use the privy.

"What is it, my darling?" she asked in her chambers.

"I was down at the harbor," I said. "Your father's men have found a Granthian trader with a piece of paper that shows he delivered a shipment of daggers to your brother Elizar."

Zariya sat down on the divan and covered her mouth, eyes wide with surprise. "Elizar!"

"You don't think him capable of it?" I asked.

She frowned. "I thought him resigned to the fact that our father favored Tazaresh, and Kazaran before him."

"Both of whom are dead," I said. "To the lion go the spoils."

"Unless the lion gets caught," Zariya said. "The question is, what do we do with this information? Is there any advantage to being the first to possess it? I might warn Adinah and earn my way out of her bad graces," she mused. "If Elizar did it, she had to be involved. She's the ambitious one; he cares more for his precious collection than the throne. But then, if Elizar is guilty, then he is guilty of sedition and behind the attack on the wedding procession as surely as the Mad Priest. No." She shook her head; "I think we do nothing with this knowledge, my heart. It will be out soon enough."

"Perhaps," I said. "The trader was uncooperative."

"Granthians are notoriously stubborn," she noted. "And you said there was a record of the shipment in the manifest. I daresay the ambassador will be called in to sort it out in short order."

Zariya was right. By the day's end, the details had reached the women's quarter. Prince Elizar had been accused of purchasing a shipment of Granthian daggers and using them to arm the Children of Miasmus.

Under duress, the trader had confirmed that the daggers matched the weapons used in the attack. He reported that the purchase was arranged by a representative of the prince and produced a letter of commission stamped with Elizar's personal seal, an intricate stamp familiar to dozens of traders who had procured curios for his collection over the years. Elizar adamantly denied the charges and claimed that the stamp must have been stolen from him, even as another precious item had been stolen from him. A search of his quarters determined that the stamp was in his possession.

Since the evidence was strong, but not conclusive, King Azarkal had his eldest son thrown in the royal dungeon.

The women's quarter was buzzing like a hornets' nest, and Queen Adinah was in a towering rage. That evening the king paid a visit to her chambers, and it was not the sort of conjugal visit of which she would boast on the morrow; her sharp accusations and the king's angry rebuttals rang throughout the quarter. To drown them out, Zariya played softly on the little whistle that Dozaren had given her, coaxing sleepy chirps and trills from her birds in their wooden cage.

My heart was uneasy.

In a mere two weeks' time, the candidates for the throne of Zarkhoum had dwindled from five to three: Prince Tazaresh slain, and now Prince Elizar disgraced and imprisoned. No one had seen what befell Tazaresh in the chaos of the attack, but he had died with a dagger planted between his ribs.

Elizar could not have done it. He was mounted, and his horse had not been hamstrung. Any blow he would have struck against his brother would have been a slashing blow from on high.

It might mean nothing. If he was behind the arm of conspiracy that drove the Children of Miasmus, he could easily have commissioned an assassin to dispatch Tazaresh in the heat of battle.

I sat on the carpet listening to Zariya play a lilting tune and thinking dark thoughts. The whistle was carved so that the wooden bird's wings rose and fell with each note she played. It was indeed very cleverly wrought.

Zariya's profile in silhouette against the dusk falling in the lush green garden behind her was very pretty.

I had not forgotten what she said to me about desire. I was yet uncertain what I felt about it.

Some bitter resolution must have been reached in Queen Adinah's chambers, for the arguing voices that echoed through the quarter fell silent.

Zariya lowered her whistle and contemplated me. "What is it that you're thinking? It feels weighty."

"You will not like it," I warned her.

Her gaze was unwavering. "Perhaps not, but I would hear it nonetheless."

I took a deep breath. "The only proof that Elizar commissioned this purchase of weapons is the stamp of his personal seal. And there is a thing that your brother Dozaren said that troubles me."

Zariya raised her brows at me. "Which is?"

I nodded at the whistle. "He met a cunning carver in the market one day."

She was silent for a long moment. "So you think he had a copy of Elizar's seal made? Why would he let such a thing slip if he were guilty?"

"Brother Yarit once told me that one of the greatest challenges a thief faces is keeping his mouth shut," I said. "That there is an almost irresistible temptation to boast after a successful job, to have one's skill and cleverness admired."

"It would be a damnably subtle boast." Zariya's tone was neutral and I sensed she was displeased.

"Your brother Dozaren is a subtle fellow." I raised my hands palms-upward. "It is only a thought."

Zariya hesitated, then shook her head. "I could find it easier to entertain the notion if you and I had not been targeted in the attack," she said. "I am aware that Dozaren's kindness toward me may have begun as an attempt to curry favor with our father, but I do believe he has grown genuinely fond of me."

"I do not think the Mad Priest's actions were under anyone's control,"

I said. "I suspect he made for an unpredictable ally at best." She said nothing. "Are you angry that I said so?"

"No." Her reply was swift and sure. "For telling me the truth when it is exactly what I asked of you? Of course not, my darling. It is only that I hope you are wrong."

For her sake, I hoped so, too.

But I didn't think I was.

THIRTY

As though to mock my suspicions, the following morning I received a missive from Prince Dozaren making good on his request to spar with me.

We met in the courtyard adjacent to the Hall of Pleasant Accord, where he professed himself interested in the two-handed technique of wielding a *yakhan* and *kopar* unique to the Brotherhood of Pahrkun. I did my best to instruct him, but it was a difficult thing to master, and all the more so when one had years of training in a completely different fighting style to overcome. Still, I learned in the process that Dozaren had been overly modest. He possessed more than a little skill with a single blade; certainly enough to have dispatched his brother in the thick of battle.

I wondered if he meant for me to know it.

I wondered if I was right about him.

"How can you be but sixteen years of age?" he exclaimed in a good-natured tone when we had finished. "You fight like a seasoned warrior in his prime! No, belay that. You fight like no one I've ever seen, Khai of the Fortress of the Winds." He gazed at me beneath his long eyelashes. "It's a pleasure to watch you."

Only a few days ago, his regard would have made me uncomfortable; now, I felt differently, armored against his charm by what I suspected. "I am what I was trained to be, Your Highness."

"And nothing more?" Dozaren inquired. "Is that your sole purpose in life? It seems . . . wasteful."

"Do you seek a dalliance?" I asked him bluntly.

It startled him into laughter. "Does it appear thus? I suppose it must. As

Zariya noted, I have a habit of flirting." He shrugged and sheathed his blade. "You are a stranger to me, chosen, a stranger who in the blink of an eye became closer to my favorite sister than any other living soul beneath the starless sky. Do you blame me for wishing to know you better?"

"By sparring?" I said.

Dozaren gave me a disarming smile. "It seemed to me that steel is the language you speak most fluently. But I would certainly *welcome* a dalliance. Do you fear for your honor? Such things can be managed discreetly, you know."

"The only dishonor I fear is failing in my duty to Zariya," I said to him. "Your Highness, I do not know what game we are playing. I do not care whether or not the king names you his successor, and I do not care . . ." I paused, wanting to give voice to my suspicions without stating them outright. "If I were a whit less skilled, if I had not had Vironesh as a mentor, Zariya would have been abducted or killed in that attack. Only tell me this. Do you mean her harm for any reason?"

He drew in a sharp breath. "No! Gods, no!"

His response was as swift and sure as hers had been last night, and I gauged it genuine. Once again, Zariya was right; he did care for her.

But I was right, too. I felt it in the silence that stretched between us, the balance of power shifting back and forth. I summoned Pahrkun's wind and looked into the spaces between inside him; between what was said and left unsaid, between ambition and affection, between resentment and resolve, between calculation and risk, and I saw the truth written there.

Dozaren was guilty.

I knew it.

He must have seen the knowledge reflected in my face. Breaking my gaze, he looked away from me. "Your suspicions do me an injustice, chosen. I could never wish to harm Zariya."

"And yet the Mad Priest sought to do so," I said, edging closer to the unspoken truth. "*Kill the shadow, seize the princess.* That's what he said."

"There is a reason they called him the Mad Priest," Dozaren said dryly. "He also claimed that Miasmus will swallow the world in darkness. As I told you, I am sincerely grateful for your service that night."

So I was right about that, too. The Mad Priest had been a weapon no one could control. I wanted to ask him more, but I sensed that this was a moment that could easily go awry, so I chose my words with care. "Why do you suppose he wanted me dead and Zariya seized?" I asked. "Have the physicians learned anything about the man and that . . . thing inside him?"

"No." Dozaren shook his head. "I only know sailors' gossip. There are rumors that it's happened elsewhere. Apparently he was a perfectly ordinary fellow, at least for a pirate, until the thing afflicted him. His shipmates abandoned him here after he began raving."

"And found an eager audience for his message in the poor quarters of Merabaht," I murmured. "A tinderbox awaiting a spark."

Dozaren glanced around to confirm no one else had entered the garden while we were engaged in conversation. "Chosen, I do not believe my sister Fazarah and her husband are wrong in their estimation of the realm's troubles," he said in a low voice, and it seemed to me that the mask of his casual charm had been replaced with something more serious. "And I will tell you this: My brother Tazaresh would have been a ruler in exactly the same mold as our father."

It was as close, I thought, as he would come to an outright admission of guilt. "And Elizar?"

"Elizar would be worse," he said.

"And you would be a reformer in the mold of your rebel sister?" I asked, keeping my tone light.

"If you're asking if I would dismantle the monarchy to install a system of governance in accordance with the code of Obid the Stern, no." He summoned a wry smile. "It is a little *too* stern for my taste. But if you are asking if I would seek a better balance between the people of Zarkhoum, yes."

I studied Dozaren, thinking that he could not have done this on his own. "Do you count Fazarah as an ally?"

He laughed. "My sister Fazarah would make for a dangerous ally. You have seen there is no love lost between her and our father."

So not Fazarah; no, of course not. Her grief at her brother's death had been genuine and she would not have countenanced a plot to kill him. And yet someone with ties to the lower levels of Merabaht had to have been involved to organize such an attack, to identify three hundred men desperate enough to undertake it, to distribute weapons enough to arm them.

Brother Yarit had taught me to throw *zims* blindfolded; with Pahrkun's wind yet stirring within me, I threw out a question like a dagger in search of a target. "What of her husband?"

Something subtle shifted in Dozaren's expression. "Tarkhal is a good man who believes in the work he does, but he holds no sway in the House of the Ageless. What use would he be as an ally?" He cleared his throat and steered away from the topic. "I would gladly count our dear Zariya as one, but she has made it clear that she does not wish to play at politics. Still, if her heart were to change, I would welcome it."

"I do not know if she could condone your methods," I said to him.

"To the lion go the spoils." He fixed me with an intent gaze. "She knows that as well as I do. Tell me, chosen, how will you relate this conversation to her?"

I hadn't the faintest idea.

"I do not know, Your Highness," I admitted. "But your sister and I have sworn to be honest with each other."

"It is an admirable goal," he said mildly, his manner suggesting such a thing was impossible.

"It is an extension of who and what we are," I said. "In and of ourselves and to each other, Sun-Blessed and shadow. I do not expect you to understand it."

Now Dozaren's expression held a complex and undecipherable mixture of emotions. "Should I envy or pity you for it, Khai of the Fortress of the Winds?"

"I do not know that either, Your Highness," I said. "But if you are asking if I will share this conversation with anyone save Zariya, if I will give voice to what I think we have said without saying here today . . ." I shook my head. "No. I will not. I told you, I do not care about the succession. My duty is to Zariya, and Zariya alone. I think she loves you too well to betray you, and I am glad of it, for it means neither you nor I need attempt to kill the other over this conversation."

He offered me a half-mocking salute. "At least not yet. I confess, I would not relish the prospect. Are we done here?"

I paused. "Do you know who was responsible for infecting Zariya with Dhanbu fever when she was a child?"

"So she suspects as much?" He shook his head. "Not for certain, no. But I'd wager on Queen Adinah."

"Whose fortunes have been brought low with her eldest and last surviving son's fall from grace," I observed.

"Yes." There was no apology in his voice.

I returned his salute. "Now we are done."

Knowing that Zariya would be in equal measure grieved by our separation and curious about my encounter with Dozaren, I should have returned to the women's quarter to report to her, but my heart and mind were too full. Instead, I departed from the palace and took to the streets of the city, enduring the aching hollowness engendered by my Sun-Blessed charge's absence in exchange for the solace of solitude. The knowledge that I had gained this day felt like a series of stones cast into a deep well.

One . . .

Two . . .

Three . . .

Dozaren was guilty; Dozaren had helped orchestrate the attack and was responsible for one brother's death, for another brother's imprisonment.

In this, I gauged there was a good possibility that he was in fact aided by his sister's husband, Tarkhal, who was well connected in the impoverished quarters and might have believed strongly enough in his cause to engage in a conspiracy to murder his own wife's brother.

The Mad Priest's reasons were his own.

Although I had no conscious destination in mind, my feet carried me to the harbor, which was relatively quiet today. Without thinking, I had ventured out fully armed in my desert woolens; realizing I had done so, I left my face bare. Today, I wanted to be myself. Folks who would not have spared me a glance as a veiled woman saw the marks of Pahrkun on my face and saluted me. I did not venture into Three-Copper Quarter, and no one in the vicinity of the wharves had ever hissed *shadow* at me.

In the harbor, I found an empty pier and made my way to the end of it, sitting on the edge and letting my feet dangle. I gazed at the sun sparkling on the water and watched crab fishermen in the bay drawing up their pots. It reminded me that I had not yet sent word to my family in their coastal fishing village, a notion that was still immensely strange to me.

And I could not begin to think what I would say to them.

Dear Mother and Father, whom I remember not at all, I am well and serving as Princess Zariya's shadow in the Palace of the Sun. Today I learned that her favorite brother is behind a deadly conspiracy. Do I have any siblings? If so, I hope they are not in the habit of murdering each other.

It was going to be a hard thing to tell Zariya; hard because she did not want to believe it, and hard because it was difficult to explain my certainty. I had no proof. Dozaren had not actually admitted his guilt.

Then again, if he had, it would have been a dangerous piece of knowledge to possess.

I thought about these things.

And I thought about desire, a subject we had not discussed since the day that Zariya broached it.

Do you not know that most of the royal women, including my own mother, are convinced I've already taken you as a lover?

Of course I had not known, but it seemed to me that there was a question beneath the question. On the surface, it was a question posed by my far more worldly and sophisticated Sun-Blessed princess, who already knew the answer, to prod me out of my naïveté. Ah, but underneath, it was a question posed by an uncertain young woman who had been taught to believe herself damaged goods by cruel women jealous of her father's affection for her.

Am I worthy of desire?

And that was knowledge that made my heart ache for Zariya. She was oh, so very beautiful to me, and her strength and courage and daring vulnerability only made her the more so. Since she had posed me the question and I had begun to look at the world through different eyes, I had begun to see that it would be a profound and wondrous thing to explore with my soul's twin, to discover my body as an instrument of pleasure and not merely

a well-honed instrument of death. But I thought that it would be a dangerous thing, too.

I sat in contemplation until I had reached a conclusion, well past the
beginning of the midday rest.

When I returned to the palace, I found Zariya reclining on the divan in
her sitting room and reading.

"I thought to see you back ages ago, my heart!" She pushed herself upright. "Is everything all right? You didn't quarrel with Dozaren, did you?"

"Quarrel?" I shook my head. "No. But I have two things I must tell you,
and neither one is easy."

"Well, *that* sounds ominous," she observed.

I sat beside her on the divan. "First, there is something that I very much
want to do." Taking Zariya's face in my hands, I leaned over and kissed her,
hoping I was doing it right. It caught her by surprise; she stiffened slightly,
then softened and returned my kiss with unabashed ardor. Her skin was as
smooth as silk and her lips were the softest thing I'd ever felt.

It was so sweet and lovely it grieved me to end it, but I did.

Zariya regarded me gravely, her dark eyes luminous, a faint furrow
etched between her brows.

"I have been thinking." My voice was a bit unsteady. "We are already so
much more than lovers, you and I. In some ways, what would it matter to
take one more step? We know each other's hearts and minds. Why should
we not know each other's bodies as well? But I do not think it is the purpose
for which Pahrkun and Anamuht joined our souls at birth, and there is
this." Vironesh had been broken and devastated by Prince Kazaran's death;
how much worse might it have been if they were lovers? I clasped my hands
tightly together in my lap. "Zariya, if you were to become any more precious to me, I fear my heart truly *would* shatter into a thousand pieces."

Outside, the sun shone brightly. The birds in their cage hopped about
and chirped merrily.

Zariya gave me a quiet smile filled with love and regret and understanding. "You are wise beyond your years, my darling. Now, what is this second
difficult thing you must tell me?"

I told her about my conversation with Dozaren.

She listened without comment, and when I had finished, rose from the divan, retrieved her canes, and hobbled into the garden.

I waited a moment before following to stand patiently behind her, seeing from the angle of her head that she knew I was there.

"I did not want it to be true," she said presently.

"I know," I murmured.

"You're sure of it?"

"Yes."

"I suppose I should be grateful that he does not wish me harm," she said in a flat tone. "Since it seems he is very good at inflicting it. You bring me information like a cat dragging a dead sparrow across my doorstep, and once again, I do not know what to do with it. A great many men lost their lives to this plot." She paused in thought. "The honorable thing to do would be to inform Father. But we have no proof, and I fear that making an enemy of the one contestant for the throne who cares for me is not the wisest course."

"I could kill him," I said quietly.

Zariya rounded on me. "And be executed for it? You will do no such thing!"

I swallowed. "I could do it in such a manner that no one would ever know. There are ways."

"No." Her voice was adamant. "There has been altogether too much murder among the Sun-Blessed. Even if I were willing, I would not allow you to sacrifice your honor over this. And to what end? To protect me? And yet Dozaren would make alliance with me, and I am safe so long as I say nothing. To punish him for his betrayal? And yet he is playing by our father's rules. To avenge Tazaresh? Tazaresh played by the same rules. To exonerate Elizar? I think not."

"The guards were innocent," I reminded her. "And the poor folk who were slaughtered little better than tools."

Zariya sighed. "Would that I'd been born a man," she said with rare bitterness. "I could contest for the throne myself."

A thought came to me. "Your father has lost three sons," I said to her. "He could replace one. He could declare you *bhazim*."

She stared at me. "Oh, my darling! It's a bit late for that, don't you think? And I doubt I'd live out the week if he did. Rashina would drown me in the bath the first time you turned your back on her."

"I'd never leave your side," I promised her.

"You're serious." Zariya shook her head. "Khai . . . perhaps it would be different if I had been raised to it, but I wasn't. And Dozaren and the twins have decades of experience on me. When all is said and done, I'm a sixteen-year-old girl with absolutely no knowledge of governance."

"Yes, and a very clever girl with quick wits, a scholar's soul, and a kind and brave heart," I said. "I'd wager that Liko of Koronis or one of his ilk have some profound observations on governance to impart to you. And your father might well live for another hundred years."

"Not if Anamuht fails to quicken the *rhamanthus*," she said soberly. "And to that end . . . do not mistake me, dearest. I adore the fact that you believe me capable of such a thing. And I will consider it, although I have no idea whatsoever what my father might say if I posed it to him. Regardless, I will do nothing until Nizara returns from the desert, for it is in my heart that if the Sun-Blessed cannot find a way to regain Anamuht's favor, all of this is moot."

I inclined my head to her. "And Dozaren?"

"Dozaren." Zariya sighed again. "What he did troubles me deeply, and I am not prepared to ally myself with him. But I will send him an innocuous note, something to let him know I do not intend to betray him." She gave me an apprehensive look. "Does that disappoint you?"

Did it?

I thought about that night of blood and fire, the Mad Priest and the crawling thing in his chest, and there was a part of me that was shocked to the core by the notion that Prince Dozaren might suffer no penalty for having orchestrated it. But while I could mourn the innocent lives lost, I could not grieve for the death of Prince Tazaresh, who was likely a murderer in his own right, and I could not grieve for the wrongful imprisonment of Prince Elizar, who had had his chamberlain executed when the Teardrop was stolen from him; the one thing I had not told Zariya despite the honesty of which I'd been so quick to boast.

Above all, I could not condemn any decision that led to her safety.

Honor beyond honor.

"No," I said honestly to Zariya. "All that matters to me is that you are safe. In that regard, I think you have chosen wisely; and I think it is wise, too, to await Sister Nizara's return."

"I am glad." She smiled at me. "And I thank you, my darling."

"For suggesting a course of action that would earn you the enmity of your entire family or for dragging unwelcome information across your doorstep like a cat with a dead sparrow?" I inquired.

She flushed. "For the kiss."

THIRTY-ONE

Some two weeks later, Sister Nizara returned.

Her entourage had departed without fanfare, but folk in the city had taken notice of it and word of their return spread quickly when their party was sighted along the River Ouris. Despite her comments regarding dead sparrows, Zariya was impatient enough for knowledge that she sent me to observe their reentry into the city.

People turned out to line the streets and watch. No one threatened violence against the High Priestess of Anamuht or the escort of Royal Guardsmen flanking the procession, but the mood was strained.

Sister Nizara wore the tall crimson headdress and the veil, so I could not read her face or the faces of the priestesses accompanying her, but from the way she held herself in the saddle, shoulders braced as though carrying an unexpected burden, I knew something had transpired.

"Elder Sister!" someone called out. "Why has Anamuht the Purging Fire forsaken the Sun-Blessed?"

She raised one hand and her entourage halted. "Anamuht has not forsaken us," she said from behind her veil, her voice hoarse. "I will say no more until I have taken counsel with King Azarkal and my kindred."

I trailed the party for a few blocks, then seeing neither new information to be gained nor danger averted, slipped past them to return to the palace to engage in pointless speculation with Zariya.

What had transpired in the desert, we learned soon enough, for Sister Nizara convened a meeting that evening in the Hall of Pleasant Accord with the king and all the members of the House of the Ageless present.

"Well?" King Azarkal was as impatient as his youngest daughter. "Tell us, what have you learned? Are there amends that must be made? Will Anamuht grant us a harvest or not?"

She bent her gaze toward him. Her unveiled face looked gaunt and sun-scorched, the sockets of her eyes hollow. "On the advice of the Seer, I held a vigil in one of the high places of the desert. On the third day, the Sacred Twins appeared in the distance. I waited and Anamuht the Purging Fire approached me, a column of flame as tall as the plateau on which I sat, and spoke to me."

The fine hair on my forearms rose at the memory of her presence. Beside me, Zariya reached for my hand.

Sister Nizara took a sip of water scented with orange blossoms and cleared her desert-parched throat. Her gaze shifted to Zariya and me, and there was sympathy in it. "Anamuht the Purging Fire said to me that the Sun-Blessed have grown too insular here in Zarkhoum," she said softly. "And that the youngest of our number must wed a foreigner and venture forth from our shores. Once the nuptials have been agreed upon and the betrothal an-nounced, then, and only then, will Anamuht quicken the *rhamanthus*, and three thousand seeds shall serve as the dowry for this marriage."

There was a moment of silence, and then Zariya's mother let out a wail of anguish. A dozen other voices rose. "Three thousand seeds wasted on a foreign dowry!" one muttered in disgust. "It's a travesty."

I felt Zariya's pulse quicken against our clasped palms and stole a glance at her. "Across the *sea*, my darling!" she whispered to me, her eyes shining. "Think of it!"

Someone exclaimed; something else had transpired.

"Ah, no!" King Azarkal was holding out his hands as though to implore the gods, and beneath his ageless brown skin, the steadily beating pulse-points of *khementaran* glowed at his wrists and the sides of his throat. It had happened. The moment of *khementaran* had come upon him at last. "Not Zariya. Please, not my little lion-hearted daughter! Has she not suffered enough for one lifetime? I beseech you, do not take her from me. Say it is not so."

"Oh, Father!" Tears stood in Sister Nizara's eyes. "Forgive me. But I can-not gainsay the will of the Purging Fire."

It felt to me as though the world was tilting like a hawk soaring on angled wings. All around the hall, glances were being exchanged as the Sun-Blessed assessed the significance of this turn of events, the one-two punch of them landing like thunder and lightning; Zariya to wed a foreigner and depart Zarkhoum, and the king entering *khementaran*.

"I am not afraid, Father!" Zariya said in a clear voice. "I will do my duty with honor."

"Of course you will, my heart," he said. "And yet I am afraid for you."

"But I have Khai," she said simply. "It must be for this that the Sacred Twins joined us."

The king gazed at his empty hands, at the glowing pulse beating at his wrists. "I have lived too long," he murmured. "Nizara, tell me, did Anamuht say *whom* Zariya must wed?"

"No, Father," she said quietly. "Only that it must be a foreigner and she must leave these shores."

He lifted his head and there were tears in his eyes, too. Whatever his flaws, King Azarkal was a man who loved his youngest daughter. "Then I will send word to our nearest allies in Barakhar and Therin," he said in a firm tone. "Neither realm is so terribly far away, and I can endure the thought of Zariya living in either one if I must."

"What of Granth, Father?" It was one of the twins who posed the question, his brow knit. "We always have need of their steel. And wasn't our brother Kazaran betrothed to a Granthian woman?"

"Do not speak to me of Granthian steel!" the king said sharply. "And that is a different matter altogether. Women are not treated with honor in Granth. Your brother was a warrior who meant to become the Kagan. Your sister would be nothing more than a valuable broodmare with an invaluable dowry."

The thought sickened me. "I would kill anyone who treated you thusly," I murmured to Zariya.

"I know you would, my shadow." She looked a bit less undaunted. "But even you would find it difficult to dispatch an entire realm."

King Azarkal rose and surveyed the Sun-Blessed, who fell silent beneath his regard. "Today is a bittersweet day," he announced. "Eldest daughter,

Nizara, Elder Sister . . . I am grateful to you for the quest you undertook. You have endured great hardship for the sake of the Sun-Blessed and brought new hope and a path toward a harvest." He saluted her. "For this, I thank you. Youngest daughter, Zariya . . ." He paused, then continued in a rough voice. "I honor your courage. I will see to it that you are given a voice in the choice of your bridegroom."

That engendered not a few murmurs of envy; no other daughter had been afforded the same luxury. Zariya pressed her palms together and offered her father a graceful salute in silence.

"I *have* lived too long, have I not?" King Azarkal mused. "Ah, Kazaran, my son! You were the best and brightest of us. Why did *khementaran* not come upon me when you were slain? And yet it did not, and now it has, and I must make a choice." His gaze fell upon his eldest son in the hall. "Prince Dozaren of the House of the Ageless, Sun-Blessed son, come and kneel before me."

Dozaren obeyed. I glanced at Zariya again. Her lips were compressed in a thin line, but she gave me a slight shake of her head.

King Azarkal laid his hands on Dozaren's shoulders. "In the presence of all here assembled, in the name of the Sacred Twins, Anamuht the Purging Fire and Pahrkun the Scouring Wind, beneath the all-seeing eye of Zar the Sun, I name you my heir and the successor to the throne of Zarkhoum."

Dozaren bowed his head. "I know I was neither your first nor second choice, Father," he said humbly. "But I accept this honor nonetheless, and I will do my best to see that you have no cause to regret it."

It was done.

The swiftness with which events had transpired left the hall stunned. Dozaren stood and took a deep breath. "A bittersweet day indeed, Father. It is in my thoughts that it would be apt to mark it with a grand gesture to demonstrate to the folk of Merabaht that the Sun-Blessed are magnanimous in retaining Anamuht's favor. Scores of relatives of our attackers languish in prison with no proof that they collaborated in treason. Perhaps we might declare clemency for them, and oversee a distribution of grain in quarters of the city experiencing famine? It could be done in honor of

Zariya's sacrifice," he added. "For I think that will touch their hearts as deeply as it does mine."

"Do as you like," the king said indifferently. "I cannot find it in my heart to care about the wretched of Merabaht today." His attention returned to Zariya. "By the standards of our long-lived house, you are young for marriage. We're not like common folk who breed at the first sign of fertility. We have always had the luxury of time. No longer. It would be best if this were arranged swiftly."

"I understand, Father," she said.

King Azarkal inclined his head to her. "Before you depart from these shores, you will partake of the *rhamanthus*." His eyes glistened. "For that, too, you are young, my heart; but if there is a chance that it will allow you to enter into marriage whole and hale, I would give it to you."

Zariya caught her breath. "Thank you, Father. And Khai, too?"

"So it must be according to lore, Father," Sister Nizara said when the king hesitated. "It will be a great harvest when it comes."

"Then it shall be so," he said. "Is there aught else that you need impart to me, Nizara?"

"No, Father," she murmured.

He turned his hands over and looked once more at his wrists, at the faint blood-red light of mortality throbbing there. "Then I shall go take counsel with my advisors and ambassadors," he said. "Dozaren, come. You will assume all duties befitting your new status."

In the wake of their departure, the Hall of Pleasant Accord burst into a cacophony of conversation: speculation, indignation, despair, gloating. Beside me, Zariya rested her head against my shoulder and I shifted to put my arm around her. Since the matter of desire had been settled, there was a new measure of ease and comfort between us. "Tired?"

She nodded. "It's only that it's a great deal to take in for one morning, my darling. I feel rather as though the earth itself has shifted beneath me."

"I know." I glanced at Sister Nizara. "Elder Sister, did you speak to Brother Yarit of the Mad Priest?"

"I did." The High Priestess looked bemused. "He's quite a character, isn't he? Very . . . blunt and plainspoken. Not at all what I expected of the Seer, though you did try to tell me as much. It all struck a chord with him, but he would not deign to say why. I assume he could not."

"Did he have any words for me?" I asked her.

"He said to thank you for what you said about Belisha," she said. "And he said, 'Tell the kid I believe in him, but he might want to consider learning how to swim just in case.'"

Despite everything, it made me smile. "That sounds like him."

Upon returning to the women's quarter, Zariya and I retreated to her chambers, where she perused her books and chose a volume. "Did you know that in Therin it's considered impolite to say exactly what you mean?"

"No," I said. "Why in the world?"

Reclining on her divan, she paged through the book. "Therin lies under the aegis of Ilharis the Two-Faced. It's considered a sign of respect to the god to say one thing, and mean quite another. That would take some getting used to, don't you think?"

"I do," I said. "But women are treated well there?"

"Women are reckoned the equal of men in Therin, for one of Ilharis's faces is male and the other female," Zariya said. "Rather like you! Therinians are also fond of games of chance, and all manner of dalliances are permitted without shame. In Barakhar, where Lishan the Graceful sheds drops of dew that imbue her chosen with surpassing grace and beauty, artistry is prized above martial skills and women are reckoned superior to men." She put her finger between the pages and looked thoughtful. "I must say, either would make an interesting change."

I thought so, too.

In the days that followed, I learned a fair bit more about Barakhar and Therin as Zariya read me passages from her favorite books, trying to guess at what our future might hold. I took heart from the fact that, as the king had suggested, I could endure the thought of Zariya living in either realm.

I considered Brother Yarit's advice, too. It may have been offered partially in jest—at a distance, I could not be sure—but he had a point. If I were to accompany Zariya across the sea, it would behoove me to learn how to swim; only I did not know anyone capable of such a feat, and of course, there were the never-ending issues of propriety in the royal court.

When I said as much to Zariya, she had an unexpected suggestion. "What about your family?"

I looked at her in surprise. "My *family*?"

"Well, they're fisher-folk, aren't they?" she said pragmatically. "I imagine they must know how to swim. Khai, I know you've wrestled with the notion of what you might say to them. Why not simply send for them instead?"

"And ask them to teach me to swim?" I said.

Zariya shrugged. "Well, I wouldn't *lead* with it, my darling. Get to know them first."

I had no idea how such a thing could be accomplished. "How would I even send for them?"

"I'll ask Father to arrange it," she said simply.

All things are possible with wealth and power, and King Azarkal was minded to give his youngest daughter anything within his reach.

In a week's time, I met my family.

The king dispatched a quartet of Royal Guardsmen to escort them to Merabaht; my mother and father and two brothers, one older than me and one younger. Although the village was a mere two days' ride from the city, there was some delay when it transpired that none of them had ever sat a horse, and my mother flatly refused to do so. After some bartering, a wagon and cart-horses were procured. Once they reached the palace, my family was given lodging in quarters used to house visiting diplomats. Zariya argued that as they were of my blood, they were honorary kin and might be received in the Hall of Pleasant Accord; and to this, too, her father acceded.

It is an awkward business to meet one's family as strangers. They stared about them as the Queen's Guard ushered them into the hall, no doubt looking as dumbstruck as I had when I first entered the palace. All four of them wore cotton garments in a checked pattern of white and red and black, which I later learned was a pattern specific to our village. My father was a tall man and a rather handsome one, his eyes lined with crinkles from squinting against the sun. My older brother took after him, while my mother was short and plump, and my younger brother thin and wiry.

"Khai?" my mother whispered, her eyes wide over the strip of black cloth that served as her veil. "Oh! Look at you! Such a warrior the brothers have made of you!"

I had chosen to dress in my desert woolens. "It's good to meet you, Mother," I said, offering her a respectful salute. "It's good to meet all of you."

"Your Highness." My father saluted Zariya, who was already seated prettily on a cushion at the head of the great carpet, which was set with the customary array of tea and delicacies. Blood kin or not, we had determined it best if my family remained unaware of her affliction for now. The king was anxious that word not leak before a betrothal was arranged. "We thank you for this."

"Oh, my darling man!" She smiled at him. "Of course Khai must have the chance to meet his family. But you must be weary from your journey, and this is all so strange, is it not? Come, sit, take refreshment. Let us make each other's acquaintance. Tell me, what is life like in the village where my beloved shadow was born?"

Although I was their flesh and blood and Zariya was one of the royal Sun-Blessed, it put them at ease in a way that nothing I could have said would have done. In a quarter hour's time, she had them eating and drinking and chatting with an animated blend of enthusiasm and awe.

From my father and mother, Zariya elicited the story of how the priestesses of Anamuht had found me by my birth record, and how they had traveled by wagon-train across the desert to the Fortress of the Winds. I learned that of the thirteen babes identified as potential shadows, I was the only girl-child; and I learned too that my parents had known that I was to be raised *bhazim*.

It stung a little, an echo of that old betrayal; but my parents had no way of knowing. It seemed I had a distant cousin who was raised the same way, only she knew all along. So had another girl in a nearby village.

It was not an uncommon practice. I was only unusual in that I had wholeheartedly believed the fiction . . . and that I had not been required to resume an identity as a girl when I reached adolescence.

"But of course you couldn't," my father said in an understanding manner. "You have your duty."

"Oh, Khai is a perfectly lovely girl when he wants to be," Zariya said airily.

My mother, who had long since unpinned her veil, gave me a wistful smile. "Is that so? I would like to see it just the once. Just the once, I would like to see the woman my baby girl grew into."

"Then next time, I shall wear a dress," I promised her.

"I wouldn't if I were you!" my younger brother, Dinesh, announced, his eyes bright and his mouth full of pastry. "The guards told us stories. They told us you killed a hundred men single-handed!"

My older brother, Kephos, fetched him a mild smack. "I told you not to speak of such things."

"It's all right," I assured him. "I do not know if it was a hundred men, only that there were many of them."

Zariya shuddered at the memory.

My father cleared his throat. "We have also learned of Anamuht's decree," he said quietly. "I do not know if this is a thing that may give comfort to you, Khai—indeed, I do not know if you are in need of comfort—but although you are desert-raised, the sea is in your blood. Mind you, none of us have ventured far from Zarkhoum's shores; still, it is our element."

"It is good to know, Father," I said.

"Speaking of which . . ." Zariya cocked her head. "May I ask if you know how to swim?"

My father smiled. "Like a fish, Your Highness."

I could not imagine how or where such an undertaking might occur, but Zariya had thought this through, too. Less than a league to the north was the king's private retreat on the coast of the sea, known as the Villa of Heart's Ease. It had a more vulgar name, too, for it was where he had arranged dalliances with his mistresses, many of whom had gone on to become his junior wives; Zariya knew of it from her own mother's descriptions. The walled villa could be easily guarded and it perched on a terrace above a fine lagoon. King Azarkal was not enamored of the notion, but he saw the wisdom of it. A sea voyage was an uncertain thing, and I daresay the vision of a capsized ship, his favorite daughter Zariya floundering in the waves and me unable to save her, haunted him as much as it did me.

So it was that the next day we journeyed to the Villa of Heart's Ease, disguised as a family of wealthy traders and their household escorted by mercenary guards. It made me uneasy to venture onto the streets of Merabaht with Zariya, but our guise had been a wise precaution. No one suspected our company's true identity nor troubled us, and by the afternoon, we were ensconced in the king's retreat.

Behind the high walls surrounding the estate, it was a delightful place. There were outlying barracks for the guards. In comparison to the Palace of the Sun, the villa itself was small and modest. Zariya and I were housed in the king's own chambers, which opened onto the terrace with a wide slate stairway that led down to the lagoon. The breeze was cleaner than those that reached the upper tier of the city, smelling of saltwater and frangipani blossoms.

Gazing at the shining sea, Zariya drew in a long, slow breath. "Oh, I could live here, my darling! Couldn't you?"

"Your father gave us three days," I reminded her.

"I know," she said. "Let's try to make them last."

Although I trained harder in those three days than I had since leaving the Fortress of the Winds, it was an idyllic time. The members of the Queen's Guard who had accompanied us were uneasy about the arrangement, but they determined soon enough that my family presented no threat, and I was grateful for their presence during the long hours I spent in the lagoon.

It was a blessed relief to be free of the tedium of the women's quarter, to immerse myself in the quest to master a new skill. At first I struggled, flailing against the water, my mouth filled with the taste of salt and my eyes stinging while my brothers dove and splashed like porpoises; but my father was a patient teacher, and by the day's end, I learned to trust the water to buoy me. For the sake of modesty, I bound my breasts and wore a sleeveless cotton tunic and a pair of breeches cropped at the knee. Even so, my older brother, Kephos, was careful to avoid looking directly at me. I understood. I'd felt the same way in the baths.

On the first evening, after I'd washed my salt-stiffened hair and the faint gritty rime from my skin, I suffered Zariya to braid my wet hair and paint my eyes with kohl before donning the orange silk dress with the gold border.

At dinner, my mother's eyes shone at the sight of me, and she clapped her hands together involuntarily. "Oh, I did so miss having a daughter!" Her voice softened. "You look beautiful, Khai."

I had only done it to please her, but unexpectedly, I felt my throat tighten. "Thank you."

"I like you better as a boy," Dinesh informed me.

I raised my brows at him. "Don't worry, I can kill in skirts as well as I can in breeches."

He grinned.

"So this is what it's like to have a normal family," Zariya remarked. "A family not bent on plotting against one another. I quite like it, my darlings."

One . . .

Two . . .

Three . . .

It seemed I was always counting something; here, it was the fleeting days. I learned that the members of my family were honest and good-hearted; still a bit awed by these sudden circumstances, but stalwart and kind. Sometimes I could almost imagine what our lives together would have been like; but then I would catch Kephos averting his gaze when we swam, or my mother frowning in perplexity at the glinting slashes of the marks of Pahrkun on my cheekbones, and I would remember.

Still, it was glorious.

And I learned the sea, or at least what I might of it in the sheltered lagoon of the Villa of Heart's Ease. I could not hope to acquire the skill of a lifetime in three days, but I was a swift learner. I learned to dive so as to part the waters as cleanly as a blade, and I learned to propel myself through the waves with long arm-strokes and a steady kicking rhythm. Every day I trained to the point of exhaustion, reveling in the familiar languor in my muscles when at last I stopped.

"Never fight the sea, Khai, for she will always win," my father counseled me. "Do not seek to swim against the current, great or small. If the tide takes you, drift and be patient. The sea is as fickle as Eshen the Wandering Moon, but if you let her aid you, she may."

"I will remember," I promised him.

All too soon it was over. With regret, we donned our merchant guises and returned to the Palace of the Sun.

When Zariya's mother enfolded her in a weeping embrace upon our return to the women's quarter, I assumed Queen Sanala was merely indulging in a flair for the dramatic.

I was wrong.

"What is it, Mother?" asked Zariya, who knew her mother far better than I did. "What's happened now?"

It was Queen Adinah who answered in a gentler tone than I'd ever heard her use before. "The Granthians have gotten wind of Anamuht's decree," she said. "And they're demanding the right to contest for your hand."

THIRTY-TWO

Not only was Granth demanding the right to contest for Zariya's hand—and the prospect of the invaluable dowry of *rhamanthus* seeds that would accompany it—but they were threatening to declare war over the issue.

The news struck me like a blow to the gut.

"What does Father mean to do?" Zariya asked, her face pale, but her voice steady.

"He hasn't decided, dearest," Queen Adinah said, still in that unwontedly gentle tone. "It's not a simple matter."

It seemed that outright refusal was not an option. If the king had been confident that the Sun-Blessed yet enjoyed the full favor of the Sacred Twins, it might have been another matter. Hundreds of years ago, when Granth sought to conquer Zarkhoum, it was Pahrkun the Scouring Wind who drove the winged stink-lizards with their deadly acid bile from the sky, and the desert tribesfolk who united under his banner to drive the Granthian warriors from our shores.

But even if King Azarkal were willing to risk all-out war, with Anamuht's favor contingent on Zariya's betrothal to a foreigner, he could not be certain that Pahrkun would come to our aid if he refused to entertain a foreigner's suit.

The debate raged for days, during which time my family took their leave of Merabaht.

Zariya offered them the opportunity to stay, assuring them that a place would be found for them. I think she had developed a genuine fondness for them during our time at the Villa of Heart's Ease. Although they thanked her profusely for the offer, they declined it.

"If you and Khai were not leaving, I would consider it, Your Highness," my mother said shyly. "But the city is very big and full of strangers. As splendid as it is here, I miss my home."

"You could stay until Zariya's betrothal is arranged," I suggested. "And perhaps even see Anamuht herself striding through the city to quicken the *rhamanthus*!"

"Or the riots if the harvest fails," my father said quietly; he was a man who listened to what was said around him. "Or the fighting if Granth does not get its way. No." He shook his head. "It is best that we go. I pray that what I have taught you serves you well, Khai." He offered Zariya a heartfelt salute. "Your Highness, we are undeserving of the honor you have showered upon us."

She smiled at him. "You are deserving of every honor for giving me Khai, my darling man."

I embraced my mother and clasped forearms with my brothers, and last of all my father. His grip was firm and his palms were as callused from hauling nets as mine were from squeezing rocks and hilts.

"My daughter-son." The lines fanning from his eyes crinkled. "I am proud to call you mine."

Again, my throat felt tight; I had not expected to be so affected by meeting my blood kin. "And I to call you Father."

The day after their departure, King Azarkal called for a summit in the Hall of Pleasant Accord. Since *khementaran* had come upon him, the weight of his years showed more visibly.

"I have made a decision," he announced. "Two Granthian suitors will be allowed to seek Zariya's hand in marriage." A dozen voices rose in a chorus of protest, and the king raised his hand to silence them. "Abide," he said grimly. "The Kagan of Granth demanded that we hold an open tourney. This, I deemed unacceptable, as do the ambassadors of Barakhar and Therin, each of whom have named a worthy suitor. But in keeping with the customs of Granth, I have agreed to allow two competing suitors from their damned bloodthirsty realm to duel for the honor in Zariya's presence."

She took a quick, shallow breath. "To the death, Father?"

"It is an unpleasant compromise that will result in an unseemly spectacle," the king said with distaste. "But in exchange, Granth has agreed to my stipulation that the final choice of whom you shall wed resides with you, and you alone."

A faint line etched itself between Zariya's fine brows. "Why would they do that?" she mused.

King Azarkal smiled humorlessly. "From the wives of the Kagan to the lowliest peasant, any status Granthian women enjoy derives from their husband's skill at arms. Granth expects you to be overwhelmed by the victor's prowess."

Zariya gave me a sidelong glance. "In that, I suspect that they are very much mistaken."

Once the matter was decided, things moved quickly.

We learned that the suitor that Barakhar had put forth was one Prince Heshari, the queen's second-born son, only three years older than Zariya. As a man, he was not eligible to inherit the throne, but he was well placed in the royal court and had been blessed as a child by Lishan the Graceful herself.

The Therinian suitor, Lord Rygil, was known as the Keeper of the Keys, which Zariya explained to me was a hereditary title that meant he held the keys to the royal treasury and the ability to allocate funds, a position that carried a considerable amount of power, prestige, and wealth in Therin. He was young for the post, having inherited it at twenty-four when his father was killed in a fall from a balcony.

It gave me pause to hear it, for if such a thing had occurred in the House of the Ageless, doubtless it meant the man had been pushed, but the Therinian ambassador had offered assurances that it was an accident and no conspiracy was involved.

Of the Granthian suitors we knew nothing, for Granth had chosen to hold the open tourney they desired to select the two warriors who would be given the honor of dueling to the death in Zarkhoum.

"I do not like to think about how much blood will be spilled in my name," Zariya murmured when we learned this piece of news.

"They are not doing it for your sake," I observed. "They are doing it for their own notion of honor and the possibility of three thousand *rhamanthus* seeds."

Each prospective bridegroom would present his suit before King Azarkal in the throne hall. As the royal heir, Prince Dozaren would stand at his father's right hand. A great fretted screen was erected beside the sunburst throne, its apertures carved at cunning angles so that one could see through it from the back, but not the front. This would allow Zariya—and her mother, Sanala, who had demanded to be included—to observe and participate in the proceedings while remaining discreetly unseen.

"I should like to know what they say when I'm *not* present, my heart," Zariya said thoughtfully. "And people will speak freely in front of servants. How would you feel about attending their entourages?"

I smiled and saluted her. "I am yours to command, Your Highness."

The Barakhan embassy was the first to arrive, a vast ship of state docking in the harbor. After being offered hospitality and a day to refresh themselves, they were escorted into a sitting room to await their audience with the king. Clad in the long white linen robes, veil, and gold sash of an upper-echelon palace servant, I greeted them in the traders' tongue and bade them make themselves comfortable and partake of food and drink.

I had always admired the nimble grace of Barakhan sailors in the harbor, but the members of the royal family made them look crude by comparison. Prince Heshari was tall and lissome. Like most Barakhani, his skin was a brown so dark it was almost black, with a deep violet undertone. His hair was sheared close to his scalp, which served to emphasize the elegant shape of his skull and the perfect symmetry of his features. His eyes were large and lustrous, his lips full; and yet there was nothing feminine about his beauty.

He was beautiful, so much so that I was hard-pressed not to stare. There was grace and elegance in every move he made, large or small, in the way he seated himself on a cushion, in the way he reached for a goblet.

Anything can be a weapon, kid, Brother Yarit had once told me. *Grace and guile can be deadlier than a stink-lizard's bile, and luck can change any outcome.*

I wondered if it had been prophetic, though he had said it before he became the Seer.

The queen's sister and prince's aunt, Lady Onesha, was the head of their entourage, and she was every bit as beautiful as he was, her head wrapped in a colorful silk scarf, but her features proudly bare of any veil. I knew without being told that she too had been blessed by their goddess. All of them wore robes of Barakhan silk draped in folds that flowed like water in bright jewel-tones that glowed against their skin, and smelled of subtle, pleasant fragrances. They lounged at their ease and conversed in their own tongue, which was full of soft syllables and lilting tones like music.

That, I realized, was the flaw with Zariya's plan. Still, if I could not listen, I could watch. I circulated with a ewer of orange-blossom-scented water, offering to refill empty goblets. I thought myself nigh invisible, but when I reached Lady Onesha, she took me by surprise, addressing me in the traders' tongue.

"You move well for a Zarkhoumi." Her hand circled my wrist, her touch deft, delicate, and discomfiting. "Were you trained as a dancer?"

"No, honored one," I murmured.

"A pity." She regarded me. "Tell me, this Princess Zariya, is she possessed of any graces?"

I suppressed a flare of anger, wondering how these grace-touched members of Barakhan royalty would regard Zariya if they knew of her affliction. "Her Highness is possessed of beauty, a keen wit, and a kind heart."

Prince Heshari said something to a comrade in their tongue, but I heard the word *rhamanthus*. His comrade laughed.

"Your loyalty to the House of the Ageless is to be commended," Lady Onesha said, releasing my wrist.

When the Royal Guard came to escort the Barakhan embassy into the throne hall, I followed, ducking unobtrusively behind the screen to join Zariya and her mother. We listened to the prince present his suit to King Azarkal, along with a bolt of iridescent silk so fine and intricately woven that it seemed to hold all the colors of the rainbow.

"This silk is woven especially for members of the royal family, Your

Majesty," Prince Heshari said respectfully. "It is my hope that your daughter will wear it on our wedding day."

"Oh, he's lovely!" Zariya whispered to me.

I took her hand and squeezed it. "Ask him your questions before you lose your heart."

This was a protocol to which the king had agreed. After a further exchange of pleasantries, he raised one hand. "Prince Heshari of Barakhar, my daughter Zariya will pose you three questions."

The Barakhan prince looked slightly bewildered, but only for an instant. He touched his brow in a Zarkhoumi salute, imbuing the gesture with humility and grace. "Of course, Your Majesty."

Behind the fretted screen, Zariya leaned forward on her curve-sided stool. "Tell me, Prince Heshari, what do you value most in the world?"

He hesitated, and his aunt gave him a nod of encouragement. "All such beauty as makes my heart sing, Your Highness," he said firmly. "Whether it be the curve of a woman's cheek, the light of the sun setting on the waves, or a lone petal falling from a tree. All that fills me with joy, I value."

"And what do you most despise in the world?" Zariya asked him.

"Despise?" Prince Heshari knit his brow. "It is an unattractive word for an unattractive emotion. Perhaps it is only that I am young and fortunate, but I can think of nothing I despise."

Zariya posed her final question. "What do you fear the most, Your Highness?"

"Fear?" Again he echoed her; again he paused. "Death, I suppose. Does not everyone?"

"I do not know," Zariya said. "That is why I ask. Thank you for your candor, Your Highness."

There was much discussion of the Barakhan prince in the baths of the women's quarter that afternoon. The mood in the city was calmer since Prince Dozaren had followed through with his beneficent gesture, and several of Zariya's sisters had dared venture from their own households to visit the palace, eager for gossip and details. They exclaimed over the gorgeous silk and exchanged opinions, heedless of whether or not there was any basis for them.

It did not surprise me that Queen Sanala was already urging her daughter to accept the prince's suit.

"He's young and virile and ever so handsome, dearest," she said to Zariya. "And you would live a life of luxury as a junior princess in Barakhar!"

"I live a life of luxury here, Mother," Zariya commented. "And I do not always find it stimulating." She glanced at me. "You're very quiet, my darling. What did you think of Prince Heshari?"

"I think he is very nice to look at," I said. "But I think he is callow. And it troubles me that the Barakhan place such importance on physical grace."

Zariya regarded her legs. "Which I perforce lack."

I nodded reluctantly.

"Oh, but the *rhamanthus*!" Queen Sanala said with fervent hope. "And . . . and even if it doesn't work, my heart, the prince wouldn't know until after the betrothal. Your father will make certain the terms are unbreakable."

That was not my concern; my concern was that Zariya would be reckoned less than her worth in Barakhan society. I opened my mouth to say as much, but Zariya silenced me with a hand sign. "Well, we must hear out the other embassies before I make any decision."

Her mother shuddered. "Surely you're not considering Granth!"

"Of course not," she said. "But they must be given their chance to make their suit."

Although Granth was nearer, the second embassy to arrive was from Therin; presumably because the Granthians were still slaughtering one another to choose their suitors.

Once again, I donned the attire of a royal servant and attended their retinue while they awaited their audience with King Azarkal.

Despite the fact that they were clearly suffering in the heat, clad as they were in ornate jackets and close-fitting breeches, the Therinians were a lively bunch, chattering in their own tongue and uttering quick bursts of laughter at regular intervals. They were as fair-skinned as the Barakhan were dark, with straight hair that they wore shoulder-length or longer, tucked behind ears that tapered almost to a point at the top. By the way the others deferred to him, I guessed Lord Rygil was the ranking member of his entourage. He had sharply etched features that were not displeasing, eyes that were neither brown nor green but a mixture of the two, and hair the reddish-gold color of apricots. With his alert, curious gaze, he put me in mind of a bright-eyed desert fox, although I daresay the desert was the last place he'd care to be.

When I refilled his goblet with water, he thanked me courteously for it, adding in a humorous tone, "Though I cannot imagine why in the world you think I might look thirsty, my good lass!"

I paused, for it was obvious that he was flushed and sweating; then remembered what Zariya had told me about Therinians saying the opposite of what they meant. "You are unaccustomed to the heat, my lord. I will send for servants to fan you."

Lord Rygil waved a dismissive hand. "Oh, no need! Why, I don't mind the heat one bit."

The others laughed, but there was nothing cruel in it; their laughter had the sound of fellowship. I smiled and sent for servants and fans, and the Therinian embassy did look measurably less overheated when the Royal Guard came to escort them into the throne hall.

"Well?" Zariya murmured when I rejoined her behind the screen.

"It's difficult to say," I admitted.

The Keeper of the Keys presented his suit to King Azarkal. "I don't suppose your daughter would care to leave the embrace of Zar the Sun for the cooler climes of Therin to wed a poor fellow below her royal status, Your Majesty," he said in a diffident manner. "Still, I've coin enough in my purse to ensure she had plenty of warm blankets and furs if she were willing to chance it. Naturally, she would be accorded every honor at my disposal, though I imagine she would find such honors as I have to bestow upon her as the wife of a lord of Therin beneath her."

"Is the man mad?" Queen Sanala whispered.

Zariya shook her head. "Shhh."

Lord Rygil beckoned to a member of his retinue who came forward with a small casket. "In any case, I brought a small token for Her Highness. A gift to thank her for her consideration." His man opened the casket and someone—I think it was Dozaren, standing beside the throne—drew in a sharp breath.

Behind the screen, all three of us leaned forward, craning to no avail to see what the casket held.

"If that's what I think it is, it's a great deal more than a mere token," King Azarkal said in a flat voice.

"Well, it is a tear shed by Ilharis the Two-Faced, Your Majesty." Lord Rygil sounded almost apologetic. "A fate-changer, we call them; though I'm afraid there's no telling which way it will sway one's fate, which is why it's been in my family for generations." He shrugged, tucking a stray lock of hair behind one ear. "Call it a piece of whimsy on my part. Fate-changers are indeed scarce, but it's not as though it's a teardrop from the Lone Tree of the Barren Isle."

For the first time in many months, I fought the urge to feel at the back of my neck.

Unlike the Barakhan prince, Lord Rygil did not hesitate when Zariya posed him her first question and asked what he valued most in the world; indeed, he seemed to quite relish the challenge.

"Why, my integrity in my role as the Keeper of the Keys, of course," he answered lightly. Members of his entourage murmured, and he grinned. "I do but jest. Above all else, I treasure a witticism that cuts like a double-edged blade."

Zariya frowned, trying to parse his answer. "And what do you most despise, my lord?"

"Tedium, Your Highness," he said promptly.

"Lord Rygil hews close to the bone of truth!" someone called out merrily. I would have called it disrespectful and irreverent . . . and yet this strange badinage *was* a form of reverence for them.

"Very well, my lord," Zariya said. "What is it that you fear the most?"

He wiped his sweating brow with the cuff of his brocade jacket and laughed, turning the gesture into a salute. "At this very moment, it is that I will disgrace myself by fainting in the heat, Your Highness."

I did not know what to make of him. Neither did Zariya, although her mother was quick to take offense at his manner, as were the other royal ladies when they heard the scandalous details. While they clicked and clucked and exclaimed over the exchange, Zariya and I tried to make sense of it.

"I think there *were* some true things he said, my darling," she said to me, lying on her belly while Soresh massaged her legs. "Not those answers that were wholly flippant; those were not so much falsehoods as a veil to disguise whatever deeper truths lay beneath them. No, the true answers were the ones he undercut with a jest or a dismissive comment."

I thought back over the audience. "Which would mean that he truly does value his integrity and intend to offer you every honor at his disposal."

"*If* I read his answer rightly," she agreed.

"This would be a great deal easier if he'd simply speak plainly," I grumbled.

"At least that's one thing we can count on the Granthians to do, my heart," Zariya said wryly. "What do you think Lord Rygil meant by his gift?"

Like the bolt of silk before it, the fate-changer in its inlaid enamel casket had been delivered to the women's quarter. The gem itself was a strange thing, round as a pearl, yet clear as a diamond. I had more than half expected it to glow from within like the Barren Teardrop or the *rhamanthus* seeds, but the only light it held was the light it reflected, which shifted in its depths in subtle, aqueous patterns. There was a note penned on vellum in the casket, informing Zariya that to invoke the fate-changer, one dashed it on the ground and shattered it with the words, *Ilharis, change my fate!*

It had been passed around and admired, but so far no one had dared touch it out of an irrational fear that it might break by accident and unleash an uncertain change of fate.

"I don't know," I admitted. "Do you have any thoughts on the matter?"

Zariya shook her head. "Only that he called it a piece of whimsy on his part, which means it was no such thing."

I said nothing, thinking that it seemed to me a considerable coincidence that each of us, Sun-Blessed and shadow, now possessed a tear shed by one of the children of heaven. As always, I felt a pang of guilt at keeping the secret from her; and yet I feared to tell her here in the Palace of the Sun. Even with her brother Elizar the collector languishing in the dungeon for a crime he hadn't committed, it was a dangerous thing to know.

Perhaps when we departed from the shores of Zarkhoum, I thought, I would divulge this last secret. The thought heartened me.

Two days passed before the embassy from Granth arrived. It had been determined that both prospective bridegrooms would present their suits before dueling on the morrow. One, who was known as Varkas Long-Arm—all Granthian warriors, Zariya told me, were given nicknames—was actually the son of a former Kagan, though it signified nothing, for the title could only be claimed by winning the seven-year tourney. The other Granthian suitor was known as Sandrath the Quiet, and when I attended to their retinue in the sitting room, I had no trouble guessing which was which.

The Granthians were an imposing lot, brown-skinned and black-haired like us, but tall and broad-shouldered to a man, their bodies thick with muscle. All of them were warriors in their prime. Although they were not permitted to wear weapons in the king's presence, they flaunted the wealth of their realm's resources in the form of steel chest-plates, gauntlets, and greaves.

I found them loud and boastful, especially Varkas Long-Arm, who stood half a head taller than any other man in the room. It was clear that his reach would give him an advantage in battle. He had features that fell just short of handsome: his eyes too far apart, his mouth too small for his face. When I turned away after filling his glass, he gave me a hard pinch on my left buttock.

I froze.

He laughed and made a comment in his own tongue; the others laughed, too. With anger coursing through me, I clutched the handle of my pitcher tight and repressed the desire to whirl around and rain down thunder and lightning upon him.

"Do not judge us all by the same measure," the only Granthian seated said in a low tone. Sandrath the Quiet. Like the others, he wore his black hair cropped short and steel armor over his attire; unlike the others, his gaze was thoughtful. "We are not all ill-mannered brutes."

I filled his glass. "And yet one of you will kill the other tomorrow without just cause."

He raised his glass to me. "Is the hand of your Princess Zariya not a cause worth dying for?"

I shrugged. "Her Highness or her dowry?"

Sandrath the Quiet's gaze was unflinching and his answer was simple and direct. "Both, of course."

At that moment the Royal Guard came to escort them into the throne hall, sparing me the need to answer. I trailed behind them and once again slipped behind the fretted screen.

Zariya gave me a curious look. "You're agitated, my darling."

I shook my head. "One of them is despicable. The other is . . . not what we expected."

Varkas Long-Arm was the first to present his suit. "In a year's time, I will be Kagan," he announced. "Like my father before me. I *will* win the tourney." He slapped the empty scabbard that hung from the thick leather belt slung over his hips. "My gift is my sword. I pledge it to your daughter's honor, King Azarkal. She will be the first and foremost of my wives and bear me many sons. With her at my side, I will rule for a thousand years."

When it came time for Zariya to pose her questions, Varkas Long-Arm scowled, disliking the entire process and answering each question with a single curt word.

What did he most value? Victory.

What did he most disdain? Cowardice.

What did he fear? Nothing.

And then it was Sandrath the Quiet's turn. He stood at his ease before the throne, an unremarkable-looking man with a warrior's bearing. "I make no bold claims, Your Majesty," he said. "I, too, hope to be Kagan; I, too, will fight in next year's tourney." He took a slow, deep breath. "I would like the chance to shape Granth's destiny. This I believe your daughter and I might do together. I have made inquiries. I believe we are like-minded. And to that end, I have brought a small token with which to present your daughter."

It was a book; and not just any book, but a rare volume by Liko of Koronis that Zariya did not possess.

"Oh!" she whispered.

Against all odds, I found myself wondering if this Granthian suitor could actually win her heart.

Sandrath the Quiet's answers to her first two questions were as brief as his countryman's, but they were thoughtful: what he valued most in the world was wisdom; what he most despised was cruelty born of willful ignorance. His answer to her final question was longer.

"You have seen, I think, that Granthians are not given to fear, Your Highness; or at least not to confessing it," he said. "And yet no man in full possession of his wits is truly fearless. What do I fear most in the world? I cannot say there is one thing. But I can tell you that today, what I fear most is that you have already hardened your heart against my suit, and that my words fall upon deaf ears."

I had to own, it was an awfully good answer.

THIRTY-THREE

Zariya was quiet and withdrawn after the Granthian audience. I let her be and did my best to keep her mother and aunts and sisters from pestering her. It wasn't until we were alone in her chambers that evening that she shared her thoughts with me.

"His words did not fall on deaf ears," she said. "Yet I find myself wondering if he merely said what I wanted to hear."

"I do not think any Granthian in history has ever done such a thing," I said dryly. "And he spoke gently to me despite supposing me an ordinary servant."

She smiled a little. "True. I find myself at cross-purposes, my darling. Prince Heshari . . . I will not deny it, his beauty appeals to me. The intriguing and maddening Lord Rygil piques my wits. But much to my surprise, it is Sandrath the Quiet who spoke to my heart."

I nodded. "I know."

"There is no guarantee that he will emerge victorious in tomorrow's duel," she mused.

"No."

"And if he does, he means to stand for Kagan at next year's tourney," she continued. "There is no guarantee that he will win that battle, either. I could find myself a widow in a year's time."

"You could," I agreed.

"To be young and widowed in Granth . . ." Zariya shuddered. "I am not too proud to admit that the prospect terrifies me."

It did me, too. Zariya was right, I could not stand against an entire realm.

"You needn't choose yet," I said to her. "There's no point in it. You can wait until after the duel."

She shook her head. "Yesterday, the duel was a pointless, bloody exercise I must endure for the sake of diplomacy. Today, it is different. I need to know my own mind, my shadow."

I understood. "If Sandrath the Quiet is victorious, will you consider his suit in earnest?"

Zariya was silent for a moment, then nodded. "I will."

Granthians were not known for wasting time; the duel took place the following morning before the heat of the day became too oppressive.

It was held in an arena on the grounds of the palace, where in happier times, Zariya told me, theatrical performances were staged. There was even a special box for the royal women, fitted with curtains of gauze that were easier to see through than the fretted screen in the throne room. The mood among the royal women was a blend of resolve and disdain. I daresay they would have been mortified if they knew Zariya was willing to entertain the notion of wedding a Granthian if Sandrath were to win; and to be honest, I wasn't sure whether I wanted him to or not.

I leaned forward on my seat, peering through the gauze as two men clad in steel armor entered the arena.

A vast shadow passed over the sandy ground of the arena and a harsh, shrill cry sounded overhead. It was a stink-lizard, bigger than the one I'd seen at the harbor. It descended to perch on the lip of the far edge of the arena, folding its leathery wings.

Zariya caught her breath. "Did Father agree to its presence?" she asked no one in particular.

Looking pale, Queen Adinah shook her head. "I don't believe so, my dearest."

Save for the poison sac pulsing at the base of its throat, filled with the foul-smelling bile for which the stink-lizards were named, it was motionless, powerful talons gripping the stone rim. It was here, I thought, to observe;

and I remembered Brother Yarit telling me that the stink-lizards were the offspring of Droth the Great Thunder, the dragon under whose aegis Granth lay. They may have been the Kagan's to command, but they belonged to the god. Moving in unison, Varkas Long-Arm and Sandrath the Quiet turned to offer the perched lizard a salute, raising clenched fists above their heads.

In that moment, I understood that the Granthians did not duel out of sheer bloody-mindedness.

No; for them, this was a sacrament.

The knowledge made my skin prickle, and I felt the beginning of Pahrkun's wind stirring within me.

The Granthian suitors offered a salute in the direction of the royal boxes and the duel commenced.

They fought with two-handed longswords, steel clashing and sparks skittering at the force of the blows exchanged. Both men were strong, skilled fighters. As I had guessed, Varkas's long-armed reach gave him an advantage, but Sandrath's footwork was superior, deft and evasive. The royal women winced and exclaimed at the violence, averting their eyes. Zariya clutched my hand, breathing in short gasps, her nails digging into my skin. On and on it went, the Granthians going back and forth across the arena, battling each other in a state of grim exultation, both of them bleeding from half a dozen nonfatal blows.

As the battle wore on, I saw Sandrath the Quiet's steps begin to drag and Varkas Long-Arm taste victory.

When the end came, it was swift. Parrying a slow overhead blow with ease, Varkas Long-Arm dropped to one knee and drove his longsword upward at an angle beneath Sandrath's breastplate. Standing, he withdrew the blade, the length of it slick and red with blood. Sandrath the Quiet crumpled and lay motionless in the final silence of death. Zariya let out a low sound of dismay.

Behind the faceplate of his helm, Varkas's eyes were shining and wild. "Behold, people of Zarkhoum!" he shouted, opening his arms wide. "I am victorious! Who here is man enough to stand against me? Therin? Barakhar? Or are you but fearful weaklings?" He pointed the tip of his bloodstained sword at the royal women's box. "Princess Zariya, will you truly accept a lesser suitor?"

Oh, Pahrkun's wind was rising within me.

"Name me your champion," I murmured to Zariya. "Send me into the arena against him."

She gave me a stricken look. "Are you sure, my darling?"

I nodded.

Grasping her canes, Zariya pulled herself upright. "Varkas Long-Arm of Granth!" she cried in a clear, carrying voice. "I will acknowledge your claim if you are able to defeat *my* champion!"

Varkas Long-Arm laughed deep in his chest. "Gladly! Does His Majesty King Azarkal consent to this?" he called into the stands.

The king hesitated, glanced toward our curtained box. Clenching my fists, I willed King Azarkal to feel Pahrkun's wind stirring and grant his permission. "Yes," he said at length. "Let it be so."

There was a susurrus of murmurs, comments, dissent; I paid heed to none of it, parting the gauze curtains to vault over the edge of the royal women's box and make my way to the arena. I felt light and lithe and keen, a hawk unchained. I was glad I'd worn my desert woolens.

This was what I was.

This was what I had trained for. I pressed my thumbs to my brow in salute. "Well met, Varkas of Granth."

For a moment, the battle-fever dimmed and he looked confused. "You're a mere stripling."

I angled my head so that the sun caught on the marks of Pahrkun etched on my cheekbones. "I am Khai of the Fortress of the Winds," I said to him. "The chosen of Pahrkun the Scouring Wind and shadow to the Sun-Blessed Princess Zariya of the House of the Ageless. Do you refuse my challenge?"

"I refuse no challenge," Varkas said grimly. "What little challenge you present, I accept."

"So be it." I turned to offer a salute to King Azarkal in the greater of the two royal boxes. The king gave me a grave nod and returned it.

It was the wind on the back of my neck that warned me; the shouts of alarm would have come too late. Varkas favored his right hand, so I dove to my left, somersaulting beneath the level sweep of his longsword that would have parted my head from my shoulders.

In the stands of the arena, the crowd shouted their indignation and disapproval.

"Would you have slain me from behind as I yet stood unarmed?" Bounding to my feet, I drew my *yakhan* and *kopar*. "I did not think to find you a dishonorable fighter, Granthian."

Behind the faceplate, his gaze was hard and ruthless. "I would have given you a swift, merciful death. Instead it seems I have given you a lesson. Never turn your back on a Granthian on the battlefield."

I inclined my head to him. "I will not do so a second time."

Until the duel began in earnest, I do not think Varkas Long-Arm imagined that he might lose. When I parried his first blow with ease, he looked incredulous. He had the height and reach of me; his forearms and shins and torso were covered in steel armor, and a steel helm protected his head. But his armor was heavy, the sun was rising high overhead, and he had already fought one difficult battle today and sustained minor injuries in it. And I had a lifetime of training and Pahrkun's wind coursing through my veins, showing me the spaces *between*; between the powerful blows he leveled at me and the time it took him to resume his guard; between the gaps in his armor and the leather straps and buckles that held his breast- and back-plates in place; between the surety of an easy victory and a rising awareness that he was fighting for his life.

In the stands, someone began chanting my name—I never learned who—and others took it up.

"Khai, Khai, Khai!"

If I had needed buoying, it would have buoyed me, but I needed no encouragement today.

Today, I fought for Zariya's honor and the honor of Zarkhoum.

I will not say it was an easy bout, for Varkas Long-Arm was the premier warrior of his generation, and I had never fought an armor-clad opponent. Knowing that Zariya was watching, I was more cautious than was my wont, taking no risks that might cause her undue alarm. Still, Varkas did not press me as hard as Vironesh had in our many hours of training. Growing desperate, he attempted a mighty overhanded blow. I caught his blade in the tines of my *kopar*, stepped inside his guard, and drove the point of my *yakhan* into his unprotected armpit.

The Granthian staggered backward with a grimace and dropped his blade, and I was reminded of the last battle I'd fought in the Hall of Proving. That, too, had ended with a disabling injury.

That man, I had killed in accordance with Pahrkun's will. I was not sure whether or not I ought to kill this one.

Varkas Long-Arm fumbled left-handed with his helm, prying it loose and flinging it from him. It bounced on the sandy soil of the arena, landing near the lifeless form of Sandrath the Quiet. Beneath the helm, Varkas's short-cropped black hair was soaked with sweat. Blood coursed the length of his right arm, dripping from the fingertips of his gauntlet. Lifting his chin with a jerk, he nodded at me. "Kill me. You've earned it."

The stands had gone quiet. In his royal box, King Azarkal leaned forward and steepled his fingers. On the far side of the arena, the motionless stink-lizard watched with yellow eyes.

I hesitated, then shook my head. "I am Princess Zariya's champion. That decision belongs to her."

The Granthian's gaze burned. "Then ask."

I addressed the royal women's box. "Shall Varkas Long-Arm of Granth live or die, Your Highness?"

The gauze curtains twitched.

"Let him live, my shadow." Once again, Zariya's voice rang out strong and clear; I knew what an effort it was for her to project it so. "Let Varkas Long-Arm live to tell the tale, so that all the realms beneath the starless skies might know that the hand of one of the Sun-Blessed is not to be won by mere strength of arms."

I sheathed my weapons. "You live."

I cannot say he evinced any particular gratitude for the gift of his life; indeed, it may be that the culture of Granth was such that it would have been preferable to have perished than to return defeated and disgraced. But the thing was done and it could not be undone. The remainder of the Granthian retinue were escorted into the arena by the Royal Guard, accompanied by one of the palace physicians. I kept a wary eye on them, as well as the stink-lizard. If the Granthians sought to avenge their countryman's death, it would be an ugly battle.

If the stink-lizard attacked . . . well, that would be another matter altogether. I eyed it thoughtfully, trying to determine if its wingspan was too great to be taken down by a *heshkrat*.

Probably, yes.

But no, it seemed the Granthians had only come to retrieve their dead. Varkas Long-Arm shook off the physician's offer of assistance and stalked from the arena, leaving a trail of blood-drops behind him. His comrades lifted the fallen figure of Sandrath the Quiet and followed him. A strong breeze skirled around the arena, raising small dust devils, a reminder that this was the realm of Pahrkun the Scouring Wind. With a raucous cry, the stink-lizard launched itself into the sky, flapping away toward the harbor.

I let out a sigh of relief.

It was over.

The Granthians wasted no more time in delaying than they did in dueling. By the time the midday rest was over and the royal women were convened in the baths, we learned that their ship had set sail within the hour.

"And good riddance to them," Queen Rashina said distastefully; with the ascendance of her son Dozaren, she was enjoying her role in the women's quarter as the mother of the king's heir. "Tell us, dearest, now that the chaff has been winnowed, who will you choose?" she said to Zariya.

"I have not decided," Zariya murmured.

Her mother blinked at her. "Oh, but Prince Heshari . . . my darling, you cannot be unmoved by his beauty!"

"I am not unmoved, Mother," she said in a sharp tone. "Any more than I am unmoved by the fact that a man died today seeking my hand in marriage. Will you not allow me a moment of peace to consider that fact?"

Queen Sanala made a dismissive gesture. "Merely a Granthian brute, my heart. Anyway, they are all here for the promise of *rhamanthus* seeds. Why not choose the most pleasing suitor?"

"Any one of your sisters would have been grateful for the opportunity to have such a voice in the decision," Queen Adinah observed.

Zariya said nothing.

"It was his choice," I said softly to her. "Mourn for him if you will, but know it was not your fault."

She shot me a grateful look. "Did I mention that you were absolutely splendid and terrible in the arena today, my shadow?"

I smiled at her. "Several times."

That night, Zariya was restless and unable to sleep, tossing and turning on her bed. I lay sleepless on my pallet before the door to her bedchamber, watching her through half-lidded eyes. At length she rose and grasped her canes, hobbling through the doors into the garden.

I followed her.

In the starless sky, all three moons were visible overhead in differing states of fullness, shedding their varied radiance; silvery, bloody, bluish and dappled. Seated on a low bench, Zariya craned her neck to gaze at them. "Father expects a decision from me on the morrow," she mused. "We might live a pleasant life together in Barakhar, might we not? Filled with song and music and dance?"

I sat cross-legged on the flagstones before her. "It's possible. If the *rhamanthus* heals you, it may even be likely. Is that what you want?"

Setting her canes aside, she clasped her hands together. "What I want? Oh, but this has all happened so fast. I feel as though I'm standing on the corner of a precipice with no idea which way to jump. Barakhar or Therin? What of the matter of Dozaren? Once the decision is made, do I continue to maintain my silence? Do I wait to see if Anamuht will in truth come to quicken the *rhamanthus*? And the *rhamanthus* . . . what if it *does* heal me? What if it doesn't?"

"You have but one decision to make tonight," I said to her. "It is a very large one, but the rest can wait. What does your heart tell you?"

"After today, I fear my heart has little to say," Zariya murmured. "And so I find myself thinking instead, and there is one thought to which I keep returning. Prince Heshari gave me a bolt of silk; admittedly, a very fine one.

But Lord Rygil gave me a fate-changer, a tear shed by Therin's own god, Ilharis the Two-Faced. *Why?*"

I shook my head. "You know I've no more idea than you do. But whatever you choose, I will stand beside you."

"Yes, of course." She met my gaze in the moonlight. "I belong to you, and you to me. We have known this since first we laid eyes on each other. Therefore I beg you, do not offer me platitudes, dearest. Speak plainly to me and say what is in *your* heart."

I hesitated.

"Say it!" she repeated.

"Therin," I said quietly. "I don't wish to speak of the possibility that the *rhamanthus* may fail, but it is there nonetheless, Zariya. And I fear that if it does, these grace-touched Barakhani who are so very nice to look at might hold you in poor regard when they learned of your affliction."

"But it might *not* fail," Zariya said, and there was a plaintive note in her voice that made my chest ache.

"And I pray with all my heart that it doesn't," I said. "But whether it does or not, to my mind, a royal court that values grace over character is undeserving of your presence in it." Clearing my throat, I repeated myself. "And that is why I think you should choose Therin and Lord Rygil's suit."

Zariya sighed, and I sensed she was letting go of some pleasant vision. "Although they are a confounding folk, I suspect that you're right, my darling." Leaning forward, she brushed my cheek with her fingertips. "And I thank you for your honesty."

I nodded, wishing her touch would linger. "Always."

THIRTY-FOUR

On the morrow, Zariya gave voice to her decision in the throne hall in the presence of both embassies.

She had consulted with her father prior to the audience and he had approved her choice, but he permitted her to announce it herself from behind the fretted screen. The Therinian embassy cheered and let out great gales of laughter, as though Zariya had just uttered the cleverest witticism one could imagine. Lord Rygil offered a sweeping bow in our direction.

"A choice you shall no doubt come to regret, Your Highness," he called out gaily. "Still, we shall endeavor to make the best of it!"

"I pray I *don't* come to regret it," Zariya whispered to me. "For I fear attempting to parse his meaning makes my head ache."

"No doubt we will become accustomed to it," I replied with an assurance I did not feel.

Lady Onesha of the Barakhan embassy wasn't willing to accept Zariya's decision as final. She offered a graceful Zarkhoumi salute and took a few respectful steps toward the throne, the folds of her robes swaying around her, then extended both hands palms-outward in a gesture of supplication. Inclining her head, then lifting her chin in a manner that bared the length of her throat, she addressed the king. "Your Majesty, might I not be granted leave to speak privately with the young princess?" she inquired in a tone of humility and eminent reason. "Woman to woman?"

On his throne, King Azarkal hesitated, and I saw his uncertainty reflected in Zariya's expression.

It was difficult to say what made Lady Onesha's request so compelling;

one only knew that it *was*. Her stance, her tone, the elegance of her pale palms and fingers, the vulnerable line of her throat . . . somehow all these things combined to instill in one a powerful desire to accede to her wishes.

"Oh, by all means, Your Majesty!" Lord Rygil said lightly. "Only I would ask that you extend the same courtesy to my sister the Lady Marylis." He gave an apologetic shrug. "You see, my sister and several of her women accompanied our embassy, hoping to offer your daughter a measure of familiar decorum, but they stayed aboard the ship in the doubtlessly misguided notion that unveiled women in the throne hall of Merabaht might offend your sensibilities."

"Oh, he's clever," Zariya murmured, and I wondered if the peculiar Therinian practice of saying the opposite of what they meant armored them in some manner against the combination of Barakhan grace and guile.

Whether or not it was so, the exchange sufficed to harden King Azarkal's resolve. "My daughter's choice is made," he said firmly. "I regret to refuse you, Lady Onesha, but there will be no further debate."

She was wise enough to know herself defeated and accept it with the same grace, bowing her head once more; once toward the king, once toward Lord Rygil, and once toward the screen behind which Zariya was concealed. "Then I congratulate you and wish you every happiness."

"Of that I have not the slightest doubt, my lady," Lord Rygil said in a cheery tone, causing the faintest of wry smiles to crease her smooth cheeks.

So it was decided.

The marriage contract was drawn up that very day, and although in this Zariya had no say, she was privy to the terms of it, for it was contingent on the *rhamanthus* harvest. The Therinians had agreed to a waiting period of thirty days. If Anamuht the Purging Fire came to Merabaht to quicken the seeds within that time, all would be executed in accordance with the contract. Zariya and her stupendous dowry of three thousand seeds would sail to Therin and wed Lord Rygil, the Keeper of the Keys.

If Anamuht failed to make good on her promise in that time, the betrothal would be rendered null.

With the ink on the marriage contract not yet dry, King Azarkal sent couriers throughout the city of Merabaht and to the far reaches of Zarkhoum announcing the betrothal. How long would it take, I wondered, for word to reach Anamuht's ears? Had a goddess need of mortal couriers? It seemed unlikely to me; and yet, I suppose the king but did what he could.

Later, I would look back on the events leading to this interminable waiting period and remember once again Brother Yarit scratching in the hard-packed sand with the point of his dagger and muttering to himself, *So if* this, *then* that; *but if* this, *then* that.

If Varkas Long-Arm had not defeated Sandrath the Quiet . . .

If I had not spared Varkas's life . . .

If Lord Rygil had brought some lesser offering . . .

If King Azarkal had granted Lady Onesha's request . . .

At any given crux of events, the outcome would have been different. Or *might* have been different.

It was all very complicated; but at the time, I could do naught but endure the tedium of waiting. The day after the betrothal was arranged, Zariya dispatched me to invite Lord Rygil's sister Lady Marylis to call upon her at the palace, an errand I undertook gladly. Since it was a formal visit she decided I should dress in formal attire, and for the first time I ventured into the city clad in a dress, veil, and sleeveless over-robe befitting one of the royal women, escorted by a quartet of the Queen's Guard.

The Therinian ship of state was an enormous vessel, dwarfing every other ship in the harbor. Upon stating our business, we were ushered aboard with prompt, albeit irreverent, courtesy.

Lady Marylis received me in her private cabin with several of her women in attendance. It was a spacious, well-appointed room with woven hangings on the walls and ornate furniture in a style unfamiliar to me. If it weren't for the fact that the furniture was bolted to the floor of the ship, I would never have guessed we weren't on dry land. Lord Rygil's sister didn't share his reddish-gold hair—hers was a light brown—but I could see the resemblance in her sharp, foxlike features and the bright gaze that regarded me with lively curiosity.

"Greetings, my lady." I offered her a salute. "I am Khai of the Fortress of the Winds, Her Highness Princess Zariya's shadow, and I come bearing an invitation."

"Doubtless it is my ignorance of your culture speaking, but I could very nearly swear I've heard that name before." Lady Marylis's expression was one of genuine perplexity. "Although I was not privy to the battle of the Granthian suitors, my brother spoke of a young Zarkhoumi warrior who served as the princess's champion with, shall I say, unexpected results. I don't suppose he's kin to you?"

I smiled and unpinned my veil, revealing the marks of Pahrkun. "Not kin, my lady, no. We are one and the same."

"Here in Zarkhoum, of all places!" She laughed, and her attendants laughed with her, sounding for all the world like a flock of twittering birds. "You surprise me into candor, Khai of the Fortress of the Winds. Tell me, what is a *shadow*, and how is it that the young princess comes to possess one?"

I explained the lore surrounding our twinned moment of birth at the height of the eclipse, adding only that I spent my life being trained to protect Zariya.

She exchanged glances with her attendants, who seemed more like companions than servants. "Well, now, that's a tale to pass the time on a dull day, isn't it! But I suppose it must be common here in the realm of the Sacred Twins?"

"No, my lady," I said. "Princess Zariya is the first of the Sun-Blessed to be born with a shadow in over a hundred and fifty years, and the only daughter of the House of the Ageless to be thus honored."

"Ah, you disappoint me!" Lady Marylis said. "It pleased me to imagine that Zarkhoum was hiding an army of fierce warrior-women born on the cusp of a lunar eclipse."

Unsure how to receive the comment, I said nothing.

"Does Granth know?" one of her women inquired. "I confess my heart bleeds to think of the mortification of their champion—what was his name? Farkas?—upon learning that he was defeated by a mere woman."

"I do not know." I could not keep a trace of stiffness from my voice. "But I am no mere woman."

"No, of course not." Relenting, Lady Marylis spoke kindly to me in a forthright manner. "Forgive us, Pahrkun's child. Our feckless banter must sound strange to your ears. Tell Her Highness that although I am unworthy of the honor, I accept her invitation with pleasure."

I inclined my head to her. "A litter will be sent for you on the morrow."

The following morning, the royal women of the House of the Ageless entertained Lady Marylis and one of her companions, introduced as Lady Cyrgilen, in the Hall of Pleasant Accord, where a great feast of delicacies had been laid out. As she had done with my family, Zariya received them already seated; supposing it a Zarkhoumi custom, they took no offense at it.

"What a lovely little thing you are!" Marylis exclaimed, pressing one of Zariya's hands in both of hers. "It's a pity you've chosen to wed my brother. I fear you'll find him a simple fellow."

"Meaning he's not?" Zariya inquired. "Forgive me, but in Zarkhoum we speak plainly."

"*Zariya!*" her mother whispered urgently.

Her betrothed's sister smiled, tucking her hair behind her ears. "Obviously, I am terribly offended."

"But you *can* speak plainly if you wish to, can you not?" Zariya asked her. "You did so to Khai yesterday."

"Well, it's not *impossible*. But our manner of discourse gives honor to Ilharis the Two-Faced, as I suspect you know." Lady Marylis tilted her head, studying Zariya with her bright eyes. "You've a curious mind, Your Highness. Tell me, do you regard Therin as a riddle to be solved?"

Zariya frowned in thought. "A riddle? I'm not sure. And yet there is one question that plagues me. I would know why your brother gifted me with a fate-changer, my lady."

"Oh, that!" Marylis laughed. "Why, it's been in our family for ages. A useless trinket, no doubt. Do you imagine there is some prophecy that one day a great darkness will rise in the west, and the fate of all existence might hinge on a tear shed by Ilharis the Two-Faced?"

I drew in a sharp breath.

For all her bold spirit, Zariya looked taken aback. "If it were so, I would still ask why your brother gave it to *me*."

"A whim, a gamble, a dream's prompting sent by Ilharis . . . any or all or none of those things may be true, Your Highness." Lady Marylis lifted her shoulders in a careless shrug, reaching for a honey-soaked pastry. "Who can say?"

If there was an answer to that question, we did not learn it. Seizing the reins of the conversation, Queen Adinah guided it toward a more banal exchange. We learned about the games of chance Therinians favored, which involved carved dice or painted playing cards or anything on which one might conceivably wager; Lady Marylis inquired with roundabout discretion about the challenges involved in managing such a large household composed of members who did not age. All the royal women chuckled ruefully at the question and shared their favorite stories, some of which stretched back over centuries.

It was toward the end of the visit when Marylis broached a more serious topic in her confounding manner. "Passing through the city today, I saw signs that the scourge of Miasmania has reached even Zarkhoum's shores," she said in a casual tone. "I trust you find it as delightful as we do in Therin."

"Miasmania?" Queen Adinah echoed in confusion. "I've never heard of such a thing."

Lady Cyrgilen laughed. "Oh, 'tis a term we coined to name the phenomenon. Perhaps you know it by another name, for we saw the black star painted on a number of walls. There was a small disturbance in Merabaht quite recently, was there not? We heard rumors."

I was not deceived; I suspected they knew exactly what had transpired. An attack on the royal entourage and the death of a crown prince of the House of the Ageless was not something that could be concealed. "You speak of those calling themselves the Children of Miasmus," I said. "Have there been attacks in Therin? Mad Priests inciting people to violence?"

"Oh, well." Marylis waved a dismissive hand. "There has been some unpleasantness. Mad priests . . . you speak of the Harbingers of Doom, I imagine?" She shuddered. "Yes, we were graced with one such not six months ago. Such a tiresome fellow, always droning on about darkness rising to swallow the world."

"Oh, I don't know," Lady Cyrgilen said complacently. "It made for an interesting change, don't you think?"

"You said one such," I said to Lady Marylis. "Are there others? What do you know of these Harbingers?"

She shrugged. "There are always ghastly rumors coming out of the west, aren't there? Though I imagine you've been insulated from them here at the far end of the world. I suppose we might have had two if one counts the harbormaster. Do we count the harbormaster?" she asked her companion.

"Well, I think the harbormaster deserves to be counted," Cyrgilen replied judiciously. "If it weren't for him, we wouldn't know that those industrious little parasites can take a new host and drive it just as mad as the first. I'm sure he'd be charmed to know his death wasn't in vain."

"Can we not speak of more pleasant matters?" Zariya's mother pleaded. "This ought to be a happy occasion."

Zariya and I exchanged a glance.

"Ah, but there is an inquiry pending!" Marylis fixed me with her bright gaze. "And to my everlasting chagrin, I find myself forced once more to candor. Pahrkun's child, I cannot tell you what I do not know. I believe the coursers of Obid are investigating the phenomenon, but if they have learned anything, I have heard nothing of it. We in Therin are as confounded by the Harbingers as everyone else beneath the starless sky."

"Though I'm sure it's of absolutely no cause for concern whatsoever," her companion added in a cheerful tone.

Later, in Zariya's chambers, we discussed the conversation at length, both of us frustrated by the opacity of its nature, neither of us coming to any satisfactory conclusion save that *something* was happening, and it seemed no one knew enough to piece together the puzzle. All I could do was hope that Vironesh would return from his sojourn to seek the coursers of Obid sooner than expected with answers in hand.

And then three days after our meeting with the Therinian women, we received news that put the entire matter clear out of our minds.

Anamuht the Purging Fire was emerging from the desert on a course toward Merabaht.

A combination of exhilaration and panic gripped the city.

King Azarkal gave Prince Dozaren leave to command the City Guard and rally the Fire Brigade, which had not been deployed for an entire generation; it seemed Anamuht's infrequent ventures into Merabaht were not without their incendiary hazards. From what I could ascertain, Dozaren did a good job of preparing the city for her arrival, a fact that both reassured and galled me.

"My darling, I think I need to be there," Zariya said to me, her gaze strange and distant. "You've come face-to-face with the Scouring Wind and pledged your loyalty in a moment of perfect trust. Should your soul's twin offer less to the Purging Fire? Whether Anamuht asks it of me or not, I would do the same."

I nodded. "Then you shall do so."

It was not as simple a matter as I had supposed, for by tradition no one save Sister Nizara and the senior priestesses were allowed to be present in the Garden of Sowing Time when the harvest was quickened. After a morning's hurried negotiations, Sister Nizara combed through the temple's archives. Although she found no precedent, she concluded that the tradition owed more to sensible precaution against theft than any edict uttered by Anamuht, and agreed to allow us into the garden.

So it was that with Anamuht the Purging Fire bearing down upon the city, the Queen's Guard escorted Zariya and me into the Garden of Sowing Time, lowering her litter beneath an awning of water-soaked leather that had been erected on the lowest tier.

"Not here," Zariya said, craning her neck and gazing toward the summit of the stepped mountain. "Keep going, please. We'll make our stance on the uppermost tier."

Captain Tarshim didn't respond to her request, glancing at the High Priestess instead.

"It's too dangerous," Sister Nizara said firmly. "You'll be safer here, Zariya."

Zariya pointed. "That's exactly why I need to be *there*."

Sister Nizara hesitated, and I could see refusal gathering in her concerned frown. "You sought and found Anamuht in the high places, Elder Sister," I said to her. "Even as I found Pahrkun in the deep desert. Now the Purging Fire comes because Zariya has obeyed her decree. Will you deny your sister the same chance?"

She sighed and reached into a nearby tub to pull out a waterlogged piece of hide. "The *rhamanthus* burns as it quickens and falls," she said in a grim tone. "Have a care, for her safety lies upon your head, chosen."

I accepted the hide. "Do you think I do not know that, Elder Sister?"

Ignoring my rebuke, Sister Nizara carried on with her preparations, ordering buckets filled and placed around the perimeter of the temple. At Captain Tarshim's command, the Queen's Guard hoisted Zariya's litter once more and made the arduous climb to the highest tier. I followed, carrying the dripping hide.

"You'll be on your own for the descent, Your Highness," the captain warned Zariya as he assisted her out of the litter. "We won't be allowed back into the garden until every last seed has been gathered and tallied."

"I know," she said breathlessly. "Khai and I can manage. Oh, look!" Clutching my arm, she pointed toward a fiery glow on the eastern horizon. "She's coming!"

My pulse quickened. "I see." I turned to Captain Tarshim. "We'll be fine, thank you."

He gave me a wry salute. "I daresay you will."

The view from atop the summit was splendid and bizarre. The crowns of the *rhamanthus* trees on the lowest tier were on a level with us, forming a ring of vibrant green foliage, as though we stood at the center of some unearthly lagoon; the tall silver-grey trunks on the other levels stretched above us in concentric circles. We could not see the temple for the foliage, but the sprawling city far beneath us looked as small as a child's toy in the distance.

Zariya leaned on her canes, her gaze fixed eastward. As we watched, the glow resolved itself into a column of flame.

Anamuht was coming.

It happened faster than I would have reckoned, her great strides eating up vast amounts of ground. One moment it seemed the Purging Fire was a candle-flame in the distance, the next a blazing torch, the next a roaring bonfire; and then Anamuht crossed the River Ouris in a single stride and entered the city of Merabaht, a column of flame taller than a *rhamanthus* tree.

Zariya hobbled to the edge of the tier and I followed her, the soaked hide in my arms.

Beneath her robe of fire, Anamuht's feet were bone-white and skeletal, each one as wide as a street and as long as a city block. She placed her bony feet with care, ascending the tiers of the city. The skirts of her fiery robes brushed against buildings, leaving a trail of sparks and igniting fires in her wake. We could hear faint shouts as members of the Fire Brigade raced behind her, tiny figures passing buckets from hand to hand.

Closer and closer to the Garden of Sowing Time came Anamuht the Purging Fire, looming ever larger. My blood hammered in my veins and I could hear Zariya's ragged breath.

And then Anamuht was *there,* her flame-veiled face framed by the tallest of the silvery trunks on the upper tiers. Were the flames a veil or her face itself? I rather thought it was the latter. The flames danced and shifted, crimson and gold, as expressive in their own way as human features. The heat blasted my skin and my mouth was as dry as the desert; as in Pahrkun's presence, I had the urge to fling myself to the earth in prostration.

But no, I had withstood that ordeal. I had endured the sting of serpent and scorpion; I bore the marks of Pahrkun's favor on my cheeks. I was Zariya's shadow, and my soul's twin stood unwavering despite her canes, her face alight with a fearsome ecstasy.

Anamuht the Purging Fire bent toward her. *"Zariya, youngest of Azaria's lineage, you do not lack for courage."*

Zariya's voice caught in her throat. "I am quite terrified, my lady."

"And yet you are here." The veil of flame dipped in my direction. *"You and your shadow, who bears my brother's mark and carries the breath of the desert within him. Is it my blessing you now seek?"*

Hands gripping her canes so hard her knuckles whitened, Zariya lifted her chin. "I am here to pledge myself to you, my lady."

I would not have thought such stillness possible in the heart of the city; and yet, we were high above Merabaht. Below us were shouts and cries, distant and meaningless. Here there were only the three of us, the soft crackling of Anamuht's flames as she regarded Zariya, and Zariya's arms trembling as she supported herself on her canes and returned the goddess's regard, her face uplifted and adamant, the silent majesty of the *rhamanthus* trees surrounding us all.

I wanted to assist her, to help hold her upright, but everything within me told me that this was her moment.

"I heed you, youngest." Anamuht's face blazed brightly, and she echoed the words Pahrkun had said to me. *"Life and death. Fire and wind. These are the things over which my brother Pahrkun and I hold dominion in Zarkhoum. If the time is upon us, these are the gifts you and your soul's twin will carry to the end of the earth. These are the gifts you will summon, Sun-Blessed and shadow. Remember this."*

"I will remember," Zariya said in a steadfast tone, then gave me a side-long glance. *"We* will remember."

I nodded.

The corona of flames that was Anamuht's face flared again. *"Then give me your hand and receive my blessing."*

Taking a hoarse breath, Zariya shifted both her canes into her left hand and extended her right.

Anamuht's immense hand reached through the *rhamanthus* trunks, skeletal and white, bony index finger pointing. Blue-white lightning ran the length of her arm, then leapt from her pointing finger to Zariya's palm.

Zariya let out a cry of pain; for a moment, it seemed that fire limned her entire being, and then she dropped her canes and fell to the ground, cradling her right hand close to her body.

I dropped to my knees beside her. "Are you all right?"

"I'm fine, my darling," she murmured. "It stings, that's all."

"You suffered more at my brother's hands, Khai of the Fortress of the Winds," Anamuht said above us, straightening. *"And now, the harvest."*

In my naïveté, I had imagined that here atop the summit, we were beholding Anamuht at her full height. I was wrong. The column of living fire that was the goddess surged skyward, her head rising above the crown of the tallest tree. She reached out her arms and held forth both hands, bony fingers splayed. Lightning raced down her arms and forked from the tips of all ten fingers, once, twice, and again, crackling in the crowns of the *rhamanthus* trees, illuminating their massive green fronds. The fist-sized clusters of seeds began to glow and pulse.

Zariya and I stared in wonder. It wasn't until the first cluster burst with a resounding detonation that I thought to grab the waterlogged hide and raise it over our heads, holding it outstretched with both hands.

Rhamanthus seeds rained down from the sky, pattering on the hide. They fell around us in a red-hot hail, creating tiny craters in the earth, smoking as they cooled and kindling fires when they fell on dry grass. Zariya pulled herself closer to me, tugging her legs beneath the shelter of the hide. Now, I would have assisted her if I could, but I didn't dare free a hand to do so. All I could do was hold the soaked leather in place and pray that it provided sufficient protection. I could hear seeds sizzling atop it, threatening to burn through the hide.

I stole a glance at Zariya to see if she was frightened. Instead, her eyes were wide and shining. "It's wonderful, isn't it!"

I smiled. "It is."

It lasted no longer than a spring rain squall in the desert. When the seeds ceased to fall, I lowered the hide cautiously.

All around us, crimson *rhamanthus* seeds glowed in their miniature craters. Here and there, small fires burned. The tall trees stood unmoved, their leaves and trunks impervious to the lightning and flames that had quickened their fruits.

"It is done," Anamuht the Purging Fire announced far above us, her form dwindling from the unthinkably immense to the merely gigantic. Turning her face away, the goddess began making her descent.

Beside me, Zariya drew in a slow, deep breath and let it out carefully, flexing her right hand. "May I see?" I asked her. She held it out wordlessly to me. Taking it gently, I saw an intricate tracery of red marks etched into her palm and the back of her hand, feathering their way up her wrist and arm. "Does it hurt?"

She shook her head. "Not as it did, no. Only a little. What do you suppose it means, my heart?"

I pressed the softest of kisses into her palm before releasing it. "Beyond Anamuht's blessing, I cannot say."

"Life and death," Zariya mused. "Fire and wind."

"To the end of the earth," I added.

We sat in silence together for a moment, our shoulders touching, an untold wealth of *rhamanthus* seeds cooling around us. Anamuht the Purging Fire was receding in the distance, retracing her steps through the city of Merabaht, faint shouts of joy and alarm in her wake.

"We should go down," I said presently. "Sister Nizara will be worried. Shall I carry you?"

"Let me attempt it on my own." Zariya eyed the nearest *rhamanthus* seed, so close she had but to pluck it from the ground. "You know, I didn't think I'd be tempted."

"Are you?" I inquired.

"To steal one?" She smiled wryly. "I may be too young yet to fret over my youth and longevity, but the thought that a single seed might heal me of this affliction . . . yes, I am tempted." She clasped her hands together as though to ensure that they did not disobey her. "But it is not a temptation to which I will succumb. I do not hold my honor lightly, dearest. And Father has promised. We will know soon enough, you and I."

THIRTY-FIVE

Five thousand, one hundred and sixty-three.

That was the final tally of *rhamanthus* seeds announced by Sister Nizara, looking weary and hollow-eyed with the effort of coordinating the harvest, at the gathering of the House of the Ageless in the Hall of Pleasant Accord.

All save Princess Fazarah were present, and one might suppose the mood would be a celebratory one, but no. Now that the long drought had ended, there was increased displeasure at the fact that over half the harvest would be committed to Zariya's dowry, while the rest of the seeds would be divided between the king's wives and remaining children and their households.

I listened to the complaints and protestations with half an ear, reasonably confident that King Azarkal would not seek to circumvent Anamuht's edict. Indeed, he looked impatient at the bickering. I wondered how he had stood it for so many centuries, but I could not find it in my heart to pity him. If he hadn't taken so many wives and gotten so many children on them, it wouldn't be an issue.

Then again, he if hadn't . . . Zariya would never have been born.

That was a sobering thought.

Sister Nizara had not had a chance to consult the archives, but so far as she knew, the blessing that Anamuht had bestowed on Zariya was unprecedented. So, too, was the fact that Zariya had sought it.

"Enough!" the king said at length, silencing the grumbling. "We do not quarrel with the gods and the matter is not open to debate. Zariya's dowry stands. In three days' time, she will board Lord Rygil's ship and set sail for Therin." He paused a moment, then continued in a firm voice. "Along with her shadow, Khai, and a score of Royal Guardsmen, I will accompany her myself."

The announcement was greeted with a startled outburst from almost everyone save Prince Dozaren.

King Azarkal raised one hand, the pulse-point of *khementaran* beating at his wrist, a reminder that he had returned to a state of mortality. "My mind is resolved. If it is Anamuht's decree that my youngest must wed a foreigner, I will see it done with honor and respect."

"But as your heir, surely it's Dozaren's place to represent you," Queen Adinah protested. I had no doubt that she was eager to get him out of the way for a good length of time.

"Dozaren will rule in my stead until my return," the king said calmly, and Prince Dozaren inclined his head. "He has proved himself able in these past weeks." His gaze shifted to Zariya. "On the eve of her departure, Zariya and her shadow will partake of the *rhamanthus*."

"I trust the seeds will be counted against her dowry," Queen Rashina said tartly. "It's hardly fair otherwise."

King Azarkal compressed his lips in a grim line. "I will not shortchange the terms of a dowry dictated by Anamuht herself." Plucking the crown from his head, he drew his belt-knife and pried two *rhamanthus* seeds from their settings before anyone could comment. "Eldest daughter, I give these into your custody," he said to Sister Nizara, who accepted them with a silent salute. The king glanced around at the disgruntled members of his fractious household. "That is all."

Two days until Zariya and I would partake of the *rhamanthus*; three days until we set sail for Therin.

I will own, I was apprehensive. In the absence of Vironesh, who had seen so much of the world, I would have welcomed a visit from Brother Merik and his stalwart presence, or Brother Yarit and his crude, sage advice. On the cusp of this pending adventure, attendant with portents and prophecies, I felt my youth and ignorance keenly. I knew the desert and I knew fighting. I did not know if that was enough to keep Zariya safe in a strange land across the sea where no one said what they meant, in a world beset by the threat of a rising menace.

And then there was the matter of Dozaren. I knew it was preying on Zariya's mind.

"I have been thinking," Zariya said to me the day after the king's announcement. "And I have come to a conclusion."

I raised my brows at her. "Oh?"

She didn't look happy about it, but her voice was steady. "We need to tell my sister Fazarah about Dozaren's involvement in the attack and what we suspect of her own husband."

"Are you sure?" Despite everything, she yet harbored a fondness for Dozaren.

She nodded. "It started to come clear to me yesterday listening to the wretched lot of them squabbling over the *rhamanthus,* and Dozaren doing his best not to look smug at the chance to rule in Father's stead. Perhaps he's earned it; to the lion go the spoils and so forth. Perhaps he'll even be a tolerable ruler. After all, he's made a decent start. But I could not help but consider Fazarah's absence and think to myself that my dear old nurse Soresh is right. Fazarah is the best of us. She deserves to know."

"It seems to me that your sister and her husband have an uncommonly happy marriage," I said. Although I did not want to dissuade Zariya, I wanted to be certain she was aware of the ramifications of her choice. "This may destroy it."

"There are people in this world who would prefer a pleasant fiction to a painful truth," Zariya said. "I do not believe my sister is one of them." She spread the fingers of her right hand and turned it this way and that, contemplating the tracery of marks. "We venture into the unknown, my heart. I do not wish to regret leaving with this particular truth untold."

I saluted her. "I will call upon your sister on the morrow."

I cannot say that Princess Fazarah was pleased to see me, arriving as I did without an invitation, but she received me graciously enough.

"Once again you surprise me, my sister's shadow." She poured a cup of mint tea for me. "Should you not be preparing for your departure to Therin?"

"There is something that I must tell you, my lady." I accepted the cup and set it down, lowering my voice. "It is not an easy thing. And you may wish to ensure that there are no servants present."

Her mouth took on a stubborn set. "Unlike the rest of the House of the Ageless, I have earned the privilege of trusting every member of my household."

I said nothing.

After a moment, Fazarah rose and spoke quietly to the servants in attendance. They saluted and departed, and she returned to sit across from me. "Tell me."

I did.

I think there must have been a part of her that suspected something was amiss, for she betrayed no surprise nor did she question Dozaren's guilt or my suspicion of her husband Tarkhal's complicity.

No, her response was a mixture of quiet grief and slow, simmering anger. "What, exactly, does Zariya expect me to do with this knowledge?" she asked me with knife-edged precision. "Shall I accuse my husband of plotting my own brother's murder? Confront Dozaren? Carry the tale to our father, who bears little love for me, while she sails blithely away with her dowry of three thousand *rhamanthus* seeds? It is an unkind parting gift with which my sister has burdened me."

An answering anger stirred in me. "Zariya has no expectations," I said. "She merely thought you would prefer a harsh truth to a pleasant lie and deserved to know it. But perhaps she was mistaken."

Fazarah looked away. "Why did she not tell our father herself? He favors her. He would listen to her."

"Perhaps," I said. "Or perhaps not. Perhaps she will yet tell him on the passage to Therin, for he means to accompany her. But there is no proof, and your father the king himself allowed and abetted this endless conspiring." I gestured around. "You have your own household, my lady, peopled with servants you trust. Zariya is confined to the palace and has no one but me. Prince Dozaren is the nearest thing to an ally she possesses among the serpents' nest of her siblings. What do you suppose her life would be worth if she betrayed him?"

It was Princess Fazarah's turn to be silent. "Forgive me my harsh words, my sister's shadow," she murmured at length. "I know Zariya's lot is not an easy one, and I am not ungrateful for her candor. But this is a bitter pill to swallow. Dozaren's actions come as no surprise, but I thought my husband and I were in greater accord. Your revelation carries the sting of betrayal."

I bowed my head in understanding. "I beg your pardon for burdening you with it, my lady."

After that there was little left to say. I drank my tea and Fazarah escorted me to the door, her expression grave and distant.

I hesitated before taking my leave of her. "My lady . . . there is one more thing. Thus far, having secured the succession, Prince Dozaren has acquitted himself well. It may be that he will prove himself a capable ruler and a suitable heir in your father's absence. But if he does not, you are not without recourse. If it should come to it, you might seek the support of the desert tribesfolk. They would rally to the banner of the Brotherhood of Pahrkun."

Fazarah offered me a salute. "Thank you, Khai of the Fortress of the Winds. I will bear it in mind."

So it was done, and I was glad to have it done and behind us.

I did not know if it would make any difference, nor did I especially care. My duty was done and discharged. My world was pivoting on its axis and pointing westward, toward Therin and the unknown.

But all that mattered to me was Zariya.

The remaining days counting down to our departure were marked with a flurry of domestic activity in the women's quarter. New clothing was designed by the royal seamstresses, fabric was draped and measured and cut and sewn, trunks of belongings were packed, unpacked, and packed again. Messages flew back and forth between the palace and the Therinian stateship docked in the harbor.

Was there room aboard the ship for Zariya's little feathered friends in their wooden cage?

Yes, of course, but they might not adapt well to Therin's cooler clime.

Need we commission warmer attire?

No, it would be Lord Rygil's honor to provide it.

The one thing of which Zariya and I did not speak was the *rhamanthus*, although it was always there between us. I knew how much she yearned to believe it would heal her, so much so that she scarce dared give voice to it.

I did, too.

It was a measure of the strength of the bond between us that I gave precious little thought to the effects of the *rhamanthus* seed on my own person. I was young and hale; it would allow me to continue to be young and hale. Ah, but Zariya . . . there was so much more at stake for her.

On the eve of our departure, the ceremony took place in the Hall of Pleasant Gathering. As she had done at the wedding, Sister Nizara held the seeds forth on a padded cushion of gold silk.

"Each of these seeds has been quickened by Anamuht the Purging Fire," she said to Zariya and me. "Each bears a spark of the sun's fire; each represents a year of enduring youth and vitality. Partake, my Sun-Blessed sister, and lead a long and virtuous life. Partake, my sister's shadow, and enter the House of the Ageless."

Despite the glowing spark in their garnet depths, the seeds were cool to the touch; still I could not help but remember seeing the harvest fall like burning rain, sizzling on the ox hide and smoking on the ground.

"Will you go first, my darling?" Zariya's voice held a tremor. "I am frightened."

"The *rhamanthus* will not harm you," her sister the High Priestess reassured her.

"It is not harm I fear," Zariya murmured. "It is failure."

"I will go first," I said to her. "But if the *rhamanthus* does not heal you, it is no failure of yours."

I put the *rhamanthus* seed in my mouth, feeling it cool and smooth on my tongue, then swallowed. For the space of a few heartbeats I felt nothing, then warmth blossomed in the pit of my belly; a wondrous, radiating warmth as though I had indeed swallowed a drop of pure sunlight. It spread through my limbs, infusing my entire body with health and energy and vigor until it seemed it must burst forth from my tingling fingertips. I could have fought a hundred duels or leapt to the top of the palace wall. I felt glorious, as though Anamuht herself were smiling upon me, the Purging Fire cleansing away any impurities.

"Oh, Zariya!" I gasped; though it might be a breach of protocol, I could not help myself. "It's *wonderful*!"

She took one of her slow, careful breaths and glanced around the hall at the smooth, ageless faces of her family. Her mother's expression was suffused with painfully obvious hope; her father's was stoic. The others ran a gamut, but Prince Dozaren wore a look of tender concern that sparked a faint pang of guilt in me, as well as annoyance at the eternal scheming and maneuvering of the House of the Ageless that pitted them against one another.

Although, having partaken of the *rhamanthus*, I understood it a bit better. It was a powerful experience, one I could imagine being anxious to ensure was not taken from me if I understood it to be my birthright.

With my blood still singing in my veins, I watched Zariya place the seed in her mouth and swallow.

It would heal her.

I was sure of it.

I saw the moment of awe strike her, heard her inhale sharply and fully. Her eyes widened. Canes braced in her left hand, she straightened. *Now,* I thought in exultation; *now* is the moment when Zariya will cast aside her canes and stand squarely on her own two feet, her body purged of the fever's lingering damage.

But no, I was wrong.

Instead, Zariya raised her right hand; a girl's hand, delicate and manicured, yet strong from a lifetime of gripping her canes. The gold-embroidered sleeve of her crimson silk gown slipped downward, baring the intricate traceries of Anamuht's blessing that trailed up her slender forearm.

The marks were alight with a golden glow, flickering with a beat that owed nothing to her heart. Her raised hand was limned in brightness. The mica-flecked scars on my cheekbones itched and prickled with a strange sympathy and I felt a breeze stirring around me.

"Is it *khementaran*?" someone asked uncertainly. "So soon?"

Sister Nizara shook her head wordlessly; whatever it was, it was nothing she'd seen before.

"It's not *khementaran*." Zariya's voice was thick with awe. "It's nothing of the sort, but I don't know what."

Beating more rapidly, the golden glow sputtered and died like a new-kindled flame starved for air, leaving behind the faint red marks that laced her hand and climbed her arm like a vine. With a sigh, Zariya lowered her hand. I felt the breeze around me die, too. Averting her head, she shifted one of her canes back into her right hand and leaned on both of them.

My heart ached for her, and even though I knew the answer, I had to ask the question. "Your legs?"

Lifting her head, Zariya met my gaze. Her luminous eyes were filled with a mixture of wonder and profound regret. "I'm afraid those limbs remain unchanged, my darling."

THIRTY-SIX

There was a great deal of speculation in the wake of the *rhamanthus* ceremony, none of it leading to any conclusions. At a loss to explain the phenomenon, Sister Nizara pledged once more to scour the archives.

Zariya was quiet and withdrawn, offering little to the discussion. I felt her disappointment as keenly as the edge of a blade, but she bore it with dignity during this last night on Zarkhoumi soil.

It was not until we were alone in her chambers that she allowed herself to weep, curled tightly into herself atop her bed, her shoulders shaking and her breath hitching in her chest. I climbed onto the pallet behind her and held her in my arms, offering what meager comfort my presence afforded her, my throat tight with sympathy.

Still, it was not long before Zariya turned to me. Her face was wet with tears, but her expression was fierce. "No more!" she breathed. "That is the last time you'll hear me weep for my affliction, my darling."

I touched her damp cheek. "It is the only time, and you are more than entitled to your grief."

She shook her head. "It was hope that made me weak. Now I must be strong. And I must remember I have been given gifts I never dared dream of. Tomorrow, we set sail across the sea, you and I."

I smiled at her. "I daresay you are a bit more excited by the prospect than I."

"You will be a wondrous sailor," Zariya said in a firm tone. "As you are wondrous at so many things, my heart. And if there is in truth a darkness rising against which I must stand, I will do so because I have you to lean upon."

"And I will be beside you to the end of the earth," I said. "No matter what may come."

"Miasmania." She gave the word a wry twist, pulling herself upright and scrubbing at her tear-stained face. "I think the Therinians are right, we have been isolated here in Zarkhoum. And I do not believe that they will be so quick to dismiss the signs of prophecy."

I sat and crossed my legs beneath me. "Nor the notion that you might have a role to play."

"You and I, my shadow," Zariya corrected me. "Wind and fire. You felt it, didn't you?"

I nodded.

She spread her fingers, then clenched her hand into a fist and regarded it. "In the moment, I truly felt I might summon the lightning like Anamuht herself. But then . . ." She opened her hand again as though to release some fragile, ephemeral thing in her grasp. "The moment passed."

"Then it will come again," I said.

"But will I be ready when it does?" she inquired. "You are Pahrkun's chosen, capable of channeling his wind, and your life has been honed to a single purpose. All I have done is manage to survive my family."

I thought about it. "Well, it seems to me that Anamuht considered that quite sufficient."

It won a smile from her. "A fair point, and perhaps it is so. It is to be hoped that we will learn more of what the Therinians know on our journey."

"We can but try," I said dryly, making her smile again.

Zariya glanced toward the doors onto the enclosed garden. "The hour grows late and we ought to sleep, dearest." Her voice changed and took on a vulnerable note. "Would you mind staying with me tonight instead of taking to your pallet?"

I shook my head. "Of course not."

Nim the Bright Moon was three-quarters full and high overhead, the sole occupant of the starless skies that night, spilling silvery light into the bedchamber in the small hours before dawn. I held Zariya close, tucked into the curve of my body, feeling her ribcage rise and fall beneath my arm.

She slept like a child, perfect and trusting. I gazed at her profile, lips sweetly parted, eyelids yet swollen from her bout of tears.

I thought about the fact that at the end of our journey, she would wed the Therinian Lord Rygil. We would always belong to each other, Zariya and I. But it would be different.

"You are my life," I whispered to her in the moon-silvered darkness. "You are my heart and my home. You are my honor. And I promise you, this will never change."

She murmured an unintelligible affirmation in her sleep.

At length, I slept, too.

In the morning, Zariya set her birds free.

I did not know what she was about when she asked me to bring the three-tiered wooden cage into the garden, though of course I did so willingly. Her little friends chirped and cheeped and clung to their perches, beating their wings in confusion. Zariya followed on her canes. "There," she said breathlessly, and I set the cage down on a bench. With deft fingers, she opened the door.

The yellow songbird that Prince Dozaren had given her was the first to venture across the threshold, taking wing with a trill. The others made more tentative forays, but one by one, they took flight. One fellow with iridescent green feathers circled the garden multiple times, returning to chatter at us, but in the end even he vanished over the high wall.

With a sigh, Zariya closed the door of the empty cage. "Onward, my darling."

I picked up the cage. "Onward."

Members of the Queen's Guard came to fetch Zariya's trunks and cart them to the ship, accompanied by her maidservant Nalah, who would attend to Zariya during the journey.

There was to be a formal procession from the palace to the harbor, but among the royal women, only Sister Nizara would accompany it. She waited with me, carrying a steel-bound coffer in her arms, while Zariya bade her final farewells to her mother and aunts and those of her sisters who had come to be there on this last morning. For my part, I would miss Zariya's birds more than her kin, but I kept my mouth shut on that thought, only asking Sister Nizara if she had found aught of significance in the archives. She shook her head with quiet regret and promised to continue searching.

Somehow, I did not believe there was anything to find. Whatever was happening, I doubted there was a precedent for it.

Once again, I wished Brother Yarit was here. But no, the Fortress of the Winds was far away; and today, I would leave it even farther behind me, taking with me only the lessons and the training that had been instilled in me there.

When the procession gathered, Sister Nizara made a ceremony of opening the coffer she carried to display the bounty within it, an incalculable wealth of *rhamanthus* seeds glowing like a great pile of embers.

"Zariya of the House of the Ageless, Sun-Blessed sister, here is your dowry," she said formally to Zariya. "Three thousand seeds tallied by my own hand." Closing the lid, she turned to the king. "My liege and father, I give this into your keeping that it may be kept under guard at all times until the wedding takes place." King Azarkal accepted the coffer, then turned it in his hands. Sister Nizara removed a key strung around her neck on a golden chain and locked the coffer, then presented the key to Zariya, already seated within her litter. "My sister, I give this into your keeping as a token that the dowry is yours and yours alone to bestow upon your household."

"May it be given into Khai's keeping instead?" Zariya inquired.

Her sister hesitated, then gave a decisive nod. Beckoning me forward, she placed the chain around my neck. "I can think of no safer place for it."

I tucked the key beneath my tunic, and with that, we were under way.

The procession wound its way through the streets of Merabaht, flanked by a double line of mounted Royal Guardsmen, a score of whom would be accompanying us to Therin. As before, I walked beside Zariya's litter, trusting more to my skills afoot than on horseback.

I would not say the mood in the city was peaceful, but it was calmer than it had been since I had first set foot within it. Prince Dozaren had taken measures to quell the unrest he had exploited. The Mad Priest was dead and gone and Anamuht the Purging Fire had trod its streets for the first time in living memory for many of its denizens, who were waiting and watchful, mindful that she had renewed the longstanding pledge of favor that the Sacred Twins had bestowed upon the Sun-Blessed.

I daresay no one wanted to invoke a goddess's wrath, and for that, I did not blame them one whit.

The Therinian state-ship was even larger than I remembered it. A vast barge four stories tall, it bore rows of massive oars that protruded from its lower levels. Atop the uppermost deck were four masts affixed with myriad furled sails, pennants in the cool blue and green colors of Therin fluttering atop them.

Lord Rygil hailed us from the top deck. "King Azarkal, I am unworthy of the honor!" he called merrily. "I pray you and your daughter, my most dearly betrothed, will accept our humble excuse for hospitality on our sojourn together."

The king and his honor guard and other members of the entourage dismounted, and there was a flurry of farewells there in the harbor, the sea breeze blowing from the west.

Somehow, I found myself caught up in an unexpected embrace from Prince Dozaren.

"My dear Khai," he murmured against my temple. "I *am* sorry about the way matters fell out." His strong hands flexed on my shoulders, his black hair falling over his brow and his dark gaze intent upon my own. "Promise me that you will keep my sister safe?"

By all the fallen stars, he confused me.

I gave him a brusque nod. "Honor beyond honor, my lord. All that is within my power, I will do."

Dozaren released me with a final squeeze and a sigh, turning to part the curtains of Zariya's litter and plant a kiss on her veiled cheek. What they said to each other, I did not hear.

And then there were no more farewells to be said. Sister Nizara lifted her hand in a formal blessing. "May the Sacred Twins grace and guide your journey, and Zar the Sun, the father of us all, ever light your path."

The king and half the guards boarded first. I walked behind Zariya's litter up the wide boarding ramp, the remaining guards bringing up the rear. Above us, Lord Rygil saluted us and called out a welcome.

Zariya and I parted ways with the king's entourage when cheerful attendants directed her bearers to a private chamber allotted to us on the third
story of the ship, where Nalah was arranging Zariya's trunks and unpack-
ing some of her things. It was even more richly appointed than the chamber
in which Lady Marylis had received me, and I was pleased by the indication
that the Therinians meant to treat Zariya with the respect due her stature.

Once the bearers had departed to stow the litter, Zariya sank into one of
the tall, high-backed chairs, allowing her eyes to close briefly. "Are they
treating you well thus far, Nalah?"

"Well enough, my lady," her maidservant said uncertainly. "I've been
given a berth to share with the other ladies' maids. They are not unkind but
their manner of speaking is . . . strange."

"So it is." Zariya opened her eyes. "But I trust we will all become accustomed to it. At least you no longer need spy upon me and carry tales to
Queen Adinah."

Her maidservant flushed. "It was never out of spite or malice, my lady."

Zariya regarded her. "The women's quarter of the Sun Palace was not
an easy place to be a child, and I daresay in most ways it was more difficult
to be a servant. Let us make a clean start of it, shall we?"

Nalah offered her a fervent salute. "Yes, my lady."

There was a knock at the chamber door, which was unlatched and swung
open before Nalah could answer it; moving without thinking, I spun and
drew my weapons, *yakhan* and *kopar* singing free of their scabbards.

Lady Marylis blinked at me. "Oh, my! Is that a traditional Zarkhoumi
greeting?"

I scowled at her in response and sheathed my weapons. "Of course not."

Ignoring my rudeness, she addressed Zariya. "Your Highness, if it might
amuse you to watch the departure, there is a deck at the rear of the ship on
this level secured for your privacy."

"That is kind of you," Zariya said to her. "You need not go to such measures to accommodate our customs."

"Your customs." Lady Marylis pursed her lips. "Such a quaint word, is it
not? Such a *small* word for the differences between us. We are, shall I say,
unaccustomed to such segregation between women and men in Therin. If you

would care to join my brother on the top deck, I suspect he would not mind in the least."

Zariya smiled wryly. "I do appreciate the invitation, but perhaps it would be best not to scandalize my father on our first day at sea." She hesitated, then added, "And I fear I might find it difficult to make the ascent without assistance. You see, I suffered Dhanbu fever as a child, and it has left me with . . . certain limitations."

I saw Marylis take in the implications, saw her bright gaze dart to Zariya's canes propped nearby. "Ah. I infer that you and my brother will not dance the wild gavotte at your wedding."

"No." Reaching for her canes, Zariya levered herself to her feet and lifted her chin. "Does it matter?"

A series of complicated expressions crossed Marylis's face. "Call it a selfish whim, but my brother *is* desirous of an heir, Your Highness."

"Of course." Zariya inclined her head. "The physicians assure me that I'm perfectly capable of bearing children."

"And Zariya's dowry of three thousand *rhamanthus* seeds is also assured," I muttered. Although I liked the woman well enough, I was mindful of the fact that no matter what manner of man her brother was, he would never have sued for the hand of the least daughter of the House of the Ageless were it not for her staggering dowry.

This comment, too, Lady Marylis ignored. "I suspect it was not your choice to withhold this piece of information," she said to Zariya. "Thus I shall flout convention and thank you for your candor in the hopes that it will encourage you to likewise flout custom, for my brother is eager to make greater acquaintance with his bride on this journey." Her expression softened. "Doubtless it escaped your notice, but we in Therin value quick-wittedness over physical prowess. The game of questions to which you put your suitors surely demonstrates the former." She paused. "Indeed, I made mock of my brother for being so foolish as to wonder whom you might have chosen had the other Granthian proved victorious."

It was clear that the comment was a question, and Zariya frowned as she considered how best to answer it in a manner both truthful and diplomatic. "I cannot say, my lady. The opportunity to make that choice was taken from me, and though it cost a man his life, perhaps I must be grateful for it. I do not deny that Sandrath the Quiet's gift and his answers moved me, but I am not sure I would have been happy in Granth. The questions were not the only test," she added. "Khai donned the guise of a palace maidservant that he might observe my suitors as they awaited their audiences. Your brother spoke courteously to him."

Lady Marylis let out a delighted laugh. "Ah, well! You shall be downright miserable in Therin." She gestured. "But for now, Your Highness, shall we witness your departure from the shores of Zarkhoum?"

"I would like that," Zariya admitted.

It was a sight to behold.

Twin sets of oars on either side of the state-ship dipped and hauled, churning the water and propelling the mammoth barge out of the harbor. Standing beside Zariya, I watched the coastline recede. Above us, I heard the rush and snap of sails unfurling and catching wind. We picked up speed, although not a great deal of it. As I understood, the inbound journey from Therin had been swift and smooth, the ship riding the great eastern current. Our return would be neither, for now we must navigate the complicated labyrinth of smaller counter-currents and eddies closer to the Nexus and rely more heavily upon wind- and oar-power.

Even so, although I misliked this business of traveling on the open sea, it was exhilarating.

Our journey had begun.

SEA

THIRTY-SEVEN

On the first day, Lord Rygil issued an invitation to Zariya to join him and his sister and her father for the evening meal in his stateroom; an invitation she politely declined, as she did when it was repeated the next day.

When the third invitation arrived, she sent word to her father that she wished to speak to him.

I daresay I was in large part the cause. Our chamber was pleasant enough and the secluded viewing deck afforded hours of entertainment watching the seabirds and dolphins that trailed in our wake. Left to her own devices, Zariya might have been content to pass the journey in a manner respectful of Zarkhoumi customs. But I was restless at the confinement. At least in the women's quarter of the palace, I'd had the outlet of sparring with the Queen's Guard. Aboard the ship, I was all the more the caged hawk that Zariya had once named me; and although she urged me to fly free and explore, I was reluctant to leave her side. The Therinians *seemed* honorable, but I was unwilling to entrust Zariya's life to that assumption.

And, too, Zariya was curious.

"I am betrothed to a Therinian lord," she said to her father. "Men and women commingle freely in Therin, and I shall have to adopt their ways sooner or later. Is there any point in delaying?"

King Azarkal scowled. "You're not wed yet, daughter."

Zariya raised her brows at him. "Do you doubt that I shall be, Father?"

In the end, the king acceded to her wishes, only stipulating that I must continue to attend her at all times—a stipulation with which I wholeheartedly agreed—and that Zariya must continue to wear a veil in her betrothed's presence in a concession to Zarkhoumi modesty.

So it came to pass that on the third evening of our journey, we dined with Lord Rygil.

Steep ladders conjoined the ship's decks, but mindful of Zariya's limitations, Lady Marylis had ordered a sling devised by which attendants might raise and lower her between the levels.

I will own, when we first emerged onto the uppermost deck beneath the open sky, I felt myself able to breathe freely for the first time since we had boarded. I craned my neck to stare up at the tall masts and their myriad sails, yearning to scramble up the rigging as I'd seen Barakhan sailors do in the harbor, yearning to flex my muscles and pit myself against something, anything.

Knowing my mind, Zariya gave me an affectionate look. "Perhaps tomorrow, my darling. If you might trust me safe while in plain sight and attended by my father's guards for a moment's time?"

I gazed fixedly at the tall masts that appeared to bob and sway against the sky. "Perhaps."

Between the king's discomfort at the breach of protocol, the confounding manner of Therinian discourse, and the tall table and uncomfortable high-backed chairs they favored, it was a stilted meal; still, I preferred it to dining in the company of the House of the Ageless. I could not always tell what was said in jest and what in earnest, but at least I wasn't forced to endure an endless exchange of false endearments between family members likely plotting murder or mayhem. And it grew easier as the evening wore on, aided by the liberal application of a tart-tasting wine pressed from a fruit called a grape. Although I partook sparingly of it, I found myself relaxing as King Azarkal lowered his guard.

"I'd have wagered good coin that I first saw you in the arena, Khai, but my sister swears otherwise," Lord Rygil remarked. "Yet I'm sure it can't be true that the delightful maidservant who took pity on a party of miserable, sweating Therinians is the same dauntless warrior who defeated Granth's champion."

"I assure you, we are one and the same, my lord," I said to him. "And you claimed you did not mind the heat a bit."

He laughed, and beneath her veil, Zariya smiled into her wine cup. "Well, then, it seems I must believe!" Lord Rygil offered me a sincere salute. "As a son of Ilharis the Two-Faced, I acknowledge your dual nature."

In the days that followed, I was happier than I'd been since our time at the Villa of Heart's Ease.

I liked the Therinians.

For all their confounding ways, I sensed no malice in them. Nothing about them made my skin prickle in warning. In their own oblique manner, they were kind—not just Lord Rygil and his sister and her companions, but the attendants and the sailors and oarsmen, too. Once King Azarkal consented to allow the Royal Guard to attend Zariya when she ventured to the uppermost deck, I allowed myself to partake of a degree of the greater freedom she urged me to enjoy.

There was a viewing platform atop the second mast called a crow's nest—a crow being a Therinian bird of some sort—that I liked best of all the places aboard the state-ship, high above the sea, reaching toward the sky like the crown of a *rhamanthus* tree. There the sailors kept watch for uncharted fluctuations in the counter-currents and eddies, or obstacles like patches of strangling kelp that might bring down even such a vast ship as ours. The lookouts posted in the crow's nest seemed pleased by my company when I clambered up the rigging to join them, engaging me in genial conversation and pointing out such sights as there were to be seen.

Once, I saw a flock of seabirds drifting on the waves take alarmed flight as a winged shark launched itself from beneath them, twisting in the air, its great maw opening like a trap and snapping shut on its prey. Vironesh had mentioned such a thing to me. I wondered where he was, what he had learned, and how long it would take him to find us in Therin, but it did not seem so pressing as it once did. Although we had not yet succeeded in drawing out the Therinians in the matter of prophecy, there was ample time on the journey and there were no strange signs or portents to trouble my thoughts in the meanwhile.

The coffer of *rhamanthus* seeds resided in the king's quarters, guarded at all times; the key resided around my neck. There were no indications that anyone meant to make an attempt on either.

The air grew cooler, but it was yet mild enough for comfort.

By all appearances, Lord Rygil was genuinely taken with Zariya, delighting in her quick wit and showing no signs of being troubled by her affliction or the fact that it had not been divulged to him. It seemed his sister's reassurances regarding Therinian values held true, and I was grateful for it. Perhaps I could not rejoice wholeheartedly at the prospect of Zariya's marriage, but her safety and happiness were the most important things in the world to me. And, too, I was the one who had advocated for him over the Barakhan prince. It reassured me to think I'd chosen wisely.

Even King Azarkal seemed as close to happy as I'd ever seen him. The further we got from Zarkhoum, the easier his demeanor grew. Despite the onset of *khementaran,* he actually looked younger to my eyes, the unnaturally smooth cast of his features becoming more expressive and vibrant.

Zariya thought so, too. We had been at sea for a week's time and were within a day of reaching Granthian waters when she remarked upon it. Her father smiled, the corners of his eyes crinkling. "Oddly enough, I find myself remembering what it feels like to be a young man for the first time in many, many years, my heart."

"I'm glad," she said simply.

"It was not my choice to surrender to mortality, but there is a certain relief to it," he mused. "So I was always told, and now I find it is true."

We were standing beside the railing of the uppermost deck, where we had been watching a capricious pod of dolphins. Zariya glanced around, but since I was with her, the guards hung back at a respectful distance. "I hope you no longer feel that you have lived too long, Father."

King Azarkal was silent for a moment, the wind ruffling the hair of his uncrowned head. "The thought of you being exiled from my presence broke my heart," he remarked presently. "But this Lord Rygil seems a fine enough fellow for all his double-talking ways. If I live to see you happily wed, I have not lived too long."

Zariya smiled at her father. "Then I am glad of that, too."

"I will remain in Therin long enough to be sure it is so," he promised her. "And then . . ." He laughed, an unexpected sound. "Who knows? Perhaps I will sail the four great currents and see the rest of the world. Why return to the serpents' den I hatched? Dozaren has proved himself an able enough ruler. Having surrendered immortality, why not surrender the throne?"

Furrowing her brow, Zariya shot me a look, her fingers moving in a silent question. *Should I tell him?*

I shrugged helplessly in response, spreading my hands. *I don't know.*

It was a calm day, the twin banks of oars two decks beneath us dipping and splashing as the state-ship wended its way along the lesser counter-currents. "Father," Zariya said carefully, "you should know that I am fairly certain Dozaren orchestrated the attack that killed Tazaresh and arranged that Elizar should take the blame for it."

The king looked at her, all traces of good humor vanishing to leave his expression impossible to decipher. "Yes, I suspected it was possible," he said in a tone as unreadable as his expression. "I've always underestimated him. But he wasn't caught at it."

"Is that all that matters?" Zariya asked quietly. "To the lion go the spoils?"

Her father looked back at the sea. "And who would you have me name in his place? Elizar?"

"No." Zariya hesitated, and I knew her sister Fazarah's name was fore-most in her thoughts. I watched her gauge whether or not it was worth her while to speak it, and determine with regret that it was not. "At least Doza-ren has an ounce of kindness in his soul," she said instead. "But I suppose at some point, you might consider persuading him to have Elizar pardoned for the crime he did not commit."

"At some point," the king agreed dryly. "Elizar has plenty of other sins on his head."

The guilty urge to finger the back of my neck surfaced, but it passed as Zariya deftly turned the conversation to other matters.

I thought to myself that perhaps that night I would break my silence and tell her the one secret I'd withheld from her, but when Nalah had been dismissed for the evening and we were alone, it was the conversation with her father that Zariya wished to discuss.

"Do you think I did the right thing, my darling?" she asked me. "Should I have said more? Or said nothing at all?"

"I think you did exactly what you could," I said honestly. "I think you said what was needful. I do not think he would have listened to more. And I am quite sure he wouldn't have entertained the notion of appointing your sister his heir."

"That's what I thought." Zariya sounded relieved to have it confirmed. "I tell you, this is the last I will speak of the matter. I am *done* with the endless intrigues of the House of the Ageless as surely as I am with tears." Her tone turned adamant. "Tonight, here and now, I leave it behind me. I shall wed Lord Rygil and learn to be a proper Therinian wife and mother. I shall learn to speak lightly of the things I hold dear, and somberly of frivolities. I shall learn to play games of wit and guile with painted playing cards, and wager on the outcome of the most trifling of matters . . ."

I closed my eyes, listening to her carry on. The state-ship rocked gently beneath us. At first the motion had disturbed me, but now I found it soothing. The sea anchors had been dropped for the night that we might not drift far astray or run afoul of another ship. In the days of old, the sailors had told me, it was said that such a thing would not be necessary, for they might continue to navigate by the myriad stars of the children of the heavens, each of whom occupied a fixed territory in the night sky. Now there were only the wandering moons to light the starless sky.

I should tell Zariya about the Teardrop, I thought to myself; but no, now was not the time.

Instead I let her talk and talk, her voice lulling me to sleep.

In the morning, Lady Marylis conveyed an invitation from her brother to join them atop the uppermost deck as the realm of Granth came into view.

The wind had picked up overnight and we were making good progress past the Granthian coast. Traveling on the counter-currents, we were too far away to make out many details except their own tall lighthouse, but from our vantage point one could see that Granth was a mountainous land with forested slopes stretching down toward the sea. Above the tree line, a great range of barren peaks towered over the interior.

"Oh!" Zariya pointed toward the highest peak, from which a plume of dark smoke trickled into the blue sky and trailed westward. "Is that what I think it is?"

"That would be the abode of Droth the Great Thunder," Lord Rygil said lightly. "Belching smoke and dreaming of crushing peasants beneath his mighty claws, no doubt. Once every seven years, he awakens and descends to bind his offspring into the service of the newly victorious Kagan."

I was considering climbing to the crow's nest for a better view when a shout of alarm came from that very vantage point. Glancing up, I saw the lookout pointing across the waters between us and Granth. At first I couldn't make out what the sailor was pointing at; then I thought it must be a flock of seabirds following a fleet of fishing vessels, and wondered why he'd bothered to raise an alarm. It wasn't until they grew close that I realized the creatures flying in a cloud above and around the ships were far too large to be birds.

"Watery hell," I heard myself say, my heart sinking into the pit of my stomach. "Those are stink-lizards, aren't they?"

"Yes, and those are Granthian war-ships." It was a flat, declarative sentence, and I understood that for Lord Rygil, it was the equivalent of a strong curse. "We're under attack."

THIRTY-EIGHT

There were six Granthian war-ships angling across the great eastern current on a course to intercept us, accompanied by a flock of stink-lizards that darkened the sky; a decision had to be made swiftly.

Lord Rygil conferred with the ship's captain, who informed him that our cumbersome state-vessel stood no chance of outracing the Granthians on the winding counter-currents. Our choices were threefold. We could stand and fight, outnumbered though we were, and pray that the Granthians were merciful in victory. We could offer up the prize of the *rhamanthus* seeds and pray it satisfied them. Or we could turn tail and flee, letting the southern current carry us back toward Zarkhoum and pray that the wind shifted in our favor.

"I am not willing to see anyone else die for the *rhamanthus* seeds," King Azarkal said, his expression stark. "There is too much blood on the hands of the House of the Ageless. I say we negotiate."

"I agree," Lady Marylis murmured.

No one asked my opinion, but I remembered the hatred in the eyes of Varkas Long-Arm when I spared his life at Zariya's behest. "I do not think we may count upon the Granthians to be reasonable, my lord," I said. "There is one at least with a grave slight to his honor to avenge."

Zariya nodded, gripping her canes so hard her knuckles were pale. "The ship is under your command and the decision is yours, my lord. But I believe Khai is right, and I am loath to become a Granthian captive."

"This is an act of outright war sanctioned by the Kagan himself," Lord Rygil said grimly. "I fear the odds against mercy are long."

So we fled.

Even with the wind in our faces, the state-ship picked up speed when it swung into the broad path of the great eastern current and the unseen oarsmen in the lower decks bent their backs, their blades churning the water. For a time, we put some distance between us and the Granthian fleet. But the oarsmen were only mortal and it took a prodigious amount of strength and endurance to propel a ship this large; as their efforts flagged, the Granthians in their small, deft, single-masted vessels gained upon us.

"Oh, I would that the wind would shift." Zariya eyed the sails, slack and fluttering in the headwind. "My darling . . . is there any way in which you might beseech Pahrkun's aid?"

"And summon the wind?" I asked bitterly, clenching my hands into fists. "To fight, to see between places, yes. Then, I *am* Pahrkun's wind. This is different."

"Zariya!" her father roared at her. "Go below and take shelter!"

"He's right," I said; Lady Marylis had long since done so. "The doorway to your chamber is narrow. I can make a stand there."

Her gaze was steady. "Ah, but for how long, my darling? Not even you can hold out forever."

Bit by bit, the distance between us and our attackers was dwindling. The only thing that had saved us thus far was the fact that the stink-lizards had a limited range of flight and must pause to roost on the Granthian prows and sterns from time to time. But now a shadow passed over the ship, accompanied by a raucous cry; a stink-lizard, a smallish one, darting ahead of the others. From below it, I saw the sac at the base of its throat pulsing; I saw it part its jaws and open its mouth to spew a gout of stinking acidic bile over the ship and its occupants.

I moved without thinking, shoving Zariya out of the course of the falling bile, diving and rolling, my hands untying the cords knotted around my waist. Coming to my feet with my *heshkrat* in my hands, I whirled it and threw. It fouled the flying lizard's left wing and the creature crashed onto the uppermost deck, floundering there. Sailors shouted and scrambled; someone was screaming in pain. The fallen stink-lizard rolled a baleful eye at me, its free wing flapping wildly. Drawing my *yakhan*, I severed its head from its leathery neck and retrieved my *heshkrat*.

Oh, but there were more coming, so very many more. And the distance between us was closing.

"Khai!" Somehow Zariya had retained her canes and gotten to her feet. *"Khai!"* Her expression was fierce and intent. "We are not beaten yet, my shadow, but I have need of your swift, strong legs. Go to my chamber and fetch the fate-changer."

I stared at her. "You're sure?"

She nodded. *"Go!"*

I sheathed my *yakhan* and ran.

How long did it take? Not long, I think; I ran like the very wind I could not summon. Below deck in Zariya's chamber, Nalah was cowering and begging to know what transpired. Although I felt guilty at it, I said tersely that we were under attack and then ignored her, rummaging through Zariya's trunks until I found the coffer. Stashing it beneath one arm, I scrambled up the ladders.

Atop the uppermost deck, everything was chaos. Stink-lizards circled the masts, spewing bile.

Men screamed in agony, clawing at skin that bubbled and dissolved in broad patches beneath the viscous yellow bile. There were holes in the sails, acid-eaten and fraying lines swaying loose in the wind. The Granthian war-ships were crowding close. Both King Azarkal and Lord Rygil were attempting to rally their respective guards, but the stink-lizards made it impossible to mount any kind of cohesive defense.

Zariya was nowhere to be seen and I panicked, cursing myself for having left her side; but then I saw one outstretched wing of the dead lizard I'd slain shift and Zariya beckoned to me from beneath it.

I raced across the deck and slid in beside her. "Thank all the fallen stars you thought to take shelter!"

"I'd read that the lizards' hides are impervious to their own bile." Her breath came in short gasps; at close range, the stench was even worse. "But my darling, I fear I must stand to do this properly."

"Wait." I handed her the coffer. Clambering from beneath the lizard's wing, I drew my *yakhan* once more. Even a small specimen was large enough that it took several strokes to cleave the lizard's other wing from its body, but being composed of nothing but leathery membrane stretched over hollow bones, it weighed surprisingly little. I held it above my head, just as I'd done with the soaked hide during the harvest. "Now."

Zariya crawled out from beneath the remaining wing. Opening the coffer, she levered herself upright and held the fate-changer aloft. For a moment, it sparkled in her palm, and then she closed her fingers around it. "Ilharis, change my fate!" she shouted defiantly, dashing the gem upon the planks.

It burst.

It burst in a blast of brightness, and there was a pause like an indrawn breath before everything changed.

Lightning forked down from the cloudless sky, sowing panic in the circling stink-lizards. The wind shifted, springing up behind us. It filled our myriad sails, and even with the damage they'd sustained, it was enough to lend increasing momentum to the state-ship, which began pulling away from the Granthian fleet. Slowly but steadily, the gap between us began to widen.

King Azarkal strode across the deck. The skin of his face and throat was blistered and seeping where droplets of bile had struck him, but he appeared heedless of the fact. "Are you harmed?"

Zariya shook her head, her veil swaying. "No, Father."

"Thanks be to all the children of the heavens." His hands gripped her shoulders. "Do you know what you've done?"

"Well, of course not. That's the nature of a fate-changer, isn't it?" Lord Rygil limped over to join us; a splash of bile had eaten through the calf of his left boot and the flesh beneath it. "One never *does* know. But in this case, it seems my trifling courtship gift came in handy."

Zariya let out a ragged laugh. "I'm sorry to have used it without consulting you, my lord."

"It was yours to dispose of as you wished, Your Highness," he said lightly. "Your courage in doing so humbles me. I suppose my left leg and I can but wish you'd done it sooner."

King Azarkal glanced astern, frowning. Behind us, the Granthians were beginning to regroup, their intent to continue their pursuit manifest. "How long can we expect this wind to last?"

"Expect?" Lord Rygil laughed, but there was a shadow behind his bright eyes. "That is a very definitive word with which to speak of the favor of Ilharis the Two-Faced, Your Majesty." He tucked his hair behind his ears. "The face that has smiled upon us today may yet change, and Granth is nothing if not persistent. But if I'm not terribly mistaken," he continued in an apologetic tone, "I suspect the injured and dying might appreciate our attention. Once they've been tended to, perhaps we might venture to consider our next course of action."

So it went, the massive Therinian state-ship running before the fate-changer's wind, the deft Granthian war-ships pursuing at a distance.

I tried in vain to persuade Zariya to rest belowdecks. Having set this course of events in motion, she was adamant about seeing it through.

"I'll do as you say if the Granthians overtake us," she promised me. "But until then, I can't bear the thought of being closeted away in ignorance."

For that, I could not blame her; and in truth, I'd rather witness our fate unfold than be closeted away myself. And so I found an out-of-the-way spot on the leeward side of the forecastle where Zariya could rest and catch her breath.

It was a grim scene. Two Therinian sailors and one of our own guardsmen were dead, and there were scores of grievous injuries. The ship's physician ordered a cask of wine brought from the hold and washed their wounds with a sponge dipped in it, for the astringent liquid was the only thing that would dissolve the thick bile and counter its effects.

In an hour's time, the worst of the human damage had been addressed and the Granthian fleet was only a smudge on the horizon. Those sailors who were uninjured or hale enough to work set about repairing the worst of the damage done to the lines. Patching the sails would have to wait until we made safe harbor in Merabaht, assuming we were able to do so.

What we would do after that was another matter.

I'd already begun to give thought to it, and when I saw the sailors attempting to wrestle the stink-lizard's carcass to the railing and heave it overboard, I hastened to halt them.

Lord Rygil, his injury bandaged, came to intercede. "I understand that you want your trophy, young dragon-slayer, but it's taking up a considerable amount of space," he said to me.

"I want its hide," I said. "They're proof against their own bile. I thought we could use it. If we had a dozen skilled archers with some measure of protection, they might be able to handle the stink-lizards."

He stared at me a moment. "So says the young warrior who brought down the dragon with a bit of string and some rocks. Very well, start skinning. I imagine that will be a treat."

It was a messy, arduous business, but once I'd cut out the bile sac with my belt-knife, taking care not to puncture it, it was no more difficult than skinning an exceptionally large goat. The segments of membrane in the veined wings were the easiest, so I dispatched those first. I worked as quickly as I could on the body of the creature, periodically glancing to make sure Zariya was safe, wishing I were a man that I might strip to my breeches to avoid gore soaking my tunic. When I was done, a handful of sailors did just that and disposed of the skinned carcass.

I was in the process of scraping the hide when the wind faltered.

It didn't die or shift course, only slowed; still, it was cause for alarm. I listened with half an ear to Lord Rygil and King Azarkal consulting with the ship's captain in worried tones. Folding the stink-lizard's hide into a sloppy bundle, I dragged it over to Zariya, who wrinkled her nose at it. "You do bring me the most unlikely gifts, my darling."

"You sound like a Therinian," I informed her. There was a bucket of sea-water used for sluicing the deck nearby. I pushed up my sleeves, unbuckled my brace of *zims*, and plunged my arms into it, scrubbing away the gore.

"I shall take that as a compliment." Her voice was light, but her eyes were grave. "What did you overhear? Even with the great current, we must be some days' journey from Merabaht. Do they think we might reach it before the Granthian fleet catches us?"

I wiped my hands on my breeches. "It will be close. Nothing is certain."

Zariya closed her eyes briefly. Her knees were drawn up and her arms wrapped around them. "Perhaps I used the fate-changer in vain," she murmured. "Perhaps I should not have done it."

I shook my head. "Don't say that. It's done. Would you rather the Granthians had caught us? There's no point in second-guessing."

There was another cry of alarm from the lookout in the crow's nest; two unfamiliar Therinian words, high and shrill.

Zariya's eyelids flew open.

Hastening to buckle my brace of throwing knives in place, I peered around the forecastle toward the stern; but no, the Granthian fleet was still barely visible in the distance. I returned to find that Zariya had levered herself to her feet, her gaze fixed on the lookout, who was pointing toward the south.

What or who under the starless sky might be threatening us from the *south*?

The two Therinian words were repeated, echoed from sailor to sailor. King Azarkal's voice rose hard and commanding above the fray, demanding someone, anyone translate the alarm into the traders' tongue.

At length someone did.

Wyrm-raiders.

Zariya's gaze met mine, her pupils huge and fearful. "Oh, Khai! By all the fallen stars, what *have* I done?"

"I don't know," I whispered.

THIRTY-NINE

They came swiftly toward us, a lone ship arrowing its way across the currents.

"Why such a panic over one little raiding ship?" There was an edge of contempt to King Azarkal's tone. "Surely our fighting men outnumber theirs by a goodly measure."

"I assure Your Majesty, I am quite capable of counting." Sweat beaded on Lord Rygil's brow. "In this case, the number that matters is two."

"The sea-wyrms," Zariya murmured.

"Quite so," her betrothed agreed. "It seems we've the interesting dilemma of being caught between lizards and serpents."

"But I thought Dulumu the Deep gave the Elehuddin command of the sea-wyrms." Zariya looked pensive. "And Liko of Koronis wrote that the Elehuddin were a peaceable folk. He said nothing of wyrm-raiders."

"'Tis a more recent fad, I suspect," Lord Rygil said wryly. "Still, it's said they prefer robbing to killing. If we cooperate, we may even have the good fortune to survive long enough for the Granthians to catch us."

"I'm so sorry." Zariya's voice broke. "This is all my fault."

The ship was drawing nearer, an odd single-masted vessel with a steep, sharp keel that rode high atop the water. I could make out the heads of the sea-wyrms above the waves; nothing of their bodies was visible save a long trail of wake. "We're going belowdecks," I said to Zariya. "Now."

"No."

"You *promised*," I reminded her.

"I promised to do so if the Granthians overtook us, which has not happened yet, my darling." Below the edge of her veil, the set of her jaw was mutinous. "This is *my fault* and I *will* stand and face it."

"You most certainly will not." King Azarkal grabbed his daughter unceremoniously about the waist and slung her over his shoulder, her veil falling over her eyes and her canes clattering to the deck. I could sense the bone-deep humiliation piled upon Zariya's fear and remorse.

Honor beyond honor.

Here on the open seas, the tang of salt water on my lips, I could feel the arid breath of the desert stirring within me. With a certain sense of regret, I drew my weapons. "No, Your Majesty. Zariya is right. If she wishes to stay, she stays."

The king stared at me. "Are you mad? *Do your duty, shadow!*"

"You do not understand my duty," I said gently to him. I could see the spaces *between* within him; between his love for his daughter and his fear for her safety; between the guilty knowledge that he had ruled unwisely and his desire to make amends for it. "Only Zariya and I and the Sacred Twins themselves understand it. In the name of Pahrkun the Scouring Wind, I am telling you, put her down or I will cut your legs out from underneath you."

Lord Rygil glanced back and forth between us and held his tongue.

King Azarkal set Zariya on her feet, holding her upright. "Why must you break my heart, little lioness?" he whispered to her.

I sheathed my weapons in silence, retrieved her canes, and handed them to her.

"Why do you ask me to be less than you have named me, Father?" Zariya answered quietly, supporting herself.

And then there was no time for an answer, for the raiding ship was nigh upon us, closing the gap with incredible speed.

The heads of the sea-wyrms reared high above the water on sinuous necks, larger at close range than I could have imagined at a distance. I had an impression of shimmering blue-green scales; round, iridescent eyes; long snouts with flared nostrils; and jaws parted in toothy grins to grip something like the bit on a horse's bridle before the sea-wyrms vanished, plunging beneath the waves. One impossibly long shadow passed beneath our state-ship.

I drew my weapons again and shot Zariya a look. "Will you at least stand behind me?"

This, she obeyed.

One of the sea-wyrms burst from the waves in a shower of dripping water to launch itself skyward, wrapping two lengths of muscular blue-green coils around the prow of the ship. It no longer gripped its bit, and its powerful jaws were closed in what looked like a secret smile. A ridge of translucent pale blue fins fanned out along the nape of its neck, and there were smaller fins framing its jaws and the length of its body.

There was a great deal of shouting and trampling as sailors fled toward the stern of the ship. I ignored it and considered how I might best kill the sea-wyrm.

"Hail, Therin!" a clear voice shouted, speaking the traders' tongue with a strange, fluting accent. "That's a mighty big ship you have there, but I'm guessing it will sink all the same if Eeeio breaks off the bow. Which he will do if anyone raises a hand against us, so let's not do that, yah?"

"At the risk of stating the obvious, Your Majesty," Lord Rygil observed, "*this* is why one does not seek to engage wyrm-raiders in battle."

"Do you understand, Therin?" the voice called. Timbers creaked in protest as the wyrm tightened its coils.

"Yes, I daresay we do!" Lord Rygil called in response. "We're in a bit of a hurry. May I ask what you want?"

The second wyrm surfaced between our massive state-ship and the smaller vessel, offering up an obliging loop of coil. Several figures stepped onto it, swaying comfortably atop its mass as it rose to our level.

Elehuddin.

I guessed it must be so; they had sleek, greenish-tan inhuman skin speckled with darker brown, vertically slitted golden-yellow eyes, manelike heads of green hair, and narrow, pinched nostrils. But there were others among them, too; foremost the speaker, who had skin almost as dark as a Barakhan's; long, glossy black hair; and light silvery-grey eyes.

"Oh, well, whatever you have," he said carelessly. "Are you prepared to be reasonable?"

"*Are* we?" Lord Rygil inquired pointedly.

King Azarkal gritted his teeth. "Have we any choice?"

"Well, we might let them sink our ship and take our chances with the wyrms," the Therinian lord offered. "It's not a choice I'd recommend, mind you." At the king's dour nod, he addressed the speaker. "Yes, messire pirate, provided you're prepared to leave us in peace if we comply. We *do* outnumber you."

"Numbers and swords won't do you any good at the bottom of the ocean," the speaker said cheerfully. One of the Elehuddin added a whistling series of notes and a warbling trill. "Oh yah, unless you're Elehuddin. Anyway, we're prophecy-hunters, not pirates." He leapt from the wyrm's coil to land lightly atop the deck, followed by the others. "Give us your valuables and you'll come to no harm."

Behind me, I felt Zariya startle at the words "prophecy-hunters," and my skin began to prickle.

"Funny, that sounds a lot like piracy to me," Lord Rygil said in a dry reply.

The speaker shrugged and gestured to the others, who fanned out: three Elehuddin; a tall, fair-skinned man with a bald head and a thick black beard; a wiry brown-skinned figure whose skin was inked with designs. Long knives hung from their belts, but they bore no other weapons, and my palms itched with the knowledge that I could easily have taken all six of them by myself. "Prophecy doesn't fill our bellies. But maybe you *do* have something special we want, Therin." He scratched his chin. "A fate-changer, maybe?"

"Oh, I do hope you'll appreciate the irony of this," Lord Rygil said. "Because that's exactly what put us in your path."

The speaker's insouciant manner vanished. *"What?"*

"This is ridiculous." Pushing past the Therinian, King Azarkal strode forward to confront the speaker. "Listen to me," he said in an impatient voice infused with the unmistakable command born of three hundred years of rulership. "I am King Azarkal of the House of the Ageless, Sun-Blessed

King of Zarkhoum, and this ship bears what was to be my daughter's wedding party." He pointed toward the stern. "However, there's a Granthian
war-fleet with a full contingent of stink-lizards not a league behind us.
Unless you want to tangle with them as well, I suggest you be on your way."

Whatever response the king was expecting, it wasn't the one he got. The
speaker's silvery eyes widened in awe; one hand flew to cover his mouth and
the other to clutch a pendant at his throat.

"Jahno . . ." the tall man whispered, tears in his eyes. "We found them."

The Elehuddin whistled to each other in sharp, surprised tones. Only the
tattooed figure—whom I realized with a shock was a woman—remained
impassive.

"I know," the speaker—Jahno—whispered to the tall man. "I heard." He
turned to the king, his voice trembling. "Your Sun-Blessed Majesty . . . do
you perchance possess a *shadow*?"

King Azarkal frowned. "I do not."

Their faces fell.

Leaning on her canes, Zariya emerged from behind me. "*I* do."

Letting go his pendant, the speaker stared at her in disbelief. "*You?*"

"She is the Sun-Blessed Princess Zariya of the House of the Ageless," I
said grimly. "I am her shadow, chosen by Pahrkun the Scouring Wind himself, and I swear to you, if you lay a hand on her, you will die."

Jahno spread his hands in a forfending gesture. "I mean her no harm.
But you must come with us, both of you. Now."

"She will do no such thing," her father said.

The speaker Jahno ignored him. "You have *rhamanthus* seeds, yah?" he
said to Zariya. "And you used the fate-changer?"

"Why does it matter?" Zariya asked steadily.

There was another shout from the crow's nest; the Granthian fleet was
beginning to close the distance between us.

"Warriors and stink-lizards coming fast," the tattooed woman remarked.
"Lots of 'em."

The wyrm-raiders' speaker took a deep breath, his intent gaze fixed on
Zariya. "'From the south comes the Seeker; from the north the Opener of
Ways; from the west the Thunderclap; from the east Sun-Blessed and Shadow,

bearing the seeds of Zar's fire,'" he quoted. "So says the Scattered Prophecy. And it says that the children of Droth the Great Thunder will drive the defenders of the four quarters together, but their course will be determined by the intervention of Ilharis the Two-Faced. A dark tide *is* rising, my lady. Right now, it is only a trickle, but it will grow. All those who are destined to stand against it must band together."

It could have been a ploy, of course; but no, I knew in my bones that the speaker believed what he was saying.

If it was true, then the time of the prophecy was upon us.

I thought of Brother Yarit scrawling frantically on the desert floor with the point of his dagger. If *this,* then *that*; but if *this,* then *that.*

No wonder the Seer nearly lost his wits attempting to chart the unlikely series of events that had brought us to this juncture. Once again, the plane of the world was tilting beneath me.

Zariya studied the speaker; his dark skin and light eyes, the elongated lobes of his ears, the clay cylinder knotted around his throat. "You're Koronian, aren't you?" she whispered in amazement. "I thought you were all dead."

He bowed to her. "I am Jahno, son of Teris, son of Moro, son of Liko the scholar. Koronis sank beneath the waves, but I was born and raised on Elehud, and I ask you, do you have *rhamanthus* seeds?"

"Yes."

The sea-wyrm alongside the ship lifted its massive head, water cascading from it as it parted its jaws and let out a long, keening trill. The other sea-wyrm shifted its coils and echoed the cry.

Jahno held out his hands to both of us. "Fetch them and come with us. Now!"

"I forbid it!" King Azarkal thundered.

Zariya glanced at me. There was a ringing sound in my ears and the blood was beating in my veins. It seemed as though we stood atop a high crag with an unfathomable abyss yawning beneath us, and this wyrm-raiding pirate, this great-grandson of her beloved Liko of Koronis, was telling us to jump.

I knew Zariya's heart and mind. She meant to do it.

"Fetch the *rhamanthus* seeds," I said to the nearest Royal Guardsman.

"Don't you dare," the king snapped, and the guard stayed put.

Lord Rygil cleared his throat. "Unless I'm very much mistaken, this ship is still under my command," he said in his deceptively dismissive manner. "And we are speaking of a dowry to which I am entitled, are we not?"

"Forgive me, my lord," Zariya murmured to him. "I did not intend this."

The Therinian lord laughed, his eyes bright. "I should be quite awestruck if you had, my lady," he said lightly. "Your Majesty, it seems that destiny has claimed your daughter today. I humbly suggest you accede with grace and let it have her, for whatever destiny has in store for her, I would wager good odds that it's preferable to being a Granthian captive."

We had been long enough among the Therinians to know that Lord Rygil was in deadly earnest. Something in his words reached the king, and I saw the moment His Majesty's will broke within him and bowed before fate.

"Fetch the *rhamanthus*," he said quietly to the guards. "And have the attendants bring Princess Zariya's and Khai's things."

Tears filled Zariya's eyes. "Thank you, Father."

He folded her in an embrace. "May all the gods be with you, my little lioness," he murmured against her hair. "I never meant to question your courage."

Once set in motion, matters progressed swiftly. Our trunks and my battered satchel were brought from our chamber. Two of the Elehuddin set about transferring the trunks to their ship; the satchel I slung over my shoulder and kept. Under the circumstances, the matter of piracy was largely abandoned, but the remaining raiders made a cursory examination of the upper deck.

"Is that what I think it is?" Jahno wrinkled his nose and pointed to the stink-lizard's hide.

"Quite possibly," Lord Rygil said. "That delightful trophy rightly belongs to Khai, our resident dragon-slayer."

The Koronian shot me an impressed look. "Huh. We'll take it with us."

The *rhamanthus* seeds were the last item to arrive; the guards on duty refused to believe King Azarkal meant to hand them over without a fight, and the king himself had to go belowdecks to order them to obey.

Meanwhile the Granthian fleet was drawing alarmingly close.

"They're after the *rhamanthus,* yah?" Jahno said to Lord Rygil, who inclined his head.

"And the princess, I imagine." He looked apologetic. "One of them may have a bit of a quarrel to settle with her shadow."

"A bit of a quarrel," Jahno echoed wryly; clearly, he had experience with Therinian understatement. "But not with you, Therin? No? Good, you run up a white parlay flag. You tell them we have the seeds and the Sun-Blessed and her shadow, that we laughed and said, 'Come and get them.'"

"What do you suppose the odds are that it will work?" Lord Rygil mused. "I'd rather not die today."

The Koronian shrugged. "Better than none. We've never crossed paths with Granthians, so they don't know what speed the wyrms are capable of. We'll go slow and follow the great eastern current for a while, let them think they have a chance of catching us."

"I do hope you won't be offended if I say that's surprisingly decent of you," Lord Rygil remarked.

Jahno grinned. "I told you, Therin, we're prophecy-hunters. And you just delivered an important piece of the puzzle to us. The world may yet owe you a great debt for it."

And then King Azarkal was there with the coffer of *rhamanthus* seeds, and there was an awkward moment as he attempted to give it unto Zariya's keeping and realized she could not carry it and manage her canes at the same time. The raiders would have taken it, of course, but the king was adamant that it remain in the hands of the House of the Ageless, so I shoved it into my satchel along with the lock-picks, thieves' lantern, and grappling hooks that I had brought from the desert.

"I'm sorry, my lord," Zariya said to Lord Rygil, her veil fluttering in the breeze. "I daresay we might have been happy together."

"And I daresay you and your fearsome shadow would have found your lives in Therin terribly dull," he said ruefully. "May Ilharis the Two-Faced forgive me, I am not even sure if that is a true statement or a lie. My lady, might I ask a boon?" She nodded. "I would see my betrothed's face before I lose her to fate."

Holding both canes in her left hand, Zariya unpinned the right side of her veil, hesitated, then ripped it loose. Her silk head-scarf came with it, her elaborately braided locks spilling over her shoulders. There were gasps from the Zarkhoumi guards, but her father the king merely nodded to himself as though he had expected no less.

Lifting her hand, Zariya let the wind take veil and scarf alike.

Lord Rygil bowed to her in a silence that spoke more than words.

"Thank you for your kindness, my lord," she said to him. "And I beg you thank your sister for hers. I pray you will be well."

There was time for King Azarkal to give his daughter one last fierce embrace, then no more; the Elehuddin were whistling urgently and the sea-wyrms were uttering trills of alarm.

For all her courage, Zariya blanched at the prospect of climbing onto the wyrm's coil. "Will you go first and steady me, my darling?"

Jahno beckoned to the tall man, who stepped forward obligingly. "Tarrok will carry you. It will be easier."

"No." Zariya may have abandoned her veil, but not her dignity. "I believe you, messire, else I should not be doing this. But I am a princess of the House of the Ageless of Zarkhoum and you are strangers to me. I will not suffer anyone but Khai to lay hands upon me."

I vaulted atop the railing and braced myself with one foot astride it and the other on the slick surface of the wyrm's coil. I expected the latter to dip beneath my weight, but it was so immense and strong, one more person made no difference. Maneuvering my satchel out of the way, I reached down to Zariya. "Give him your canes and clasp my arms."

She obeyed and I clasped her forearms in turn, lifting her over the railing. It took a considerable amount of strength, but I'd be damned if I'd let her dignity suffer. I slid an arm around her to support her and stepped onto the wyrm's coil. Atop the slippery scales, I envied the barefoot raiders.

"Oh!" Zariya clung to me, her unveiled face suffused with wonder.

The others followed suit. One of the Elehuddin let out a piercing whistle, and the sea-wyrm lowered its coil.

The raiders leapt lightly to the deck of their odd little ship, and I helped Zariya down.

The great-grandson of Liko of Koronis handed her canes to her and offered another bow. "Welcome aboard, Sun-Blessed and shadow," he said to us. "Welcome to the defenders of the four quarters."

FORTY

The Elehuddin whistled and trilled, and the sea-wyrm wrapped around the bow of the Therinian state-ship unwound its coils and poured its length into the sea. Both wyrms vanished beneath the waves, emerging at a distance. I could not see the bits they gripped in their mighty jaws or the lines attached to metal hoops on either side of the ship's bow, but I felt the ship move as the lines grew taut.

Behind us, the Therinian state-ship raised the white parlay flag. Zariya and I watched with our hearts in our throats as the first stink-lizards arrived to circle its masts, sighing in relief as the lizards withheld their bile, at least for the moment.

"Do you really think there's a chance the Granthians will spare them?" Zariya asked Jahno.

"Oh, yah." He was watching, too. "No reason not to now that the prize has slipped away. They must have wanted it bad to risk all-out war with Therin. Unlucky things happen to people who cross the children of Ilharis the Two-Faced." He glanced at us. "How many *rhamanthus* seeds, anyway?"

Unobtrusively, I took a tighter grip on the satchel.

"Three thousand," Zariya replied calmly.

The Koronian sucked in a sharp breath. "Three thousand! No wonder. A Kagan could hold the throne for a long time with three thousand *rhamanthus* seeds." He caught the eye of one of the Elehuddin and gave an inquiring trill; the Elehuddin whistled in response. "Don't worry. We'll dawdle along the eastern current long enough to draw out the Granthians."

"You speak their tongue," Zariya observed.

He nodded. "I do as a courtesy, for I was raised among them. Even so, some sounds are difficult for human lips and tongue and throat to shape."

We resumed watching in silence as the Granthian fleet reached the state-ship. The wyrm-raiders' ship jounced over the rippling waves. Zariya was wavering with the effort of keeping herself propped upright and I could hear her breath wheezing in her lungs, but I refrained from telling her she needed to rest. Among others, her father was aboard that ship. I knew she would not rest until she knew their fates.

It wasn't long before we saw the Granthian ships glide past the state-ship, all oars out in pursuit of us.

"Thanks be to all the gods," Zariya said in a fervent tone. "And to you, messire, for conceiving of the ploy. Are you *quite* sure they can't catch us?"

"Yah, unless the wyrms run into a huge patch of strangling kelp or some such," Jahno said. "But they're pretty wily and we keep a good lookout." He made an expansive gesture. "And we can cut across the currents anywhere we want, anytime we want. Once we do that, no ship powered by wind or oars can keep pace with us."

"And where will we be going once we do, Captain?" I inquired.

"Captain!" He laughed. "Is that what you thought? There's no captain among us; the Elehuddin wouldn't stand for it. We're all brothers and sisters alike. But since I'm the Seeker, I get more say when it comes to prophecy-hunting. As soon as we've put enough distance between Granth and Therin back there, we're heading to the Nexus to consult the Oracle, among other things."

Behind us, the massive Therinian state-ship was changing course. I wondered what sort of reception they would find upon returning home.

"I have a thousand questions for you, messire, and of course I wish to make the acquaintance of the others in this company of which we have so unexpectedly found ourselves members." Zariya's skin looked ashen and her voice was faint. "But it's been a taxing day, and I fear I must rest for an hour or two and recover my strength." She glanced around. "Is there a quiet place out of the sun where I might lie down?"

Jahno hesitated. "Not a private place, Sun-Blessed. Like brothers and sisters, we share a berth. But I will see that you and your shadow are undisturbed for now."

Zariya swallowed. "Then it will have to do."

The ladder was steep, but it was short enough that she could manage the descent. I went first, her canes tucked under my arm. At the bottom, I caught myself short, a startled sound escaping me.

The interior of the ship was *alive*. Vines laced the walls and ceiling, elongated orange fruit growing from them. Pale green moths flitted among the vines, shedding a dim luminescence. Here and there, furry white cocoons clung to the vines. I was so astonished, I left Zariya clinging to the ladder until she reminded me to give her canes to her.

Both of us stood staring as Jahno descended to join us. "What *is* this?" Zariya asked him.

"You like it?" He smiled. "The ship's part of an *ooalu* tree. They grow in salt water. It was my grandfather who had the idea of cultivating one for a vessel." He plucked one of the fruits from a vine and took a bite. "Good to eat, too. Help yourself. The moths pollinate the flowers," he added. "So leave them be."

"Of course," Zariya murmured.

The sleeping berth was toward the front of the ship and consisted of nothing more than a dozen rope hammocks slung from the beams. I eyed them askance, thinking how very, very different this was from the seclusion of the women's quarter in the Palace of the Sun. There were nets affixed to the walls containing an array of clothing and other personal items; Zariya's trunks had been secured therein, taking up a considerable amount of space.

Jahno pointed toward the hammocks nearest them. "Those have been reserved for your usage, Sun-Blessed."

"Thank you." Her voice shook slightly; whether from weariness or shock at the circumstances in which we found ourselves, I wasn't entirely sure. "I will just rest for a bit."

He inclined his head. "Then I will leave you to do so." He turned to go, then paused. "Sun-Blessed, shadow . . . I see that this is all very strange to you, and I know it has happened with great suddenness. But I promise you that no one aboard this ship will harm the least hair upon your heads, and you need not guard the *rhamanthus* with your life, shadow. No one will steal them from you. The seeds are a piece of the Scattered Prophecy."

"The Scattered Prophecy." Despite her exhaustion, Zariya could not help but give voice to her curiosity. "Have you assembled all the pieces?"

"Not yet," Jahno said. "But there is time to speak of these matters. Sleep; rest and refresh yourself."

I got Zariya settled in one of the hammocks. Her eyelids fluttered closed almost immediately. "Thank you, my darling," she murmured. "I suppose you're not the least bit weary after all this excitement."

"No," I admitted. "But I will stay with you."

"I see no point in it," she said. "For better or worse, our fate has been changed, and we must learn to accept it. Go, and learn what you may about our strange new companions. And perhaps you might see about rigging a sling," she added. "For I fear I'll not be able to climb the ladder."

"In a little while," I said.

It was a matter of minutes before Zariya was fast asleep, her features softening in repose. I stayed with her a while longer, debating whether or not to take her at her word, debating whether or not I dared leave my satchel with the coffer of *rhamanthus* seeds unguarded.

In the end, I did.

Zariya was right. Our lives had changed in what felt like the blink of an eye. If we could not trust our new companions, we were doomed, for although I could defend us against any human threat aboard this peculiar vessel, the sea-wyrms were another matter. So I stowed my satchel behind the netting, plucked an *ooalu* fruit, and went abovedecks to investigate.

For all that we were being pursued by Granthian war-ships, the atmosphere was surprisingly relaxed. The square sail on the single mast had been hoisted and one of the Elehuddin was standing lookout in the crow's nest, but the bulk of the effort of sailing the ship—or towing it, I should say— was done by the sea-wyrms. Jahno and two of the Elehuddin were consulting in the structure that I learned was the charthouse, poring over maps of the currents. In the shadow of the charthouse, the tattooed woman and another of the Elehuddin were playing some sort of game with a board and pegs.

The tall man hailed me. "Tarrok of Trask," he said by way of greeting, thrusting out a big hand to clasp my forearm.

I clasped his arm in turn. "Khai of the Fortress of the Winds," I said. "Of, um, Zarkhoum."

He grinned, his teeth strong and white in the thick nest of his beard. "Welcome. I take it you've seen signs of the rising, else you wouldn't be here."

"The rising?" I echoed.

Tarrok of Trask raised his heavy brows. "The children of Miasmus? The sign of the black star?"

"Yes."

He nodded his bald head. "Trask lies in the far west. We were the first to be afflicted."

Over by the charthouse, one of the Elehuddin let out a victorious trill and raised both arms overhead. The tattooed woman overturned the game board in disgust and stomped over to join us.

"Evene of Drogalia, the Opener of Ways." She looked me up and down with impersonal curiosity. "Are you man or woman, shadow? I confess, I am uncertain. And what is it that ails your mistress?"

I took a deep breath. "As to the latter, Her Highness the Princess Zariya contracted Dhanbu fever as a child. As to the former . . ." I paused, weighing my answer, and surprising myself in the process of delivering it. "Both, I think."

It felt good to say it aloud.

Both of them nodded as though unsurprised, as though it were the most natural thing in the world. Until that day, I had not realized how much I had missed the fellowship of the Brotherhood of Pahrkun; how much I had missed the very notion of fellowship.

I fell into an easy rhythm with my new fellows.

I met the Elehuddin, whose names I struggled to pronounce. They laughed at my efforts, their laughter a curious sound like a cat sneezing. Although their physiognomy made it even more difficult for them to speak the traders' tongue than it was for me to speak theirs, all of them understood it. One procured a spare length of rope for me, and I set about knotting it into a sling with which to hoist Zariya from the berth below.

Jahno came to join us, sitting cross-legged on the sun-warmed planks of the decks, tilting his face skyward, his silver-grey eyes half-lidded.

"How did all of you find each other?" I asked them, my hands working absentmindedly on the sling.

They took turns explaining. Thanks to Jahno's translating, I learned that it had long been prophesied by Dulumu the Deep that the Elehuddin and the sea-wyrms would play a key role in combatting the rise of Miasmus. For three generations, the Elehuddin and the remaining scions of vanished Koronis had partnered together to search for pieces of the Scattered Prophecy and those who might fulfill it; only now was it coming to pass.

I supposed that Jahno and the Elehuddin must have found Tarrok in far-flung Trask and Evene in the northern reaches of Drogalia, but I was wrong. Tarrok had been exiled by his own people for the danger he posed, for it seemed that the gift he possessed and what it might portend had drawn the children of Miasmus to their shores in ever-increasing numbers, seeking to end his life.

It reminded me with a shiver of the words of the Mad Priest.

Kill the shadow, seize the princess.

Facing execution on charges of theft, Evene had fled Drogalia. Both had found new lives in the labyrinthine archipelago of the Nexus, where they were discovered by the prophecy-hunters.

"So the Children of Miasmus haven't penetrated the Nexus?" I asked, testing my knots.

"No, I fear they have," Jahno said soberly. "But Miasmus's message of anarchy and ruin finds less purchase there than elsewhere, for the Oracle has declared it a place of sanctuary for all who seek it."

"I thought it was a pirates' haven," I said, remembering Vironesh had claimed as much. Oh, but on the first day we had met, Zariya had spoken of it, too. "But pilgrims come to seek answers from the Oracle, too, do they not?"

"It is all of those things," he agreed. "And some people just live there. It is a vast place." He rubbed the back of his neck. "If I understand the prophecy aright, the last of the defenders is meant to come from a place of birth there. 'From the Nexus comes the Quick, who will recognize his queen.'"

"What does that mean?" I asked.

Jahno shook his head. "That we do not know yet."

Mostly I sat and listened.

I learned that Evene was known as the Opener of Ways by virtue of having been graced by Quellin-Who-Is-Everywhere with the gift of being able to pass through any locked space. It was a gift she had indeed turned to thievery, albeit from what I could determine without the dedicated craft of the Shahalim Clan. She cocked a brow at me when I smiled at her revelation. "This amuses you, shadow? You think less of me for putting my gift to good use?"

"No," I said, thinking that I might as well have left behind my lockpicks. "It is only that I had a mentor who would have appreciated your gift."

I did not learn why Tarrok was known as the Thunderclap, except that it had nothing to do with Droth the Great Thunder as I might have imagined. No, Tarrok had been gifted by the god under whose aegis the realm of Trask lay, Luhdo the Loud. As to the specific nature of his gift, he merely smiled into his beard and said that it was better demonstrated than told and that now, while the Sun-Blessed princess slept belowdecks, was not the time to reveal it.

When I was not listening, I watched.

I was fascinated by the sleek-skinned Elehuddin. What I had taken at a distance to be green hair was actually masses of tendrils that stirred of their own accord. Their fingers and toes were elongated; webbed on the lower half, tipped with small black claws. They wore nothing but short breeches, and based on their smooth, narrow chests, I assumed all were male until the one who'd brought me rope—whose name sounded to my ears something like Essee—nodded and whistled at my sling, and Jahno translated. "She says you've got a good hand with knotwork."

"Thank you," I said, startled. She smiled broadly in reply, narrow jaws parting to reveal rows of small, pointed teeth. "Forgive me, I had not realized there were women as well as men among you."

"Some days more than others," Jahno said, and the Elehuddin laughed their cat-sneezing laughs. "Unlike us, they may change genders at will," he explained to me. "Though probably not in the middle of a sea voyage, yah, because it takes some time to accomplish," he added. "That was a joke."

"I have heard that the Elehuddin have a word for someone who is neither a man nor a woman," I said. "Or possibly both? Zariya said your great-grandfather Liko was unclear on the matter."

He nodded affably and made a short clicking sound, then repeated it with a slightly different inflection. "The first is for a person who is in the middle of changing between one and the other. The second . . ." Breaking off our discourse, he conferred with the Elehuddin in their own tongue. "A person who is alone, maybe a person who has lost their tribe for some reason, may choose to be both. This person may become father and mother alike to their own child."

Essee laid a long-fingered webbed hand on my knee and met my gaze, letting out a series of whistles and trills.

"She says it seems this speaks to you," Jahno translated. "And a person is a person. Even if you cannot change in body as the Elehuddin do, you may change in spirit. You must be the person you are."

I laid my own hand atop the back of her cool, smooth-skinned hand in gratitude. "Thank you. I am coming to understand that very thing."

She nodded, yellow-gold eyes bright with kindness.

"All right." Evene jerked her chin at me. "We've told you a bit of our stories. What's yours? From what the Seeker has learned of the Sun-Blessed and their shadows, we were expecting a pair of mighty warriors, not a crippled girl and a kid with a pair of swords. We know your mistress brings the *rhamanthus*. What gift do you bring to the quest? And what's with the marks on your face? Did the Zarkhoumi brand you somehow?"

"Evene," Jahno said mildly, "do not be unkind. It is also worth noting that at the least, Khai here killed a stink-lizard, and you should not be so quick to dismiss him." He glanced around. "That reminds me, did someone set its hide to soak in a tub of seawater?"

One of the Elehuddin whistled in affirmation.

"First of all, it is not a pair of swords," I corrected the tattooed woman. "It is a *yakhan* and a *kopar*. And the marks on my face were put there by Pahrkun the Scouring Wind himself. It is a long story, and I should look to see if my lady Zariya has awoken before I tell it. As to what gift I bring . . ."

I thought about how best to answer and spoke the simple truth. "I am very good at killing."

"You're very young to make such a bold claim, Khai of the Fortress of the Winds," Tarrok observed.

I shrugged. "Nonetheless."

Leaning toward me, Essee spoke intently in the Elehuddin tongue.

"She says she is sorry to hear it," Jahno murmured. "And sorrier still that it is likely our quest will require such a skill. As am I."

By the expressions on the faces of the other Elehuddin, they agreed. I had been raised in a society in which a warrior's skills were prized; I did not know how to feel about having them pitied.

"We do not all have the luxury of commanding sea-wyrms to sink our enemies' ships," I said stiffly. "Some of us must fight with our own hands. But if you will excuse me, I will look in on my lady."

Jahno lifted placating hands as I rose. "No one meant to insult you. And the Therinians are not our enemies. We are prophecy-hunters; we have no enemies but Miasmus. It is only that we saw the ship and thought it might contain a great prize." He smiled. "As it did, yah? Just not the one we expected."

Somewhat mollified, I descended into the sleeping-berth in the hold.

Zariya was awake, her arms folded behind her head, watching the luminous pale green moths flutter amongst the vines. "So, my darling," she greeted me. "How do you find our new companions?"

I sat on the hammock next to her. "Kind, mostly. A bit confounding. The woman Evene is prickly. How are you? How do you feel?" I hesitated. "Can you endure these circumstances?"

She gazed at the beams overhead. "You know, dearest, I felt so bold when I ripped off my veil and scarf. But now I will be honest. I am a bit terrified. I feel so very exposed here. Vulnerable."

"You have other scarves and veils in your trunks," I reminded her.

Zariya turned her head toward me. "That is not what I meant."

I took her hand in mine. "I know."

She took a slow breath and let it out in a sigh. "So I am to sleep among strangers tonight."

"Strangers who are not engaged in endless and ongoing conspiracies to murder members of their own family," I said. "Forgive me for finding a measure of relief in that fact."

Zariya smiled wryly. "All that I dreamed in my youthful imagining has come to pass. We are prophecy-hunters, my darling! Yet somehow, I never imagined it would come at a time that *mattered* so. Surely I did not envision the fulfillment of it all. I dreamed of a great adventure on the seas, nothing more." She cast a disdainful glance toward her legs. "And now I find even that prospect frightens me. As I promised, I will not weep for my weakness, but I cannot help but despise it."

I tightened my grip on her hand, thinking about what Essee had said to me. "You are not your body. Your spirit is strong."

She searched my face. "*Is* it?"

I nodded. "You've not even begun to realize your own strength."

Zariya squeezed my hand, then let it go, determination suffusing her features. Pushing herself upright, she lifted her legs over the edge of the hammock and reached for her canes. "Then let us confront our fate."

FORTY-ONE

I needn't have worried.

It seemed some words had been exchanged while I was below deck, and Evene was on better behavior. This was to the good, for if she referred to Zariya as a "crippled girl" again, I was minded to teach her a lesson in courtesy.

A second round of introductions was made. Zariya did better than I at mastering an approximation of the Elehuddin names; I imagined some of that came from a childhood spent poring over chronicles like that of Liko of Koronis, attempting to sound out the unfamiliar words. But she also made a point of asking each member of our new crew a simple question or two about themselves, so that by the time the introductions were done, I felt I knew them better than I had.

Behind us, our Granthian pursuers had slowed their pace, laying off their oars. The stink-lizards perched and rested in shifts. It seemed they had resigned themselves to the fact that they weren't going to catch us in an all-out chase, and were waiting for the sea-wyrms to tire, something the Elehuddin assured us wouldn't happen anytime soon.

"So tell me everything!" Zariya exclaimed to our new companions. I had brought up some blankets to make a cushioned place for her in the shade of the charthouse, and her eyes were bright with excitement. "I thought the Koronians were lost, and all their long centuries of research into the prophecy with them. How is it you came to be born on Elehud? Were each of you chosen and marked by the gods under whose aegis you dwell? What wisdom did they impart to you? What do you know of the Scattered Prophecy?

The darkness that rises . . . is it Miasmus itself or the children of Miasmus? What does it seek? How are we meant to defend against it? What role do the *rhamanthus* seeds play?"

Jahno laughed. "Slow down, Sun-Blessed! We will attempt to answer all your questions."

She gave him an apologetic smile. "Forgive me. Now that I have rested, my mind is ablaze."

He folded his hands in his lap. "First of all, you are correct. My forefathers and mothers were great scholars, but they were jealous of their secrets. Much of the knowledge they gathered regarding the prophecy vanished when the state library sank into the sea."

"Have you attempted to retrieve any of it?" Zariya inquired. "And why were they so secretive when the fate of the world might hang upon their findings?" She flushed at his sidelong glance. "I'm sorry. Please continue."

Jahno inclined his head. "Again, to answer your first question, yes. Many brave Elehuddin have dived deep beneath the waves, far deeper than is safe, to retrieve what they might. Much was ruined beyond salvaging. As to the second question, it is more difficult to answer."

The tallest of the Elehuddin—I recognized him as Kooie, whom Jahno had introduced as his nest-brother—spoke at length.

"He says the Koronians were vain of their knowledge," Jahno translated. "They believed that because Enayo the Speaking Stone declared a Koronian would be the one to solve the riddle of the prophecy, they should not share it with the rest of the world. But that is not the way it was meant to be." He intertwined his fingers and raised his hands. "We are all brothers and sisters. Dulumu the Deep has decreed it. Together we are stronger. We must share our knowledge, share our strengths and weakness, share the burden of danger and the rewards of victory."

All the Elehuddin nodded in agreement, their manelike tendrils stirring.

"That is a thing my great-grandfather recognized," Jahno added. "Because of it, he chose to settle his family on Elehud; and many who assisted him in his efforts, the cryptographers and sailors and servants, chose to do the same, with the blessing of the Elehuddin."

Essee offered a whistling commentary that ended with a satisfied click.

"And then they were not lordly scholars and apprentices and servants, but brothers and sisters alike," Jahno agreed.

"I had no idea," Zariya murmured. "Your great-grandfather wrote no more after Koronis sank. I assumed he perished there."

"Alas, that is so," Jahno said. "He was seeking to persuade the parliament of scholars to open their archives. Perhaps he might even have succeeded, but that we will never know."

Zariya pondered that for a moment. "That seems a bitter irony."

"Indeed, my lady." He tilted his head, regarding her beneath his lashes. "But tell me, how did you know me for Koronian?"

She glanced away under his regard, suddenly shy. "Your coloring and physiognomy resembles your great-grandfather's description of your people," she murmured. "And you wear a *khartouka*."

"What, exactly, is a *khartouka*, and why is this the first I'm hearing of it?" Evene interjected.

Jahno touched the clay cylinder at his throat. "It is a key for translating Koronian cryptography and likely of no interest to you," he said, answering Evene but continuing to gaze at Zariya. "You're very well read, Sun-Blessed."

She said nothing, but flushed again at his praise.

"This is all well and good, but there's time aplenty. Meanwhile we missed the midday meal and I'm griped with hunger," Tarrok grumbled. "Tell me I'm not the only one aboard this ship that feels the same?"

A cacophonous chorus of whistles and trills and human voices erupted in emphatic accord.

Jahno glanced toward the western horizon, where Zar the Sun was turning orange and beginning his descent toward the waves. "Yah," he agreed. "Let us eat and plot our course."

Meals aboard the Therinian state-ship were formal affairs. I never saw the galley where they were prepared, but it was well stocked with all manner of produce and delicacies.

Here, it was a different matter. A wooden cage filled with live fish was hauled dripping from one side of the ship. When I studied it with perplexity, trying to determine how the trap worked, Jahno laughed and told me that the Elehuddin caught the fish themselves; the cage was merely used to store them. The fish were scaled and gutted and wrapped in sheets of sea-weed that were kept under damp cloths in a basket, then grilled on a small brazier. This, along with *ooalu* fruit, formed the basis of our meal—and indeed almost every meal to follow—which we ate with our hands, seated on the ship's deck, and washed down with remarkably fresh-tasting water from the casks stored in the cargo section in the rear of the hold.

Although it was worlds away from anything she had known, Zariya endured it with good grace.

It seemed we were not the only ones hungry. Partway through our meal, the ship took an unexpected lurch to the right, then drifted slackly atop the waves for a moment before resuming its course. Members of the crew conferred amongst themselves, then one of the Elehuddin went to the bow to call out to the sea-wyrms, who whistled and hooted in response.

"Do not be alarmed if the ship is adrift on the current for a few moments," Jahno said to us. "Eeeio and Aiiiaii have just encountered a large school of fish, and the wyrms also need to feed. We will be under way shortly."

"Do the wyrms obey the Elehuddin in every particular?" Zariya asked curiously.

Essee responded to her query, her tone tinged with what sounded like mild disapproval.

"The sea-wyrms do not *obey* us," Jahno translated. "They are partners in this endeavor. Our big brothers and sisters have as much stake in this as we do. Why would you think otherwise?"

"Forgive me," Zariya said. "My understanding is based upon your great-grandfather's writings."

"And perhaps because we are currently being pursued by the children of Droth the Great Thunder," I added tartly. "Which suggests *they* have no interest in the fulfillment of the prophecy."

Jahno was silent for a moment. "My great-grandfather's understanding of the relationship between the Elehuddin and the wyrms was imperfect," he said. "As for the stink-lizards . . . do not be swift to assume you comprehend the mind of Droth the Great Thunder. It may be that the lizards have played exactly the role that was intended for them, with the Granthians all unwitting."

"By driving us together," Zariya said softly.

He nodded. "It is said that when Zar cast down the children of heaven, he gave them a prophecy. Miasmus, last-born of the children of heaven and the only one undeserving of his fate, would sleep for centuries beneath the waves, dreaming of vengeance and annihilation. One day it would wake and rise and seek to cover the world in darkness. The children of heaven are bound to the lands over which they hold aegis. We are the only weapons with which they may fight the rising tide."

"I still don't understand why the gods don't just *tell* us what to do," Evene said with annoyance.

If this, then that; but if *this*, then *that* . . .

"It's not that simple," I said slowly. "Our fates hang in a delicate balance. Anything they do might upset it." I glanced at Zariya. "Anamuht the Purging Fire decreed that you must agree to wed a foreigner, but if Lord Rygil had not given you a fate-changer, we would not be here today."

She nodded. "And if I had not bade you to spare Varkas Long-Arm's life, my darling, the Granthians might not be pursuing us in fury."

"Well, they might have done it anyway for the prize of three thousand *rhamanthus* seeds," Jahno observed. "But yah, that's the thing. The levers that turn the wheels of the prophecy are varied and subtle. If you were not caught thieving, Evene, you would not have fled to the Nexus."

"Nor I, were the people of Trask not so fearful of the rising tide as to exile me," Tarrok remarked.

"But why *us*?" Zariya inquired. "If it's true that we are the prophesied defenders, why so few to stand against something so mighty?"

Essee spoke in answer, her yellow-gold eyes gleaming ardently in the light of the fading sun.

Jahno smiled wryly. "She says we are not few, that we are symbols of the many who have a role to play, great or small, as your Therinian lord played a role in bequeathing you a fate-changer. It is only that the defenders happen to possess the skills or gifts that render us the tip of the spear."

Zariya spread the fingers of her right hand, regarding the markings etched upon it. "I should like to know exactly what those are," she said in a wistful voice.

"So should we all, yah?" Jahno wrapped his arms around his knees and gazed at the twilit sky. "A thousand years ago, we would be seeing the stars emerge, the bright eyes and flashing teeth and fierce hearts of the children of heaven shining far above us in the night sky. Now we have only the moons to light our way, and we cannot chart our path by them. But it is said that if the defenders of the four quarters prevail, Zar the Sun will return his children to their place in the heavens."

"And if we fail?" I asked.

He turned his silvery gaze on me. "Miasmus will swallow the world in darkness and it will be no more."

I swallowed. "Surely that cannot be Zar's desire?"

His shoulders rose and fell in a shrug. "If it comes to pass, I believe that Zar will create the world anew."

Evene turned her head and spat. "Fucker." There was a short, shocked silence in which she lifted her chin defiantly. "I mean it! It's not fair. Why should *we* have to do the dirty work of the children of heaven? Why should *we* have to pay for the sins of the gods if we fail?"

Unexpectedly, Zariya broke the silence with a laugh. "I cannot disagree with the sentiment. And yet it changes nothing, does it?"

"No." Evene gave her a grudging look of respect. "I suppose it doesn't."

Nim the Bright Moon was on the rise and waxing gibbous that night, laying a shining path over the waters, while Shahal the Dark Moon was a waning sliver on the horizon, and Eshen the Wandering Moon was nowhere in sight. I was glad of it, since Nim's silver-white brightness always seemed less ominous to me than the bloody light of Shahal or the fickle blue light of Eshen. Behind us, the Granthian fleet had lit their sea-lanterns. They would not be dropping anchor for the night, trusting to the wind and the great eastern current to bear them closer to us.

The sea-wyrms fed, their great sinuous bodies churning the waters before us into a small maelstrom. Once satiated, they lifted their heads and one gave a questioning whistle.

"Oh yah, that's a good idea," Jahno said. "*Ooalu*-moth cocoons," he explained to us. "It helps them see in the dark."

Kooie went below deck, returning to whistle the wyrms over, for all the world like one of the desert tribesfolk summoning their hunting dogs for a treat. It was dark enough that all I could see by moonlight was the silhouettes of their heads swaying as they snapped up the cocoons, but afterward, the wyrms' eyes took on a faint luminescent shine. Trilling thanks, they dove deep to retrieve their abandoned bits, clamping their jaws tight around them and swimming steadily, twin wakes streaming behind them.

Once again, we began inching away from the Granthian fleet behind us.

I gazed at the night sky, trying to imagine *stars*.

I could not.

It had been an impossibly long and improbable day and I was more tired than I knew, my eyelids growing heavy.

"Khai." Zariya leaned forward to touch my cheek. "Even you must sleep, my darling. And I should be ever so grateful to have you beside me."

"We would give you and your shadow privacy were it possible, Sun-Blessed," Jahno said apologetically. "I know this arrangement must seem terribly scandalous to you. But though we will sleep in shifts throughout the night, sleep we must."

"I know." She glanced around. "Is there . . . ?"

I rose, knowing what she was hinting at and glad I had already determined the answer. "I'll take you to the privy bucket."

The privy closet in Zariya's quarters in the Palace of the Sun had a door for privacy and an inlaid chamber pot of such a height that she could manage it on her own. It had been brought aboard the Therinian state-ship for her. Here, the bucket placed in the open air in the stern of the wyrm-raiders' ship was low enough that she needed my assistance to reach it.

"Oh, Khai!" Her voice broke at the indignity of it all, and my heart ached for her. "I could not do this without you, you know. Not for one heartbeat."

"That is why the Sacred Twins joined us," I said softly in reply.

"That you might help me squat over a bucket?" She waved away the comment. "Pay me no heed, my darling. It's only that I'm still a bit overwhelmed. I don't suppose there's a washbasin?"

"There's another bucket," I said.

Zariya knelt and scrubbed her hands and face with a sliver of hard soap floating in the fresh water while I lowered the privy bucket on its long rope over the railing that the sea might sluice it clean. "You wouldn't want to confuse the two in the dark, would you?" she observed as I helped her to her feet.

I smiled, glad to see that her bright spirit was unquenched. "No, you would not."

Out of respect, the crew allowed us to descend first and settle ourselves for the night. Knowing she was tired, I would gladly have lowered Zariya on my makeshift sling, but she insisted on climbing down the ladder herself, reminding me that she had done it earlier. "And on the morrow, I shall begin attempting the ascent," she said firmly. "My legs may be afflicted, but my arms are hale, and they will grow stronger with increased use, will they not?"

"Yes."

She nodded to herself. "I have led a coddled life, but that has changed. I cannot afford to accept any more assistance than is absolutely necessary." She paused. "Although . . . are we truly meant to sleep in the clothing we've worn all day? I know that was the practice in the desert where you grew up and I suppose being at sea is much the same. How many days in a row does one do such a thing?"

I watched her hoist one leg and then the other over the edge of her hammock, suppressing the urge to assist her. "You probably don't want to know the answer to that, Zariya."

She gave me a wry smile before closing her eyes. "You're probably right."

Tired as I was, I remained sleepless for the better part of an hour. I had stowed my *yakhan* and *kopar* and belt-knife, all of which caught and tangled in the hammock, but I kept the *zims* lashed to my forearm, the garrote laced in my hair, and the *heshkrat* wrapped around my waist, unable to relax without weapons at hand.

I heard the hatch door open, members of our unlikely crew descending the ladder, whispering to one another in hushed voices. I heard them settle into their hammocks, which creaked and swayed with the jouncing of the ship.

The air belowdecks grew heavy with sleep and sighs.

In the quietude, pale green glowing moths flitted here and there among the vines. One landed on the back of my hand, and when I brushed it gently away, it left behind a trace of luminous dust.

At length I slept.

FORTY-TWO

In the morning, the Granthian fleet was still visible behind us, still continuing their dogged pursuit.

Jahno and the Elehuddin conferred.

"It's time, yah?" he said, glancing around to see if anyone disagreed. "Half a day and a night, time enough for Therin to make their escape."

No one disagreed, and Tarrok suggested he might give the Granthian fleet a parting gift. "Then you will see why I am called the Thunderclap," he added.

To that end, we idled on the current for a quarter of an hour or so while the wyrms had another feed, gathering their strength for the coming dash. Seeing this, the Granthians took to their oars once more and redoubled their efforts, the stink-lizards rising to circle overhead.

They drew near enough that I was beginning to feel anxious, my palms itching for my hilts, before Essee whistled to the sea-wyrms. With answering trills, they retrieved the bits of their tow-lines.

Standing in the stern of the ship, Tarrok took an impossibly long, deep breath, his chest expanding like a bellows.

"You'll want to cover your ears," Evene advised us, fitting actions to words. Zariya had to sit to do so; the rest of us remained standing, our hands clapped tight over our ears.

Tarrok opened his mouth and let out a wordless shout.

I do not know what else to call it. His breath-swollen torso deflated all at once like a burst bladder as the sound left his lips, beating against the air in an invisible wave: a sound like a single clap of thunder or the slamming of an immense door. In mere seconds we saw the sound break like a wave over the Granthian fleet, rocking their ships and sending the stink-lizards reeling. A couple of the smaller lizards dropped like stones, stunned from the very sky. Granthian sailors scrambled in disarray. The Elehuddin whistled, the sea-wyrms responded, and our ship made an abrupt pivot to the south, cutting across the current and bounding over the waves, leaving the Granthian fleet behind us.

Tarrok bent over and braced his hands on his knees. His chest was heaving, but he was grinning into his beard.

I lowered my hands and glanced at Zariya. "Are you all right?"

"Yes." She nodded. "That's quite a gift, messire."

"Just Tarrok, my lady." He straightened with pride. "*That* is the legacy of Luhdo the Loud."

"'And the Thunderclap shall stun the armies of the risen and returned,'" Jahno murmured. "'And the Shadow's blades shall scythe through them like the wind and reap a deadly harvest.'"

"That's part of the prophecy?" Zariya inquired. He nodded. "What are the armies of the risen and returned?"

Jahno shrugged in apology. "Alas, I cannot say. It is only a fragment. Fragments are all we have."

"What *do* we know?" she asked.

Bit by bit, he laid out the pieces of the puzzle that the descendants of Koronis had assembled over the years. The rising of Miasmus would be presaged by the sign of the black star, a sign under which the prophets of Miasmus, afflicted by the dreaming god's madness, would sow mayhem and anarchy. During this time, the Seeker would attempt to assemble the defenders of the four quarters. As Miasmus awakened from slumber, the tide of the risen and returned would grow larger and stronger, and the defenders would find no safe haven from them, but must take the battle to Miasmus and destroy it.

The prophecy identifying the defenders, most of which Jahno had quoted on the state-ship, was reasonably clear. The specific details of exactly what we were to defend the world against, not to mention how, were lost or vague. In Trask it was prophesied that one bearing the gift of Luhdo the Loud would cleave the rock in the farthest reaches of the west if the time were upon us; what that meant, no one knew. Evene informed us dourly that no equivalent prophecy existed in Drogalia, where Quellin-Who-Is-Everywhere inhabited an infinite variety of forms at will and could seldom be recognized.

It seemed that Zariya and I were unique in having been addressed directly by our gods, the Sacred Twins who were the best-beloved of Zar the Sun. At Jahno's prompting, Zariya and I related our experiences with Pahrkun and Anamuht and the words they had spoken to us, which he wrote down carefully in a leather-bound journal.

"Life and death," he mused. "Fire and wind. Do either of you know what it means? Are you meant to be able to summon the elements?"

I shook my head. "Not me. Pahrkun said that to bear his mark was to carry the breath of the desert within me. I can channel the Scouring Wind, especially when I fight, but it is not the same as *summoning* it. It is a way of seeing the spaces between things."

Evene made a gesture, pressing her hands together and opening them wide. "Well, I *am* the Opener of Ways. Perhaps I'm meant to make spaces between things, to create a path for you."

"Can you do that?" I asked her.

She shrugged. "I can cause a crowd to part by . . . well, it's sort of impossible to explain. I just never saw much use in it."

"Ah, but now we are seeing possible patterns emerge," Jahno observed, making more notes. "What of you, my lady?"

"Can I summon fire, you mean?" Zariya asked ruefully. "You know, when Khai and I partook of the *rhamanthus,* there was a moment where it almost felt to me that it was possible, that I might call lightning from my fingertips like Anamuht the Purging Fire herself. But the moment passed."

He made a note of that, too. "We will keep seeking answers."

"What of the coursers of Obid?" I asked him. "My mentor told me that they had a prophecy that when the children of Miasmus sowed darkness, they would help stem the tide."

Jahno nodded. "Yah, that is so. Although they are not named among the defenders of the four quarters, it is clear that they have a role to play." He looked somewhat abashed. "We, ah, do not enjoy the best relationship with the coursers of Obid."

"I'm not sure we can afford to let old hostilities color our judgment," Zariya murmured.

"No, of course not, my lady," he replied. "But we also cannot afford to be hauled to Itarran and thrown in jail for past crimes by the self-appointed policers of the world."

It occurred to me that they might have given that more consideration before deciding to augment prophecy-hunting with piracy, but I supposed the former wasn't exactly a profitable career. Even a company as relatively self-sufficient as the wyrm-ship needed some material goods. Later, I learned that they also used stolen goods to exchange for tales or rumors regarding the Scattered Prophecy.

"The coursers of Obid sent a scouting party to investigate when the children of Miasmus first began to appear," Tarrok said soberly. "It was before I was exiled. They never returned."

"To investigate what?" I asked.

He glanced at me. "Miasmus."

"The Abyss that Abides." I remembered Brother Yarit muttering the words, Brother Ehudan telling me the tale of Miasmus. "I've heard tell that it's capable of swallowing entire ships."

"Oh, it's true enough," Tarrok said. "We in the far west know better than to sail near the Maw, but there are always those foolish enough to pursue rumors of glory or treasure."

Zariya was frowning in thought. "So when you speak of the children of Miasmus, are you speaking of the cursed sea-spiders?"

"Yah, for now." Jahno nodded. "But we think it's only the first wave. Worse is coming."

"Coming from where?" she asked.

"Coming from the Maw of Miasmus itself," he said. "It is a guess, for no one can confirm it, but it is an informed one." He hesitated. "You asked about the armies of the risen and returned. The prophecy is unclear, but I do have a theory. I think perhaps dark-dreaming Miasmus begins to spew into the world all those creatures it has devoured over long centuries. Now it is only the sea-spiders that carry its message. That will change as Miasmus awakens."

"And do they seek us out, these children of Miasmus?" Zariya inquired, glancing at Tarrok. "I understand you were exiled from Trask because your presence drew them to its shores."

He inclined his bald head to her. "That is so, my lady. Those afflicted by the children of Miasmus spoke of end times and fomented rebellion, but they also sought to incite my death."

"As the Mad Priest sought yours, my darling," Zariya murmured to me. Her mouth quirked wryly. "Though he merely exhorted them to *seize* me. Do I pose so little a threat?"

"With respect, my lady, I do not believe the children of Miasmus convey clear motives," Jahno said. "Now it is yet a thing as nebulous as a dream. Now they are capable of carrying its message of annihilation and destruction. They are capable of using their hosts to rouse the populace to overturn whatever order exists; and yah, they are capable of recognizing those of us chosen as defenders, and seeking to destroy us." He looked apologetic. "If you had been seized by this mob and given over to the most savage and base desires incited within them, it would have fed their frenzy to a greater degree than if you had merely been slain."

She took a slow breath. "And I should have been no less destroyed by it."

He nodded.

"I would *never* let that happen!" I said fiercely.

"No, I should hope you'd kill me yourself first, dearest." Zariya reached for my hand and squeezed it. "Well, this has been most informative."

Despite the talk of prophecy and impending doom, the mood aboard the ship was calm and prosaic. Now that we had left the Granthian fleet far behind, the sea-wyrms slackened their pace and chose their course with more care, and the ship did not jounce so over the waves. I would have been glad to make myself useful, but there was little to do. I checked on the stink-lizard hide curing in its tub of salt water and changed out the tainted water for new.

At Zariya's request, I washed my hands and set about undoing her wind-frazzled braids and combing out her hair. Re-creating the elaborate Zarkhoumi braided coiffure was beyond me, but I offered to twine it in a single plait.

"I'll try if you like, my lady," Evene offered in a gruff manner. "I had a name among the other girls at the Inn of Ten Palms for being skilled at braid-work." I looked at her in surprise, both at the unexpected offer and because her own hair was cropped nearly as short as a Granthian warrior's.

Zariya gave me the hand sign for *be quiet*. "That's very kind, thank you."

I made way for the tattooed woman, who sat behind Zariya and began plaiting her hair with deft fingers. Her face relaxed as she concentrated on the task. I'd guessed her age to be somewhere in her middle forties, but now I saw that she was some ten years younger than I'd reckoned.

"I'm not familiar with the Inn of Ten Palms," Zariya remarked.

"You wouldn't be," Evene said shortly. "It's a boarding house on Arisinia in the Nexus. Cheap, but clean. I served drinks at a tavern down the street." Her fingers went still. "Don't suppose you've ever mixed with the likes of me before, eh?"

"I've led a very sheltered life," Zariya said in a light tone. "I've never met the likes of *any* of you. Tell me, if I were able to read Drogalian symbols, would I have seen your profession etched on your skin?"

"No. Gods, no. I'm not ashamed of it, but I'm not proud of it, either. Anyway, I'm a long way from home." Evene resumed her work. "You know what the tattoos mean, then?"

Zariya nodded. "I think so."

"I don't," I said.

"I told you that Quellin-Who-Is-Everywhere can take any form, yeah?" Evene smiled. "He's a prankster, an awfully naughty one. In the old days, he would take the form of, say, a boy's mother, set him a task that would land him in trouble; take the form of a woman's husband and steal into her marriage bed."

It seemed distinctly ungodlike behavior to me, but then, I was beginning to suspect I knew little about the children of heaven as a whole.

"But the one aspect of another's appearance that Quellin-Who-Is-Everywhere couldn't duplicate was the markings, is that not so?" Zariya said.

"Yeah, that's how it began." Evene slapped her left shoulder, bare in a sleeveless jerkin. Both her arms were covered with elaborate whorls and symbols and her throat was circled by something that resembled the noose of a rope. "Folk found if they got tattooed with signs that meant 'I am Evene, daughter of Edsal and Varia' they could make sure a person was who they looked to be. Once begun . . ." She shrugged and extended both arms. "In Drogalia, you know a person's history at a glance. The entire lineage of my family is written here. Not that it's anything to boast of, but if you were Drogalian, you would know exactly who I am, who my people were, where we came from, and what we are known for."

"But not the whole of *your* history," Zariya said quietly.

"No." Evene touched the nooselike tattoo around her throat with one finger, her face hardening. "This is the last piece of my history from the realm of my birth, when I was sentenced to be hung. All criminals are marked."

Essee happened to be passing and laid a long-fingered hand on Evene's close-cropped head in a brief gesture of sympathy; I was grateful for it, since I had no idea what to say in response to her disclosure.

"You did well to escape, then," Zariya offered. "And we must be grateful for it, since it brought you to us."

"Yeah, well." Evene gave a mirthless laugh. "It's not as though the dungeon could hold me. The guards were another matter. But luckily for me there was one guard . . ." Something in her expression changed, tinged with realization, apprehension, and dawning awe. "Oh, watery hell!"

Zariya and I looked at each other and held our tongues.

"He offered to look away while I made my escape in exchange for . . . well, the obvious favor," Evene said, remembering. "He wore sleeves, long sleeves. Now that I think of it, he kept his shirt on throughout. You know, I never put the pieces together. But that guard, he was the one who said to me, 'If I were you, I'd make for the Nexus.' And so I did, whoring my way across the seas since I'd no coin left to my name. But he set me on that path. Now that I think of it, I bet it *was* him." She shook her head in something like admiration. "Fucking *Quellin!*"

"If it is true, his methods seem a bit . . . unkind," I said cautiously.

Evene fixed me with a hard stare. "Oh, and pray tell, shadow, was it kinder of Pahrkun the Scouring Wind to score your face with stinger and fang, to fill your veins with venom, and leave you to live or die in the desert?"

To that, I had no answer.

Were the children of heaven kind or cruel or indifferent? Did they care for us or merely their own fates?

I did not know.

That evening, while the sun yet hovered above the horizon, the Elehuddin dropped the sea anchors and whistled to the wyrms. They came arrowing across the water, heads held high. At close range, their upraised heads towered above the ship. While they had been about the hard work of towing us, I had forgotten exactly how enormous they were.

Kooie spoke, gesturing toward Zariya and me.

"We have not had a chance to make a proper introduction," Jahno translated. "Eeeio and Aiiiaii, this is Her Highness Princess Zariya of Zarkhoum and Khai of the Fortress of the Winds, Sun-Blessed and Shadow of prophecy."

The sea-wyrms dipped their heads in acknowledgment. In the lowering light, their iridescent scales gleamed ruddy and copper. I folded my hands and pressed my thumbs to my brow in salute.

"Oh!" Zariya's voice was filled with wonder. "You're both so very beautiful."

Eeeio, the larger of the two wyrms, stroked the underside of his long jaw along the other's crest of fins, which flattened and rose under his attentions. He lifted his head on his long, sinuous neck and let out an inquiring trill, luminous eyes bright with inhuman curiosity.

Jahno smiled. "Eeeio and Aiiiaii are a mated couple," he explained. "He asks if you are also."

Zariya glanced at me and smiled. "Perhaps not as they would understand it, I think," she said. "But yes, Khai is my soul's twin."

Aiiiaii whistled and lowered her head, resting her chin on the ship's rail.

"Then you are blessed," Jahno translated.

Transferring her canes into her left hand, Zariya flattened her palm against the sea-wyrm's mighty jaw. "Indeed, my darling," she murmured to Aiiiaii. "I do believe we are greatly blessed."

Some yards away, a winged shark breached the water, its body thrashing in midair as it gulped at a seabird. The wyrms' already bright eyes brightened further, and Eeeio gave a short, sharp whistle.

Kooie whistled in reply.

I watched the sea-wyrms peel away from the ship in pursuit of the winged shark, blood frothing the waters as they made their kill, long necks arching against the sky while they tossed down bite after bite of shark.

Truly, we had entered a new world. I could only be grateful that Zariya and I had entered it together.

FORTY-THREE

We were at sea for a month.

For all the portents attendant upon our journey, it was an uneventful one. Sometimes we passed island realms in the distance and Jahno would point them out and describe them to us, but we made no stops.

With each day that passed, Zariya grew a bit more at ease with our unexpected circumstances and our strange new companions, and she proved deadly serious about her goal of climbing the ladder unaided. I knotted a couple lengths of rope around the ship's railing that she might practice hoisting her own weight. The first days left her sore and aching, for it required the use of an entirely different set of muscles than those she used to support herself on her canes, but that soon passed and by the end of the second week she had developed sufficient strength to climb the ladder unassisted—as well as to use an additional fixed rope to lower and lift herself to and from the privy bucket without my help, a development that may have been even more welcome.

Zariya's unalloyed delight in these new measures of personal freedom filled my heart with gladness. She also spent long hours in conversation with Jahno, the Koronian allowing her to pore over the journal in which he had recorded every confirmed scrap of prophecy as well as rumors and folklore relating to it. They were kindred spirits, the two of them, and while I could not help but feel a twinge of jealousy at the rapport they found in studying oblique texts, what mattered most was that Jahno treated her with respect and Zariya was happy.

Still, I did take the precaution of ensuring that everyone aboard the ship knew that if Zariya was harmed in any way, I would happily chop them into pieces and feed them to the sea-wyrms, a sentiment with which Essee declared a surprisingly emphatic agreement. She may have been a pacifist, but I had learned that she was also a mother who had lost her only child, and Zariya in particular evoked a maternal tenderness in her.

I began to understand bits and pieces of the Elehuddin tongue, but it was difficult to make progress save when Jahno was available to translate until I hit on the idea of teaching Shahalim hand signs to the Elehuddin. It gave us a common language we could both use to communicate, and the Elehuddin took to it readily, long fingers flickering fluently. Jahno was intrigued, for it was a cultural phenomenon that no one had ever documented, and he pressed me for details.

Since there seemed no point in concealing my skills from the company, I told them about my training.

"Think what I could have done with that," Evene said wistfully.

"Yah, but we might never have found you if you'd been a better thief," Jahno reminded her.

I managed to get the stink-lizard's hide crudely tanned with salt water and scraped clean to a reasonable measure of pliability. I learned to play the board game clatter-peg and lost innumerable matches to Keeik, who was the youngest of the Elehuddin, an outgoing and lively fellow always ready with a toothy grin.

The one thing I wished for was a suitable sparring partner, for I worried that my skills would grow rusty for lack of practice. Tarrok indulged me on occasion, for he had been a blacksmith before his exile and knew his way around a blade, but he was far too slow to give me any real challenge. So for the most part, I simply practiced on my own against an imaginary opponent, replaying sparring matches with Vironesh in my memory, flowing through long series of strikes and thrusts and parries.

The crew gave me a wide berth when I did so, and Evene offered a grudging apology for having called me nothing more than a kid with a pair of swords. If nothing else, at least the ship's incessant bobbing motion forced me to improve my focus and balance.

At last we reached the outermost verge of the Nexus.

Even at first glance, I could see it was vaster than I could have imagined. Jahno informed us that there were over a thousand islands in the entire archipelago, each with its own deity.

"We will make for Verdant Isle first, to refill our water-casks," he said, pointing to a distant green island with mountain peaks wreathed in mist. "It lies under the aegis of Ishfahel the Gentle Rain."

Once we entered the Nexus, it was apparent that the currents and counter-currents were swift, strong, and complicated. Conventional ships dependent upon sails and oars fought to navigate them, carried this way and that by the unpredictable waterways. I will confess, I felt a certain smug satisfaction as we arrowed our way past them toward the harbor of Verdant Isle, Eeeio and Aiiiaii's heads held high in triumph, the neck-ridges of their fins proudly fanned.

Jahno named the islands we passed. "Bottle Isle, so called for the shape of its harbor; Coopers' Isle, nice strong trees for building casks; Grapevine Isle . . . that one lies under the aegis of Aardo the Intoxicated." He smiled at a private memory. "You can have quite a time there, but it's good fresh water we're after today, yah?"

Zariya leaned on her canes, swaying with the ship's motion. "We'll reach the Caldera by tomorrow?"

He nodded. "Or today yet. In time to consult the Oracle the next day, if we're lucky. If he has any counsel for us."

"Kephalos the Wise," she murmured. "I pray he does."

In the harbor of Verdant Isle, we queued in a line of ships seeking to take on fresh water. If a wyrm-raider ship had entered the harbor of Merabaht, folk everywhere would have been gaping in amazement; here, Eeeio and Aiiiaii's presence merely drew mild interested glances from the folk ashore and envious ones from the other sailors. The sea-wyrms dipped their heads beneath the waves, blowing out fine blasts of misty seawater through their nostrils.

One by one the ships in line ahead of us refilled their casks, which were raised on platforms and slings by means of a large winch-and-pulley system and filled ashore by a team of men hoisting massive water-skins with spouts, the process overseen by the local dockmaster, who collected payment in advance. At last it was our turn. Intent on watching our empty and near-empty casks being transferred ashore, I did not see what was happening inland.

Zariya caught my arm. "Oh, Khai! Look!"

I looked and my skin prickled.

Ishfahel.

One does not need to be told when one is in the presence of a god or goddess. Ishfahel descended from the mountain peaks with purpose and grace, trailing rain clouds in her wake. Her appearance was greeted with shouts of delight and the Verdant Islanders offered their own unique salute, lifting up both arms in praise and lowering them, fingers wriggling in a gesture meant to emulate the falling rain. Children followed behind Ishfahel, dancing in the rain showers, faces raised to the sky in joy.

The dockhands ceased their labors as Ishfahel approached. Like Anamuht and Pahrkun, Ishfahel the Gentle Rain was taller than a *rhamanthus* tree. Her smooth skin was a pale blue-grey the color of slate, shining rivulets of water running over it. Tendrils of mist cloaked her body and wound around her head. Her face was beautiful and serene, her eyes closed, the curl of her lashes breaking like great waves against her cheeks.

The rain clouds surrounding the goddess drifted forward as she came to a halt in the harbor, drizzling softly over the ship. It smelled indescribably clean and pure and good, and the sensation of it against my skin was so refreshing, restorative, and uplifting, I wanted to dance like the children in the streets. It felt as though the rain's touch washed away not only weeks' worth of grime, but every unworthy thought or impulse I'd ever had.

"Oh!" Zariya gasped, her face turned to the sky. "I feel *clean* for the first time in ages!"

I licked my lips, and the taste of the rainwater was sweet, sweeter than honey, making the rivers of blood that ran in my veins leap for joy. "I know."

"Seeker," Ishfahel murmured, and the sound of her voice was as soft and gentle and comforting as the susurrus of the falling rain. Her eyes remained closed, the smooth, graceful curves of them like polished stones. *"You and your company face a long and arduous journey."*

"Yah, my lady." Jahno's voice trembled a bit. He stepped forward and offered her a Koronian salute, folded palms spreading open like the pages of a book. "You grace us with your presence. Do you have counsel for us?"

"I have a blessing." She beckoned to the dockhands. *"Bring forth one of the empty vessels."* They hastened to obey, rolling one of our empty casks in place before the goddess. Ishfahel's mouth opened impossibly wide, her unhinged jaw lowering, and suddenly the landscape of her face was transformed; no longer did she resemble a beautiful woman, but a smooth-faced mountain, the cavern of a spring opening beneath the dome of her brow and the ridge of her nose. She raised cupped hands to her waist and inclined her head. Silver-bright water spilled forth from the well-spring of her mouth, shining even beneath the clouds. It filled her cupped hands, now like a pool surrounded by crags worn smooth by falling water; spilled in a sparkling stream to fill our empty cask.

I caught my breath at the sheer beauty of it.

At length the well ran dry; Ishfahel hinged her jaw and closed her mouth, her features rearranging themselves into something resembling a beautiful woman's face once more. *"Breach the cask only in your time of greatest need,"* she said, and it seemed her close-lidded glance touched each and every one of us. *"May it sustain you when all else fails."*

All of us saluted; everyone in the harbor and the neighboring ships offered their version of a salute. The sea-wyrms raised their heads and trilled a note of gratitude in unison.

A smile touched Ishfahel's lips, all at once gentle and sorrowful and hopeful. *"I wish you well upon your quest."*

Don't go, I wanted to cry out, only because the goddess was so gracious and lovely; but she was already turning, tendrils of mist swirling around her as she made her retreat, taking the rain clouds with her, laughing children chasing after her in vain as her strides grew longer.

"Well!" It was the dockmaster's voice that broke the reverie. He scratched his head. "Never seen *that* before." He glanced up at our ship. "What's the nature of this quest of yours anyway?"

We looked to Jahno to answer. He might not be our captain, but he was the Seeker, and it was him whom Ishfahel had addressed.

Jahno drew a deep breath. "Well, we're still piecing it together," he said apologetically. "But I *think* we're the defenders of the four quarters who are meant to slay Miasmus upon its rising."

The dockmaster gave us another once-over, looking dubious. "Good luck to you, my friends. I reckon you'll need it. We're clean here on Verdant right now, but I've seen the poor mad fuckers infested by those things."

The remaining casks were filled and nailed shut in short order and hoisted back aboard the ship. I helped in the effort of wrestling them into the cargo hold, marking the lid of the barrel that contained Ishfahel's blessed water with a bold *X* with the point of my belt-dagger.

"So at least we've got a barrel full of god-spittle," Evene remarked. "That's something, isn't it?"

I gave her a cool look, misliking her irreverent tone. "Do you imagine such a jest commends your character?"

The tattooed woman opened her mouth for a tart reply, then shivered unexpectedly and wrapped her arms around herself. "No," she whispered. "I envy you your surety of purpose, shadow; I envy your training and the bond you share with your Sun-Blessed princess. I have none of those things. I am a failed thief, an escaped convict, and a reasonably good barmaid, none of which remotely qualifies me for attempting to save the world." In the dim green glow shed by the flitting *ooalu* moths, her gaze was bitter and shadowy. "At least your god gave you words of prophecy and the gift of status. As you so kindly noted, *my* god fucked me under false pretenses and sent me on my merry way." She shivered again, searching my eyes. "At first it was a lark to imagine myself chosen for a higher purpose. But the more real this business of the Scattered Prophecy becomes, the more terrified I am. Do you blame me?"

I sheathed my belt-dagger, feeling guilty. "No. But Ishfahel's blessing was meant for all of us."

"It was, wasn't it?" Evene mused.

"Yes."

She gave me a crooked smile. "I'll try to remember it. Thank you, shadow."

I nodded.

That day we sailed past another several dozen isles. Rejuvenated by the rainfall, the wyrms swam strongly, heads low, the bits clamped tight in their jaws, the action of their powerful tails leaving twin trails of wake behind them. Date Palm Isle, Forked Rock Isle, Mussel Isle . . . I lost track of the names of the islands and the gods and goddesses who held aegis over them, although I daresay Zariya committed each and every one of them to memory. I did not think I needed to do the same. We were bound for the Caldera at the very heart of the Nexus, a hollow semicircle ring of an island, the basalt husk of a volcano that had exploded long ago, before the children of heaven had fallen from the skies. There in the deep ocean in the center of the Caldera, the Oracle of the Nexus abided: Kephalos the Wise.

There we would seek the Oracle's counsel.

We reached the Caldera before nightfall. Myriad small, deep harbors were staggered all around it, nestled at the bottom of steep crags with switchback trails leading to the top of the ring.

After conferring with the Elehuddin, Eeeio and Aiiiaii simply made for the nearest harbor.

There was a Mad Priest there on the wharf.

A prophet of Miasmus, I suppose I should call him; at any rate, he had been afflicted. Who he had been before it happened, I never knew. The prophet held up one hand as we glided into a berth in the harbor, and his entire palm was suppurating with the mark of the black star, lines extending up his fingers and wrist, angry red infectious streaks rising the length of his arm. "They come!" he cried in a shrill voice. "Sun-Blessed and Shadow, Seeker and Thunderclap and Opener of Ways! Kill them and seize their spoils as your rightful prize! Kill them *all* and let the blessed darkness rise!"

Everyone ignored him. The Nexus was a place all unto itself and the Caldera all the more so. Those who dwelled here wished to preserve it as it was; those who came as pilgrims had no desire to alter it.

Even so, I was uneasy. "Shall I kill him?" I asked Jahno, fingering the hilts of my weapons.

Essee clicked in disapproval.

"No." Jahno frowned. "He has offered us no violence, shadow, only words. We cannot kill him for words."

"It might be a mercy," I suggested.

He gave me a sidelong look. "Perhaps, but it would be a violation of the decree that Kephalos the Wise has laid over the Nexus. All are welcome here. There are many harbors. Let us seek another."

As we made our way around the coast of the Caldera toward the south, Aiiiaii looped her coils around to lift her head and call out an apologetic trill. "She says they should have recognized the smell of corrupted flesh," Jahno translated. "They will make sure there are no such afflicted souls in the next harbor."

At the next harbor, however, the wyrms raised an alarm; and the next two harbors afterward. It was not until the fifth harbor we attempted that we found a safe berth for the night.

"That seems rather a lot of Miasmus-afflicted," Zariya said soberly. "Is that usual here?"

"No." Jahno looked troubled. "But as you saw, their message has gained no purchase here."

"That would not matter if there were enough of them to attack us in strength." I turned to Tarrok. "How many assailed Trask's shores at once?"

The tall man shrugged. "No more than a dozen at any given time. Trouble was their message *was* finding an audience." He scratched his bearded chin. "And I worry that it still is. There hasn't been any news out of Trask for a year or more."

Kooie spoke, his yellow-gold eyes catching the setting sun's light to gleam crimson, his fingers augmenting his words.

"He says things are growing worse and this is only the beginning," Jahno said. "But we need to do this, and together we are strong and courageous and compassionate, my brothers and sisters."

I was still thinking about the prophet. "What if I'd just cut his arm off?" I held up my hand, forestalling Essee's disapproving glance. "No, I mean, is it possible to free one of the afflicted from the children of Miasmus if the spider isn't lodged in his vitals?"

"I've seen it attempted," Tarrok admitted. "But I fear that the afflicted never recover their wits, and you have to be damned quick about killing the creature afterward, because they only need a minute or two to recover and seek a new host, and they move lickety-split once they do. And it takes fire to put an end to them."

Remembering Vironesh and myself stooping over the pulsing sea-spider, I felt a little sick.

Keeik glanced toward me and whistled, hands signing too swiftly to follow in the lowering light.

"He says that we will harm no innocent victims unless our hands are forced," Jahno translated. "But if the prophets of Miasmus do attack us, we must let Khai kill them. Yah, I agree. But no one is killing anyone tonight," he added. "Tonight we rest aboard the ship and give thanks to Ishfahel the Gentle Rain. Tomorrow, we will seek to consult the Oracle of the Nexus, come what may."

Everyone nodded in agreement, even Essee, the tendrils of her mane stirring with quiet sorrow.

FORTY-FOUR

In the morning we ventured ashore.

It was a matter of considerable debate whether to take the *rhamanthus* seeds with us or leave them aboard the ship. Although I was reluctant to leave them, the coffer was awkward to carry, and bringing it was likely to draw more attention to it. In the end it was the sea-wyrms who decided the matter, assuring us that one or the other of them would attend the ship at all times.

Thus reassured, we set out. There were a dozen porters with sturdy little donkeys offering to transport pilgrims or traders—honest or otherwise—up the steep, craggy paths and across the island to the Oracle. We hired one for Zariya, who was quite taken with the novelty of riding astride.

"It's almost as though I've got my own strong new set of legs, my darling," she remarked to me. "Why did I never try this before?"

I smiled at her. "I doubt you would have been permitted. I don't recall seeing any women save your sister and her priestesses riding in Merabaht."

"True." She looked pensive. "My entire family would be utterly appalled by everything about this journey. I only pray I have the chance to share the scandalous details with them one day."

The narrow streets were lined with shops and taverns and thronged with all manner of people. I tried to keep a sharp eye out for any prophets of Miasmus, but it was nigh impossible in such a crowd. Simply keeping track of our companions was difficult enough. We made one stop at a fabric shop, where Jahno and Evene haggled over the sale of the bolt of Barakhan silk that had been Prince Heshari's courting gift, for the chance to consult the Oracle didn't come cheap. Zariya looked a bit wistful at seeing the iridescent fabric vanish into the depths of the shop, but it had been her idea to sell it when she learned that our company was short of funds.

"And now I suppose one might say that Barakhan has contributed its piece to the fulfillment of the prophecy," she remarked when Jahno and Evene emerged with a considerable purse.

"*If* we get counsel," Jahno cautioned her. "It's always a gamble, yah? We've sought it before and received none."

Zariya patted her donkey's neck. "I'm feeling hopeful, my darlings."

It took a good half an hour to navigate the winding maze of streets and arrive at the large square known as the Pilgrims' Plaza, where at last the crowd thinned. I began scanning once more for prophets or pickpockets. Out of the corner of my right eye, I saw a blurred figure darting toward Zariya.

By all the gods, it was *fast*! The startled porter let go of the lead-rope and the donkey shied; Zariya slid sideways in the saddle. Even if she'd been an experienced rider, her legs lacked the strength for a proper grip.

"Catch her!" I shouted, drawing my weapons and placing myself between Zariya and the figure.

A young man blinked up at me; but no, he was looking past me. He'd flung himself to his knees and his arms were outstretched, a long, slender sword lying on his upturned palms.

"My queen!" he cried in ecstasy. "I've found you! I pray you accept my sword into your service!"

I stared at him in pure astonishment, the weapons in my hands momentarily forgotten. The young man's sparkling eyes, which were gazing fixedly at Zariya, were the aquamarine hue of the sea. His skin was tan, his long hair a shining gold. He wore a leather vest without a back and a double set of narrow, transparent wings sprouting from his shoulder blades vibrated on either side of him with a low humming sound.

"I should have guessed," Jahno said in disgust behind me. "It's a god-damned *mayfly*."

I had absolutely no idea what that meant.

Flexing my hands on my hilts, I took an offensive stance. "Who are you and what do you want?"

The young man tore his gaze away from Zariya and met mine with an effort. "I am Lirios of Chalcedony Isle," he said humbly. "And I do but seek to find my one true queen and serve her. The blessed goddess Selerian the Light-Footed, daughter of Eshen the Wandering Moon, bade me seek her in the presence of the Oracle." He transferred his gaze back to Zariya, smiling a broad white smile. "And here she is!"

At a loss, I glanced over my shoulder at Zariya.

She was still upright in the saddle, steadied by Kooie and Tarrok, and looking bewildered.

Jahno came forward. "May I ask how old you are, Lirios of Chalcedony Isle?"

The young man cast his gaze downward. "I am very nearly nine years of age," he admitted. "I know it is old to be mated."

"Yah." Jahno blew out his breath. "Well, I don't think you're meant to be *mated* to your queen, my young friend."

Lirios glanced up, crestfallen. "No?"

"'From the Nexus comes the Quick, who will recognize his queen,'" Jahno quoted wryly, putting out his hand. "I do believe you have just completed the company of the defenders of the four quarters. And as the Seeker of the Scattered Prophecy, I offer you welcome."

Lirios ignored his extended hand. "My queen?" he asked Zariya. "Do you accept my service?"

Zariya glanced at Jahno, her brow furrowed. I felt an unwarranted pang of jealousy that it was to him, and not me, that she looked for counsel; but no, that was foolish. He was the Seeker and I knew nothing of mayflies. "I confess myself on uncertain ground."

Jahno nodded. "Yah, my great-grandfather never had the chance to write about Chalcedony Islanders," he said. "The lifespan of the males is three times shorter than that of the women. Their lives are short and fast. Everything about them is . . . well, quick." He grimaced. "And very, very energetic and earnest."

"Once we have found our queens, we are loyal unto death," Lirios added humbly, still kneeling and offering his sword on outstretched palms. "I do not know yet how I am meant to serve you if we are not to be mated, but

Selerian the Light-Footed does not make mistakes. I know that you are my queen, my true queen. Do you accept my service?"

"Ah . . . yes, of course," she said in a bemused tone. "Thank you, Lirios."

He bounded to his feet and sheathed his sword, narrow wings vibrating at an excited pitch that made my eardrums itch. "Thank *you,* my queen!" He paused. "How shall I call you?"

"She is Her Sun-Blessed Highness Princess Zariya of the House of the Ageless," I informed him.

He gave me a sunny smile. "Then I shall call her that."

"Zariya will suffice," she said in a reserved manner.

So it was that our company increased by one before consulting the Oracle of the Nexus.

The number of pilgrims who might consult the Oracle at any given time was eight. As the Seeker, Jahno decreed that the six chosen defenders—Seeker, Sun-Blessed, Shadow, Thunderclap, Opener of Ways, and the Quick—should be among them. The Elehuddin debated amongst themselves and chose Essee and Kooie to complete our company of pilgrims.

Priests and priestesses of Kephalos the Wise escorted us to the innermost ridge of the Caldera. Below us, in the cupped hollow of the isle, the blue sea looked calm and serene. We descended the path to the ledge below with care, Zariya yet astride her donkey, the porter leading it impassively. I helped her dismount when the priest indicated she should do so.

I would have stayed by her side, but a robed priestess shook her head at me and urged me onward.

"I will be fine, my heart," Zariya said breathlessly, propping herself upright on her canes. "Go, and learn what you may."

One by one, we arrayed ourselves along the ledge. The sea beneath us began to churn as the Oracle rose from its depths.

Although Jahno had described it to us, and I had seen many octopi caught by the Elehuddin in our weeks at sea, nothing could have prepared me for the sight of Kephalos the Wise. An octopus, yes; but one as vast as a mountain, looming out of the sea, water streaming from the mottled red skin of its great, bulbous head. Tapering tentacles as thick as tree trunks at their base arched into the air with sinuous grace, their pale undersides lined with a double row of hundreds of suckers, each one larger than my hand. It had eight eyes, as black as ink and deep with wisdom, and eight beaked orifices ringing the edge of its underbelly.

All eight tentacles streaked out at once, and it took a considerable effort not to reach for my weapons as one wrapped around my waist. Although Kephalos was gentle, I could sense the tremendous strength in its limb. The pale suckers flexed and moved independently of one another, but didn't latch on to me.

We had been told to search our hearts for the question we most desired answered, that we might pose it to the Oracle. "How can I best protect my lady Zariya from harm?" I asked; at the same time I spoke, I heard bits and pieces of other questions, the words overlapping with clicks and whistles from Essee and Kooie.

". . . meant to use the *rhamanthus* seeds?"

". . . find the key piece missing from the Scattered Prophecy?"

". . . hell am I doing here?"

". . . destroy Miasmus?"

". . . serve my queen?"

The Oracle of the Nexus closed its eyes, taking in our questions, then opened them once more. One deep black eye regarded me, and Kephalos the Wise opened the beak in its nearest mouth-orifice and loosed its tentacle from around my waist. *"The tools you need have been given to you. For you I have no counsel."*

Disappointed, yet oddly unsurprised, I listened to the overlapping bits and pieces of its answers.

"A way is not always a door. Remember this."

"For you I have no counsel."

"No."

"That which you seek lies in the possession of those whose lifeblood is trade, and value the worth of a thing more than the thing itself."

"The answer to your question abides in the words of the Scattered Prophecy."

"For you I have no counsel."

It was to Zariya whom the Oracle spoke at greatest length. I shook my head, trying to clear out the cacophony of its eight-fold response and concentrate on the words it spoke to her.

"Your childhood illness has impaired the flow of energy that would allow you to channel the sun-fire of the rhamanthus. *You must seek healing among those who dwell amidst a thousand forms of death."*

One by one, the remaining tentacles unwound themselves from around our waists and retreated, waving in the air above the sea. The Oracle's eight eyes closed once more for the space of a few heartbeats, then opened ink-black and blazing, all eight of its beaked mouths speaking in unison.

"Miasmus awakens!" Kephalos the Wise cried in a voice that rang out across the Caldera. *"Flee!"*

The sea erupted.

Sea-spiders, the firstborn children of Miasmus; hundreds of them, crawling forth in a great black wave.

"To the ship!" I shouted, already racing along the ledge in retreat. "Everyone! *Now!*"

I paused long enough to hoist Zariya into the saddle by main force, tucking her canes under one arm. "Hold tight to its neck," I said. She nodded and obeyed without a word. The porter was wide-eyed with terror. "Run," I advised him. "I'll turn the donkey loose later."

He nodded, too.

Behind us, the Oracle of the Nexus flailed its powerful tentacles, sweeping dozens of sea-spiders into the water with every blow; but there were simply too many of the small creatures, scrambling up the crags in a rising tide. I grabbed the donkey's lead-rope and hauled, dragging it behind me.

A great shout split the sky behind us: Tarrok the Thunderclap. I stole a glance over my shoulder and saw the tide of sea-spiders momentarily stunned. Other members of our company streamed past us.

"Fire!" Jahno shouted at the priests and priestesses of the Oracle. "Fetch torches! Oil! You need fire to kill them for good!"

Evene was panting.

Lirios's wings were buzzing in agitation. "What can I do?"

I tossed Zariya's canes to him. "Carry these."

He caught them deftly and whipped up the steep trail; I saw him pause at the top, silhouetted against the sky. "Oh, no."

Prophets of Miasmus.

There were at least two score of them arrayed in the Pilgrims' Plaza; men and women, young and old, armed and bare-handed, every single one of them marked in some part, arms and legs and torsos and even one on her face, by the suppurating sign of the black star. It struck me that there was a deadly clarity of purpose to them that I had not seen before, and I thought it must be because Miasmus was no longer dreaming, but awake and watching through their eyes. The pilgrims and ordinary folk in the plaza had retreated to avoid them, giving them a healthy berth.

I halted beside Lirios, the rest of our company fetching up behind me.

The oldest of the prophets pointed at us with a gnarled forefinger. "Defenders of the four quarters," she said in a quavering voice that was all the more disturbing for the fact that it was almost kind. "You have found one another, but your cause is in vain. Miasmus awakens and the darkness rises, ready to drown the world and you with it. Today is the day you die."

"Do what you must, my darling," Zariya murmured, her arms still twined in a death grip around the donkey's neck.

I handed the lead-rope to Essee and glanced at Lirios. "Can you fight, Quick?"

He nodded and drew his narrow blade, tossing Zariya's canes to a startled Jahno. "I think so. I have trained at it, anyway."

Pahrkun's wind was rising, skirling around my ankles, blowing through me. "Then let us do so."

Innocents.

There was a part of me that grieved at the necessity of killing so many folk whose only crime was having the bad luck to be afflicted; and yet it was clear there was no other way. I drew my *yakhan* and my *kopar* and cut a swath through them; one step, two steps, three steps. I targeted those with weapons, doing my best to avoid the unarmed prophets. The mayfly's wings buzzed, his thin sword darted. He fought with more speed than skill, but his speed was enough.

We made a path.

Essee plunged into it, hauling the donkey behind her. Zariya clung to its neck. One by one the others followed, shouting at the milling pilgrims and spectators and vendors to run, flee, get away.

Behind us, the sea-spiders recovered and climbed.

Between *this* and *that*, I killed a score or more of the afflicted, their blood staining my blades.

It was enough to allow our company to pass. Lirios and I fled along the path that we'd forged. Panic began rising behind us as people realized what was happening and sought to flee the square.

"Should we not stand and fight?" Lirios inquired; he was not even the slightest bit winded from his exertions. "Is that not our duty?"

I shook my head grimly. "The children of Miasmus are drawn to our presence. The greatest gift we can give the people of the Caldera is our absence."

It was a thing easier said than done, for panic had outraced us and now that we had left the square behind us, the narrow, crowded streets were a solid press of people. I could see Zariya's head a block ahead of us, higher than the rest of the crowd thanks to her mount, and could only trust the others were with her. A surging mass of bodies separated us from our companions.

There was a sign hanging from a stout iron rod protruding from a tavern to my left. Moving without thinking, I sheathed my weapons, grabbed the rod, and hoisted myself atop it, catching my balance and propelling myself to the rooftop. The roofs were fairly flat and the buildings close together. I ran along the rooftops, leaping over the gaps between them.

Lirios the mayfly pulled alongside me. "May I ask what your plan is?"

"I don't have one." I hadn't exactly meant to leave him behind, but I hadn't expected him to keep up with me, either. "Any suggestions?"

"No," he admitted. "I am very new to this."

"You're nine years old." Now I was close enough to see with relief that our company had kept together, closed in a protective knot around Zariya atop her donkey; however, the way before them was completely blocked. "You're very new to everything."

"My every year is as three of yours," Lirios said with a touch of wounded dignity. "I am older for a man of my people than you, I think."

I ignored him, my mind ticking over the possibilities. Jahno and Tarrok were shouting for people to give way and let them pass, but everyone was pushing and shouting by now and their words were lost in the din. I almost wished Tarrok hadn't used the Thunderclap on the sea-spiders. It was a formidable weapon, but he had told us it took at least an hour to recoup the prodigious amount of energy it expended. Then again, if he hadn't bought us time, this might already be over.

Could Lirios and I haul our entire company to the rooftops? If we'd had rope, maybe. Without it, no.

I could kill everyone blocking the way and create a mountain of corpses for us to clamber over in pursuit of our escape. It was a course of last resort and not a pleasing prospect.

We caught up with our crowd-stranded company. Zariya saw me atop the roof and lifted her face, dark eyes pleading. Behind us there was screaming. The children of Miasmus were coming, scuttling along the cobblestones.

Coming for *us*.

I ground my teeth in frustration, my hands balling into fists. Unexpectedly, I heard Brother Saan's voice in my memory.

Let your mind be like the eye of the hawk . . .

I found a point of stillness, my thoughts drifting, and then it came to me; a solution so simple and obvious that it struck me like a slap to the face.

"Evene!" I shouted from the rooftop. "Opener of Ways!" She did not hear me, but one of the Elehuddin did and gave her a sharp poke in the arm with one clawed fingertip. Evene shot me a stricken look, her features blank with terror. I mimicked the gesture she had once made, folding and opening my hands. "A way is not always a door! You said you could part a crowd. Do it!"

Gradual understanding replaced her expression of paralyzed fear; I watched her close her eyes and gather her concentration, placing her palms together, then opening them as though she were lifting a great weight. And slowly, slowly, the crowd before our trapped company parted, folk plastering themselves to the walls, confused looks on their myriad faces.

I let out a whoop of triumph.

"I do not understand what is happening," Lirios said in bewilderment. "Why are the people doing that?"

I grabbed his forearm and squeezed it. His skin was warm to the touch, warmer than ordinary skin. "Later. Are you with us?"

His aquamarine eyes blazed. "Yes!"

"Come, then."

We ran along the rooftops, following as our company fled down the path that Evene had opened; fled through the narrow streets, the sound of screaming growing fainter behind us as we neared the verge of the town. On the final rooftop, I hung from my fingertips and dropped to solid ground. Lirios followed suit, landing soundlessly. This early in the day, the descending path to the small harbor we had chosen was clear. We scrambled down it, passing porters and donkeys and pilgrims going the other way and calling out warnings to them. The Elehuddin whistled sharply to the sea-wyrms in the harbor, who raised their heads and trilled alarmed answers.

"Go, go, go!" Jahno urged us, although no one needed urging.

"My lady, forgive me, I mean no disrespect," Tarrok said to Zariya, scooping her bodily from the saddle and cradling her in his arms.

"I take none," she assured him, her breath raspy with the effort of speaking.

On the wharf, I drew my weapons and made a stand to guard our retreat. Lirios joined me unbidden. Behind us, the Elehuddin scrambled to untie the mooring lines. Before us, a rivulet of sea-spiders was pouring down the path, sowing fresh panic in their wake, finding horrible purchase in the bodies of those humans unable to flee in time.

I pitied their victims, but it was the fast-moving stream of the children of Miasmus that worried me. There wasn't a blessed thing that Lirios and I could do against hundreds or thousands of the creatures. If they reached us, we would all be numbered among the afflicted and the battle lost.

"They're coming fast," Lirios observed, his wings whirring.

"I know." I turned my head to shout over my shoulder. "Are we nearly ready to cast off?"

"Yah!" Jahno shouted in reply. *"Now!"*

The ship's prow was already angling out to sea. Kooie clung to the boarding ladder on the stern, prepared to cast off the last line. Seeing our pounding approach, he wasted no time, unhitching the rope and swarming up the ladder. Taking it as a sign to depart, the sea-wyrms leaned into their bits and the ship began to pull away from the dock. There were sharp trills and whistles and cries of "Go back!"

I stole a glance behind us. The sea-spiders had reached the wharf, the black tide advancing toward our fleeing heels.

"Keep going!" I shouted, shoving my weapons into their sheaths and praying that Lirios was as agile as he appeared to be. I rounded onto the dock without slackening my speed, sandals slapping the wooden planks, and launched myself toward the stern of the retreating ship, catching the railing and vaulting aboard.

The mayfly's leap wasn't graceful, but it was prodigious. He hung suspended in the sky, arms and legs akimbo, his translucent wings spread and his sword still gripped tight in his left hand before catching the uppermost rung of the boarding ladder with his right hand and dangling there.

Sea-spiders reached the edge of the dock and began spilling into the sea. Leaning over the railing, I caught Lirios's wrists, avoiding his flailing blade with an effort. His feet found the rungs, and I helped him aboard.

Kooie let out an ear-piercing whistle and the ship leapt forward like a bee-stung horse, sending Lirios tumbling to the deck, the sword he yet clutched nearly severing one of Kooie's tendrils. Kooie grimaced, drawing his tendrils tight to his head.

I looked back over the stern.

Fast though the children of Miasmus might be, they were no match for the sea-wyrms in open water. Distance opened between us and the black tide that trailed in our wake.

We were safe, for now.

But I shuddered to think of the carnage behind us. Miasmus was rising. It was no longer an abstract possibility, but a reality. Hundreds of innocent lives would be lost today, perhaps thousands; and this was only the beginning. I felt an emotion as unfamiliar and unwelcome as jealousy.

It was fear.

FORTY-FIVE

"We need to talk." Jahno's tone was grim.

We had gathered in the shadow of the charthouse where Zariya was resting, eyes closed and back propped against the wall, her chest rising and falling in shallow breaths.

"She needs time to recover," I said pointedly.

Lirios knelt beside her. "Is that what you need, my queen?" he inquired anxiously. "I am here to serve you."

Zariya cracked open one eye and gave me a wry look. I tugged the mayfly to his feet. "Give her room to breathe."

Essee gave an apologetic click and whistled, her fingers signing.

"Yah, she's right," Jahno agreed. "There's no time to rest just yet. Miasmus has awakened, and we need to plan our actions and chart a course based on what the Oracle told each of us."

"You will not like what I have to report," Zariya murmured. "It is a rather terrifying piece of counsel."

He sat cross-legged opposite her and fetched out his leather journal. "Tell me."

Allowing her eyelids to drift closed again, she quoted Kephalos the Wise. "'Your childhood illness has impaired the flow of energy that would allow you to channel the sun-fire of the *rhamanthus*. You must seek healing among those who dwell amidst a thousand forms of death.'"

Tarrok sucked in a sharp breath, turning pale. *"Papa-ka-hondras?"*

"So I fear," Zariya said. "I can think of no other place that fits the description."

Jahno glanced around. "Who else received counsel that might affect the course of our journey?"

Heads shook. "The Oracle had no counsel for me," I admitted.

Essee spoke, signing, *It had no words I welcome.* Somehow I suspected that the Oracle's simple *"No"* was in response to her question, and I wondered what that question had been.

"The Oracle told me to remember that a way is not always a door." Evene glanced in my direction. "Which I completely failed to do. It wasn't exactly the answer to the question, 'What the hell am I doing here?'"

"But was it not the exact answer you needed?" Zariya pushed herself to a more upright position, a measure of color returning to her cheeks. "You were splendid. We owe you all our lives."

Evene raised her brows at Zariya. "Are you jesting? I froze in terror. If Khai hadn't prompted me, we'd have been spider-bait."

"Yes, but he did, and you *were* splendid." Zariya glanced at Kooie. "What did you say the other day? 'Together we are strong and courageous and compassionate.' Truer words were never spoken." She paused a moment to catch her breath, one hand signing thanks for our patience. "Today several of you saved all of our lives, and you were *all* splendid, my newfound brothers and sisters. But our task has only just begun, and though all that lies beneath the starless skies is at stake, others pay the price for the continuation of our quest. So, pray tell, who else among us received counsel from Kephalos the Wise?"

Kooie had received none.

Lirios, to my surprise, pointed at me. "I asked the Oracle how I was meant to serve my queen if not in the customary manner of the men of my people. It told me to follow her companion's lead."

"I cut to the quick of the matter and asked how we might destroy Miasmus," Tarrok said bluntly. "For what it's worth, the Oracle said the answer lies in the words of the Scattered Prophecy. I'd certainly rather it had just *told* me."

"Because it doesn't know the answer," Jahno said, tugging absently at his right earlobe. "Not even the Oracle. *None* of the children of heaven possess the whole of the prophecy. Their father Zar the Sun's words shattered and fell upon their ears in scattered pieces as they fell from the heavens. No one knows more than a part; no one can see the whole of it."

"You know this to be true?" Zariya asked him.

He lowered his silvery gaze. "It is a theory."

"It's a worthy one," she said. "What did you ask the Oracle and what counsel was offered?"

Jahno hesitated. "I asked where I might find the key piece missing from the Scattered Prophecy." He inclined his head toward Tarrok. "Which I believe is the answer to the question of how the defenders of the four quarters are meant to put an end to Miasmus, my brother Thunderclap."

My friend Keeik, denied by circumstance the chance to seek the Oracle's counsel, whistled and signed impatiently, *Where is it?*

"If I had to guess, I'd say the Tukkani have it in their possession," Jahno said. "Kephalos the Wise said, 'That which you seek lies in the possession of those whose lifeblood is trade, and value the worth of a thing more than the thing itself.' No one comes close to the Tukkani when it comes to trading." He frowned. "But where would they have come across a piece of the Scattered Prophecy no one else possessed?"

"From their god, surely?" Zariya offered. "Was there not something in the fragments you recovered regarding Galdano the Shrewd?"

"Yah." Jahno tugged his earlobe again. "'When one way is closed, an acolyte of Galdano the Shrewd will point to another.' There was nothing in the Tukkani prophecy about destroying Miasmus." Kooie whistled an inquiry too lengthy for his vocabulary of hand signs, and Jahno gave him a look of horror. "You think a Koronian scholar could have *traded* them a copy of the secret archive? No, no, that would have been unthinkable."

"Well, Kooie thought it," Zariya said in a reasonable tone. "And if it were written in Koronian cryptographs, the Tukkani wouldn't have been able to read it without a *khartouka*."

"Then it would be useless to them," he said. "So what would be the point?"

"Ah, but it would be of immeasurable worth to us," she replied. "And the Oracle said they value the worth of a thing more than the thing itself. I do believe that was decreed by Galdano the Shrewd himself." She shrugged. "My eldest half brother has a mania for collecting items of great value. I do not pretend to understand it, but I have seen it at work. For him, it would be enough to possess the item, whether it was of use to him or not."

I couldn't help it, I rubbed the back of my neck; but now was definitely not the time for confessing my secret.

"Will someone please tell me what passes here?" Lirios asked in a plaintive voice, his wings wafting uncertainly.

Essee patted his shoulder and spoke gently to him. "Yah, of course. She says just give us a few moments," Jahno translated. "There is much to explain, but first we must make an important decision. So." He glanced around at us. "The Oracle has given us two possible destinations. And I am sorry to say it, but . . ." He swallowed, suddenly looking young and unsure. "We are a great deal closer to Papa-ka-hondras than we are to Tukkan. If we are journeying toward Miasmus . . ." He did not finish the sentence. "I may be the Seeker, but this choice I cannot make alone."

Papa-ka-hondras, A Thousand Ways to Kill. It seemed like a lifetime ago that Nazim the apothecary first told me about the place while I studied poisons in the Fortress of the Winds.

No one spoke. No one wanted to give voice to the decision.

It was Zariya who broke the silence, her voice unsteady. "The children of Miasmus claimed a great many lives today. If I were able to use the *rhamanthus* to summon the sun's fire, as it seems I'm meant to do, I might have saved them. And this is only the beginning. My darlings, I fear our choice is plain. But you need not place your lives in jeopardy because of *my* infirmity," she added, her voice growing stronger. She glanced at Jahno. "According to your great-grandfather, it is the interior of the island that is the most deadly. If you put us ashore, Khai and I will venture inland alone and seek the folk who dwell there."

I nodded.

Lirios's wings whirred. "Oh, but *I* will not leave your side, my queen."

Essee gave a soft trill; she would not suffer us to make the attempt on our own, either.

Evene sighed. "You know, if we're journeying toward Miasmus, like as not most of our damned lives are forfeit anyway. Papa-ka-hondras can't be worse, can it? What the hell, let's do this."

So it was decided.

Our destination determined, Jahno and the Elehuddin consulted their charts to set our course, the sea-wyrms adjusting obligingly and angling across the swirling counter-currents toward the southwest. Zariya went below deck to rest and regain her strength.

It fell to me to explain to Lirios the situation into which fate had unexpectedly thrust him.

He listened attentively, his chin propped on his fists, the twin blades of his translucent wings folded on his back, his expression one of wonder. "So I am to be like Astarion the Noble, a Great Protector?"

"Ah . . . I'm not familiar with Astarion the Noble," I said.

Lirios looked astonished. "No? The great hero of the Goat Isle War?" I shook my head. "He held the entrance to the Palace of Ten Thousand Bells against hundreds of Goat Islanders until help arrived," he said reverently. "He died saving his queen, who was *the* queen of Chalcedony Isle, though they never had the chance to be mated. It is a most romantic story. I am surprised you do not know it."

I smiled. "Well, Zarkhoum is a very long way away. You probably haven't heard our stories, either. But let's not make dying in Zariya's service a goal, all right? Our goal is to protect her."

"Yes, Khai." He tilted his head. "I saw that you are very good at fighting. Can you teach me to be better?"

"Absolutely," I promised.

In the weeks it took us to sail to Papa-ka-hondras, I did just that.

At times I sympathized with the dismay that Jahno had evinced upon discovering the identity of the Quick. The mayfly's unflagging energy could be wearing. Lirios might be a mature adult by the standards of his folk, but he possessed a childlike earnestness and enthusiasm. Subtlety and nuance often evaded him, and he had no understanding of the concepts of sarcasm, irony, or cynicism. He would have been utterly lost among the double-talking Therinians. But as I came to know him better and learn more about the culture of Chalcedony Islanders, wherein the women lived ordinary mortal lifespans and might take three or more mates over the course of their lives, I thought that it wasn't the brevity of Lirios's time on earth that engendered such earnest naïveté—surely there were children begging in the markets of Merabaht who had an unwelcome grasp of cynicism by the age of nine—it was the speed with which it passed.

By the time he reached Jahno's age, Lirios would be an old man; by the time he reached Evene's age, he would be dead. The men of his people had no time to waste on such things, but sought to live every moment of life to its fullest.

And by all the fallen stars, he *was* quick. I fancied myself fast, but Lirios could very nearly run rings around me. It frustrated him that it wasn't enough to defeat me when we sparred, and I could not help but remember my own frustration at being unable to utilize my own speed and agility to get past Vironesh's deceptively impenetrable guard in those early days.

I couldn't teach Lirios to channel Pahrkun's wind, but I could teach him to improve his footwork and his strokes. Bit by bit, he attained enough skill to press me in our bouts, the number of openings he left narrowing. I was glad of it, for the challenge of sparring with the mayfly sharpened the skills I feared were suffering from neglect.

At first, Zariya was unwontedly reserved with him, not wanting to lend false encouragement to his ardor. "It just doesn't seem fair, my heart," she murmured to me. "It's not like it is with you and me. The Sacred Twins didn't join us at birth. I don't feel what he feels."

"I know," I said. "He understands. The men of his folk don't expect their queens to feel as they do."

She glanced at Lirios practicing his footwork, his wings a happy blur. "I just wish he wasn't *quite* so excited about the notion of dying in my service."

I nodded in rueful agreement. "We're working on it."

Zariya and Jahno spent a great deal of time conferring together, pooling their shared knowledge of everything they'd ever read about Papa-ka-hondras, which lay under the aegis of Shambloth the Inchoate Terror, about whom little was known except that it was a deity that instilled mind-rending fear in unwitting trespassers. They discussed the thousand ways the island might kill a person and speculated on ways we might avoid its myriad pitfalls.

The first of those was the death-bladders.

It was a clear morning when we drew within sight of the isle, which lay on the outermost verge of the great western current. From a distance, it looked a pleasant and uninhabited place with an apron of empty white sand beaches ringing its shores and a lush, green interior. It was only as we drew nearer that we could see that the calm seas surrounding it were filled with the translucent violet sacs of death-bladders bobbing in the water, stinging tentacles dangling beneath them. From time to time, one of the death-bladders would stir below the surface of the water, its deft tentacles entangling a darting fish.

The sea-wyrms dropped their bits and dove, burbling, underwater. Our ship drifted untethered.

Eeeio surfaced to raise his head and give an inquiring trill; Kooie nodded emphatically, his tendrils waving, and whistled in reply.

Jahno looked hopeful. "Eeeio thinks these funny little cousins might listen if they ask them nicely to move, yah?"

I would not in a thousand years have described the death-bladders thusly, but move they did at the sea-wyrms' polite request, the deadly violet sacs drifting languorously to the east and west to clear a path to shore, tentacles trailing in their slow wake. I supposed that our crew meant to draw as near to shore as possible, then anchor in the shallow waters, whereupon we would have to swim for the shore as best we could, since we had no smaller secondary vessel. In this I was mistaken, for the wyrm-raiders had a unique method of beaching their unusual ship.

Can you swim? Keeik signed to me as we neared the shore.

"Yes," I said. "But should we not discuss how we're to transport the items we need? Not to mention my lady Zariya?"

He gave me one of his toothy grins, flicking his fingers in dismissal. *No, you will see. Come.*

So I stripped down to the sleeveless tunic and cropped breeches I'd worn swimming at the Villa of Heart's Ease, following the Elehuddin and Jahno as they dove into the sea with careless grace. Those who could not swim, which included Evene and Tarrok and Lirios with his fragile, useless wings, remained aboard the ship.

Upon reaching the shore, we set about digging a long, deep trench in the gritty white sand, the considerable task made easier by the speed with which the Elehuddin were able to scoop sand with their large, webbed hands.

"This wouldn't work with any other kind of ship," Jahno informed me as he dug. "But because of the sea-wyrms and because *ooalu* wood is so buoyant, we can beach it here. The trench will stabilize it."

"So the wyrms will pull it ashore?" I asked.

Jahno shook his head, wiping his sweating brow with one forearm. "No, they cannot survive on land; the weight of their bodies is too great to allow them to return to the sea. They will sling it ashore."

Swimming as close as they dared, the wyrms lifted their heads to inspect the trench, whistling when they gauged it sufficient and returning to the ship to take up their bits. I'd grown accustomed to Eeeio and Aiiiaii and come to think of them as friends in their own right, but I had to own, it was intimidating to stand on the shore and see them bearing down on us at full speed, heads reared against the sky, the ship riding high and skimming over the waves behind them. At the last minute, they dropped their bits and veered left and right.

Borne by momentum, the ship cleared the shore, grinding to a halt in the trench we'd dug for it.

"I don't suppose reversing the process will be easy," I observed.

"Easier than this," Jahno said confidently. "When the time comes, we will move the tow-lines to the stern and Eeeio and Aiiiaii will pull us back into the water." Kooie added something, laughing his cat-sneezing laugh. "Yah, as long as we didn't make a mistake and do this at low tide! Otherwise we'll be floating soon and have to do it all over again."

The ship secured, the others descended. Zariya was quite adept on the boarding ladder, though it was a large enough drop from the final rung that she suffered me to lift her down.

Lirios, following her, halted in astonishment at the sight of me, his mouth agape. "Khai!" He pointed at me. "You're *female!*"

I glanced down at myself, at the thin soaked cotton clinging to my shallow breasts, which I hadn't taken the time to bind. In all this time, it had not occurred to me that Lirios didn't know I was *bhazim*, and I didn't know if I was proud or indignant that he hadn't noticed.

"Khai is whatever he wishes to be," Zariya said firmly, testing the sand with her canes. "There are more important things at hand."

He turned his wide-eyed gaze to her. "But she is someone's *queen!*"

"Or *he* is someone's prince," Evene said in an impatient voice. "Can we not get on with this?"

Essee whistled softly for peace, signing a reminder that we were all brothers and sisters here.

"Yah, we need to take stock of the situation." Jahno dusted sand from his hands and glanced around. "Quiet here, eh?"

It *was* quiet on the beaches of Papa-ka-hondras; unnaturally so. Behind us, the sea lapped the shore, death-bladders drifting soundlessly in the calm waters, the sea-wyrms feeding amongst them. A hundred yards before us, the green interior of the isle lurked in waiting silence. Here on the white sands, nothing grew; not grass or trees. No crabs scuttled underfoot, no mollusks burrowed beneath the sand. Not even seabirds flew overhead.

"Are we sure it's inhabited?" Tarrok inquired.

Jahno and Zariya exchanged a glance. "My great-grandfather Liko met them." He gestured toward the tree line. "He got half a league or so into the forest and lost a dozen men in the process. The Papa-ka-hondrans found them and led them back to the safety of the beach. There, the elders spent two weeks among what remained of my great-grandfather's company learning the rudiments of the traders' tongue, and when they did, they told him to go away and never come back."

"Well, *that's* encouraging," Evene remarked.

"It was a different time," Zariya murmured. "We are here out of necessity, not curiosity. Let us pray that it makes a difference. But let us take a closer look at what we're up against, shall we?"

"I'll fetch the stink-lizard's hide," Jahno offered. "Maybe we can test our theory."

After he had done so, we ventured together to the verge of the interior.

Here, the silence ended.

The forest of Papa-ka-hondras was alive, rustling and whispering with quiet menace. Tall trees with broad crowns of spatulate green leaves trembled and released showers of acrid dew that left smoking holes in whatever it touched; unseen insects buzzed and whirred, hidden frogs croaked in an ominous chorus. Prickly vines writhed and contorted with an anguished hissing sound, tendrils reaching out blindly, causing us all to take a prudent step backward.

Things I could not name made sounds I could not identify.

I did not like this place. Everything about it conspired to say, *You do not belong here, you are not welcome here.*

Beneath the tall green canopy, the terrain was sprawling with fallen logs dense with emerald moss, thick with shrubs and vines, dotted here and there with saplings. "I fear that's going to be difficult for me to traverse," Zariya commented.

"Yah," Jahno agreed. "We'll have to rig something to carry you." He glanced at Evene. "Is there anything the Opener of Ways can do to forge a passage?"

She frowned in concentration, at length shaking her head in regret. "No. I'm not sure if I can explain, but this forest . . . it's not just an assortment of trees and plants. On a level we can't see, it's one single living entity. There's no way to part it. I'm sorry I'm of no use," she added in misery. "I probably could have managed the death-bladders."

A small animal with bright bulging eyes scampered down the trunk of a tree; a large plant with clamshell-shaped leaves snapped shut upon it. There was a short agonized squeal, and then viscous material oozed from the plant's needle-edged lips.

My flesh crawled.

"Well, we'll just have to manage." Zariya eyed the weeping bile-trees. "Lirios, are you quick enough to spread this hide under one of those without getting any of those drops on you?"

"Of course, my queen!" He looked pleased at being assigned a task. The stink-lizard's hide was actually in three pieces; it was one of the smaller wing segments that Jahno had brought. Lirios leapt over the writhing vines and darted under the canopy of the nearest bile-tree and opened the stiff hide beneath it, darting back to join us. The tree's leaves trembled and a shower of droplets fell to patter harmlessly on the hide.

"Ha!" Jahno grinned and clapped a hand on my shoulder. "So we have found a good use for your prize, dragon-slayer. We're going to need poles, though," he mused while Lirios retrieved the hide. "Lots of them."

I pointed at the scattered saplings, which looked to be immature bile-trees. At least none of them were weeping yet, and I hoped it would stay that way. "How many?"

He scratched his chin and conferred with Seeak, one of the older Elehuddin. "Two long ones sturdy enough to use for a litter. We can use smaller ones for the hide shields. Maybe six of those?"

"Shall I attempt it, Khai?" Lirios inquired, not quite looking at me.

"No," I said, drawing my *yakhan*. The mayfly's slender sword didn't have the cutting heft this task would require, and his blade strokes lacked the acuity to wield mine effectively. "But follow me and retrieve what I cut."

"I can fetch my blade and assist," Tarrok offered.

I shook my head, gazing into the forest, quieting my thoughts and feeling Pahrkun's wind stirring in me. "I can see a path between one danger and another, brother. Let us do this."

He didn't protest, and I didn't blame him for it.

"Be careful, my darling," Zariya said softly.

It went well enough at first. One need not be able to name a danger to sense and avoid it. I avoided the reaching vines, I dodged around the verdant shadows of weeping bile-trees, I gave the carnivorous clam-shell plants a careful berth. I stooped and slashed low and my wind-cutter sang in my fist, the curved blade severing the slender trunks of saplings at their base with a single stroke. One great, two small; another great, three more small. I let them fall and kept moving between one thing and another, trusting Lirios to gather them.

And then it changed when I ventured deeper into the forest for the sixth small sapling. Out of the corner of my eye, I saw a shadow; a shadow of something immense and only vaguely glimpsed moving in the green dimness.

For reasons I could not name, it made my bowels clutch and tighten, my breath come short.

"Khai?" I turned. Behind me, Lirios's arms were filled with saplings. Pinpoints of glistening bile were gathered on their leaves, not profuse enough to collect and fall in droplets. The whites of his eyes were showing and his wings vibrated at a terrified pitch. "Oh, Khai! I think it's coming for us."

Somewhere to our left, the unseen thing let out a deep cough and a low guttural growl. A questing vine wrapped around my ankle, stinging prickles sinking into my flesh. I wrenched my foot loose, severing the vine with my *yakhan*. My skin stung as though bitten by fire ants. The vine's remnants clung to me, writhing.

"Run!" I said to Lirios.

We ran, the both of us; him with his arms filled with saplings, me with my naked blade clutched in my fist. *You should not be here,* the forest whispered behind us. *You do not belong here.*

We burst out of the forest onto the white sand of the beach, Lirios flinging his bundle of saplings to the ground at our companions' feet.

"There!" I pointed behind us. "Did you not hear it? Do you not see it?"

No one did; nothing was there. The forest had fallen silent.

"What did you see, my heart?" Zariya asked me.

I shook my head. "I don't know. Something. I'm not sure." I was ashamed to find my voice trembling. "I think we just encountered Shambloth the Inchoate Terror."

FORTY-SIX

We did not begin our journey into the interior of Papa-ka-hondras that day, but retreated to the beached ship.

After I pried the vine loose, the flesh of my ankle swelled and burned like fire, but it subsided within the hour, as opposed to the weeks of agony that Liko of Koronis had reported. Like Vironesh, I possessed a measure of immunity to toxins. I should be grateful, I supposed, that I did not turn purple.

Instead I was frightened, which was yet an unfamiliar state for me. I had been afraid since the children of Miasmus boiled out of the Nexus, but for the first time, I could no longer conceal it.

Zariya sat on the beach beside me, watching Jahno and the Elehuddin use shears, awls, rope, and saplings to cut the stink-lizard's hide and fashion crude parasols while I sharpened my *yakhan* with my whetstone, smoothing out minor nicks. "This is going to take all of the courage we possess, isn't it, my darling?"

"Yes."

She touched the back of my hand. "I've never seen you scared before. Do you wish to speak of it?"

I shook my head. "I do not know *how* to speak of it, Zariya. But for all the dangers of this place, it seems to me that our own fear—or the fear that Shambloth instills in us—may be our worst enemy."

"Then we shall have to conquer it," she said simply.

I summoned a wry smile. "Just like that?"

"No." Zariya shivered and leaned her head against my shoulder. "I am terrified to the marrow of my bones. But we have no choice."

I put my arm around her. "I know. At least it seems that we've outrun the children of Miasmus."

"For now," Zariya said. "I fear they will be seeking us."

"Even they might think twice about assailing Papa-ka-hondras," I said.

For all that I made a jest at her simple declaration, I did draw courage from our conversation. If Zariya needed me to brave, brave I would be. Honor beyond honor demanded it of me, and the fate of the world might hang in the balance. I could behave as nothing less than the warrior I was trained to be. When Jahno reported that several additional saplings were needed, I ventured back into the forest to procure them; seeing me emboldened, Lirios found a new measure of courage of his own, although he continued to look askance at me. This time our foray was uneventful.

Our company slept that night aboard the ship, and it seemed strange to me to sleep in a hammock that did not sway with the sea's motion, but hung still and motionless, all of us suspended from the beams of our beached ship on the quiet sands of Papa-ka-hondras while the *ooalu* moths flitted around us.

In the morning, we made our plan.

There were not enough hide parasols to outfit our entire company, and three people would have to remain with the ship. Jahno proposed a lottery, but Essee pointed out with quiet dignity that unlike the rest of us, the individual Elehuddin didn't have a specific role in the prophecy.

"That doesn't make you *expendable*!" Zariya exclaimed in horror.

No, but she is right, Kooie signed.

"Yah," Jahno said with regret. "We need the Elehuddin and the sea-wyrms, but it only takes one person to fulfill the bond of Dulumu the Deep, and it does not matter who. If we lose the Thunderclap or the Opener of Ways, there is no one to take their place."

So it was determined that Tarrok and Evene would stay behind, and the Elehuddin held a discussion amongst themselves and chose Tiiklit, who had a bad knee.

We would carry with us water-skins, *ooalu* fruit, and strips of dried fish that the Elehuddin had spent the past weeks preparing. Each of us had a crude hide parasol for protection from the weeping bile-trees, and several of us wore ropes knotted around our waists that we might retrieve anyone unlucky enough to step into a hidden sinkhole.

Once again, the *rhamanthus* were the subject of debate. It was Jahno who declared that the choice should be left to Zariya, since it was she who must learn to use them. Zariya elected to bring a handful of the seeds in a leather purse tied about her waist. The sling that I had devised for her was lashed to the two sturdy poles, which four of our company would carry over their shoulders. It would be a cumbersome way to travel, but it was the best solution anyone could find.

"According to my great-grandfather's records, the Papa-ka-hondrans were always accompanied by yellow-crested kingfishers," Jahno reminded us. "Pretty violet birds with a bright yellow belly and crest, makes a call like a person laughing. So we keep our eyes and ears open for them, yah?"

It wasn't much to go on, but it was all we had. Out in the ocean, Eeeio and Aiiiaii gave trills of hope and encouragement. The others remaining behind accompanied us to the verge of the forest, where we said our farewells.

"Come back safely, all of you," Evene said, giving me a fierce and unexpected embrace. "That's all we ask."

"We'll do our best, my darling," Zariya murmured, sinking into her sling and settling her canes across her lap as the pole-bearers hoisted the contraption onto their shoulders.

It would be necessary for all of us to trade places and share our burdens over the course of our journey, but for now, Jahno and I took the lead, Seeker and shadow, while Essee and Lirios brought up the rear, scoring trees so that we might find our way back. Alone, I could duck and dodge between dangers; now, I must chart a course broad enough for three to walk abreast— or more rightly, for the pole-bearers with Zariya swaying in her sling between them, clutching the shaft of her parasol with her right hand. It was impossible to avoid passing beneath the bile-trees, and I was grateful for our hide shields as the caustic droplets pattered down like rain.

At twenty paces, it felt as though the forest had swallowed us. It was a living, breathing thing that did not want us there, and I felt its warm, moist breath panting against the back of my neck.

You should not be here . . .

You do not belong here . . .

Slithering vines reached for my ankles as though eager to taste my flesh a second time. I steeled my will and slashed at them with my *yakhan,* clearing a safe path for our company.

Bile-trees wept.

There were bright blue poisonous tree frogs to be avoided, swift scarlet-banded snakes that could kill with a single strike, broad-capped mushrooms that released toxic spores, and venomous spiders lurking in webs they spun across any semblance of a passage. I was grateful that we had the benefit of knowing what to look for, else we surely would have suffered casualties. The ground was soft and spongy underfoot and I tested it with every step before putting my full weight down, grateful for Brother Yarit's long-ago tutelage in the art of walking silently, my muscles remembering the long hours of training. At one point our path was blocked by a great fallen log covered with emerald moss, and when I could find no way around it through the dense surrounding underbrush, we clambered over it, the Elehuddin pole-bearers coordinating their efforts with whistles and grunts, Zariya's sling lurching wildly between them. Black beetles rose from the log in a whirring cloud; stinging midges assailed us.

We kept going.

An hour, another hour . . . it was difficult to say in the green murk of the forest, the sun hidden by the canopy high overhead. There was no time here, only day and night; and I dreaded the prospect of night. I did not hear or see any sign of Shambloth the Inchoate Terror, but the mere possibility of it, coupled with the constant need for vigilance, kept me on edge.

Beside me, Jahno kept half an eye on the canopy, searching for signs of a yellow-crested kingfisher, and I suppose it was no surprise that he encountered the first hidden sinkhole.

It happened in the blink of an eye; one moment he was walking beside me, in the next, he was waist-deep and sinking fast, mouth agape in shock, casting a terrified gaze up at me.

I dropped my blade and my hide parasol, whipping the rope around my waist free and tossing one end to him. "Hold fast!"

Above us, leaves trembled and droplets fell.

I hunched my shoulders and braced myself for the scalding bile; but no, Lirios was there, impossibly quick, hurtling past the pole-bearers to hold his own parasol aloft and shield the both of us. I hauled Jahno free of the sucking mud, drops of weeping bile blistering his flesh.

The Koronian grimaced. "My thanks, shadow."

There were nearly a dozen leeches attached to his legs, their bodies already growing swollen with blood. One by one, I pried them off. At least the leeches weren't poisonous, but I wished we had soap with which to wash the seeping bites.

We traded places on the poles and persevered, our progress slowing further as Kooie struggled to wield my *yakhan* effectively, his forearms getting ensnared in the stinging vines in the process. At length we were forced to acknowledge that it was for the best if I remained in the lead position and that Lirios, with his speed, was best suited at the rear where he could see and react to any threat.

By the time Jahno called a halt at midday—or our best guess at midday—our company was in poor shape. Kooie was miserable, his arms in agony. We were bitten, stung, blistered, scratched, and scraped, exhausted and dispirited, and it had only been half a day. At least I had succeeded in finding a small glade surrounded by towering palm trees that thus far appeared harmless, so we might set aside our hide shields to eat and drink.

"Seeker, I do not mean to intrude upon your role," Lirios said apologetically. "But if the Papa-ka-hondrans found your great-grandfather's company, might we not simply wait for them to find ours?"

The Elehuddin exchanged glances and said nothing.

Jahno took a deep breath, rubbing dried mud from his calves. "It is a fair question, mayfly, and I am not confident of my answer. I know only that the Seeker's job is to *seek*."

I drank from my water-skin. "Lirios and I might scout ahead," I offered, though the notion of being parted from Zariya in this place filled me with dread.

"No." Zariya was drawn and short of breath, but her face was set with a look of stubborn determination. "The Oracle of the Nexus was clear. Anyone who wishes to wait or turn back may do so, but I will persevere if I have to hobble every step of the way on my own two feet."

Essee opened her mouth to reply, and at that moment, something violet and yellow flashed through the air beneath the canopy.

"Ha-ha!" A yellow-crested bird perched on a palm frond high above us, bobbing its head. "Hahaha-ha-ha!"

Jahno leapt to his feet. "It's a kingfisher!"

Hope infused us with fresh energy. Gathering our things, we set out in pursuit of the bright flitting figure.

Alas, hope also made us careless. Keeik was walking point alongside me when we came upon a bog. The kingfisher soared across it, darting low to snatch up a small fish with its long red beak. Intent on charting a course around the bog, I didn't notice Keeik skirting too close to the edge, shading his eyes to keep the kingfisher in sight.

I do not know what to call the grey-green creature that lunged out of the depths of the muddy bronze water, immense jaws agape to reveal a double row of jagged teeth, only that it snatched up Keeik as deftly as the kingfisher caught the minnow, dragging him beneath the water.

With a furious shout, I plunged after it, knee-deep in muck and sinking, slashing wildly with my blade where I thought the creature's body ought to be, but it had vanished as quickly and thoroughly as it had struck. Behind me there was more shouting, and hands tugging at the back of my tunic.

"Khai, *no!*" It was Zariya's voice that reached me, fraught with fear and anguish. "It's too late, my darling!"

I let Lirios haul me to solid ground; mercifully for the both of us, we weren't under weeping bile-trees.

The bronze waters of the bog returned to stillness.

Zariya was lying sprawled on the forest floor; Kooie and Essee had dropped their poles. The Elehuddin keened in grief, a high-pitched whistle I had never heard before. Jahno covered his face with his hands.

I grieved with them, my throat too tight to swallow.

Somewhere to the right of us, something enormous rustled in the undergrowth and let out a deep cough and a low roar, and I felt a creeping terror in my bowels.

The kingfisher chortled.

I hated this place.

Using her canes, Zariya struggled to her feet, her eyes ablaze. "Is that you, Shambloth?" she cried. "Shall we speak of *terror*? Miasmus is awake! The Abyss that Abides is rising, and it *will* swallow the world in darkness! Is that not worth the price of aiding us?"

There was no reply.

"Come," Jahno said wearily. "Let us continue while the light lasts, and seek a place to make camp for the night."

Step by torturous step, we persevered, following the darting kingfisher. Zar the Sun was sinking low in the west, filling the forest with slanting golden light, when we came upon a second palm glade filled with enormous butterflies feeding on the orchid flowers that grew on the trunks of the palms, their gold and black wings as wide across as the length of my arm. By all the fallen stars, I thought it a happy omen.

"All right," I said, lowering my blade beneath the green-gold shadow of a palm tree. "We'll make camp here."

Something fell upon me from above.

It was thick and damp and heavy, knocking me to the floor of the forest. I felt bristles pierce the back of my neck, injecting my flesh with poison. Once again, there was a great deal of shouting. The heavy thing was wrestled from me, but my entire body had seized and I was unable to draw breath. Someone rolled me onto my back. On the ground beside me, an enormous green caterpillar writhed, its body bloated and segmented, bristles waving in the air.

"Khai!" Jahno's face swam in my vision, silvery eyes wide with fear. He slapped me. "*Khai!* Breathe!"

My lungs strained in vain, my heart thudding in my chest like a trapped animal. Spreading darkness began to blur the sight of Jahno's features.

". . . paralysis . . ."

". . . can't breathe he'll *die*!"

It would pass; it had to pass. I had been stung by serpent and scorpion, and I bore the marks of Pahrkun the Scouring Wind etched on my cheek-bones to prove it; I was not going to be killed by a gods-bedamned cater-pillar.

And then Zariya was there, her hands cupping my face. "Don't you leave me, Khai! Don't you *dare* leave me!"

I willed my mind to stillness, seeking a path between one thing and an-other. My racing heart slowed. My fingers twitched and the poison's iron grip on my lungs eased a measure. I drew a slow, careful breath, sipping the air like it was the finest wine; one sip, then another and another, until the darkness retreated.

Lirios ran the caterpillar through with his blade, flinging it some dis-tance away. Zariya helped me sit upright. "You mustn't terrify me like that, my darling," she said somberly. "We've already suffered a grievous loss."

"I didn't mean to," I croaked. "Everyone. Out from under the trees. Now."

There was no truly getting out from under the trees in that place, but we gathered in the center of the glade where the canopy was thinnest and no green sacs of caterpillars were visible overhead. It was a piece of luck—the only one in a grim day—that no one else had been attacked. After what had transpired, none of us would have chosen to make camp there, but the light was fading fast. I left the cautious work of collecting firewood and dried palm fronds to the others, still regaining my strength. Bit by bit, the last of the paralysis left my body.

We made a small campfire, sitting around it in a circle, and it seemed a woefully inadequate thing in the face of the blackness that descended with nightfall. The butterflies took to the trees. The kingfisher we had been fol-lowing had long since vanished. If one of the moons was overhead, it was invisible beneath the canopy. The benighted forest began to whisper and stir in a different way, filled with slithering sounds and a sense of terrible menace, as though something unspeakably vast hunted us.

Shambloth.

Fear crept into the marrow of my bones. Every fiber of my being told me to run, to flee from this place where I was unwelcome, and I could see the same urge reflected in the fire-lit eyes of my companions.

Flee.

But if we fled, the forest could surely claim us; Liko of Koronis had lost several members of his party that way.

Unexpectedly, Essee gave an imperative whistle and extended both arms, gesturing for all of our circle to clasp hands around our inadequate campfire. We did so, each of us drawing a measure of reassurance from the contact. Looking each of us in the eye, she spoke at length, a tremor in her voice. "The enemy of fear is not courage," Jahno translated for her. "The enemy of fear is love, for it is in loving others that we set aside our own personal fears, holding their safety and well-being as our highest regard. Tonight I am afraid, but I take heart from the love I bear for each of you, and for our beloved brother Keeik, whose sacrifice we grieve and honor. For your sakes, I abide. For you, I endure. And when I bear this in mind, this baseless fear loses its power over me. Remember this."

Humbled, I bowed my head to her.

"We had great need of that reminder," Zariya murmured, squeezing my hand hard. "Thank you, Essee."

It was a long and dreadful night, and I am not sure our company could have endured it unbroken were it not for Essee's admonition. We took turns keeping watch and tending to the fire, the others grasping at fitful sleep. The sounds of the forest around us were unrelenting.

At times it was the slithering sound, a great heavy rasping accompanied by the cracking of trees, *sss-sss-sss-kraak.* My mind conjured images of a giant serpent circling the perimeter of the glade. At other times it was the sound of something impossibly immense padding through the forest, twigs snapping beneath its weight; the panting breath, the hoarse cough, and the guttural roar.

You should not be here . . .

You will die here.

The panicked buzzing of Lirios's wings was a near-constant counterpoint to the sounds of the forest, stringing our frayed nerves nearly to breaking. Unable to control it and a light sleeper at the best of times, he could but mumble apologies. Kooie's forearms were swollen and burning from his encounter with the stinging vines and he thrashed and whimpered in his sleep, scratching himself with his claws. Zariya's breath was labored, wheez-ing painfully in her chest, and for all her determination, I feared her body might lack the strength to fulfill the promise of her will. When I closed my eyes and sought sleep, I saw behind my eyelids the creature that had snatched Keeik, its gaping jaws, its double rows of teeth.

And yet impossible as it seemed, I did sleep in fits and starts, my body in dire need of healing rest.

I awoke in the grey light of dawn to Lirios shaking my shoulder.

"Khai!" he whispered, pointing. "We are not alone."

A kingfisher laughed.

FORTY-SEVEN

There were half a dozen figures on the southern verge of the glade: human in form, but strangely stooped, with long arms and protruding muzzles. A dusting of grey fur covered their skin and they wore knee-length skirts of woven fiber.

I reached instinctively for my weapons, then hesitated. The figures appeared to be unarmed.

"Wake up," I said in a low voice. "We have company, my brothers and sisters."

My companions stirred, waking from their various nightmares. The silent figures watched us, and out of the green dimness of the forest, three more figures emerged: great cats that stood as high as a man's waist, with dark, mottled fur.

Perhaps the Papa-ka-hondrans did not need weapons.

I drew mine. "We mean no harm!" I called. "We are here at the bidding of the Oracle of the Nexus."

The Papa-ka-hondrans advanced, the cats pacing alongside them. "We do not know what that means," one of the humans said, speaking the traders' tongue in a slow, careful tone. Like the others of his company, he had round, brown eyes that appeared almost luminous in the dawn light. "But it may be that this meeting was foretold, for you have passed the test of Shambloth. Is there one among you who seeks healing? One who desires to wield the gift of fire?"

Zariya levered herself to her feet with her canes, her braided hair disheveled and twig-snagged, a nasty scrape marring one cheek. "I do."

The leader beckoned to her. "Come."

She shook her head. "Not alone."

The Papa-ka-hondrans conferred with each other in their own tongue. "We are a peaceful folk who seek to be left alone," the leader said at length, pointing at me. "We will suffer no violence here."

I sheathed my weapons. "We will offer none."

They conferred again, nodding in agreement. "Come, then," the leader said again. "All of you." His nostrils flared. "Leave your lizard-hides behind. You will have no further need of them."

We collected the rest of our things and straggled after them, Jahno and the Elehuddin shouldering the poles that bore Zariya's sling.

The forest in the company of the Papa-ka-hondrans seemed a different place altogether. They knew its ways; and in turn, the forest seemed to give way gracefully before them, allowing them passage. Giant butterflies flitted harmlessly and no caterpillars dropped from the palms. They found routes between the bogs and sinkholes and weeping bile-trees that appeared impassable. I cursed myself for not seeing them, though I wasn't entirely sure they existed until the Papa-ka-hondrans approached. Even the writhing vines retreated at their advance, the great cats stalking alongside our new-found companions with a profound lack of concern.

"So you say that this meeting was foretold?" Jahno inquired, laboring to catch his breath. "What was this foretelling? We should make proper introductions, yah, and share our knowledge."

The leader turned on him. "I am called Onditu. The ancestors remember your folk, Koronian. They sought to intrude here."

Jahno was taken aback. "Only in pursuit of knowledge."

Onditu glowered. "They were not welcome here."

"Well, it's quite clear that *no one* is welcome here, my darling," Zariya commented with considerable asperity; it was the first time one of her care-less endearments carried the barbs so common among members of the House of the Ageless. "Still, I do think we might benefit from pooling our knowledge. Or do you imagine Miasmus will spare Papa-ka-hondras in its quest to annihilate the world?"

He lowered his head in a gesture of acknowledgment, the whiskers sprouting from his muzzle drooping in apology. "No, we do not. But it is for the Green Mother to say. Let us reach the village, where we may speak in peace."

Padding alongside us, the great cats with their mottled coats purred in agreement and menace.

At midday we halted to take food and drink, and the Papa-ka-hondrans regarded our strips of dried fish with quiet horror. Onditu informed us that they did not eat the flesh of animals.

"Your imposing friends here have no such qualms," Zariya observed, having coaxed one of the cats to take a bit from her hand.

"The cats are as Zar made them," Onditu said stiffly. "It is their nature. It is not ours."

Kooie clicked and whistled in irritation, baring his sharp teeth in a pointed gesture.

"He says one of your forest creatures ate one of our brothers," Jahno translated. "So do not be so quick to judge us. And do not tell an Elehuddin not to eat fish, for we are as Zar made us, too."

"The forest takes its toll on those who intrude upon it," Onditu said to Kooie. "And that, too, is its nature. But you are in pain and angry. I cannot ease your grief, but I can ease your discomfort." He spoke to one of the others in their tongue. The fellow trotted into the underbrush, returning presently with a broad, fleshy leaf oozing a clear, viscous liquid, which he smeared on Kooie's inflamed forearms, affording him a considerable measure of relief.

Thus fortified, we continued onward.

Two more hours into our journey, it was clear that the forest didn't merely seem a different place; it *was* a different place. The flesh-seeking vines vanished. The number of creeping, crawling poisonous things dwindled. The bile-trees thinned, increasingly replaced by myriad varieties of palms and fruit-bearing trees. Bogs and sinkholes gave way to the occasional sparkling stream. Dragonflies hovered over the water, iridescent wings shimmering. It grew easier to walk three abreast and we made swifter progress, all of the defenders taking turns as pole-bearers.

"It's quite beautiful here after all, isn't it?" Zariya remarked in wonder. "I would never have guessed it."

Onditu glanced at her. "It is the true heart of Papa-ka-hondras. You are the first not of our folk to see it."

Swaying in her sling, she steadied her canes and folded her palms, touching her brow to offer him a Zarkhoumi salute. "And we are honored by it."

He studied her for signs of insincerity; finding none, he nodded in satisfaction. "That is good."

Although it had seemed at the outset that our journey into the heart of Papa-ka-hondras would be interminable, under the guidance of our escort, we reached the village before nightfall. It was an unexpectedly joyous place. A dozen palm-thatched buildings on low stilts were scattered alongside a small river. Papa-ka-hondran children with dark fur and bright eyes raced to greet the returning sojourners. The children examined our company with intense curiosity, hooting and chattering in their own language, stroking the great cats' mottled coats with absent-minded fearlessness. The cats stretched and preened at their regard, arching their backs and parting their jaws to yawn with curled tongues.

"Tonight you will sleep in the big lodge," Onditu said, pointing to the largest structure. "Tomorrow you will meet with the Green Mother."

"So this foretelling—" Jahno began.

"Tomorrow," Onditu said firmly. "It is for the Green Mother to say, as it should be."

That night we slept in peace, and never in my life had I been so grateful for a thing I had long taken for granted.

I do not know—nor did I ever learn—how the Papa-ka-hondrans determined who amongst their tribe should sleep in the big lodge on any given night. Our time among them was scant; later, I would be unsure whether I was grateful or regretful for this. We ate fruit and nuts gathered by the scampering children, who used their long arms and dexterous feet to climb trees with an effortless speed that I envied. Afterward, we collapsed into sleep on woven mats. Zariya lay curled against me, her breathing still labored.

Even Lirios slept deeply, his wings stilled in exhaustion.

At some point I awoke. Nim the Bright Moon was high overhead, its silvery light piercing the thatch. Zariya's arm was flung across me and her head was tucked into the curve of my throat, her breath soft against my collar-bones; something, child or cat, I could not tell, was nestled warm at my back.

"Please," I whispered to Nim or whatever gods were listening, not even sure what I was asking. "Oh, *please!*"

Then I slept, too.

In the morning, we met the Green Mother.

Her fur silvery-white with age, she hobbled into the big lodge, her body so bent-backed and stooped that her knuckles brushed the ground, but for all the infirmity of her body, her voice was strong and deep.

"So!" she called out. "I am Yaruna. Which of you is the damaged child of the sun's fire?"

"That would be me, my lady," Zariya admitted. "I am here at the bidding of the Oracle of the Nexus."

Yaruna made a dismissive gesture. "Why and how does not matter. You are here because of the foretelling. But if I am to play the role that is or-dained, I must examine you first."

"May we *please* hear of this foretelling?" Jahno asked with a stymied scholar's anguish. "It may matter a great deal."

The Green Mother fixed him with a stern, rheumy gaze. "You would place words before deeds?"

Jahno set his jaw. "Words may matter as much as deeds. I am the Seeker. I would *know.*"

Unexpectedly, Yaruna relented. "Perhaps you are right." She beckoned. "Gather and hear."

The Papa-ka-hondrans, young and old, arrayed themselves in a circle around the perimeter of the big lodge, sitting with long arms looped over bent, bowed legs, round eyes bright and attentive.

We did our best to emulate them, and Yaruna the Green Mother low-ered herself to the floor in the center of the lodge. "Once upon a time, the children of heaven rebelled against their parents and were cast down from on high," she said, and there was a series of soft echoes as various elders translated her words for those who did not speak the traders' tongue. "But there was one who was cast down undeserving: Miasmus, whose mother,

Eshen the Wandering Moon, cloaked her child in darkness and hid it from his father, Zar the Sun."

Heads nodded; this tale was familiar to them.

"The god-child Miasmus took no part in the rebellion, but it was punished for it nonetheless," Yaruna continued. "For a thousand years, Miasmus has slept, knowing nothing but darkness, betrayal, and solitude. Because it was kept hidden, it had no knowledge of folk. It had no folk to nourish its heart." She made a slashing gesture with the side of one leathery palm. "Only nothingness."

There were sharp indrawn breaths, and the Elehuddin exchanged glances of understanding.

"Long ago, Shambloth the Great Protector, whom you know as the Inchoate Terror, told our ancestors that one day, Miasmus would awaken in righteous anger," Yaruna said. "And when it did, it would seek to destroy the world to which it had been banished." She lifted one gnarled finger. "But there would be those who were destined to stand against it. And if they are wise and kind and cunning and courageous, they may find a way to restore Miasmus to the very heavens from which it was unjustly expelled."

Jahno frowned in concentration, his brows furrowed, and I knew he was wishing he had his journal at hand to jot down notes. "So we are not meant to destroy it?"

Yaruna shrugged. "What is destruction, scholar? The children of heaven are meant to occupy the skies and Miasmus to shine among them."

"And we are to restore them?" he asked.

"I do not know," she admitted. "Only that there *is* a way, and that way requires kindness and love. That is the knowledge we have been given to impart to you."

"And the matter of healing?" Zariya inquired.

"Yes." The Green Mother's filmy eyes were grave. "I am descended from a long line of healers. I will examine you and see what might be done, sun's child. It will not be easy. I see you bear the mark of a god on your hand. Do you also come bearing seeds of fire?"

"I do." Reaching into the purse tied to her sash, Zariya held forth a handful of *rhamanthus* seeds. "Do you require them?"

"No." Yaruna shook her head. "I do but seek assurance that this effort will not be in vain." She heaved herself to her feet and beckoned. "Come."

I helped Zariya rise. "Where she goes, I go."

The Green Mother nodded. "As you will."

We followed her to a thatched hut on the outskirts of the village. There was a Papa-ka-hondran woman I guessed to be of middle years there, bustling about and tending to various salves and oddments contained in clay jars and dried gourds and stored on shelves around the hut.

"My apprentice, Shulah," Yaruna said by way of introduction. She gestured at a raised platform in the center of the hut. "Remove your clothes and lie upon your belly, sun's child."

With my assistance, Zariya obeyed. I had grown accustomed to nudity in the baths in the women's quarter, but here her exposed body looked particularly fragile and vulnerable to my eyes.

Consulting in their own tongue, the two Papa-ka-hondran women laid a series of cloudy crystal fragments down the length of Zariya's spine. As they drew warmth from her skin, most of the crystals began to pulse with an inner light; most, but not all. The Green Mother and her apprentice conferred at length. I sat cross-legged on the floor at the front of the platform, my gaze on Zariya's.

"Here and here, there are blockages." Yaruna touched two of the dull, unlit crystals with her forefinger, one in the center of Zariya's back, one at the base of her spine. "Old damage from the fever. It is the reason your energy does not flow through the proper course of its channels."

"Can you fix it?" Zariya asked, her chin propped on her fists.

"It is possible." The Green Mother hesitated. "There is a way to clear the blockage. But I must tell you that it will be painful. Very painful."

"Oh, pain! Well, I have known pain all my life," Zariya murmured. "We are very well acquainted, pain and I. I can bear it. But tell me this; shall I be able to walk when it is done?"

"No." There was a world of sympathy and understanding in one single syllable, a word as heavy as a stone. Yaruna's leathery palm flattened on the base of Zariya's spine. "That damage I cannot undo, and I am sorry for it. But you will be stronger. You will be able to breathe more freely. And you should be able to wield the seeds of fire."

Focused on survival, we had not spoken of hope; but it had been there all along, frail and persistent creature that it was.

Zariya looked away, no tears falling. She had made a pledge. "It is enough and more. Do what you must."

Yaruna inclined her head. "It is best if you remain unclothed for the process."

First came a strong purgative.

The less said about that, the better, I suppose. I do not know what vile liquid Zariya gulped with a grimace, but it had the intended effect. Over the course of the next hour, I helped her hobble to and from the hut's privy hole and drink fresh clear water from the stream until her body was flushed clean.

Second . . .

I will own, I caught my breath at the sight of the creature Yaruna fetched forth from a clay jar with a pair of wooden tongs. It was a centipede of sorts, its segmented crimson body writhing and sparking, its myriad legs flailing in the air.

"They dwell in the trunks of trees struck by lightning," Yaruna said, regarding the creature with reverence. "If you allow it to pass through your body, it will undo the blockages."

Seated on the platform, Zariya paled. "I must . . . swallow it? I thought you did not consume the flesh of living creatures."

The Green Mother's face was oddly impassive. "You will find it agonizing, but the creature will pass unharmed."

Zariya eyed the twitching, sparking thing. This was no softly luminescent insect like the *ooalu* moths; this was a creature of fire and lightning. "I fear I may require your assistance to accomplish this."

Yaruna nodded to her apprentice, who stood behind Zariya, strong hands tilting her head back and holding her mouth open. Ah, by all the fallen stars! If I could have taken this upon myself, I would have done it in a heartbeat.

Instead, all I could do was watch helplessly. Yaruna dropped the crawling thing into Zariya's open mouth and Shulah closed her jaw on it, her other hand moving swiftly to pinch Zariya's nostrils shut. Zariya's body seized and Yaruna leaned over to press hard on her shoulders, holding her firmly in place.

I surged to my feet. Above the hands clamped over her face, Zariya's eyes were stretched wide with pain and horror; and yet she signed adamantly with her right hand for me to stand down.

At last her throat convulsed in a swallow and a faint glow was visible at the hollow of its base, a vile mockery of the gentle pulse of *khementaran*. It moved lower and vanished. Exchanging nods, Yaruna and Shulah released her.

Zariya let out a scream of raw agony, her entire body contorting with horrifying violence. Her back arched like a drawn bow, so hard I feared her spine might snap, and her head was flung back, the cords of her throat standing out.

My weapons were in my hands. "If she does not survive this, I swear, I will carve you from limb to limb!"

Both of the Papa-ka-hondran women gave me that strange, impassive look. "You would offer us violence and death in exchange for healing," Yaruna said beneath the sound of Zariya's screams. "Do not wonder that Shambloth shows one aspect to her people and another to the rest of the world."

Meanwhile Zariya's screams continued unabated. Outside I heard racing footsteps approaching, so swift it could only be Lirios. He burst through the door of the hut, his wings vibrating, his blade drawn.

"Zariya, my queen!" His voice was frantic. "By all the fallen stars, what are they *doing* to her?"

I sheathed my own weapons and wrestled him out the door. Zariya would not want him to see her thus. "It is the healing process," I said to him. "We were warned it would be terribly painful."

The others came at a run. "This sounds like no healing I have ever encountered," Jahno said grimly, and the Elehuddin whistled in concerned agreement. "Are you sure of this, shadow?"

I was sure of nothing except that my entire body was rigid with sympathy and terror; but what could I do if this were a terrible mistake? Cut the creature from Zariya's poor anguished body? It would kill her. "No," I whispered. "But I fear that there is no way to halt the process once it has begun."

Essee gave a sober trill, signing, *Then we will wait and pray.*

There was nothing else any of us could do. Around the village, the Papa-ka-hondrans went about their business, chatting and weaving and gathering fruit, as though it were of no interest that my soul's twin was lying in a hut screaming in agony. I did not know whether to draw reassurance from their lack of concern or conclude that there was something subtly monstrous about these strange, isolated folk.

Both, perhaps.

I returned to the hut to bear vigil. Zariya thrashed and convulsed and screamed, her skin and hair soaked with sweat, insensible to anything but the agonizing process of the creature inching its way through her body. If she'd been wearing a gown, it would have been rent to pieces. Her eyelids fluttered, showing the whites of her eyes. Yaruna and Shulah tended her as best they could, laying damp cloths on her brow that were thrown off seconds later by the next seizure. As the hours passed, her screams grew hoarse, dwindling to moans; bit by bit, the convulsions weakened as she sank into an unconscious state.

"What's happening?" I asked the healers in a fever of anxiety. "Is this good or bad? Is it almost over? Is she dying?"

The Green Mother held up one finger, gazing intently at Zariya's limp, twitching figure. "Watch."

The intricate traceries of red marks that adorned Zariya's right hand, the hand that had received Anamuht's blessing, began to shine with a faint golden light, tendrils creeping up her wrist and forearm.

"*Now*," Yaruna said to her apprentice. Between the two of them, they levered Zariya into an upright sitting position. Shulah pried her mouth open to pour some concoction from a hollow gourd into it. Zariya's eyes opened, looking blind and unfocused, but she swallowed obediently. Yaruna shook her shoulders. "Now you must allow the creature to pass from your body, sun's child. Do you understand?"

Zariya's lips moved in a silent yes.

A clean pot had been placed beneath the privy hole; the Papa-ka-hondran healers slung Zariya's arms over their shoulders and hauled her to it, supporting her as she squatted over it, her head hanging low. Sweat-drenched braids fell over her brow, half-undone and snarled. I heard the faint *plink* as the crawling, sparking centipede exited her body and fell into the clay pot below.

I stood uncertainly.

With an effort, Zariya lifted her head and met my gaze. Her lips formed a rueful smile; she tested her voice, paused, and tried again. "Forgive me, my dearest," she rasped. "I did not mean to subject you to such indelicacy. Thank you for not killing anyone."

Alive.

My soul's twin, my lion-hearted princess, was alive and whole and *herself*, no matter how damaged. My legs gave way beneath me, my weapons clattering as I sank to my knees. Unsure whether to laugh or weep or give thanks to the children of heaven, I did all three.

The Papa-ka-hondran healers helped Zariya back to the platform. She sat with her head hanging low, bare legs dangling.

I rose and approached her. "How do you feel?"

Her head lolled. "Rather like I've been tortured in my father's dungeon," she mused. "Perhaps that's apt."

"You should rest now," the Green Mother advised her. "Sleep and allow your body to heal."

"No." There were bruised hollows beneath her eyes and she couldn't raise her voice above a hoarse whisper, but there was steel in it. "Not yet. Khai, bring me my gown and canes and fetch the *rhamanthus*."

The Green Mother and her apprentice were silent as I eased Zariya's gown over her head, the scarlet and gold silk snagged and shredded by the forest, and helped her down from the platform. I was not sure at first if she would be able to walk unaided, but sheer determination impelled her to do so, leaning on her canes as she dragged herself forward step by step.

Outside the hut, our company was waiting, faces filled with a mixture of dread and hope. Lirios cried aloud for joy at the sight of Zariya, and Jahno and the Elehuddin offered heartfelt salutes.

But Zariya was not finished. "A single seed, if you please, my darling," she murmured, gathering her canes in her left hand and holding out the other.

I fished in the pouch and placed a glowing crimson *rhamanthus* seed in the palm of her right hand.

Zariya closed her fist around it, and the now-golden traceries on her skin blazed into brilliant light, evoking soft gasps of awe. Her lips moved in a silent prayer as she raised her hand overhead, her gaze following it, swaying with the effort of remaining upright.

I held my breath.

Zariya opened her clenched fist and blue-white lightning leapt from her palm, forking and crackling in the sky above her, drenching our surroundings in a sudden shock of white light.

The spent seed fell to earth, dull and lifeless. I let out my breath in a fierce shout of triumph.

It had worked.

FORTY-EIGHT

Afterward, Zariya did sleep, profoundly exhausted by her ordeal, lying curled on the floor of the big lodge with her head pillowed in my lap. While she slept, I did my best to pick out her tangled braids. Some of them, I thought, would have to be cut loose, but it could wait for Evene's touch.

Honor beyond honor.

Never before had Zariya been more precious to me. With her screams of agony yet echoing in my ears, my heart ached at the thought that I could have lost her in this place; and while she slept, a simple realization settled into my bones.

I loved her.

I truly did love her with all my heart and soul; not just as Sun-Blessed and shadow, but in all the ways that one person could love another. I was a fool not to have realized it sooner, blinded by my own sense of duty.

"She has great strength of will," the Green Mother observed.

"Yes," I said. The weight of Zariya's head cradled in my lap filled me with tenderness. I stroked her tangled, sweat-soaked braids with my fingertips, regarding the Green Mother. "You don't like us very much, do you?"

"I do not like *you*." The lips of her muzzle drew back, revealing broad, worn teeth. "Killer of men! Your weapons stink of old blood. We do not even have a word in our tongue for what you are."

I leaned my head against a lodge post. It was true. I was a killer; but it was the destiny to which I had been born. "Fair enough. But I, too, am as Zar the Sun made me; Zar and Pahrkun the Scouring Wind."

Yaruna gave me a grudging nod. "As it seems the world has need of you, I will pray for your survival."

We passed another night among the Papa-ka-hondrans. At daybreak, Onditu and the other scouts escorted us through the forest, skirting all the pitfalls it had to offer, the great cats pacing alongside them. I supposed we ought to be grateful for their aid, for we would surely have lost more of our company without it; and yet I could not quite bring myself to feel thankful. Still, such was our speed under their guidance that it meant that we need not spend the night beneath the canopy, and for that, at least, I was glad.

I do not know how much of the journey Zariya was aware of, for her attention was turned inward, her body yet healing from the internal violence wrought upon it. Despite the jarring nature of her mode of transport, at times she dozed in her sling. Whenever I took a turn on the poles—my skills in the vanguard of our company no longer paramount—she woke long enough to summon a smile.

We reached the beach before nightfall, and there, alas, two pieces of unhappy news awaited us.

"Gods be thanked!" Evene gasped at our arrival, scarce taking notice of the Papa-ka-hondrans. "Oh! It seems a lifetime since you left."

Jahno glanced around. "Where's Tiiklit?"

"Gone," Tarrok said in a sober tone. "Yesterday afternoon he went in search of firewood. We never even saw what took him."

One of the great cats purred. Sitting on its haunches, it licked one paw and flicked it deliberately over an ear.

I really, really did not like this place.

The Elehuddin keened in grief, and Evene surveyed our company. "Where's Keeik?"

"Also gone," Jahno said in a bleak voice. "We will speak of it later." He pointed toward the northern horizon. Beyond the circle of death-bladders that ringed the island, the surface of the sea was black and swarming. "What passes there?"

"Ah, well." Tarrok shrugged his broad shoulders in a defeated gesture. "It seems that the children of Miasmus have found us."

Kooie gave a sharp whistle; the heads of Eeeio and Aiiiaii surfaced amid the floating death-bladders, trilling in response. The sea-wyrms sounded frightened, which was enough to make all of us anxious. He reported and Jahno translated. "They are afraid of the spiders, for they do not know if they are vulnerable to them. But it appears that the stinging bladders are not. The spiders are loath to venture into their midst and are content to wait for us to depart. Is there yet an open passage to the east or west?" he added. Kooie relayed the question and response, and Jahno looked unhappy. "They say the island is encircled. The spiders have been coming and coming since yesterday. Perhaps our guides wish to return to their village in haste?" he suggested, looking around again. "I do not know if the spiders will seek to penetrate the forest, but . . . where *are* our guides?"

We were alone on the barren beach. Our guides and their feline companions, it transpired, had vanished back into the forest without a word of farewell.

"The Papa-ka-hondrans have fulfilled their duty," Zariya said hoarsely, easing herself out of the sling. "If we are able to depart, I suspect the children of Miasmus will follow and leave the isle in peace for now." Her gaze settled on Evene. "You said you could have managed to part the death-bladders, my darling. Could you do the same for the spiders?" She looked tired, but alert. "I will aid you as best I can."

"You will aid me . . ." Evene's voice trailed off. "By all the fallen stars! When I saw you in the sling, I thought surely our quest had failed." She looked uncertainly at Zariya's canes. "But you found healing among the Papa-ka-hondrans?"

"I found an ordeal hideous beyond the telling. But yes, although my legs remain as they were, the necessary damage elsewhere was undone." Zariya raised her gold-traced right hand, flexing her fingers. "I can wield the *rhamanthus*."

"She can summon *lightning!*" Lirios added in awe, his translucent wings shivering with delight.

"Though we do not know how much that will avail us against thousands and thousands of the creatures," Jahno cautioned us. "Nor if it is the true purpose of the *rhamanthus*. So it falls to you, Opener of Ways."

Out in the ocean, Eeeio gave an urgent trill, his immense head and sinuous neck silhouetted against the sky's fading glow.

"The wyrms do not think we should wait until dawn," Jahno said reluctantly. "Too many spiders are coming."

"You want us to attempt this in the *dark*?" Evene looked aghast.

I pointed toward the west. "Nim is rising and more than halfway full. There will be light."

"Not enough," she said in a panic, wrapping her arms around herself. "I cannot do it in the dark! Seeker, please do not make me."

"No one will force this upon you," Jahno assured her. "If we leave at first light, do you think you might manage it?"

"I will stun them for you," Tarrok added, laying one hand on Evene's shoulder.

She hesitated, then nodded. "I will do my best."

It was another long, terrible night. We slept in shifts, or at least attempted to do so, nerves wound taut. Eeeio and Aiiiaii slept not at all, patrolling the border of death-bladders with fearful vigilance, eyes gleaming under the influence of *ooalu* moth cocoons.

In the grey light before dawn, we waited for the tide to rise high enough to allow the sea-wyrms to swim close enough to shore to haul our ship back out to sea. Jahno and the Elehuddin busied themselves with switching the tow-lines from the prow to the stern of the ship.

Quiet waves lapped on the shore.

Death-bladders drifted.

Beyond the living barricade they formed, an enormous, shapeless army of the children of Miasmus awaited us. Evene paced back and forth along the shore of Papa-ka-hondras, arms crossed to grip her tattooed biceps so hard her knuckles paled, shivering at the prospect of what was to come. At a significant nod from Zariya, I fell in beside her, joining her as she paced.

"Shadow." Evene glanced at me. "I am afraid of failing."

"I know."

"I was not raised to be a hero."

"I know."

She grimaced. "Tell me I can do this. Lie if you must."

I caught her arm, halting her. "I do not need to lie. You can do this, Evene. You *will* do this. We will do this together."

"I pray you're right," she said.

The sea-wyrms eased the ship along the trench to the edge of the shore. Once we had boarded it, they towed it backward into the water until it was floating freely. The Elehuddin returned the tow-lines to the ship's prow and Eeeio and Aiiiaii took up their bits, great bodies undulating through the water.

I brought up the coffer of *rhamanthus* seeds and unlocked it. We gathered in the fore of the ship, and under the gilded rays of the rising sun, as far as the eye could see before us, the sea beyond the barricade was black, its surface surging and roiling with thousands upon thousands of the children of Miasmus.

"Eeeio will ask the bladders to move," Jahno murmured to Tarrok. "Send your voice as narrow and deep as you may, Brother Thunderclap."

The tall man nodded in understanding, his chest swelling as he drew an impossibly long breath, bringing his cupped hands to his mouth. At Eeeio's muffled trill, the death-bladders moved to the east and west, opening a passage onto the black sea. A river of sea-spiders flowed toward us into the opening, and we covered our ears.

Tarrok hurled his ear-splitting shout into the midst of the children of Miasmus like a man casting a spear. The river ceased to flow, stunned sea-spiders adrift on the waves; but it would not last long, for already the seas on either side of the path of his thunderclap were crawling.

"Evene, *now!*" Jahno cried.

Evene pressed her palms together so hard that her hands shook; her entire body trembled with the effort of opening them, the muscles of her upper arms taut and straining. Zariya plucked a *rhamanthus* seed from the coffer I held, the tendrils of gold lacing her hand coming ablaze with light.

Slowly, slowly, Evene's palms opened and the tide of sea-spiders before us parted. Needing no encouragement, the wyrms leapt forward and the ship began jouncing over the narrow path.

A strident and panicked whistle came from Tliksee, stationed in the stern of the ship.

"They're closing behind us!" Jahno shouted.

Turning pale, Zariya slung her arm around my neck. "Get me there, my darling. Fast!"

I shoved the coffer at Jahno. "Bring the seeds!" He scrambled ahead of me as I slid my arm around Zariya's waist and hauled her the length of the ship, her feet dragging behind her.

There were sea-spiders crawling over the railing. Lirios was whirling like a dervish, his blade a blur.

"Stand back!" Zariya cried, her clenched right hand aloft as I held her upright. Lightning forked from her fist as she opened her hand, nearly scorching the mayfly's wings as it passed. The black sea behind us sparked and sizzled, but there were more sea-spiders coming and Zariya dared not set the very ship afire. One fell to the planks and Tliksee made an instinctive move to stamp on it with his bare foot.

"No!" Lirios shouldered him out of the way, stabbing it with his blade and flinging it overboard. "Do not let them touch your flesh! Khai! Help me!"

With a sharp, commanding trill, Essee came to take my place, supporting Zariya as she plucked another seed from the coffer Jahno held out for her.

I drew my weapons and plunged into the fray.

I do not know how long it took us to traverse the narrow path that Evene held open for us, only that it felt like an eternity. Lirios took the starboard side of the stern and I took the port, hacking and slashing and stabbing at the crawling things, the Elehuddin doing their best to aid us with the squirming and still-dangerous remains, while blue-white lightning crackled over our heads, leaving a growing trail of dead, charred sea-spiders in our wake.

At last we broke into open water.

Nothing had ever looked so sweet to me as the sight of that black tide receding behind us. Kooie stabbed one last wriggling remnant of a sea-spider with his belt-knife and flicked it away with a contemptuous whistle. In the prow of the ship, Evene let her hands fall and slumped to the deck in boneless exhaustion, resting her brow on her knees. The rest of us examined

ourselves and each other; miraculously, we had suffered no further casualties in our escape from Papa-ka-hondras.

"Whither now, Seeker?" Tarrok asked Jahno in a deep, calm voice.

Zar the Sun was not so very far above the horizon; it had taken a great
deal less time than it seemed to effect our escape.

Jahno gazed at the rising sun, its light reflected gold in his silvery eyes.

"'That which you seek lies in the possession of those whose lifeblood is
trade, and value the worth of a thing more than the thing itself,'" Zariya
murmured. "I do believe we are bound for Tukkan."

Jahno nodded. "Yah."

FORTY-NINE

Now our course turned toward the west, following the great western current in the direction of Tukkan, which was situated at the confluence of the great western and northern currents.

At least this time we were not venturing into the unknown, for Jahno and the Elehuddin had sojourned there before. Tukkan was a proud and prosperous nation ruled by merchant-lords who guarded their wealth zealously, but even the poorest of its citizens flaunted whatever finery they had to display, promenading before the temple of Galdano the Shrewd and boasting of the favor they received in exchange for ostentatious offerings to the god.

Even if our supposition was correct, Jahno warned us, we could not expect the Tukkani to hand us the missing piece of the Scattered Prophecy, but would be expected to haggle for it, something that struck me as incredibly foolish and short-sighted under the circumstances.

"It is not sheer mean-spiritedness, my heart," Zariya explained to me. "Galdano the Shrewd decreed long ago that the worth of a thing could only be determined through trade. For the Tukkani, it is a form of worship." She glanced at Jahno. "And you have traded with them before, have you not?"

Kooie whistled and signed, and Jahno nodded in agreement. "Yah, but we only ever traded stolen goods on the black market. Tukkan is not a great pirate haven like the Nexus," he added, "but they're not particular about where a thing came from, and they will not allow the coursers of Obid to interfere with trade. This will be different. We will have to go before the Gilded Council."

The Gilded Council, I learned, were the twenty-one wealthiest merchant-lords and -ladies in the nation. If such a thing as a copy of the Koronian collected prophecies existed, it would almost surely belong to one of them.

Zariya and I went through the trunks of her belongings, selecting items from her wedding trousseau that might serve us well in trade.

"It's odd to think how much such things seemed to matter once, isn't it, my heart?" she remarked wistfully, holding up a pair of dangling golden earrings with ruby teardrops. "It seems so very long ago. I wonder how Lord Rygil fares, and if my father has returned to Zarkhoum."

"I wonder if Prince Dozaren yet governs in Merabaht," I added. "And how my brethren in the Brotherhood of Pahrkun fare."

I did not give voice to the thought that we might never see them again, but I saw it reflected in Zariya's gaze. If we failed in our quest, the world as we knew it would no longer exist.

In the days immediately following our flight from the shores of Papa-ka-hondras, Zariya had spent long hours dozing in her hammock, allowing her body to continue healing. She had confided to me that she was passing blood in her stool, and I knew she was in considerable discomfort. But it seemed that the Green Mother had not misled us, for day by day, Zariya's pain eased and she grew stronger. Her breath came more freely and her stamina increased accordingly; it was, she told me, as though a painful vise that had gripped her lungs since she'd been a fever-stricken child had at long last loosed its hold on her.

I cannot put into words how glad this made me, and I daresay everyone on the ship rejoiced, too.

The ordeal had changed her in other ways. I had always known Zariya to be kind and thoughtful, and those qualities had deepened to a new level of maturity. I noted it particularly in her dealings with Lirios, for she set aside the unease that his relentlessly enthusiastic ardor evoked in her and treated him with a more characteristic degree of openness and respect; in turn, it had a calming effect on him.

"I know my queen does not love me, Khai," Lirios said to me in his earnest manner. "But I think she understands now that this is well enough; it is our way, the way of the children of Selerian the Light-Footed, not your way, with your Sacred Twins. Your way . . . in her heart, it will always be *you* that she loves best, and although it is strange to me, I know it is so."

I smiled wryly.

At the moment, Zariya and Jahno had their heads bent together, poring over his journal. Since my realization in the wake of the terror that I might lose her on Papa-ka-hondras, it had struck me that I bitterly regretted having kissed her only the once as a sweet affirmation. It seemed in hindsight a lost time of innocence and possibility, when it would have been unthinkable for a princess of the House of the Ageless to consort unveiled with a man who was not kin to her and prophecy was merely the stuff of daydreams, not a deadly reality.

Though if I had dared more, perhaps I could not have endured her betrothal. Either way, it was a thought I had kept to myself.

"We are Sun-Blessed and shadow, our destinies twined at birth, and only death can break that bond," I said to Lirios. "Zariya's life and her honor are more dear to me than my own. But I think that is a thing both deeper and different than mortal love, my brother." I nodded at Zariya and Jahno. "She has the heart and mind of a scholar, and they are well suited to each other."

Lirios gave me a sidelong glance, his aquamarine eyes glinting. "*I* think you are mistaken."

I shrugged. "There are greater matters at hand."

"This is very true," he agreed.

Just how great, we learned some ten days into our journey to Tukkan when it seemed the entire world . . . shuddered. I do not know how else to describe it. I felt it, the sea-wyrms felt it, we all felt it, the impact as profound as Tarrok's thunderclap of a shout, only infinitely more vast.

Somewhere in the world, something had happened. We exchanged wild looks, all of us.

"What *was* that?" Evene demanded.

No one knew.

A day later, the skies darkened, a cloud of ash blotting out the sun and raining down upon us, covering our ship's deck and drifting in gritty piles, making a dense film on the surface of the water.

"'And the skies shall grow as dark as night and ash shall rain from the sky,'" Jahno quoted, reading from his journal. "'And the world shall know that the Abyss that Abides is no more, for Miasmus has risen.'"

"Does it say what form Miasmus will take, my darling?" Zariya inquired.

He shook his head. "No."

She fixed her gaze on the western horizon. "Well, I suppose we shall find out, shan't we?"

For three days and nights, the ash continued to fall. Zariya and I shared our head-scarves among the company so that every member might wrap a length of cloth over his or her mouth and nose, filtering the air that we breathed. Even so, all of us were coughing and miserable.

On the fourth day, the skies cleared and the wave struck.

It seemed to come out of nowhere, for the sea was placid that day. When the wyrms trilled an early alarm, their senses far keener than ours, none of us knew what to make of it. Kooie dove overboard to assess the currents with his own sensitive tendrils, surfacing to scramble up the boarding ladder, whistling in urgent haste.

"Very, very big wave coming," Jahno translated. "Everyone hold tight!"

A few minutes later we saw it, a wall of water rushing down upon us, blue-green and glassy, as tall as a tower. I wrapped my right arm around the ship's mast and the other around Zariya's waist, and she wound both arms around my neck.

If *ooalu* wood had not been so extraordinarily buoyant, I am not sure we would have succeeded in riding out the impact of the wave unleashed by the violent uprising of Miasmus. It was a wave without a crest and it surged beneath us without breaking. Our ship bobbed atop its face like a cork at a pitch that felt well nigh vertical. For the space of a heartbeat we hovered atop it; then plunged, careening down the backside of the great wave into the trough below. Flung forward by the abrupt change in momentum, I strained to keep my grip on the mast, my arm feeling half yanked from its socket, while Zariya clung to me for dear life. Our vessel jounced and shuddered as it struck the trough, cast adrift, for the sea-wyrms had dropped their bits under the onslaught.

Behind us, the wave rushed onward. Beneath us, the sea returned to a state of calm placidity.

Zariya released her death grip around my neck. "Thank you, dearest," she breathed. "I expect I shall owe you my life several times over before this is finished."

I rubbed my aching shoulder. "Is it just the one wave, do you think?"

She shivered. "I hope so. At least the wyrms will warn us if another is coming."

Counting heads, Essee whistled in alarm; Seeak and Lirios were missing.

Without a word, the Elehuddin dove overboard to search for them. Seeak surfaced some distance from the ship with a reassuring trill; the un-expected plunge would do him no harm.

The mayfly was another matter.

The rest of us leaned on the railing and watched helplessly; even the best swimmers among us could do nothing to assist the Elehuddin in the water. In the end it was Aiiiaii who found Lirios, surfacing and swimming toward the ship with her head held high, holding him as tenderly as possible in her mighty jaws, his limp body dangling on either side.

Jahno and Tarrok raced to meet her, lowering Lirios to the ship's deck, careful to spread his sodden wings beneath him. The mayfly's golden skin was tinged with pale blue and he wasn't breathing. Jahno turned Lirios's head to the side and some water came out of his mouth. "I'm going to breathe for him," he said to Tarrok. "One, two, three, four, five, then you push on his chest, one, two, three, yah?" The tall man nodded and Jahno suited actions to words, pinching Lirios's nostrils closed and clamping his mouth over the mayfly's.

Gripping the railing with one hand, Zariya slid her free hand into mine, gripping it hard.

I squeezed back, fearful for our mayfly, whom I had begun to consider something of a brother, albeit a peculiar one.

On the third round of ministrations, Lirios's chest rose. He vomited forth a copious amount of seawater, gasped, and began breathing. With a sigh of relief, Jahno sat back on his heels, wiping his brow with his forearm.

"Thanks be to all the children of heaven!" Evene breathed beside us. "He's not terribly bright, but he's far too pretty to die."

"I'm glad you have your priorities in order, my darling," Zariya murmured.

Evene nudged her. "Oh, you know I don't mean it."

Tarrok helped Lirios sit upright. The mayfly coughed and sputtered, fanning his drenched wings experimentally. "I am sorry," he said in a contrite manner, his voice a bit ragged. "That was more difficult than I expected." He rubbed his hands over his face, lifted his gaze toward Aiiiaii, and offered her a Chalcedony Islander salute, thumbs hooked and fingers spread wide. "Thank you."

The sea-wyrm dipped her enormous head graciously and gave a low series of whistles in response.

Jahno smiled wearily. "She says you are welcome and try not to fall overboard again. Onward, yah?"

Onward.

As before, we avoided making landfall. Prior to the giant wave, we had seen other ships here and there sailing the great western current and given them a wide berth as we passed, our wyrm-drawn ship capable of greater speed than those forced to rely on wind and current alone. Now we saw the wreckage that the immense wave had left in its wake, flotsam floating on the water all that was left of ships that had been swamped or capsized by it. I'd been right: We did owe our lives to the buoyancy of the *ooalu* wood, and the realization of what a near thing it had been was a sobering one. We kept a sharp eye out for survivors, but saw none.

It was a grey day when we drew in sight of the tall lighthouse that marked the harbor of Yanakhat, Tukkan's capital city, rain drizzling from the cloudy skies. The sea-wyrms signaled that the harbor was mercifully free from corruption by Mad Priests. Jahno had declared that we would take lodgings at a fine inn, something necessary to impress the Gilded Council, and I confess, even I was immeasurably glad to hear it.

By our reckoning, it had taken three days for the children of Miasmus to follow us from the Nexus to Papa-ka-hondras. It wasn't a great deal of time with which to work, but at least it would afford us a night or two of comfort.

Nearing the harbor, we found it barricaded by a line of Tukkani tradeships, and the captain of a ship with the black-and-white-striped sails of the coursers of Obid the Stern in apparent negotiation with them. A pang of excitement gripped me, and I could not help but wonder if Vironesh was aboard it.

Considerably less pleased by the sight, Kooie whistled an inquiry to Jahno, who shook his head. "No, we're here on trade, we've every right to be here and the Tukkani will uphold it," he said. "And the coursers can't remand us for things we *might* have done in the past. Not without proof, anyway."

Zariya was gazing intently at the coursers' ship. "I don't think the coursers of Obid are here on a matter of justice," she said quietly. "Not this time."

She was right.

As we drew closer, I saw that the entire ship was crammed with people; not sailors or warriors, but ordinary men, women, and children, most of them fair-skinned and dark-haired, crowded shoulder to shoulder on the deck. Some of them clutched bundles of belongings. All of them looked stricken and frightened, as though the world had dropped out from under them.

Essee's hands flew up to cover her mouth, her eyes bright with sympathy.

Tarrok drew a sharp breath, the unexpected sight hitting him hard. "Ah, by all the fallen stars! Those are Traskans."

"Pull alongside them," Jahno ordered.

There was shouting as we did so, and the ship's crew shoved passengers out of the way, coming to the starboard railing to burnish long barbed spears with which to repel the sea-wyrms. Eeeio and Aiiiaii angled prudently away.

"We are here on a matter of trade and mean no harm!" Jahno called to the ship. "What passes here?"

The ship's captain pushed her way through the throng. "Miasmus has risen and Trask has fallen," she said bluntly. "*That* is what has come to pass while you gallivanted about the seas, wyrm-raider."

Tarrok leaned over the railing. "What do you mean when you say Trask has fallen, lady?"

The captain's expression changed. "Forgive me, friend. The Risen Maw spews forth all that it has devoured, and I fear an army of the dead and drowned overruns your nation. The coursers of Obid do but seek to repatriate the survivors." She spat on the crowded deck. "And these sons of bitches will take no further refugees."

"Tukkan has taken its share!" an official shouted from the barricade. "It is all we can do to protect our own."

Tarrok paled. "Have you word of the family of Alara, daughter of Kadar, and her twin sons?"

"That is his wife and children," Evene murmured. "His family refused to accompany him into exile. Our Thunderclap does not like to speak of it."

The revelation struck me like a blow to the gut. All these months at sea together, and I'd had no idea.

The captain conferred with her crew and heads shook. "There is no such family in our manifest. Perhaps they found refuge on another ship, but I can make no guarantee. It is a time of death and chaos."

Tarrok bowed his head.

The official in charge of the barricade line made a shooing gesture. "Carry on toward Khent; you may find a welcome there."

The captain glared at him, but she gave an order, and the ship's oars began to churn the water, propelling it backward.

"Wait!" I shouted. "Have you word of Vironesh of Zarkhoum? He sailed among you!"

"The purple man, the great warrior?" The captain nodded and pointed toward the west. "He fights in the vanguard against the army of the risen dead, buying time for the rest of us to rescue whom we might. Trask has fallen, but Kerreman yet holds forth resistance. But make no mistake," she added grimly, "the armies of Miasmus are coming for all of us."

"Not today, they aren't," the official retorted. "So take your wretched human cargo elsewhere!"

Our ship drew back and we watched the coursers of Obid take their leave, navigating the swirling conjunction of the currents to head northward, our mood somber as the black-and-white sails dwindled in the distance.

"Hey!" the official shouted at us. "Will you dawdle all day, wyrm-raiders? State your business!"

Jahno clapped a sympathetic hand on Tarrok's back. "We're here on a matter of trade."

"Stand by to be boarded," the official replied with a nervous glance at the sea-wyrms idling patiently in the water. "Assemble your crew. No one passes until we're sure there are none of the afflicted among you."

We obeyed.

The inspection was accomplished swiftly and the official returned to his own vessel. Oars out, the ships forming the barricade moved and parted, and the official gave us a magnanimous salute. "Welcome to Tukkan."

FIFTY

Three days.

We were acutely conscious of the limits of the time allotted to us to achieve our goal, all of us. Upon securing a berth in the harbor of Yanakhat, Jahno sought out lodgings in the finest inn the city had to offer, securing a porter for our trunks and a hired palanquin for Zariya using the funds remaining from the sale of her Barakhan wedding-cloth in the Caldera. As soon as we were ensconced, he sent a messenger to the Gilded Council requesting an audience on a matter of utmost and urgent concern. At Zariya's suggestion, he sent it in her name as a royal princess of the House of the Ageless of Zarkhoum.

It proved a good suggestion, for the council responded that very day, granting us an audience the following morning.

With the exception of Essee, the Elehuddin had elected to remain aboard the ship, more comfortable in a harbor than a city. The sea-wyrms would patrol the ocean for signs of the children of Miasmus, and we had agreed that if the vanguard was spotted, they would send Tliksee to alert us and flee to the far side of the isle, where we would reconvene as swiftly as possible. Tukkan was considerably larger than Papa-ka-hondras, but a great deal smaller than Zarkhoum, and we thought we could outpace the sea-spiders by crossing overland if need be.

After so long at sea with our small company, Yanakhat seemed crowded and busy to me. The Tukkani folk were loud and brash, favoring garish colors and ostentatious displays of jewelry. At first, overwhelmed by the clamor of the city, I thought that other than the barricade on the harbor, one might suppose its inhabitants to be oblivious of the looming menace in the west; upon looking more closely, I saw that there was a forced quality to their brazen behavior. People were frightened all right, they were just doing their damnedest not to show it.

At least the inn was a pleasant place, boasting spacious rooms that opened onto a central courtyard. There was no bathing chamber such as one might find in a wealthy Zarkhoumi home, but the room that Zariya and I shared sported a tub in which one person might sit to bathe, and solicitous maidservants brought hot water for us, as well as a platter of dates stuffed with rice and ground meats.

We opened our trunks to select attire for the morning's audience, and at Zariya's request, a maidservant lit the room's brazier and set to work pressing our wrinkled garments with a heated flat-iron.

Essee and Evene joined us, the former adorned with an intricate set of necklaces of polished shells that constituted Elehuddin finery. When Evene reluctantly confessed that she possessed no suitable attire, I insisted on lending her a gown of turquoise silk edged with a deep gold-patterned violet and a matching outer robe. It was a bit too large for her, but Zariya's clothing would be too small. It would serve.

Evene's eyes shone as she twirled in the sumptuous garments. "Are you sure? It's so very nice!"

"Yes, of course." There was no way I would venture unarmed into this audience, so I would wear the gold silk brocade tunic and breeches tailored for Izaria's wedding what seemed so very long ago, painstakingly laundered clean of bloodstains.

She stroked the soft silk. "Thank you, Khai. But I suppose such garb was little to your liking."

I didn't answer right away, remembering the first time I had seen myself in the mirror attired as a woman; remembering the light in my mother's eyes when she had seen me thusly as the daughter for whom she had yearned. I did not think these were things Evene could fully understand, even if I were able to articulate my own conflicted feelings. "That is not entirely true."

Jahno rapped on the door of our chamber and poked his head in. Seeing

Evene in my gown, he let out a low whistle of appreciation. "You look very beautiful tonight!"

Evene flushed and curtsied, turquoise silk pooling around her ankles. "Thank you, Seeker."

"We are taking Tarrok to a tavern, Lirios the mayfly and I," he said. "Brother Thunderclap is distraught at the day's news, and understandably so. We will attempt to help him drown his sorrows. But we will convene in the morning, yah?"

Essee clicked in affirmative response and signed our agreement, and Jahno withdrew.

Zariya was watching me, her luminous gaze soft and gentle. "You know that you may be whatever you wish, my darling. I adore you regardless."

Grateful for her understanding, I smiled at her. "I know. But it is best if I am prepared for danger."

She nodded. "As long as you know."

We spent some hours fussing over clothing and cosmetics and hair before retiring for the night. Aboard the ship after our escape from Papa-ka-hondras, Evene had largely succeeded in unsnarling Zariya's hair without cutting much from its length; now, she brushed it out and braided it in intricate loops. The solicitous maidservants brought platters of roasted fowl, heaps of stewed squash, and a flagon of date-palm wine.

At length we retired to our respective chambers and slept.

It was a clamor in the courtyard that awoke me; voices raised in fierce argument. Jahno's and Lirios's were on the high end of the spectrum, fierce and familiar, contending with many others that were strange to me; Tarrok was singing in a low counterpoint in his native tongue, belligerent and drunken.

I vaulted from my pallet.

Zariya sat upright. "What passes?"

"I don't know, but I'll find out." Lashing my sash around my waist and thrusting my weapons into it, I flung open the door and darted barefooted into the courtyard.

Nim the Bright Moon and Shahal the Dark Moon were hiding their faces tonight; only Eshen the Wandering Moon was present in the sky. Under the speckled blue light of the fickle moon, Tarrok swayed and sang what sounded like an elegy or a song of mourning, his face raised to the night sky, bald head gleaming.

How was it that I had known so little of what he lost when he was exiled? My heart ached anew at the knowledge. Uniformed figures clung to the tall man, dragging at his limbs: Yanakhat's version of the City Guard, seeking to bear him down. Jahno and Lirios were yelling on the outskirts of the skirmish and brandishing weapons.

"Peace!" I cried. "Let him be, he means no harm!"

Everyone ignored me.

Tarrok shuddered as though surprised to find himself beset and glanced around. His chest swelled as he drew breath.

I clapped my hands over my ears.

The shout Tarrok unloosed broke like a veritable thunderclap over the courtyard, broken and jagged and filled with anguish. The guards dropped, stunned into unconsciousness, and Jahno with them; Lirios had been quick enough to drop his blade and cover his own ears in time.

Tarrok fell to his knees and buried his face in his hands.

"We came upon a family of Traskan refugees begging in the square," Lirios explained. "Tarrok became very upset upon speaking to them and began shouting. The Seeker and I did our best to get him away, but these guards followed us, threatening to jail us if we did not pay a fine."

I frowned down at the unconscious figures, thinking.

"Forgive me," Tarrok murmured, lifting his head. "I did not mean to cause trouble. But what they spoke of, what they have seen and endured . . . I fear it filled my heart with an agony too terrible to bear."

Essee and Evene had emerged to join us; with a low trill of comfort, the former put her arms around Tarrok, crooning to him. Still kneeling, the tall man clung to her waist and she stroked his shaking shoulders. Hobbling on her canes, Zariya came to investigate the silence in the aftermath of the fray.

"Well, if it's a bribe the guards were after, I say we give it to them," she said in a pragmatic tone when Lirios repeated his explanation. "Haul them outside the courtyard gate and leave them a purse for their troubles. I should think they ought to count themselves lucky."

The guards were beginning to stir and moan as Lirios and I set about dragging them out of the courtyard one by one. The last one was alert enough to stumble between us without protest.

I pressed the small knotted cloth of coins that Evene had procured into his hand. "You sought to extort money from a powerful man in the throes of great grief," I said to him. "Take it and be grateful you suffered no worse a bargain in the exchange." He stared at me, dazed; I suspect his ears were ringing too badly to hear. Nonetheless, his fingers closed on the purse, and when Lirios clanged the gate shut behind us, none of them seemed inclined to pursue the matter.

Jahno was sitting upright and rubbing his temples when we returned. "I fear we didn't handle that so well," he said in an overly loud voice. "Brother Tarrok, we are so very sorry. Will you share with us what you learned from your unfortunate compatriots this evening?"

The tall man shook his head with quiet dignity. "Begging your pardon, Seeker, not tonight. Let us confront the task that awaits us on the morrow first."

The matter closed for now, we returned to our respective chambers in search of sleep.

In the morning, we donned our finery and proceeded through the streets of Yanakhat to Council Hall, drawing stares along the way; I daresay the likes of our company had never been seen before in Tukkan. Zariya sat straight-backed in her hired palanquin, gowned and veiled, her eyes heavily lined with kohl, looking every inch the Zarkhoumi princess that she was. The rest of us walked alongside her litter, doing our best to appear imposing, although Jahno and Tarrok had bloodshot eyes and looked a bit worse for the wear after the night's ordeal. Upon reaching the ornate building situated at the end of one of Yanakhat's major thoroughfares, a company of impassive armed guards escorted us into the presence of the Gilded Council.

Twenty-one members, every single one of them wealthy beyond telling, none of them young. They sat at a long table, ten on either side flanking High Councilor Dauvin, a gaunt-faced man in garish robes, an ashen cast to his fair skin, his bony fingers dripping with rings.

He looked unimpressed. "I take it there is one among you who claims to be a member of Zarkhoumi royalty?"

Zariya lifted her chin. "I am the Sun-Blessed Princess Zariya of the House of the Ageless, youngest daughter of King Azarkal of Zarkhoum, and I thank you for granting us this audience, High Councilor."

Members of the Gilded Council raised bejeweled fans and murmured to each other behind them.

I had a bad feeling about this audience.

The High Councilor raised one finger, an emerald the size of his knuckle glinting on it. "State your business."

Zariya inclined her head to him. "Allow me to defer to my companion, Jahno of Koronis."

Jahno stepped forward and cleared his throat. "My lords and ladies, I am a prophecy-hunter by trade," he announced in too-loud tones. "I am the great-grandson of Liko of Koronis, whose name I hope you recognize as a respected scholar."

One of the women seated at the table winced. "Would you mind lowering your voice, messire?"

"Yah, forgive me." Jahno lowered his voice. "My lords and ladies of the Gilded Council, as I am sure you know, Miasmus, the Abyss that Abides, has risen. We live in dire times. The children of Miasmus are abroad sowing chaos; the armies of the returned dead advance upon us, isle by isle. Darkness threatens to swallow the world. But there is a prophecy that details the ways in which the gods' chosen may avert this devastation. It was the life's work of my people, the scholars of Koronis, to assemble the scattered pieces of this prophecy. In this we failed, for we were too jealous of our knowledge. Koronis sank beneath the waves, and the knowledge we gathered sank with it." His voice grew stronger, impassioned. "But the great Oracle of the Nexus, Kephalos the Wise, has told me that it was not lost." His bloodshot eyes flashed, his voice rising. "The Oracle tells me that a copy of the gathered pieces of the Scattered Prophecy abides among you! This, my lords and ladies, is what we seek."

It was a speech worthy of cheering, and it fell upon indifferent ears.

"Supposing such a thing exists, what do you offer in trade?" the High Councilor inquired.

Jahno beckoned.

Lirios stepped forth, holding a tray in his outstretched arms. "A wedding necklace fit for a Zarkhoumi princess," he announced, opening the tray.

It was a glorious piece, a collar of linked gold plaques inset with rubies. It was also the most valuable item that Zariya yet possessed, and she and I had selected it for its impact.

Out came the jeweled fans again, and the members of the council whispered behind them. It seemed to me that the conversation eddied most strongly around one corpulent fellow in a lemon-yellow robe. I wondered if he were the owner of the copy of the prophecy. It seemed strange to me that the entire Gilded Council should negotiate the trade of an item owned by a single individual, but according to Jahno, the members believed their numbers gave them a position of greater strength.

Well, if they could converse in secret, so could we. I caught Zariya's eye and signed, *Watch the fat man.* She gave me a slight nod of acknowledgment.

Members lowered their fans, and the High Councilor leaned back in his chair and steepled his fingers. "It has come to our attention that your company found itself in a spot of trouble with the city's Orderkeepers last night," he remarked. "An unfortunate thing when you come seeking our aid."

"The book of the Scattered Prophecy is worthless to you," Jahno said. "We offer an item of great value in trade for it."

"You ought to know better, Koronian. The book is worth what it is worth to *you*," High Councilor Dauvin commented. "Let us propose a counteroffer. It is passing strange to find a Zarkhoumi princess in such unsavory company, but these are strange times. Rumor reached our ears some weeks ago that the youngest daughter of the House of the Ageless was betrothed to a Therinian lord and set forth bearing a dowry of three thousand *rhamanthus* seeds. Supposing such a thing exists, *that* is an offer that the Gilded Council would entertain."

A shocked silence fell over our company.

"No." Jahno shook his head. "That you cannot ask of us. We need the *rhamanthus* to defeat Miasmus."

The High Councilor arched one brow. "Defeat Miasmus? How do you propose to do so?"

"I do not know!" Jahno retorted in frustration. "The answer lies in the book of prophecy!"

A woman raised her fan and whispered to the High Councilor. "And your motley lot fancies yourselves destined," he observed. "How quaint."

"It is not *quaint*," Tarrok grated, his hands clenched into fists at his sides. "My people are refugees. Those you have not turned away, you suffer to beg in the streets for sustenance. Do you suppose the same will not befall you in time?"

High Councilor Dauvin shrugged. "We have named our price."

My palms itched for my hilts. In that moment, I would have enjoyed killing every last one of the members of the Gilded Council.

"My lord Councilor." Zariya took a step forward, her voice soft and imploring. "You speak the truth, our claim is outrageous; and yet I believe it is a true one. For better or worse, it seems that we *are* the defenders of the four quarters of whom the Scattered Prophecy speaks. And to this end, the *rhamanthus* seeds were entrusted to me by Anamuht the Purging Fire herself. I cannot barter with them."

Fans were raised; speculative whispers ran back and forth along the length of the table. The High Councilor regarded Zariya with hooded eyes. "How do you know that this is not exactly the purpose for which the seeds were intended?"

Taken aback by the question, Zariya furrowed her brow and hesitated.

"Because my queen can use the seeds to summon lightning to her hand and destroy the children of Miasmus!" Lirios said fiercely, his wings buzzing in agitation. "Because she paid a terrible price to be able to do so!"

"Life and death, wind and fire," Zariya added. "Anamuht told me that these are the gifts my soul's twin and I are meant to carry to the end of the earth if the time is upon us. For this I require the *rhamanthus*."

"And do you claim one among you can summon the wind as well?" the High Councilor inquired.

I scowled at him. "Pahrkun's wind is not a wind such as you understand it."

"Oh, of course not," he said in a bland manner.

Essee spoke at length, her golden eyes fixed on the High Councilor's face. Jahno nodded. "She says you cannot afford the luxury of doubt. Whether or not you believe us, it is true that the children of Miasmus found us in great numbers at the Oracle of the Nexus; they found us in greater numbers on the shores of Papa-ka-hondras. Even now, they pursue us, and I fear we have but two days at best before they find us here, and threaten the entirety of your realm. Of what use is longevity to you if your lives are already forfeit? Do not be proud and stubborn and foolish. Be wise and accept this trade that we have offered in good faith."

I still had an eye on the fat man. For a moment, his face softened, and for the space of a few heartbeats, I thought perhaps Essee's words had reached him, perhaps there was hope. But no; the fans rose. Behind them, whispers and nods ensued. The fat man's expression hardened.

High Councilor Dauvin raised his bejeweled hand. "You seek to threaten us with dire consequences if we fail to accede to your terms," he said. "This we find unacceptable and a violation of the principles of trade. You have made a request; we have named a price. You have a day to make your decision."

With that we were dismissed.

FIFTY-ONE

"Fuckers!" Evene spat on the ground outside Council Hall.

I did not disagree with the sentiment.

Jahno rubbed his face. "It is likely that they expect us to counter with a lesser number. I suspect that they might settle for as few as a thousand seeds. But to me it seems that even one seed is unacceptable. Are we agreed that the *rhamanthus* must not be used for bargaining?"

"Absolutely," Zariya said firmly. "I cannot believe for an instant that Anamuht entrusted them to me as a bargaining chip." She shuddered. "Especially not after Papa-ka-hondras."

I felt helpless. "What do we do? Counter with another offer?"

"There is Ishfahel the Gentle Rain's gift," Tarrok murmured. "Though we do not know its purpose."

"No." Jahno shook his head. "Ishfahel said to breach the cask only in our time of greatest need. It is to sustain us when all else fails. That time has not yet come. But at least we may be certain that a copy of the Scattered Prophecy exists," he added. "Else they would not have bartered for it." Our Seeker came to a decision. "The Tukkani portion of the prophecy says that when one way is closed, an acolyte of Galdano the Shrewd will point to another. We will go to the temple."

The temple of Galdano the Shrewd was located in the heart of Yanakhat, an immensely tall building with a gilded roof. The square outside the temple was thronged with petitioners, all of them in their best finery, all of them clutching offerings for the god. On the outskirts, vendors had set up awnings and hawked skewers of grilled meats and cool fruit juices in singsong voices.

We took our place in the throng, waiting while the sun climbed higher into the sky. All of us, especially Zariya's patient Tukkani litter-bearers, sweated beneath it. At Zariya's behest, Lirios gave the tray containing the necklace into Jahno's keeping and darted away to purchase fruit juices served in watertight cones of thin bark for everyone. Inch by slow inch, we moved closer to the temple, until at last we were ushered through its doors and into the shade within. Inside the temple, there remained a crowd of petitioners between us and the god himself, but now I could see our destination.

Galdano the Shrewd.

It was the first time I had encountered a fixed god, one who did not roam the land or inland seas over which it held aegis. Galdano was no less awesome for being permanently ensconced in his temple. He sat cross-legged on a plinth in the center of the central chamber, his gilded skin gleaming. The top of his head brushed the roof of the temple, and there were two great coffers of treasure on either side of the plinth. His golden face was impassive, jeweled eyes gazing across the sea of petitioners, but he had eight arms that were in near-constant motion; one plucking forth offerings from outraised hands, placing some in a scale he held in another hand, placing others in the coffers of treasure to either side of him. One hand held sheets of vellum and another an inkwell; a third scribbled notes upon the vellum. Other hands fished within the coffers, bringing forth various items.

Some petitioners received written responses for their offerings; others received items in trade. Some rejoiced, while others went away disgruntled or confused by the god's response.

The poorest petitioners, those who had nothing of value to offer, paid a single copper coin to green-robed acolytes to light a candle in Galdano's honor, placing it on an iron rack. It seemed they received nothing in response save hope that the god might hear their prayers.

I daresay all of us hoped that one of those very acolytes might approach us in accordance with the prophecy, but although several gave our company curious glances, none came forward.

Zariya leaned forward in her litter. "Well, it seems we must make an offering. What shall it be?"

Jahno gave an uncertain shrug. "I do not know what is fitting."

"May I say something, my lady?" the litter-bearer on the left front pole inquired, looking over his shoulder.

She blinked in surprise. "Of course."

"You sought something in trade from the Gilded Council and did not receive it," he said. "Do you think it wise to offer less to the god in exchange for his favor?"

"No, my friend," Zariya said after a moment's pause. "I think you make a very good point, and we are grateful for it." She offered him a sincere salute. "Thank you."

He inclined his head to her. "Most patrons do not think to offer refreshment to the day-servants they hire."

It was another hour before we reached the base of the plinth. From this perspective, Galdano the Shrewd loomed even larger. The sole of his gilded right foot on the plinth before me was taller than I was. I had to crane my neck to see his impassive face, lost in the rafters.

"State your desire and make your offering," a green-robed acolyte said to us, the words sounding rote.

We exchanged uncertain glances, and Zariya nodded to Jahno. "Seeker, I believe this yet falls to you."

Jahno took a deep breath. "Galdano the Shrewd, we seek the gathered pieces of the Scattered Prophecy that were lost when Koronis sank beneath the waves!" he called, opening the tray. "Here is our offering."

The god did not deign to look at us; but then, he deigned to look at no one, his jeweled gaze fixed on the distance. One enormous golden hand descended to pluck the necklace from its tray. It draped over his fingers, intricate gold links and inlaid rubies glinting in the shadowy light. Behind us came murmurs of awe and envy, for it was by far and away the most valuable offering anyone had made that day. Beside the plinth, another acolyte scrawled notes in a ledger he held, recording the nature of our offering.

Galdano the Shrewd placed the collar in the scale it held in another hand, weighing its worth, then transferred it to the coffer to his left, heaped with offerings—necklaces, bangles, anklets, bejeweled mirrors, goblets, sacks of grain. I held my breath, hoping to see one hand dip quill into inkwell and write an answer on a sheet of vellum.

It was not to be.

Instead, another hand reached into the coffer to his right and drew forth a simple wax taper, the kind of candle the acolytes were selling for a single copper coin to impoverished petitioners.

This, the god offered us in exchange for a necklace worthy of a Zarkhoumi princess's wedding dowry.

The recording acolyte startled, then made note of it in his ledger.

I will own, my heart sank; I daresay all of ours did. Jahno let out his breath in a weary sigh, accepting the candle. The petitioners behind us whispered in sympathy or restrained glee at the poor trade we'd gotten.

"This way," the presiding acolyte said, ushering us out of the presence of the god. She nodded toward the iron rack. "You may light the candle in homage if you wish ere you depart."

"I suppose we might as well," Jahno muttered, dejected. He handed the wax taper to Zariya, still seated in her litter. "It was your dowry, my lady. Since it seems we have spent it unwisely, you may as well have the honor."

The bearers lowered her palanquin and I helped her climb forth, holding the taper for her while she got her canes beneath her. The rack was a simple affair of concentric circles with crude sconces for the tapers, and one thick column of a candle in the center from which to light the offerings. Zariya lit our taper and placed it carefully in the nearest sconce.

"It's true!" a voice behind us murmured in awe. "You *are* the ones who were foretold!"

I turned to see the acolyte who had been recording transactions beside Galdano's plinth, an ordinary-looking young Tukkani man, no longer carrying his ledger. "What do you mean?"

"You're together, all of you?" He beckoned when I nodded. "Follow me. Leave your hired bearers behind."

Our company exchanged quick glances, but it appeared that a piece of the Scattered Prophecy was falling into place after all, and the matter wasn't in question. I gestured to him. "Lead on."

We followed him through a door in an alcove that led to another wing of the temple, this one sized to an ordinary human scale; the spaces where the acolytes slept and ate and did whatever else it was that acolytes of Galdano the Shrewd did. He escorted us to a small study, the walls lined with ledgers, and closed the door behind us.

"I am Badu, son of Ranalos," he said expectantly. "And you are here in answer to my petition."

Jahno gave him a puzzled look. "*Your* petition? No, you sought us out in answer to ours. Do you not have counsel for us?"

"I?" Badu the acolyte looked stricken. "No, my friends, not I. Can it be I have made a mistake?"

"More likely we have," Evene said in a sour tone. "And a damned expensive one at that."

"Yes, that's the thing," Badu said. "Galdano the Shrewd wrote a response to my petition. 'Enter my service and those with the power to grant what you seek will come. By this you will know them: They will receive the least in trade for the greatest offering, and a candle flame shall be their sign.' I have spent years in his service tallying the offerings, and never have I seen such disparity as with your offering today." He tugged at his short, dark hair. "Does none of this mean anything to you?"

Heads shook.

I held up one hand. "Not yet, but wait. Perhaps it will become clearer. Tell us, what is it you seek?"

Badu's face darkened. "Revenge. Revenge against my former master, Lord Solinus. My sister and I were sold into debt-slavery in his household. He subjected her to all manner of depravity; he got her with child, and sold the babe when she displeased him. She took her own life because of it, and I fled his service."

All of us winced, and Essee whistled in horror and sympathy.

"I am terribly sorry," Jahno began. "But I do not see—"

If this, then that; but if *this*, then *that*. What had transpired in the temple could not be a mere coincidence. I interrupted our Seeker. "Badu, your former master, is he a particularly fat man? Does he sit on the Gilded Council?"

A cautious look of hope dawned on the acolyte's face. "Yes."

I took a deep breath. "Then I think it is possible that he has something we desire very much."

"It would be a book, or possibly a lengthy scroll," Jahno added, his voice charged with renewed urgency. He untied the cylindrical *khartouka* bead knotted around his throat and passed it to Badu. "Written in these symbols. Did you ever see such a thing in his possession?"

The acolyte studied the clay bead. "Oh, yes. I recognize the symbols. It is a scroll. He keeps it locked in his treasure room, but I have seen it many times when I dusted there."

"So it is confirmed," Tarrok murmured in his deep voice. "But I do not see how that helps us or how our purposes align."

I did. "Badu, this scroll contains the only known copy of the lost prophecies gathered by the scholars of Koronis. Although it is useless in the wrong hands, in the right ones, it may very well be the most valuable item beneath the starless skies. We sought this item in trade and the Gilded Council offered us unacceptable terms. If it were stolen from your former master, would you consider it sufficient revenge?"

Badu knit his brows as he considered my question; at length, he gave a reluctant nod. "It is not the revenge I would have chosen," he admitted. "I wish to see Lord Solinus suffer, as he made my sister suffer. However, it is true that this would humiliate him in the eyes of his peers and the eyes of the realm, and perhaps that is a greater revenge than I could have imagined." He shook his head. "But this theft would be a very, very difficult thing to accomplish."

I felt Pahrkun's wind stirring within me. "Why?"

"There is an outer gate that is locked; the manor is locked; the treasure room is locked," Badu said. "There are guards on duty at all hours. There are even bells on strings stretched across the treasure room itself to sound an alert lest any servant attempt to sneak past the guards in an effort to steal from their master in the small hours of the night, and their position is changed every day at sunset."

I laughed.

He eyed me. "It is not a jest."

"I can open the outer gate for you," Evene said to me. "But I'm *not* going any further."

"Nor should you," I replied. "By all accounts, you're a lousy thief."

"And you a brilliant one in training and theory, my darling." Zariya's gaze was troubled. "But you've never actually done this before, have you? And knowing that we seek the scroll, this Lord Solinus may have doubled his guard or taken other measures you cannot anticipate."

"There are twenty-one members of the Gilded Council," I said. "The fat man has no reason to suspect that we have attained certain knowledge that the scroll is in *his* possession."

"The Gilded Council will be expecting a counteroffer," the acolyte added. "Not an attempted theft."

Zariya shuddered. "Do not think me weak and foolish to confess that the prospect nonetheless terrifies me."

"I would never think such a thing," I assured her. "You are one of the bravest people I know, Zariya. But Brother Saan defied the other elders of the Brotherhood of Pahrkun to ensure that Brother Yarit taught me the arts of the Shahalim Clan, dishonorable though they were reckoned. Brother Saan Saw that it might be necessary. If not for this, then what?"

She gave me a wistful smile of surpassing sweetness. "I fear you are right, of course."

I turned to Badu. "Can you draw a map of the manor and the grounds for me?"

The acolyte unstoppered an inkwell, smoothing a piece of vellum on the table before him. "Most certainly."

FIFTY-TWO

Nightfall.

With the likely arrival of the children of Miasmus only a day in the offing, we dared not delay.

Lord Solinus's estate was situated on a hillside some half a league from the center of the city. A tall wall that stretched from the base of the hill surrounded it, with a single entrance marked by a large pair of fretted iron gates.

I wore close-fitting dark attire, smudges of kohl darkening the glittering marks of Pahrkun that slashed across my cheekbones. In the satchel slung across my torso, I carried a set of lock-picks and a light grappling hook and line. My belt-dagger was thrust into my sash and a thieves' lantern hung from a cord around my waist. I had a handful of pebbles in the pocket of my breeches.

I had committed Badu's map to memory. I felt light, alive, vibrant; though I felt, too, the keen ache of separation from Zariya. Lirios and Evene had accompanied me. Hunkered across the way in a dense copse of trees, we waited for darkness to fall.

Shahal the Dark Moon was full and rising bloody overhead; for once I took it as a good omen. We watched as lamps and candles were extinguished in the estate, windows turning dark one by one until there was only the faintest glow from within. Atop the hillside, I could make out two guards with torches patrolling the grounds, circling the manor in opposite directions. I waited, timing the circuit of their rounds until I was certain of it.

"Now!" I whispered to Evene.

We crossed the cobbled thoroughfare. I could feel her trembling as she laid her hands upon the iron gates. The lock gave way silently, the gates creaking slightly as she pushed them ajar.

I nodded to Evene. "Go." The remainder of our company was already aboard the ship and we had agreed that it would be for the best if Evene were to join them as soon as her part here was done. If I were caught or roused pursuit, it would be safer.

She touched my arm. "Good luck, shadow."

I saluted her and slipped through the gates, pulling them not-quite-closed behind me.

In truth, the wall would have posed little difficulty for me and I would sooner have had Evene's aid in opening a door into the manor, but any risk eliminated was to our benefit. There were tall trees lining the paved approach to Lord Solinus's manor. On silent feet, I darted from shadow to shadow, working my way closer. The acolyte Badu had suggested that the entrance to the servants' quarter would be the easiest one to access and the most lightly guarded course within the manor.

I waited for the guards to cross paths, then stole behind the one patrolling clockwise as the shadow of a sun's dial moves, following him to the rear of the estate. The door to the servants' quarters opened onto a terraced garden carved into the hillside. I waited for the guards to cross paths once more, then assailed the door.

It was locked with a simple padlock. My fingers had not forgotten their skill; I could have picked it in my sleep.

Inside the servants' quarters, it was pitch dark at first. I closed my eyes and breathed slowly, my skin alert to any stirring of air; but no, all was still and silent. When I opened my eyes, I could see that the banked embers in the stoves of the kitchen ahead of me alleviated the darkness.

I crept past the kitchens, placing each foot with care as I had been trained to do, breathing in silence.

The stairway that led from the servants' quarters to the upper stories was steep and narrow, but Badu was right, it was unguarded. I traversed it in darkness, my fingertips brushing the walls with the lightest of touches. I found the first landing by feel. That would be the second story, where the merchant-lord and his family members had their bedchambers.

The treasure room was located on the third story; and there, Badu had as-sured me, a guard would be posted, but his attention would be bent toward the formal staircase, not the servants' approach.

I emerged from the stairwell's darkness into dim light, following the light's source until I came upon it. A single torch burned in a wall sconce outside the treasure room. Beneath it, a lone guard leaned against the wall, his arms folded over his chest, his eyes blinking sleepily. I squatted on my heels in the shadows, rested my chin in my palms, and considered him.

The easiest thing, the simplest and safest thing, would be to kill the guard. It would be a dishonorable killing, for he had done nothing to de-serve it, but it would be in the service of honor beyond honor. It would be in the service of saving the world from the rising darkness.

Ah, but Zariya had asked me not to kill any innocents unless it was ab-solutely necessary. Was it?

The guard looked to be some thirty-odd years of age. Like as not he had a family, perhaps a wife and children like Tarrok; hopefully, they cared for him more than it seemed that Tarrok's had. His eyelids flickered, heavy with the desire for sleep, his chest rose and fell in long, peaceful breaths.

I should kill him.

I didn't, though.

In the end it was both the thought of the quiet disappointment in Zariya's eyes and the notion that killing an innocent servant of the household would be a poor kind of vengeance for Badu's sister that swayed me. Untying the garrote from my hair, I fetched a pebble from my pocket and tossed it past the guard. He startled fully awake with a gasping snort, hand seeking the hilt of his sword as he peered in the direction I'd thrown the pebble. I fell upon him from behind, whipping the garrote over his head and throttling him. I kept up the pressure past the point of unconsciousness, easing him to the floor. When I touched the soft place beneath the joint where his jaw met his throat, I felt a faint pulse yet beating.

The lock on the treasure room door was considerably more difficult to pick than a simple padlock. I knelt and worked at it patiently, hearing Brother Yarit's voice in my memory exhorting me.

At last it gave way.

I pushed the door open a cautious fraction. No bells rang. I glanced back at the guard, who was still unconscious. I was not sure how long he would remain that way. I slid sideways through the door, my skin tense and alert.

In the treasure room, I unshuttered the thieves' lantern. It was a cunning device, holding a single glowing knot of oil-wood in a nest of a particular lichen that was impervious to flame. It did not shed a great deal of light, but it shed enough. Brass bells glinted on the tight strands of thin rope that crisscrossed the treasure room. It gave me a pang of nostalgia for my days of training in the Hall of Proving. If this had been an exercise, Brother Yarit would have scoffed at the ease of undertaking such a challenge without a blindfold.

According to Badu, the scroll was displayed in an open coffer on a pedestal in the southwest corner of the room. I worked my way soundlessly in that direction, crawling under and stepping over the bell-strung ropes, raising the thieves' lantern to examine the contents of every pedestal I encountered.

I found it on the fourth pedestal, a large scroll on two spindles nestled in a velvet-lined case of inlaid wood that appeared to have been made especially for the item. I examined it carefully until I was certain that the unfamiliar characters in which it was written matched the unfamiliar characters on Jahno's *khartouka*. Satisfied, I closed and latched the case and stowed it in my satchel, working my way back through the bell-lines. Shuttering the thieves' lantern, I exited the treasure room.

In the hallway outside, I found the guard I'd garroted was awake. He was sitting splay-legged on the floor, his gaze blurred and uncertain. Until the moment I emerged, I daresay he'd no idea what had befallen him.

Our eyes met.

Panic and anger flashed in his; he tried to cry out, a strangled sound emerging from his bruised throat. Somewhere on a floor below us, I heard a shouted query, followed by the sound of pounding feet on the stairs.

If the entire household was roused, it would be pandemonium. Best not to chance the servants' quarters, I thought, else I'd find myself carving a path with the point of my dagger. I called up my memory of the map Badu had drawn and dashed down the corridor to the south.

One turn to the left, another to the right, then yes; there was a window. Here on the third floor, the shutters weren't even closed. I hopped onto the window ledge and fished the grappling hook from my satchel, sparing a quick glance below to see if either of the guards was patrolling beneath me. Seeing none, I hooked the grapple over the ledge, leaned back and set my feet, then raced backward down three stories of the vertical face of the manor so fast that the friction of the rope abraded my palms.

In the manor there was shouting; lights were being kindled. I flicked the line in an attempt to free my grappling hook and failed. It was a skill that took a certain amount of practice to maintain. A pale, furious face appeared in the window high above me, and I thought it best to abandon the effort.

"Hey!" One of the guards patrolling the grounds raced around the corner of the manor, flames streaming from his torch. "You! Stop!"

This had not gone entirely as I'd hoped.

Unlashing my *heshkrat* from about my waist, I slung it low. It entangled the guard's legs and he fell hard, grunting at the impact. "We've got an intruder!" he shouted, fumbling to free his legs. "Over here!"

Eschewing the gates, I ran down the slope of the estate toward the outer wall, dodging trees, and launched myself in a high leap. My fingertips found purchase and I scrambled inelegantly up the wall, the weight of the satchel strapped across my torso dragging on my right hip.

"To the gates!" the guard shouted behind me. "He's going over the wall! Cut him off!"

Beneath the bloody light of Shahal the Dark Moon, Lirios danced anxiously from foot to foot on the cobbled thoroughfare, his narrow sword glinting in one hand. The short, lightweight cloak he had donned tonight to conceal his distinctive wings fanned around him. "Khai! Here, Khai, here!"

"Hush!" I dropped into the shadows alongside the wall, wincing a bit at the impact. There were guards emerging from the gate; now, I wished I'd let it close behind me. Unlocking it would have delayed them a few more seconds. I pulled the case containing the scroll from my satchel and tossed it to him. "Go!" I said in a fierce whisper. "Sheathe your weapon and *go*, brother! I'll meet you aboard the ship!"

Lirios caught the case with his free hand, and obeyed, darting down the street at an impossible speed. Catching sight of him, the guards shouted and gave chase. Beneath the wall, I crouched unseen in the shadows and smiled to myself with grim satisfaction. Lord Solinus's guards would not catch Lirios; no one could catch the mayfly in flight.

Overhead in the night sky, the Dark Moon loomed, crimson and full.

Behind me, I hoped, the unsavory merchant-lord was awaking to the knowledge that he had been robbed of his most valuable possession, that the treasure upon which he and the Gilded Council had placed too high a price at the uttermost worst time had been stolen from him.

I saluted Shahal. "Thank you, my lady."

It took me the better part of an hour to work my cautious way back to the harbor where our ship was docked, avoiding the despondent guards returning to report their failure.

"Gods be thanked!" Zariya gasped. "Oh, my darling, I was starting to worry terribly."

"I was only being careful," I assured her. "Did we succeed? Does the scroll contain the missing pieces of the prophecy?"

"It looks like it." Jahno's face was suffused with a scholar's wonder at the discovery. "Though I still do not understand how such a thing may be. But I will not know for certain until I have time to decipher it."

Alongside the ship, Aiiiaii raised her dripping head and gave an inquiring trill and Kooie whistled in response. We had determined that if we were successful, it would be best not to wait for dawn to depart Tukkan. A lack of evidence notwithstanding, suspicion would fall on our company. If Lord Solinus swallowed his humiliation and summoned the Orderkeepers to search our ship, we might find the scroll and the *rhamanthus* alike confiscated, and ourselves imprisoned.

There was still the matter of the barricade across the mouth of the harbor, vessels anchored for the night. Aiiiaii and Eeeio took up their bits and drew us within hailing distance of the flagship. Tarrok cupped his hands and shouted—not a thunderclap of a shout, but one loud enough to rouse anyone within. "Ho, Tukkani navy! We seek passage!"

It took a few moments for a sleepy official to emerge and squint at us. "You can wait for daybreak like civilized folk!" he called.

Tarrok folded his arms across his chest and the sea-wyrms raised their heads to imposing heights, sinuous necks swaying, *ooalu* cocoon–enhanced eyes glowing against the blood-dark sky. "It's an emergency." He jerked one thumb at the towering wyrms. "Do you really want to quarrel with *them*?"

The official most assuredly did not. With a considerable amount of grumbling and cursing, the sailors aboard the flagship woke and emerged to hoist the anchor and man the oars, moving the vessel just enough to allow us to pass through the barricade. Eeeio and Aiiiaii arrowed gleefully through the gap, heading for open sea.

Standing in the stern, I watched the lighthouse of Yanakhat recede until it was a single pinprick in the distance. I wondered if that was what the stars in the night sky had looked like. Zariya came to join me, propping herself on her canes in her left hand, linking her right arm with mine. I drew comfort from her presence.

"Do you suppose that's what a star looks like?" she mused.

"I was just wondering the same thing," I said. "Zariya . . . we don't know exactly where we're going, do we?"

"No." She shook her head. "Toward the west, toward Miasmus. Toward death and destiny, or perhaps both. We'll know more once Jahno has the chance to decipher the scroll." She paused. "Were you able to procure it without killing anyone?"

"Yes." I didn't tell her that it had resulted in discovery and pursuit, as well as the loss of my grappling hook and *heshkrat*. The decision had been mine and I would take ownership of it.

"I'm glad." Zariya rested her head on my shoulder. "The scroll was the most important thing, but killing some poor guard who was only doing his duty would have been rather contrary to the notion of avenging an innocent woman."

"I thought so, too," I said. "I'm only sorry we didn't have a chance to thumb our noses at this Lord Solinus and the Gilded Council on Badu's behalf. It would have made his revenge a great deal more satisfying."

"Oh, but we did." She smiled against my shoulder. "You recall the litter-bearer who so wisely, as it transpired, advised us in the temple? I paid him to deliver a missive to the Gilded Council in the morning once he confirms our ship has sailed. Don't worry, I didn't name the acolyte as an accomplice," she added. "I only said that Galdano the Shrewd himself provided us the knowledge we required in exchange for the offering they refused in trade, and if they have an issue with *that* bargain, they may take it up with the god himself."

I laughed. "You've an unexpected knack for twisting the knife."

Zariya squeezed my arm, then released it. "Well, I certainly saw enough of it in the women's quarter to know how it's done, my darling." Her voice took on a more somber note. "You know it's quite possible none of this will make any difference in a matter of months?"

"I know."

We watched the lone point of light on the horizon vanish from sight. I was grateful to have succeeded, grateful that there was no innocent blood on my hands tonight, and grateful beyond telling for Zariya's warm presence beside me; yet at the same time, a deep sense of foreboding filled me. We were sailing into the unknown, where death or destiny awaited us. Whether we triumphed or failed, either way, the world would be forever changed.

That night I dreamed of stars.

FIFTY-THREE

When I awoke the following morning, Jahno was already hard at work translating the scroll and Zariya assisting him, jotting the notes in his journal as he murmured to her. I could not help but notice again how very well suited they were to each other, how much she enjoyed working with him; now, the thought was like a dagger to my heart. But this was no time to dwell on such matters, so I set the thought aside.

While breaking my fast, I learned that the company had decided we would set a course for the western isle of Kerreman, the realm reported to be yet holding out against the army of Miasmus. There we would learn what we might.

I was glad, for it meant there was a chance of reconnecting with Vironesh, assuming my mentor yet lived.

Depending on what Jahno learned from the scroll, depending on the news we garnered from any ships we encountered on the way—for no longer would we seek to avoid others, but actively engage them—our course might change. But at least for now, it was set.

Once I had eaten, Tarrok cleared his throat and made an announcement. "My brothers and sisters, if you would hear it, I am ready to share with you what I learned from my countrymen."

Not looking up from the scroll, Jahno flipped a hand at him. "Yah, tell us."

"The matter deserves your full attention, Seeker," Tarrok said in quiet reproach. "Surely reality has as much bearing on the challenges we face as does prophecy?" Chastened, Jahno returned the scroll to its case, while

Zariya closed the journal and stoppered her inkwell. "The sea-wyrms ought to hear it, too."

Kooie whistled to Eeeio and Aiiiaii, who abandoned the tow-lines and came to join us, leaning their great jaws on the railings on either side of the drifting ship, stilling it with their weight.

Tarrok folded his hands in his lap. "The risen dead come from the sea, dragging themselves ashore. They require neither food nor sleep, and there is no obstacle that can stop them for long. They slaughter all that lies in their path, and fight onward despite receiving wounds that would kill a mortal being. They fall only when their heads have been severed from their bodies. They are human and inhuman alike, and all of them are *changed,* for they have not succumbed to bloat and decay, but have been hardened and preserved, like corpses in a peat bog. Creatures that should not be able to walk on land have sprouted limbs that allow them to do so." He took a deep breath, rubbed his eyes with the heels of his hands, then continued grimly. "And where the army of the risen dead treads, the earth itself dies beneath their feet. Grass withers, trees shed their leaves and become barren. Such creatures that attempt to graze the land, sheep and cattle, perish; such creatures as feed upon their fallen corpses perish. Luhdo the Loud could not stand against them. Trask was a land of sweeping moors and great forests," he added. "Now it is a dead, barren place haunted by the mournful cries of its god."

We sat in silence for a moment.

"How are we to fight against such an enemy?" Evene asked at length in a tone of disbelieving wonder.

"The answer lies in the Scattered Prophecy," Jahno said doggedly. "And we *will* find it."

I prayed it was so.

We sailed onward.

Deciphering the prophecy was a slow, painstaking process, and much of the information Jahno and Zariya translated proved redundant. Jahno spent a great deal of time spinning his *khartouka* and muttering to himself; Zariya aided him with tireless patience. I sparred with Lirios, wishing we faced an enemy I could simply kill. The mayfly's swordsmanship continued to improve.

Some five days after our flight from Tukkan, we encountered a vast fleet of all manner of ships escorted by the coursers of Obid, distinctive black-and-white-striped sails bobbing against the horizon. The ships rode low in the water under the weight of human cargo they carried.

This time, it was not Traskans.

"Kerreman has fallen," the flagship's captain responded wearily to our hail. "Now the armies of Miasmus assail Yaltha. We're just trying to save whomever we might. This is no time for piracy, wyrm-raiders. If you've any sense, you'll turn back and flee toward the east."

Hollow-eyed refugees nodded in agreement.

"What of Vironesh the purple man?" I called. "Does he yet live to fight against them?"

The captain nodded and pointed. "In Yaltha, yes, assisting with the evacuation effort there."

We readjusted our course.

On the seventh day, Jahno and Zariya's efforts bore fruit.

The Koronian summoned us to a meeting. He was fairly vibrating with the excitement of his discovery, silvery eyes gleaming. "Yah, so, we have an answer!" he said triumphantly, one finger tracing the text. "Only that, too, is a riddle, eh? So let us try to solve it. Fire and wind, life and death. This portion of the Scattered Prophecy says that the defenders of the four quarters will carry a drop of ichor shed by the nameless god to the end of the world; and this Miasmus must swallow, for it is the seed of ending that is to be ignited by the seeds of beginning and bring about a new order." He frowned at the scroll. "The seed of beginning is surely the *rhamanthus*, yah? It must be so. But what is the seed of ending? I can think of no nameless god."

My skin prickled; I touched the back of my neck.

"What of the Lone Tree of the Barren Isle?" I whispered. "I've never heard it called by a proper name."

"Nor have I," Evene agreed. "And the Barren Isle lies near enough to Drogalia that nigh every man, woman, and child in the realm has dreamed of being lucky enough to harvest a teardrop of everlasting amber from the Lone Tree." She gave a short laugh of despair. "And once every one hundred years, someone is. By all the fallen stars, Seeker! You might as well ask us to pluck one of the moons from the sky."

"Not quite," Zariya murmured. "My brother the collector actually had such an item in his possession, but it was stolen from him . . . to think it was so near! Do you suppose it *could* be what the prophecy means?"

"It's possible," Jahno said reluctantly. "One might consider the sap of the Lone Tree to be the ichor that flows in its veins, and not a teardrop at all, as people have named it. But if that is true, Evene is right, too; at this moment, such a thing is as unobtainable as the moon."

I drew a shaking breath, filled with a strange mixture of elation and terror. "That's not true," I whispered. "I have one."

Everyone stared at me.

"What?" Zariya's voice held a tone I had never heard before, a tone like a whip-crack. She stared at me as though I had become a stranger to her.

"I'm sorry." My throat felt too tight; I swallowed with an effort. "I'm so very sorry, Zariya. I meant to tell you. I meant to tell you a hundred times. I never wanted to keep a secret from you. But at first, I thought it was too dangerous; I only wanted to protect you from the knowledge. You see, it *is* your brother's teardrop, the one that once belonged to a courtesan-queen of Barakhar."

"The one that was stolen," she asked in a flat voice. "How do you come to possess it?"

I closed my eyes briefly. "Brother Yarit had a vision. He Saw that I would need it. He wasn't sure why; he thought to keep my woman's courses at bay, perhaps. Or perhaps he did See the truth and withheld the knowledge from me lest it upset the balance of fate. One never knows with the Seer. At any rate, he had a member of the Shahalim Clan steal it for me."

Lirios rustled his wings. "But this is *good* news, is it not?" he asked plaintively. "Why are you so angry, my queen?"

"I broke her trust," I said to him, knowing he couldn't begin to understand what a betrayal that was between us, Sun-Blessed and shadow. "I'm sorry," I said again to Zariya. "I meant to tell you, I truly did. But Brother Yarit . . . he told me to do my best to forget about it entirely lest I give myself away, and I did just that. For days on end, weeks at a time, I never thought of it."

"And yet when you did, you chose not to mention it to me," she observed. "Long after the knowledge posed any threat."

"It was never the right time," I murmured. "And then the moment would pass, and I put it out of my thoughts."

Zariya raised her eyebrows at me. "Where have you been hiding this infamous item all this time, my darling?"

"Here." I touched the back of my neck. "It was sewn into my flesh when I was thirteen years of age."

At that, she gave a faint shudder. "I see." She was silent for a moment. "Well, in light of this discovery, I think we may consider this particular riddle solved, Seeker," she said to Jahno. "And it *is* good news, wondrous news. I am very well aware that the fate of the world might hang upon it." To me, she said, "I am not angry, Khai, but I am hurt. From the moment we laid eyes upon each other, my soul's twin, you have been the one person I trusted with every part of my being; and growing up in the House of the Ageless, that was no small thing. So you will forgive me that I cannot yet rejoice to learn that you kept such a grave secret from me."

I had no excuses. All I could do was bow my head in acquiescence.

It made for a tense mood aboard the ship for the next few days, and Zariya's coolness toward me made my heart ache. I should have entrusted her with the knowledge from the beginning; trusted her to be strong and clever enough to ensure no whisper of it passed her lips. But that had been a different time, when talk of darkness rising in the west was a pure abstraction and talk of prophecy an idle daydream, far from the increasingly grim reality we faced.

That reality was brought home to us when we reached the shores of Yaltha.

There had been fierce debate about the wisdom of making landfall there. Jahno had unlocked another piece of the prophecy and was afire with eagerness to pursue it—we knew now how we were meant to seek Miasmus and what we were to do. Tarrok, mired in hopelessness, agreed for his own reasons. Evene was adamantly in favor of anything that delayed the inevitable confrontation, and I was equally insistent in my desire to locate Vironesh and get his counsel.

"I understand that this man was your mentor, but he's just one man," Tarrok said to me in a tone that bordered on dismissive. "What difference can one man's counsel make?"

"Vironesh is the greatest warrior of his generation; one of the greatest warriors of any generation," I pointed out. "And he's actually spent these past months fighting the armies of Miasmus. If these risen creatures have weaknesses I may exploit, he will know them. His counsel may prove invaluable."

"I agree with Khai," Zariya said unexpectedly; I would have thought she would side with Jahno. She gave me a sidelong glance. "Khai is the only one among us who has trained from birth to fight this battle."

Yaltha was a small island with a single large settlement on a good-sized harbor. We had passed refugees on our journey there and more were amassing. Later, we would learn that these were the inland dwellers from smallholds and hamlets, the last to be evacuated. The harbormaster ordered us to turn back, disgusted by our presumed purpose and so harried he couldn't even summon fear at the sight of the sea-wyrms.

"Are you fools?" he shouted at us. "We're fleeing for our lives here! Don't waste our time!"

"We mean no harm," I assured him. "We are not pirates come to prey on refugees. We come seeking the coursers of Obid and a warrior who fights among them; Vironesh, the purple man."

"Why?" The harbormaster paused and shook his head. "You know, I don't care. Dock on the northern quay and stay out of my way." He pointed toward the west. "The city's on the verge of falling. You'll find the allied forces fighting to hold a trench beyond the outer wall."

We docked the ship and disembarked. Although I had it in mind to go alone, Zariya insisted on accompanying me. "I know it will slow our progress, but I must see these creatures for myself." She touched the pouch of *rhamanthus* seeds that now hung from her waist; not the whole of our remaining store, but a goodly arsenal. "And remember, I may be our greatest weapon against them."

Mindful of my recent betrayal, I did not attempt to dissuade her. Once that was determined, nothing would do but that Lirios come, too. The others chose to remain with the ship. Tarrok's thunderclap was a formidable weapon in its own right, but in a pitched battle, it would harm friend as well as foe.

The city was largely deserted, shops and inns and trade-stalls stripped of goods. A thin stream of refugees trickled through the streets toward the harbor, all of them looking stunned and numb, clutching their worldly goods. Here and there, abandoned livestock and livery-horses wandered. I caught the bridle of a placid cart-horse, procuring transportation for Zariya. She accepted it without comment, refusing assistance to clamber awkwardly into the cart. The horse plodded through the city with the same numb obedience as in the faces of the fleeing refugees.

Outside the western gates of the city walls, we could hear the sound of battle raging, but not a battle such as I had ever imagined. In addition to the shouting and clashing of weapons, there were inhuman sounds—deep roars, high-pitched squeals, and unholy gnashing and clicking sounds.

At the gates, a pair of soldiers so filthy I couldn't begin to guess their origin were urging refugees to pass through swiftly and continue to the harbor. They looked at us in disbelief as we approached and sought passage toward the battleground.

"Are you out of your fucking minds?" one shouted at us. "Get out of here!"

Holding to the cart's railing with her left hand, Zariya had her head high. "We are the defenders of the four quarters," she announced, a claim that would have sounded ridiculous had she not reached into her pouch and drawn forth a *rhamanthus* seed. The golden traceries on her right hand and arm flamed to life as she held it aloft, and lightning crackled around her fist. "And we are here to fight against the darkness that rises in the west."

The soldiers stared, mouths agape.

"We seek Vironesh," I added. "Let us pass. We can aid you in this battle." They did.

Beyond the gates was a scene out of a nightmare. A vast trench had been dug before the wall, spanned by a lone bridge of knotted rope. The last handful of refugees struggled to cross it, and a line of defenders fought to allow them the chance to do so. The army against which they fought . . .

Tarrok's secondhand description had not done justice to the army of the risen and returned. At first glance, it seemed a vast sea of darkness pressing forward. My mind refused to see its parts; then it began to pick out details, and I nearly wished it hadn't. There were things that had been men, once; blackened, leathery, skeletal things with greenish corpse-light glowing in the empty sockets of their eyes, obsidian blades clutched in their hands. There were things that had swum in the sea—fish, eels, dolphins—that had sprouted segmented legs; there were enormous crabs and lobsters scuttling across the ground and waving calcified black pincers.

There were things I could not name, things from the deepest trenches of the ocean, things with round, grasping mouths frilled with feelers. There was a winged shark that waddled on thickset legs, a gleaming black carapace armoring its torso. It stood taller than a grown man, its maw lashing from side to side, its teeth red with blood.

"Oh, dear gods," Zariya whispered in horror.

It seemed impossible that a mortal army could stand against these creatures; and yet they were attempting it, holding a line of defense that the last of the refugees might cross the trench.

Although the defenders had their backs to us, I could pick out Vironesh by his bulk and his fighting style; unhurried, deliberate, and deceptively deadly. He stood before the rope bridge, his swirling blade carving out a space around him.

The last of the refugees scrambled across the wavering bridge on wobbling legs, a mother dragging a child by the arm.

"Fall back!" a commander on the far side of the trench shouted. "Yalthans, fall back and flee!"

They tried.

The undead army of Miasmus surged forward. I saw the legged and winged shark-thing making for Vironesh, and my palms itched; I longed to race across the bridge and join the fray, to fight alongside my mentor. But no, I did not feel the rush of Pahrkun's wind rising in me.

This was not my fight, not yet.

"Khai!" Lirios cried, his wings humming. "What do we do, Khai? How do we aid them?"

I looked up at Zariya in the cart. "Unleash the lightning. Let us see if it will kill these undead creatures."

She opened her clenched fist.

Blue-white lightning crackled forth, arcing across the trench, arcing across the heads of the mortal soldiers. Shrieks and groans and wails of fury arose from the vanguard of the army of Miasmus.

Shouting wildly, the mortal soldiers rushed across the swaying rope bridge. The soldiers at the gate hustled the refugees through, clearing a path for the retreating army. On the far side of the trench, Vironesh stood his ground, the strokes of his weapons slowing. He was growing weary.

The armies of Miasmus plowed forward with the legged and winged shark-thing leading the charge.

"Again," I murmured to Zariya.

She nodded without looking at me. Again and again and again, Zariya rained lightning down upon the armies of the risen and returned, leaving the smallest of them scorched and dead and stinking, and the larger injured and held in abeyance. It was not enough to defeat them—no, nowhere near—but it was enough to safeguard a retreat. Spent *rhamanthus* seeds dropped like pebbles from her hand, rattling against the bottom of the cart.

On the far side of the trench, Vironesh fought his way backward on the rope bridge, the last man standing. Once the bridge was clear, with two deft strokes of his *yakhan,* he cut through the support lines.

Lirios gasped.

The rope bridge gave way, swinging violently across the deep trench. His sword in his right hand, Vironesh clung to the bridge with his left, holding on for dear life as it struck the near side of the trench. I heard my mentor grunt at the impact, then begin the difficult task of dragging his exhausted body up the length of knotted net.

I raced to aid him, leaning over to grab his wrists, bracing myself and pulling hard. Vironesh grunted his thanks, not glancing at me until I'd succeeded in hauling him to safety. His eyes widened and he covered his mouth with his free hand. "Khai!" Tears glistened in his eyes, something I'd never thought to see. "By all the fallen stars! Is it true?"

I saluted him. "Yes, brother."

Vironesh's gaze moved to Zariya, still standing in the cart, lightning wreathing her upraised fist as she kept a watchful eye on the forces arrayed on the far side of the trench. She looked at once terribly young, and yet age-less. Vironesh approached her and dropped heavily to one knee. "Your Highness," he said humbly. "I know now that you *are* the Sun-Blessed war-rior who was foretold. Forgive me my disbelief."

Not taking her gaze from the army of the risen dead, Zariya inclined her head to him. "Thank you, my darling. I can't honestly say I blame you for it."

FIFTY-FOUR

We stayed outside the city gates long enough for the mortal army to make their retreat. The risen dead amassed at a distance, wary of Zariya's lightning.

"They are relentless," Vironesh warned us. "The trench will not stop them for long once we cease to guard it. If we took the battle to them, do you have the capacity to destroy them, Your Highness?"

"I fear not," Zariya said with regret. "There are not sufficient *rhamanthus* seeds to destroy an army this vast; and that is not the task with which the defenders of the four quarters are charged by the Scattered Prophecy."

"Our quarry is Miasmus itself," I added. "But I seek your counsel in killing the risen dead, for the prophecy tells us that we shall have to fight our way through those left behind to guard their creator."

"Then I will come with you," Vironesh said simply.

"What of the coursers of Obid?" I inquired.

"They are doing their part to stem the tide," he said. "But they are fighting a losing battle. Trask has fallen. Kerreman has fallen. Yaltha will fall before Zar the Sun sets on this day, for once the armies of Miasmus cross the trench, the wall will not hold them. And then they will move onward to the next isle, and the next and the next, until there is nothing left." He shook his head. "No. I will accompany you. I should have kept my word and returned to Zarkhoum as soon as I learned what was happening."

If this, then that, but if *this*, then *that*.

"You would have found us long gone," I said. "Fighting alongside the coursers was the right choice."

We retreated through the city, the streets empty save for the wandering livestock, sheep and cattle lowing plaintively. In the harbor, human refugees were crowding onto ships and rowboats that wallowed low in the water. I helped Zariya descend from the cart and unhitched the horse from its traces. It gazed at us with pricked ears and plaintive eyes.

"It's going to die, isn't it?" Zariya murmured. "Like every living creature left behind here."

I nodded. "I'm afraid so. Those not slain will starve."

"Oh, Khai!" Her eyes were bright with tears. "It's so very terrible. How are we supposed to bear this?"

"I don't know," I admitted.

She took a deep, shuddering breath. "Well, we must try."

There in the harbor, Vironesh parted ways with the coursers of Obid. While the coursers regretted the loss of his fighting skills, his addition to our company was not met with universal acclaim.

Jahno in particular was troubled. "Nothing in the Scattered Prophecy speaks of *two* shadows," he said fretfully.

"Nothing speaks against it, either," Zariya reminded him.

"Yah, but—"

Essee whistled forcefully, her fingers signing.

I watched her carefully, translating for Vironesh's benefit. "She says that there is nothing in the prophecy that speaks of numbers. Six of the Elehuddin set forth on this quest; four remain. I do not expect to survive. None of us should. Who are we to refuse this warrior who seeks to aid us?"

The Seeker sighed, relented, and saluted her with respect. "As you say, nest-mother. Let it be so."

By the time we set sail, Yaltha had fallen; the armies of the risen and returned had swarmed over the walls. We heard the brief screams or lowing cries of abandoned livestock slaughtered in their path. We saw the vast army of undead creatures pour into the harbor, plunging into its waters in pursuit of the refugee fleet, the rising dark spreading ever eastward.

Us, they did not pursue.

Westward lay our course; westward, ever westward, a lonely ship beating its way against the tide of fate.

Two days after we departed Yaltha's shores, a grave new problem arose: The seas were dying. At first, we saw a few dead fish and sea creatures here and there floating atop the ocean, but the farther westward we sailed, the more we saw, until the air stank with their effluence. I suppose it shouldn't have come as a surprise. If the passage of the armies of Miasmus caused the land to fall barren, it stood to reason that the same would hold true of the sea. It was only that it took longer due to the vastness of the sea and the greater complexity of the system of food and prey; a system that, alas, included all of us. We dared eat nothing save our small store of dried fish. The *ooalu* vines withered, the fruit rotted and had to be thrown overboard. The fuzzy bodies and pale papery wings of *ooalu* moths littered the floor of the hold.

It was the worst for the sea-wyrms, who could not avoid contact with the tainted sea and whose massive bodies and prodigious expenditure of energy required vast amounts of food. Although Eeeio and Aiiiaii carried on valiantly, their strength began to flag visibly as their scales lost their luster, growing dull and flaky. We gave them the last of the dried fish, a paltry amount compared to what they required. Jahno and the Elehuddin consulted maps in the charthouse in low, worried voices.

If our ship had been an ordinary vessel, we would simply have sent the wyrms back toward unspoiled seas and sailed onward without their aid, but such was the design of the ship that it was dependent on them. Without the sea-wyrms, it sailed poorly and slowly, and Jahno reluctantly concluded that we would starve to death before we reached Miasmus.

The thought that we could come so close to our goal and fail filled me with helpless anger.

We had gone two days without food and were not yet in sight of Kerreman, all of us listless and hungry, the sea-wyrms swimming sluggishly through floating shoals of dead fish at a fraction of their usual speed, when Jahno reached a decision.

"It is time to breach the cask of Ishfahel's gift," he announced. "As the Seeker, I say that our hour of greatest need is upon us."

A spark of hope kindled in my breast. We hauled the marked water cask from the hold and lashed it in place, prying the lid loose. The water within gleamed in the incongruous sunlight and a sweet, clean odor rose from it, dispelling the omnipresent stink of dead fish.

Kooie clicked and pointed in the direction of the sea-wyrms. "Yah," Jahno agreed, whistling them over. "Eeeio and Aiiiaii should drink first."

It was painful to see how slowly the sea-wyrms moved through the water, how difficult it was for them to lift their heads to rest their long chins on the ship's railings, their iridescent eyes filmy.

"Their courage and determination shames me," Zariya murmured beside me.

"It shames us all," Vironesh said quietly.

Jahno filled a dipper. Careful not to spill a drop, he approached Aiiiaii, who opened her mighty jaws. He poured the dipperful of water into her mouth, and she tilted her head on her sinuous neck and swallowed. The transformation was instantaneous; Aiiiaii's blue-green scales turned bright and glistening, and the dim clouds were dispelled from her eyes. She let out a gleeful trill and plunged through the waves, the vast length of her body undulating with exuberant energy.

I offered a silent salute of thanks to Ishfahel the Gentle Rain.

Eeeio drank; we all drank. A dipperful for each of the wyrms, a sparing sip for the humans.

A sip was enough.

I felt my body come alive, no longer hoarding its resources, renewed strength coursing through my veins; I saw the same restored vibrancy reflected in the bright eyes of my companions.

We sailed onward through the dying seas, doling out Ishfahel's water parsimoniously.

We passed the isle of Kerreman, all barren shores and high cliffs. There Johina the Mirthful had held aegis, and we saw the goddess as we passed, or what the goddess had become in the aftermath of the armies of Miasmus. According to Zariya and Jahno, Liko of Koronis had described her as a joyous figure, always in motion, feet dancing, eyes sparkling, laughter on her lips; her skirts a blanket of flowers, a crown of blossoming branches atop her head, birds nesting and singing amongst them.

No longer.

The figure we saw was silent and somber, sitting cross-legged atop a cliff, its head crowned with dead branches. I might have thought it a statue had Johina the Mirthful not acknowledged us as we sailed past, slow hands rising in a salute, fingers forming the shape of a blossom.

The children of heaven themselves were depending on us to prevent darkness from swallowing the world.

It was a terrifying truth.

Jahno finished the work of translating the scroll. The Scattered Prophecy remained incomplete, for there were pieces of the puzzle yet missing, but we had as many as the Koronian scholars had assembled over the centuries. We knew that Miasmus dwelled within the hollow of a volcano, its entrance sealed by a great boulder. That was the rock that Tarrok was to cleave, and the final way that Evene was to open. We knew that an army of the risen dead awaited us, and that my blades—and now Vironesh's—were meant to scythe through them. We knew Miasmus must be enticed to swallow the seed of ending—the Barren Teardrop, the blood of the nameless god—which Zariya must ignite with the seeds of beginning.

How many seeds, we did not know, and the rate at which the *rhamanthus* seeds dwindled while being used in battle was alarming. Nor did we know what form Miasmus took, nor what would happen if we succeeded in restoring Miasmus to the heavens and ushering in a new order.

To the frustration of Lirios, his role in the Scattered Prophecy remained a mystery, for none of the pieces explained what the Quick was meant to do.

We passed the isle of Trask, every bit as barren and dead as Kerreman, the terrible cries of the unseen Luhdo the Loud echoing over the empty hills.

And then there were only the dying seas between us and our final destination.

It was a strange time. Behind us, the army of the risen and returned was spreading death and destruction in its wake, but our company was alone at the end of the world, sailing toward an unknown fate. Ishfahel's gift continued to sustain us, and the longer we subsisted on nothing but the Gentle Rain's water, the more I felt at once hollowed out and filled with a peculiar lightness and brightness, as though radiance as well as blood flowed in my veins.

I should have thought that Vironesh and I would spend a great deal of time sparring in those final days, honing our skills to a fine edge; and yet, neither of us were inclined to do so.

Vironesh shared with me—and with all of us, for every hand capable of wielding a blade would be needed—the knowledge he had gained in fighting the risen dead. They fought without strategy or regard to their own safety, weaknesses that could be exploited so long as one remembered that an injury that would kill a mortal foe was a mere inconvenience to them. Many of them were slow to react, relying on their own inexorable forward momentum and terrifying numbers. Contrary to what the Traskan refugees had told Tarrok, it was not necessary to behead them to slay them, merely to sever their spines. Once slain, they did not rise again. Unlike the sea-spiders, the risen and returned were not capable of inhabiting and animating their mortal victims.

It was a small mercy.

On the day that we sailed past Trask, Vironesh cut the Barren Teardrop from my flesh, reckoning that it would be best if I had a few days to heal.

"Such a small thing on which to hinge the fate of the world," Zariya murmured, seeing the seed of ending glowing amber and bloody in the palm of my hand. "I'm sorry I was so angry at you, my darling."

"You said you weren't angry," I reminded her. "Only hurt."

Her lips curved in a faint smile. "I may have lied a bit."

I wished . . .

I wished so many things. All of us did. During those final days, we made our collective peace with death and shared the hopes and dreams of what we wished we might do if we survived.

"I would like to show you the desert in springtime with all the flowers blooming," I said to Zariya.

"I would like to see it, my heart," she said.

Tarrok wished to see his wife and his twin sons, praying that somehow they had survived the fall of Trask.

Kooie wished to sleep without nightmares.

Jahno wished to see a Barakhan dancer perform.

Everyone had wishes. The sea-wyrms wished to lay a clutch of eggs and raise a family together.

Lirios wished to be mated.

Tliksee wished to dive deep into clean seawater and eat fresh fish until his belly was near to bursting.

Essee wished for a world in which kindness prevailed over cruelty and bloodshed was unnecessary.

Vironesh confessed in a low voice that he wished to find redemption and a final chance at attaining honor beyond honor.

Evene wished to learn to play the lute, a surprising choice that she blushed upon admitting.

I kept my truest, deepest wish to myself, for I wished to tell Zariya that I loved her with all my being, that I was a fool for not understanding it sooner. At the end of the world, it did not matter, or so I told myself.

Of death itself, we did not speak. The specter was with us always. The hopes and dreams and simple small pleasures of which we spoke seemed so very distant, like something from another lifetime, memories that brought us comfort in the sharing. Some days we went for hours at a time without speaking, each of us occupied with our private thoughts. Some days it seemed as though we were caught in a never-ending dream; that there had never been anything but this, sailing across the dying seas on an endless quest, and never would be.

It wasn't true, of course. A week's time after we had sailed past Trask, the isle of Miasmus came into view on the horizon. We gathered in the prow of the ship to observe it. At a distance, the isle was a dark smudge with a smoking peak at its center, casually darkening the skies. Now I felt the first stirrings of Pahrkun's wind rising within me, a harbinger of the battle to come.

"This is it!" Jahno said in a reverent voice. "We have reached the farthest west."

That day we drew near enough to ensure that we could anchor at a safe distance, yet make landfall the following morning.

Under the starless night skies, we could make out glowing rifts in the isle's rocky surface. The scent of ash and sulfur hung in the air, and not even the sweet, clean aroma of Ishfahel's water could dispel it.

We took turns standing watch that night, unsure if the army of the risen dead had the capacity to go on the offensive and take the battle to us. It seemed it was not so. The isle of Miasmus awaited us, silent and smoldering. The ship's hold was dark and unwelcoming without the gentle glow of the *ooalu* moths flitting from vine to vine, and it stank of rotting vegetation; nonetheless, I slept soundly after my watch, my body readying itself for the coming battle.

At dawn, Kooie, who had stood the last watch, poked his head into the hatch, tendrils stirring, and whistled us on deck.

Zariya hung back to let the others precede and I waited patiently behind her. Once the remainder of our company had climbed the ladder and exited the hold, she handed me her canes and pulled herself up the first rung, her arms grown strong and sinewy by dint of long effort and practice.

I tucked her canes under one arm and prepared to follow, but Zariya paused and turned back toward me, holding herself in place with her left hand. Her lustrous eyes shone with purpose and her delicate features were set with determination. "Khai, my darling, come here."

Perplexed, I obeyed.

With her free hand, Zariya clasped the back of my head, fingers sinking into my hair.

She kissed me, and there was nothing sweet about it. It was hard and searing and urgent and possessive; the press of her soft lips against mine, the thrust of her darting tongue into my mouth. It sent a bolt of desire through my body as galvanizing as the lightning that forked from her fist.

I gasped when Zariya released me, my heart thudding against my ribcage.

"I am *not* venturing into near-certain death without kissing you properly at least once," she said in a fierce whisper. "And if by some miracle we survive, I intend to do a great deal more."

A wild laugh escaped me.

Zariya raised her brows at me. "Does that amuse you, my shadow?"

"No." I shook my head. "No. But I thought, you and Jahno . . . you are so well suited."

"I am fond of Jahno," she said. "And if, again, by some miracle we survive this undertaking, I may very well ask him to father my children. But I am not in *love* with Jahno. Only you. Only and always you." She studied me. "Have you anything to say?"

I gazed at her. "Just that I love you with all my heart and soul, but it is only since Papa-ka-hondras that I truly understood it."

Zariya smiled. "Good. Let this be the end to any dishonesty between us, my darling."

I climbed after her in a daze.

Above deck, Jahno was ladling out dippers of water. This time, all of us drank deep, including the sea-wyrms.

I touched my fingers to my lips, still feeling the hot, urgent press of Zariya's lips against them.

I felt Pahrkun's wind rising in me, rising and rising. I would channel it. I would cut down the army of the risen dead, my weapons like a scythe in a field of wheat.

Honor beyond honor.

And here at the end of the world . . . love.

Essee uttered a sharp, shrill trill and Eeeio and Aiiiaii took up their bits, towing our ship toward shore.

Closer and closer we drew toward the isle of Miasmus, until we could make out the restless figures of the army of the risen dead awaiting us. Jahno consulted with Vironesh on the best place to attempt to make landfall, both of them arguing and pointing.

That was when the dying sea erupted.

It was a sea-wyrm larger than either Eeeio or Aiiiaii, and like all of the creatures that Miasmus the Risen Maw spat forth, it had been transformed. Its scales were black and dull, and the ridge of fins that ran the length of its neck was in tatters. A sickly green light glowed in the hollow sockets of its eyes. Here and there chunks of flesh were missing and white bones showed in the ragged wounds; but it was filled with all the animating force of Miasmus, and it was coming straight for our vessel, jaws parted in a silent hiss.

After the uneventful night that had passed, it caught us unprepared, all of us having come to trust that the battle would begin on land.

Eeeio and Aiiiaii dropped the tow-lines, heads rearing. Zariya fumbled for a handful of *rhamanthus* seeds.

The black wyrm dove deep, plunging beneath the ship.

If it got its coils around the ship, we were doomed before the battle even began. I raced to the stern, drawing my weapons, and leapt atop the railing, balancing there. The black wyrm surfaced, coiling in on itself. Its tail lashed out in an effort to swat me loose. I jumped high, high enough to let it pass beneath me, slashing downward as it did so, the blade of my *yakhan* glancing off its hardened scales. I caught myself and balanced, the ship swaying on the waves of the wyrm's passage.

The air was filled with whistles and trills. I ignored them, waiting for the black wyrm to make a second pass.

Instead it surfaced on the port side of the ship, its head looming high, preparing to lunge across our width.

With a fierce shout, Zariya unleashed the lightning. The black wyrm's scales were scorched and singed, but it was undeterred; not by one strike, not by two, not by three, and I realized it could sink us before it would succumb to the lightning.

But then Eeeio was there, launching himself at the black wyrm, his massive jaws closing around its coiled midsection.

"The sea-wyrms say to stay out of it, Khai!" Jahno was shouting at me. "This is their fight!"

I had no choice. Eeeio dragged the black wyrm away from the ship; twisting its sinuous neck, the wyrm savaged him in turn. Aiiiaii darted into the fray, the entire length of her body undulating frantically. In the desert of Zarkhoum, I had seen nests of serpents intertwining until I could not tell where one ended and another began. In the desert of the dying seas, the sea-wyrms' battle was a similar sight writ large, tangled coils churning water that began to run red with Eeeio's blood.

"I can't see where to strike!" Zariya said in frustration, impotent sparks crackling from her hand.

"They're too knotted up," Jahno said soberly. "Strike one and you'll harm all three."

All we could do was watch in horror.

At last Aiiiaii succeeded in entangling the black wyrm's jaws in her coils. With an impossible effort, Eeeio lifted his head, the undead wyrm's midsection still clamped between his own jaws. Arching his powerful neck, he brought his head down hard, crashing against the surface of the sea, severing the creature's spine.

It sank beneath the waves.

Eeeio swam painfully over to the ship, resting his chin on the railing. The nictitating membranes that covered his eyes were closed, and blood streamed from the myriad gouges that rent his flesh, too many and too deep to hope they were not mortal. Aiiiaii crooned and stroked her chin along the length of his ridge.

There would be no clutch of nestlings for them to raise. My eyes stung with hot tears, but cold anger rose within me.

"She says rest well, great warrior," Jahno murmured. "You have made Dulumu the Deep proud today."

Eeeio sighed, his chin sliding from the railing, the shining length of his body slipping beneath the waves.

Aiiiaii and the Elehuddin keened in grief.

"I hope you are planning on killing a great many of those gods-bedamned undead creatures today, shadow," Evene said to me, her voice thick.

My teeth were clenched so tight that my jaw ached. "I am."

FIFTY-FIVE

Aiiiaii towed us toward the isle alone.

For as much as we had made our peace with death, it was different now that one of our number had died, the first casualty our company had suffered since Papa-ka-hondras. Now the final battle had truly begun.

On the shore, the army of the risen dead awaited us. There were at least a thousand of them, human and inhuman, armed with blades of obsidian or such weapons as nature had gifted them.

There were eleven of us to stand against them.

It seemed that such a thing must be impossible; and yet we were no ordinary mortals. We were the defenders of the four quarters, Sun-Blessed and Shadow and Seeker, the Thunderclap and the Opener of Ways, the Quick. We carried wind and fire, the seeds of life and death.

And we did not have to defeat the entire undead army, only fight our way through them to gain Miasmus.

The isle of Miasmus was not large. I gauged the smoldering mountain at its center to be no more than a league away, but it would be the hardest league any of us had ever traveled. Simply making landfall would be the first challenge. Upon drawing closer, we saw that the shoreline consisted of a vast sprawl of uneven fingers of jagged black basalt protruding into the sea, all of them lined with the risen dead. Even if we hadn't lost Eeeio, it would have been impossible to attempt the slingshot maneuver that had worked so well at Papa-ka-hondras.

At least the army of Miasmus did not venture into the sea after us. It seemed that while they were able to traverse the sea's floor, with the exception of the terrible black wyrm, the transformations wrought upon them rendered them fit only for fighting on solid ground.

Aiiiaii investigated warily, returning to report that the waters surrounding the outermost spit were deep enough that she could get sufficiently close to form a living bridge for us to traverse. The problem, of course, was that we were likely to get slaughtered in the process. We needed to create space.

"I know you must conserve your energies to face the final challenge," Jahno said reluctantly to Evene and Tarrok. "But the way must be opened long enough for us to disembark, and the army of Miasmus held at bay long enough for us to regroup."

"I will find a way to do what is needful if it takes the last breath in my body, Seeker," Tarrok said in an implacable tone.

Evene lifted her chin, the noose tattooed around her throat stark in the morning light. "So will I."

All of us checked our weapons one last time. I wore my desert woolens, dingy and frayed and familiar. My *yakhan* was whetted to a razor's edge, the central tine of my *kopar* honed to a keen point. A length of rope was wound around my sash. I carried the Barren Teardrop, the seed of ending, in a pouch knotted on a thong around my neck. Zariya carried the last of the *rhamanthus* seeds in a pouch at her waist. All of us carried water-skins of Ishfahel's gift.

Zariya's bearers would be the most vulnerable members of our party. We had modified the sling that we had built on Papa-ka-hondras so that instead of four poles, it now consisted of a double yoke that two people could carry, the sling hanging between them. Seated in it, Zariya would have sufficient freedom of movement to wield the *rhamanthus*. Those bearing the yoke, however, would have little or no means of defending themselves.

Our course of action decided, Vironesh and I conferred. There was a large part of me—and I daresay of Vironesh, too—that wished to argue that we should take up positions on either side of Zariya and her bearers, to protect her at all cost. Protecting our Sun-Blessed charges was the destiny to which we had both been born, the thing we had been trained and shaped to do; and though Vironesh had failed with Prince Kazaran, he now saw a chance for redemption in assisting me in attaining honor beyond honor.

But this was the end of the world, not the snake pit of plotting and betrayal that was the court of the House of the Ageless.

Honor beyond honor meant something different now. Zariya was not defenseless. The fate of the world might depend upon her survival, but it also depended upon our company winning our way across the jagged plains through an army of the risen dead. We could not afford to be less than strategic in our approach. I knew Evene could not part the army of Miasmus forever; I knew from our experience in the flight from Papa-ka-hondras that they would fall upon us from behind.

"I will take the rearguard, little brother," Vironesh said to me. "The vanguard is yours."

I saluted him.

Nearer and nearer to the isle we drew, Aiiiaii swimming doggedly, the bits of both tow-lines in her jaws. All too soon, it was upon us.

"My brothers and sisters!" Jahno cried. "Today we fight for our fallen brethren, for Eeeio and Keeik and Tiiklit! We fight for fallen Trask and Kerreman and Yaltha, and for all the lands that lie beneath the starless skies!"

Essee whistled softly and signed, *We fight for hope.*

"Just so, my darling," Zariya murmured.

The outermost spit was fast approaching. Members of the army of the risen and returned clustered upon it, gnashing teeth and waving weapons, lifting feelers and clicking claws, parting jaws to reveal teeth capable of tearing and rending.

"Now," Jahno said to Evene. Closing her eyes, the tattooed Drogalian woman took a deep breath and placed her palms together, opening them with an effort.

Bewildered, the army parted. Wasting no time, Aiiiaii snaked her head forward, her chin resting on the basalt spit, her tail rising to loop around the railing of the prow.

I vaulted atop her back and ran the length of her spine, leaping ashore.

Behind me, Evene's hands trembled.

"Go, go, go!" I urged my companions.

They came as best they could: Evene stumbling and concentrating on holding the way open, Tarrok watchful and awaiting a command to release the thunderclap. Essee and Tliksee served as sling-bearers, Zariya swaying between them; Jahno was scowling in an effort to read the battlefield and guide us in his role as Seeker. Kooie and Seeak dove overboard and swam ashore with Elehuddin deftness. Lirios raced light-footed, wings humming at his back, narrow blade in hand, and stalwart Vironesh brought up the rear. We had gained the shore.

Ah, gods, but we had so far to go!

Aiiiaii retreated to the safety of deeper water, towing the ship with her. We set out toward the distant mountain.

The first fifty yards or so of our journey were strange and surreal, like something from a dream. Evene continued to hold the way open and we progressed over the rocky black terrain, a cacophonous chorus of frustration and fury rising on either side of us. It could not last, of course, and it didn't. Behind us, both flanks of the army of the dead converged on the rearguard.

"Now, Tarrok!" Jahno shouted, and all of us covered our ears. Vironesh stepped out of the way as the tall man drew one of those impossibly deep breaths and released the thunderclap on the army behind us. I glanced backward to see hundreds of them stunned in our wake.

It bought us a few more precious minutes, but only a few, for Tarrok's thunderclap had little impact on the hordes yet before us, only those behind and around us. Soon the battle was enjoined on three fronts, and I heard the sound of Zariya's lightning unleashed behind me.

Before me, the way remained open.

The breath of the desert was rising in me like a sirocco and I yearned to turn it loose, yearned to join my companions in their fight; but no, glancing over my shoulder, I could see them holding their own, see Evene's trembling hands beginning to fold. She caught my eye with a wild glance. "I can't hold it open anymore, Khai!" she gasped. "I need a respite!"

I nodded.

Evene's hands folded.

The open corridor before me collapsed, and hundreds of undead creatures, human and inhuman, rushed toward me.

I was Khai of the Fortress of the Winds, Pahrkun's chosen. I had caught the hawk's feather in my fist.

With a high, fierce cry, I loosed the wind, letting it flow through me. My weapons in my hands, my feet moving sure-footed over the harsh terrain, I began killing.

One . . .

Two . . .

Three . . .

And then there was no counting, only killing. It was what I had been trained to do. It was what I was good at. I caught a descending obsidian blade in the tines of my *kopar*; I beheaded the undead soldier who wielded it with a single stroke of my *yakhan,* the wind-cutter that had once belonged to Brother Jawal. Whirling, I severed the neck of a slow-crawling tortoiselike thing with a sharp beak that was angling for my ankles. I was the point of a wedge driving deep into the army of Miasmus, the army of the risen and returned. I flowed into the spaces *between* them, killing left and right, carving out a path. Shrunken leathery flesh parted under my blade, blackened bones gave way. Corpse-light in hollow sockets flickered and died; the risen dead died again.

Time seemed to hold still.

I caught glimpses of the battle behind me as I fought, enough to see we were still alive, still fighting. Evene was behind me, hands still folded, lips moving in a silent prayer; Tarrok was at her side, a longsword in his hand. Essee and Tliksee staggered onward beneath their yokes, Zariya's sling lurching between them, Jahno and Kooie and Seeak and Lirios defending them.

Again and again, lightning crackled from Zariya's fist, driving the attackers back from our column.

Vironesh fought at the rearguard, calm and unhurried and deadly.

I do not know how long we fought nor how much ground we gained. Enough that the smoldering mountain had grown closer. Enough that Evene regained sufficient strength to part the army again. We made haste in the gap that she opened. The exhausted yoke-bearers switched places, Jahno and Kooie taking a turn while Essee and Tliksee drew their long belt-knives.

Tarrok unleashed another thunderclap, his lungs roaring like a bellows. The risen dead behind us fell back.

We made haste, covering as much ground as we could.

Onward.

And then Evene gasped out another warning, her hands folding once more; and again the army of Miasmus fell upon us.

As I fought, I saw something wading through the ranks of the undead from afar, its humped back rising high above them. Nearer and nearer it drew, and as it came, the ranks of the risen dead parted to make way for it, sickly green light gleaming in their eye sockets. Weapons in hand, I waited on the balls of my feet, the desert's scouring wind blowing through me.

It had been a tusked whale, once; a sea creature of enormous bulk and grace, as tall as a two-story building and as vast as a mountain. Now its shrunken, skeletal form stumped forward on unnatural legs that threatened to crush us all, long ivory tusks framing an immense toothy maw opened in a guttural roar of fury and anguish.

It had not chosen this. For the first time, I was struck by the thought that none of the risen dead had chosen this perversion of existence. My heart ached at the knowledge, and I recalled the words of the Green Mother on Papa-ka-hondras. Here at the end of the world, kindness and love were required of us. The only kindness I had to offer was death; but perhaps it *was* a form of kindness.

I hoped so, since it was all I had to give.

I sheathed my weapons as the whale-thing charged on its ungainly legs, its massive head lowered. I caught one tusk in both hands. Its clawed feet plowed the stony ground and its massive body flexed, its head flinging upward in an effort to dislodge me. I let go, vaulting into the sky and somersaulting, landing on its back. If the tusked whale had been alive, I would have stood no more chance of slaying it than whittling down a mountain, but its bones were visible through its withered and rent flesh. Drawing my weapons, I plunged my *yakhan* into its spine, finding the space *between* one huge vertebra and another and parting them. "Find peace," I whispered.

It shuddered and died beneath me, its massive form crashing to the ground.

My perch atop the dead whale's back afforded a good vantage point.

Glancing toward the west, I saw what must surely be our destination. Half-way up the smoldering mountain a great boulder blocked a recess. It appeared only a few scattered members of the army of Miasmus held posts on the steep and jagged slope to defend it.

Behind me, one of the Elehuddin let out a shrill whistle of pain. I scrambled down from the whale's back to find Seeak clutching his thigh, thick pulses of blood spurting between his long, webbed fingers, while Lirios defended him in a furious blur. A large stilt-legged fish with a long, saw-toothed bill lay dead at his feet.

The creature's sharp bill had severed an artery. Seeak would bleed out and die. I saw the knowledge reflected in his golden eyes.

"Khai, what do we do?" Lirios cried. "We can't *leave* him!"

"We have to," I said quietly beneath the clicking, screeching din of the army surrounding us.

His gaze on mine, Seeak gave a single sharp whistle and drew one finger across his throat.

I understood.

Seeak tilted his head back, baring his throat for the mercy blow. I made it swift and sure.

The Elehuddin keened in grief.

The armies of Miasmus were pouring around the corpse of the fallen whale. Zariya drove them back with lightning.

"They're pressing hard from behind, little brother," Vironesh called grimly. "Keep going!"

Somehow, we did.

Step by step and yard by yard, we fought onward; all of us fighting, Zariya's lightning crackling around us. The stench of death and decay, scorched flesh and acrid smoke filled our nostrils. There was no more if this, then that, but if *this*, then *that*. All that was prophesied had come to pass. There was only the here and now. There was only the eternal battle. It felt as though it had been raging forever. It felt as though it would never end.

Pahrkun's wind blew through me, fraying my essence until I could not tell where the wind began and Khai ended. I was a creature of flesh and bone; I was the hot breath of the desert made manifest at the end of the world. One thing bled into the other. I sustained wounds I did not feel, none of them mortal. Like the wind, I flowed *between* one thing and another, finding the smallest of gaps, forging a path forward.

I killed and killed and killed, offering death as a benediction to the unwilling risen dead.

I was Khai.

I had caught the hawk's feather in my fist.

It came almost as a shock when we gained the base of the mountain's slope, and I shook my head to clear it, gazing upward.

The scattered defenders glared down at me: long-limbed apes of some sort, suited to traversing the steep terrain. Later, it would occur to me to wonder how they came to be sucked into the maw of Miasmus, whether they were unfortunate cargo or members of an unfamiliar species, but at the time, I thought only of dispatching them.

Behind us, the army of Miasmus pressed forward.

"Hold them back!" I shouted to Vironesh. "I will clear the way!"

I leapt from crag to crag. Above me, the undead ape-things hooted in challenge and launched themselves at me, long yellow eyeteeth gnashing, inhumanly strong fingers grasping at me. But I had been raised in the mountains, and I would cede nothing to them. My weapons in my hands, I flowed like the wind, danced on the mountainside, and killed them.

One by one by one, I cut them down, until there were no more left.

The slope was ours.

Now I fell back to join Vironesh in the rearguard and grant the others safe passage up the mountainside. My mentor the broken shadow shot me a dire look. "Let us build a wall of corpses, little brother."

Together, we did.

Our blades rose and fell, and the undead died a second death, the wall of withered corpses mounting. Above us, our companions scrambled and panted; climbing, climbing. Zariya's sling lurched wildly on its yoke.

The wall would not hold long. Already, the risen dead sought to clamber over and around it. Still, it would slow their passage. Vironesh and I retreated, following our companions. Here and there, we were forced to make our way around deep crevasses from which sulfurous smoke arose.

By the time our company gained the ledge, Zar the Sun was sinking on the far side of the mountain. All three of the moons were rising. We stood in shadow, gazing at the enormous boulder that sealed the entrance. In my mind's eye, I envisioned the whale bending its tusks and its might to the task of rolling it into place.

Jahno glanced behind us. The risen dead were coming, crablike creatures scuttling in the vanguard, pincers clicking, the more dangerous enemies following at a slower pace. "We do not have much time, Brother Thunderclap," he said.

Tarrok nodded. "I understand, and I will do my best, Seeker. For the wife and children I have lost, for fallen Trask, I will do my best. Cover your ears."

We obeyed, and Tarrok drew breath, deeper and deeper, his chest expanding until it seemed it must burst his ribcage, shattering it like the staves of a barrel. He paused and held it at the apex, his face darkening, then loosed it in a shout, a shout like no other, a shout that struck the boulder and reverberated all around us. I felt the earth tremble beneath my feet as the impact drove us to our knees, hands pressed over our ringing ears; it stunned the armies of Miasmus behind us.

With a resounding *crrrack*, a split ran the length of the boulder. Tarrok swayed on his feet, then crumpled to the ground.

Lirios was the first to reach his side. Wings buzzing with agitation, he rolled the tall man onto his back. Tarrok's eyes gazed sightlessly at the lowering sky, the whites red with ruptured blood vessels. "Brother, no!"

Moving stiff-gaited from unseen wounds, Vironesh joined him and felt for a pulse. "I fear the effort has burst his heart," he murmured. Gently, he closed the tall man's eyes. "May his sacrifice not be in vain."

There were tears in Zariya's eyes. "We must continue."

Jahno turned to Evene. "Now it falls to you, Opener of Ways."

Once again, Evene lifted her chin, the noose that she had escaped tattooed on her skin. *I was not raised to be a hero,* she had said to me on Papa-ka-hondras. But now, I thought, she had found a place beyond fear.

A petty thief, an exiled blacksmith, a scholar, a sheltered princess, peaceable fish-loving Elehuddin, an earnest mayfly yearning for a mate . . . who were we to be anointed the defenders of the four quarters?

And yet here we were at the end of the world, chosen by the Scattered Prophecy to do the impossible.

Evene placed her palms together and closed her eyes.

I watched the cords of her neck draw taut. Her hands shook with the effort of opening them.

With a low, grating groan, the two halves of the sundered boulder parted to reveal a passage lit by a sullen glow.

The final way was open.

FIFTY-SIX

One by one, we passed through the narrow aperture, Zariya abandoning her sling to hobble on her canes.

"How many *rhamanthus* seeds are left?" Jahno asked her quietly.

Her eyes reflected the dim glow. "A handful."

I prayed it was enough.

We didn't know. None of us knew.

It was hot and close inside the tunnel, the air thick and acrid. Behind us, the aperture opened onto a glimpse of twilight.

"The dead will be coming for us," Vironesh said in a pragmatic tone. "Opener of Ways, can you close them, too?"

Weary to the bone, Evene gave her head an exhausted shake. "I do not possess that gift."

Vironesh's broad shoulders rose and fell in a faint shrug. "Then my role here is clear. I am not one of the chosen defenders. I will not accompany you on this final journey, but remain here and guard the passage."

"Are you hale enough to do so?" I asked, suspecting his injuries were more grave than he was letting on.

A crablike thing advanced through the opening, eyestalks waving in the dim light. Vironesh crushed it underfoot, then drove the tip of his *yakhan* through its broken shell. "Hale enough, little brother. The big ones can only come at me one at a time." His bruise-colored face was tranquil. "Khai, I wish to thank you. You gave me purpose when I had none. Your Highness . . ." He offered Zariya a one-handed salute. "You gave me hope. All of you give me hope. If we fail here, it will not be for lack of courage and per-severance."

"I owe you a great deal, my mentor." I took a swig from my water-skin, feeling the sustaining water of Ishfahel the Gentle Rain restore me, and glanced down the length of the tunnel. It appeared empty, but I wanted to be sure. "Brother Lirios, will you scout ahead with me?"

His wings hummed. "With pleasure."

"Be careful, my darlings," Zariya cautioned us.

Weapons in hand, Lirios and I ventured into the tunnel. It twisted and turned as we went deeper into the mountain, the heat rising and the sullen glow intensifying the farther we went. I unwound my head-scarf to wrap a length of woolen fabric over my mouth. There were no members of the un-dead army to oppose us. Nonetheless, a strong feeling of menace pervaded the place. There was a sound, a low deep susurrus, as though an immense being breathed in and out at impossibly long intervals. The walls around us seemed to pulse with life, and I had a sense that we were being watched at every step along the way.

Some hundred yards into our journey, the tunnel opened onto a massive pit, jagged ridges funneling down to a churning pool of red-hot lava far, far below us. It pulsed like the beating of a heart.

"Khai?" Lirios's voice was small and shaken. "Khai, I think we are *inside* Miasmus."

"I think so, too," I whispered.

We made our way back to report. Already, the battle had been enjoined in our absence, Jahno and the Elehuddin defending the opening to give Vironesh a respite before the final effort.

"We dare not waste time," Zariya said firmly. Essee whistled and hoisted one end of the yoke, and Zariya shook her head. "You have done enough and more, my dearest. Let everyone among us fend for themselves. Let me manage this last bit on my own, and stand against the rising tide in accor-dance with prophecy."

"It is fitting," Jahno agreed somberly.

Before Papa-ka-hondras, such a thing would have been unthinkable, but

Zariya's mettle had been tempered on that deadly isle. The healing she had found had come at a steep price, but her lungs were strong now. Step by step, she dragged herself forward, her chest rising and falling steadily, freed from the vise that had gripped it since childhood. We walked the tunnel together, all of us, and if our progress was slow, it was sure.

Behind us arose the renewed sound of combat. Vironesh the broken shadow was holding the way.

Before us . . .

The pit yawned, magma seething. Far below us, flaming gouts rose and fell, splashing and returning to molten formlessness. All around us rose the walls of the hollow mountain, and high above us were the starless skies, lit with the light of three moons.

We ranged ourselves along the ledge.

My useless weapons sheathed, I touched the pouch strung around my neck containing the Barren Teardrop; the seed of ending that had been lodged in my flesh for so long. Such a small thing on which our fates depended.

"Miasmus!" Jahno cried. "We are here!"

For a moment there was nothing; and then there was laughter, deep and dark and bitter, arising all around us and thrumming through our bones. On the walls surrounding us, stones and pebbles cascaded as a series of four glowing eyes blinked open, roiling with magma. An enormous round mouth like that of a lamprey, ringed with row upon row of teeth, emerged from the lava, swaying above it.

"The defenders of the four quarters." Miasmus's voice reverberated all around us, dripping with contempt. *"Such a pathetic lot my father Zar sends against me at the end of the world! How pathetic that my brothers and sisters cannot fight their own battles, but must send these puny children of theirs!"*

My ears hurt.

Against the god, I felt small and impotent. How were we to defeat a living mountain?

"We are not here to do battle with you," Jahno said. "We are here to usher in a new order."

Again, that dark, bitter laughter shook the inner walls of the volcanic hollow, seeming to come from nowhere and everywhere. *"You understand nothing, mortal! My mother shrouded me in darkness. My brothers and sisters raised their hands against our father; and for their sins he cast me down."* Eyes blazed all around us. *"I want them to suffer!"*

The word broke over us like one of Tarrok's thunderclaps, the very air trembling at Miasmus's rage.

Let your mind be like the eye of a hawk . . .

I willed my thoughts to stillness.

Somehow, Miasmus must be induced to swallow the seed of ending. I had no powers of persuasion. I could only assess what *I* could do. I gauged the distance to the swaying lamprey-mouth of the Risen Maw, trying to determine if I could hurl the Teardrop into its gullet.

No. It was too far.

I peered over the ledge. If I'd had a rope twenty times longer than the paltry length tied around my waist, I might be able to descend far enough, if the forge-breath of the lava didn't kill me first. But I had no such thing. I needed another plan.

Essee was speaking.

". . . take your rightful place in the heavens?" Jahno translated for her. It was for our benefit, not the god's; it was a scholar's reflex and I was not even sure he was aware he was doing it. Even so, he caught something of her sympathetic tone. "For if we understand rightly, that is the truth of the gift we offer you."

"No."

A single syllable, cold and dark, falling like a stone and shattering whatever frail hope we held.

The lava far below us surged and flared in accordance with Miasmus's mood; the basalt walls expanded and contracted in harsh pants. *"Understand this, defenders of the four quarters. My army is on the march. Trask and Kerreman and Yaltha have fallen; as we speak, Tukkan falls. Elsewhere, my firstborn children, my spiders, spread my gospel, and your puny folk turn against one another. But in time, all will fall. All will die."* Its voice rose to a crescendo. *"The earth and seas will die beneath the trampling feet of my army; all will become death and decay and barrenness. My brothers and sisters will be left alone, alone as I have always been, to mourn the loss of all that they held dear beneath the starless skies,"* Miasmus thundered, and the walls shook around us, rocks showering down. *"Nim the Bright Moon and Shahal the Dark and my fickle mother Eshen the Wandering may join my arrogant father Zar the Sun to gaze down upon the devastation I have wrought and know regret!"*

The silence that followed his soliloquy was deafening. Into it, Essee gave a low, plaintive whistle, asking a simple question. "But will it make you happy?" Jahno translated in a soft murmur.

On the walls, Miasmus's glowing eyes regarded her, and somehow for all their molten glow, their gaze was cold; cold and cruel. Its gaze shifted to take in all of us in our collective impotence. *"Shall I tell you what will make me happy?"* the god inquired with malice. *"Your despair."*

The living wall behind Essee shifted. A long, vertical ridge peeled loose and lifted, becoming a clawed limb. Before any of us could react—even me, even Lirios—it grasped Essee around the torso and flung her into the pit. Her sharp trill of sudden terror was cut short as the lamprey-mouth of the Risen Maw shot into the air to devour her in a single gulp.

There was another silence, this one stunned. Evene began to weep quietly and hopelessly.

Let your mind be like the eye of a hawk.

Clarity descended upon me.

". . . was your conscience, was she not?" Miasmus was saying in a taunting voice, for all the world like a cruel child lashing out. *"Shall I send her back to you, risen and returned, and force you to slay her? Yes, I think I shall."*

Kindness and love would be needed, the Green Mother had said on Papa-ka-hondras, but all the gifts of Papa-ka-hondras were double-edged. I think among us only Essee had a heart vast enough to find within it love and compassion for this mad god, this neglected vengeful god-child who sought to destroy the world, who would torment us here at the end of all things like a mortal child pulling wings from flies for mere sport. And Miasmus had repaid her with cruel death; death and further perversion yet to come. But Essee's unwitting sacrifice had shown me what must be done.

Pahrkun's wind blew through me, steady and sure. I backed up a few steps to get a running start. It would take a prodigious leap to gain the pit and the Risen Maw within it, but then, I was a prodigious leaper.

Zariya's head swung around, her dark eyes wide with horror. She knew my mind; she knew my heart better than I did.

"I am sorry," I said to her; and I was *so* very sorry. Sorry for the opportunities wasted, sorry for the dishonesty and the secrets withheld, sorry beyond words that here at the end of the world, honor beyond honor demanded that I leave her. "I'm so sorry. Just be ready, my soul's twin."

Her eyes filling with tears, my lion-hearted princess nodded her understanding. Leaning one-handed on her canes, she reached for the remaining handful of *rhamanthus* seeds.

The others were turning, slower than Zariya to grasp what was happening, to grasp my intention.

In the fiery pit, the gullet of the Risen Maw belched forth a lone figure, depositing it on the ledge below us.

It began to climb.

Essee.

Kooie let out a low moan of anguish, and Jahno averted his gaze.

I took a deep breath, the gift of Ishfahel the Gentle Rain yet coursing through my veins, and gathered myself.

In the periphery of my vision, there was a darting motion. "For my queen!" Lirios shouted, his voice high and fierce and wild as he snatched the pouch containing the Barren Teardrop from around my neck, yanking it hard enough to break the thong and send me staggering to one knee. *"For my queen!"*

"No!" The shout left my throat raw, but it was too late.

One step, two, three; Lirios launched himself from the ledge, his narrow sword in his right hand and the leather pouch clutched tight in his left. The mayfly was a prodigious leaper, too. For a moment it seemed he hung in the air, a shining figure, his translucent wings spread wide. And then he fell, still shining; shining like the vision of a star falling from the heavens, his golden hair catching fire and his wings shriveling in the heat.

Below us the Risen Maw of Miasmus dilated, the round opening lined with row upon row of teeth. Swaying, striking like a snake, it snatched Lirios in mid-fall, tossing him into its gullet and swallowing him whole; swallowing the seed of ending he clutched in his left fist.

Later, I would grieve.

Now, I leapt to my feet. "Zariya! *Now!*"

Zariya raised her fist, golden traceries alight, her expression set with grim fury. Blue-white lightning forked from her fist in all directions, striking the walls around us with their watching eyes, striking the swaying trunk of the Risen Maw, crackling into the starless sky above us.

Oh, my brothers and sisters . . .

Lightning laced the rock, lightning laced the lava; here at the end of the world, the lightning of Anamuht the Purging Fire was turned loose. The seed of ending met the seeds of beginning. Wind and fire, life and death. These were the gifts we carried, Sun-Blessed and shadow.

There was a sound.

A wail, call it; rising and rising and rising, a wail of agony. Miasmus was dying or ending. The walls of the volcanic hollow began tumbling around us, the ledge crumbling beneath our feet.

"Fall back!" I shouted, thrusting Zariya behind me. "Everyone! Fall back and flee this place!"

It was easier said than done.

Kooie was closest to the tunnel. He slung one arm around Zariya and began hauling her by sheer force, her feet dragging; Tliksee hurried to help him. Evene extended her hand to me, her face rigid with terror as the rocks gave way beneath her, and behind her, Jahno gave a shout of alarm and vanished from my sight.

I lunged to catch Evene's hand and only barely succeeded, our fingertips curved like hooks. I could feel her slipping. There was no time to think. I took one step closer to the crumbling ledge, loose rocks sliding under my feet, and grabbed her wrist with my other hand, yanking her to safety. "Go!"

She stumbled past me in a daze, cradling her right arm.

Jahno.

I had to look, and as impossible as it seemed, our Seeker had not yet plunged to his death. He dangled from the crumbling ledge, knuckles ashen, his hands shifting in an ongoing effort to maintain purchase on the rock eroding beneath them. I whipped the length of rope from around my waist. Lying on my belly, I managed to pass it beneath his arms, gathering both ends in my hands and rising.

I had scarce gained my feet when another great section of ledge gave way, forcing me to scramble backward. There was no time to brace for the impact of Jahno's full weight on the rope.

It nearly dragged me down with him, but stubbornness and rage fueled my determination. I tightened my grip on the rope, set my feet, and continued to work my way backward, racing the crumbling rock. I hauled Jahno out of the abyss, bruised and battered, but alive.

With the living mountain groaning and shaking itself to pieces around us, we raced after the others, dodging falling rocks. Our company had passed through the aperture before us, all save Vironesh, who stood slumped against the wall of the tunnel, his sword held loosely in his right hand, his left pressed to his belly. Crumbling corpses littered the ground at his feet.

I shoved Jahno toward the egress, and he staggered out. "The risen dead?" I gasped at my mentor. "Do they yet await us?"

Vironesh gave me a smile of surprising peace. "No, they have turned to dust and decay. I held them off long enough for you to succeed, little brother; and against all odds, it seems you have done so. But I fear I am done for."

I shook my head. "No."

He did not protest as I looped his arms around my neck, only grunted with pain as I wriggled through the aperture, the bulk of his weight draped over my back.

Down . . .

Down . . .

Down . . .

The ground trembled beneath our feet. The gorge we had traversed was clogged with desiccated corpses. We tripped and stumbled over them as we descended the slope. I struggled under Vironesh's increasingly slack weight, my steps coming hard, taking comfort from the sight of Zariya in the vanguard before me, swaying in the sling that Kooie and Tliksee had retrieved in the course of their flight.

Behind us, Miasmus's wail of anguish rose, spiraling higher and higher into the starless sky.

Above us, the three moons moved into conjunction: Nim the Bright, Shahal the Dark, and Eshen the Wandering, the mothers of all of creation, all of them full and shining here at the end of the world.

We gained the plain, staggering a distance away from the mountain. The Elehuddin released Zariya, who braced herself on the canes she had somehow retained on our flight. I lowered Vironesh to the ground.

The jagged cracks of lightning ran all through the mountain now. Overhead, a thousand beams of light shot downward and outward from the conjoined moons, bright and milky against the night sky, mottled with traces of red and blue. One plunged into the depths of the hollow mountain, and in that instant, the endless rising note of Miasmus's anguish changed to something altogether different, a shimmering sound of exultant crystalline purity.

The living mountain exploded into the sky.

I flung myself over Zariya without thinking, bearing her down to the corpse-littered ground and covering her body with my own. When the hail of debris I anticipated failed to fall, I stole a glance over my shoulder. What I saw made me roll onto my knees and stare, Zariya sitting upright beside me.

A transformed Miasmus was ascending into the heavens. The shattered chunks of the living mountain coalesced into something different, an immense being of surpassing darkness and unbearable brightness, such brightness that I had to shield my eyes with my hand to gaze upon it.

"Look," Jahno said in a hushed whisper, pointing toward the east.

It was not only Miasmus.

All the children of heaven were ascending, a thousand thousand points of light rising into the night sky, shedding their inhuman immortal forms shaped by sea and earth, desert and forest, temple and mountain and tree, and all the myriad creatures that dwelled beneath the starless skies to become something other, brilliant and dark, terrifying and incomprehensible. The chiming note of Miasmus's ascendance became a vast chorus of soul-aching beauty.

Tears stung my eyes at the sheer beauty of it; and at the unfairness, too. Lirios, earnest Lirios, had shone like a star as he fell. For failing to destroy the world, Miasmus was rewarded with a homecoming to the heavens from which he had been unjustly banished.

But the minds of the gods were unknowable. Perhaps it was unfair; or perhaps it was fitting in a way that none of us puny mortals, we puny mortals who had fought the children of heaven's battle for them—for it *had* been a battle—and won, could comprehend. All we could do was watch and wonder.

Beside me, Zariya slid her hand into mine.

I squeezed it in silent reply.

Together, we wept for those who had paid the cost for this victory: for Lirios; for valiant Eeeio and stalwart Tarrok, who had given his last breath; and for the peaceable Elehuddin, and most especially Essee. We wept for those who had passed before them, for the dead lands and the dying seas, and for the thousands upon thousands of victims whose names we would never know.

Above us, the stars shone brightly in the night sky.

FIFTY-SEVEN

Vironesh died at dawn.

All of us knew it before the end. His injuries were too numerous and he had lost too much blood to survive.

"Khai." He whispered my name with an affection I'd never heard before, beckoning me to his side with a feeble gesture. "Do not grieve for me, little brother. You granted me a gift I never thought to find."

I nodded. "Redemption."

His eyes closed, a faint smile curving his lips. "Exactly."

Soon afterward, his breathing ceased.

"What do we do now?" Evene asked, glancing around. The world had not ended after all, but for us, it might as well have. We were battered and exhausted, grief-stricken and diminished, stranded on a barren isle amidst dead seas in a world bereft of gods.

Kooie heaved himself to his feet and let out a low, inquiring whistle. When there was no reply, he whistled a sharper series of notes that carried across the corpse-cluttered landscape.

At length there came a faint trill in distant reply.

Aiiiaii had not deserted us.

Kooie bared his pointed teeth in a grin, clicking and signing. *We go home.*

Evene gazed at him with dull eyes. "And where is that?"

I wondered, too.

Jahno roused himself. "We do not know how we will find this changed world, and we can only pray that there is enough of Ishfahel's gift remaining to sustain us for long enough to escape the dead seas." He exchanged glances with Kooie and Tliksee, who signed agreement. "But of this I am sure. You are family, all of you. There will always be a home for you on Elehud."

"Thank you, my darling." Zariya pushed disheveled braids back from her face. The golden traceries on her right hand and forearm had turned silver-bright. "Let us first see if we might survive this bitter victory."

I had not counted the toll of our day-long battle. Now Pahrkun's wind no longer blew through me, nor did I know if it ever would again. Now my mortal flesh and bone and muscle felt the price of what I had done.

I hurt.

I hurt everywhere.

But so did we all, and we were alive. So we trudged uncomplaining, the brittle corpses of the unwilling risen dead crumbling under our feet, Zariya suffering herself to be carried in the sling, all of us taking turns at the dual yoke. It took us the better part of a day, but there was no urgency. The battle was over.

With Aiiiaii's assistance, we boarded the ship. We tended to our myriad injuries and partook of the sustaining water of Ishfahel the Gentle Rain. After Aiiiaii had drunk her dipperful, the sea-wyrm took up both bits in her jaws and began towing the ship toward the east.

The black basalt shores of the isle of Miasmus receded behind us. The world had not ended, and we were journeying toward that which remained.

Slowly, slowly, we traversed the dead seas, Aiiiaii performing the heroic work of two. Our wounds began to knit, our aching bodies to heal.

Our hearts were another matter.

Of all the losses we had endured, it was Lirios's death that affected me the most, for I felt he had died in my place. I was Zariya's shadow, trained from birth to defend my Sun-Blessed charge. I had caught the hawk's feather in my fist, but it was the mayfly who had taken the sacrifice upon himself. I heard his final words ringing in my ears, and saw him shining as he fell, his hair streaming flames and his wings, his useless, lovely wings, shriveling into nothingness.

Zariya sensed I was troubled and drew it out of me, her brows furrowed with concern as she listened.

"It troubles me, too, my darling," she murmured when I had finished.

"It was in my name that he died. I had done nothing to be worthy of such a sacrifice on his part."

"You speak of the mayfly, yah?" Jahno said, overhearing us. He shook his head. "It was his destiny."

"But you didn't know his role in the prophecy," I said.

He was silent.

"You *did* know, didn't you?" Zariya said to him. "You left that part untranslated on purpose."

Jahno drew a deep breath. "'And in the darkest hour, the Quick shall bear the seed of ending into the Risen Maw and pay the ultimate price,'" he quoted. "Yah. I did not think it was fair to put that burden upon Lirios. I thought the choice, if it came, must be his own." He shrugged his shoulders and turned his palms upward. "I am the Seeker. It was my decision to make, and I made it."

I thought about it for many days.

In the end, I thought that Jahno made the right decision. If Lirios had known his sacrifice was foreordained, it would have taken away from the grand and terrible romance of his gesture. He had sacrificed himself for his queen, just like the hero of the Goat Island War he had idolized. It made me smile to remember his astonishment that I was unfamiliar with the tale; smile, and fight the sting of tears.

In time I made my peace with it, and Zariya did, too.

Neither of us had forgotten what had transpired between us on that final day when the battle was enjoined. Her kiss, so searing and surprising. It lay between us, a promise waiting to be fulfilled one day when we were alone together, Sun-Blessed and shadow.

But not now, no.

Now our grief, and the grief of our companions, was too raw. It left no room for joy.

Someday, perhaps.

If we survived.

There were days when that seemed an impossibility. We were alone in the world, sailing endlessly over the dead seas. At night, the bright stars in the sky seemed to mock us. We sailed past Trask, the barren isle of Tarrok's birth fallen silent, no longer haunted by Luhdo the Loud. The water in the cask given us by Ishfahel the Gentle Rain dwindled and dwindled.

Ah, but then . . .

We were two days past Trask when Aiiiaii dropped the tow-lines and dove deep into the water, leaving our ship adrift. The sea-wyrm surfaced with a mouthful of gleaming fish that she showed us between her foot-long teeth before tossing her head and gulping them down, whistling with happiness.

"She says the sea is coming back to life!" Jahno shouted, and Kooie and Tliksee dove overboard.

The world had changed, but it had not ended.

We sailed past Kerreman and Yaltha, and if the islands were blasted and sere, there were fish in the sea. Aiiiaii and the Elehuddin feasted on them raw in great quantities; the rest of us ate as much as we dared, wishing we had wood or coal for the grill.

Ten days after Aiiiaii's announcement, the ship's hold began sprouting new *ooalu* vines, pale green and tender.

Hope.

There was hope.

To make plans seemed like an act of daring, and yet we could not sail purposelessly forever, dependent on Aiiiaii's dogged endurance.

"Do you wish to go home to Drogalia?" Jahno asked Evene, for we had caught the great eastern current, and such a thing now seemed like it might be possible. "To see your family?"

Evene smiled wryly, tracing the noose tattooed around her throat with one finger. "Do you suppose my people would believe a word of my tale? That they would conceive glorious new markings to celebrate the fact that I helped save the world? No. I will sail with you to Elehud and learn to play the lute."

The Seeker nodded. "And you?" he said to Zariya.

She tilted her head and considered. Reaching into her pouch, she drew forth the last remaining *rhamanthus* seed, one lone seed that had been hidden in a fold of her leather pouch. It had changed, too. No longer crimson but white, it shone as brightly as a star in her palm. She closed her fingers around it, and lightning wreathed her fist, sparked along the twining silver pattern etched on her arm.

The children of heaven might have abandoned this earthly plane, but the gifts they had bequeathed us remained. I had discovered that I could yet summon Pahrkun's wind, and it, too, had changed; no longer the hot, acrid breath of the desert, but something cold and crystalline and different.

Zariya opened her fist, the lightning unspent, and the sparks faded. "Who are we to be in this new world?" she asked in a philosophical tone. "I have seen and done more things than I ever dared dream. Some of them were wondrous, and some of them were terrible beyond all imagining. And yet I think I should like to do and see more. I should like to go to Therin and tell Lord Rygil what his fate-changer wrought, and why I cannot honor our betrothal. Like our Seeker, I should like to visit Barakhar while those touched by Lishan the Graceful yet live, and witness their arts." She tucked the *rhamanthus* seed away. "I should like to visit Chalcedony Isle and tell their people of Lirios's sacrifice," she said quietly. "And I should like to seek Tarrok's family among the Traskan refugees, so that his children might know their father perished a hero."

It shamed me that I had not thought of those things. "Wherever you go, I will be at your side."

She smiled and gave me a significant sidelong glance. "That, my darling, is not in question."

Kooie whistled and signed an inquiry, his golden eyes grave. *Then will you not join us in Elehud, sister?*

"In time, yes," Zariya said. "I think so. We *are* family, our bonds forged in horror and loss, in a wondrous and bitter victory. It is a thing that no one outside our company will ever understand."

"It is what Essee would have wished for us," Jahno said. "It is what she would have wished for all of us."

We were silent for a moment.

"A world where kindness prevails over cruelty, and bloodshed is unnecessary," Zariya murmured. "It was her wish at the end of the world, was it not? It is the legacy I think we must embrace."

I cleared my throat, feeling awkward. "It is not a legacy to which I am suited, Zariya."

"You *are* very good at killing things," she agreed. "None of us would be here if you weren't. And I do not suppose that is a skill that will be unnecessary in our lifetimes. But you have a kind and loving heart, too, and perhaps that is all that is needful." She took my hand in hers, her gaze intent on mine. "And we have not spoken of *your* wishes, Khai. Do you still wish to show me the spring desert in bloom?"

I nodded. "I do."

Zariya nodded, too. "That is where we will begin, then. I am a Zarkhoumi princess who has never seen the desert. If Aiiiaii and the rest of the company are willing, I ask that you deposit us at Merabaht, where we may discover what my murderous family has wrought in our absence, and I will tell them of our impossible deeds. And then we will venture into the desert, you and I. I shall meet this importunate Seer of yours, and the brotherhood who raised you, and follow in the footsteps of Anamuht the Purging Fire and Pahrkun the Scouring Wind."

So it was decided.

We continued to sail along the great eastern current. The cask of Ishfahel's gift ran dry, but fish became more plentiful. In the ship's hold, the *ooalu* vines thickened, twining around the desiccated husks of cocoons I had supposed dead, which latched onto the vines and grew plump.

One moth hatched, then two, then three, flitting pale and glowing amidst the vines, which brought forth blossoms.

Some days later, we came upon a vast flotilla of Tukkani refugees floundering along the current, shepherded by a lone ship with the now-familiar black-and-white-striped sails of the coursers of Obid. The refugees in their extravagant and ridiculous Tukkani finery were gaunt-faced and hungry, having prized possessions over foodstuffs as they fled. Such was a measure of their desperation that the coursers' ship did not take alarm at the sight of Aiiiaii, but hailed us; or so I thought until we drew nearer, and I caught sight of a familiar figure among them, bearded and handsome and newly weatherbeaten, the pulse-lights of *khementaran* beating at his wrists and his throat.

Zariya leaned on her canes and stared in disbelief. *"Father?"*

From the deck of the ship on which he served, King Azarkal offered his youngest a weary and profoundly sincere salute, his eyes bright with tears. "Oh, my little lioness! Do you yet live? I did not dare to hope!"

It was a strange and joyous reunion, and it brought home to me the fact that Zariya was right. No one could ever understand what our company had witnessed, what we had endured. And it was strange, too, after being alone for so long, sailing beneath the unfamiliar starlit skies, to be among others.

But there was merit in it, especially for the suffering refugees. Aiiiaii provided for them, diving deep beneath the sea, gulping at shoals of fish and depositing them in gleaming heaps on the decks of their ships to the grateful cheers of the hungry refugees.

While she did so, King Azarkal came aboard our ship. "There were more of you, were there not?" he asked quietly, glancing around.

"Yes," Zariya said. "There were."

Jahno told our tale, and the king listened with wonder, scarce able to encompass the story. "My little lioness," he whispered. "My little lioness at the end of the world with lightning in her fist."

"We did what was needful," Zariya said soberly. "All of us; and some of us paid the final price. But how do you come to be amidst the coursers of Obid, Father?"

"Ah, well." He gave a rueful shrug. "After you left with the wyrm-raiders, I didn't know what to do with myself, heart of my heart. And so once we made landfall in Therin, I bethought myself of your brother's shadow, Vironesh, who set sail among the coursers. I thought they might help me track down this mad crew of yours. Instead, Miasmus rose, and I found myself engaged in an effort to manage the tide of refugees flooding from fallen realms. It is worthy work," he added, glancing down at the beating pulse of his wrists. "Worthier work than I have done in all my years as the king of Zarkhoum."

"We are bound for Merabaht," Zariya said to him. "At least for a time. Will you come with us?"

King Azarkal hesitated, then shook his head. "I think not, my lioness. You have no need of me. These people do. Let me be of use for once in my very long life." His gaze fell on Evene, whose tattoos evinced her origins. "You know, we are bound for Drogalia. Thanks to your great wyrm's aid, we ought to reach it without starving. Would you care to sail with us?"

Evene's face hardened. "I expect to find no welcome there."

"The world is not what it was," the king said gently. "I expect you should find a hero's welcome, especially with a grateful horde of refugees and the King of Zarkhoum vouching for your deeds."

She stared at him open-mouthed, flushing at the unexpected offer. "You would do that for me?"

"It would be my honor," he said.

Jahno and the Elehuddin conferred. "I think you should consider it," the Seeker said to Evene. "We have seen that the past haunts you, and there are things you would undo if you could. There will always be a place for you among us. But this may be a chance to find a measure of redemption."

Evene opened and closed her mouth again, her color still high. "I will do it," she said in a rush. "Only let me get my things, such as they are."

"Does this mean you're formally abdicating the throne, Father?" Zariya inquired as Evene left to retrieve her possessions.

King Azarkal frowned. "I suppose it does." He worked a large signet ring free from his right forefinger and handed it to Zariya. "If you find that Dozaren has governed well in my absence—better, I pray, than I did—you may give this to him with my blessing. Tell him it is my decree that aught you require shall be given to you. If you find he has not . . ." His voice faltered.

Transferring her canes into her left hand, Zariya tucked the signet ring into her pouch, then reached for my arm, linking hers through it. I stood beside her, her shoulder brushing my arm. "If we find that he has not, well, we will do something about it, my shadow and I," she said firmly.

Her father gave her a faint smile. "I do believe you will." Gazing at the two of us, something in his expression changed. "And I don't suppose you're going to wed Lord Rygil after all, are you?"

"No." Zariya's tone was unapologetic. "It is far too late for me to be the dutiful daughter I once was, Father, and I have endured far too much to gainsay the truth of my own heart."

King Azarkal—or just Azarkal now, I supposed—bowed his head and kissed his daughter on the brow. "Then I wish you and your shadow every happiness, my young lioness. I misspoke when I said I had done nothing of use prior to this in my very long lifetime, for I begot you."

FIFTY-EIGHT

We parted ways ere the sun set on that day.

A reunion unlooked-for; a separation unexpected. Before she departed, Evene surprised me with one of her hard, fierce embraces. "You were the one who gave me the courage to believe in myself, Khai. For that I thank you."

My throat felt tight. "We owe you our lives, Opener of Ways. All of us do."

"And you," she said. "We owe one another, all of us, and we owe those who are lost to us."

I grasped her tattooed arms in my hands. "I will never forget."

"Nor I," she said steadily. "And one day I pray we will all reunite in Elehud. Until then, be well."

"And you."

Onward.

Our course lay due east, while the flotilla angled across the great current toward Drogalia in the northeast.

The world had changed.

The world endured.

The further eastward we sailed, the more distant and dreamlike the events behind us seemed; and yet at night the stars in the sky overhead proved otherwise, and it was different. I had nightmares; all of us did. We fought that terrible battle over again in our dreams, the risen dead clicking and screeching and gnashing, their desiccated corpses crumbling under our feet. We sweated and trembled in the green depths of Papa-ka-hondras while Shambloth the Inchoate Terror slithered or padded or crawled unseen around us. We saw our brothers and sisters die; we heard Zariya's screams of agony and the taunting voice of Miasmus ringing in our ears.

These things, I thought, would always be with us. We endured them because we had no choice.

We kept to the center of the great current where it flowed the strongest and saw little in the way of other ships. The army of the risen dead had not made it past Tukkan, but it seemed the chaos spread by the sea-spiders, Miasmus's firstborn children, had provoked sufficient unrest in the isles that all sea trade had halted. Jahno was reluctant to put ashore, but in time our stores of water—ordinary fresh water—ran low and we were forced to do so. We made landfall at the small island realm of Hahrn. They were primarily fisher-folk and had a reputation for holding the Elehuddin, who were surely the ultimate fisher-folk, in high regard.

Indeed, they welcomed us warmly enough, starved for news. Ours were the first foreign faces they had seen in months. Hahrnians clustered on the dock, barefoot boys racing with buckets to the nearest well and back to refill our casks, while we told them what had befallen the world.

In turn, they told us of the waves of sea-spiders that had crawled upon their shores, afflicting hundreds, turning brothers and fathers and sisters and mothers against one another. It had not ceased until the night the children of the heavens ascended, and they reckoned half their number had died.

The Hahrnians would accept no payment for the water, but instead made us gifts of the abundant fruit that grew on the isle and, when they learned we had none, firewood for the brazier. I was grateful, for I had grown heartily sick of raw fish.

We sailed onward, Jahno pointing out and naming the myriad lands that we passed. Not wanting to lose my edge, I trained alone on the ship's deck, retracing the steps and feints and strikes of duels and sparring matches and battles I remembered, summoning Pahrkun's wind and feeling it flow through me, cold and distant, at once star-bright and black as night.

I thought about Vironesh, and how we would not have survived had he not been there to hold the passage behind us.

If this, then that, but if *this*, then *that*.

We gained the northern waters and shivered in the chilly air, donning multiple layers of clothing.

We passed Therin, a vast green smudge of land on the northern horizon, and Zariya looked thoughtful. "The girl I was might have been happy there," she murmured. "But I am not the same girl who walked into the Green Mother's hut on Papa-ka-hondras."

"She is not the girl you were meant to be," I reminded her. "A different destiny awaited you."

"And you." Zariya slid her arm through mine and tilted her head up at me. "When did you know? About us, I mean."

"After the Green Mother's hut." I did not like to remember her agony and my bone-deep terror of losing her. "When did *you* know?"

She gazed at the horizon. "I don't know, my darling. It wasn't all at once. After I ceased to be my father's dutiful daughter, I realized bit by bit, day by day, that it was you, and only you, whom I loved. I mean, I adored you from the beginning, of course. You remember, you understand. We are Sun-Blessed and shadow, each other's soul's twin, our fates linked from the moment we were born. But I thought you must be right, that *love* wasn't the purpose for which the gods joined our fates." She paused. "And I suppose perhaps it isn't."

"Fuck the gods," I said, thinking of Evene, although I did not spit on the deck as she would have done. "We have done all that they asked of us. Now it is time for us to live for ourselves."

Zariya laughed, a clear, joyous sound, her dark eyes shining. "Yes, *exactly*!"

If we had been alone . . .

We weren't, but one day we would be.

Therin faded in the distance behind us; next we sailed past Granth. Remembering the attack that they had launched on the Therinian state-ship, I could not help but feel apprehensive, but the tall mountain where Droth the Great Thunder had made his home no longer trickled smoke, and no stink-lizards darkened the skies above us as we passed. I wondered if they were no longer bound to the Kagan's service.

Aiiiaii swam doggedly, towing our ship toward Zarkhoum and the uttermost east, aided by the great current and a following wind that filled our square sail. The temperature rose, and we shed layers of clothing. It was a matter of mere days before we spotted the tall lighthouse in Merabaht's harbor. Although the Zarkhoumi had never been sailors, Merabaht had always been a significant port of call for traders, and it was strange to see the harbor empty of aught but small fishing vessels.

It had not occurred to me that our arrival might be hoped for and heralded, but it was. But of course, King Azarkal and the Therinians would have sent word of what had transpired when we fled from the Granthian attack, encountered the wyrm-raiders, and answered the call of the Scattered Prophecy. It was likely that the guards and servants who sailed with us had returned, carrying their own versions of the tale. Many of the Zarkhoumi people were aware that it was prophesied that one of the Sun-Blessed would stand against the darkness.

They knew that the children of heaven had ascended, they knew it meant that against all odds, their young princess must have succeeded.

And it was very highly unlikely that anyone else would be sailing into the harbor on a wyrm-drawn ship.

Fishermen setting out crab pots rose to their feet in shallow-bottomed boats and cheered as Aiiiaii glided into the harbor, her head held high, and I will own, my heart was gladdened at the sight and the sound.

A crowd gathered on the quay. Interspersed among them were members of the City Guard, though not the City Guard as I remembered them, for they sported new crimson-and-gold-striped sashes over their white tunics.

I felt grubby; I daresay all of us did. Zariya shot me a rueful look. "I was not expecting to arrive to fanfare, my darling."

"Neither was I," I admitted.

With graceful care, Aiiiaii guided our ship to a berth. Kooie and Tliksee set about securing the lines as Aiiiaii dropped the tow-lines and slipped free, angling out to deeper waters.

On the quay below us, a guardsman with a gold collar of office around his neck stepped forward, his gaze respectfully averted from Zariya's unveiled face. "Is it possible that I have the honor of addressing Her Highness

Princess Zariya, Sun-Blessed daughter of the House of the Ageless?" he inquired.

"It's more than possible," Zariya said dryly. "Who asks?"

He dared a covert glance at her and offered a salute. "Captain Ranesh of the Steward's Watch."

Zariya frowned. "The Steward's Watch?"

"Your own honored sister, the Princess Fazarah, was named the Steward of Merabaht by your brother Prince Dozaren." He turned to one of his men. "Send word to her household and the palace." Clearly, there had been change in our absence. "Ask the palace to send a litter for Her Highness," the captain continued.

"Actually, I'd prefer to ride," Zariya said. "Bid him send mounts for my companions and me."

Captain Ranesh stole another glance at her, taking in her canes. "Is Her Highness quite sure?"

"Quite," she said firmly. Kooie whistled and signed. "Ah, although it seems the Elehuddin prefer to go on foot."

The crowd grew, but it was a peaceable assembly, staring at us with fascination. While we waited, we learned that Zarkhoum, too, had been assailed by a plague of the children of Miasmus, the attacks centering on Merabaht. But thanks to Princess Fazarah's stewardship, the damage was contained and the prophets of Miasmus, the poor afflicted, had not succeeded in inciting a second uprising among the common folk.

At length we saw a procession winding down the tiered streets of the city, a squadron of Royal Guards led by Prince Dozaren astride a handsome black horse. *Khementaran* had come upon him in our absence, the pulse-points beating in the hollow of his throat, visible at his wrists where he gripped the reins. We disembarked as he dismounted and strode the length of the dock, the guardsmen parting the obliging crowds for him.

"So you did it," Dozaren said in a wondering tone, gazing at his youngest sister. "You actually did it."

"*We* did it," Zariya said.

"Oh, my heart!" He folded her in an embrace, then wrinkled his nose. "By all the fallen stars, you stink to the heavens."

"It's been a very long and arduous journey," I said.

"My sister's shadow," Dozaren said in acknowledgment. "I owe you a vast debt of gratitude." His gaze took in Jahno and the Elehuddin. "I suspect we owe you *all* a vast debt of gratitude."

Tliksee clicked in wry agreement, making us laugh: gallows laughter with a shadow of pain and loss beneath it. It struck me again that no one outside our company would ever, ever understand what we had endured.

Prince Dozaren, I think, was shrewd enough to realize that this was the case. He offered a salute. "Welcome home, my dearest sister and her shadow, and allow me to welcome your companions to Zarkhoum. Let us offer you hospitality, and then let us gather in the Palace of the Sun to hear your tale." He raised his brows at Zariya. "My sister, do you truly intend to ride through the streets of Merabaht bare-faced and brazen?"

She lifted her chin. "I do."

Unexpectedly, he laughed. "It's a bold choice. I like it."

FIFTY-NINE

Merabaht had changed.

There were fewer people in the streets and no beggars in the squares. Although some of that was due to losses suffered, there was a sense of order and purpose, and I sensed Princess Fazarah's hand in this.

Mindful of the fact that the entirety of Zariya's riding experience consisted of traversing the Caldera on donkey-back, I kept a careful eye on her. It was fortunate that there was a mounting block in the harbor yard high enough that I'd been able to lift her into the saddle with a reasonable measure of decorum, and she had been sensible enough to allow one of the guards to lead her mount.

Zariya sat tall and proud in the saddle, her head held high. Her unveiled face was bare of cosmetics and her unbraided hair hung lank down her back, but if she did not look like a pampered and sheltered Zarkhoumi princess, she looked every inch of what she was: a heroine. Folk lining the street gazed at all of us in wonder—especially at the Elehuddin, whose people had never set foot on these shores—but it was Zariya to whom they offered heartfelt salutes, tears in their eyes.

"You've not remarked on Father's absence," Prince Dozaren observed. "I confess myself surprised."

"I am well aware that our father is aiding the coursers of Obid," Zariya said. "Our paths crossed on the return journey, and indeed, I bear a message for you. In turn, my brother, I confess myself surprised to find that you have appointed Fazarah to the stewardship of Merabaht."

Dozaren gave her a look. "Ah, yes. Well, my hand was somewhat forced.

It seems our sister was in possession of some potentially damaging information and an interesting plan of action did I not accede to her will. Threats
were made." Zariya's eyes narrowed and my hands went to my hilts.
"Peace, sister mine." He turned out one palm, showing the pulse of *khementaran* at his wrist. "In hindsight, it is one of the wisest choices I made. We
are changed, my dearest. The House of the Ageless and its endless intrigues is no more."

Eyeing him, she drew in a sharp breath. "*Khementaran* came upon all of
you?"

"All of us," he agreed. "But not you."

Zariya shook her head. "No."

I wondered what it meant.

We wound our way up the tiered streets of the city to the Palace of the
Sun, dismounting in the courtyard. Zariya leaned over trustingly in the saddle
and I lifted her down, acutely conscious of the length of her body sliding
against mine. She gave me a secret smile that brought a flush to my cheeks.
Kooie bowed and presented her with her canes.

Captain Tarshim of the Queen's Guard saluted her. "Allow us to escort
you to the women's quarter, Your Highness."

Zariya's delicate nostrils flared. "No."

He blinked. "I beg your pardon?"

She propped herself on her canes. "I am not returning to the women's
quarter, not now, nor ever. My people and I will take lodging in the royal
ambassadors' suites."

The captain looked scandalized.

Prince Dozaren smiled broadly and snapped his fingers, enjoying this
breach of propriety. "It shall be so."

So it was done.

One suite of rooms was given to Jahno and the two Elehuddin; another,
to Zariya and me. After so long, luxury was a strangeness, as strange to me
now as it had been when I first came to court. Veiled handmaidens brought
refreshments and an array of clean attire to our suite while the bathing
chamber was made ready.

I had assumed that Zariya and I would bathe together, as was the custom in the women's quarter, but she surprised me. "Given that you have quite literally helped me piss in a bucket, there is precious little mystery left between us, my darling," she observed. "But now that we have declared ourselves to each other, I would at least preserve the semblance of some."

I inclined my head to her. "You are as wise as you are beautiful, and there are things about you that will always be a mystery to me, Zariya. I cannot fathom the source of your courage and determination."

She laughed a bit self-consciously. "Are you quite sure, my shadow? For I owe the greater part of it to you."

"No," I said to her. "It was always there. It has been there since the beginning, when the gods joined our fates."

Zariya slid her hand into mine and squeezed it.

Since there was but one bathing chamber for royal guests, I went to join the others in their suite while Zariya was bathed and plucked and oiled, massaged and painted and braided by assiduous attendants.

Tliksee and Kooie were immersed in a game of clatter-peg, having brought the board with them. After the innumerable games all of us had played on the ship, I'd have thought they never wanted to see it again, but there it was. Jahno, poring over silk tunics and breeches, gave me a shrewd look. "She has banished you while she makes herself ready, yah?"

I sat cross-legged on the carpet. "So it seems."

He set aside a striped tunic. "Tonight you will be alone together for the first time in many months. And although you are both very young, Zariya has waited a very long time for this, I think."

I shrugged, not ready to hear it stated so openly. "How long will you stay in Merabaht?"

Jahno whistled a query to the Elehuddin; Kooie clicked and signed in reply. "Only tonight," he said. "We will set sail on the morrow. We are anxious to be home, all of us, and especially Aiiiaii." His silvery gaze was gentle. "Will you come find us one day?"

I nodded. "Yes, I believe so. I don't know how yet, but we will find a way." I gave him a rueful smile. "You ought to know that Zariya may ask you to be the father of her children."

His lips parted in surprise, and he ran a hand through his hair. "Oh! It would certainly be an honor."

"I can think of no one better," I said honestly. "The two of you are so alike, I thought . . ." I shrugged again.

"Zariya could have been Koronian," Jahno said in acknowledgment, and it was clear that it was high praise. "She has a keen and curious mind, yah? In that we are alike. But it has always been you that she loves, Khai. I have seen it; we have all seen it." His voice took on a somber note. "You may be young in years, but none of us can ever truly be young again after what we have seen and endured, can we?"

I shook my head. "No."

Leaning forward, he laid one hand on my knee, his eyes grave. "Lirios had fewer years upon this earth than any of us, and he saw it clearer than anyone. Seize whatever joy the world yet affords you. Do not let the mayfly's sacrifice be in vain."

I swallowed hard. "I won't."

Twilight was falling over the city of Merabaht by the time we were summoned to the Hall of Pleasant Accord, all of us now scrubbed and scoured and shampooed, anointed with fragrant oils and attired in fine silk garments.

Zariya glowed.

It was said that the fire of Zar the Sun ran in the veins of the Sun-Blessed, and tonight I believed it. Her brown skin glowed, and her dark, lustrous eyes glowed with fierce assurance. Far above us the stars emerged one by one, and their silver-bright light was reflected in the intricate patterns traced on her right hand and forearm, her grip firm and determined on the handles of her canes.

We entered the Hall of Pleasant Accord, and it seemed almost a quaint thing; this place, these people. The royal women peered over their veils, eyes wide at the sight of the bare-chested Elehuddin, necklaces of pearlescent shells shimmering against their greenish-brown skin; at the sight of Jahno, a strange human man in their midst; at the sight of Zariya, unveiled and unabashed. They came forward to embrace her in wonder and dismay, and her mother, Sanala, fell weeping on her neck.

"Oh, my daughter, my darling daughter, what have you endured?" she sobbed. "We thought you lost to us!"

Zariya slipped free of her mother's grip. "You shall hear all in time," she promised. "But come, will you not meet our guests? We have journeyed to the end of the world and back, and they are as family to me."

The gathering was a strange one.

Our Seeker, Jahno, told our tale while we enjoyed a repast. I would have sooner he told it to the fishermen in the harbor who cheered our return, for I daresay they would have relished it more. Here in the Palace of the Sun, far above the streets of Merabaht, they were so very sheltered from the events that had nearly destroyed the world, I am not sure most of them credited it, save for Prince Dozaren, Princess Fazarah, and Sister Nizara, who was the only one of the lot I was certain was wholeheartedly glad to see us. Prince Elizar, pardoned for the crime he hadn't committed and freed from the royal dungeon, could do nothing but glower at the news that his precious Teardrop had played a role in determining the fate of all existence, although Jahno was careful to note that no one knew how the Seer had obtained it.

"Peace, brother," Dozaren said in a warning tone. "Be glad the world yet stands and let the matter drop." He turned to Zariya. "It is a wondrous tale, my sister. But you said you bore a message from our father?"

"I do." She glanced at her sister Fazarah. "Do you say that Dozaren has governed wisely and well in Father's absence?"

Princess Fazarah smiled wryly. "Not without some strong encouragement, my dear, but against all odds, yes, I do say so."

"Then I am to give you this with our father's blessing." Zariya removed the signet ring that hung loose on her forefinger and handed it to Dozaren. "In turn, he decrees that you give me aught that I require."

Surprised and awed, Prince Dozaren slid the ring onto his own finger, admiring it. "And what is it that you require?"

"A ship," Zariya said firmly. "Nothing large, but small and sturdy and agile. I require a ship with which to sail the world, a captain to sail it, a crew to man it, and sufficient funds on which to survive."

Her brother laughed. "Is that all?"

"Very nearly."

"It will take some time," he said. "We Zarkhoumi are not exactly ship-wrights and sailors."

"There is time," Zariya said. "Khai and I mean to journey into the desert. For that, we will require mounts and supplies."

Prince Dozaren inclined his head to her. "Those you shall have."

"I don't understand," her mother said fretfully. "You're home and safe! Why do you seek to abjure your family? Why do you forsake all modesty? Zariya, I should think you of all people would honor Anamuht the Purging Fire, and not venture bald-faced into the world!"

Zariya gazed at her mother. "Do you believe that Anamuht the Purging Fire veils her face with flame?" she asked gently. "You are wrong. And that is a thing we failed to understand, all of us." Lifting her right hand, she opened it with a graceful gesture, and sparks of blue-white lightning danced in her empty palm. "The very essence of Anamuht *is* fire."

I caught my breath.

There was no *rhamanthus* seed; there was only Zariya, the sparks reflecting in her dark eyes. Kooie gave a soft trill of awe and appreciation in the startled silence that fell over the Hall of Pleasant Accord.

Now, they believed.

Sister Nizara cleared her throat. "To that end, I bear a gift for you, my youngest sister." She brought forth a coffer and opened it, revealing hundreds of star-bright seeds shining like diamonds. "The last of the *rhamanthus* seeds."

Zariya closed her hand and the lightning vanished. "For what purpose?" she inquired humbly.

The High Priestess of Anamuht shook her head. "I do not know. I do not even know if these changed *rhamanthus* will continue to bestow the gift of longevity. Only that you are the living avatar of the Purging Fire herself, one of the last vestiges of the Sacred Twins to walk the earth, and these belong to you." She gave us a slight smile. "It is well that you're bound for the desert. Perhaps Khai's truculent Brother Yarit will have some counsel for you."

"If the Brotherhood of Pahrkun yet stands," I said, thinking it might have already disbanded.

"The Sacred Flame yet burns in Anamuht's temple and the Brotherhood of Pahrkun has not abandoned the Fortress of the Winds. Brother Yarit is the Seer," Sister Nizara said. "If he has Seen aught that might aid you, he will abide."

I hoped so.

It was a relief when the interminable gathering ended, and we were escorted from the Hall of Pleasant Accord. We said our goodnights to Jahno and the Elehuddin, promising to see them to the harbor tomorrow that we might bid them and Aiiiaii a final farewell until we met again. In our own luxurious suite of chambers, a veiled maidservant bustled around, turning down sheets and lighting lamps.

"Is there anything else you require, Your Highness?" she asked Zariya.

"No, thank you." Zariya was watching me. "You may take your leave and see that my shadow and I are undisturbed."

And then we were alone together in the lamp-lit darkness, a soft breeze blowing through the room.

I felt Pahrkun's wind stir within me in answer, black and crystalline and distant. My body was strung taut with desire; I was tongue-tied with it. Zariya sat on the bed, arranging her legs. She beckoned to me, sparks flickering around her fingers. "Come here."

I went to her, knelt on the bed before her, and cupped her face in my hands. Her skin was so very soft. "Zariya, I know nothing of lovemaking."

She smiled. "Nor do I, my darling, but I have sixteen years' worth of gossip in the women's quarter on which to draw. It ought to be good for something."

I laughed and kissed her.

She wound her arms around my neck and kissed me in return, and sparks crackled in my hair.

It was exhilarating.

I kissed her lips, kissed her eyelids, kissed the soft skin beneath her delicate earlobes and the hollow of her throat, the places where the pulse of *khementaran* might beat one day; but not today, no. Pahrkun's wind flowed through me, flowed through Zariya, into all the spaces between us, until there were no more spaces. My skin came alive under the cool fire of her touch. Piece by piece, I removed her garments, revealing her deceptively fragile beauty; and I was glad, now, that we had not shared the bath, for her nakedness seemed new and wondrous. With deft fingers, Zariya did the same.

It was only when I was stripped bare of my attire that self-consciousness descended upon me.

Clothed, I knew myself: Khai the boy, Khai the warrior. I had even made a tentative peace with Khai the girl, the stranger in the mirror who made my mother smile. Naked, I was unsure of myself.

Zariya understood. She had always understood.

She stroked the mica-flecked scars on my cheekbones with her thumbs, her dark eyes grave, her lips swollen with my kisses, then placed one hand on the hard plane of my breastbone, spreading her fingers. Gazing intently at me, she clicked her tongue softly in the rising and falling Elehuddin intonation for a person who is both male and female at once.

A tight knot in my chest eased, and I felt tears prick my eyes.

"Your body is a beautiful weapon, my darling," Zariya whispered, lowering her gaze and tracing my collarbones. "Oh, such a very beautiful weapon! But I will teach it to sing a different song."

Oh . . .

I was wrong, I think, to believe that the gods had not joined us for the purpose of love, for surely their blessing was upon us that night. It was fierce and tender, frenzied and wild and sweet, and if I thought I knew nothing of lovemaking, my hands and lips and tongue and every part of me said otherwise. We were ourselves, we were Khai and Zariya, so very young even though our youth had been lost to us in a hut on Papa-ka-hondras, lost to us fighting our way across the plain of Miasmus toward the end of the world, weapons singing in our fists, lightning crackling from our hand, the corpses of the risen dead crunching beneath our feet.

We were Sun-Blessed and shadow, born within a heartbeat of each other, born into destiny.

We were star-fire and night wind, each of us fraying into the other while the children of heaven danced above us.

At length we slept, mortal again.

In the morning, I could not stop smiling. Zariya was sleepy-eyed and amused by my buoyant energy.

"There is one thing I did not ask you," I said to her, and she raised her eyebrows at me in inquiry. "Did you know you could summon the lightning without the aid of the *rhamanthus*?"

She laughed and shook her head. "No. I didn't think about it. I just *did*. Though I do not think I could unleash it unaided," she added. "But perhaps we might keep that to ourselves."

That, I thought, was wise.

Along with Prince Dozaren—soon to be King Dozaren—and a contingent of Royal Guards, we escorted our companions back to the harbor. A crowd gathered, watching at a respectful distance as Kooie called to Aiiiaii and the great sea-wyrm emerged from the deep waters and glided to the quay, her head held high and her blue-green scales shimmering beneath the morning sun. The *ooalu*-wood ship that had been our home for so many months bobbed atop the rippling water.

It hurt to say farewell, and I could not help but think of our fallen comrades. I could only hope they were proud of us.

"I will miss you all so very much," Zariya whispered, leaning one-handed on her canes and embracing Kooie and Tliksee and Jahno in turn.

Jahno gripped her shoulders. "We are family," he said simply. "We will always be family. Come find us when you are ready."

"We will," she promised.

Aiiiaii stretched her sinuous neck and laid her great chin on the dock, iridescent eyes luminous, making the gathered crowd murmur in wonder. I hugged as much of her as I could reach.

"Thank you," I said to her. "We owe you our lives, all of us; you and Eeeio." The sea-wyrm gave a soft trill in response, her vast, scaled cheek sliding along mine, her folded fins tickling.

Hand in hand, Zariya and I stood on the quay and watched them sail away, bound for Elehud.

Two days later, we departed for the desert.

Prince Dozaren sought to persuade us to delay our departure, as did Princess Fazarah, arguing that as a heroine of the realm, Zariya ought to stay for the coronation ceremony and see her brother take the throne, lending her prestige to the formal proceedings. Zariya heard them out patiently, and in the end, refused. "I do not think you understand," she said to them in a calm tone. "I am done with your expectations. I am done with obligations. We have fulfilled the will of the gods, Khai and I, and now we will do as *we* see fit."

Her half brother Dozaren, charming schemer, amoral murderer, and surprisingly adept ruler, offered her a rueful salute. "Then I wish you well."

So.

They sought to impose an escort on us; this, too, Zariya refused. "There at the end of the world, Khai carved a path through the armies of the risen dead," she said in her new resolved and implacable manner. "My shadow is all the escort I have ever needed."

In the end, she got her way.

We crossed the River Ouris on the ferry, our fellow passengers gazing speculatively at Zariya's unveiled face and the marks of Pahrkun on mine. For two days, we journeyed alongside the river. I had chosen a gentle horse for Zariya and she swayed upright in the saddle, one hand on the pommel and the other gripping the reins, grateful to have four strong legs beneath her.

On the third day, we turned toward the east and the desert, leaving the world behind us.

It had been a long time.

A very long time.

I breathed deep of the desert air, filling my lungs. Spring was nigh, and I could taste the promise of rain.

We traveled in the cool morning hours and the twilit evenings, taking shelter during the midday heat. At night the sky was impossibly vast, the stars scattered like diamonds over the black canopy, the flashing eyes and teeth and the fierce beating hearts of the children of heaven shining above us.

It was strange, though, to sojourn across the desert and think that never again would I catch sight of a column of wind or a column of fire in the distance; that never again would I see the Sacred Twins striding across the sandy plains.

On the fifth day, I said as much to Zariya.

She loosened the length of scarf wrapped around the lower part of her face to reply. "I have been thinking the same thing, my heart," she said thoughtfully. "I have seen Anamuht the Purging Fire in her glory, but I shall never see the Scouring Wind; nor shall any child born since the ascension. The world is changed. Generations will pass and memories will fade. One day, folk will find it impossible to believe that the gods once walked the earth and showered mankind with their gifts."

I nodded. "It saddens me."

"Me, too." Zariya favored me with a smile. "But I have also been thinking that it gives us a purpose."

"Oh?"

She fixed her gaze on the eastern horizon. "Let us collect their stories, you and I. *All* the stories. Let us collect them and preserve them and write them down, so that one day our grandchildren's grandchildren shall know what trial Khai of the Fortress of the Winds underwent at the behest of Pahrkun the Scouring Wind; so that they shall know what counsel Kephalos the Wise, the Oracle of the Nexus, offered the defenders of the four quarters; what horrors Shambloth the Inchoate Terror engendered in the forests of Papa-ka-hondras; what tricks Quellin-Who-Is-Everywhere played in Drogalia, and what bargains Galdano the Shrewd offered in his temple."

"All the stories," I echoed.

"Yes."

"It will be a considerable undertaking," I observed.

Zariya gave me a sidelong glance, her eyes sparkling. "Yes, but who better to undertake it, my darling?"

"No one," I said slowly, thinking about the coffer of *rhamanthus* seeds stowed in the satchels our patient and plodding packhorse carried. "It is the work of a lifetime; perhaps a very, very long lifetime. But what happens when we have outlived mortal memory, Zariya? What tales will we tell then?"

She laughed, and the wind caught her laugh, sending it skirling across the empty desert floor, raising acrid puffs of ochre dust. "When there are no more tales to tell, we shall invent our own, my dearest. We shall invent such gods as no one could have imagined, inspiring hope and courage and dreams of honor beyond honor."

I smiled at her. "Then let us do so."

Zariya smiled back at me, her eyes as bright as the stars in the night sky. "Oh, but we have already begun."

ABOUT THE AUTHOR

Jacqueline Carey is the author of the *New York Times* bestselling Kushiel's Legacy historical fantasy series, as well as the Sundering epic fantasy duology, postmodern fables *Santa Olivia* and *Saints Astray,* and *Miranda and Caliban*. Carey lives in western Michigan.